YURY NAGIBIN
The Peak of Success and Other Stories

Edited by Helena Goscilo

Ardis, Ann Arbor

Yury Nagibin, *The Peak of Success*
Copyright © 1986 by Ardis Publishers
All rights reserved under International and Pan-American
Copyright Conventions.
Printed in the United States of America

Translated from the original Russian

Ardis Publishers
2901 Heatherway
Ann Arbor, Michigan 48104

Library of Congress Cataloging in Publication Data
Nagibin, Iurii Markovich, 1920—
The peak of success and other stories.

Translation from Russian.
Bibliography: p.
I. Nagibin, Iurii Markovich, 1920—   —Translations,
English.   I. Goscilo, Helena, 1945—   . II. Title.
PG3476.N34A2 1986   891.73'44   85-18696
ISBN 0-88233-800-5 (alk. paper)

In memoriam
Tatuś, who had the courage to be tender
and
Dan Armstrong, who was integrity incarnate.

CONTENTS

Introduction

Throughout an uninterrupted career of forty years, Yury Nagibin's talent as a fictionist has defined itself almost exclusively in the genre of the short story *(rasskaz)* and the short tale *(povest')*. The single exception, and one that the author recalls unenthusiastically, is the novella *Pavlik*. Fully cognizant that his abilities are geared to the small form, Nagibin confesses that *Pavlik*—both the finished product and his recollection of working on it—reduces him to "shivers of alienation."[1] For reasons that elude logical explanation, large-scale canvasses are organically alien to him, just as in his youth those sports that demanded physical endurance rather than speed or agility proved incompatible with his athletic prowess. As a prosaist, then, Nagibin favors the short sprint, usually preferring ten to twenty pages for the length of his narratives, and rarely exceeding fifty. The majority of his longer works belong to the 1970s.

Although his reputation rests principally on his stories and tales, Nagibin has also written essays, adaptations, travelogues, reviews, and over thirty film scripts and scenarios, many of them based on his own fiction.[2] His most memorable scenario, for the prize-winning movie *Dersu Uzala*, earned international accolades and, indeed, surpassed the average Soviet film in virtually every respect, though it might have benefited from more rigorous editing.[3]

By contrast to writers who withdraw behind a screen of reticence, enigma, or subterfuge when queried about their art (e.g., Nabokov, Oates), Nagibin does not hesitate to make his critical judgments and his working habits public through interviews, essays, and personal reminiscences. A curious and disarming blend of contradiction in his conversation and his published commentary alike, Nagibin moves fluidly between confident generalizations that border on *ex cathedra* pronouncements and a genuine tolerance for multiple and conflicting viewpoints. While delivering categorical opinions on the one hand, he insists, on the other, that what obtains for one writer need have no relevance whatever for another. Individual inspiration and subjective circumstance guide the direction and mode of literary creation, so no universal rules—except the most elastic and general—can possibly govern all art. One author's ideal may be anathema to someone whose creative impulse springs from a different source. What matters finally, he contends, is that each writer's choice always work for, and not against, his art.

In his unpretentious readiness to acquaint readers with everything that concerns his professional activities, Nagibin has divulged some surprising details about his own creative process. For instance, his compositions as a rule start with the conclusion, which comes to him in a sentence, a paragraph, or an entire page.[4] That conclusion, he claims, predetermines the remainder of the story. On the basis of that information one might reasonably anticipate narratives whose resolution hinges on a *pointe*. Yet Nagibin's almost never culminate in that epigrammatic twist which characterizes, for example, the bulk of de Maupassant's and Maugham's tales, and those that do end with a reversal have elicited, ironically enough, sharp—and deserved—criticism for flabby or contrived motivation (e.g., the husband's abrupt decision to return to his family instead of joining his youthful mistress in "Needed Urgently—Gray Human Hair"). According to Nagibin, his unorthodox method of composition derives indirectly from an observation made by Chekhov, for whom Nagibin cherishes a boundless adoration: Chekhov once recommended that immediately upon finishing a story a writer eliminate its beginning and end, for authorial lies proliferate in those two places. For the sake of the story's integrity, those falsehoods should be expunged. Presumably by lies Chekhov means the inclusion of elements, such as cheap effects, that violate a text's inner unity—the aesthetic consistency within the framework of a given narrative that makes the whole convincing, whether the original concept be rooted in recorded fact or untrammelled fantasy.

The issue of dishonesty clearly bears little relation to whether a specific event or situation could occur in real life. In Nagibin's case especially, the question of external probability seemed immaterial at least until 1960 and the story "Echo," for by his own admission before then he had been utterly incapable of invention, and drew all his material from his own life experiences. His stories recreated actual situations in which he had played the role of observer, minor participant, or focal figure. Apart from anything else, this admission suggests what a richly-textured and intensely felt existence Nagibin led. Yet for years his avowed lack of imaginative powers distressed him. Then he learned that Leskov, one of his esteemed favorites, had suffered from the identical complaint,[5] and the coincidence reconciled Nagibin totally to what had impressed him earlier as a crippling drawback. And in 1960, with "Echo," he gingerly loosened the reins on his imagination in his portrayal of a girl who collects echoes. The story's unqualified success (it is second in popularity only to "Winter Oak" with Soviet readers) gave Nagibin the self-confidence for a bolder exploration of his imaginative resources, and several of his later works evidence a decreased reliance on actual incidents (e.g., "Somebody Else's Heart" and some of the artist stories of the 1970s).

Many of Nagibin's disclosures about himself and his literary tastes confound expectations born of a general familiarity with his oeuvre. Stylistically Nagibin belongs to a tradition in Russian prose that harks back to Turgenev and extends through Chekhov and Bunin to Paustovsky, Kazakov, Antonov, and to some degree, Tendriakov. Yet Nagibin unhesitatingly cites Dostoyevsky, Gogol, and Leskov as his idols, and in an essay devoted to the language of fiction, declares a preference in no uncertain terms for Dostoyevsky's "chaotic" and Tolstoy's "ponderous" language over Turgenev's universally praised "crystal pure, clear, sonorous, poetic" prose.[6] For Nagibin, good language denotes precise wording, an author's ability to make the means of expression correspond absolutely to his insight. A complete grasp of a phenomenon automatically guarantees the appropriate wording; if a writer cannot articulate what he perceives, his perception must be partial or flawed. Echoing his protagonist from "Muteness," Nagibin maintains that words are not merely words, but essence, just as writing is not simply an exercise, but a heuristic process that leads the writer to a richer comprehension of life itself. His observations converge with Joyce Carol Oates's assertion that to write is to "consciously arrange and re-arrange reality for the purposes of exploring its hidden meanings."[7]

The question of language unavoidably raises the related issue of brevity and compactness. Apropos of verbal economy, Nagibin defines laconism as the absence of "emptiness," of "dead verbal material that doesn't do any work."[8] By that definition, Proust, Dostoyevsky, Tolstoy, and Bunin (his wealth of adjectives notwithstanding) are all succinct, whereas a provincial imitator of Hemingway commits the sin of verbosity even in a twenty-word story, for all twenty words are superfluous. Verbal deadwood, not length, is brevity's true enemy. Emaciated sentences borrowed from the West, with phrases stripped to the bone à la Hemingway, should not be confused with brevity. Such an imitative pseudo-laconism, in Nagibin's opinion, merely betrays an absence of personal style, and regrettably, it has seduced many a young inexperienced writer. Particularly telling in light of Nagibin's high regard for Hemingway as a writer,[9] this view testifies to the Russian's professional integrity and powers of discrimination. Which does not imply that Nagibin's narratives exemplify a prose free of deadwood; on the contrary, the extraneous often encumbers his stories. But whatever Nagibin's practice, what he preaches is essentially sound. And in general Nagibin's theoretical and critical pieces number among his best writing—shrewd, insightful, and to the point.[10]

In response to an official questionnaire circulated among a large cross-section of Russian prosaists in the 1960s, the overwhelming majority listed Hemingway as the primary foreign influence on their style.[11] Although Nagibin agrees with those critics who presume a profound subtext beneath Hemingway's mannered simplicity, he considers a Russian's adoption of Hemingwayesque terseness especially ill-judged because of the discrepancy between the fundamental nature of the two languages. And to Nagibin's credit, he pinpoints precisely what negates the possibility of a successful Russian copy of Hemingway. The strict limitations that Hemingway imposed upon his fund of vocabulary (particularly the verbs and epithets), when transferred into Russian, rob Russian of its inherent energy, color, and expressiveness. The result is terminal linguistic anemia. Nagibin further asserts (and the point is perhaps too platitudinous to need stating) that imitation of any type is fatal; a writer should take up his pen only when seized by an uncontrollable drive to express his own, unique apprehension of life. Otherwise, he should abandon all intention of writing. One would hardly characterize Nagibin as a proponent of the sacerdotal school of writing, which credits literary genius with divine origin and purpose. But he unequivocally acknowledges inspiration as a normal and necessary ingredient in the creative process. As Nagibin's own prose testifies, he meets his stated requirement of a personal vision—one, moreover, that he feels compelled to transmit to the largest possible audience, through both his fiction and his cinematic projects. Much as Nagibin may have learned from someone like Platonov, whom he freely recognizes as his teacher, Nagibin cannot be accused of emulating his 'master's' dramatic, often startling, verbal effects. Nagibin's literary voice unmistakably belongs to him alone. And, paradoxically, Nagibin resembles least those writers he most admires.

Nagibin's stories tend to draw on a repertoire of subjects which the author himself has categorized: war ("The Last Assault," "Vaganov," "In Early Spring"); children ("Komarov," "Echo," "Children Build Snowmen"); sports ("The Unbeatable Arsenov," "The Winner," "World Champion"); hunting and fishing ("The Last Hunt," "The Test," "At the Quiet Lake"); village life ("Pages from the Life of Trubnikov"); art ("Muteness," "The Typist Lives on the Sixth Floor"); life abroad ("My Venice," "Weimar and its Environs," "The Soldier"); love ("Whatever You Say, Aurelio," "The Newlywed," "The Peak of Success"); and historical personalities ("The Island of Love").[12] Such a catalogue suggests a clear-cut demarcation line that cannot actually be drawn precisely without reduction or oversimplification, and one should view the majority of Nagibin's stories as belonging to one or more of these categories only for the expedient of an orderly discussion. Certain subjects absorbed Nagibin more during the early phase of his career, only to recede and vanish later when his attention transferred to other themes. For example, almost all his war stories belong to the early and mid-1940s, and his narratives about children, sports, hunting and fishing, to the 1950s and 1960s; his fascination with the psychology and unofficial biography of artists to whom contemporaries denied just recognition increased noticeably in the 1970s, when the past suddenly opened up to him new areas of creative exploration: in the last decade he has written "The Runaway" and "Island of Love" about Trediakovsky, "The Fiery Archpriest" about Avvakum, "A Morning at Tsarskoye Selo" about Pushkin, "At the Krestov Ferry" about Pushkin and Delvig, "Death at the Railroad Station" about Annensky, "Christopher Marlowe's Epitaph," "A Dream about Tiutchev," and "Where the Table Was Laid with Food"—a narrative about Rachmaninov, Scriabin, Verdi, and Wagner.[13] With the years Nagibin has moved steadily away not only from certain topics, but also from the subjectivity and free-flowing lyricism of his youthful prose. Most of his biographical stories absorb the language of the period and personality depicted. "The Fiery Archpriest," for example, linguistically recreates the seventeenth century, and incorporates phrases from Avvakum's autobiography, just as Tiutchev's inner monologues in "A Dream About Tiutchev" are couched in the lexicon of Tiutchev's lyrics.[14]

Possibly because the birth of Nagibin's writing career in 1939 coincided with the outbreak of World War II, his first endeavors (see the collection entitled *A Man from the Front,* 1943) strove to bolster national morale by lauding Russian bravery at the front and resilient stoicism at home. Although very few of these narratives treat actual battle scenes, they reek of optimistic patriotism occasionally delivered in a quasi-virile sentimental key.[15] Most compare unfavorably with his later stories and reveal, if not consonance with the demands of Soviet orthodoxy, then a perspective and tone that could be interpreted as such. Nagibin's prose evinces no desire to challenge, violate, or depart from the manner and values advocated by official Soviet ideology.[16] His acceptance of the system, or perhaps his allegiance to some of the beliefs that inform the system, manifests itself not in his subservience to the dictates of socialist realism, but in his apparent indifference to controversial issues which more unorthodox prosaists, such as Aksyonov, tackle, and in the political shibboleths (affirming socialism's superiority over other forms of government or stressing a writer's love for the masses) that occasionally pepper his prose. But to make of Nagibin a committed spokesman for any given way of life is to misrepresent his concerns, which transcend temporal and geographical boundaries to confirm universal human problems. Psychology, not social causes, animates his art; it is not by accident that one of his favorite writers is Marcel Proust.

Although a high percentage of Nagibin's narratives end on an irresolute note, the values they repeatedly champion unmistakably adhere to the humanist tradition. Above all else Nagibin esteems courage; tenderness and kindness; fidelity to a tested personal code of ethics that is tempered by tolerance and generosity; clear-sighted honesty in facing life's complexities; receptivity to love, beauty, and to any experience that enriches one's appreciation of life by giving one access to some unknown facet of human existence; and skill in one's profession or occupation. No traits arouse Nagibin's revulsion more than cruelty, deception, shallowness, irresponsibility, smugness, and myriad forms of philistinism. Yet he conceives of those who suffer from these defects as pitiful and circumscribed rather than villainous. Perhaps it is Nagibin's refusal to condemn the weak and misguided that makes his readers instantly aware of the human sympathy and understanding that emanate from both the author and his narratives. If bitterness and vicious resentment motivate a character in Nagibin's world, their sharpness is blunted by the author's undisguisedly compassionate attitude toward his sufferer.

As Atarov,[17] Porter,[18] and Nagibin himself have pointed out, a discovery of some sort forms the pivot for countless Nagibin stories, especially in the early and middle periods. For instance, "Winter Oak," "The Newlywed," and "Shurik" all build up to a climax of illumination that reverses facile or premature assumptions or enables the narrative's central consciousness to understand something that (s)he never suspected. The revelation, which Nagibin likes to place at the story's conclusion, presumably marks a crossroads in each discoverer's internal life. Elsewhere—e.g., in "The Night Guest," "Olezhka Got Married," "The Peak of Success," and "The Outsider"—the revelation dawns gradually. A series of small clues whose individual significance seems negligible steadily accumulate until at some juncture they collectively effect a moment of awareness in the protagonist. Often a protagonist's blindness in the face of truth stems from a too rapid and superficial judgment or from a reluctance to acknowledge the frailty and pettiness of human nature or of a specific individual. Not all such revelations are momentous *per se,* but they carry far-reaching implications that force the reader to re-evaluate the story in retrospect. A sizable percentage of Nagibin's stories implicitly caution against an overly simplistic interpretation of human personality on the basis of visible data.

Nagibin's use of epiphany relies on a device that dominates his style and accounts for the best and the worst in his prose: qualification on an epistemological, thematic, and linguistic level. When people's perception of, and attitude toward, an individual or situation undergo gradual modification, the device of verbal qualification proves effective, since it accords neatly with the process itself. In "The Night Guest," for instance, most of the characters in the story experience a shift in their view of Pal Palych, but it is primarily the narrator's assessment of the man that guides our judgment. As the narrator's feelings change under the impact of a succession of disillusioning episodes, capped by the loss of the knife and Pal Palych's uncharitable reaction to the misfortune, they color the reader's attitude accordingly. The exposure of the attractive, seemingly good-natured sociable intruder as a self-centered opportunist comes in stages which force both the narrator and the reader to make constant adjustments in their original impression. When the scales finally fall away from all eyes, the picture acquires an edge in the contrast drawn between the central epiphany and a smaller but comparable one involving Nikolay Semyonovich. Described at the outset as a gruff man of unprepossessing physical appearance interested solely in fishing, Nikolay Semyonovich turns out to possess acute human understanding and tenderness, and actually notices and interprets correctly much more than does the narrator. The entire story is a lesson in qualification which assumes a triple form— we are obliged to re-evaluate Pal Palych, Nikolay Semyonovich, and the narrator, while keeping in mind that Pal Palych does have the likable traits with which most of the story's participants credited him earlier, along with the selfish egotism he later betrays. Nagibin manipulates readers' responses through a skillful use of modification here and in other stories that employ the same device more or less successfully: "Olezhka Got Married" and "The Outsider." But when the device is compressed into a single paragraph and used in descriptions, particularly of setting and emotions, it sometimes misfires, partly because its usage produces the verbal deadwood that Nagibin criticizes in his essay. Then the relentless modification through adjective clusters, series of near-synonyms, and nets of subordinate clauses throttles the prose without refining the basic idea or image. Instead of complexity, perplexity results. See, for instance, the irrelevant details regarding the horse tethered to the carriage that Pushkin hires for his day's jaunt with Delvig in "At the Krestov Ferry":

> The horse was old and gaunt, but neither the hollows above its eyes nor the rawboned buttocks and protruding ribs, nor the balding spots beneath the harness, could debase the noble physique of a purebred Orlov steed, and one could divine some melancholy equine mystery behind this aristocrat harnessed to a "Guitar," as Petersburgians called the small carriage on which one sat astride.[19]

Unless the horse is intended as a rather crude parallel for Delvig, the particulars serve no valid function, and merely splinter the reader's attention. The same defect detracts from the quality of several scenes in

"Needed Urgently—Gray Human Hair," where Nagibin indulges in a description of Leningrad that seems too minute for the story's needs.

A slightly different form of deadwood weighs down the narrative when Nagibin does not allow the reader to draw his own inferences, but even after making the implication of an event or a relationship fairly clear he goes on to elaborate his point in explicit terms. An instance of such redundancy occurs in two stories included in this collection: by the end of "The Newlywed" the blatant shortcomings of Voronov's life and the contrasting intangible rewards of Vaska's are established beyond all doubt. to articulate the 'moral lesson' as thought in Voronov's mind is gratuitous; it weakens the story irreparably. That Nagibin had justified qualms about the ending may be seen in the two versions he produced: whereas the first concludes with the expendable explanation of the obvious,[20] the second (rendered here) wisely omits it, thereby gaining in strength. A similar error in judgment flaws "Shurik." There the narrator's regret and compassion for the imaginative little boy's death can safely be assumed, whereas by voicing them directly Nagibin degrades the conclusion into a maudlin anticlimax. These two endings, as well as that of "Needed Urgently—Gray Human Hair" and of several other stories (e.g., "At Night"), bear out the observation by Chekhov that Nabigin likes so much—that authorial lies invade narratives at their start and finish. However conscious Nagibin may be of that truism, his conclusions in several cases constitute the least satisfying part of his narrative.

The commonplace that Russian novels tend to neglect plot to dwell on psychology certainly holds true for Nagibin's fiction. Dramatic events—or incidents that breed immediate excitement and curiosity, causing the reader to wonder 'what happens next,' as (s)he might when reading a work by Wilkie Collins or Charles Dickens, or even E.T.A. Hoffmann, for that matter—occur infrequently. With few exceptions, Nagibin prefers to depict the everyday, focussing on the inner significance of seemingly mundane actions and occurrences. To a high degree Nagibin possesses what one critic, speaking of Somerset Maugham, succinctly called "the ability to see the ordinary extraordinarily well."[21] "Before the Holidays," for example, traces a girl's transition into early womanhood through portraying with remarkable sensitivity and naturalness the onset of her menstruation; the external action of "The Abandoned Path" may be summarized as a short exercise in weeding; "Komarov" merely shows an irritable, vinegar-hearted governess rounding up her charge—an inquisitive little boy enamored of pine-cones, frogs, and sundry objects that strike the average adult as nondescript or unimportant. These can scarcely be considered earthshaking events, especially when presented in a highly descriptive mode. Melodrama and colorful effects hold scant appeal for

Nagibin, whose palette contains mainly delicate pastels. If "Elijah's Day," which is somewhat reminiscent of Chekhov's "Peasants" (Muzhiki), deviates from this rule, it does so only in the sense that its hues are unrelieved black and gray. And the devastating portrayal of drunkenness depends for its effects not on a heightened melodramatic tone but on the startling contrast between the brutal events and the matter-of-fact low-key narrative voice.

Of all Nagibin's narratives, the early war stories and a few of the historical sketches have a minor claim to drama—for obvious reasons. Yet even there Nagibin perceives the greatest significance in the most inconspicuous, even banal, acts. "In Early Spring," for example, rather than graphically dramatizing the horrors of World War II, quietly unfolds the diverse reactions of a motley group to the food shortage during the war years; "Vaganov" offers a partial portrait of a war hero, but instead of showing him in combat, it spotlights his frenetic dancing and his reluctant rejection of a young woman who makes advances to him. Even the potentially dramatic suicide of Guy, the protagonist of "The Peak of Success," becomes defused through Nagibin's avoidance of a description of the act itself (he confines himself to the preparations) and though the rather tranquil responses of Guy's friend(s) to the self-inflicted death. Grand gestures and stirring incidents have too conspicuous an exterior to seduce a writer with Nagibin's distrust of surface glitter.

Nagibin's plots tend to stretch out minor episodes, not to crowd a lot of action into a small space. And they rarely deal in the fantastic or improbable. "The Peak of Success" posits the fantastic situation of a researcher's discovery of a cure for cancer, which he identifies as a virus. But the improbability of that event does not generate additional situations that challenge one's credulity; the rest of the narrative proceeds to trace calmly and matter-of-factly the history and dissolution of his marriage. "Somebody Else's Heart" likewise, despite its farfetched notion that the human heart is literally the source of all human feelings and memory, develops in a quite mundane fashion. A rare exception is "Among Professionals," which establishes a parallel between a tennis player of waning powers and a prince consort tormented by his inability to produce a male heir to the throne. Both salvage their reputation and their self-respect when the player wins his match and the prince's wife give birth to a boy who—and here fantasy boldly intervenes—resembles the tennis champion. Such an unexpected touch (possibly borrowed from Goethe's *Elective Affinities*) is not typical of Nagibin, nor does he allow it to tip the entire story over into the realm of the fantastic.

Whatever heights Nagibin's handling of dialogue, exposition, or narration may attain in isolated cases, there can be no doubt that on a steady basis his forte is description, and above all, description of setting. Although several of his stories transpire abroad or in cities, most take place in the midst of nature (especially in the Meshchyora region that he knows and loves)—in the woods, in the taiga, at the beach, beside a river, or along a country road. That gift of an extraordinarily penetrating eye and acute ear for nature's sights and sounds with which Nagibin credits Bunin he himself unquestionably possesses. His sensitivity to fine and telling detail and his solid knowledge of meteorology, trees, grasses, flowers, fish, birds, and wild animals lend his stories a concreteness that enhances their credibility, their authenticity. Particularly in outdoor settings Nagibin has a flair for capturing mood, for communicating to the reader the odors, sounds, colors, and textures of a given locale so vividly that (s)he has the illusion of being transported to that spot. Those stories that deal with hunting or fishing evidence Nagibin's thorough knowledge of the two sports, and the details and specificity of his descriptions lure the reader into a rapid acceptance of the location portrayed, and by extension, the events that transpire there. Edith Wharton, herself a formidable mistress of the short form, declared that "one of the chief obligations in a short story is to give the reader an immediate sense of security."[22] Skillful description usually discharges that obligation in those Nagibin stories that win the reader's credulity and instant trust in the author's competence. In their assured command of descriptive elements, Nagibin's fishing and hunting tales recall the early Hemingway's Nick Adams stories. But Nagibin rarely permits details to obtrude as Hemingway does whenever obsession with the conventions of a sport (e.g., bullfighting in *The Sun Also Rises)* leads him to digress needlessly and to betray naively his pride in "knowing" the ins and outs of a game. On those occasions when Nagibin's taste does fail him, however, he, too, errs on the side of excess, as in the lengthy catalogue of items cluttering the protagonist's desk in "The Peak of Success." But the merits of his descriptions normally outnumber their flaws.

Settings in Nagibin's prose—and notably the outdoors—fulfill a rich variety of functions. In such stories as "The Chase," setting attains the dimensions of a major character, almost rivalling the protagonist, Anatoly Ivanovich, whose unwitting antagonist it becomes. In narratives like "The Test" nature becomes moral teacher. Elsewhere it provides a metaphor for or contrast to the human domain (e.g., "The Outsider"). For the most part, the world of nature constitutes a testing ground, unleashing forces or erecting obstacles that furnish a reliable measure of an individual when he attempts to cope with them. For instance, the spiritual strength, the goodness of Vaska in "The Newlywed," Putyatin in "Outsider," Nikolay Semyonovich in "The Night Guest," Bolotov in "Olezhka Got Married" and Savushkin in "Winter Oak" cannot be separated from their proximity to the natural world, to which they are attuned and for which they have a profound respect. The failure of Pal Palych, Olezhka and his friends, and Burenkov ("The Chase") to appreciate and harmonize with natural surroundings signals a more meaningful inability on their part to live according to decent standards.

Not only nature but proficiency in a chosen specialization is used to gauge a man's caliber. Particularly in those stories that treat sports, hunting, and fishing, Nagibin shares Hemingway's habit of distinguishing between the *bona fide* aficionado, the man who proves himself through his commitment and skill, on the one hand, and the amateur who yearns to 'belong,' yet is doomed to rejection because he lacks something essential if unidentifiable in his makeup. Skill coupled with grace counts for a great deal in Nagibin's world, and often provides a dependable clue to a person's moral stamina and worth. Gushchin's professional expertise in "Needed Urgently—Gray Human Hair," for example, shows up the handsome young poet, with his half-hearted dabbling in judo, poetry, and acting, as a dilettante.

Few contemporary Russian prosaists match Nagibin in the diversity of characters he portrays. His gallery of figures includes people of both sexes and of all ages and professions, ranging from soldiers and engineers to actresses. Children (e.g., Komarov, Savushkin, Vitka) tend to be shown as charmingly responsive to those treasures of life that adults are too preoccupied or corrupt to notice or prize. Because they intuitively value the essential in life, Nagibin's children, like Tolstoy's, often unconsciously serve as a potential lesson for adults, as a means to a spiritual rebirth or awakening. Although Nagibin casts a lyrical glow over many of his youthful characters, he can also be soberly realistic about their shortcomings. The children's world in "Echo" and "Shurik," for example, is inhabited by the vices and weaknesses that we customarily associate with adulthood: the group mentality, envy, callousness, injustice, and the like. Even the child narrator in "Shurik," who in the course of the narrative gains a precious insight into Shurik's and his own inner self, cannot escape the negative side of human nature.

Adults as a rule are prey to pettiness and frailties of one kind or another. Very few of them qualify as haloed paragons or irreclaimable villains; most come in various shades of gray. A small minority of Nagibin's men, however, verge on sainthood: Vaska in "The Newlywed," for instance, is blessed with practically all desirable virtues—generosity o spirit, a capacity for intense and abiding emotion, naïveté, purity, supreme modesty, professionalism, vitality, good looks, etc. Guy in "The Peak of Success" likewise seems to lack any undesirable traits, and Gushchin's only faults—if they can be called such—in "Needed Urgently—Gray Human Hair" are inordinate compassion and almost virginal innocence.

In view of Nagibin's closeness to Hemingway, the insight and warmth the Russian brings to his characterizations of women is surprising. Like the men, they are mixed, varying in age, appearance, profession, and temperament from one story to the next. Their psychology preoccupies Nagibin somewhat less than that of their male counterparts, but whenever Nagibin elects to concentrate on feminine motives and impulses, he does so with intelligence and understanding (see "The Outsider," "The Runaway," and "Whatever You Say, Aurelio"). A few of his narratives even stem from a feminine point of view ("Before the Holidays," "Winter Oak," "Whatever You Say, Aurelio"), which Nagibin controls most ably, especially for a man who seems to believe that sexual identity determines temperamental traits, and that women act and think differently from men because of their gender. In the main Nagibin manages to avoid the narrowness of sexual stereotyping that often leads to imbecilic conclusions.

Relations between the two sexes figure prominently in Nagibin's fiction, assuming the form of nascent love ("Whatever You Say, Aurelio"), illicit adult liaisons ("Olezhka Got Married"), or marriage ("Elijah's Day"). Nagibin's treatment of the marital theme changes with different narratives: while a piece like "The Newlywed" shows marriage in an ideal light, "The Outsider" and "Needed Urgently—Grey Human Hair" focus more on the insoluble problems and limitations that can accompany a legal union; "The Runaway" depicts a wife who remains faithful and loving in the face of overwhelming temptations and suffering, while "The Peak of Success" (somewhat in the manner of Chekhov's "The Grasshopper," to which "At the Krestov Ferry" also bears a resemblance) offers a contrasting glimpse of an engaging but irresponsible and unappreciative wife whose infidelities end only when she abandons her husband for no apparent reason other than unspecified boredom, a "spiritual disease of modern times." Rather than advocating a consistent philosophy of marriage, Nagibin examines individual cases of happy, troubled, or indifferent couples from many different perspectives. Unlike Pasternak, who tends to idealize women, and Tertz, who clearly mistrusts and fears them, Nagibin simply regards them as a species very dissimilar to, but on a par with, men. A number of his male protagonists may see the women they love in a poetic light, but Nagibin as author does not.

It is chiefly the psychology of his couples, the hidden motives behind their behavior rather than the behavior itself, that absorbs Nagibin. Some commentators have claimed that, with the exception of his fishing and hunting stories, Nagibin's works about Soviet adults "contain much fine writing but generally strike one as contrived," whereas "his stories about childhood ... are generally good."[23] Yet Nagibin's childhood narratives frequently flounder in bathos, while those narratives that delve courageously into relations between the two sexes attain, at their best, a high level of psychological and stylistic sophistication. "The Outsider" affords a prime example of a work that tackles complex adult dilemmas with unflinching honesty and a degree of finesse. The title's outsider is Vera Dmitrievna, the 'younger woman' whom Putyatin, one of the protagonists, marries. To do so, he divorces his overpoweringly affectionate first wife Lipochka, thereby alienating his closest friend Kungurtsev and Kungurtsev's undemonstrative spouse Maria Petrovna; both resent the interloper out of loyalty to Lipochka. The story traces a day-long outing in the taiga, during which the Putyatins and Kungurtsevs entertain a famous film director and his staff, trying to impress him with Siberian hospitality. Because Kungurtsev's point of view dominates the first half of the story, the reader more or less accepts his version of the events (even though much of it is conjectural) and sympathizes with his consequent dislike of Vera Dmitrievna, his dismay over Lipochka's departure, and his puzzled disappointment with Putyatin. Lipochka, who remains a hearsay character throughout, seems a victim of Putyatin's incapacity to appreciate her true merit and of Vera Dmitrievna's wiles. As the story progresses, however, that picture becomes clouded by the unexpected truths that emerge: Kungurtsev's sympathy, however authentic, mingles with regret at the loss of Lipochka's wonderful cooking and the fear that the group activities of the two couples will cease. Moreover, though he is Putyatin's best friend, Kungurtsev's selfish prejudice blinds him both to the genuine love and mutual respect that unite Putyatin and his second wife, and to Putyatin's horror at the prospect of Lipochka's return—for which there must be a reasonable explanation. Vera Dmitrievna proves not a youthful and casual seductress, but a responsible courageous woman who fulfills Putyatin, even if she cannot load his stomach with the delicacies that Lipochka could prepare so effortlessly. By the story's conclusion the reader is forced to revise his opinion of Kungurtsev as narrator and friend, Putyatin as husband, and Vera Dmitrievna as individual. The drift of the narrative also strongly implies that one can never understand another person's relationships with others that all human behavior springs from very mixed motives—ideas that surface also in "The Runaway" and "Needed Urgently—Gray Human Hair."

"The Outsider" is one of Nagibin's best adult stories, maybe in part because Nagibin divests the situation of sentimentalism and sagely withholds certain information from the reader—for example, did Lipochka leave because Putyatin fell in love with Vera Dmitrievna or did unsatisfying relations between the Putyatins make Putyatin susceptible to Vera in the first place? Why does the possibility of Lipochka's presence beside him fill Putyatin with such revulsion? Nagibin keeps the reader as much in the dark as he does Kungurtsev, and his reticence enhances the theme of complex motives and the impact of the conclusion. Moreover, the story does not adduce readymade panaceas to predicaments for which real life has no easy solutions. Although Putyatin seems to be a likable man of principles and integrity, his obvious guilt before Lipochka and his impotent commiseration with her plight have a solid basis in his own withdrawal of affection. Similarly, Lipochka may be universally loved and eager to please, but Putyatin's nightmare hints that something very fundamental went awry in their marriage. As Wharton notes, "exactly the same thing never happens to any two people, and . . . each witness of a given incident will report it differently."[24] Without exploiting shifting viewpoint to its full capacity, Nagibin nevertheless allows it to underscore the notion that truths vary according to the psychology of their observers, and only a synthesis of diverse and conflicting perspectives can begin to approximate what we call objective reality.

Nagibin's most successful stories overcome a weakness that marks not only some of his writing, but much of Soviet prose in general: sentimentalism.[25] In his war stories Nagibin yields to mawkishness when his nationalism gets out of hand; in his stories about children, sentimentalism grows out of unchecked tenderness or pity for a child's distress; elsewhere it surfaces when Nagibin fails to distance himself sufficiently from a character who indulges in regretful reminiscences or succumbs to a flood of emotion (e.g., Gushchin's bittersweet flights when he walks with Natasha to her apartment after a visit to her friends in "Needed Urgently—Gray Human Hair"). When Nagibin stands removed from his characters he fares better, for then the temptation to linger in mournful contemplation over a moment whose affecting power should speak for itself is reduced. Nothing leavens bathos as effectively as humor—a lesson that Byron's *Don Juan* and Pushkin's *Eugene Onegin* drive home with dexterity and zest—but aside from an occasional flicker of irony, Nagibin does not incline to humor as a device. His characters take themselves and each other as seriously as Nagibin depicts them.[26]

In his reluctance to admit the comic into his prose Nagibin breaks with the long Russian tradition sustained by some of his favorite fictionists— Gogol, Dostoyevsky, and Chekhov. But in most respects Nagibin continues the traditional line in Russian prose, eschewing the experimental and aggressively modernist techniques that so dearly appeal to innovators like Aksyonov, Tertz, and Bitov.[27] Although he does not belong to the literary avant-garde, Nagibin does not reject its talented exponents. Nor does his traditionalism place him alongside the troglodytes of Soviet prose; in "The Peak of Success" and elsewhere, for instance, he frequently abandons conventional narrative for a modified stream of consciousness and has no qualms about disordering time sequence. If one judges Nagibin on the strength of his best works, one cannot deny him a permanent place in Russian letters as an adept practitioner of the short story. It is not unfair to say that Nagibin offers an example of a relatively rare phenomenon—some Western critics might even call it oxymoron—a good Soviet writer. Many readers in the Soviet Union consider him the best author of short stories alive today.

* * * * *

The selection of stories for the present volume was made with Nagibin's assistance, primarily though not exclusively on the basis of quality. So as to provide the reader with an accurate if general notion of Nagibin's development as a writer, the collection includes his best and most characteristic narratives from the 1950s, 1960s, and 1970s. Despite certain misgivings, I finally decided to omit Nagibin's earliest efforts and his war stories for the simple reason that they strike me as inferior to his maturer creations. Furthermore, the three decades from which the narratives are drawn are represented unequally: the emphasis on the 1970s seems justified by the availability of translations of the early fiction, which have appeared intermittently in the United States in journals and anthologies and in Russian in 1958 as a separate book. By contrast, his most recent work is known only to the Slavic specialist.

Steady contact with Nagibin's prose for over two years has persuaded me that its charm defies translation, for in the transition from Russian to English the muted richness of his language—and particularly the imagination he brings to his use of verbs and the fine distinctions he draws through the discriminating juxtaposition of near-synonyms—diminishes significantly. His epithets and verbs are much more evocative than their equivalents suggest.

Since seven individuals have contributed to the translation section of the volume, the English versions undoubtedly bear the imprint of seven different styles of translation. In my capacity as editor, I have checked each text carefully without, however, trying to eliminate the distinctive features of each translator's particular 'voice.' Responsibility for errors, awkward phrasing, or Briticisms naturally lies with me alone.

All notes appended to the translations and biography are mine unless indicated otherwise. They are intended to supply information that will clarify or enrich the reader's understanding of the stories and the commentary. Where such information appears to serve little purpose (e.g., details about villages or areas in the Meshchyora region, with which even many Russians are totally unfamiliar), it is excluded.

For all stories but the three published after 1973, the Russian text used is the two-volume 1973 edition, Iurii Nagibin, *Izbrannye proizvedenniia* v dvukh tomakh, M. 1973. Two of the post-1973 stories, "Elijah's Day" and "The Outsider," are translated from the collection *Berendeev les,* M. 1978, while the third, "The Runaway," is taken from *Nash sovremennik,* No. 10 (1978), 71-113.

Instead of following consistently any single transliteration system elaborated by Professor Shaw, I have opted for a combination of two in the interests of practicality. To enable readers with no knowledge of Russian to pronounce proper names as closely to the original as possible with a minimum of effort, I have adopted a modified form of Shaw's System I throughout. Shaw's System II has been used only for original titles of Russian works or publications and for bibliographical data that can be of interest or aid only to speakers of Russian. Hence Nagibin is Yury in the introduction, but Iurii in a bibliographical citation. Those names whose spelling has been established by convention, e. g., Krushchev, Rachmaninov, appear in their traditional form.

Russian punctuation has been altered to conform to standard American usage except in those cases where unorthodox punctuation seems inseparable from a specific stylistic effect, presumably intended by the author.

From the moment he learned of my wish to undertake this project Nagibin has been a model of eager cooperation, for which he has my most respectful gratitude. Thanks are also extended to everyone who helped in the preparation of the book: to Nagibin's wife Alla, to the translators and contributors, to Bozenna, Brit, Davey, and Nina—and to the American Enterprise Institute, which together with a grant from the National Endowment to the Humanities, provided working conditions conducive to the completion of the volume.

Washington D.C./Pittsburgh   Helena Goscilo
1980

Notes

1. Iurii Nagibin, "O svoem remesle," *Literaturnye razdum'ia* (M. 1977), pp. 72-3.

2. For a complete list of Nagibin's scripts and scenarios, see the comprehensive bibliography compiled by Ellen Cochrum, "A Bibliography of Works by and about Jurij Nagibin: 1940-1978," *Russian Language Journal,* XXXIII, No. 115 (1979), 159-160.

3. Nagibin claims that he had difficulties at first adjusting to the slow pace of the film set by Kurosawa, which must have affected the pace of the scenario too.

4. The 'write-it-backward' method was advocated by Edgar Allan Poe, who encouraged its usage as a preventative against a limp conclusion.

5. Nagibin, "O svoem remesle," pp. 17-18.

6. Nagibin, "O svoem remesle," pp. 5-6.

7. Joyce Carol Oates, "The Nature of Short Fiction; or the Nature of My Short Fiction," *Handbook of Short Story Writing,* ed. Frank A. Dickson & Sandra Smythe (Cincinnati, 1970), p. xii.

8. Nagibin, "O svoem remesle," p. 46.

9. As both a prosaist who forged his own inimitable language and a big-game hunter, Hemingway for a long time was the object of Nagibin's awed respect. In recent years, however, Nagibin increasingly has expressed qualms about some of Hemingway's values and pronouncements. See Nagibin's comments on *The Green Hills of Africa* in Iurii Nagibin, "Keniiskie zametki," *Pereulki moego detstva* (M. 1971), pp. 392-5.

10. See particularly the slim volume entitled *Literaturnye razdum'ia,* which contains general remarks about literature as a craft and chapters on Leskov, Chekhov, Andrey Platonov, and others.

11. I learned this fact from a writer friend of impeccable integrity in Moscow last year (1979).

12. Nagibin, "O svoem remesle," p. 15.

13. See the article by Richard N. Porter, "Jurij Nagibin's 'Istoricheskie rasskazy,'" *Russian Language Journal,* XXXIV, No. 118, 127-135, and the review by Munir Sendich, "Carskosel'skoe utro," *Russian Language Journal,* XXXIII, No. 115, 243-9.

14. Sendich's review gives a brief but helpful analysis of Nagibin's linguistic interpolations in these stories. Sendich, 247-9.

15. On the issue of sentimentalism, see note 24 below.

16. As exceptions to this rule, Western critics have cited "Light in the Window" and "The Khazar Ornament," published in *Literary Moscow* (1956). Nagibin's relatively unrestricted travels abroad, however, indicate that he enjoys the Soviet government's confidence.

17. N. Atarov, Introduction to Iurii Nagibin, *Izbrannye proizvedeniia* v dvukh tomakh (M. 1973), I, 14.

18. Richard N. Porter, "The Uneven Talent of Jurij Nagibin," *Russian Language Journal,* XXXII, No. 113 (1978), 104.

19. Iurii Nagibin, *Ostrov liubvi* (M. 1977), p. 438.

20. "But I know, the words formed in Voronov's mind, and the unpleasant feeling that had gripped him took on a clearly defined shape. It was an acute despondent envy, as oppressive as anger. He, Voronov, was a beggar beside this lad. He had been robbed of the most precious thing in life. He could have known joy, pain, anxiety and jealousy, even defeat—and he had preferred to all this the niggardly poverty of a peaceful life." Translated by Robert Daglish in Yury Nagibin, *Dreams* (M. 1958), p. 39.

21. Ruth Engelken, "Writing with Description," *Handbook of Short Story Writing,* p. 75.

22. Edith Wharton, *The Writing of Fiction* (New York/London, 1925), p. 37.

23. Porter, "The Uneven Talent of Jurij Nagibin," 108.

24. Nagibin himself calls this tendency "heightened sensitiveness, emotionalism" *(povyshennaia chuvstvitel'nost', emotsional'nost')* and sees it not as a defect, but as an inherent feature of the dominant current in Russian prose. To dub Soviet prose sentimental, he maintains, is to adopt a purely American stance. I strongly disagree, in the conviction that heightened emotion denotes an intensity of feeling that a given situation seems to warrant, whereas sentimentalism is the *excessive* indulgence in sentiment that errs more on the side of quantity than of degree.

25. Wharton, p. 45.

26.   Yet in person Nagibin reveals a lively, often dry, sense of humor that accounts for some of the appeal of his conversation. According to Nagibin, humor permeates many of his stories, e.g., "Elijah's Day" and "My Venice." I have not been able to find it.

27.   Nagibin perceives himself as belonging only partially to the 'classic' Russian tradition, pointing out that the inner monologues and time displacements as well as the speculative fantasy of his "modern fairytales" (e.g., "The Peak of Success") prevent him from fitting comfortably into the traditional mold. See Dragan Milivoević, "Nagibin's Views of American and Soviet Literature: An Interview," *Russian Language Journal*, XXXIII, No. 115 (1979), 128.

Biography

Yury Markovich Nagibin was born in Moscow on April 3, 1920, the only son of Ksenya Alekseyevna Konevskaya and Mark Yakovlevich Nagibin. His family lived in a large apartment building facing the corner of three streets, Armenian Lane (Armyansky pereulok), Cricket Lane (Sverchkovy pereulok), and Telegraph Lane (Telegrafny pereulok), a short distance from Clear Ponds (Chistye prudy). This is an old section of Moscow named after a pond located on the Boulevard Ring (Bulvarnoye Koltso), a broad thoroughfare that encircles the center of Moscow, creating a large park area. As a young boy, Nagibin spent his leisure hours boating in an old shallow dinghy, fishing, swimming, and diving from the piles. Here Nagibin began to experience nature as his classroom and second home, and he vividly describes this period in his book of childhood reminiscences, *Chistye prudy*.

Nagibin grew up under the influence of his mother and his paternal grandparents. By the time he was seven his mother had familiarized him with various stories by reading them aloud to him. Dumas's *Three Musketeers*[1] was the first book he tackled on his own, finding to his profound delight that the world created by Dumas was so clearly related to life as to make it difficult for him to distinguish fiction from reality.

Nagibin's father, an engineer-economist by profession, was rarely in Moscow, and his son seldom saw him. His earliest memories of his father go back to the long journeys he undertook with his mother across broad rivers and wide-open steppes, through villages and towns with strange-sounding names so as to keep in touch with the peripatetic Mark Yakovlevich. The boy learned his geography while keeping track of his father's moves from one part of the country to another to work on various construction sites. Young Nagibin used to brag to his friends about his father's incredible strength and courage, and this frequently-voiced pride in his father's toughness helped him to cope with his constant absence. Mark Yakovlevich's small height did not prevent him from participating in World War I from 1914 to 1917 and being decorated with two St. George Crosses, one of the higher badges of honor in the pre-Soviet army. The first

27

Cross was awarded for his role in an attack with bayonets, the second for replacing the commanding officer when the latter was killed in battle.

With his father gone from home so much of the time, Nagibin grew very close to his grandfather, a physician of some repute and skill. In fact, the word 'grandfather' still evokes many fond memories of learning to ice skate, hoisting himself up on gymnast's rings, and working out with weights. The growing youth would turn to his grandfather for his first man-to-man discussions about fights or the girls at school, and would listen for hours when his grandfather regaled him with stories from his own past. All that ended shortly before the boy turned ten: his grandfather died, bequeathing a sum of money to the remaining family members.

At about that time, Mrs. Colbert, a 'real' Englishwoman, appeared in the Nagibin household and the boy embarked on learning English. Although he never mastered the language completely, he learned and retained enough to be able to read English today. He can handle, though not without difficulty, Shakespeare, Dickens, Hemingway, Fitzgerald, Salinger, and George Painter's two-volume biography of Proust in the original, and in a lighter vein, admits to a fondness for Agatha Christie in English.[2]

Rummaging through his father's library one day, Nagibin came across a volume with the intriguing title of *Mémoires de Monsieur D'Artagnan*. A little earlier Nagibin had started studying German at school, and now he began reading the book laboriously in German; it dealt, after all, with his favorite literary hero already known to him in Russian from the reading sessions with his mother. However unconscious Nagibin may have been of it, literature was already molding his life.

At school Nagibin excelled in all subjects—a consequence of his having no particular preference for any one subject, he claims[3]—and seemed fond of languages. Like most other boys, he played soccer, and showed such an aptitude for the sport that his coach even foresaw a professional soccer career for him. But his mother, who by then had remarried, had other plans for her son. At her instigation, the boy's stepfather, the writer Yakov Semyonovich Rykachyov, persuaded Nagibin to write something.

His first story, about a class skiing trip, was very poor, and after reading it his stepfather did not encourage him to write any more. And yet Nagibin believes that his impulse to write dates from this first feeble attempt. He recalls: "With profound surprise I discovered how from the mere necessity of putting down on paper a few simple impressions of the day and of people I knew, all the emotions and observations connected with this unassuming exercise became strangely deeper and more extensive. I saw my school friends in a new light and began to notice the unexpectedly complex, subtle and intricate patterns of their relations."[4] He discovered, too, that writing meant learning to understand life, and this realization determined the course of his future literary path for the first twenty years of his career: not to invent, but to take everything from life became his creative rule. It was only much later that he cautiously allowed himself to rely more on his own imagination.

Whatever discovery this neophyte creative effort yielded, it failed to transform Nagibin instantly into a committed writer. After high school, he, like Chekhov and Bulgakov before him, decided on a medical profession. His contact with medical studies, however, was brief, and he soon enrolled as a student at the Institute of Cinematography. He did not abandon writing, though, and in 1940 his first story, "A Double Mistake" (Dvoinaia oshibka), was published in the popular magazine *Ogonyok*.

At the outbreak of World War II, Nagibin volunteered for front-line service. His knowledge of German enabled him to publish a German newspaper and to make frequent trips to the front with a mobile radio unit to conduct broadcasts in German to enemy soldiers. In his spare time he wrote stories about communications men, truck drivers, translators, political workers, and soldiers at the front. These narratives later were collected in the first anthology of his works to be published, *Man from the Front* (Chelovek s fronta, 1943). Toward the end of the war Nagibin suffered a contusion, but he remained with the Russian army until 1945 as a war correspondent for the newspaper *Trud* (Labor).

Obviously Nagibin's early prose must have made some impression on his fellow-writers, for while still at the front he was accepted to the Writers' Union.[5] The entire incident transpired with amazing simplicity. At the meeting for initiates in March 1942, one of Nagibin's war stories was read aloud and Aleksandr Fadeyev[6] recommended: "He's a writer; let's admit him into our Union."

Back in civilian life, Nagibin began working as a travelling correspondent for the newspaper *Socialist Farming* (Sotsialisticheskoe zemledelie). His assignment was to gather information about and impressions of village life. Although he had never studied farming or agriculture, he had first-hand experience of rural life, having spent his boyhood summers in the village. One of his trips to the village now was to play a significant role in his literary career.

In 1947 Nagibin happened to meet Tatiana Petrovna Diachenko, the chairwoman of a prosperous collective farm in the Kursk region. A severe drought had parched the Kursk lands the year before, disabling even the tractor-repairing stations. Collective farm workers were forced to plow the fields with their cows or, in extreme cases, to hitch themselves to the harnesses. Yet in the Kursk region near the town of Sudzha Nagibin suddenly stumbled onto a wealthy efficient farm where the people had everything; they ate geese and freshly-baked bread at a time when the surrounding countryside was lucky to have soured milk. It all seemed to be the result of good organization, management and selfless labor on the part of Diachenko, who inspired the kolkhoz workers.

Profoundly impressed by the woman's extraordinary ability to succeed so dramatically where others were failing, Nagibin first wrote a sketch of her life, which turned out so well that it was serialized into a three-day radio presentation. Then Nagibin shaped the sketch into a film scenario called "Women's Kingdom" (Bab'e tsarstvo). Next he reworked the screenplay into a long short story *(povest')* with the same title, after which it became a play, *The Madonnas from Sudzha* (Sudzhanskie madonny), which ran for ten years in the Lenin Communist Youth Theater (Teatr Leninskogo Komsomola). Finally, the story served as the basis for an opera entitled *Russian Women* (Russkie zhenshchiny) that was performed in the Kremlin Grand Palace. Later he incorporated some of the heroine's character traits and some of the motifs into another *povest'* about collective farm life called "Pages from the Life of Trubnikov" (Stranitsy zhizni Trubnikova), which he subsequently turned into a script for the film *The Chairman* (Predsedatel'). The movie caused quite a stir and Ulyanov, the leading actor,[7] won the Lenin Prize for his performance (1966). That pattern was to be repeated with a series of works which first saw the light of day as stories and soon after were transformed into largely successful films.

By the mid-fifties Nagibin had achieved some reputation as a writer, and a handful of his narratives, such as "Winter Oak" (Zimnii dub) and "Komarov," enjoyed immense popularity with the reading public. But then, as ever, Nagibin was constantly on the lookout for new material, and found precisely what he was searching for when a friend took him hunting to the Meshchyora region, a forested area dotted with lakes and situated on the border between Moscow and Ryazan, some 120 miles southeast of Moscow. To someone raised in the city, Meshchyora is a revelation. Its inhabitants lead a hand-to-mouth existence, and conditions are so harsh that the local peasants are forced to poach game and fish to survive. The heritage of want in the area persists so strongly that children have to quit school at the age of ten, particularly the boys, who are essential to the economy. A swamp that isolates its people from the rest of the world for months on end, Meshchyora is an ideal place for hunters, and they flock there from the capital during their free time, traveling the distance in several hours. But the separation between the permanent dwellers of Meshchyora and any city cannot be measured by these rabid sportsmen. A letter from Meshchyora to Moscow travels ten days, and only three individuals from the region have ever traveled to the capital, and even then they went because of army duty. Among this community of hardworking simple folk Nagibin discovered a hunter's paradise, became an enthusiastic hunter, and between 1954 and 1964 produced a cycle of thirteen stories about hunting and fishing

Faithful to the practice he had established in the formative stages of his career, Nagibin in the cycle relates only those episodes that he actually witnessed or heard reported by others. He even retains the real names of the places and people in Meshchyora: the villages of Podsvyate and Faleyevka, the river Pra and the Great Lake (Lake Velikoye); Anatoly Ivanovich Makarov, who functions as a moral standard of sorts against which others are measured, Dedok, the oldest hunter in the area, whose full name is Mikhail Semyonovich, and Petrak, the over-burdened family man who doggedly strives to curb Valka Kosoy's outrageous lies. Many of the characters appear in several stories: for instance, Anatoly Ivanovich is the protagonist of "The Decoy" (Podsadnaia utka), "The New House" (Novyi dom), "The Chase" (Pogonia), and "When Ducks Are in Season" (Kogda utki v pore); and in six other Meshchyora stories he either fulfills the role of secondary character or has participated in an incident that pertains to the current events. The repeated appearance of these well-defined personalities clearly enhances the unity of the cycle, and a certain sameness of style, narrative tone, and description of setting further binds the individual units together. "Elijah's Day," however, composed some seven years after the other stories in the group, stands apart. In it Nagibin revisits Podsvyatye and gains a different and disturbing perspective on its inhabitants during the celebration of Elijah's Day. A depressing orgy of senseless uncontrolled drunkenness, then an aftermath of bewildered shame, reveal to him a moral decay that he had not even suspected before. With this story, in which the idyll of the 1950s and 1960s has degenerated into debauchery, one gets the impression that a disillusioned Nagibin has put an end not only to his hunting days in Meshchyora but also to a phase of his literary development as the enthusiastic portrayer of that area, its population, and its mores.

After the Meshchyora period, Nagibin returned to the childhood theme, treating it in a rather more sophisticated fashion than he had in the *Chistye prudy* collection. These narratives, written over the years 1967-71, comprised the volume *Book of Childhood* (Kniga detstva).

Ever since his student days at the Institute of Cinematography, Nagibin maintained his connections with the moving picture industry. Starting with the 1950s, he was involved periodically in a variety of film projects, often recasting his own works into scenarios: *The Chairman* (Predsedatel'), based on *The Madonnas from Sudzha, The Night Guest* (Nochnoi gost'), based on the story with the same title, and *Komarov*, likewise based on an identically named narrative. With *Echo*, the order was reversed: the scenario materialized first, followed by the story. Some scenarios bore no direct relation to Nagibin's prose: *Chaikovsky,* the enthusiastically-received biography of the composer, and *Dersu Uzala,* the joint Soviet-Japanese production directed by Akira Kurosawa that received the American Academy Award for Best Foreign Language Film in 1975. By and large the films with which Nagibin has been affiliated in some way have fared well with the Soviet public.

When not engaged in writing, Nagibin loves to gather data for future stories. He has travelled widely both in the U.S.S.R. and throughout the rest of the world, gathering material wherever he goes. In 1961 he published a collection of travel impressions of Hungary, and at regular intervals has published extensive travel stories about Africa, Eastern Europe, Asia, and the Middle East. His more recent travelogues deal with writers, notably in Holland, Australia, Norway, and the United States, e.g., Arthur Hailey. Last year Nagibin visited the United States for two months, lecturing, giving interviews, and conducting seminars in universities across the country.[8] Some of his stories about that trip have already appeared in Soviet periodicals and he is currently working on a volume scheduled for 1982 entitled *Study of Foreign Travels* (Nauka dal'nikh stranstvii), which will include previously-published travelogues along with many new sketches.

Nagibin's professional activities keep him constantly on the go. Perhaps the absence of a large family enables him to keep up the remarkable pace that he accepts as a norm. His mother died in the mid-1970s and he has no children, though he does have a wife, Alla Grigoryevna. Nagibin has been married five times: one of his wives was the popular variety show dancer known on stage as Adelaida Vladimirovna Paratova. In 1960, he married Bella Akhmadulina, the controversial Russian-Tatar poetess. They were divorced in 1967, and the following year he wed Alla Grigoryevna, an intelligent and charming woman with a linguist's training, who helps Nagibin by taking care of the practical aspects of his life and by offering useful criticism of his work.

Today Nagibin occupies a solid, respected position in the Soviet literary world. Published in practically every literary journal and paper in the Soviet Union, he appears on television, attends various official functions, and gives interviews on a regular basis. Although he resides in the countryside outside of Moscow, he also owns a comfortable roomy apartment in the city; he lives inconspicuously, but well. His contacts with the West are many: in addition to travelling abroad frequently, he entertains foreigners extensively and generously at both his residence in the country and in the city.

A cultured and exceedingly well-informed individual, Nagibin can be an engaging and receptive conversationalist, quick to respond perceptively and often wittily to his interlocutor's comments. The humor that his prose lacks surfaces in his personal exchanges, while the sentimentalism that weakens some of his stories by contrast, never emerges. That occasional bathos is one of his failings Nagibin himself recognizes all too well. Sensible and clear-sighted in his judgments, Nagibin has the relatively rare ability to pinpoint the strengths and limitations of his own works, and dismisses several of his early stories as too syrupy (e.g., "The Night Before Battle" [Noch pered boem], which originally was slated for this volume, and which the editor was happy to exclude at Nagibin's request).

As he frequently iterates, time has wrought many changes in Nagibin; it has dispelled his illusions about the hunting that so enchanted him in his younger years—man should preserve life, he contends now, not destroy it—and it has brought him to a more passionate love of literature, art, and music. Perhaps the inner shift accounts partially for his increased concentration in the 1970s on a fictional treatment of famous composers and literati. What the 1980s hold for Nagibin is impossible to predict. To commemorate his sixtieth birthday in April 1980, the Soviets decided to publish a four-volume edition of his collected works. On the basis of that, at least, one can safely say that Nagibin's niche in the Soviet literary establishment is quite secure. What he plans to do from that position of security remains to be seen.

Ellen Cochrum

Notes

1. *Les trois mousquetaires* (1844) by Alexandre Dumas, père (1802-70) is the first of three swashbuckling pseudohistorical novels that chronicle the exploits of the four famous musketeers, D'Artagnan, Athos, Porthos, and Aramis. "L'action et l'amour" were the staples of all three volumes, both treated with immense gusto and historical inaccuracy.

2. Nagibin volunteered the information during an informal chat with me in March 1979 at the University of Pittsburgh.

3. Yuri Nagibin, "A Word About Myself," preface to "Somewhere Near the Conservatoire," *Soviet Literature,* No. 8 (1974), 27.

4. Ibid.

5. The Writers' Union (Soiuz pisatelei) is a government-sponsored organization of Soviet writers, conceived in 1932 and created in 1934. It fully supports and enforces to the best of its ability decisions made by the Party, meets regularly to discuss politico-literary questions, etc.

6. Aleksandr A. Fadeyev (1901-56), author of *The Rout* (Razgrom 1927) and *The Young Guard* (Molodaia gvardiia 1945), a leader of RAPP (1926-32), and secretary of the Writer's Union from 1946 to 1954, committed suicide in 1956

7. Mikhail A. Ulyanov (1927-   ) is a Soviet actor who from 1950 has been a member of the Vakhtangov Theater, played the title role in a staging of Shakespeare's *Richard III,* and starred in such films as *The Brothers Karamazov* and *Flight* (Beg).

8. For Nagibin's discussion of the trip, various American universities' reaction to his visit, a complete bibliography of his works and commentary on them, an interview with him, and an essay on his latest stories, see *Russian Language Journal,* Vol. XXXIII, No. 115 (1979), 99-204.

Winter Oak

The snow that had fallen during the night covered the narrow path leading from Uvarovka to the school, and its course could be surmised only by the faint broken shadow on the glistening carpet of snow. The teacher trod cautiously in her small fur-trimmed boots, ready to withdraw her foot if the snow proved treacherous.

It was only a half-kilometer to the school, and the teacher had merely thrown a short fur jacket over her shoulders, and tied a light woollen kerchief on her head. It was bitter cold, and there was a fierce wind besides, which swept the freshly-fallen snow off the frozen snow crust and showered her with it from head to foot. But the twenty-four-year-old teacher liked all that. She liked it when the frost bit her nose and cheeks, when the wind blew under her fur jacket and stung her body with the cold. Turning her back to the wind, she saw behind her the thick footprints of her pointed shoes, like the tracks of some wild animal, and that, too, appealed to her.

The fresh January morning, saturated with light, awakened in her joyful thoughts about life and about herself. It was only two years since she'd come from college, and already she'd acquired the reputation of a competent, experienced teacher of Russian. They knew and appreciated her everywhere—in Uvarovka, Kuzminky, Black Gully, the peat settlement, and the stud farm—and they respectfully called her Anna Vasilyevna.

A man was coming across the field in her direction. "What if he won't step aside to let me by?" thought Anna Vasilyevna with lively apprehension. "Two people can't fit onto the path, and if you step aside you sink into the snow in a second." But she knew inwardly that there wasn't a person in the district who wouldn't step aside for the teacher from Uvarovka

They drew level. It was Frolov, a warden at the stud farm.

"Good morning, Anna Vasilyevna!" Frolov raised his fur hat above his solid, close-cropped head.

"What are you doing! Put it back on, it's freezing!"

Frolov probably wanted to pull his fur hat over his eyes himself, but now he delayed on purpose, wanting to show that the cold didn't affect him at all. A sheepskin coat fitted his trim light body snugly, and in his hand he held a slender snake-like whip with which he kept hitting his white felt boots, which were turned down below the knee.

"How's my Lyosha? He's not acting up?" Frolov asked deferentially.

"Of course he is. All normal children act up. Just so it doesn't go too far," replied Anna Vasilyevna, conscious of her pedagogical experience.

Frolov grinned:

"My Lyoshka's quiet, he takes after his father!"

He stepped aside and, sinking up to his knees in the snow, he looked no taller than a fifth-grader. Anna Vasilyevna nodded condescendingly to him and went on her way...

The two-story building, with its wide windows painted with frost, stood behind a low fence right beside the highway; its red walls cast a reddish light on the snow all the way up to the highway. The school had been built on the road on the side away from Uvarovka because it was attended by children from all around: from the nearby villages, from the stud farm, from the oilworkers' sanatorium, and from the distant peat settlement. And now along the highway from both directions hoods, kerchiefs, caps, hats, earmuffs, and bashlyks streamed toward the school gates.

"Good morning, Anna Vasilyevna!" sounded every second, some of the greetings ringing and clear, others muffled and barely audible beneath the scarves and kerchiefs bundled up to the eyes.

Anna Vasilyevna's first lesson was with the fifth-grade "A" group. The shrill bell signalling the beginning of classes hadn't ceased ringing when Anna Vasilyevna entered the classroom. The children rose together, greeted her, and sat down in their seats. It took a while for it to get quiet. Desk tops banged, benches creaked, someone sighed loudly, evidently bidding farewell to the carefree morning mood.

"Today we'll finish analyzing parts of speech..."

The class grew quiet, and one could hear a heavy truck crawling and skidding along the highway.

Anna Vasilyevna remembered how nervous she used to get the previous year before classes began, and she used to repeat to herself like a schoolgirl during an exam, "A noun is a part of speech... a noun is a part of speech..." And she also remembered how a strange fear had tormented her: what if they won't understand?

Anna Vasilyevna smiled at the recollection, adjusted the pin in her heavy knot of hair, and in a calm, even voice, feeling her calmness like a warmth through her body, began:

"A noun is a part of speech that denotes an object. In grammar an object is the name for anything about which one can ask who or what it is. For example: 'Who is he?' 'A student.' Or 'What is it?' 'A book' . . ."

"Can I come in?"

In the half-open doorway stood a small figure in worn felt boots on which sparkles of melting frost were dissolving. His round face, stung by the bitter cold, glowed as though rubbed with beets, and his eyebrows were silvered with frost.

"Late again, Savushkin?" Like the majority of young teachers, Anna Vasilyevna liked to be strict, but right now her question sounded almost plaintive.

Interpreting the teacher's words as permission to enter the classroom, Savushkin quickly stole to his seat. Anna Vasilyevna saw the boy put his oilskin bag in the desk and ask his neighbor something without turning his head—probably what she was explaining.

Savushkin's lateness grieved Anna Vasilyevna as an annoying little incident that ruined a day which had begun well. The geography teacher, a small, dried-up old lady who resembled a night moth, had complained to her that Savushkin kept coming in late. She complained a lot in general— about the noise in the classroom, the students' inattentiveness. "The first morning lessons are so difficult!" the old woman had sighed. "Yes, for those who can't hold their students' attention and make their lessons interesting," Anna Vasilyevna had thought then with self-assurance, and had offered to change hours with her. Now she felt guilty before the old woman who was perceptive enough to have sensed a challenge and a reproach in Ann Vasilyevna's obliging offer.

"Is everything clear?" Anna Vasilyevna addressed the class.

"Yes! . . . Yes! . . . " the children chorused in response.

"Fine. Then give me examples."

It was very quiet for a few seconds, then someone said hesitantly: "Cat."

"Right," said Anna Vasilyevna, instantly recalling that the year before the first example had also been "cat." And then all bonds seemed to break loose:

"Window! Table! House! Road!"

"Right," said Anna Vasilyevna.

The class seethed with happy excitement. Anna Vasilyevna was surprised at the joy with which the children named objects that were familiar to them as though they perceived a new, unusual significance in them. The range of examples kept expanding, but during the first moments the children stuck to the most familiar tangible things: wheel . . . tractor . . . well . . . starling's nest . . .

But from a desk in the back where fat Vasyatka was sitting there came the thin but insistent sound of:

"Tack . . . tack . . . tack . . . "

And someone said tentatively:

"Town . . . "

"Town—good!" Anna Vasilyevna approved.

And then they were off:

"Street . . . Subway . . . Tram . . . Film . . . "

"That'll do," said Anna Vasilyevna, "I can see you understand it."

The voices died down somehow reluctantly; only fat Vasyatka still kept on droning his unacknowledged "tack." And suddenly, as if roused from sleep, Savushkin rose from his desk and cried out clearly:

"Winter oak!"

The children burst out laughing.

"Quiet!" Anna Vasilyevna slapped her palm on the desk.

"Winter oak!" Savushkin repeated, without noticing either his classmates' laughter or the teacher's peremptory shout. He said it differently from the other students. The words burst from his heart like a confession, like a joyful mystery which his brimming heart hadn't the strength to hold back.

Anna Vasilyevna couldn't understand his strange excitement, and hiding her irritation with difficulty, she said:

"Why 'winter'? Simply 'oak'!"

"What's an oak! A winter oak, now that's a real noun!"

"Sit down, Savushkin. That's what lateness does. 'Oak' is a noun, but we haven't yet studied what 'winter' is. Be so good as to come to the teachers' room during the main break."

"So much for your winter oak!" tittered someone at the back desk.

Savushkin sat down, smiling at his own thoughts, totally unaffected by the teacher's threat.

"A difficult boy," thought Anna Vasilyevna.

The lesson continued.

"Sit down," said Anna Vasilyevna when Savushkin entered the teachers' room.

The boy sank into the soft armchair with pleasure and rocked several times on its springs.

"Be so good as to explain why you invariably come late to school."

"I really don't know, Anna Vasilyevna." He spread his hands in an adult gesture. "I leave a whole hour before school starts."

How difficult it was to arrive at the truth in the simplest matter. Many of the children lived much farther away than Savushkin, and yet none of them spent more than an hour getting there.

"You live in Kuzminky?"

"No, at the sanatorium."

"And you're not ashamed to say that you leave an hour before class? It's a fifteen-minute walk from the sanatorium to the highway, and it doesn't take more than half an hour to get here from the highway."

"But I don't use the highway. I take a short cut, throughn the forest," said Savushkin as though he himself was quite surprised at the fact.

"'Through,' not 'throughn,'" Anna Vasilyevna corrected him mechanically.

She suddenly felt upset and sad, as she always did when she came up against a child's lies. She remained silent, hoping that Savushkin would say: "I'm sorry, Anna Vasilyevna, I got carried away playing snowballs with the other kids,"—or something just as simple and ingenuous, but he only regarded her with his big gray eyes as if to say, "So we've cleared it all up. What else do you want from me?"

"It's sad, Savushkin, very sad! I'll have to talk with your parents."

"There's only my mother, Anna Vasilyevna," Savushkin smiled.

Anna Vasilyevna blushed slightly. She remembered Savushkin's mother—"a shower nurse," as her son called her. She worked at the sanatorium hydrotherapy section—a thin timid-looking woman with hands that were white and flaccid, as though made of cloth, because of the hot water. She was alone (her husband had been killed during World War II), and she fed and brought up three other children besides Kolya.

Savushkina undoubtedly had enough worries without this business.

"Do come, Anna Vasilyevna, she'll be glad to see you!"

"Unfortunately, nothing of what I have to say will make her glad. Does she have the morning shift?"

"No, the second, starting at three,"

"Very well, then. I finish at two. You'll take me there after class..."

The path along which Savushkin led Anna Vasilyevna started right at the back of the school grounds. As soon as they entered the forest and the heavily snow-laden fir branches closed behind them, they were transported into another, enchanted world of peace and quiet. The magpies and crows flying from tree to tree shook the branches, knocked off the cones, and from time to time broke off the brittle dry twigs that they caught with their wings. But nothing made any sound.

It was totally white all around. Only high up the crowns of the tall weeping birches tossed by the wind stood out, and the slender branches seemed drawn in Indian ink on the blue mirror-like surface of the sky.

The path ran alongside a stream—now on a level with it, obediently following all the windings of its course, now climbing up high to wind along the sheer steep slope.

Occasionally the trees would part to expose sunlit cheery clearings, crisscrossed with hares' tracks that resembled a watchchain. There were larger tracks too, in the form of a shamrock, which belonged to some large animal. The tracks led into the innermost depths of the forest, to the wind-fallen wood.

"An elk's been through here!" said Savushkin, as though he were speaking of a good acquaintance, when he saw Anna Vasilyevna's interest in the tracks. "Don't be frightened," he added in response to the glance the teacher cast at the dense forest. "Elks are peaceful."

"You've seen one?" Anna Vasilyevna asked excitedly.

"An elk? A real live one?" Savushkin sighed. "No, I never had the chance to. I've seen his little pellets."

"What?"

"Droppings," Savushkin explained shyly.

Gliding under the arch of a bowed willow, the path ran down to the stream again. In places the stream was covered by a thick blanket of snow, in others, it was trapped in a sheer armor of ice, and occasionally amid the ice and snow free-flowing water peeped out with dark eyes.

"Why isn't it completely frozen?" asked Anna Vasilyevna.

"There are warm springs gushing in it. Look, can you see them spurting?"

Bending over the unfrozen patch of water, Anna Vasilyevna made out a thin thread extending from the bottom; it burst into tiny bubbles without reaching the water's surface. The very slender stem with its small bubbles resembled a lily of the valley.

"There are simply tons of these springs here!" said Savushkin enthusiastically. "That's why the stream runs even under the snow."

He brushed the snow aside, and some pitch-black but transparent water became visible.

Anna Vasilyevna noticed that the snow that fell in the water didn't melt, but thickened instantly and sagged in the water like gelatinous greenish algae. She liked that so much that she started knocking snow into the water with the toe of her boot, feeling happy when especially intricate shapes formed from a large lump of snow. She'd begun enjoying herself, and didn't immediately notice that Savushkin had gone on and was waiting for her. He'd sat down high in the fork of a branch that hung over the stream. Anna Vasilyevna caught up with Savushkin. At that point the activity of the warm springs ended; the stream was covered with a thin film of ice. Swift light shadows rushed about along its marbled surface.

"Look how thin the ice is, you can even see the current!"

"What do you mean, Anna Vasilyevna! I rocked the branch, and that's the shadow moving."

Anna Vasilyevna held her tongue. Perhaps here in the forest she'd do well to keep quiet.

Savushkin set off again, walking in front of the teacher, bending slightly and gazing about him concentratedly.

And the forest led them on and on with its complicated tangled paths. There seemed no end to the trees, snowdrifts, silence, and twilight shot through with sunshine.

In the distance a smoky blue chink appeared unexpectedly. The trees thinned out and it became open and fresh. And then the chink turned into a wide clear space which appeared in front of them flooded with sunlight; something glittered, sparkled, and warmed with icy stars.

The path skirted a nut bush and the forest immediately opened up in all directions. In the midst of the clearing, in white glistening garments, stood an oak as enormous and magnificent as a cathedral. The trees seemed to part respectfully to allow their older companion to spread out in full force. Its lower branches stretched out in a tent over the clearing. The snow had filled the deep crevices of the bark, and the trunk, which was so wide that it would have taken three men to get their arms around it, looked as if it were shot through with silver thread. It had hardly shed any of the foliage which had dried up during the fall; the oak was covered with snow-capped leaves to the very top.

"There it is, the winter oak!"

Anna Vasilyevna stepped timidly toward the oak and the mighty magnanimous forest sentinel quietly shook a branch to her in greeting.

Totally unaware of what was passing in his teacher's heart, Savushkin was messing about at the foot of the oak, treating the oak simply as his old acquaintance.

"Look, Anna Vasilyevna!"

With an effort he pushed aside a lump of snow whose underside was plastered with earth and the remains of rotting grass. There in the hole lay a little ball wrapped in rotting leaves as thin as a cobweb. Sharp points of needles protruded through the leaves, and Anna Vasilyevna guessed that it was a hedgehog.

"He's wrapped himself up well!"

Savushkin carefully covered the hedgehog with its modest blanket. Then he dug up the snow at another root. A tiny grotto with a fringe of icicles on its opening was revealed. A brown frog was sitting in it as if it were made of cardboard; its skin, tightly stretched along its bones, looked as though it were lacquered. Savushkin touched the frog, but it didn't stir.

"It's pretending it's dead," Savushkin laughed, "But just let the sun warm it up a bit, and boy, will it jump!"

He continued guiding Anna Vasilyevna through his world. There were many other guests who'd taken shelter at the foot of the oak: bugs, lizards, insects. Some were hiding under the roots, other had burrowed in the cracks of the bark; grown thin, as though they were hollow, they were hibernating through the winter. The powerful tree, brimming with life, had gathered around itself so much vital warmth that the poor creatures couldn't have found themselves a better dwelling. Anna Vasilyevna was staring with joyous interest at the secret life of the forest, so unfamiliar to her, when she heard Savushkin's anxious exclamation:

"Oh, we'll be too late to catch mother!"

Anna Vasilyevna quickly lifted her hand to look at her watch—it was a quarter past three. She felt as though she were caught in a trap. And mentally begging the oak forgiveness for her petty human deceit, she said:

"Well, Savushkin, that only shows that a short cut isn't necessarily the best way. You'll have to start taking the highway."

Savushkin didn't answer, merely lowering his head.

"My God!" Anna Vasilyevna thought painfully, "What clearer way of admitting my impotence?" She remembered that day's class and all her other classes: how poor, dry, and cold were her comments on the word, on language, on those things without which man, helpless in his feelings, is mute before the world—on their beautiful language, which was as fresh, beautiful, and rich as life was bounteous and beautiful.

And she considered herself a competent teacher! She'd taken no more than one stride, perhaps, along the path for which a whole lifetime isn't sufficient. And where was it, this path? To find it wasn't simple or easy, like finding the key to a miser's casket. But in the joy with which the children had yelled out "tractor," "well," and "starling's nest," a joy she now understood, the first landmark was dimly visible to her.

"Thank you for the walk, Savushkin. Of course, you can take this route too."

"Thank you, Anna Vasilyevna!"

Savushkin blushed: he badly wanted to tell the teacher that he'd never be late again, but he was afraid of lying. He raised the collar of his jacket and pulled the cap with earflaps lower over his eyes.

"I'll walk you . . . "

"There's no need, Savushkin, I'll make it by myself."

He glanced doubtfully at the teacher, then picked up a stick from the ground and breaking off its bent end, held it out to Anna Vasilyevna.

"If an elk jumps out, let him have it across the back and he'll run for all he's worth. Better still, simply wave the stick, and that'll be enough for him. Or else he'll get offended and leave the forest for good."

"All right, Savushkin, I won't hit him."

After she'd gone a short distance Anna Vasilyevna for the last time glanced around at the oak, lightly pink in the rays of the sunset, and saw a small dark figure at the foot of it: Savushkin hadn't left, he was watching over his teacher from a distance. And suddenly Anna Vasilyevna realized that the most wonderful thing in the forest wasn't the winter oak, but the small person in the worn felt boots and the patched cheap clothes, the son of a shower nurse and a soldier who'd perished for his country—a marvellous and mysterious citizen of the future.

She waved her hand to him and quietly made her way along the winding path.

1953   Translated by Helena Goscilo

The original ("Zimnii dub") first appeared in *Novyi mir,* No. 3 (1953), 114-120. The present translation is of the edition included in the two-volume collection, Iurii Nagibin, *Izbrannye proizvedeniia* v dvukh tomakh (M. 1973), I, 34-43.

The Night Guest

He arrived late in the evening, almost at night. The door swung open, the black wedge of night blew in a cold wind, shadows wavered on the walls as though all the objects in the room had all at once swayed back from the door, and the gust of wind swept in his lean, graceful figure, clad in a short coat and narrow striped slacks.

There was nothing surprising about his arrival at our lodge on the lake. During the early spring every dwelling around Pleshcheyev Lake, down to a broken-down barn or a dugout half-flooded with melted snow, drew the fishermen. Besides, our cottage stood right on the water's edge, close to the mouth of the stream where the roach came to spawn. I too had arrived about a week earlier, drawn by the caressing light of the two small windows behind the dense wattle-fence of alder undergrowth. That's how my roommate, the elderly taciturn Nikolay Semyonoich, an inveterate fisherman, also came there. Many other people also stopped by the place at this time. But there was a difference in the way they all arrived. Each new guest first stamped about in the entrance hall for a long time, knocking the dirt off his boots and shaking out his wet clothes; the heavy oilskin waterproof that was obligatory apparel for every real fisherman rustled with a tinny sound as he shrugged out of it. At the sound, Granny Julia, the mistress of the cottage, would come out into the entrance hall with a candle-end, shielding the thin tongue of flame with her hand. After a short exchange they came to an agreement, the door opened, and first one saw a rod, nets, and other fishing gear, then the owner of the tackle himself, shuddering, chilled through, with a face red from the wind. Depositing his tackle in a corner and smiling at the samovar that never left the table in the evening, the fisherman said in a deep voice, "Tea and sugar!"—laid out his food supplies, and started drinking down glass after glass of tea.

But this particular late guest materialized without a sound, without any preparation, and without any luggage whatsoever, as though a gust of wind had blown him into the house like a rotten leaf, a piece of paper, or a dry blade of grass. And his whole appearance in his light city clothes gave the impression of flightiness, of his not being firmly attached to the ground.

The guest, however, immediately explained the reason for his rather strange appearance. He'd been driving by car with a group to the Nerl area to fish for perch, but some passerby had told them that the road there was terrible—nothing but potholes, dirt, and marshes. "Now, I came along to fish, not to push a car," explained the guest with a smile. And when he noticed the lights of our house, he left his friends: let them worry about getting there, if that's what they wanted; he'd be happy to fish here.

"What are you planning to fish with?" Nikolay Semyonovich asked the guest. "Your pants?"

There was a distinct tinge of hostility in his question, which surprised me. In the week I'd spent with him I'd become convinced that my neighbor was utterly indifferent to everything except fishing. He never sought any contact with anybody—including the hostesses, me, and the fishermen who were staying there. All he did was fish. Elderly—close to fifty—solidly built, massive, weather-beaten, with eyebrows that resembled mustaches, he succeeded in making himself totally unobtrusive. We had immediately pooled our food supplies, we slept in the same bed, went fishing together, froze and shivered together in the wind, but I didn't know his profession, nor where he worked or lived. I only knew that in the Fishermen's Sports Club he was a specialist in pike perch. That's a special characteristic of human relations in fishing and hunting. A man can share his possessions down to the last item (except, of course, live bait and cartridges), he can pull you out of the icy water at risk to his own health, but sometimes you won't even know his name. And why should you—all are equal before the god of the hunt.

Upon hearing the abrupt question coming from the shadowy corner of the room, the guest stretched out his neck in embarrassment, as though he felt choked, and something childishly helpless flashed in his light blue, slightly protruberant eyes.

"Surely someone must have a spare rod," he said dispiritedly.

The mild blueness of his eyes instantly settled the question. I immediately offered him the choice of one of my rods. He selected a short flexible rod with a nylon line, a feather-float and a small sharp hook.

"If you could give me another hook," he said plaintively, "They come off so easily . . ."

I had a lot of those too. I gave him an extra line with hook, float, and sinker, and several more hooks of various sizes. The guest cheered up at once, and exclaimed, "There are good people in the world!" and quickly took off his coat, revealing a woollen jacket with a leather back—a trifle worn, but elegant.

And he wasn't bad-looking himself: slender, lean, with long dark hair brushed back, and a finely-shaped bony nose. Only his mouth flawed his looks—it was too small and narrow-lipped, like the seam on a fold; it lent his face an old-womanish look. But when the guest smiled, he revealed two rows of strong white teeth. His age was uncertain: anywhere from thirty to forty. He was either a well-preserved mature man or a somewhat worn young one.

Feeling at home and taking a good look around in the dimness—the room was illuminated by a weak kerosene lamp—the guest exclaimed:

"But this is really a Biblical setup! Only the old Dutch masters knew how to convey this wonderful crowding together of people and animals!..."

And in fact it was crowded in the lodge. A space of ten square meters, of which the Russian stove took up a good third, accommodated the old hostess, her older daughter with her three children, and us, the lodgers. Penned in behind a plywood partition, a calf was breathing noisily; two long-legged chickens and a rooster without a tail roamed among the pots and pans, their claws tapping loudly.

"Won—derful!" Granny Julia picked up on the guest's exclamation. She was standing by the stove, bent over the boiling samovar, and in the dimness one could see her fiery black eyes, which the years hadn't cooled, sparkling. "Fancy saying won—derful!..." And the old woman burst out laughing, so that the wrinkles on her face moved in a lively fashion.

Her daughter Katerina echoed her mother's laughter. She was lying on the bed, covered up to her chin with a patchwork blanket. The children looked at their mother and grandmother, then gave a laugh too.

"We all have a strong character, that's why we can stand it," continued the old woman. "Anyone else would have gone under a long time ago!"... And she burst out laughing unrestrainedly until her eyes filled with tears.

I already knew that now she'd start telling the story of how all her family came to be crowded together in such a small place according to the saying "the more the merrier." She regaled practically every guest with the story, apparently deriving some satisfaction from it.

Granny Julia had gotten the cottage from her late husband, the lake watchman. Until recently she'd lived there along with her younger daughter Lyuba. Lyuba wasn't home now; she'd cycled over to see her boyfriend, who was serving in a sapper unit stationed nearby. Katerina, the older daughter, had lived with her husband in an apartment in the peat settlement. In short, they'd had a lot of room. But about a year ago Katerina's husband had taken up with a woman from the settlement and when Katerina found out about it, she took the children and moved in with her mother. She abandoned everything: the apartment, the housekeeping, and the estate. She started working as a tie-layer on the narrow-gauge railway. It was a five-kilometer walk to work and the same distance back. Her husband probably thought that she wouldn't be able to stand it for long, and decided to stand firm and wait it out. When he realized that her decision was firm, he came to ask her forgiveness. But Katerina was deaf to his pleas...

When Granny Julia reached this point in her narrative, the guest raised his eyelids with their sparse lashes in alarm and exclaimed:

"That's really going too far! I'd have gone back in her place!"

"But she's strong-willed!" the old woman informed him happily. "It's all right, we'll be patient for now, and then—who knows, maybe she'll get a stone mansion! Right, daughter?"

Katerina didn't answer, merely laughing as she wrapped the blanket tighter around her.

"In other words, stick to your guns, even if you burst!"

"That's right! Ah, you're a lively guest!... What's your name?" asked the old woman, wiping her tears with a corner of the kerchief on her head.

"My name's simple, Granny, but you won't be able to say it without teeth. Call me Pal Palych..."

"That's fine with me! What's your job?"

"You're inquisitive, Granny," replied the guest with a gentle smile. "Look, the samovar will boil over..."

"That's right, too! Pull up a chair, Pal Palych, and have some hot tea!" And lifting the humming samovar that was whistling faintly off the floor with a vigorous movement, the old woman set it on the table.

"Tea—that's marvellous!" said Pal Palych joyfully. "And I have a treat for you!..." He took a paper bag of candy out of his pocket and started passing it around to all those present. "'Golden Key,' I love this candy. Take some, Granny, take some and give it to the kids. Grab a few, little feller!..." He then approached Nikolay Semyonovich, who was puffing away gloomily in the corner. "Take some to suck on—it's the best cure for smoking!..."

"But I'm not planning to give up smoking," was the rather ungracious response.

"To each his own!" said Pal Palych goodnaturedly and with a sweeping movement spilled the remaining candy out of the bag onto the table. "Help yourselves!" he said to all those present in the room.

There was no doubt that apart from the candy he had nothing to eat with him. He'd shared all he had so generously and easily that it was impossible not to reciprocate. I didn't bother asking my roommate's permission and laid out all our food supplies on the table: canned food, pork brisket, sausage, butter, and sugar.

"Oh, this is great!" Pal Palych rubbed his hands with joy. "Come on, my dear hostesses, let's get to it!"

"You eat, we'll eat later," replied Granny Julia.

"No arguments!" retorted Pal Palych firmly. "Or else we won't eat either!..."

For some reason it had become the custom for our hostesses to eat supper after we had ours. We'd thought that they found it more convenient and hadn't tried to change the established order of things. But seeing how willingly Granny Julia yielded to Pal Palych's persuasions, with what gay eagerness she drew her stool up to the table, I had doubts about how right the previous arrangements had been. Katerina also didn't need much cajoling; she quickly pulled her slender light body off the bed, adjusted her dress with an imperceptible movement, smoothed her hair, and sat down at the table.

Pal Palych took a knife out of his pocket and started deftly spreading the sandwiches. Sipping from the saucer that she held in her widespread five fingers, Granny Julia told her responsive guest the facts of her life.

"We bought a cow last year. We got it cheap, and it was with calf. We don't need it ourselves, but you can understand the children do," said the old woman, her startlingly lively young eyes sparkling. "We built a cattleshed for it, but there wasn't room for the calf, so we had to squeeze it in here. If we had a man in the house it'd be different, but you know womenfolk have no gift for carpentry. But I tell you, that's all right. The Town Soviet promised Katerina to help with the building. Come see us in a year, be sure to come, and you'll see how well we're living then. Isn't that right, Katerina?"

As usual, Katerina only answered with a burst of her quick, quiet, shy laughter, and looked away. In her silence, her reserve, and the laughter that came so easily to her lips, one sensed an integrated and unspoiled nature.

"So you'll come?" said Granny Julia again, as though they were talking about an urgent matter.

But Pal Palych was no longer listening. He was gazing as though enchanted through the window at the black expanse of lake which was live with wisps of red flame. The fires drifted slowly over the lake like mobile airborne campfires.

"What are those mysterious lamps?" asked Pal Palych.

"Those are the men who went out with torches," replied Granny Julia.

A ragged uneven flame flared up not far from the house. The flame left the ground, rose in the air, and whirled about in long tongues of fire, then suddenly, as though giving up, sank, crept up around an invisible focal point, and was transformed into the strong steady light of a torch. Under it were outlined two figures: a man and a young boy. They moved slowly along the black oily water, and soon it was possible to make out that the young boy was carrying the torch on a long punting pole, pressing the other end of the pole against his stomach. The fire was reflected in the water in a narrow reddish circle, and at intervals the man stabbed the circle of light with a fish spear. With a measured, solemn step they passed by the windows and vanished from sight.

"Listen, there's something mystical in this!" said Pal Palych ecstatically. "One would think they're performing some ritualistic act!... Ah, how I wish I could try it!"

"Why can't you?" said Granny Julia gaily. "We have a fish spear. True, it's wide, for pike, but that's all right—the roach are big right now, and I saw the 'cage' in the attic recently. And there's tons of resin wood in the entrance hall. I find it very good to use as kindling."

"Oh, do let's arrange it, do let's!" Pal Palych clapped his hands.

"Mind, if the guards catch you, they'll fine you and take away your fishing gear," observed Nikolay Semyonovich from his corner.

"But why—it's so beautiful!"

"It's forbidden to spear fish here."

"But we'll only try it a bit!" said Pal Palych in a childlike voice. "It's not the fish that appeal to me, but the strange nocturnal beauty of the spectacle!..."

I've seldom met such a lively responsive old woman as Granny Julia. So as to please a guest who'd caught her fancy she mobilized the entire household. There was Katerina dragging an old torn 'cage' from the attic— a metallic cage attached to a long pole; there was Katerina's older daughter carrying resin wood—finely-chopped pine root stems—from the entrance hall in her skirt; and Granny Julia herself was cutting up with a kitchen knife an old galosh, which is always placed in the resin wood to make the torch burn better. In a few minutes everything was ready, the fish spear was sharpened, the cage stuffed to capacity with resin wood and pieces of rubber from the galosh. And then we realized that PalPalych had nothing suitable to wear for fishing. He himself drew attention to the sad fact with a comically mournful expression.

"That's no problem!" Granny Julia smiled, "Nikolay Semyonovich has some extra boots!"

In fact, Nikolay Semyonovich did have some waist-high boots of rubberized silk that he never used, preferring his ordinary tarpaulin boots with their Wellington rubber soles. In response to our request, he growled:

"You're welcome to them." And Pal Palych pulled on the unusual light-weight boots with thick rubber soles, elegantly fastening the laces crisscross.

Granny Julia made him put on a rather greasy but warm padded jacket, and hung the fishbag around his neck.

And at that point our venture almost fell through.

Pal Palych had already taken the fish spear in his hand, I'd lifted the heavy clumsy cage, when suddenly the door swung open and Granny Julia's younger daughter Lyuba walked in, with her bicycle on her shoulder. As usual, she wore a thick padded jacket and a woollen kerchief was wound around her head and entwined around her neck; she had soft goatskin boots on her feet, which were shoved into galoshes. Lyuba greeted all of us, hung her bicycle on its hook, removed her boots, took off her padded jacket, and with her customary rapid movements unwound her kerchief and tossed it on the stove, emerging from her rough clothing like a butterfly from its cocoon. This sight was one of the small miracles of our life there. Slender, strong, with a delicate and rather indolently insolent face, Lyuba was so beautiful that when she simply looked at you and smiled, you wanted to thank her as if for a favor.

Pal Palych put the fish spear aside.

"Listen," he said seriously and sincerely, "You should live in Moscow!"

"As if people can live only in Moscow!" Lyuba smiled lazily. She knew the uncalculated power of her charm and was used to not being surprised by anything. "We like it fine here!"

"Fine, you say?" Granny Julia echoed peevishly. "And yet you're planning to go to the virgin soil region."

"And I will go," said Lyuba defiantly, "I'll wait until Vasily can come, and we'll go together."

"No, Moscow's the only place for a girl like you," replied Pal Palych with conviction.

"You don't say! ... " drawled Lyuba and went behind the stove to get a drink of water from the tub.

Pal Palych followed her.

"Your house is full of surprises," came his excited voice. "I feel as though I've stepped into a fairy tale! You're a delightful little fairy... "

Lyuba didn't make any effort to be quick and clever. To all his flowery speeches, in between sips of water—which was very cold—she answered in a drawl,

"You don't say! ... "

"Now I'm convinced I didn't leave the car and my friends by chance when I saw the lights from your house. Some unknown power was driving me. It's possible that somewhere in my subconscious I knew I'd meet you... "

"Hey, young man!" Nikolay Semyonovich's loud voice was heard. "I thought you were getting ready to go spearfishing. The fellow's waiting for you!

Pal Palych poked his head out from behind the stove.

"Yes...yes..." he said in confusion. "I'm coming, I'm coming...
We'll see each other again?" he said tenderly to Lyuba.

"Why not, seeing you're staying here," replied Lyuba, coming out
from behind the stove.

"So, have you had enough water?" said Granny Julia peevishly, as
before. Lyuba's daily visits to the sapper made her angry. But for some
reason I thought the old woman was angry merely for appearance's sake,
and in her heart of hearts she was as proud of Lyuba's selflessness as of
Katerina's steadfastness, seeing in the one and the other the manifestation
of that familial strong character that so gladdened her heart.

"What do you think—is she a virgin?" Pal Palych asked me when we'd
left the house.

I didn't like the question and pretended not to hear it.

"Don't think anything bad," Pal Palych assured me hastily, "She's
such a charming creature!... She's got someone, I gather?"

I replied that she had a fiancé, a sapper, and that she rode over twelve
kilometers daily on her bicycle to visit him.

"And that's after work, mind you."

"The old woman apparently isn't very well disposed to him?" Pal
Palych asked thoughtfully.

We reached the water. The lake seemed boundless, although countless
fires marked the other shore with a chain of lights. I struck a match and lit
the resin wood. It didn't take immediately. A flame ran from one chip to
another and suddenly disappeared, as if getting lost in the center of the pile,
then it broke through in several places simultaneously. Soon the little
tongues of flame merged in a single solid sheaf, the rubber hissed and began
to smell, releasing a powdery spark, a flame shot up in a bright red swirl
that was stifled by the wind, and the surrounding area seemed to be cut off
instantly; impenetrable blackness closed in around us like a wall. We
entered the water. In the tiny area that was visible there was only the water,
heavy and thick as black oil, and the sparse boughs of bushes that were
submerged in the spring flood. Sparks from the cage fell like stars into the
water and out of the dark depths other sparks flew skyward to meet them.

Our eyes soon adjusted, and the water became transparent. The sandy
bottom covered with little mother-of-pearl husks, slender quivering
waterweeds, looked yellow and smooth as a palm in one place, like a
washboard in another, and overgrown by some underwater flowers in a
third. And then the first roach was suspended by a thin gray little filament
in the spot of light.

"Get it!" I whispered to Pal Palych.

He struck. A big roach, its silver side glittering as if a mirror had risen
to the water's surface, dashed aside, striking my boot as it passed.

"The teeth are too wide apart," remarked Pal Palych.

Depressed, I thought that I was dragging the heavy cage from which my back was already aching for nothing. To handle a spear takes skill, agility, patience, and quick reflexes, and one could hardly expect a novice to possess all these qualities.

And then another roach appeared in the water as though anchored by its nose to a reed, and alongside it another one at right angles to it. I didn't have time to shout when Pal Palych struck, and struck so hard that the fish spear got stuck in the bottom, stirring up the sand.

"I didn't take the angle of refraction into account," he said calmly.

He freed the fish spear but didn't take it out of the water. And he was right not to, because the next second, with a short, accurate movement, he speared a roach. I didn't have time to congratulate him on his success when he jabbed again with the fish spear and again dropped a fish into the bag. I'd underestimated my companion. He turned out to have a sniper's eye and a sure hand. We'd gone into the grass where the roaches were swarming by the dozens. His narrow mouth tight, his eyes staring, he struck left and right, hitting not only the blinded motionless fish, but by some amazing unerring instinct, also getting those that were moving in the pitch darkness.

He interrupted his activity for just a second to pass me the bag of fish that hampered his movements. Although it wasn't easy for me to carry about the cage as it was, right then I was so astonished at his skill that I didn't start arguing.

The red circle on the water shrank perceptibly and dimmed—the 'torch' was burning out. I plunged the cage in the water, and the resin wood hissed, then went out. The black walls moved apart, and we again found ourselves in the middle of an enormous space marked by points of fire.

"What, already?" said Pal Palych in disappointment. "I was just beginning to enjoy myself."

But I was so tired from holding the cage that I categorically refused to fish any more.

When we returned home everyone was asleep. Nikolay Semyonovich had bedded down on the floor, leaving the bed for me to share with Pal Palych. On the wide double bed Katerina was sleeping with her three children; Lyuba was sleeping on the stove, her leg in its twisted silk stocking dangling uncomfortably; on a narrow pallet Granny Julia was curled up like a pretzel. The family slept, gathering strength for a new arduous day. I thought that we too would follow their example, but Pal Palych got a yearning for fried fish.

"Don't wake up the old woman for that." I tried to make him see reason.

"But I've dreamed so much of eating fresh fish that I'd caught myself!" he said plaintively.

"You'll be eating so much of it, you won't want to look at it!"

"It doesn't take long to fry up a few fish on the primus stove, does it? Granny will be happy to eat some herself."

He went up to the sleeping woman and gently shook her by the shoulder, but it proved difficult to wake up the old woman, who'd worn herself out with the day's work.

"Wake up, Granny!" said Pal Palych affectionately, bending over the old woman's large ear. "Granny!..." Without raising his voice or changing intonation, he continued calling to her for two or three minutes, and finally achieved his aim. Granny Julia started up from the pallet, sat up, rubbed her eyes, returning their customary lively sparkle to them, and burst out laughing when she learned why she'd been awakened.

"You're a persistent fellow, aren't you!" she said, her bare feet feeling about for her boots. "It's easier to resurrect the dead than to wake me up."

But I think she found Pal Palych's persistence to her liking. Apparently she knew how to appreciate 'character' in others too.

"All right, give me the fish! Look at that, how many you got! A real pro!"

Lyuba moaned softly in her sleep. Pal Palych got up on the bench and carefully, with a purely feminine deftness, tucked her leg in.

"He's thoughtful!" Granny Julia nodded at him.

The disemboweled and cleaned roach was soon hissing in the frying pan, but Pal Palych didn't have occasion this time to taste any fresh fried fish. He'd fallen asleep on the edge of the bed and was sleeping so sweetly and soundly that he didn't wake up when Granny Julia pulled off his boots. And we didn't make bold to wake him.

2.

In the morning it wasn't so much smoky as rather foggy in the cottage. The corner farthest from the stove had gotten cold and had accumulated a grayish vapor; tobacco smoke spread under the ceiling and dark dust floated in the slanting ray of the sun that penetrated the small window facing east. Waking up in the morning, especially early, is a difficult time of day: one has to harness oneself anew to the coach of life and to assume anew all its cares, labors, and unfinished business. But this family started its day with a fine unshaken cheerfulness. Granny Julia fed the calf and gave fodder to the poultry, carried in the water, lighted the stove, and poked at the samovar, which in the mornings absolutely refused to start boiling. All the household utensils—buckets, dustpans, oven prongs, pans—were amazingly docile in her hands. She never dropped anything, never clattered, banged or splashed anything; she worked practically without making a sound.

Katerina fed the baby. He was an extraordinary baby: he demanded to be breast fed in the morning and evening, but during the day he was quite satisfied with the pacifier. While she fed him, Katerina kept an eye on her six-year-old daughter, who was a very absent-minded creature. The little girl didn't have time to assimilate one impression when life offered her another, even more wonderful, one. The big beetle in its shiny black coat of armor that ran out from behind the stove, the kitten, which started a game with a yellow powdery moth, the accumulation of dirt with the spangles of fish scales on Pal Palych's boots—all in turn captured her attention. All one could hear was her mother shouting:

"Put on your other stocking! . . . Leave that alone—it's Granny's boot, yours is under the bed! . . . "

Lyuba, washed and tidy, had already taken the cow off to the shed, and now was taking care of Katerina's second son, who was her favorite. She combed his hair, tied a piece of calico around his neck like a tie, and made some toys out of rags and chips for him so that he'd be amused for the day.

As usual, Katerina was the first to leave for work, with her food tied up in a bundle; then Lyuba left on her bicycle—she worked in town at the flax mill. After a quick breakfast of fried fish we followed, setting out for our fishing.

During the night the surrounding area had become wonderfully transformed. The alders that had still been bare the day before were now covered with a tender fluffy down of foliage; an asp growing on the rise behind the alders had acquired some leaves, and all the newborn little leaves were trembling. The world that had still been penetrable the previous day, transparent on all sides as far as the eye could see, had closed up, curtained off with a green curtain that screened from all eyes the narrow-gauge line along which the small peat 'steam engine' ran and the cobblestone road behind it, and the forester's cottage to the right, and the old willows along the banks of our stream. There was open space only in the direction of the lake, where hills with ancient belfries rose high behind the broad pale stretch of water brightened slightly by the rising sun.

We set off along the bank covered with soft fleecy young grass. Seagulls flew screaming above the frozen icy center of the lake, a flock of mallards passed by at an alarming height in a cranelike formation and were reflected in the depths of the lake.

At first we walked alongside open water, and then the creeks overgrown with sedge and rushes started. An incessant chirring was audible, as though little files were tirelessly working away there.

"You hear that?" Nikolay Semyonovich turned to me.

"Are you talking about the chirring?" Pal Palych picked up on his words.

He was equipped as yesterday, only a waterproof raincoat that one of Granny Julia's regular 'lodgers' had left behind hung over his shoulders. "There's something unearthly about it, as if it were the mysterious whisper of some invisible underwater creatures, don't you think?"

"What's so unearthly!... " Nikolay Semyonovich responded irritatedly. "It's simply the fish rubbing against the grass. It helps them."

"That means the springlings have come," I said. "The winterlings spawned a long time ago."

"Winterlings, springlings—how great that sounds!" Pal Palych was delighted. "How much poetry there is in the word—springling!"

"They're also called blackfish or mudfish," Nikolay Semyonovich informed him.

"Why are you picking on him?" I reproached Nikolay Semyonovich when Pal Palych got entangled in the long raincoat and fell a little behind.

"And why's he hiding behind words?"

"That's nonsense! He simply sees a lot of things differently from us."

"Know what?" replied Nikolay Semyonovich angrily, "Let's not talk about elevated matters. We're here to fish."

And quickening his pace, he went ahead.

In the meantime Pal Palych had deftly tucked the flaps of his raincoat under his belt, cavalryman style, and caught up with us. He asked me for a glove; his hand had gotten cold while he was carrying the rod, and he still had to do some fishing. I took the glove off my left hand and he pulled it onto his right one, as a result of which his hand looked as though it were broken at the wrist. Unable to control myself, I asked him how he'd dared set out so ill-equipped.

"You know, when you come to people with an open heart they'll always help you. I'm prepared to set out even for the Kara Kum desert,[1] even for the ends of the earth with nothing but a handkerchief for baggage—and I'm convinced that I'd make it!"

I glanced at Pal Palych, at his blue, somewhat protruberant eyes, in which there was something exalted at the moment, as though he were expressing an elevated thought that was, moreover, very important to him; at his finely-molded bony nose with its flaring nostrils; at his whole delicate face, spoiled only by the wrinkled seam of his old-womanish mouth, and I suddenly felt as though I'd met him somewhere before. Somehow the gaze of those blue eyes and even the sincere intonation of his voice were familiar to me. But following Nikolay Semyonovich's wise rule, I told myself:

"It's not worth racking your brains over it, we're here to fish."

We picked a spot close to the mouth of the stream. Higher up, where the shores were overgrown with willows, the fishermen's campfires were shooting up sparks as far as the railroad bridge; apparently the mudfish had managed to get high up the river. But Nikolay Semyonovich liked to have room when he fished and preferred a place that wasn't protected from the wind but was deserted to one that was more sheltered but crowded.

The chirring that had accompanied us en route grew louder and denser here. The fish were rubbing themselves violently against the grass, at times splashing against the leaves of the water lilies, sometimes leaping right out of the water and inscribing a short sparkling rainbow in the air before disappearing underwater again. At the very edge the newborn fish were teeming, and suddenly, as they became frightened by something, they made a dash in a slanting line for the sedge.

We fixed the length of our lines and cast them together, aiming for the border of the sedge. I had a bite as soon as the float touched the water. It wasn't just a bite, but the line was pulled as it usually is when it's a good fish. I hooked it and pulled out a fat mudfish over three inches wide, shot with navy blue; it was very rough, as though someone had run a knife a couple of times the wrong way along its scales—in short, it was bursting with roe.

Untill noon we continued to have incredible fishing, the sort you dream about. The fish practically bit when there was nothing on the line, as fishermen say. I no longer threw the fish I caught into the bucket, but simply tossed them on the shore, intending to pick them up later.

By midday the fishing slackened. And although the chirring in the grass didn't quiet down, more and more frequently now we'd get thin flat male fish and dry silvery winterlings that had already cast off their roe. But that first greedy sense of challenge that fishing arouses was satisfied. I was already considering taking a rest when the seagulls screamed above the yellowish sand bank by the mouth of the stream and Nikolay Semyonovich said tersely:

"They're coming!"

A fresh shoal was coming. Evidently it divided at the very mouth of the stream, for some of the seagulls turned off in a different direction while others flew on over our heads, losing the shoal that entered the river undergrowth. And again the fat roe-packed mudfish was blessedly heavy on our lines. And again bite followed bite so quickly that our wrist and backs ached and everything spun before our eyes. Now, however, we fished as though we had a second wind, more calmly, without our earlier self-oblivion.

True, that couldn't be said of Nikolay Semyonovich. He fished with the same concentration, standing up to his knees in water in his tarpaulin boots with their Wellington rubber soles. He didn't change his position once, as if he were sucked in by the bank mud. Strange thing! We all found ourselves in different situations: we had the same rods, the same hooks, bait from our common supply, we were even fishing in the same small area—

and yet he caught the biggest fish. You'd have thought that the roach intentionally chose his hook, preferring to be the catch of a real pro.

Pal Palych didn't fail to notice this. He'd already changed his place more than once, had gone to the sand bank and fished in the lake, where the catch was much worse than at the mouth of the stream. Finally he positioned himself close to Nikolay Semyonovich. Their floats hung so close to each other that from where I was it was impossible to distinguish which was whose. This dangerous proximity was bound to cause their lines to get tangled—through Pal Palych's fault, of course. Without saying a word, Nikolay Semyonovich disentangled his fishing line and calmly continued fishing. But a short while later the same thing happened. Nikolay Semyonovich took out a knife and just as calmly cut Pal Palych's line. Pal Palych looked at him with some surprise, and with the end of his rod tried to fish out the line, which had fallen in the water, but he buried the rod in the silt. Carefully pulling it out, he came up to me and asked me to tie on a spare line.

I had observed the wordless duel with interest, and suddenly realized that Nikolay Semyonovich's calm was feigned—his big ears were purple with the blood that had raced to his head—whereas Pal Palych's tranquillity was perfectly genuine.

While I was fastening on the spare line, twisting it into tiny loops and immediately letting them slip, my fingers froze. Pal Palych had entered the water, seized an armful of weeds, jerked them out, and thrown them on the shore together with the sand, silt, and close to ten small roach that were caught in the grass.

"Now that's fishing!" laughed Pal Palych. "Seven at one go!"

"You have no conscience!" wailed Nikolay Semyonovich. "They're good, clever fish. Why frighten them?"

"I'm not frightening them—I'm fishing."

"What's the idea of this tomfoolery? The fish will go away!"

"No, its better that I go away!" Pal Palych winked at me, and resting his rod on his shoulder, moved off upstream.

Pal Palych's restlessness and frivolousness, manifesting themselves as they did after he'd shown himself such a good fellow the night before, came as an unpleasant surprise. But he apparently didn't find in fishing with a rod that intense pleasure that spearfishing gave him.

We fished for about three or four hours, but Pal Palych didn't come back. The sky was flooded with the glow of sunset, then it faded, and the bluish shadows of the earth settled along the horizon. The water in the lake turned white and thickened like cream, and seagulls flew over the edge of the shore with loud, panic-filled screams, as though they were out of their element.

The fish kept on rubbing, hitting against the sedge and reeds as before, but they had stopped biting. A cold wind arose. We started collecting our catch: two full buckets. Besides that, it turned out that Nikolay Semyonovich had put the largest roach in a net—it looked as if there were no fewer than fifty of them.

"Not bad!" I remarked.

"That's nothing," responded Nikolay Semyonovich. "You should have seen what it was like in other years!..."

I've never yet met a fisherman who doesn't think that in past years the fish were bigger, the catch richer, but to this day I can't understand why; is it said for fear of putting a jinx on their luck or because of a quirk of human memory?

"And where's—that fellow's fish?" asked Nikolay Semyonovich.

"Must be here, with ours."

"Okay, let's go!"

And seizing the heavy buckets, we made our way back home.

3.

We saw Pal Palych as soon as we reached the cottage. In the transparent bluish dusk of the new moon he was standing in front of a rotten haycock, reading poetry. As we got closer we discovered Lyuba's petite figure in the haycock; she had buried herself so far in the hay that from a distance she was completely invisible.

> Hasten! The flood of joy
> Will sweep over us, but won't divide us...[2]

"You don't say!" was Lyuba's familiar response, but there wasn't any of yesterday's casual laziness in her voice; there was interest and a trace of coquetry in it.

"It'll be a pity if he turns her head," growled Nikolay Semyonovich. "She's a fine innocent girl."

This remark had nothing to do with fishing, and I gazed at my companion in surprise. Nikolay Semyonovich knitted his bushy brows, which resembled mustaches, coughed behind his fist, and quickly went into the house.

Before supper Pal Palych announced that there would be dancing later that day. It seemed that he'd discovered an old gramophone and a selection of records in the house. Apparently it had all been settled before we arrived. The children were put to bed early, and Katya and Lyuba dressed up: they put on dresses of crêpe de chine, silk stockings, and high-heeled shoes. With the usual solemn aura of our dwelling was mixed the subtle scent of something feminine: powder and perfume.

Katya was endearingly embarrassed by her attire, as though she had no right to wear it. She kept avoiding our eyes and emitted short shy bursts of laughter for no reason. Lyuba, on the other hand, was dignified, sedate, and extremely solemn; a dance is a serious affair when one's eighteen!

I realized that she wouldn't be cycling over to see her sapper today, and I felt a trifle upset, as though I too were guilty of disturbing the customary mode of life here. But the gramophone wheezed and started playing, a sobbing male voice sang of a lone gypsy, Pal Palych caught hold of Lyuba, and her moist eyes showed such profound enjoyment that the unpleasant feeling left me immediately.

Granny Julia probably also noticed the touching expression of joy on her daughter's face.

"Go ahead and dance, dance, my dears . . . " said the old woman in a soft kind tone.

Katerina turned the record over so quickly that Pal Palych and Lyuba didn't have to interrupt their dancing. And now a cheerful bravura melody sounded, and the dancers' movements became fast and abrupt. Pal Palych danced wonderfully, leading his partner as easily and confidently around the small cottage crowded with benches and tubs as if they were in a ballroom. Lyuba's face became flushed and her eyes acquired a distant transported look.

But the melody ended in a tinny wheeze—it was time the needle was changed. Pal Palych kissed Lyuba's hand and she responded with a look of gratitude.

"Ah, the only thing missing is a glass of something to drink!" exclaimed Pal Palych, his shining eyes roaming over the cottage. And then he caught sight of the neck of a bottle on the cluttered window sill.

"And there you are, sweetheart!" He dashed over to the window sill and with a deft movement removed the bottle.

"That's my vodka!" came Nikolay Semyonovich's somber voice. He was sitting in his usual place in the dark corner, smoking his pipe, blowing the smoke out of a crack in the broken window.

"Now that's wonderful!" responded Pal Palych. "Ladies, please join me!" With extraordinary speed he got cut-glass tumblers and cups from the cupboard, knocked the stopper out with a sharp blow of the fist on the bottom, and poured the vodka in the 'glasses.'

Both Lyuba and Katya protested, of course, claiming that "they never touched it," but to resist Pal Palych's bulldozing insistence was impossible. He even got Granny Julia to drink some of it, which set the old woman laughing uncontrollably. Only he didn't drink for some reason, although he zealously treated everyone.

And the music started up again...

I'm a bad dancer, but, warmed by the vodka, I decided to invite Katya to dance. For a long time she refused—acting frightened and angry, seriously protesting that "she was too old"—, pulled her hands away and hid them behind her back when I tried to pull her out of her chair, but finally, blushing furiously, she agreed and held out her small, firm, rough hand. As she danced she kept looking at her feet, choosing the best spot to place them, and she placed them in such a way that from time to time I trod on her toes, and forestalling me, she'd immediately say: "Excuse me."

And Granny Julia, standing at the stove, looked at us cheerfully and greedily as if she herself were ready to start dancing, and wiping her laughing lips with her hand, she kept saying:

"Eh, you little devils! ... "

Of course, one is quite justified in treating a fisherman without a rod with irony, but at that moment a thought involuntarily occurred to me: and what had Nikolay Semyonovich and I given these people? So many people passed through that cottage, but no one was interested in anything but fishing. Pal Palych, however, proved to be very different, and in the hostesses' memory he would likely remain associated with the warmth and gaiety that he'd brought into their lives...

Those were my thought as I rested after another painful dance with Katya. Pal Palych and Lyuba seemed capable of dancing indefinitely. Now he was leading her in the smooth insinuating catlike steps of the Boston waltz and whispering something in her ear. Lyuba held herself aloof from his whispering, throwing back her head to expose her soft, slender neck, which looked transparent. Suddenly she freed herself from Pal Palych's arms and, giving him a severe look, retired to stand by the wall.

"That's fine with me!" said Pal Palych in disappointed muffled tones. "I'll ask Katya!"

He led Katya off, and under his skillful guidance Katya starting moving much more fluidly and gracefully then she had with me.

And all of a sudden everything was thrown into confusion. Doors banged, bringing the cold from the outside into the cottage. Granny Julia kept running to and from the hallway. The nimbus of flame in the lamp, deflated and inflated by the gust of wind, dimmed and flared brightly.

"Katka's disgrace has turned up," said Lyuba contemptuously.

"I hope we haven't done anything wrong?" said Pal Palych uneasily, hurriedly releasing Katya.

"Well, let him come in. Why's he making people feel uncomfortable for nothing?" said Katya severely.

But he came in of his own accord without waiting for an invitation— small, red-haired, with despairing eyes. Whatever feelings possessed him, they weren't kind. But he had no time to give expression to what he'd carried with him through the night and bad weather to the house that sheltered his beloved. Pal Palych's disarmingly sweet, resolute manner instantly entrapped the newcomer, distracted him, seated him at the table, and forced him to drink enough to soften his heart.

He himself probably couldn't understand how it happened that he was eating and drinking in that house, and clinking glasses with his wife, and gently running his fingers through his sleeping daughter's hair, and dancing, his knee touching the ground until his bones cracked...

But everything comes to an end, and the late hour of itself somehow silenced the music and whispered to the people: "Enough is enough." Katerina's husband had to go back through the night, the bad weather, and the impassable roads. What had he achieved in coming here? He seemed to feel cheated and the earlier despair of someone at bay appeared in his eyes. He reached for his cap with a timid convulsive movement, but Pal Palych wouldn't let him leave.

"Do stay," he urged, putting an affectionate arm around his shoulders. "How can you go anywhere when it's so dark?"

The husband looked sullenly but hopefully at his relatives' faces, which had become estranged, closed once again. Katerina was making the bed, her back turned to her husband.

"Do stay, really, you can leave together in the morning. One can't drive a man out, my friends!..."

I admit that I followed this bold interference in the complex, subtle, difficult life of other people with some trepidation. But it all turned out to be amazingly simple.

"As far as I'm concerned, he can stay," Katerina said very calmly.

"Give me the mattress," Granny Julia was as calm and businesslike in her turn, "I'll make a bed for him on the benches."

A few minutes later everyone was in bed, Granny Julia had extinguished the lamp, and I immediately heard Pal Palych's gentle, quiet breathing beside me. He had the habit of falling asleep instantly, like a child.

I woke up in the night, awakened by someone's voice.

"Have you gone crazy?! You'll wake the child!..." I heard Katerina's voice, strange, unfamiliar, and strained.

There was a scuffle in reply, then a man's broken whisper:

"Am I your husband or aren't I?"

"Get away from me, do you hear!... I thought you were a human being...Get away!..."

"Kate!..."

"Forget it—don't even think of it... Never...now it'll never be!"

There was a silence, then a sharp curse through clenched teeth. Lighting his way with a match, the man rushed to the door, and for a moment I saw the pale face under the cap of red hair; the door banged, cutting off the light, and in the darkness a woman broke into muffled, cautious, and angry sobs.

In the morning no one mentioned the unsuccessful attempt at a reconciliation; everyone acted as though nothing had happened. It was only after her daughters had left for work that Granny Julia said to Pal Palych:

"You're some peacemaker!" But she sounded sad, not reproachful.

4.

The weather that day was bad. The wind that had been blowing the night before drove the ice inshore, and to escape suffocation the roach left the coastal inlets for the open water. It looked as though winter had decided to make a last attempt to pit its strength against spring. The shores were green with young grass, the alders all curly with leaves, but blocks of ice covered with rough granular snow were pressing in from the lake, emitting a violent chill. Fragments of ice slithered out onto the bank and piled up one on top of another. The low gray sky over the lake slowly stratified, sinking increasingly lower toward the water. The strip of shore that was still light was shrinking before our eyes and by the time we reached the stream the boundary of light area had shrunk to the foot of the trees, and then the young green dress of the alders that were shadowed became leaden in hue. Spring retreated into the distance behind the horizon.

The stream was cold and forlorn. The wind lashed the water, covering it with quivering ripples, stirred the bare twigs of the bushes, and blew about their swollen buds, which were ready to burst; they looked naked and dead. The sedge darkened and shrivelled, the reeds where the familiar exciting chirring had fallen silent were flattened. They weren't biting, of course. We caught only a few thin bleaks with the dull sheen of herring and we threw them back in the stream.

We moved slowly from the mouth of the stream to the railroad bridge, choosing the most sheltered spot among the old willows hanging over the water, but with no result. Nikolay Semyonovich finally had some luck. On a small clear patch among the water-lily leaves, almost at the shore, he pulled out one after another about a dozen big mudfish full of roe. This gave us the surge of encouragement to fish fruitlessly for another three hours. Pal Palych, the most impatient of us three, had already gone as far as the bridge and returned, but without success.

A thickish wet snow started to fall. It melted almost as soon as it touched the ground and in the course of a few minutes the banks had turned to slush.

"Well, there's no point in hoping for anything now," said Pal Palych, hunching up as the snow trickled down his collar.

"That's obvious," agreed Nikolay Semyonovich, pulling out a bream.

"I went all the way to the bridge without getting a single bite!" said Pal Palych, turning to me.

He clearly wanted me to keep him company on the way back, but Nikolay Semyonovich pulled out a striped perch right after the bream, and I told Pal Palych that I wanted to fish some more.

"I wish you luck!" replied Pal Palych with his usual kindness, and turning up his jacket, he moved off down the bank.

For some reason I thought we wouldn't see him any more. He'd exhausted what round of local pleasures he could find and would disappear as easily as he'd come the night before without troubling himself about a conventional leavetaking.

But I was wrong.

When we returned home in the evening we found the whole family engaged in a search. Lyuba was standing on a bench searching the stove, going through the mattress, blankets, and bedding; Katerina was rummaging under the sideboard; and Granny Julia was inspecting the bed.

Kateria's funny absent-minded little daughter, dressed in a long homespun coat that didn't fit her, was feeling around all the corners of the room. Her younger brother was similarly engaged. Apparently he didn't know what they were searching for, and with a joyful look on his face would in turn bring Granny a matchbox, then a candle-end, and the kitten. He'd receive a gentle cuff as a reward and then he'd resume the search with renewed enthusiasm.

The baby was also searching. But he was searching for his mother's breast; she was so engrossed in the search that she'd completely forgotten about him. Our arrival brought her to her sense. Dusting off her knees, she sat down on the bed and took the baby in her arms. He immediately found what he needed and abandoned himself to his task, oblivious to everything else in the world.

With an absent-minded, abstracted took, Pal Palych loafed aimlessly about the cottage, only getting in people's way. His peculiar expression of aloofness from all the commotion at once made me think he was the one who'd suffered the loss.

"What's happened here?" I asked Pal Palych.

"My knife's disappeared," he answered in an injured tone.

The insignificance of the misfortune was so disproportionate to the people's efforts and the owner's chagrin that I wanted to answer with a joke, but Nikolay Semyonovich forestalled me.

"How annoying!" he said seriously.

Such unexpected sympathy on Nikolay Semyonovich's part surprised me. But it was probably the result of a professional respect for the tools of his craft: a knife is the most basic necessity outdoors, especially for a fisherman or hunter.

Nikolay Semyonovich also joined in the search. First he felt through his clothing, then searched the window sill where our food was kept, then the shelf with the dishes, and finally he went through the pockets of our raincoats and jackets, which were hanging by the door.

"You've really lost it," he said, sitting down at the table. He took out his splendid five-bladed knife and started slicing the bread for supper.

"Well, we simply can't find it!" said Granny Julia, kneeling by the bed under which she'd just been looking. Her face was red from the blood that had flowed to her head. "If you want, take our knife!"

"Which one—the kitchen knife? Come on! My knife was in a sheath. A small, elegant knife in a leather sheath," said Pal Palych, puckering his narrow mouth piteously.

"We've never had such a thing happen before!" sighed Granny Julia miserably. "How many people have stayed here ... God, what a thing to happen!"

I felt uncomfortable in front of the old woman and her daughters on account of this crude fuss. It was clear that they'd been searching for a long time, rummaging in every nook and cranny, knowing they wouldn't be able to find the knife, yet continuing their senseless efforts out of a sense of delicacy and embarrassment.

"Forget it!" I said. "After all, it's hardly the family jewels . . ."

"Excuse me, but it *is* my knife," Pal Palych's tone verged on the haughty.

"But why are you so sure you lost it right here? You could have dropped it by the stream, on the way there ... "

"I'm too careful with things for that to have happened," came the reply.

Both Granny Julia and Lyuba, however, took my interference as a signal to stop searching. Lyuba sank down on the bench and stretched luxuriously, Granny Julia, her spine doubled up in pain from her frequent bending down, took up her usual place at the stove, pressing her back against its warmth. Imitating the adults, Katerina's daughter also stopped rummaging about the cottage, went and joined Granny and stood beside her, propping up her cheek with her fist in an adult manner. Only her little brother couldn't settle down and was already carrying some new find in his little fist when his mother cried angrily at him,

"That's enough! Stop it!"

And that sharp peremptory cry showed me how bad the hostesses felt, how unpleasant the loss was for them. If only Nikolay Semyonovich would say something. But true to his habit of not interfering, he was getting the supper ready in silence. Pal Palych, on the other hand, said with an obstinacy that was blind to everything else:

"Perhaps the children took it?"

"They've never done such a thing in their lives," Granny Julia answered sternly. But with the conscientiousness of an old person she stooped down to her granddaughter, who was standing beside her, and turned out all the pockets of the shabby homespun coat. Her hand failed to catch the knife that fell with a clatter as the ring hit the floor. Pal Palych leaped up joyfully, picked up the knife, took it out of its sheath as if to make sure that the knife hadn't suffered any damage, replaced it, and put it away in his pocket.

"Why did you take someone else's property?" said Granny Julia in a stern voice and breathed "Ah!" in a terrible manner.

Granny gave the little girl a violent slap in the face with the back of her long flat brown hand, traced with veins. Indentations appeared on the pink rounded cheek from which rays of white spread out, to be flooded abruptly with crimson. It was as if a maple leaf had been branded on the child's cheek.

Katerina made no move to defend her daughter—Granny ran the house—but her face turned stony.

Granny raised her hand and swinging her arm from the elbow to the wrist, slapped the little girl just as sharply on the other cheek.

"You're not to take someone else's things!... You're not to take someone else's things!... "

It must have hurt the little girl, but she didn't cry and didn't even utter a word of excuse. It could have been stubbornness, a callousness of her little heart, or that same 'strong character,' but most probably she was simply trying to grasp the meaning of what was happening.

She'd evidently taken the knife to play with, then had put it in her pocket and forgotten about it. And now new associations were forming in her little mind: someone else's property doesn't become yours because you've taken a fancy to it; if you take it, you get humiliated and slapped hard for it. This internal effort, which taught her something new, absorbed all the powers of her tiny being and drove away the tears.

"Don't you dare take someone else's things!"—and Granny raised her hand again.

"Oh, please don't!" exclaimed Pal Palych, his face puckering.

"What do you mean—don't?" asked the old woman sternly.

"Wait," said Pal Palych quickly. "Maybe in the dark I put the knife in her coat myself. It was hanging by the door beside my jacket!"

"You should have thought of that earlier!" cried Lyuba angrily.

Yet the real significance of Pal Palych's belated intercession didn't immediately dawn on me; in the first moment I even felt relief. But then I saw the little girl's eye's. Two large round eyes with dilated pupils were fixed on Pal Palych with an expression of distressing, unchildlike hatred.

"No," Nikolay Semyonovich's loud voice was suddenly heard, "I saw her playing with the knife myself. You did play with the knife, didn't you?" he addressed the little girl in a kind voice.

"Ye-es . . . " came the squeaky whisper.

"There you are, then!" said Granny Julia in relief, and taking her granddaughter by her blonde tuft of hair, tugged hard at it two or three times, saying: "You're not to take someone else's things! . . . "

Apparently the little girl had assimilated that fact; the concentrated expression which looked so tense and stubborn to me disappeared from her face, which became simple and childlike.

"I won't, Granny!" she started crying, and Granny replied pacifyingly: "Well, get along, then . . . Wait, let's blow your nose!"

The little girl blew her nose thoroughly on the hem of Granny's skirt, and a minute later life in our crowded dwelling had returned to its customary routine. Katerina was feeding the baby, Granny Julia was stoking the samovar with the help of an old boot, and the young 'culprit' was teaching the kitten the piece of wisdom that Granny's kind hand had hammered strongly into her. She kept putting a ball of wool on the floor, and whenever the kitten sank its paws into it, she'd shake it by its fur, saying:

"You're not to take someone else's things! . . . You're not to take someone else's things! . . . "

Lyuba was silently dressing in preparation to go out. She pulled on her padded jacket, tied a kerchief around her head, winding it several times around her neck; she was apparently getting ready to visit her sapper.

"What, you're going?" Pal Palych turned to her. "But we agreed . . . "

Lyuba silently lifted her bicycle down from its hook.

"Go on, go on, daughter," said Granny Julia in a warm voice. "He must be impatient with waiting."

Pushing the door open with the front wheel of the bicycle, Lyuba went out into the entrance hall. Pal Palych gazed after her and heaved a sigh. The outer door banged. Pal Palych lit a cigarette with an absent air.

"Nikolay Semyonovich," he said unexpectedly, walking up to the table, "You really know that the little girl . . . took the knife?"

Nikolay Semyonovich was opening a can of food at that moment that must have been made of roofing iron judging by the way his large fat face had grown damp and red from the effort. He answered only after the blade of the knife had slid smoothly into the rim of the can.

"No."

"But you saw her playing with the knife?"

"That's not important," said Nikolay Semyonovich slowly and with seeming reluctance.

"But, excuse me!" For the first time I saw a look not of rapturous, but of serious, even rather perturbed, wonder on Pal Palych's face. "Then I don't understand you... What the hell is this!..." he began with uncertain indignation—and broke off.

Two dark eyes with yellowish whites that had seen a great deal in their time were fixed steadily on him—tired eyes as keen as a soldier's, kind and merciless. And the stout heavy-set specialist in pike perch who was indifferent to everything except fishing said with a strange expression of gentleness and anger:

"You didn't notice how the little girl looked at you when she'd already paid for her unwitting wrong and you decided to play at being noble? That's what it's about! There are some things that are beyond a child's understanding... There'll come a time when she'll learn to loathe people like you..." And he added very quietly: "You worthless, greedy, ingratiating parasite..."

"Ah, so that's it!" was all Pal Palych said with a vague and thoughtful expression. Yes, thoughtful. There was no sense of anger or resentment or indignation or even regret in his tone, only a faint hint of weariness, the weariness felt by a traveller when he is aroused too early from his rest. "When does the train come through here?" he asked Granny Julia politely and calmly.

"Not until dawn, no earlier," answered Granny without turning her head.

"And how far is it to town?"

"About ten kilometers."

Pal Palych dressed unhurriedly, pulling his travelling cap over his eyes, raised the collar of his coat, and made for the door. Now I could see him as if through a magnifying glass: he obviously hoped that someone would stop him. When nobody did he pushed the door open. The night with its darkness and cold stared Pal Palych in the face. Closing the door carefully, he took off his outdoor clothes and sat down on the bed.

"After all, everyone has the right to stay the night," said Pal Palych without the slightest defiance or bravado, and plumping up the pillows, he settled down to sleep.

Nikolay Semyonovich let me have half his mattress and I nestled down at my neighbor's warm side...

In the morning Pal Palych was gone from the cottage, evidently having left on the first train. He'd gone forgetting to pay for his lodging. But everything of ours that he'd used—Nikolay Semyonovich's boots,

Granny's raincoat and padded jacket, my rod, the extra hooks, the can of
bait, the glove—was neatly piled on the bench, showing all too clearly that
Pal Palych couldn't be held accountable for any legal crimes.

1953   Translated by Helena Goscilo

Excerpts from the original ("Nochnoi gost") were first published in *Ogonek*, No. 4
(1955), 10-16. The story in its entirety first appeared in *Rasskazy 1955 goda* (M, 1956), 466-
490. The present translation is of the edition included in the 1973 two-volume collection, I, 80-
106.

Notes

1. The Kara Kum desert is located in the southwestern part of the Soviet Union in Asia,
largely in Turkmenistan, south of the Aral Sea.
2. According to Nagibin, the lines are from a forgettable poem by a second-rate poet
whose name he does not recall.

The Last Hunt

When Dedok paddled up in his old dug-out to the "landing"—as the Podsvyatye hunters call the bit of shore on the Great Lake that is suitable for mooring boats—it was already crowded with people. Hunting wasn't permitted until the next morning, but evidently no one could bear to wait at home.

"Dedok, you alive?" said Anatoly Ivanonich. "And here we were thinking of having a good time at the wake."

"What an idea!" laughed Dedok.

Anatoly Ivanovich looked at Dedok's face: it was gray, as though lightly covered with ash, with white lips under the little brush that was his sparse, scraggly mustache, and sunken, caved-in cheeks, covered with a soft growth of grey beard.

"How is it the old lady let you go?" he asked in a tone of mild reproach.

"As if she could keep me from going!" replied Dedok, avoiding the hunter's persistent look, while his gnarled hands, disfigured by gout, automatically moored the boat. "I don't waste words with my old lady."

"Well, carry on, Dedok," said Anatoly Ivanovich, as if admitting him with these words into the hunters' fellowship.

The hunter's words reminded Dedok about his preparations for the hunt, and about the pitiful and humiliating experience he'd had to go through before setting off.

When they'd banned hunting the spring before, Dedok seemed to fall apart all at once. The weariness he'd accumulated over the long years, the lack of sleep, all the cured and uncured ailments, all the cold he'd stored up in abundance during the raw spring and frosty autumn dawns—all of it attacked his body, which was withered with age and twisted by an exhausting rheumatic pain that was especially sensitive to cold. Dedok moved his bedding to the top of the tiled stove, from which he climbed down only to relieve himself or when his old woman made him eat some hot soup. During the day he would doze and hear in his sleep the oven tongs clanging in the old woman's hands, the door in the entryway banging and creaking on its rusty hinges, the stove pipe swinging back and forth in the

71

shed and suddenly hitting the wooden wall with a hollow thud; and then at night he would suffer from insomnia. As Dedok looked into the coal-black darkness above the stove, there arose before his eyes with an insistent and rather frightening clarity the faces of people living and dead, near and distant: the face of his aging daughter and of his already aged son, both of whom had long existed apart from Dedok, and then the face of his other son, who had been killed in World War II, and those of his twin daughters, who had died of measles in childhood, and—most often—the face of his old woman, which would appear sometimes in its present state, covered with wrinkles, and sometimes young and smooth.

Their annoying uselessness tired and upset Dedok. What good were they if they couldn't answer the only important question facing Dedok now: what was the point of all his past if now there was only this stove, this mortal weakness and indifference to everything in the world? No matter how often Dedok questioned them, his night visitors kept silent; they seemed to be busy with their own concerns and unwilling to help Dedok. So during the day he tried to ask his old woman about this somehow, but either he couldn't find the right words, or else his old woman didn't wish to understand him. She started swearing and spouting a lot of spiteful, womanish nonsense, and Dedok hid from her on the stove.

With the spring, the ringing sound made by the drip of thawing snow ceased, the door in the entryway stopped banging and creaking; now it was always wide open, letting into the house summer warmth and smells that Dedok barely sensed, and could only guess at. In July the thunder stopped rumbling, and summer suddenly leapt into fall: August began to look more like October, with its morning frost and gray drizzle and its rare clear, sunny days. Once when she came home from the farm, the old woman found Dedok sitting on a bench. This was so unexpected that she froze to the spot.

"Where are you off to, old man?" she asked with an effort.

"It's time I was on my way," replied Dedok, looking off to the side.

The old woman's legs gave way under her.

"Already?" was all she was able to get out.

"Take a look at the calendar. Two days till the hunt and nothing's ready, the gun's not cleaned, the cartridges aren't filled."

And then the old woman noticed the gun barrels lying on the bench in a case made from one of her torn stockings, and on the windowsill she saw the blackened stock of a rifle with wire wound around it, and a leather belt, shiny from having rubbed so much against Dedok's body and looking as if it had been waxed on the wrong side—it was his bandolier.

Then the old woman realized that Dedok had put off dying and intended to go on the hunt. She didn't argue or swear, but simply took the gun barrels and hid them. After a futile attempt to wrest them from her, Dedok realized how weak he was compared to the old woman, and sitting down on the bench, he began to weep. The tears ran like tiny streams along the bends of his wrinkles. He didn't try to stop them or wipe them away, and the old woman, who had never seen Dedok cry, was frightened and embarrassed, and hastened to return the gun barrels to him. When he got back the gun barrels, redolent of shots long past, Dedok immediately calmed down like a child, and began looking at the color of their corroded cylinders, which had long since lost their sheen.

Now the old woman actively helped Dedok in his preparations: she mended his warm cap with its worn fox trim, and his quilted coat with its ripped armholes, darned his socks, and glued rubber patches onto the tops of his wading boots. Dedok filled his cartridges, measuring the shot and powder with a tarnished copper cup.

Finally the time came to leave. Dedok pulled on a sweater and quilted trousers, and pushed his feet in their thick wool socks with reinforced heels into his rubber boots. And the old boots, which had sat around almost a year in the entrance hall, gripped his feet with such biting cold, penetrating to his heart, that Dedok seemed to shrink and shrivel, and his cheekbones acquired a sallow cast.

"What's the matter, you poor devil?" asked the old woman.

"Nothing," Dedok got out, afraid that she'd notice how he'd begun to shiver all over. "Give us some hay for padding."

The old woman brought some hay, and he packed it into the boots and put them on with an effort. The cold didn't go away; it clenched Dedok's thin calves in an icy grip and penetrated into his shin bones.

"Now it's fine," said Dedok, deceiving both the old woman and himself.

The old woman helped him pull on his quilted coat, straightened out its flaps, and pressed down the hardened collar. He felt her rough hands on him and her warm, quickened breath with its slightly bitter scent, and there arose in him a long-forgotten tenderness towards his old, life-long companion.

"Let's go, why don't we," said the old woman. "I'll take the shotgun to the boat."

When they were young, his wife would see him off on hunts quite often, proudly carrying the heavy shotgun over her round, soft shoulder. Till this day Dedok remembered the crease left by the gun's strap on that dear shoulder. But then it was just a game: even though he was short, Dedok was so robust and solidly built that it was child's play to carry not only all his hunting gear but his wife along with it.

"What nonsense!" said Dedok. "As if I can't do without guides!"

With his gun slung across his back, and over his shoulder a wicker basket in which a live decoy quacked and moved about restlessly, with an oar in one hand and a bag of provisions in the other, and girded with his bandolier, Dedok crossed over the threshold leading out of the house.

"Get ready to fix us some duck tomorrow," he said to the old woman without turning around, and immediately forgot about her. The pale-blue and green world, singed with the yellows of early autumn, opened up before him, beckoning and calling. And Dedok set off into its freshness, which was filled with strong, damp, marshy air, and headed towards the wind-blown brilliance of the river, its color a deep blue flecked with silvery sparks.

He reached the dugout without any difficulty, walking over the springy hummocks along the shore; a little out of breath, he pushed the dugout into the water, but he couldn't steer it while standing up—everything fluttered before his eyes and he felt dizzy. Resigning himself to this new, unfamiliar weakness, he settled down in the stern and, preserving his strength, quietly guided the dugout along the bank.

In Dunyashkin Creek, Dedok roused a large flock of mallards. The ducks, grown bold during the long period without slaughter, let him come up very close. They flew up out of the reeds heavily and noisily, and gathering into a flock, veered off to the side and towards the open water. There were masses of ducks. At times Dedok couldn't follow them with his eye, but he did hear the sharp warble of their ascent, the harsh whirring of their wings in their upward flight, or the sound of many little slaps merging into one, like that of a broom hitting the waves, as the flock landed on the open water. He was glad that there were many ducks, but it grieved him that he no longer had the range of vision he used to, and had to rely more on his sense of hearing to take in what was happening around him.

A gentle, low, even wind helped Dedok, and he didn't notice how he passed Dunyashkin Creek and skirting Shibayev Island, reached the Great Lake. Here the wind began to work against Dedok. No matter how hard he rowed, two old elms, whose roots lay exposed on the embankment, stubbornly loomed next to him, level with the dugout, and wouldn't let Dedok leave their side. Dedok tried to look not at them, but only at the water which flowed in smooth streams along the sides of the boat, giving the impression that the dugout was briskly moving forward. But when Dedok again cast a glance at the shore, the elms were standing level with his shoulders, just as before, and their hairy roots were stirring as if alive. And then, either because the wind had quieted down, or because it had changed direction, or else because human persistence had gained the upper hand, in place of the elms a haystack appeared on the shore, and then a little while later—blackberry bushes, and after that a birchwood followed by a nutgrove.

Dedok spotted a place for a shelter. About thirty meters from the shore there was a green islet of rushes which were as pliant as switches, with tufts of reeds sticking up in the air; it was surrounded by a semi-circle of brown duckweed—a favorite feed of ducks. In the midst of the small brownish-gray leaves, whose curled-up edges barely poked up out of the water, appeared white stalks that had been plucked at and eaten away by ducks: that meant they came there for their evening feed. Dedok pulled in to the shore of the lake and broke off a number of birch branches. Piling up the branches in the bow of the boat, he pushed off, and the wind, as if it had been waiting for just that, struck at the dense heap of branches, driving Dedok back towards Dunyashkin Creek. Getting on his knees, Dedok crawled up to the branches and pulled them down into the bottom of the dugout, but even then they rose higher than the sides of the boat, and the wind hit each little leaf as if it were a tiny sail, driving the boat farther and farther away from the islet. Bending over the side and reaching under the bottom of the boat with his oar, Dedok swung the bow of the dugout around in order to turn the fierce pressure of the wind to his own advantage. Small waves kept lashing the dugout, threatening to capsize it, but somehow, moving sideways and at an angle, the dugout gradually made its way towards the place he'd picked out, and finally Dedok grabbed the slender, rounded, dark-green switches of reed. True, the brittle reeds broke off then and there, revealing tender white plant fibers which looked like honeycomb; then Dedok seized the branch of a hazel bush. The double-edged swords of the hazel cut the skin of his palms, but Dedok nonetheless managed to pull the dugout into the thick rushes and there the wind died out as if suddenly cut off.

Dedok held his hands in the water, and when the burning pain subsided, he built a rather flimsy and drafty shelter, and then he sat for a long time without moving, waiting until he gathered enough strength to continue on his way.

Dedok had left home in the early morning and it took him till evening to reach the 'landing' that served as a gathering place for all the Podsvyatye hunters...

The unpleasant feeling aroused by Anatoly Ivanovich's words passed away as soon as Dedok stepped onto the firm edge of the shore, washed smooth and slippery by the water. At the sight of the familiar faces, and of the punt-pole to which a puny hawk was tied, and the stack of swamp grass destined to be used that day for the hunters' needs, Dedok was seized with intense emotion and a feeling of lightheadedness. He was back among his own kind, Anatoly Ivanovich on behalf of everyone had accepted him into the old fellowship, no one pestered him with sympathy, no one thought Dedok was all washed up and no longer fit for serious business.

In the meantime, more and more people were gathering on the shore. There'd be a rustle of branches, and then one after another, singly or in twos and threes, hunters would come out of the woods onto the muddy shore wearing rubber boots rolled up to below the knee, and thick quilted jackets, fur hats, and service caps with the peaks removed so they wouldn't hinder them in shooting. Each one had a knapsack with decoys on his back, and a wicker cage with a live decoy at his side; some carried their rifles across their backs, others across their chests, like tommy guns. Petrak, who had a large family, came with his quilted jacket in tatters, looking like an enormous ruffled bird; with him was his brother-in-law Ivan, dark-skinned, with black gypsy brows, in a brand new padded jacket and leather pants. Nimble little Kostenka appeared, laughing for some reason, as usual, and already arguing with someone. "I'll show you!... I'll get you!... " he cried in a thin voice, laughing merrily. From the regional center came the taciturn Zhamov, an oldtimer from the Meshchyora district, a huge, heavy man wearing two raincoats; two young hunters came: the kolkhoz bookkeeper Kolechka, and Valka Kosoy, expelled from school "because of hunting." Together with Bakun, a tall, thin, gloomy man respected for a lack of success that was hard to match and the incredible fortitude with which he withstood the troubles that had befallen him, there came Anatoly Ivanovich's handsome brother Vasily. Even from afar, one could hear him pumping Bakun for the details of his latest feat: one rainy day Bakun took it into his head to move a swarm of bees and they were so mad at the foul weather that they attacked Bakun himself as well as his mother-in-law, and stung to death a rooster and two hens. Vasily laughed loudly, showing his white moist teeth, while Bakun only smiled meekly.

The hunters threw down their bags, knapsacks, and guns and sat down on the stiff sedge, beneath which they could feel damp and warm peat. Everyone had come too early, they all felt a little ashamed of their impatience, but those who'd come earlier had already gotten over their embarrassment and teased the newcomers. Cigarettes were lit and conversations started up. Dedok wandered from group to group, listening to the hunters' talk with a warm feeling in his heart. He'd never thought that these people could be so important and dear to him. Previously, he'd thought that he had no particular liking for some and disapproved of others. But all of them were a part of that world—now nearly lost to Dedok—in which it was so sweet and joyous to be alive. And without any one of them, life would be in some way poorer.

In the group gathered around Anatoly Ivanovich, who as usual was sitting as straight as if he'd been run through with a ramrod, the conversation had a scholarly tone.

"So why, for instance, is a crane called a crane?" the kolkhoz bookkeeper was asking, his round unshaven face downy with a growth of beard.

"Well, that's easy," Anatoly Ivanovich answered scornfully. "Haven't you ever seen a 'well-crane'? A shaft with a bucket on one end that rocks up and down—like a crane standing on one leg."

"But I think the crane came before the well," Petrak noted thoughtfully. "The bird turned up first..."

"That's right, it did!" explained Kolechka, struck by the thought.

Anatoly Ivanovich shifted his flat, cold, gray eyes slightly in his direction.

"Of course it did, what kind of talk is that!" he said sternly. "Only it didn't have a name then."

"It really didn't have a name?" Kolechka exclaimed in amazement and turned his large round head.

Dedok got the urge to cut in and also say something as clever and impressive as Anatoly Ivanovich had, so that the gamewarden would squint at him with his cool gray eyes, and Kolechka would turn his large round head, but he just couldn't gather his thoughts, which kept slipping away, and he suddenly blurted out something that wasn't at all what he'd meant to say.

"And in Ryazan they say 'cheal' instead of 'teal'!"

Anatoly Ivanovich, without turning his head, got Dedok into his sights.

"Were you really ever in Ryazan?"

"What do you mean, was I ever?" gasped Dedok. "I went with your father, may he rest in peace. I've been everywhere: in Ryazan, in Klepiky, in Shilov..."

"That's right, that's what they say," Anatoly Ivanovich confirmed. "They always mix up 't' and 'ch' over there."

"That's it!" Dedok said joyfully. "And any duck to them's a 'cheal'—a teal's a 'cheal' a wild duck's a 'cheal,' and a golden eye's a 'cheal' ".

"Don't talk nonsense, old man," interrupted Anatoly Ivanovich. "A wild duck is a mallard to them, and a golden eye's called just that."

"That's right," Dedok thought to himself, as if he'd just woken up. "Why in the world did I...?"

"Where'd a name like 'teal' come from?" asked Kolechka.

Dedok walked on a little farther.

Ivan, the dark-skinned driver who looked like a gypsy, and Anatoly Ivanovich's brother Vasily were chiding Bakun for not being able to manage his wife, a stout young cattle-farm worker named Nastya. Kostenka, who liked racy talk, was also bustling about there.

"They say she's taken to going over to Zarechye," the driver was saying. "That's where your replacement must live."

Bakun wasn't offended.

"Maybe that's so, fellas," he was saying, the gaps between his teeth showing as he smiled meekly. "You can't blame her. She's a young woman, nice and plump, and me—I'm just a half-finished product."

The hunters laughed, and again Dedok wanted to impress them with something witty and daring.

"Aw, you youngsters!" he said. "Me, I'm pushing eighty, but I pay a visit to my woman once a week."

"The old man's sure strong!" exclaimed the driver, raising a dark eyebrow, and added a bad word. Kostenka snickered and Vasily smiled with pity and disgust.

Dedok became painfully embarrassed; he turned away, his shoulders drooping, and went off.

The light wind that heralded the sunset died down, and the faint ripple subsided, the smooth surface of the lake becoming as still as if a tight sheet had been stretched out over the water. Between a thin, bluish-gray stripe lying on the horizon and a heavy, stratified, chalky-blue cloud, there appeared a jagged, blood-red flame, as if the top of the guard tower had caught fire. Then something shifted in the moisture-laden air and the jagged edges merged, shaping the enormous setting sun unto a half-circle neatly cut off at the top by a cloud. A haystack blazed crimson with green and blue veins of color, as if it had been set on fire. Then the sun began sinking visibly into the bluish-gray stripe on the horizon; its golden crown lit up blindingly for one last time, and then disappeared. Into the silence of the smoldering day fell the sound of a shot—hollow, dry, and brief. After a noiseless moment, it rolled over the lake, echoing in different keys in the backwaters, and spilled like a shower of peas into the forest on Saltny Point. Everyone who was sitting or lying on the shore pricked up his ears— some raised themselves a little, others squatted down on their haunches, some stared at their neighbors with uncertain smiles on their faces.

"They're shooting in Dunyashkin Creek," said someone longingly.

In the distance could be heard the sound of two hollow shots which didn't resound in the open space.

"They're at it in Dubovo," sighed someone.

Just then Prudkov Creek answered, and Beryoza Island piped up. A large flock of mallards rose up from there, flew along the shore over the hunters' heads and, turning towards Khakhal, suddenly dissolved in the air.

"They're scaring the ducks off," noted Petrak.

"I can't stand it!" said Kostenka in a childish voice.

The driver got up with an angry look on his face and, clutching his bag with the decoy in it, he set off for his boat.

"Where you going, Vanechka?" Petrak called out after him.

"We're here yappin' and the tourists are banging away like nobody's business," answered the driver coarsely. "That does it! ... "

"He's right, you know!" chimed in Kolenka. "We've been waiting it out here till it's time, but what's the sense? ... "

The rapid whir of a motorboat could be heard through the intermittent shots.

"Lake police, from Klepiky," said Vasily.

"They're far away ... in Nalmus," said Kostenka, listening. "No, we're missing out on the best hunting for nothing."

"So why don't you give it a try," said Vasily, egging him on.

"I'm scared. What if they take away my license."

"And your gun to boot," added Anatoly Ivanovich gravely.

The firing picked up. They were shooting on the far lake and on the one nearby, and in Dunyashkin Creek; they were firing at Lake Dubovo without a let-up, and there was rapping from the shore at Prudkov. The ducks were flying quickly over the lake, but not being seriously frightened yet, were landing on the water close to the hunters' shelters.

Following his brother-in-law, Petrak went to his boat with a distracted and preoccupied look. He unlocked it and got an oar out from under the seat. He looked at the oar as if he himself didn't understand how it had gotten into his hands, and shrugging his shoulders, still with that same distracted look on his face, he pushed off from the shore.

"I'll go too, so help me God I'll go!" said Dedok, surprising himself. He hadn't meant to do that at all, but the desire to show that he was still his old self—a brave and clever hunter—pushed the words onto his tongue.

"You sit where you are!" Anatoly Ivanovich shouted at him.

It was already getting dark; the sunset, smothered with clouds, lent the lake only a little bit of reddish color, and Dedok knew he wouldn't be able to spot any game, and besides, he didn't care to break hunting regulations; but in Anatoly Ivanovich's words, and especially in his expression, there was something reminiscent of his old woman's "You poor devil!"—and that settled the matter.

The whole short distance to the shelter, Dedok reproached himself for his rashness. Cold rose from the water and as usual his bones began to ache. Dedok didn't let out the live decoy, and planted only the artificial ones. Then he rowed into the cold, damp rushes under the unsteady roof of his shelter, loaded his gun, and got ready to wait for either a long or a short time. The last red spots on the water had faded away, and it had become milky-white, the color of the sky. Soon the sky would darken and the silvery dots of the stars, barely noticeable, would begin to gleam in it, then the stars would turn a golden color, and the openings between them would fill with a shimmering blue and finally with black, and in the same way, the water would turn as black as tar, and it would be night. If only it would come more quickly so that it wouldn't be embarrassing to return to shore...

The water was smoking. Thin streams of very light, whitish smoke rose from its smooth, quiet surface, just as if underwater inhabitants were having a friendly smoke. And every little stream appeared to dissolve in the air without leaving a trace, but it wasn't that way at all: at the height of the flower clusters among the reeds, the streams of smoke fused together here and there; the tufts would barely settle and catch new streams, forming hazy clouds, and already the flower clusters, separated by them from their stalks, would sway freely in the air, as if floating over the lake while still remaining in one place. And suddenly, looming harshly and menacingly black in the still thin haze, a dugout came directly towards Dedok's shelter. In the stern towered the heavy, thickset figure of Sergey Makarych, the gamewarden. Dedok felt an unpleasant weakness in his knees, but the next moment he rowed out of the shelter towards the warden with a merry look on his face, and, conscious of his own daring, said with assumed meekness:

"And aren't you clever, Makarych! There's no fightin' it; go ahead and run me in!"

But Makarych glanced past Dedok at the shelter, as if expecting someone else to come out of it.

"Gonna take away my gun?" asked Dedok in a businesslike tone.

He imagined how he'd return to shore under Makarych's escort, how the more cautious hunters would greet him with sympathetic and respectful jokes: well, they'd say, what a stunt the reckless old man's pulled! How he'd swear to his old woman at the relentlessness of the authorities nowadays, and she'd say: when will you ever settle down, old man! But Makarych raised his oar, thrust it against the silt-covered lake bottom, and began to turn the bow of his dugout around.

"Where in the world are you going, Makarych?" said Dedok, frightened. "I reckoned the law was the same for everybody. You don't think I was against..."

But Makarych, with the same gloomy and indifferent look, was swinging the dugout around against the current. Dedok darted back and forth, trying in vain to catch the gamewarden's boat, which was slipping away, and holding out his old army gun to Makarych.

"What's this, Makarych?" he said imploringly. "You're on duty, after all. It's your job to enforce the law. How is it you can shut your eyes to poachers?"

"You stay there, we're not going to touch you," said Makarych, and added with a smirk: "Poacher!..."

Pushing off hard with his oar, he immediately placed a strip of darkened, grayish-blue smoking water between himself and Dedok.

Dedok gathered up the slippery decoys, put them on the bottom of the boat, and slowly set off in the opposite direction. When he reached the landing, it was completely dark, the hunters were busy with preparations for the night, and his appearance went by unnoticed.

Following the others, Dedok set off for the dark, heavy haystack, as high as a hill, which was about thirty paces from the shore. Stumbling into a soft, damp hole, and almost getting stuck in the sticky slime beyond the mound, Dedok reached the haystack, which had been clawed away around the bottom by the hunters, and, spreading his arms wide, he grabbed a prickly armful of hay, which gave off a sharp, stifling smell from the contact. Now he had to bring his arms closer together, energetically push himself away, and he'd have an armful the size of a small hayrick. Dedok made an effort, pushed his arms through, first up to his elbows, then up to his shoulders, so that the hollow, bristly tips got caught in his nose and beard, and he pulled back. The hay responded to his movement with a weak, mysterious rustle and suddenly drew Dedok to itself, pulling his face into its prickly dryness. He again tried to tear himself away from the haystack, and once again the haystack proved to be stronger than he, and drew him to itself. Dedok freed his arms, caught his breath and began to pluck out the hay a little at a time. "Well, that ought to do it," Dedok said to himself, knowing full well that the hay would barely be enough to put under his backside and that sleeping would be hard and cold for him.

It was very dark on the shore, and from the moonless sky, the weak light of almost invisible stars barely pierced the haze of soaring, whirling clouds which were as light as smoke; but when Dedok got into his dugout, it seemed to him that he'd gone from day to night—such was the darkness that reigned here under the embankment. Groping his way along, he moved the bag with decoys to the front of the boat, covered the bottom with a thin layer of hay, and, hindered by his own inflexible, stiff body, settled flat on his back into the narrow space.

The hunters weren't asleep; he could hear quiet talk, swearing, and laughter. The lights from their cigarettes glowed like fantastic red fireflies. Dedok lay there, sensing that even here he wouldn't be able to fall asleep, just as he'd not been able to sleep up on the stove.

"Dedok, hey—Dedok!..." he heard Kolechka's voice call out. "What's the weather gonna be like tomorrow? They say you're a walking barometer."

Cheered that he'd turned out to be useful, Dedok listened carefully to his legs, which hummed like telegraph poles when he put his ears to them, and he felt the side of the boat, which was as smooth and slippery as if it had been lathered, and looked at the dull, distant sky with its gradually fading stars.

"Cloudy, with a little wind, and then it'll clear up."

"Aw, even I could've told you that!. . ." laughed Kolechka, and his laugh died away in the darkness.

Then Anatoly Ivanovich asked in a very loud voice:

"Dedok, will you wake us in the morning?"

"Sure I'll wake you, old buddy..."

The night passed neither quickly nor slowly, as did all his sleepless nights. It probably seemed shorter to Dedok than the nights on the stove. The sky kept changing: one moment a bleak darkness was drawn across it, the next, it threw out bunches of stars; something gurgled and splashed in the water, either a pike or a water-rat; then suddenly it started to drizzle, but a wind rose and swept aside the still falling rain. Life in its diverse forms was going on in the darkness, and Dedok felt his own diminishing life and his breathing alongside the breathing of the world, and he wondered why in this pre-dawn hour, at the darkest time, when night seemed to be spending the last of its supply of darkness before it began its retreat, his deceased son, as dark as the night itself—and yet visible just the same in faint glimmering outline, sat down on the side of the boat. Dedok looked at him for a long time, then asked soundlessly, moving only his lips:

"What are you here for?"

His son didn't answer; he loomed silently and stubbornly before his father's eyes as if he wanted to remind him of something, but Dedok didn't want to understand him; right now he was alive and among the living, and rejected what the newcomer had brought with him. His son disappeared when the trees, the haystack, and the top of the barge-pole began to take shape in the darkness.

There was no wind, but all the air seemed to be shivering with an icy chill; along the edges of the shore there lit up the thinnest crust of milky-white ice, and the motionless water at the sides of the dugout was coated with a needle-like film.

"Rise and shine, boys!..." cried out Dedok in a weak voice.

However quiet his trembling voice may have been, it chased off the light sleep of the hunters. Vasily's tousled head appeared above the side of the nearest dugout; after him Anatoly Ivanovich got up and immediately began to roll a cigarette, and then Valka jumped up, wildly rolling his slanted eyes.

Dedok let his oar down into the water; a narrow, black slit yawned, and the dugout moved away from the shore.

The morning came without a sunrise; the sky was clouded over. Light didn't stream from the east, but came dimly and uniformly from the open expanse. Working at the oar didn't warm up Dedok and when he pulled out the live decoy from his bag it began to beat its wings in his cold, stiff hands. Dedok became afraid that it might knock off the band on its leg and fly away to its wild kin. The hard wings of the decoy beat Dedok across his face and eyes, but he stroked its back and its supple neck, and laughed softly in order to avoid owing up to his weakness before this pitiful rebellion. Finally he succeeded in fixing the band on its leg and he unclasped his hands with relief. The decoy fell on the water, then tore away forward and upward, but the plummet, which sank to the bottom swiftly and noiselessly, pinned it to the spot. It cried out in a high, piercing voice once or twice and then, calming down, buried its beak in its breast feathers.

And Dedok was in the shelter once more. The decoys were rocking and slowly rotating on their axes; the tufts of reed rustled, the switches of reed whistled drily and delicately; Dedok's unseeing gaze was covered with moisture: he was sleeping with his eyes open, overcome by fatigue, lulled by the monotonous song of the lake. He didn't hear the hunters' shots or the noise of the wings as flocks flew by overhead, or the brief splash of the mallards, teal, and wild ducks that would alight near his live decoy or by the fake ones. When he woke up, the sun was already high in the sky, which was clear of clouds, and the water sparkled dazzlingly, as if invisible fingers were tirelessly pouring out handfuls of gold coin.

"Looks like I had a little nap," said Dedok to himself, driving away the terrible thought that he'd slept through the best time for hunting. "Well, that's all right, I won't be left empty-handed."

Soon he had no strength left to look at the water, in whose sparkling, fatiguing glitter the decoys were rocking monotonously and lifelessly. Dedok turned away his worn-out eyes and not far away, in the rushes, he saw what looked like a mound of all kinds of refuse from the lake. It was the little house of a muskrat, made habitable and warm in time for winter. Dedok had seen hundreds of them in his day, but now he looked closely and with new interest at the simple structure.

The dead life of nature had renewed itself so many times before Dedok's eyes that he never thought of death as an ending. The feeling that he would disappear without a trace and be no more was alien to his soul. He didn't believe so much as assume that a person who'd died would return to life as some kind of animal which in turn would become a smaller creature—and so on until it all came to a tiny, invisible being that would then remain forever. He himself couldn't say where he'd gotten such a strange idea, but it pleased him, it seemed convincing, and he didn't want to part with it. But that didn't reconcile him at all with what is called death.

The human phase was the best, the most worthy time in this immortal life. Beyond it, everything would be worse, pettier, more insignificant, although each type of existence was probably not without its joys. But now, feeling that he'd worn out his human form, Dedok had nothing against beginning to live anew in the skin of a sturdy young muskrat. More than anything in life, Dedok had valued his dwelling, his home, the roof over his head. He'd been born in a hut that looked like an old bast shoe, with a rotted thatch roof tilted to one side, and a dirt floor. In that hut he'd grown and matured, and when his father gave him his inheritance after the wedding, Dedok built himself a better house, with a wooden floor and a big window, though it, too, had a thatch roof. Later on, when he was the foreman of the kolkhoz carpenters, he built three different houses before putting up the present one, a durable home with a tin roof.

The muskrat was also a builder; it was content with any burrow or lair. It had built itself a real home with a little dome roof out of pitiful building materials supplied by the lake: wood chips, dry reeds, rushes, small branches, and leaves. Dedok recalled that at Saltny, where hunters arriving from the city would regularly stay, you could find not only good wood chips, but also old jam jars and all kinds of other durable material. "I better not forget... " he ordered himself, getting confused and thinking of the time when he'd become a muskrat.

But for the time being he was still a man, a hunter; there was a gun in his hands and he was supposed to kill with that gun, to kill no matter what, because if he didn't, it meant he was no longer worth anything among people. Dedok began to look at the water again, overcoming the cutting pain in his eyes. There were reeds between him and the decoy. The supple blades trembled and shook and divided the decoy in two with their quivering movement. He had to check himself constantly so as not to mistake the decoy's double for a live duck. But there was a moment when a pulse of blood in his heart persuaded Dedok that now it wasn't an illusion: a teal had really settled near the decoy. He raised his gun and aimed carefully. Not risking a shot to the head, he took the teal from underneath, as if mounting it on the gun barrel. The teal waited patiently until the hunter's old eye, which was continuously flooding with tears, caught it in the middle of its pupil. The hard recoil of the shot struck Dedok painfully in the collarbone and almost threw him over into the water. The sweet smoky stench of the powder entered his nostrils. And before Dedok could make out the teal again, he knew that he hadn't missed. But what was going on? Instead of lying on the water in a dark stripe, the teal had turned upside down, exposing its bright belly: Dedok had bagged the decoy, taking it for a live teal. Dedok immediately grew weak from shame and grief; he put aside his gun without even removing the fired cartridge and sat for a long time without moving, cradling his head in his arms.

When he'd reloaded his gun, and the cartridge which had been thrown into the water floated up to the bow of the dugout, standing upright, like a toy soldier, a teal landed to the side of the decoy, completely separate, small, and self-important. Dedok shouldered his gun and fired, barely aiming. The teal lay down on the water obediently, its wing sticking out slightly. Dedok sighed deeply, with his whole insides, and took up his oar.

A small wave lifted the teal and carried it to the stern, almost into the very hands of the old man. In his long lifetime Dedok had shot a countless number of them. Kindly but without pity, like any real hunter, he never destroyed a living creature to no purpose, he shot birds only on the wing, and wasn't tempted by immature ducks. But he did shoot as many as he could. Yet now, when he took the compact, heavy little body of the teal out of the water and it immediately became dry because the drops ran off its waxy feathers, he felt an unaccustomed, complex feeling towards it. The teal was lying in his palm, its head hanging, and its dead, unreflecting eyes half-covered by a light-blue membrane; its bright little breast was bent in a sharp hump, and its flat back was giving up its escaping warmth of life into Dedok's palm. And Dedok felt a tenderness painful to the point of tears, an aching gratitude, towards the small, lightning-quick flier that had given its life to prolong the fading life of the old hunter.

Even if Dedok boasted to the others how deftly he'd bagged the teal, he himself knew that the teal had come of its own accord to be small game. It was stronger, quicker, more clever and wise than Dedok, and it sacrificed itself of its own free will. Dedok bent down and kissed the teal on its sharp little head, and then tossed it into the bottom of the dugout...

Without having agreed to do so in advance, the hunters met at the landing almost at the same time. The frightened ducks had made for the open water, the birds were landing on the water more infrequently, and besides, most of the hunters had run low on cartridges. Anatoly Ivanovich, Petrak, the driver, and Vasily returned with a good deal of game, but as for the rest, few did any better than Dedok, and Valka Kosoy hadn't bagged anything at all. Rolling his slanting eyes upwards, Valka swore that the birds he'd wounded had fallen to Zhamov, who'd been sitting in the neighboring shelter. It somehow became known that the police who'd come from the city had shot at Bakun's domestic ducks, taking them for wild ones. "You don't get tame ducks on the water," they informed Bakun's wife, who tried in vain to save her poultry. Dedok heard the hunters' talk and a strange lack of interest possessed him—everything had suddenly become strange, distant, indifferent...

Having tied up their dugouts and hidden their oars in the grass, the hunters set out for the woods in single file. Dedok made his way close behind the others. Wending its way among the hummocks and swampy lakes, the path ran into the forest dryland and became a wide forest road. The hunters speeded up and Dedok fell behind. Then he saw that the hunters had checked their pace, apparently waiting for him. He waved them on and turned off the road as if to go relieve himself. He stood, resting with his shoulder against the trunk of a birch tree, until the hunters' voices died out in the distance and only the rustle of leaves and the gentle tap of a young woodpecker remained to be heard around him. Dedok went out onto the road and slowly made his way forward. A large cowberry bush, the size of a cranberry bush, looked bright red in the grass, and the fruit of a great bilberry was blue, as if covered with hoarfrost. Dedok wanted to feel in his mouth the cool, bitter-sweet taste of the berry crushed under his tongue; he bent over, but there was a buzzing in his ears and a reddish fog rushed to his eyes. He straightened up and began hobbling forward quickly.

A feeling of weakness in Dedok's neck made it want to let his head drop, and a weakness in his shoulders made them want to throw off their own weight, and a weakness in his hands made them wish they could hang like the runners of a climbing plant and hold nothing, nor hold up anything, and there was a feeling of weakness in his legs: they buckled, his knees shook, his ankles twisted, his feet could no longer carry Dedok's body. He held up his whole body by the bones at the small of his back; their rigid strength was the only thing he could depend on.

A thin, bony rabbit with dirty yellow fur crossed the road boldly and without hurrying. It looked at the old man and went into the thicket, into the dryness of the fallen leaves and the verdure of live grass. Dedok envied the rabbit: those on four supports had it good; any wretched creature—a rabbit, a hedgehog, a beetle—supports itself on the ground with four extremities, but a man was given only two weak posts. Dedok wanted to drop down on all fours. "You can't," he ordered himself, although he began to feel lightheaded from weakness and the temptation to lie down and not move. He remembered and yet didn't remember where he was and where he was going; sometimes he saw and then didn't see the forest surrounding him on all sides, and the thrushes which were flying from tree to tree, as if someone were flinging small shot at them in handfuls.

Suddenly it was as if a dull green cloth had been torn apart, and the forest flew open at its edge, and something fire-red, like the fur of a fox, appeared in front. And first the fire-red something was quite close, then it moved away, freeing a space for other numerous, more subdued colors. The colors acquired shape, and became plowed land, a potato field, a wattle fence, the roofs of huts, poplars, a ribbon of river; and the red became the rowan bush, its clusters singed by autumn, that grew in his, Dedok's garden. In front of him was the village and his house, but, seeing his goal already so near, Dedok realized that he wouldn't reach it. He felt neither pain nor suffering; even the weakness which had been knocking him off his feet ceased to be something strange, hostile, hampering; it became himself. And it became quite simple and easy to not be; it was enough to drop to the ground. "You can't," Dedok told himself again. "You can't die before your time." That which had tormented him all the long days and nights spent on the stove finally found its answer: all that had been, had been only in order for him to complete this last journey.

One moment the earth rose up before him with all the trees and huts, with the bright red rowan bush, and with the blue ribbon of river, and the next it dropped swiftly; spinning, making his head reel, the earth rocked him, as the cradle had rocked him in childhood, but Dedok kept going towards his unattainable goal.

1955   Translated by Irene Kiedrowski

The original ("Posledniaia okhota") first appeared in 1955 in *Moskva*. The present translation is of the edition included in the two-volume 1973 collection, I, 131-148, where the story is misdated as 1957.

The Newlywed

Voronov learned from the old woman who ferried him across the Pra that finding a huntsman in Podsvyatye was complicated. The old woman was tall and well-built, with strong legs in short canvas boots; her khaki quilted jacket fitted snugly across her broad rounded shoulders; though it was summer, her head was covered with a warm army cap that concealed her gray hair, and when she turned her small wrinkled face away from Voronov as she wielded the pole, it was a pleasure to watch her. Time had spared her figure, but had disfigured her hands—they were dry, gnarled, and blotched; it had preserved her dark sparkling eyes, with bluish whites, in a face taut with wrinkles. Her lively unfaded eyes dancing playfully, the old woman explained loquaciously:

"You've come a little late. There's not a huntsman to be had here two days before the season, and in mid-season—not a chance!... I'm sure it used to be easier before. But now some of them have given it up totally because the collective farm has become profitable—take my youngest, Vaska, for example—and others have gone to work for the government. The best huntsmen now work at looking after the lake. Take Anatoly Ivanovich, now, my oldest. You wouldn't know about him in Moscow..." The slight shade of contempt that sounded in the last words wasn't directed at her son's limited reputation, which hadn't reached the capital, but at Voronov's ignorance.

"No, why do you say that," retorted Voronov. "I've heard of Anatoly Ivanovich more than once as the most reliable man for hunting."

"You people in Moscow aren't well informed about Meshchyora," the old woman said disapprovingly. "As if Anatoly Ivanovich had nothing to do but take you townspeople around. He looks after our region!"

"So what do you advise me to do?" asked Voronov.

Voronov liked hunting, he had endurance, a keen eye, and a steady hand, but he wasn't a real hunter, and besides, this was his first time in Meshchyora.

"I can't advise you in anything," replied the old woman, dexterously steering the nimble boat across the waves. "I'll tell you one thing: try to get one of the old men, they're free from work and they like to go off. But I think you'll be looking in vain there too."

The boat scraped along the bottom and came to an abrupt halt. It was about three or four meters from shore. Lifting the hem of her skirt as she moved, the old woman threw first one leg over the side of the boat, then the other, leaned her chest against the stern, and pushed the boat onto the sandbank.

The solid immovability of the bank caused Voronov to stagger.

He took out a ten-ruble note and held it out to the old woman.

"Keep the change," she said, and in response to his gesture of protest, "Those are our rules. The ferry's a fiver, an overnight stay is three, and a huntsman is twenty-five a day... Look, try and give that cottage there a knock. Ask Dedok, maybe you'll persuade him..."

Voronov thanked her, and set off along the bank, which was full of mounds, toward the house she'd indicated.

An old woman who bore a remarkable resemblance to the ferry woman opened the door: she had a youthful figure and a small wrinkled face with dark, lively, beady eyes. She was dressed like her too: a khaki quilted jacket, canvas boots, a cap with earflaps and corner traces of a star that had been removed. "Looks as if the old women from around here are still waging some war of their own," thought Voronov with a smile.

"No, dear, Dedok won't go, he's sick," she said. "He came from Great Lake dead beat yesterday."

Nevertheless, she let Voronov into the cottage, where the master of the house lay under a pile of overcoats on a bed with pillows. Dedok himself wasn't visible; only a gray stump of beard, yellowed from smoking, was sticking out.

"What if I pay you well?" said Voronov.

"You hear that? Eh, mother?" a weak voice emerged from the depths of the bed, and the gray stump quivered.

"Not a chance," his wife raised her voice. "He's panting steam and wants to go yet! As you can see, we're of no use to you, my dear man," she told Voronov sternly.

"So where can I find a huntsman?" asked Voronov persistently.

"Where can you find one, if there aren't any! There aren't any, and that's that!" said the mistress of the house angrily.

Had such a conversation taken place a few years ago, Voronov's Meshchyora hunting trip would have ended without having begun. In the past he'd been inclined to exaggerate the antagonistic forces of life; all obstacles, even insignificant ones, had seemed insurmountable to him. But with the years he'd acquired the conviction that there weren't any insoluble problems in life, that a calm and sober persistence could sweep aside any obstacle. His voice sounded almost cheerful when he asked:

"But where am I to find a huntsman?"

The old woman raised her sparse eyelashes nervously.

"So where can you find one, my dear?" she said, but now instead of being angry she was at a loss.

"That's what I'm asking you," said Voronov.

The old woman cast her eyes right and left, as though a huntsman really could be hiding somewhere nearby, which this Muscovite surely must know.

"I really don't know what to tell you... Perhaps you'll be able to persuade the newlywed?"

"The newlywed's not likely to go!" came from beneath the pile of overcoats.

"He'll go," Voronov answered for the old woman. "Where'll I find him?"

"The last cottage to the left of us," explained the old woman. "Go see him, dear, maybe you'll persuade him. It's just that he's given up hunting since he got married."

"He won't go," was heard again from under the coats. "He won't leave his wife."

"What's he called, the newlywed?" asked Voronov.

"Vaska," replied the old woman. "What else?"

"He won't go," reached Voronov's ears when he was already in the hallway.

He decided that the newlywed's resistance to the temptation of making easy money at hunting was one of Meshchyora's points of interest, one which the local people were proud of.

Voronov had forgotten to ask on which side of the street Vaska's cottage stood. Of the two end cottages he chose the one that looked cleaner and was decorated with an iron weathercock on the rooftop and freshly whitewashed fretted shutters. It seemed fitting that newlyweds should live in the neat dwelling which had some claim to smartness. Voronov went into the large dark hallway, which smelled of calf, rotted straw bedding, chicken droppings, and duckmeat that had turned. In the center of the hallway a decent-sized bunch of mallard and teal with tufts of grass in their tails hung on a loop of rope. "That means he hasn't given up hunting altogether," Voronov observed privately. A curly-haired broad-shouldered young man in riding breeches and white shirt with rolled-up sleeves rose from his knees—he was rough-hewing a log with an axe—and asked Voronov whom he was looking for.

"I'm looking for you," replied Voronov. The young man drove the axe into the log and led the way into the cottage. Voronov followed him. In the doorway he stepped aside, letting by a small woman with a full basin in her hands.

The newlyweds' home was as inviting inside as on the outside. A freshly-whitewashed stove, multicolored wallpaper, windowsills with pots of geraniums, and a lot of pictures from the magazine *Ogonyok* on the walls. In the corner a sideboard with a small lace cloth, on it a tumbler of cheap colored glass, two big heavy shells of the kind in which "you can hear the sea," a frame with photographs, and in the middle, as usual, a picture of the young couple.

On a bench near the door sat an old woman in a quilted jacket and canvas boots—apparently they were a must in Meshchyora households, Voronov concluded. But then he recognized the old woman as the one who'd ferried him over, and he realized that she was the mother of the newlywed Vaska. On another bench by the window sat a young woman in a kerchief which hung down her shoulders. Her large firm bosom stretched her cotton print blouse tightly and heavily.

"Well, actually I've come to see you," Voronov addressed her. "Will you let the master come with me?"

The woman turned her eyes on Voronov with surprise and lowered her gaze. She had beautiful eyes with prominent bluish whites.

"She doesn't have a master!" Vaska remarked with a gentle smile of irony. "That's my sister,"

Voronov bit his lip in vexation; he should have guessed that she wasn't the mistress of the house. She sat with the ceremoniousness of a village guest and, moreover, was strikingly like her brother: the same chestnut hair, the dark rosy complexion, the same moist languishing eyes with bluish whites.

"Well what do you say to my proposal?"

"He's got no call to go!... It's just silly nonsense!" This was said by the petite woman whom Voronov had met in the doorway. She was standing on the threshold, her head far short of the low ceiling, and holding the empty basin against her hip. Voronov noted with disappointment how plain the good-looking Vaska's young wife was. She was short in stature, and there was nothing pretty about her face; it was small, sprinkled with freckles, and had bottle-green eyes. Moreover, the young woman wasn't particularly young, she was twenty-five or perhaps more. She had on an old frock, which was narrow and short, and slippers that were worn down at the heels on her feet. But one sensed that she had character, and Voronov wasn't surprised that Vaska smiled and spread his hands in response to his wife's sharp comment.

"Grandma, as an old acquaintance you might give me some support," Voronov turned to the old woman.

"I'm not the mistress here," Vaska's mother answered.

This came out without any resentment or challenge—it was simply the assertion of a just fact, known to everyone.

Now Voronov knew what to do.

"Can I have a couple of words with you?" he addressed Vaska's wife.

They went out into the hall. Unhurriedly and in some detail Voronov explained to the petite woman that he wouldn't be taking her husband away for more than three or four days, that he knew the arrangements in Meshchyora, and he would pay well because he was a busy man and allowed himself to hunt all too rarely to be tight with his money. Finally, unlike other Muscovite hunters, he would let Vaska himself shoot...

The petite woman listened to him, her lips moving. Apparently she was calculating how much she'd get. The calculations satisfied her: she smiled, her bottle-colored eyes flashing, and with a vigorous gesture not devoid of grace, she extended her hand to Voronov.

"We're agreed!"

Her sleeve had fallen back to reveal for a moment her round, shapely wrist and rounded elbow, and Voronov, whose success predisposed him to be indulgent, observed: she does have a certain something.

"Vasily, get ready!" she called out in a firm voice. "You're going hunting with the man."

"We should ask the chairwoman..."

"I'll tell her myself. She was saying just the other day: why is it that all these men want time off, only yours acts as though he's tied to you. And I have to tidy up, wash the floors, you make a mess around here!"

Vaska looked at his wife, sighed, then, conquering something inside him, started getting ready.

The huntsman's preparations were brief. After putting some straw in his rubber boots, he wound warm flannel foot-cloths around his strong feet and pulled his boots on; he filled his cartridge-belt with old, discolored cartridges, and put on the belt, then tied some rubber and wooden dummies in a knapsack. Voronov liked watching his sweeping, careless, and at the same time very precise movements. While he made his preparations, Vaska whistled through his teeth, apparently totally oblivious of his attractive, well-knit body.

"Glad to get out of the house!" his wife remarked jealously, washing clothes behind the stove.

"If you want, I won't go," responded Vaska readily.

"Won't go! Have you turned rich all of a sudden?"

Voronov emptied his rucksack, leaving only the essentials: bread, butter, canned food, a thermos of strong tea, extra socks, and a blanket. Vasily brought a wicker basket from the yard in which a decoy duck was quacking away.

Vasily's wife came to see them off. She put on a velveteen jacket fitted in at the waist and high rubber boots, and at once became younger.

"Give me that," she said to her husband, and took the shotgun from him, "You're going to Great Lake?"

"To the small one," replied Vaska.

She raised her eyebrows in surprise. Voronov sensed something wrong here. While still in Moscow he'd heard that one should hunt at Great Lake and the suspicion that Vaska simply didn't want to go too far from home occurred to him.

"Perhaps Great Lake would be better?" he said.

"There's a swarm of people at Great Lake," replied Vaska, looking not at Voronov but at his wife.

Voronov also looked at Vaska's wife, expecting her support. But she merely shrugged her thin shoulders and quickly went on ahead toward the canoe that was visible behind the sedge. Evidently her supremacy at home didn't infringe upon her husband's authority in hunting matters.

Vasily nudged Voronov with his elbow, and smiling, nodded towards his wife: the butt of the long Tula gun was knocking against her heels.

"Only my wife and my brother Anatoly's see us off when we go hunting," he informed Voronov with a touch of pride, and added thoughtfully: "And in his case, since he's an invalid, he wouldn't be able to do it otherwise . . . "

When they reached the stream, the canoe was already untied and spread with fresh dampish hay which Vasily's wife had gathered right on the bank. Vasily put away the rucksacks, the basket and the gun, carefully covered them with his canvas jacket, and got an oar, which looked like a spade, from under the straw.

"Get in, hunting buddy. I don't know your name and patronymic!"

"Sergey Ivanovich." Voronov lowered himself clumsily into the bottom of the canoe; the muddy water, as black as tar, splashed in over the curved side of the boat.

"Take care!" said Vaska to his wife.

Glancing somberly at Voronov, in a short rapid movement she pulled her husband toward her, pressed herself against his side for a moment, gave an abashed smile, then pushed him away, and without turning round, strode off toward the house along the tall grass that rose above waist-level.

Vaska leaned against the bank with the paddle, pushed off—and the canoe slid rapidly along the narrow stretch of water, bumping gently against the snags, dividing with a dry rustling sound the razor-sharp sedge that hung over the canal.

Voronov unbuttoned his shirt collar. All his worries and anxieties were now behind him, he was moving toward his goal with the speed of an arrow. In Moscow he'd heard a great deal about the problems at

Meshchyora and the idiosyncrasies of the local people, whom one had to understand in order to see their gentle and obliging side, for they could be inflexible and stubbornly uncooperative. And how easily he'd handled the situation and attained what he wanted.

He enjoyed watching Vaska's strong deft strokes with the oar. The young fellow's powerful body, which had been inactive for a while, seemed to delight in the exercise. One could feel his taut muscles rippling under his shirt, his healthy easy breathing.

Presently the channel began to zigzag, and if Voronov still had the faint suspicion that Vaska had chosen the small lake because it meant an easier route, it vanished now without a trace. The long canoe couldn't take the sharp turns. Before every turn, using the oar as a pole, Vaska would push off with all his strength, and from the impetus the canoe would speed into the shallows. Vaska would jump into the water, lift the heavy stern, and guide it into another bend in the turn, after which he'd push its bows into the water. The canoe was very heavy, but whenever Voronov offered to help Vaska, the latter wouldn't let him.

But right before they reached the Pra, where the narrow channel flowed out into shallow free waters along the marshy shore, the canoe got stuck so solidly in the mud that Voronov had to get out and lend a hand.

"If my wife saw, oh, would I get it!" said Vaska confidentially.

"What do you mean?"

"She can't stand it when I can't handle something on my own."

Vaska laughed and Voronov asked:

"Do you love her?"

"How could I not?" Vaska said joyfully in surprise. "You saw what she's like!... Who am I compared to her?..." And he spread his hands wide.

He was standing knee-deep in water, the sleeves of his vest rolled up; as the young, hot sweat ran down his swarthy face, darkly-tanned neck and muscular arms, his skin looked varnished. Vaska was so good-looking, so pure and naive in his feelings, that Voronov thought, "Well, fellow, you're worth a damn sight more!" He didn't say that, of course, and they set off along the wooded bank of the Pra.

The Pra here bore no resemblance to a river. It fanned out into a wide lake with flat green little islands and creeks covered with rushes where the fishermen's canoes showed dark. Seagulls flew over the water, and still higher, ducks passed by singly and in flocks. A kite that had been hovering over a cloud smoothly swooped headlong into the water, and touching it with its hooked paws, soared aloft with a roach in its talons. And immediately a crow on top of a pine tore after it. It quickly overtook the kite and seized its prey. Returning to its lookout post, the crow rapidly gobbled up the roach, then waited again for the hard-working kite to fish out another one.

They turned off into a side-channel again, which, unlike the first, was as straight as an arrow. From time to time the narrow passage widened, the water spread out in patches—the channel led from one swampy lake to another. The banks were low here too, but tall sedge, taller than a man, which mingled with the bushes at the water's edge, encased the channel in a dusky dark-green tunnel. It seemed to grow dark suddenly, and Voronov began to worry about arriving too late for the evening's shooting.

"We'll get there just at the right time," said Vaska confidently.

Now and then snipe flew fearlessly right over their heads, a woodcock fluttered out of the grass, and from beneath the flat black leaf of a water lily leaped out a tiny duckling, little bigger than a fledgling, and fled from them at full speed. Not knowing that it had hatched out of its egg too late and wasn't fated to grow into a full-sized duck, the poor little thing was trying with all its strength to save its short life. Squealing pitifully and flailing along the water with pathetic flourishes of its undeveloped wings, it fled along the channel, sometimes right at the canoe's bows, and finally plunged into the undergrowth at the bank. It had barely hidden when something noisily flitted out from that spot, and for a moment in the light opening between the bushes rose the black tattered silhouette of a mallard, and at the same time the pink flash of a shot splashed Voronov's face. Before the echo died away, the duck described an arc and fell into the bushes.

Voronov was startled not so much by the unexpected shot that had rung out just above his ear as by the extraordinary speed and agility with which Vaska had managed to drop the oar and seize and aim the gun with such remarkable accuracy. For some reason Voronov thought that now, also, Vaska had made an effort in his wife's honor, and felt irritated at the exultant fellow. In his state of exultation he would get all the ducks and there'd be nothing left for him, Voronov...

"Look here, Vasily, let's agree on one thing: we can both shoot at those that are in flight, but only I can go for the sitting ones."

"All right, Sergey Ivanych!" Vaska pulled in at the bank and stepped out of the canoe straight into the tall grass. The grass closed up behind him, and when it parted again, Vasla was holding a large drake with an emerald neck in his hands.

"We've made a start, Sergey Ivanovich!"

"Yes," Voronov agreed somewhat drily.

The lake opened up suddenly and sunset-reddened clouds floated in the round mirror of water. Along the edge the water was dark and shadowy from the reflection of the line of dense firs surrounding the lake. Vaska didn't look around the reservoir so as to choose the best place, but at once guided the canoe toward the half-flooded islet at the left bank of the lake which faced the setting sun. Here he cast the dummies about, lowered the fluttering decoy duck into the water, then guided the canoe into the bushes.

"Can you see well from here, Sergey Ivanovich?" he asked.

"I can, but they can see us fine from above too," responded Voronov peevishly.

"It's all right," Vaska soothed him.

Voronov prepared himself for the long wait with which every hunting expedition usually begins, but almost immediately Vaska's quiet, calm voice sounded:

"Teal to the right, Sergey Ivanych."

Voronov started, and quickly ran his eyes over the water. But he saw only the dummies and the big decoy duck that looked somewhat unreal among them.

"By the far dummy to the right," said Vaska just as calmly.

Voronov fired with the feeling that he was aiming at a dummy. The shot lashed against the water like a broom, and one of the two equally motionless teals only swayed a little and slowly turned to show its invulnerable wooden side, while the other collapsed on the water, its neck outstretched, exposing in death the life that had pulsated within.

When they moved out to fetch it, a mallard that had already been settling soared into the air. Voronov hit it, and the duck somersaulted down into the water. It dived in, then surfaced again about thirty meters from them, and Voronov, who'd had time to reload his gun, finished the duck off.

"Good shot," approved Vaska.

But that was only the beginning. Voronov had rarely had such luck at hunting. He killed three teal with one shot, then two large birds and a pintail duck as big as a swan, one after another. Vaska also was busy. He winged three mallards in flight, but one wounded bird got away, another found cover in the rushes, and they couldn't find it in the darkness of the water thicket.

The reservoir was small, and the fierce firing frightened off the ducks, but in the ensuing lull, the self-oblivious, happy intensification of emotions for which he loved hunting so much didn't leave Voronov. He came to only when the first star pierced the sky. Small, pure, and brilliant, it was clearly reflected in the darkened waters of the lake.

"Well, Vasily, that's enough for today, buddy!"

They went down the channel to spend the night. They found a place to camp at once—at the water's edge not far from the mouth stood a wide squat rick of thick sedge hay. Vaska pulled the bows of the canoe onto the bank, unloaded the rucksacks and started to make the beds, forcefully treading down the plump hay that smelled rather pungently of the swamp.

Then they had supper and drank the tea from the thermos. Total darkness set in. The sky filled with stars, and the yellow flank of the moon swelled above the palisade of distant firs. It was still warm, though a chill wafted over occasionally from the creek, which was beginning to cool. Eating pickled perch with gusto and washing it down with the sweet tea, Voronov went over the details of the day's hunting. Vaska answered in monosyllables, more often chuckling briefly, and Voronov decided that that must be a professional characteristic, not to talk on the evening before the following day's hunt about the hunting that was over. Gradually his own excitement diminished, his sense of success stopped agitating him; it belonged to events that had already occurred, had exhausted themselves, and couldn't have any influence on the future.

A pleasant fatigue stole over his body, and peace and tranquillity filled his heart.

"Sergey Ivanych, are you married?" he heard Vasily's voice.

"Of course I am," replied Voronov and immediately caught something approaching dissatisfaction in the intonation of his own voice.

"Your wife's in Moscow?" Vaska asked carefully.

"No, she's at a resort."

"Alone, or with the children?"

"We don't have any children."

Vaska raised himself on his elbow, and looked at Voronov for a while, then said very seriously,

"How come you're not afraid—to let her go alone?"

Voronov burst out laughing. He didn't find the naive exclamation offensive. On the contrary, he experienced a pleasant sense of invulnerability: he was absolutely sure of his wife, and besides, he wasn't at all concerned about her behavior.

"You don't think you can ever safeguard yourself against that, buddy, do you?" he said with an air of superiority.

The huntsman was silent. In the darkness Voronov couldn't see his face, but he sensed that he'd lapsed into disturbed and gloomy thought.

Finishing his tea, Voronov lay down on the scented hay.

Shaking off his pensiveness, Vaska approached Voronov.

"Sergey Ivanych," he said uncertainly. "You're not afraid of spending the night here alone, are you?"

"Of course not, what's there to be afraid of?" Voronov replied, suppressing a smile. He understood that it wasn't jealousy that moved Vaska, but that sudden percing longing for the loved one which can seize the heart even during the briefest of separations. And yet Vaska seemed somewhat funny and pathetic to him now.

"I'm off for a quick visit home. I'll be back by dawn. Believe me!"

"Go ahead, go on," said Voronov, and he turned away, pulling his jacket collar over his head so that Vaska would know there was nothing more to talk about.

He heard Vaska push the canoe into the water; the bottom dragged against the sedge with a screech, the coarse sand on the bank of the lake crunched drily and sharply, then a resounding splash of water was heard, and then a gust of cold damp air penetrated under Voronov's jacket. The sound of water slapping under the bows of the canoe died away. Vaska had sailed off to see his wife. Voronov imagined the journey which Vaska would have to make along the two channels and the river, he remembered all the turns that Vaska would have to negotiate, pulling the canoe out onto the bank and guiding it into another turn, and besides that there was the sandbank which they'd had difficulty in handling together. And all this in the dark, in the damp cold of the night. The journey would take a good four hours. Four there and four back. In order to make it back before dawn Vaska wouldn't even have an hour with his wife. What power of feeling had sent him off on such a hellish journey?

Voronov sighed and drew aside the flaps of his jacket. There had been a time in his life when he, too, could run God knows where at any time of day or night at the first summons, and even without a summons. He, too, had been filled with that passionate, painful agitation that now was driving the young hunter through the night along the waterway. And then he had suddenly become afraid for himself, for his peace, and for God knows what else. Till the very break he had known that everything could be put right, he had only to trust his own feelings. But he had told himself: it's better this way, calmer, simpler. And in order to cut off his own retreat, he'd married his present wife, whom he'd known for a long time as an intelligent, kind, and loyal person. If there had been no joy, there also hadn't been any pain, and that, too, is worth something...

And now his encounter with the young fellow disturbed Voronov, caused him to remember what he disliked remembering. But then, Vaska would get over it one day, and he would see his wife as, say, even Voronov, saw her: a plain, freckled, peevish, demanding woman totally absorbed in domestic worries. Perhaps the aftermath would be bitter for him... "What am I doing?" though Voronov gloomily. "Comparing my lot with his?"

The star-laden sky hung very low. It looked as though it couldn't hold all the stars and they'd fall out. And they really were falling. Turning into green crystals as they flew down, they fell to the ground here and there, some dropping straight down, others in steep or broad arcs. Billows of warm steam rose from the earth, which had become overheated in the course of the day. And the sky with all its stars grew dim, as though it were receding one moment, and the next, coming down closer, saturated with brilliance; it seemed to be breathing.

Voronov was awakened by the sharp chill of dawn. In a single moment his clothes, the jacket that covered him, the thickly-packed flattened straw under his side, and the cap on his head—all seemed as though by agreement to have stopped preserving his body heat, and suddenly they proved cold, damp, heavy, and hostilely comfortless. Voronov twitched his shoulders, and the passing shiver that the movement aroused sent a little charge of warmth and cheer though him. He rose abruptly, already knowing that his next feeling would be annoyance at Vaska's absence. He saw a gray sky that seemed overcast but actually was clear and as yet devoid of blue, a bright band of dawn beyond the forest, the sedge gray with dew, and the black wet bows of the canoe, which was protruding over the sedge of the bank.

Voronov went up to the canoe. Sitting in the stern, Vasily was drawing the ducks they'd shot the day before.

"Hi there, Newlywed!" Voronov called out.

Vaska raised a face that was a trifle pale under its dark tan to Voronov.

"She really cursed me out, Sergey Ivanych, for leaving you!" he said with a joyful smile that was at odds with his words. "I told her that you'd sent me yourself. Don't give me away."

"Of course I won't."

Vaska gave Voronov a cautious side glance. "Don't think I don't trust her. It's simply that I suddenly had such a yearning for her . . . For some reason it struck me that she could have chosen someone else, she could be with someone else right now. And the thought was more than I could stand . . . " Vaska spread his hands in the familiar gesture of helplessness. Then he suddenly shook his curly head, smiled at a private thought, and bending forward slightly, added, "Boy, am I a fool!"

A dim, intoxicated gleam entered Vaska's dark eyes with their prominent whites.

"I expect you won't be able to hunt now," remarked Voronov. "You've exhausted yourself!"

"You must be kidding, Sergey Ivanych! There's nothing I couldn't do now! Why, I . . . "

Vaska said this with such sincerity and simplicity that no doubt remained: it was from his small harassed wife that he derived his strength and joy of life.

Irritation with Vaska stirred again in Voronov: he found his happiness tiresome, it oppressed him and almost humiliated him. He was ready to tell the young fellow that the time would come when his youthful greedy passion would spend itself, fade, but instead of doing that, he asked almost sadly:

"Why do you love her so much?"

"But how can you say that?" responded Vaska in surprise, as if the thought had never entered his head. "Who was I without her? Nothing but Vaska! And now I'm a man, a husband, you could say the father of a family. But it's not even a question of that..."

"Now wait a minute, wait," smiled Voronov, "It's a little early to call yourself the father of a family. To do that, after all, you have to have children."

"But I do have children!" Vaska laughed happily. "Katka and Vaska, the twins. And then there's Senka, though he's still a baby; he's at Gran's..."

"I don't understand a thing," said Voronov, with an unpleasant feeling. "How many years... have you been married?"

"We're old, it'll soon be six years!..."

"Then what kind of newlywed in the hell are you?" demanded Voronov roughly.

Vaska spread his hands again.

"That's what they call me, I don't know why..."

1956   Translated by Helena Goscilo

The original ("Molodozhen") first appeared in *Znamia*, No. 10 (1956), 66-74. The present translation is of the edition included in the 1973 two-volume collection, I, 107-120.

Echo

Sinegoriya, the shore, deserted in the early afternoon, a girl emerging from the sea . . . It was almost thirty years ago!

I was looking for pebbles on the rugged beach. It had stormed the day before; the waves had crept, hissing, across the beach up to the white walls of the seaside sanatorium. The sea had quieted down now and returned to its boundaries, baring a wide chocolate strip of sand shot with blue, separated from the shore by a bank of pebbles. The sand, wet and so hard that one's feet left no imprint on it, was studded with sugary pebbles, turquoise-colored stones, smooth round bits of glass that emitted a pungent iodine smell. I knew that a large breaker washes valuable pebbles ashore, and patiently, step by step, I combed the sandy shore and the newly deposited pebbles.

"Hey! Why have you sprawled out on my shorts?" a reedy voice rang out.

I raised my eyes. A naked little girl stood over me, skinny, ribs protruding, with slim arms and legs. Her long wet hair clung to her face, water glistened on her pale body, almost untouched by the sun and blue and goose-pimpled now from the cold.

The girl bent down, pulled the yellow and blue striped shorts out from under me, shook them out and tossed them on the rocks, while she herself flopped down prone on a mound of golden sand and began raking the sand toward her sides.

"You might at least get dressed . . ." I mumbled.

"Why? This way you get a better tan," the girl replied.

"But aren't you embarrassed?"

"Mama says it doesn't make any difference for kids. She doesn't let me swim in shorts—you can catch a cold that way. But she doesn't have time to bother with me."

Suddenly something flashed softly among the dark rough rocks—a tiny clear teardrop rock. I took the cigarette box from my shirt pocket and added the teardrop to my collection.

"Come on, show it to me! . . ."

The girl tucked her wet hair behind her ears, uncovering a darkly-freckled thin face, green feline eyes, a turned-up nose, a large mouth that stretched from ear to ear, and began examining the stones.

On a thin layer of cotton wadding lay a small oval rosy-transparent carnelian; another carnelian, a bit larger, that hadn't been polished by the sea and was therefore shapeless and didn't respond to the light; a few other stones in a porcelain patterned casing; two interesting fossils, one in the form of a starfish, the other with the imprint of a crab; a small 'chicken god'—a stone ringlet; and the pride of my collection—a small topaz, a patch of fog dissolved in dark glass.

"Did you find all these today?"

"What do you mean?..It's taken the whole time I've been here!.."

"It's not much."

"You just try it!.."

"Why should I?" She shrugged a skinny peeling shoulder. "Crawling around all day in the heat for some lousy little rocks!.."

"You're an idiot!" I said. "A naked idiot!"

"You're an idiot yourself!.. You probably collect stamps too."

"Yes, I do!" I replied defiantly.

"And cigarette boxes too?"

"I collected them when I was little. Then I had a butterfly collection..."

I thought she'd like that and for some reason I wanted her to like it.

"How disgusting!" She pulled back her upper lip, showing two sharp white canine teeth. "Did you crush their heads and pin them down?"

"Not at all. I put them to sleep with ether."

"It's still disgusting...I can't stand it when people kill."

"Do you know what else I used to collect?" I said, after a moment's thought. "Different makes of bicycles!"

"Oh, sure."

"Honest! I'd run down the street and ask all the bicyclists: 'Hey, what make do you have?' They'd say 'Dux' or 'Latvella' or 'Opel.' That way I collected all the models—the only one I didn't have was Endfield's 'Royal' model..." I spoke quickly, afraid that the girl would interrupt me with some mocking comment, but she looked seriously, interestedly at me, and even stopped sprinkling the sand from her fist. "Every day I would run to Lubyanka Square, once I almost fell under a streetcar, but I finally found my 'Endfield Royal!' You know, it has a violet trademark with a big Latin 'R'..."

"That's not bad," said the girl and began to laugh with her large mouth. "I'll tell you a secret, I'm a collector too..."

"Of what?"

"Echoes... I already have a lot of them. I have a clear echo like glass, one like a bronze trumpet, one with three voices, and one that scatters like peas, another one that..."

"That's enough fibs," I interrupted angrily.

The green feline eyes pierced me.

"Do you want me to show you?"

"Well, yes, I do..."

"But only to you—nobody else. Will they let you? You have to climb Big Saddle."

"They'll let me."

"Then we'll go tomorrow morning. Where do you live?"

"On Primorskaya Street, at the Bulgarians'."

"We're staying at Tarakanikha's."

"That means I've seen your mother. She's so tall with black hair?"

"Yeah, I'm the only one that never sees my mother."

"Why?"

"Mom likes to dance..." The girl shook her ashen hair, which had already dried. "Let's have a last swim."

She leapt up, all covered with sand, and ran to the sea, her pink narrow heels sparkling...

The morning was calm and sunny, but not hot. The sea after the storm gave off a cool breeze and didn't let the sun heat the air. When a wispy cloud floated past the sun like a puff of cigarette smoke and removed the blinding southern glitter from the gravel of the roads, the white walls and the tiled roofs, the area acquired a dreary look, as before a long spate of foul weather, and the cold onshore breeze immediately increased.

The path leading to Big Saddle at first wound its way through the low hills and then stretched straight ahead and sharply upward through the dense, fragrant hazelnut grove. The path was dissected by a shallow trough strewn with stones—the riverbed of one of those turbulent streams that cascade down the mountains after a rain, roaring and ringing throughout the neighborhood, but dry up more quickly than the raindrops disappear from the leaves of the hazelnut trees.

We'd already covered a sizable part of our journey when I decided to find out my friend's name.

"Hey!" I shouted to the yellow and blue shorts flashing like a butterfly in the hazelnut grove. "What's your name?"

The girl stopped. I caught up with her. The hazelnut grove thinned out here and parted, giving a view of the bay and our village—a sorry handful of wretched little houses. The immense grave sea formed a stretch of water to the horizon, and beyond it, it formed hazy dull blue bands stacked one on top of another in the sky. But in the bay the sea pretended to be gentle and small, even playful, as it stretched out a white thread along the shore's edge, bit it off, and then stretched it out again...

"I don't quite know what to tell you," answered the girl pensively. "I have a stupid name—Viktorina, but they call me Vitka."

"I could call you Vika."

"That's disgusting." She bared her sharp canine teeth as I'd seen her do before.

"Why? Vika is what they call wild pea."

"It's called mouse pea too. I can't stand mice!"

"Well, Vitka it is, then, and I'm Seryozha. Do we have much further to go?"

"You bushed? We just have to pass the forester's, and from there you can see Big Saddle..."

But for a long time still we wound our way through the harshly melliferous, stuffy hazelnut grove. Finally the path gave way to a rocky road whose sand, as fine as powdered sugar, gleamed white; it took us to a wide sloping ledge. There in the midst of the apricot trees was the forester's lodge, built out of cockleshells.

We'd barely reached the cozy cabin when the silence was shattered by a fierce barking. Two huge shaggy dirty-white dogs flew out at us, clanking the chains that hung from a long wire and reared up in the air, but choked by their collars, they rolled their pink tongues, wheezed, and fell to the ground.

"Don't be afraid, they can't reach us!" said Vitka calmy.

The dogs' teeth gnashed only half a step away from us; I saw burrs on their manes and ticks swollen to the size of lima beans on their muzzles, only their eyes were lost in their fur. Strangely enough, no one came out of the lodge to quiet down the dogs. But no matter how much the dogs flung themselves at us or pulled on the wire, they couldn't reach us. And when I was convinced of that, I became painfully happy. Our hike had taken us to rocks and caverns inhabited by mysterious voices; the only things missing were menacing guards, dragons barring courageous spirits access to the secret. And here they were, the dragons—these overgrown, eyeless hounds with their red fleshy jaws!

We wound our way again through the hazelnut grove along a tapering path. Here the hazelnut grove was not as dense as below: many bushes had withered, on others the leaves had been so eaten up by small shiny black beetles that they were cobwebs.

I was tired and angry with Vitka; she trod on, oblivious, with her slender legs that were as straight as sticks and slightly turned in at the knees. But it suddenly became lighter ahead, and I saw a slope overgrown with a short shock of grass; in the distance a gray cliff extended upwards.

"Thunderstone!" remarked Vitka without stopping.

As we approached, the gray rocky projection rose higher and higher—it seemed to grow disproportionately as we neared it. When he stepped into its dark cool shadow it became monstrously huge. This was no longer Thunderstone, but Thundertower—gloomy, mysterious, unassailable. As if answering my thoughts, Vitka said:

"You know, so many people wanted to climb it and no one made it. Some fell to their death, others broke their arms and legs. One Frenchman made it, though."

"How did he do it?"

"He just did... But he couldn't get back down and went crazy and then starved to death... But still, he was a great guy!" she added pensively.

We'd come right up to Thunderstone, and Vitka, lowering her voice, said:

"Here it is..." She took several steps back and shouted, but not loudly: "Seryozha!.."

"Seryozha..." a mocking, insinuating voice repeated right in my ear as if it were coming from the bowels of Thunderstone.

I shuddered and couldn't help moving away from the cliff; and then from the sea there clearly splashed in my direction:

"Seryozha!.."

I froze, and somewhere above came the wearily bitter moan:

"Seryozha!.."

"What the devil!.." I uttered in a constrained voice.

"What the devil!" rustled above my ear.

"Devil!.." breathed the sea.

"Devil!.." echoed in the heights.

In each of these invisible mockers one sensed a stable and sinister nature: the whisperer was a maliciously ingratiating goody-goody; the sea's voice belonged to a cold jovial person; in the heights hid an inconsolable and hypocritical weeper.

"Well, what are you waiting for?.. Yell something!.." said Vitka.

And my ears were invaded by a whisper that interrupted: "Well, what are you waiting for?"—then clearly, and with a grin: "Yell,"—and as if through tears: "Something."

With an effort I mastered myself and shouted:

"Sinegoriya!.."

And I heard the three-voiced response...

I shouted, talked, and whispered a lot more of all kinds of words. The echo had very acute hearing. I pronounced some words so quietly that I could hardly hear them myself, but they invariably evoked a response. I no longer felt terrified, but every time the invisible one whispered into my ear a chill ran down my spine and the sobbing voice wrung my heart.

"Good-bye!" said Vitka and began walking away from Thunderstone.

I rushed after her, but the whisper overtook me, maliciously and insinuatingly rustling the words of farewell, and the distant sea shouted with laughter, and the voice above moaned:

"Good-bye!.."

We walked in the direction of the sea and soon found ourselves on a stone precipice overhanging an abyss. To the right and to the left rose the spurs of the mountains, and below us gaped the abyss in which one's gaze drowned. If Thunderstone were to fall through the earth, it would leave just as huge and terrifying a hole. In the depths of the pit jutted out sharp clammy cliffs like a giant's fangs, and the dark sea with its inky hue beat against them like a battering-ram. A bird, stretching out wings that were motionless, as though they were dead, was falling slowly in circles into the abyss.

Something still seemed to be unfinished here; the menacing forces that had ripped this gigantic shaft of stone out of the bowels of the earth, broken the mountainous firmament with this monstrous well, sharpened its bottom with thorny cliffs and forced the sea to lacerate its tender tongue against them, had not reached a state of equilibrium. The entire stone mass around and below was precarious, unstable, in a concealed inner tension that was straining to the limit... Of course, I couldn't then name the tormenting and uneasy feeling that gripped me on the precipice of Big Saddle...

Vitka lay down on her stomach at the very edge of the precipice and beckoned to me. I stretched out beside her on the hard and warm smooth stone surface, and the sucking icy pull of the abyss disappeared, and it became quite easy to look down. Vitka leaned over the precipice and shouted:

"Oho-ho!.."

There was a moment of silence and then a deep thundering voice rumbled blaringly:

"O-ho-ho-o ... "

There was nothing terrifying in this voice in spite of its loudness and deepness. Evidently a good giant, who didn't wish us harm, lived in the abyss.

Vitka asked:

"Who was the first maiden?"

The giant, after giving it some thought, answered with a laugh: "Eve!"[1]

"And you know," said Vitka, looking downward, "No one has been able to climb from Big Saddle to the sea. One guy got half way down and got stuck there... "

"And starved to death?" I asked mockingly.

"No, they threw him a rope and pulled him up... But I think it's possible to get down."

"Should we give it a try?"

"Let's!" Vitka answered promptly and simply, and I realized she was serious.

"Some other time," I laughed it off awkwardly.

"Then let's go... So long!" Vitka shouted into the abyss and jumped to her feet.

"Long!.." roared the giant.

I wanted to talk a bit more with him, but Vitka dragged me on.

A new echo—"clear as glass," in Vitka's words—was nestled in a ravine so narrow that it might have been cut by a knife. The echo had a thin shrill voice that reduced even a word uttered in a bass to a squeal. And what was even more revolting, the echo didn't stop after squealing its reply, but continued squeaking like a mouse for a long time in some of its crevices.

We didn't linger at the gorge and went further. Now we had to clamber up a steep incline that was alternately covered by a mass of coarse grass and burrs, and then bare, polished, and slippery. We finally emerged on a projection heaped up with huge boulders. Each boulder resembled something: a ship, a tank, a bull, the head which Ruslan vanquished,[2] a fallen warrior in armor, a coastal gun with the barrel broken off, a camel, the jaws of a roaring lion, as well as parts of the body of a giant who'd been torn apart: an aquiline nose, an ear, a bearded jaw, a powerful fist that was still clenched, a bare foot, a forehead with curly locks...

All of these petrified creatures, parts of creatures, objects dressed in stone, bandied a word among themselves as if it were a ball, their sides making the sound reverberate with lightning speed and abrupt brevity. It was here that the 'peas' echo dwelled...

But the most amazing echo was one about which Vitka had told me nothing. We didn't walk up to it, but crawled up a steep slope, clutching onto the juts, the lichens, and the dry shrubbery. Pebbles crumbled under our feet and hands, dragging larger stones behind them, so that a continuous rumble was created behind us. When I looked back I marveled at the trifling height that had made us so dizzy there on the precipice. From here the sea no longer seemed to be a mirror-like surface: infinite, boundless, it merged with the sky, forming a single sphere—a vault that reigned over the entire visible expanse. And Thunderstone, emphasizing our height, once again dwindled to a small projection.

Vitka stopped by the semicircular dark gap leading into the heart of the mountain. I glanced inside and when my eyes became somewhat accustomed to the darkness I saw a vaulted cave with smoothly rounded bearded stone icicles. The walls shimmered green, red, and blue; the mustiness of a crypt exuded from the cave, and I involuntarily recoiled.

"Hello!" shouted Vitka after poking her head inside the hole.

And as if empty barrels were exploding as they collided, beneath the vault there heavily resounded: "Boom!" It rattled around the corners and finally escaped outside in a low groan, as if the very mountain were giving up the ghost.

I looked at Vitka with respectful amazement. This skinny, freckled girl with disheveled ashen hair, sharp canine teeth in the corners of her mouth, and shining green eyes now seemed to me as fantastic as the secret world to which she'd introduced me.

"Go on, shout!" ordered Vitka.

I bent forward and shouted into the mountain's small dark mouth. Again there was an echo, a squeal, and then an unearthly putrid coldness breathed in my face. A terrible loneliness suddenly seized me—loneliness and helplessness in this world of sheer stone, steep inclines and deep ravines inhabited by mysterious, wild voices.

"Let's go," I said to Vitka, betraying my unease. "Let's get out of here!.."

The walk from then on seemed to me like an interminable downward fall. On our way the rock cemetery, Thunderstone, the sickly eaten-away hazelnut tree, the forester's dogs wheezing asthmatically and rearing up on their chains, and the other hazelnut tree, full of life, all flashed by again. Our fall suddenly ended in a dry gorge that skirted the town from the direction of the mountains.

"Well, did you find it interesting?" Vitka asked when we stepped into our street.

I felt myself in the placid ordinary world again and Vitka no longer appeared to me as the fantastic keeper of the mountain spirits. Just a bony plain girl who didn't have all of her front teeth. And I'd played the coward before this very girl!

"Yes, it was interesting..." I answered lazily. "But what kind of collection is that?"

"Just because you can't put it in a box inside your shirt pocket?"

"No, that's not why... It's just that an echo will answer anybody, not just you."

Vitka gave me a rather strange lingering glance.

"Well, and so what, I don't mind!" she said with a toss of her hair, and set off for home...

Vitka and I became friends. Together we climbed all over Temryuk-kaya and Wedding Mountain. We found a croaking echo in the cavern of

Wedding Mountain, but Temryuk-kaya with its spurs, mighty cliffs and peak that sharply pierced the sky, turned out to be completely barren...

We were almost never apart. I got used to Vitka's swimming naked—she was a good guy, a buddy, and I didn't see a girl in her at all. I vaguely understood the nature of her immodesty: Vitka considered herself hopelessly ugly. I've never met a person who admitted her plainness so simply, openly and with such serene dignity. When she was telling me once about one of her girlfriends from school, Vitka suddenly interjected: "She's almost as ugly as I am..."

Once when we were swimming near the fishermen's dock a gang of boys poured down from the high bank. I knew them slightly, but my timid attempts to get closer to them had come to nothing. These boys had vacationed in Sinegoriya before, so they considered themselves old-timers and didn't admit strangers into their gang. Their ringleader was a tall strong boy named Igor.

I had already come out of the water and was standing on the shore drying myself with a towel, but Vitka continued playing in the water. Catching a wave and bobbing high, she'd ride the crest on her stomach. Her small buttocks glistened.

The boys answered my greeting in an offhand way and were about to walk by when suddenly one of them, wearing red trunks, noticed Vitka.

"Hey, guys, look, a naked girl!"

Then the boys started in having fun: shouting, whistling, hooting. To give Vitka her due, she didn't pay any attention to the boys' carrying-on, but that only added oil to the fire. The boy in the red trunks suggested playing wheelbarrow with the girl. The suggestion met with enthusiasm and the boy in the red trunks waddled down to the water. But then Vitka bent down with savage speed, felt for something in the water, and when she stood up she had a heavy rock in her hand.

"Just make one move!" she said, baring her sharp canine teeth, "And I'll smash your face in!"

The boy in the red trunks stopped and tested the water with his foot.

"It's cold..." he said and his ears grew redder than his trunks. "I don't feel like going in..."

Igor went up and sat down on the sand at the very edge of the shore. The boy in the red trunks understood his leader without a word being said and sat down next to him; the rest of the boys followed his example. Their human chain cut Vitka off from the shore, her clothes, and the towel.

Vitka tried their patience for a long time. She would swim far off and then come back, then dive and splash around in the water, and then sit on a submerged rock, fanning the waves over her with her hands. But the cold at last took its toll.

"Seryozha!" Vitka shouted. "Give me my shorts!"

All this time I'd been towelling myself dry, not even aware of what I was doing. My skin, rubbed rough, burned as if scalded, but I continued to rub and rub my already dry body as if I wanted to rub a hole in myself. In the wretched and humiliating embarrassment that had overcome me my one distinct wish was not to be implicated in Vitka's disgrace.

"Seryozha, give your lady her shorts!" the boy in the red trunks squealed mockingly.

Igor, who was propped up on his elbow, turned round and said to me threateningly: "Just try!.."

It was an unnecessary warning—I wouldn't have moved from the spot anyway. Vitka realized that there was no point in looking to me for help. Squirming pathetically, trying to pull her entire body into her skinny stomach and covering it with her arms, she crawled out of the water, purple and goose-pimpled from the cold, with a grimace on her face, and ran sideways to her shorts while the boys laughed and whistled. What she in the chasteness of her heart had attached no importance to, now appeared vile, debasing, and shameful to her.

Hopping on one leg, and repeatedly missing the leg of her shorts with her other one, she somehow got dressed, grabbed the towel off the ground and ran off. Suddenly she turned around and shouted at me:

"Coward!.. Coward!.. You pathetic coward!.."

Of all the words that Vitka could have used, she chose the most vicious, offensive, and unfair one. But she evidently wanted to disgrace me utterly in front of the guys.

I don't know if it was the whim of a ringleader who didn't want to be led by somebody else in the gang, or if something about Vitka interested Igor, but he suddenly asked me in a friendly and confidential tone:

"Hey, is she crazy?"

"Of course she's crazy!" I yielded completely to his kindness.

"Then why do you hang around with her?"

Wanting only to protect myself and not even thinking of defending Vitka, I answered:

"She's fun to be with, she collects echoes."

"What?" asked Igor in surprise.

In a base fit of grateful frankness I revealed all of Vitka's secrets on the spot.

"Now, that's something," remarked Igor excitedly. "This is the third summer I've been here, and I've never heard anything like that."

"You're not exaggerating?" asked the boy in the red trunks.

"Want me to show you?"

"Everything!" said Igor with authority, once again becoming the leader. "Tomorrow you'll take us there!.."

It had been drizzling since morning, the mountains were hidden by grayish-white clouds that seemed made of soap, and to the sullen noise of the raging sea that was the color of mountain grass was added the roar of the swollen streams and rivulets.

But Igor's gang had decided not to retreat. And once more the already familiar path wound along beneath my feet, but now in the middle of it a turbid yellow stream rushed along, scooting the gravel with it. The hazelnut tree no longer smelled honey-sweet with a lightly burnt scent, but smelled instead of rotting fallen leaves, of sour eroded soil in which something was decomposing and emitting a vinegar-wine smell. The going was rough, our feet kept slithering on the wet ground and slipping on the rocks...

The watchdogs by the forester's house greeted us with their usual heart-rending barking, but their bark sounded softer, more hollow in the damp air, and the dogs themselves no longer seemed so threatening with their fur wet and tousled. You could see their black eyes, which looked like olives.

And then came the sickly hazelnut tree struck down by beetles; the wind and rain had torn off its frail, perforated leaves, and the tree stood stripped and sad and through it one could see the gloomy darkness of the sea.

Thunderstone, hidden by the clouds, did not come into view for a long time, then its peak loomed black at an inaccessible height, disappeared, revealed itself for a moment in all its magnitude, and then in an instant vanished completely in the swirling air. Curiously enough, the wind raged seaward, but the clouds, light as steam from someone's mouth, were drifting away from the sea. They floated right along the ground, covered us with mist and quickly disappeared, settling like dew on the slopes.

At last Thunderstone rose again from the cloudy haze and barred our way.

"So, let's have your marvelous tricks," said Igor unsmilingly.

"Listen!" I said solemnly, and feeling the familiar sensation of a chill down my back, I cupped my palms and shouted:

"Oho-ho!.."

In reply there was only silence, no sinister insinuating whisper, no laughing splash from the sea, no plaintive voice from high up.

"Oho-ho," I shouted again, stepping closer to Thunderstone, and all the boys joined in my cry.

Thunderstone was silent. We shouted again and again and didn't get even the faintest echo. Then I rushed toward the precipice, the boys behind me, and yelled with all my might into the swirling depths. But the giant didn't answer either.

I hurried in embarrassment from the precipice to Thunderstone, from

Thunderstone to the crevice and then back again to the precipice, and again to Thunderstone. But the mountains remained silent...

I pitifully began trying to persuade the boys to climb up to the cave—there we'd hear the echo for sure. The boys stood in front of me, as silent and stern as the mountains; Igor finally parted his lips to utter only one word:

"Windbag!"

He turned around sharply and left, taking the entire gang with him.

I trudged behind, trying in vain to understand what had happened. The boys' contempt didn't bother me now, I wanted only to penetrate the mystery of my failure. Surely the mountains didn't respond only to Vitka's voice? But when she and I had been together, the mountains had obediently answered me as well. Maybe she really had a key that allowed her to lock up the voices in the stone caves?..

The days that followed were sad. I'd lost Vitka and even my mother blamed me. When I told her the mystifying story about the echoes, she looked me up and down with the long look of a stranger studying something and said dourly:

"It's very simple: the mountains answer only those who are pure and honest..."

Her words revealed a lot to me, but not the mystery of the mountain echo.

The rain didn't stop, and the sea seemed divided into two parts: in the bay it was a muddy yellow from the sand carried out by the rivers and streams; in the distance the sea shone pure. The wind blew incessantly. During the day it tossed the rain about like a gray sheet; during the night, which was always clear and full of tiny white stars, it was dry and black, because it found itself if the dark, in the twisted boughs, branches, trunks, and angular shadows that flitted across the starlit ground.

I saw Vitka several times in passing. She went to the sea no matter what the weather was like and had been able to get a rich chocolate tan from the miserly occasional sun. From ennui and loneliness I accompanied my mother every day to the market where the local produce was sold: vegetables, apricots, goat's milk, and yogurt. I met Vitka once at the market. She was alone, a wicker bag hanging from her arm. I watched her as she walked among the trays and cans in her yellow and blue shorts, choosing the tomatoes in a businesslike fashion, slapping the chunk of meat down on the scales herself—and with a pang I felt that I'd lost a good friend.

On the morning of the first sunny day I was wandering around the garden picking up the fallen apricots that were beginning to rot, when someone called me. A girl dressed in a white blouse with a blue sailor's collar and a blue skirt stood by the gate. It was Vitka, but I didn't recognize her right away. Her ashen hair was smoothly combed and tied back with a ribbon, she was wearing a string of coral beads around her tanned neck and shoes of elk leather on her feet. I rushed toward her.

"Listen, we're leaving," said Vitka.

"Why?"

"Mama's tired of it here...So, I want to leave you my collection. It's no good to me, but you could show it to the boys and make it up with them."

"I won't show anybody!" I exclaimed heatedly.

"Whatever you want, but I want you to have it. Have you figured out why it didn't work for you?"

"How did you know it didn't work?"

"I heard...So, have you figured it out?"

"No..."

"The most important thing, you know, is where you stand when you shout." Vitka lowered her voice confidentially. "For Thunderstone—only from the direction of the sea. You probably shouted from the other side— there isn't any echo there. At the precipice you need to lean over and shout straight at the wall. Remember I bent your head down?...At the crevice shout as deep down as possible so that your voice will travel further. And you always get an answer in the cave, but you didn't get far enough. And at the rocks too..."

"Vitka!..." I began remorsefully.

Her thin face grimaced.

"I've got to run, or else the bus will leave..."

"Will I see you in Moscow?"

Vitka shook her head.

"We live in Kharkov..."

"Will you come here again?"

"I don't know...Well, so long!.." Vitka lowered her head toward her shoulder in embarrassment and immediately ran off.

My mother was standing by the gate and followed Vitka with a long fixed gaze.

"Who was that?" mother asked in a rather cheerful voice.

"That's Vitka. She's staying at Tarakanikha's."

"What a delightful creature!" said mother, her voice deep.

"What? That's Vitka!.."

"I'm not deaf..." Mother looked again in the direction where Vitka had run. "Oh, what a wonderful girl! That turned-up nose, ashen hair, striking eyes, shapely figure, narrow feet, hands..."

"What are you saying, mama!" I shouted, chagrined at her strange blindness—it somehow seemed offensive to Vitka. "You should see her mouth!.."

"A splendid large mouth!.. You don't understand anything!"

Mother made for the house, and I watched her from behind for a few moments and then tore off, dashing to the bus station.

The bus hadn't left yet; the remaining passengers, loaded with bags and suitcases, were rushing the door. I saw Vitka right away on the side where the windows didn't open. Sitting next to her was a stout dark-haired woman in a red dress, her mother.

Vitka saw me too and grasped the window latches to open the window. Her mother said something to her and touched her shoulder, probably wanting Vitka to sit down in her seat. Vitka brushed her hand away abruptly.

The motor roared and the bus slowly started to crawl along the unpaved road, a golden tail of dust fanning out behind it. I walked alongside. Biting her lip, Vitka jerked the latches and the window fell down with a crash. It had been easier for me to think of Vitka as beautiful without seeing the sharp canine teeth and the dark freckles scattered all over her face which ruined the image my mother had created and in which I'd come to believe.

"Listen, Vitka," I started speaking quickly, "Mother said you're beautiful! You have beautiful hair, eyes, mouth, nose..." The bus began to pick up speed and I started running. "Hands, feet! It's true, Vitka!.."

Vitka only smiled with her large mouth, happily, trustingly, devotedly, completely revealing her good heart in that large smile; and then I perceived with my own eyes that Vitka truly was the most beautiful girl in the world.

Sagging heavily, the bus drove onto the little wooden bridge that spanned the stream which was Sinerogiya's border. I stopped. The bridge groaned, shook. Vitka's head, with its ashen hair blown by the wind, and her deeply tanned elbow appeared in the window once again. Vitka signalled to me and powerfully tossed a silver coin across the stream. The shining streak in the air died in the dust at my feet. There was a superstition that if you threw a coin there, you'd definitely return some day...

I wanted the day of our departure to come as quickly as possible. Then I'd toss a coin too, and Vitka and I would meet again.

But that wasn't fated to be. A month later when we were leaving Sinerogiya I forgot to toss the coin.

1960   Translated by Ronald Meyer

The original ("Ekho") first appeared in *Ogonek,* No. 37 (1960), 14-17. The present translation is of the edition included in the 1973 two-volume collection, I, 198-213.

Notes

1. Vitka uses the Russian word *deva* (maiden) in her question. The giant drops the initial "d" in his answer, leaving *Eva* (Eve). (Translator's note.)

2. The reference is to the mock-heroic rescue of Ludmila by her knightly fiancé Ruslan, who decapitates her abductor, the evil magician Chernomor, thereby saving her for himself in Pushkin's Ariosto-inspired *Ruslan and Ludmila* (1820). The lighthearted mock epic later was set to music by Glinka.

By a Quiet Lake

1.

Valkov was awakened by the sudden silence, as one would be by a crash. The truck had been jolting along the cobblestone road, its loose sides clattering, the empty steel drums in the back thundering like cannons as they banged together. And the cab, too, where Valkov had been dozing rattled, creaked and clanged. These diverse sounds merged into a single, dense, ear-filling roar and, rather than disturbing his sleep, lulled him, like a lullaby. Even the jolting rocked him to sleep. He hadn't slept so peacefully and sweetly maybe since he was an infant in the cradle. He woke up, but didn't open his eyes, in the vague hope that he would be left alone, and the truck would move on again, and he could go to sleep again and get rid of the headache that had been tormenting him since last night's drinking bout.

"Hey, get up!" the driver's bony fist poked him in the ribs. "You wanted to go to Rybachye—here it is."

"Did I say I was going to Rybachye?" Valkov mumbled, and opened his eyes.

About fifty meters from the truck a large body of water extended far beyond the horizon. The lake surface was even with the low bank, which was overgrown with wild pea. A long, sharp-pointed spit, completely covered, except for the sandy point, with a dense growth of pines, jutted out into it from the right. The glare off the water obscured the lower part of the trunks of the pines, so that they seemed to be hanging in the air. Gulls circled over the lake, and two or three launches could be seen in the distance.

"I'm going to Vyazniky," Valkov said uncertainly, and climbed awkwardly out of the cab, grabbing his tool box and his saw, wrapped up in bast matting.

"They're both here, both Rybachye and Vyazniky. Over there, beyond that road!" The driver slammed the door of his cab, and the truck sped off.

Valkov followed the truck with a melancholy gaze, and headed slowly across the dewy grass to the lake. He rinsed his face, and immediately felt refreshed and invigorated. His headache disappeared magically, as if there were a curative power in the clear cold water. Valkov again surveyed the expanse of water, and discovered new details there. There was a wooden gangway to the left, with several rotund boats resembling lifeboats rocking nearby; a fishnet was drying on the shore, glistening from the fish scales caught in its mesh. A motor boat was coming toward the gangway, pulling a widely diverging double blue track behind it. A strange, vague feeling stirred inside Valkov: it was as if he had had a prevision of this clear, bright, glass-smooth lake, with all its peace and quiet, with the distant pines hovering in the air, with its fishing pier and fishnets, with its deserted air, which was not frightening, but somehow cheering. It was not at all like the lakes of his native region of Meshchyora. There the lakes, squeezed in among forested shores, are dusky and dark. They are thickly overgrown with reeds, hazelnuts, and water lilies; they are also pretty, but in a very different way.

Valkov no longer regretted now that he had yielded to the persuasion of a chance travelling companion and hitched a ride here on a passing truck. They had met somewhere in the vicinity of Orsha. He recalled a little blue roadside restaurant by the highway, a table spread with a paper tablecloth, a vase of flowers that made it hard for them to see one another. Valkov had dropped in there already a bit tight: he had had a farewell drink or two with other members of his artel, compatriots who were headed home. They all had families, but he was a bachelor, with no one waiting for him at home, and so he had separated from the fellows, as was his habit, to wander a little on his own. He wasn't sure what he and his new friend had talked about, about everything under the sun, probably. But he remembered very clearly that the friend had urged him to head for Lake Rybachye, to the village of Vyazniky, where he had come from himself, but he had married a girl from here, from Orsha, and had broken his ties with his home. And around midnight, when the restaurant was already closing, he jumped up shouting that there was a truck headed for Rybachye. Valkov got excited too, thrust money at the waiter, started to look for his tools. Then the same friend helped him into the truck, with the aid of some well-wishers. The trees, rushing out of the darkness into the glare of the headlights, flashed by his window, cat's eyes shining by the roadside, some kind of houses and cottages with dark windows. And then his awakening, and this lake . . . How much ground had he covered in the truck? At least three or four hundred kilometers.

A half-kilometer from the highway, on the other side, he could see straw and wooden roofs through the trees. That had to be Vyazniky. Valkov gathered up his case and his saw and was about to move on when he suddenly froze: a snake was crawling toward him over the dewy pea-plants, its thick and long body twisting. They had snakes in Meshchyora too, adders and grass-snakes; as a boy he had killed countless numbers of them with rocks, or with just a stick, but he had never in his life seen such a huge reptile, except maybe in the Moscow Zoo or in a movie. Valkov was not at all timid, but now, afraid to stir, he watched, transfixed, as the snake crawled toward him, leaving a bright green trace in the film of dew on the pea-plants. It came all the way to his feet before it slipped onto the water-lapped sandy edge of the shore, twitched and writhed helplessly on the sand, and with an incredible effort dragged itself to the water and disappeared at once into the depths.

Loath to give up his initial sense of serenity, Valkov, an easy-going man, immediately assured himself that it wasn't a poisonous snake after all, but a harmless local grass-snake, and set off cheerfully toward the village.

2.

The village was not very large, though it had two streets, and was very green and bright with flowers. Dahlias were blooming by every house: red, yellow, white, reddish-black, and white with red borders. Valkov marvelled at the gigantic rowan trees that lined both sides of the street. Thickly covered with crimson-ripe berries, they merged their crowns above the narrow little street, forming a shady archway. And he also wondered at the fences around the front gardens, courtyards, and vegetable gardens, made of old fishnets stretched over stakes. Clearly, he wouldn't be mending fences here, but the small, neat huts, on the other hand, stood in obvious need of him: in one place a wooden roof had rotted through, in another the shutters were sagging, in a third a door was crooked, a porch was askew, or a shed had collapsed. You could see that no carpenters had stopped by here for some time, and the local inhabitants either hadn't the time or were not accustomed to fixing up their own dwellings. It looked as if his chance companion hadn't lied to him, Valkov really would be a welcome guest here.

In the center of the small square, an iron gong hung from a post, to which a white brindle calf was tied. When it saw Valkov, the calf raised its snout and bleated, piteously and touchingly, like a child. Several tow-headed kids were trying to fly a kite with a bast tail, but the kite stubbornly hung close to the ground. There was an appetizing smell of fried fish and pine-cone smoke. A flock of thrushes landed on a rowan tree, a roller bird with a bright green back lit on top of the post. Then doves flew up and began to strut about briskly and fearlessly near Valkov. Some amazingly tiny, gaily-colored hens and an equally tiny, toy-like rooster dashed out of the nearest gate. And Valkov again felt happy for some reason, as he just had at the lake, and again it seemed as if he had had either a prevision or a dream of this little village with its neat little houses, its beautiful trees and flowers, its bold birds, its pleasant, confiding, peaceful atmosphere. Valkov always fancied, and bragged to others, that only city life was to his liking, while in fact he was at a loss in cities, especially large ones, he felt uncomfortably small and unable to attract attention to himself. And he preferred to be the center of attention...

Suddenly a little wizened old lady appeared before him with a bag full of yellow sponge-mushrooms.

"Hello, granny," Valkov said affably. "Where could I find... uh..." he strained his memory, trying to recall the name his friend had mentioned, "What's his name... Chastik?"

"Laptik, maybe?"

"That's it, Laptik!" Valkov said happily.

"Which Laptik do you need?" asked the old woman, her moist blue eyes sparkling gaily.

"Well, the main one..."

"We considered Stanislav the main one, he's the first one who settled here."

"That's probably the one."

"Well, my dear, he died before the war."

"Well, I need a live Laptik, who's here in the village."

"There's no one in the village, my dear, they've all gone fishing."

"So show me his house, granny."

"Whose house is that?"

"Laptik's house, I'm telling you, Laptik's!"

"But how can I show you, if everyone here is a Laptik."

"How's that, everyone?"

"Like I say, everyone; I'm a Laptik, and the foreman's a Laptik, and all the fishermen are Laptiks."

"Aren't you funny!" laughed Valkov, seeing the old woman's innocent game. "It's probably the foreman Laptik they told me about."

"The foreman's at the lake too, my dear, he won't be back before evening."

"Could you tell me who I could stay with?"

"Go straight to the widow Elena Laptik, the third hut from the end, she has lots of room."

"Thanks, granny... Say, your mushrooms are toadstools!"

"They might be toadstools where you come from, but here the sponge is the juiciest mushroom. You just have to know how to cook them..."

Valkov thought a bit about the whole village having the same name, and it occurred to him that the old woman might be ribbing him again. He called to the playing children, "Hey, Laptik!"

And all the children's heads turned toward him at once. Valkov grinned and headed for the hut she had pointed out to him.

On the porch, bending over a pan, a woman in a faded blue skirt and a yellow jacket was cleaning fish. Valkov looked at her firmly planted legs, with white scars from grass cuts, her strong bare elbows, her rounded neck, delicately white at the hair-line, and immediately decided that he couldn't find a better place to stay.

"Hail, missus!" he spoke jauntily. "Might a person light at your place?"

The woman turned around. She had a high bosom, broad shoulders, blue eyes, an even, clear tan on her face, and moist dimples at the corners of her full, brownish-red lips.

"Hello," the woman said without the least surprise. "Come in."

Valkov started to step up onto the porch, and stopped: snakes like the one he had encountered at the lake, only shorter and thinner, were hanging on a rope strung between the porch's columns. The snakes' bellies were cut open and spread out wide by wooden pegs.

"What kind of snakes are those?" asked Valkov.

"Eels, don't you know them?" the woman smiled. "They're just fish."

"Oh, eels ... " said Valkov. "I've eaten them."

He had never eaten eels, although he had heard that people ate them.

"Are you going to smoke them?"

"Uh-huh."

"Over alder chocks?"

"No, over pine cones."

"Where I come from they only smoke fish in alder smoke."

"There aren't any alders here. Where are you from?"

"Meshchyora. Maybe you've heard of it? The Klepiky district."

The woman shook her head.

"The Ryazan region, right near Moscow."

"Oh, there!" she said with respect. "And what wind blew you here?"

"Ahh!" Valkov said carelessly. "My kind blows in every direction! Why don't you ask where I haven't been."

There were a lot of places Valkov hadn't been: Siberia and the Far East, Central Asia and the Urals, the Caucasus and the Crimea, the Baltic area and the Far North; but on the other hand he had travelled all over the Ryazan and the Vladimir regions, had worked as a carpenter on the Volga, in the Oryol region, the Kursk region, had even got as far as Kiev once, and Moscow was practically home for him.

"And I've never been anywhere further than Kobylnik," the woman sighed.

"What the heck is Kobylnik?"

"A village, about fifteen kilometers from here; there's a Catholic church there, a village Soviet, stores, a beauty shop ... I've planned to go to Minsk all these years, but never made it."

"How come?"

"Never had time, and especially after my husband died... I had little Yazka to bring up, and no money."

"Where did your husband die?"

"He drowned," she gave a weak wave of her hand. "Five years ago. They got into a storm, the boat overturned, two were saved, but four of them were never found. Mikola was the only one of them married, the rest were young bachelors. I'm the only widow in the whole village, the men here always outlive their wives..."

"Well..." sympathized Valkov, a man of feeling, but he thought to himself that if Mikola was fated to drown, it was as well that it happened before he, Valkov, came to the village.

Elena took the eels to the smokehouse at the back of the house, telling Valkov to go in and make himself comfortable. A wooden partition divided the hut into a kitchen and a living room. In the kitchen there was a table covered with oilcloth, two benches, and a stool; a wash basin with a copper spout and a clean, unbleached towel hung on a nail by the entrance door. Valkov washed, shaved, put on a clean shirt, and went into the living room. That room was light, clean, and rather empty: two wooden beds, a chest of drawers, several chairs; a large kerosene lamp with an iron shade hung from the ceiling. In the corner, over a bed, where the icons hang in Russian village houses, a colored picture was pinned up: behind a long table, set with simple fare, sat a good dozen bearded men. One of them, young-looking and reddish-haired, had a circle above his head with an inscription in unfamiliar script. Valkov guessed that it was Jesus Christ with the Apostles. Elena, returning from the smokehouse, explained to Valkov that the picture was called *The Last Supper*. Christ had just told his disciples that one of them had betrayed him. The traitor was Judas, that was him clutching the bag with thirty pieces of silver...

"How much would that be in our money?" Valkov wondered.

The woman didn't know. As for the picture, it had belonged to her late mother-in-law; she was a believer and went to church, but the Catholics don't have icons...

Then they had a fish lunch: pike, perch, sprat, and eel that was fried, smoked, salted, boiled, and dried. Overcoming his revulsion, Valkov tried the fried eel and immediately asked for more; the fried eel turned out to be amazingly tasty, and the smoked eel was even better. Valkov said that before he left he would be sure to order himself a barrel of smoked eel. But the landlady preferred to eat the boiled sausage that Valkov fetched out of his knapsack, and he regretted that he hadn't had sense enough to fill the whole thing with sausage...

During lunch the landlady's daughter Yazya ran in. She had her mother's dark blue eyes. Seeing an unfamiliar person, she became embarrassed, and whispered something in her mother 's ear. Her mother blushed slightly and told her in a strict tone not to talk silly. The girl took a piece of bread and sausage and ran off.

"Looks like maybe she took me for her new papa?" asked Valkov.

"Some gossip told her she'd have a new one, and so she..."

"And she will, no doubt?"

"She will..." the woman answered reluctantly, but later as they drank tea, she talked more readily. There was a fisherman here, Vladislav Laptik, a friend of her late husband: his wife, Olesya, was dying of cancer. They had three children; Vladislav wouldn't be able to get along without a housewife after his wife died, and so it was assumed that he'd marry her, Elena. And to tell the truth, it wasn't easy for her as a widow; true, there was enough to eat, but then she needed clothes, shoes. Olesya wasn't against it; when she needed help in the house she always asked Elena, as the future mistress of the house. True, that didn't happen often, Olesya was still up and around, even though she was nothing but skin and bones.

"I've been around some," commented Valkov, "but I don't seem to understand. Are you having a love affair with him, or what?"

"What love affair can there be when his wife's alive?" she replied crossly. "That's not our way here."

"Well, does he love you?"

"We haven't talked about that. He's Olesya's husband: I'm Mikola's widow."

"So do you love him?"

"He's a good man and was a friend of Mikola's. But enough of that..."

And the landlady said that he, Valkov, had shown up at just the right time: she needed to replace the rotten roof of the cattle-shed, replace the partition in the pigsty, put up a shelf in the bathhouse.

"It wouldn't hurt to repair the porch too," added Valkov, "and rehang the door in the entry-way, and while we're at it, tighten the shutters. If you do a job, might as well do it right!"

"How much would all that cost?" the landlady asked timidly.

"We'll work it out; I won't cheat you."

"No, that won't do, you name me a price, maybe I can't afford it..."

"Room and board—and we'll be even!"

The widow evidently guessed that Valkov wanted to accommodate her; she flushed angrily. Then Valkov turned his limpid eyes, the color of linden blossom honey, toward the *Last Supper* and swore by Christ our Lord that that was the rule everywhere; an artisan is not supposed to accept any money from the home where he rooms and boards.

"Well, if that's how it is..."

Wasting no time, Valkov got his tools, sharpened his saw, and set to work. Kids came running from all over the village to the sound of his saw. Carpenters rarely stopped by Vyazniky, and the children followed the craftsman's methodical movements in mute rapture. They were taken with his cloth apron, and white band in his black hair, and the thin melodious whistle that escaped from his tightly closed lips, and above all the golden shavings that curled out from under his plane when he planed a board. The children whispered among themselves, poked each other in the ribs, then surrounded Yazya and began to ask her for something. Yazya kept refusing, with a frightened face, but evidently gave in to their urging, approached Valkov, and with her round cheeks blazing asked if they could each take a shaving. Valkov, touched, immediately promised to carve a sword for each of the boys, and a whistle each for the girls...

Elena came to call her roomer to dinner, and stood alongside him watching him work for some time. She knew well, from childhood, the difficult work of the fishermen, was used to their competence, skill, and courage, but Valkov's work delighted and entranced her, like a miracle. What a sharp eye and a sure hand it took to take off such an even, spider-web-thin shaving, to cut a groove so quickly and exactly, to fit one board to another so closely and firmly. She decided that Valkov was not an ordinary carpenter, but a master of his trade, and this pleased her. In Vyazniky they were mistrustful of talkative people, and Valkov seemed to be of that breed. Still, you could see that he was good at more than just working his tongue...

They were still at dinner when the fishermen passed by the house on their way back from the catch. In their canvas overalls, sou'westers, and high rubber boots, every one of them short, but stocky and thick-set, they marched by with a slow, heavy tread, to which their fatigue and water-soaked clothing lent a somber solemnity. One of the fishermen separated from his comrades, came up to the open window of the kitchen, and put a pike weighing six or seven pounds on the window-sill. His cold greenish-blue eyes slid over Valkov, who immediately decided that this must be Vladislav Laptik. Elena thanked the fisherman with a nod, and he moved off without speaking. Prompted by jealousy, Valkov sensed that in the tacit agreement that tied Elena to the fisherman, Vladislav, at any rate, was not a passive victim. The fleeting glance that the fisherman had cast at him had expressed suspicious vigilance and hostility.

They had supper at dusk. A transparent silence hung over the village; the tiny gnats swarming in the air produced an audible drone. Such feeble life dwelt in those gnats' paltry little bodies, that contact with any element coarser than air was deadly to them: those that landed on Valkov's hand or forehead died before he had time to slap them. Everyone in the village was asleep already; the fishermen had to go out again before dawn, and life in Vyazniky died down early. Only the widow's windows showed the light of a kerosene lamp. Valkov enjoyed their isolation, their seclusion, as if they were living for each other now, in a pact against the rest of the world. But he was not the kind of person to accept with quiet gratitude a modest gift of fate: the amiable and chaste presence of a young woman, easy conversation, freshly smoked eel with a golden sheen on the inside of the belly.

"Couldn't I lay my hands on a pint, landlady?"

"Are you kidding?" she grinned. "Kobylnik is the closest place you can buy vodka. And we don't make it here..."

"You mean to say the fishermen don't have any?"

"Where would they get it from? People don't drink here on workdays; just on holidays they bring a keg of beer..."

"You mean one keg for the whole village?"

"That's all our men need. They drink a mug or two, and the singing starts!"

"You don't say!" grinned Valkov. "I've never been a drunkard, you know, but with a nice snack, like our eel, I'll easily put down a dozen beers."

"The beer here is strong, it's a special brew..."

"Beer doesn't faze the likes of me," Valkov continued bragging. "I was brought up on the hard stuff!"

Valkov finally noticed that the topic didn't appeal to his landlady, and to divert her, brought up the subject of cannibalism.

"You mean it really happens?" she said in horror.

"Sure!... I'll tell you what happened to me. I was working in Siberia, in the most god-forsaken place you ever saw. Once I was making my way on shanks'-mare from one village to another, and got caught in a blizzard. And I got so turned around that I lost my way and wandered off into the taiga, into an impassable forest. And it was already late at night, pitch dark, I go along, falling into snow up to my chest, running into trees, worst mess you can imagine. And suddenly—a light, a forester's hut! Fine, I go in. The owner is a forester, big strapping fellow, pockmarked, gold rings on his fingers. You could see he traded in gold before, they go for that in Siberia. I had supper with him, we each had a glass, and went to bed. And the next morning we look out—the hut is buried in snow up to the roof, no way of getting out of the house..."

"Wouldn't you know it!"

"Yeah... So we started to dig out, kept at it the *in*tire day, but all for nothing: you heave away one shovelful, and the blizzard pours on two more. In a word, if help didn't come from outside—it'd be our coffin, with the lid on it! We lived together in captivity for about a week, played cards all the time, and ate up every last bit of grub. Toward the end we even ate his hunting dog, valuable as she was! And then one time I'm giving him the deck to cut, and he looks at my arm strangelike, and doesn't cut. I started getting suspicious. What are you staring at, I say. And he says nothing, keeps looking and licking his lips. I felt creepy... "

"How awful!... " the landlady even rose out of her chair.

"Yes, it was frightening... He had a knife and a gun, how could I go up against him with my bare hands!"

"How did you get away, then, for Lord's sake?"

"I didn't get away," he spoke sadly. "On the eighth day he gobbled me up, every bit of me... "

Another blunder: the landlady didn't even smile; it came out that her roomer was making fun of her goodwill toward him. Then Valkov began telling about the adventures that his nomadic life was supposedly full of. Now he spoke only of serious, even tragic matters. They were stories he had heard from other people in tea-houses, in trains, on ships, while walking the highways, but he generously applied them to himself, whereby they gained vividness and verisimilitude. The stories presented his life as perilous and stormy, full of amazing, fateful coincidences and cruel losses. As he talked, Valkov wondered himself why it was that all sorts of marvels happened to others, while he, as much as he knocked about the world, had not had a single adventure worth anything. A liar and a braggart, he blindly believed other people's fabrications, and seeing how his landlady's face flushed, how her eyes lit up, he didn't just narrate, but acted, with inspiration and passion.

The landlady, meanwhile, was in the throes of complicated and oppressive feelings. She felt in her lodger's tales the disturbing and tempting allure of an unfamiliar world, but she couldn't help but see that there was in all this something false, something spurious and frivolous, that robbed life of its natural, habitual seriousness. And yet the lodger was not simply lying, but exerting himself in her honor, trying to seem better and higher in her eyes, and she couldn't help but appreciate his efforts. He had never had to fish for eel on a stormy night, drag heavy nets with hands stiff with cold, be tossed on an old launch in a murderous storm,—so he was trying to prove his male virtue with words. She suddenly felt sorry for this shallow man, for his perpetual homelessness, his dependence on other people, this master craftsman who was wasting his deft skill on random and probably not always respectable work. And she asked despondently, "And do you have a family? A wife, kids?"

"Nothing of the sort," said Valkov, "I'm a free Cossack."

"Why is that?" the landlady pressed him. "Is that any way to live—all by yourself?"

Valkov started to concoct a story that there existed a certain woman doctor who, you might say, proposed to him. She had, he said, her own house near Moscow, an orchard of thirty trees, was planning to buy a motor-bike...

"Then you ought to marry her," said the landlady.

"Out of the question," Valkov pursed his lips. "That's out of the question now," and he gave her a significant glance.

The shot was wasted; it never even occurred to the landlady that her lodger was trying to involve her in his romantic life. The conversation lagged, and the silence of the village night again became audible.

"Where should I spread your bed?" Elena asked.

"In the hayloft,—I love the smell of fresh hay..."

Elena went out of the kitchen and soon called him. Valkov rose, feeling a strange dryness in his mouth. Closing the door behind him, he found himself in utter darkness. He could not see Elena, but sensed her location from her breathing, the smell of hay, the warmth emanating from her body.

"I've prepared your bed, go to sleep."

"And you?..."

"I'm going too," she yawned and patted her lips.

"With me..." he whispered, and put his arm around her shoulders.

She shoved him away silently, with a powerful motion of her hip. Then he clutched her, pinning her arms, pushed her into a corner of the entry, pressed his body against hers, and caught her mouth with his. Taken unawares, she remained motionless for just a moment, then slipped down, twisted free, and kneed Valkov in the stomach. He gasped and stepped back, and then she punched him in the nose.

"You didn't have to do that too," he said.

Elena flung open the outside door; the feeble light of the stars peered into the entry. Breathing heavily, she looked at Valkov with eyes blazing with rage, and he thought she was about to hit him again. He covered his face with his arm.

"That's enough," he said in a pained voice, sniffling slightly because blood had choked up his nose and was already running down his chin.

She went into the house and came right back, wringing out a wet towel.

"Here, apply this."

Valkov felt his nose growing, swelling, spreading all over his face.

"Put it higher, by the bridge, like this..."

"You've had experience, I see..."

His nose quit growing, it just hurt a lot. What an arm she had on her!

"How is it?"

"Better, I think. Thanks."

"Not at all," she grinned, and closed the door after her.

Valkov climbed up the short ladder into the hayloft and lay down next to the dormer-window without undressing. He thought: you can't do it without liquor, otherwise you're not determined enough, or agile enough. If he'd been drinking, he wouldn't have let her go for anything. Here she is, a thirty-year-old broad, and what's she making herself out to be! Now Vera, in Oryol, the trackman's daughter, she had just finished school, and she would come to his room every night. The foreman's wife Vasilisa, on the collective farm near Tetyushy, had jilted the agronomist for him, and the soldier's wife Nyura from Kurshchina had disgraced herself before the whole village to spend one night with him, Valkov... You'd think this one could have seen, he'd been making up to her all day long, agreed to work for her almost for nothing, and besides, he didn't start grabbing before he started talking! And what did she want, anyhow? He'd have lived with her for a month or so as if she was his wife, he would have taken care of her, pampered Yazka. Anyone else in his place would have let her have it for smashing his nose, but he put up with it, thanks to his mildness and tact...

Large, bright stars gazed into the dormer-window out of the bottomless blackness. Valkov couldn't get to sleep, and he began to gaze at the stars, at their pure, sad light; the resentment left his heart, he began to feel melancholy, lonely, and just a little bit happy that there exist such unusual people as Elena, and that tomorrow he would see her, would work for her and sit at the same table with her. "Sleep well," he said to Elena, as though she were nearby, and imperceptibly fell asleep himself.

And Elena lay and thought about her lodger. Of course, his strangeness resulted from the fact that he was a man of a quite different world, unfamiliar to her, and with different customs. Probably, among his own people he didn't seem strange at all. Maybe he had kissed other women at first acquaintance, that was his affair, but that wasn't done here. The late Mikola kissed her for the first time after the wedding, and Vladislav would kiss her after the wedding, after he had done his term as a widower. The fishermen sometimes had to be gone on expeditions for a long time, they needed peace of mind regarding their wives and fiancées, they needed to know that their property would watch over itself. This stern virtue had developed over generations, and the men here always married women of their own village. She had known from girlhood that her husband would be a fisherman, and now she had to remain a widow until another fisherman married her. But now this stranger had kissed her, and she had hit him, and hit him hard, so as to hurt, and to hurt his feelings, even though she was tired of being alone. She had shed all the tears she had for Mikola, and the only feelings she had toward Vladislav were friendship and deference. And there was nothing to be done, that was the way it had to be, clearly, for the order of life, which was more important than her woman's lot. And her lodger, obviously, was just a lout, a lecher, a rolling-stone, a bucket in an empty well. And yet he was dark-haired, while all the fishermen were reddish-blonds; dark but pale, while the fishermen were ruddy as copper, and his eyes were the color of linden-blossom honey, and not the standard blue . . .

3.

Valkov settled down in Vyazniky, there was work and to spare. The fishermen came home with a rich catch every day, and they had plenty of money. Why not use the services of an itinerant craftsman? There were jobs large and small: knocking together a stool or a bench, or raising a house that had settled so far that "the dogs came through the windows to crap."

Valkov quickly and readily entered into the sphere of local interests, which, to be sure, was pretty narrow: fish, fish, and fish, mainly eel. They also fished for pike, and perch, and sprat and roach, and burbot, and whitefish and bleak, but their conversastion, always sparing and laconic, was primarily about eels. The larger eels went for export, and the fishing collective paid twice as much for eels as for all the other fish. But then, they were much harder to catch.

Whether out of respect or out of superstition, the word "eel" was rarely spoken; they would say meaningfully "it," and everyone understood what was meant: "Today the seines made a good catch of 'it' on the Pokrovsky shoal . . . Vladislav Laptik's team had poor luck, in two catches there wasn't any of 'it' at all . . . Eh, if the wind would just rise, 'it' likes stormy weather . . . The lake is calm, it's obvious that 'it' will stay on the bottom for a long time . . . The foreman knows all 'its' habits, that's why he gets good catches: he boils the hooks and tackle in meadow-cress to take away the smell of iron and cord, since 'it' is awfully sensitive to smells . . . "

A conversation of this nature was going on in Vladislav Laptik's courtyard, where Valkov was repairing a well. Young Andrey Laptik, a sociable person who was well-disposed toward Valkov, told the following story about "it." About five years ago, envious of the constant success of Ignaty Laptik, the present foreman, their team decided to follow in his tracks. Wherever Ignaty went, they went too. And yet Ignaty invariably returned with a rich catch, and they practically empty-handed. They about sprained their brains, trying to guess why they were unsuccessful. And then they figured it out: Ignaty's team were all non-smokers, while every man-jack of their team smoked. It turns out "it" even smelled smoke in the air . . .

"Then you shouldn't have smoked while you were out," remarked Valkov.

"That's just what we did," said Andrey. "We suffered without our smokes till we could hardly stand it, and still we didn't catch anything!"

"How come?"

"There was still tobacco on our breath," explained Andrey. "Obviously, 'it' can smell that too."

"Come on now, friend, you're stretching it; Ignaty's not the only one of you that catches eels!"

"He's the only one who could with a seine; the only thing that saved us was traps."

"Sure, sure, it's just a fish. . . " Valkov started to say but Vladislav Laptik interrupted him.

"Nobody knows if it's a fish or not!" he said, as always, morosely and gravely. "Can a fish crawl five kilometers over a meadow?"

"You mean 'it' can?" asked Valkov in amazement.

"If there's a dew, it'll crawl more than that."

"And how does 'it' breathe?"

"How does it breathe. . . Learned people don't know that, so you can't expect us to."

Anything that disturbed habitual notions about life, or the immutability and permanence of any principles, evoked a glad response in Valkov. He was a breach of order himself, of that order under which a man was supposed to have a home, a family, a regular job, fixed obligations. In answer to his questions, he learned such wonders about eels from young Laptik, that it made his head spin. He found out that when the eels reach maturity they leave Rybachye and make their own way along the creeks and rivers to the Baltic Sea. Then, doubling the entire European continent, they cross the Atlantic Ocean and enter the Sargasso Sea,[1] where they spawn. When the females have finished spawning, they die there, and the young eel head back to Rybachye. . .

"But why do they go there?" Valkov asked with curiousity. "They could spawn here."

"Because that's where the males live, and here there are only females."

"Really?" Valkov replied skeptically. "Are you sure you're telling the truth?"

"That's right," Vladislav Laptik affirmed, as if throwing a heavy weigh onto the scales. "We've never in our lives caught any males."

"What do they look like, the males?"

"You think we've seen them?" said young Andrey Laptik. "Now Schultz, who was a sea-captain, lives in Kobylnik; he said the males are ten feet long and weight thirty pounds and more."

"Wow, there's an eel for you!" exulted Valkov. "And do the males croak too after the spawning?"

The fishermen's opinions differed on that point. Vladislav claimed that the males stay alive. Andrey spoke up for equality: the males must die also.

"So they're doomed to die for love," Valkov reflected. "Is that how it is?..."

At that point Vladislav's wife Olesya came out on the back porch, skinny as a fish-bone, with huge bald spots on her temples, with a bluish-yellow complexion, and cried feebly, "Vlad, call Elena, Verushka needs a bath!"

Vladislav rose, and Andrey after him.

After this Valkov would always go out to meet the fishermen returning from the catch, asking anxiously if they had caught a lot of "it," and was sincerely distressed if the catch wasn't large. Nonetheless, he remained a stranger in Vyazniky. The people here were hard to get along with; he was confused by both the men's stiff reserve and the women's good-natured unapproachability. Rejected by the widow, Valkov tried to approach Andrey Laptik's young wife, an easily amused and talkative wench who was constantly hanging around him when he worked in their yard, but he met such a rebuff, that a slap in the face would have been like a caress in comparison. Still, this did not so much upset him as puzzle him and shake his faith in some of his views on life...

Once he invited himself along on an eel-fishing expedition. When the boat moved out, Vladislav, who was standing next to Valkov, pulled out of his pocket, along with flakes of tobacco, a carefully carved wooden plug. He threw the tobacco-dust into the wind, carefully blew the plug clean, and put it back in his pocket.

"What's that you've got?"

"As if you didn't know," Vladislav replied in an unfriendly tone. "It's to plug the eels' behind."

"Come on!"

"Dummy! how else are you going to calm 'it' down? Even if you cut it in pieces—every part will flop around by itself. But if you plug its behind—it cuts off its breath just like that. Otherwise it'll crawl away..."

Valkov was ready now to believe everything, when it came to eels. Recently Andrey Laptik had shown him still another amazing trait of theirs. He took a live eel and put it on the ground near his house, with its tail toward the lake. On the spot the eel, in several powerful twists, turned its head toward the lake. Andrey returned it to the previous position, and again the eel began to thrash about until its head pointed toward the water. And the lake could neither be seen nor heard from there. Maybe the eel simply senses moisture from a distance? Andrey took the eel over to a water barrel, but the eel wasn't deceived, and again found the lake. A compass needle can be drawn away from the pole with a magnet, but there's no way you can fool an eel; no matter what you do, he'll turn his head to the lake...

Valkov tried to get a plug for himself, but no one had an extra one. He didn't have the nerve to bother the foreman; old Laptik, who was gloomy at best, looked black as thunder when on board. With some difficulty Valkov managed to find a piece of pine bark on the boat, and tried in vain to cut a plug from the rotten wood. All his enjoyment of the ride with the fishermen was ruined. It was a clear, windy day, the breakers rose, frothy and formidable, behind the propeller, gulls hung over the boat on motionless, spread wings, and suddenly slid at an angle down to the water; flocks of ducks flew in and scattered into the reeds along the shore; speckled burbots and dark pike, looking like logs, moved along the sandy bottom, which seemed near, whatever the depth—so clear and transparent was the water in the lake. But since Valkov was unable to take part in the fishing, all this was lost on him. Even the casting of the net and the placing of the traps escaped his notice...

And later, when they pulled the net up onto the deck and the long, thick, light-bellied eels were writhing on the hooks, he almost went mad from excitement and helplessness. Taking a slippery, yard-long beauty from a hook, he yelled his head off for someone to give him a plug to plug up the eel before it crawled away. The fishermen, working in silence, didn't even seem to hear Valkov; only the old foreman bellowed angrily, "Plug yourself up, blabberbox!"

Only then did Valkov notice that the eels were put into the buckets as live as could be, and although they writhed in there, and poked out their little snake-like heads, this didn't bother the fishermen in the least. It was obvious that Vladislav had played a mean trick on him, and that the others knew about the joke, too. Valkov looked apprehensively at these serious, taciturn, self-possessed people, capable of pulling such a trick. Yes, they weren't people to be trifled with!..

After they returned from the catch, the whole village found out about the prank; the women would snicker behind their hands in embarrassment at the sight of Valkov, while the kids laughed at him openly.

"How could a person believe such foolishness?" Elena said to him in vexation. She was displeased that her lodger was made the laughing-stock of the whole village.

4.

One night a storm broke on the lake. A boat returning from the catch was thrown by a wave onto the rocks in Kupansky Cove, got a hole knocked in it, and almost sank. But all turned out well: no one was injured, and they were able to repair the hole quickly. The foreman Laptik was so happy he announced a day off, and a truck was sent to Kobylnik for beer.

Near noon they unloaded the keg in the foreman's large empty courtyard, with its benches planted in the earth, and a table on one thick leg. The women set the table with beer mugs and plates of smoked eel.

When Valkov arrived, Andrey Laptik had pulled the wooden bung from the keg, and the frothy beer had begun to flow into the mugs that people were holding up. Valkov got hold of a mug and crowded up to the keg with the others.

"That's a strong plug, huh, Valkov?" Vladislav said mockingly, nodding at the bung. "I guess you could plug more than just an eel's behind with one like that."

"Yeah, even your chops," Valkov shot back good-naturedly.

"Your arms aren't long enough!" the fisherman snapped with open hostility, and walked off.

"He's alway picking," thought Valkov. "And what have I done to him? Does he notice that I like Elena? But everything's on the up-an-up between her and me. He's a canny so-and-so. He's not through with one wife yet, and he's already corralled another."

In his vexation he raised the mug greedily to his lips and drank off the cold, fresh, light beer at a gulp. His annoyance vanished into thin air; he began to delight in the fine day, and the small holiday, and the men's and women's festive dress, and a whole day's undisturbed rest. He was dressed up fit to kill too: new riding breeches of blue twill tucked into box-calf boots, a clean shirt with a white undercollar; a navy belt with a brass buckle drew in his small waist, emphasizing his slender well-knit figure. After the first mug he became especially aware of his strong, well-built body, and, so as to hold onto this feeling, he immediately emptied a second, wiped the foam from his lips, and told young Andrey Laptik, the bartender, "O.K., my lad, draw me one for the road!"

Andrey raised his bleached eyebrows: "Haven't you had enough? You'll regret it."

"That's not your worry," Valkov smiled condescendingly.

The vaunted local beer didn't affect him a bit, his head was clear, his heart warm, his body like a fully wound spring. Gazing out from behind the green edge of his mug at the women in their varicolored silk blouses, clustered off to one side, he shouted loudly, "Ladies, why are you on the wagon?"

The women laughed and didn't reply.

"It's not their place," Andrey Laptik said sternly.

No, they sure don't know how to drink in Vyazniky! The fishermen went to the keg with decreasing frequency; they crowded around the old foreman and to a lazy accordion accompaniment sang some slow unmelodious song. They appeared just a bit drunk, they swayed in time

with the music, as if on small waves; only Vladislav Laptik watched Valkov
with a sober and sharp eye.

"Shall we have a drink, Vladik?" Valkov addressed him in a
conciliatory tone.

"No need," he growled sullenly.

"Some don't, others do!" and Valkov emptied another mug.

Valkov perceived everything that happened from there on not as a
complete picture, but in individual spots that took shape from out of some
sort of drunken haze. One moment he was pestering the fishermen about
how much each had drunk, and spitting bitter-tasting saliva, boasting,
"And I've knocked back a half-dozen." The next he was interrupting
someone's conversation, the usual conversation about fish, and started
telling the story of how the forester in the taiga had eaten him. The
fishermen grinned, but old Laptik chased the children off.

"Why are you chasing them away?" Valkov said angrily.

"They shouldn't listen to lying."

"But this isn't lying, it's a tall tale!"

"All the same nonsense..."

Valkov realized that he was being insulted, but immediately forgot
about it. Then, suddenly, out of the fog, he discerned Andrey Laptik's face,
and his hand, with red hair on its fingers, taking his mug away from him.
But he had already managed to drink it, and now in place of his former
gladness, he felt a sadness intense to the point of tears: Elena hadn't come to
the party, she hadn't seen what a great drinker he was, how kindly he
treated her fiancé, how he entertained the group with his stories, how
everyone enjoyed his company except that blockhead Vladislav...

He had another mug, that he drew himself; he again gravitated to the
fishermen, every so often interrupting their tedious, endless talk about fish,
always about fish. He barely distinguished one face from another now, he
didn't hear what they were saying to him, he demanded attention, he had
seen so much more in his life than these stay-at-homes, he had something to
tell about.

"What's so great about fish?" he shouted into the weathered, ruddy
faces under their shocks of blond hair. "Birds—now there's a delight."

"What kind of birds?"

The question, put to him with sullen spite by the foreman Laptik,
suddenly fell on Valkov's ears with such clarity, as though he had been
sleeping up till then and had just awakened. He saw himself sitting on the
porch of the foreman's house, with the fishermen standing around and
waiting for his answer.

"Songbirds," he said firmly. "I have only a few birds myself: nine
siskins, sixteen goldfinches, a hundred and forty-seven canaries..."

He intended to say forty-seven, but a hundred and forty-seven slipped off his tongue. Laughing sarcastically, the fishermen all asked in unison where he kept so many birds.

"At home! Where else?"

Ah, so he had that big a house?

Yes, it was a good-sized house, and it had a loft besides. He lived in the loft himself, and left the whole main floor to the birds. The inside of the house was divided by metal netting into three unequal parts. The siskins lived in the smallest part, the goldfinches in the next part, which was a little bigger, and the canaries in the third, the biggest.

"It's an aviary!" he exclaimed, suddenly recalling a word that he had heard somewhere. "I've got all sorts of perches set up there, feeders, little watering troughs..."

By now he almost believed his yarns himself. And why couldn't it be true? Couldn't he keep songbirds on his earning? He was a fool that he hadn't thought of it before. Now he was going to build an aviary for sure, buy a bunch of canaries, and have an old lady live in the house, so that there would be someone to look after the birds when he was gone. And the birds would sing, and he would accompany them on the accordion...

The future turned into the present on the spot, and Valkov began to tell about what concerts he threw with his canaries: the whole village gathered under his windows! Some of the birds, the gray canaries, were soloists; compared to them, the yellow ones—pah, they were poor stuff! Not many people knew about that, but the gray canaries were the main ones... One of the fishermen interrupted him here: was it true that he played the accordion?

"What do you think? Since I accompany the canaries..."

Without another word they thrust some large heavy object into his hands and said: play!

Valkov inspected the object lying on his knees. "That's not an accordion, it's a concertina," he smiled scornfully, and put it aside.

Just as quickly, a small piano accordion encrusted in mother-of-pearl appeared. Valkov couldn't understand why these people were making such a fuss. Big deal—fingering an accordion! He didn't feel like playing, conversation was so much more interesting. A house full of chirping and singing birds, the soloists in their little grey frock-coats, the little yellow choir,—he saw all this with such clarity and pleasure that he began to miss his house of song, and furtively brushed away a tear.

"Get out of here with your accordion," he said gruffly and sadly to the fishermen who kept pushing the instrument into his hands. "I don't want to play, and that's all there is to it!"

And then he saw Elena standing by the fence.

"If I had a guitar, I'd play!" he said loudly, for Elena's benefit. "Where I come from, only females mess around with accordions."

"You'll have a guitar!" the foreman Laptik assured him somberly.

Valkov hadn't caught on that these serious, taciturn, honest people were giving him one last trial, before casting him out of their circle. They were tired of tolerating in their midst a ne'er-do-well, a liar, a philanderer, but they were patient and honorable, and did not want to deprive him of a last chance.

But Valkov sat there dejectedly. Why hadn't he told the fishermen right off the bat that besides the canaries, his aviary included nine little green parrots, the kind called love-birds because of their conjugal fidelity: if one of a couple dies, the other right away kicks off too. And why couldn't there be a fuzzy monkey there too. All day long it hangs head down by its tail from the electric wire. But maybe it would be dangerous to keep it there, it might eat up all the canaries and love-birds?..

Something was thrust into his hands with a muffled strum. A seven-stringed guitar, the sounding-board decorated with transfers. Strange, where would they have found a guitar, it's not their kind of instrument...

"You call that a guitar?" he said contemptuously. "Mass production, a board with strings on it. Now I've got a real guitar—a Krasnoshchekov! Its sound..."

"Well, you can play even on this one," the foreman Laptik said ponderously.

"Play," Elena said quietly, bending down to him. He hadn't noticed her approach. "Play if you can..."

Valkov responded to her unexpected gentleness with a pitiful smile.

"You want me to play?.." A vague hope lent him courage. "Shall I make it into a Havana guitar? The Havana has a moaning, flowing sound... Give me a comb!"

Elena, raising her arm slowly and gracefully, took a comb out of her bun. Valkov inserted it under the strings, at the base of the neck, and began to turn the pins. His expression was distracted and vacant. And suddenly he began to play, straight off, without playing chords to warm up, with a powerful and rich sound, confidently and easily, the way he planed boards or pounded nails. And the guitar's sound was not at all the usual one, but a special one, a "Havana" sound, with a quivering, tender, melodic wail. Valkov bent his head to the sounding board, as if inspecting the transfers,[2] and his fingers with their flat, yellowish nails raced over the strings, then he suddenly raised an almost sober face to the people and sang:

I met you, and all that was past
Came to life again in my broken heart,

> I remembered the time, the golden time,
> And my heart became so light...

He had a high, tenor voice, a bit wooden, though plaintive; he was short of breath on the upper notes, and he sang them in two breaths, but to the fishermen, who were not used to such singing, nor to such songs, it seemed like an angel singing. And Elena listened with a sorrowful and sweet feeling; it seemed to her that the song was coming from within Valkov himself, with its words and melody, that he was creating it on the spot for her...

> No, it's not just reverie,
> All of life found tongue once more,
> And you are the same vision of loveliness,
> And the same love burns within me!..

Turning his linden-blossom-honey eyes on Elena, but not seeing her, Valkov sang the final couplet and covered the strings with his palm, as if smothering the music. His head was clear now, he understood that they all liked the song, that the people were surprised and touched, and old Laptik's cheeks were wet. But he himself felt neither pleasure nor pride. For he knew the worth of his music, everyone in his village played and sang, just as everyone did carpentry and woodworking: it was a hereditary talent. Some played and sang better, others worse; he was not one of the nightingales. The same in his work—he was an ordinary skilled craftsman, not a god. But these people, it seems, hadn't even believed that he could play the guitar. What did they consider him, completely worthless? Fine, all the money he made here he'd spend on canaries, and then he'd send them pictures, or bring Andryushka there at his own expense, prove it to them...

On the other hand, what did he care about them? How many such villages had crossed his path, how many more would there be... Yes, there would be villages, and there would be cities, but without Elena. No, it wasn't just intimacy with her that he wanted now, but to live alongside her, be her husband, the father of her Yazka and of those who would come along later. And to give her all his money and be with her every night, in the house, and in the hayloft when it was stuffy in the room, and in the forest, and on the lake shore, and in the Caucasus, and in the Crimea, on the warm Black Sea. And not knock about the world, but find a job here, near her, in order to return home every evening. And they would have in their house maybe not a hundred and forty-seven, but seven canaries, and he would accompany them on his Krasnoshchekov guitar...

Without raising his head, he stared straight ahead and saw her tanned, strong, tender legs with their white scars from grass cuts.

"Here!" he said to the swarthy, white-striped legs and handed Elena the comb.

"Take it!" he thrust the guitar at Andrey Laptik. "Your 'insterment' is junk..."

He rose and sauntered off through the crowd, which parted to let him past. Someone asked him to stay and sing some more; he didn't even answer. Let them drag out their doleful songs in chorus, if they can't believe in a man, in the beauty he has in him!..

But that night Valkov got sick; he dove head first from the hayloft, but didn't make it to the door; he began to throw up his insides right there in the entry. And Elena came out to help him, in just a skirt thrown over her nightgown. He stood before her half-dressed, pitiful, sweating, and unable to say a word, only waved her away with his hand. But she didn't leave, but held his head with her palm, made him drink water from a ladle, and cursed the fishermen who had let him drink so much. Half-dead from shame and grief, Valkov understood, through his torment, that all was lost, that he had been drunk, boastful, deceitful, and pitiful, and everyone had seen that.

"All right," he finally said, hoarsely. "I'm O.K. now..."

5.

Although Valkov considered himself disgraced forever, the guitar and song had done what his loud, boastful talk had been unable to do: people began to treat him better. True, there wasn't so much as a trace of respect there; it was the attitude village people had toward those whom God had treated ill—imbeciles, hunchbacks, deafmutes. Such kindness was like a knife in Valkov's heart. He hurried to finish all his uncompleted jobs so that he could leave Vyazniky as soon as possible. He avoided Elena, and even tried to get his meals away from home.

Once Valkov heard Olesya, Vladislav's ill wife, threaten her youngest, "If you don't go to sleep, I'll call Chuchukala!"

Valkov concluded that Chuchukala was something like the house spirit or sorcerer of Meshchyora lore, and was quite surprised when he heard the word in the fishermen's conversation. They spoke it with bitterness, anger, and resignation. It turned out that Chuchukala was not some fairy-tale monster at all, but the new director of the fishery.

Chuchukala had ended up in the fishery as the result of some offense; previously he had held an important position in the republic capital. When he took over the fishery, Chuchukala decided to organize things his own way. He summoned the old foreman Ignaty Laptik, and something like the following conversation took place between them:

"Why does the eel-fishing stop long before the lake freezes?"

"The eels leave Rybachye..."

"And why should the eels leave a Soviet lake and be caught by foreign fishermen?"

"They go off to spawn..."

"And why shouldn't they spawn here, like all the other fish do?"

"Well, because only female eels live here..."

"Nonsense, no one has proved that, and meanwhile the eel quota isn't being fulfilled. Eels mean foreign exchange! The government is taking strict measures against black-market money dealers, and here we have valuable foreign exchange slipping through our fingers, and no one gives a damn. It's time to put an end to the emigration of eels, to fulfill and exceed the plan, to earn the government some gold!.."

When he found out that the great trek of the eels over the seas and oceans began in the narrow little Sapushka, Chuchukala decided to close off that stream, the only one that flows into Rybachye, and confine the eels securely in the lake. Old Laptik tried in vain to dissuade Chuchukala from this venture. He spoke in lofty, pathetic, and illiterate accents about the "cyrcle" of nature, he warned that they could completely exterminate the tribe of eels that way. In answer Chuchukala kept repeating just one thing: "We shouldn't wait for favors from nature!" The old foreman lost his patience:

"Well, and when we kill off the eels what are we going to do, catch them off your mug?.."

The director's coarse, beefy face turned red with rage, and Vladislav Laptik was appointed in the old foreman's place that very day. To be sure, no one in the village, including Vladislav himself, paid any attention to it; everything was done, as before, according to Ignaty's orders. But now it was Vladislav who would go talk to the bosses.

The fishermen called Chuchukala names: "wicked," "corrupt" a "dud"; mothers used his name to threaten disobedient children, and the only old lady in the village who attended church proclaimed that he was sent to the people of Vyazniky because of their sins. Only Valkov, who had been around, guessed the truth. No, Chuchukala was not a dolt or a dullard, but, on the contrary, very crafty. Obviously, he had come way down in the world and now he needed an opportunity to make his way back up again. A small fishery, where everything was done by hand labor, didn't provide such opportunities. It wouldn't be a simple or quick matter to increase the overall size of the catch. And Chuchukala had discovered the only sure way. He was playing a game he couldn't lose. Even if the fishermen were right, and the lake would run dry of eel, still, that wouldn't be discovered for some time, and by then Chuchukala would be safely out of reach...

In a word, Valkov felt an affinity with this new arrival, who was not afraid to meddle with the long-established order, who was ready to barge ahead for the sake of certain and immediate gain. And then the fishermen, if you think about it, were foolish to get their dander up. For now, they would catch eel right into the winter and earn a pile of money, and then they could see how it came out. Of course, Valkov didn't share his thoughts with the fishermen, it was none of his business, and besides, they apparently considered him a fool.

Vladislav Laptik kept his position of foreman for only a few days. Vyazniky was much closer to the mouth of the river than the other fishing villages, and Chuchukala called in Vladislav to demand that the Vyaznikites build a dam on the Sapushka.

"You can't do that, man!" said Vladislav with a heavy heart.

"I don't need advice," Chuchukala glowered. "That's the order—carry it out!"

"Impossible, sir."

"I'll have no insubordination!" Chuchukala slammed the desk with his fist. "You're my employees, you understand? I'll send you all packing, and you'll sing a different tune!"

"We won't and that's it," Vladislav said quietly and firmly. "If you want to exterminate the eel, scum, go do your own dirty work!.."

At that very hour, Andrey Laptik took the rank of foreman on his young shoulders. He was deeply embarrassed before his elders in age and experience, but he consoled himself that he would soon share the fate of his predecessor. But things turned out differently.

"Is there a carpenter working in your village?" Chuchukala asked when Andrey appeared. "Valkov, is that his name?"

"Yes, there is..."

"Has he got a head on his shoulders?"

"Yes..."

"Could he build a dam?"

"Ask him yourself."

Chuchukala was about to flare up, but he apparently read something in Andrey's eyes, and rapped out sullently, "You send him to me..."

Valkov was pleased and excited by his talk with Andrey: he smelled a healthy profit. The only trouble was, the fishermen obviously didn't like the idea. But then he didn't have any ties with them. In the evening he told Elena about Chuchukala's proposition, and added, "I don't have much taste for this dam, somehow."

If Elena had supported him, had shown pleasure that he was so concerned about the fishermen's troubles, Valkov would have had no trouble giving up the earnings. But she said, in a calm and distant tone, "If it's not you, they'll hire someone else, so it's all the same!"

"So I shouldn't turn it down?"

She shrugged her shoulders as if to say, "What's it to me . . ."

O.K. then, he'd build the dam, earn a pile of money, and buy a piano for her Yazka. They'd see what all of them would say about Valkov when a piano, black as pitch, with ivory keys, came rolling in from the city on a truck. She'd better watch out that she wouldn't have to take down a wall in order to get it into her crummy little house! And the rest of the dough he'd put aside for his wedding, he'd marry the lady doctor, and not some ignorant fisherwoman . . .

The next day Valkov went to the director's office. Chuchukala didn't look a bit like a sorcerer or a goblin, he had a very managerial appearance. Stocky, solidly-built, with a grayish crewcut and a black upturned mustache, he was dressed in a tunic of covert cloth and trousers of the same material, tucked into officer's boots. Chuchukala apparently understood at once that he had found the right person, he wasted no time and invited Valkov there and then to take a ride to the river so as to settle everything on the spot.

"How much do you want?" Chuchukala asked when they had sufficiently admired the narrow, muddy little stream in its low banks, overgrown with grass that was already turning yellow.

Valkov looked askance at the director's well-fed, pasty, large-pored face, remembered how wrathfully his neck and ears had flushed at every jolt of the jeep on the bumpy road, and understood that Chuchukala would stop at nothing to escape from this hole and rest his behind on the soft cushion of a Volga, and not on the hard seat of a "Goat." He named a price completely out of line: four thousand rubles.

"Can you do it?" was all Chuchukala asked.

"I've built not just weirs, like this," Valkov spat, "but regular dams!"

"Agreed," said Chuchukala.

Just as quickly, they settled the question of materials, transport, and the helpers that Valkov would need for laying the underwater part of the dam.

"Hire your helpers in Vyazniky."

"They won't do it," objected Valkov. He didn't want to deal with the fishermen.

"We'll make them!" Chuchukala spoke in a menacing voice; now for a moment one could see something of the sorcerer in him, something cold and calculating.

"No, boss, I don't want to work with forced labor . . ."

"O.K. then," Chuchukala understood something, and narrowed his eyes scornfully. "I'll give you some cannery workers."

Valkov met with Chuchukala again about two weeks later, when he inspected the completed job.

"Here's what's up," Chuchukala said gloomily as he looked over the solidly-built wooden dam. "The fishermen are talking some kind of nonsense, they claim the eels will get out anyway, on the first stormy night. Have you heard that?"

"That's a good one," Valkov grinned. "I answer for my work. You can see that for yourself, I guess, that there's no way they can get across the dam. Maybe along the bank ... "

"Like hell will I let them get away along the bank," something menacing again appeared in Chuchukala's voice. "I'll have all the grass cut, today!" He was silent for a bit. "So here's the deal, Valkov, you'll have to check out your dam yourself."

"What do you mean—check out?"

"I mean you'll stand watch on the river on a stormy night. If it's up to snuff, you'll get your money, and you can head out for wherever you like!"

"What am I supposed to do, freeze every night by the river?"

"What about weather forecasts? If there's going to be a storm, we'll let you know! Understood?"

"I did my job, you don't have the right ... "

"That's all there is to it!" Chuchukala cut him off. "You'll get half now, and the rest later ... "

On the evening the storm warning came, Valkov decided not to come back to Vyazniky after he had stood his watch. Elena was mending a landing net when he came into the kitchen and said,

"Well, I'm leaving ... Don't hold a grudge if I've ... I'm very grateful to you ... " Valkov couldn't figure out himself why all of a sudden he was using the formulas, alien to him, of village farewells. "Fare thee well ... "

"Goodbye," said the landlady, without raising her head.

"Don't take it amiss if I send your daughter a present ... " Valkov continued in the same tone, irritated with himself.

"That's not necessary," the landlady replied in a sadly scoffing tone. "You've done enough for all of us."

Valkov fell silent and backed awkwardly out of the house.

6.

There was a delicate moldy odor from the yellowing, closely mowed grass, from the dry leaves of an elm, from the willows overhanging the creek. Someone's small voices could be heard in the silence: someone was overtaken and dispatched by a stronger foe; someone escaped and was exulting in it; someone was fretting, someone was complaining, someone was muttering sleepily, as though lulling himself to sleep. This modestly soniferous silence was precarious, fragile; something clearly was coming to a head in the distance. Multi-layered steely-dark clouds were moving in from the west; the sunset was an evil-looking murky pink, and from time to time pallid, silent lightning flashed across the sunset, the rosy murk, and the dark clouds.

Seated on the ground, his back against the trunk of the elm, Valkov dozed, without entirely losing consciousness of the life teeming around him. He was aware that night had fallen and a wind had come up, that a golden moon had risen and was shining on the earth, that the sound of rising waves was coming from the lake. At the same time he was having a dream, not actually a dream, but something like a vision that kept repeating itself, like the musical beats when the needle falls into a crack on an old phonograph record. He was standing in the courtyard of Elena's house; a crow with a horse's tail was landing on the barn roof. "What's that?" Elena asked woefully. "A verticopter," he said in a soothing voice. "It's a good sign," but he knew himself that it was very bad, very sad, even fatal. Then everything went dark for a moment, then again there was the courtyard, and the crow with a horse's tail on the barn, and Elena's woeful question, and his soothing answer. And again the same, only his heart ached more each time, and, unable to bear the pain, Valkov, by a conscious effort, with a shudder, with a short moan that he heard himself, shook off this incomprehensible and uncannily sad dream...

His heart was beating hard, hollowly. Valkov shook his head, smiled, and suddenly gave a strange sob. Or rather, someone inside him sobbed, someone small and shamefully abject. "You're coming apart, fella," he said to himself. "Now you're dreaming about verticopters." But the sadness that he had felt in the dream didn't pass, it remained inside him, although what was sad about a crow with a horse's tail? It was more funny than sad.

Valkov got out his tobacco-pouch, rolled a cigarette, and lit it, sheltering the match with the tail of his jacket.

The river glimmered in the moonlight, and in its ghostly light Valkov noticed on the edge of the bank the long, writhing body of an eel that was trying to crawl around the dam on the bank. But the grass was all cut away, and the eel, gaining only a few centimeters of the bank, twitched helplessly on the short stubble.

When Valkov came out from under the elm, it was as if he entered a different night. A cold damp wind lashed him; he had had no idea, there in the shelter of the tree, that the wind was so strong. It was blowing from the lake, and driving water from there; the river was swollen on that side of the dam. The sky was covered with clouds, a blue haze kept covering the moon, but it was still light from the lightning flashes coming one after the other.

Valkov picked up the eel, which twitched like a spring and slipped out of his hands. Valkov grabbed it again, and again couldn't hang on to it: it was as if the eel sucked itself out of the man's tightly clenched fingers. Then Valkov ran over to the elm, took the crowbar he had left there, went back to the eel, picked it up under the belly, and threw it hard toward the water. The eel fell on the sandy edge of the bank, and from there it was easy to kick it into the water.

There was a thin blinding lightning flash, and in the momentary light Valkov saw that the river was swarming with eels; their black heads, sticking out of the water, showed up clearly against the light-colored mass of the dam. They looked as if they were licking the boards. Valkov felt his face go cold from an instinctive fear. Well, anyway they couldn't get over the dam; the bad part was that several more eels had flung themselves out onto the low bank by the left end of the dam. Valkov grabbed the bar—one toss, a second and one more eel, its light-colored underbelly flashing silver, disappeared into the water with a splash. But in its place other eels leapt out of the river, and among them, perhaps, was the one Valkov had just thrown into the river...

The thick wad of money in Valkov's inside jacket pocket hindered him, and he was hot besides, in spite of the brisk, cold wind. He took off his jacket, took it over to the elm, and hung it on a limb. The wind was driving water from the lake harder and harder; the quiet little stream was foaming and seething. The eels' dark heads stood out more sharply now against the white foam; it seemed to Valkov that there were many more eels than before. Of course, these boneless creatures couldn't do anything to a solid structure of thick logs, clamped fast together with iron: still, Valkov began to feel uneasy. There was something irresistible, something surpassing human calculation and will in the eels' pertinacity. He remembered the fishermen's talk: that the eels couldn't be confined, that they would leave, anyway, on the very first stormy night, that there was something mysterious about this creature, that it couldn't be compared with any other creature on earth ... Ah, that was all nonsense, pure superstition, a fish was nothing more than a fish! He was just wasting his strength, they couldn't get away from here over the bare ground anyway...

And yet he continued to throw eels into the river, not convinced that it was necesary, but neither could he bring himself to stop the fruitless, exhausting work. But then a torrent of rain began, the lightning stopped, in the ensuing darkness Valkov could no longer make out the eels; he couldn't even distinguish the bank from the river or the river from the dam. He made his way blindly to the elm; his face ran into the branches, and he bent down underneath them, pressing up against the trunk. The dry foliage was poor protection from the rain, and Valkov rolled up his jacket and stuffed it under himself, so the money wouldn't get soaked.

At this moment he seemed strange to himself. In pitch darkness, in the merged noise of the rain and the river, cut off from the rest of the world, he was sitting under a bare autumn tree, and he couldn't even understand how he had got mixed up in all this, he, an aritisan, a carpenter from Meshchyora, Vasily Valkov. Maybe this was the adventure he had dreamed about so much? He really would be glad to let someone else have it, but it couldn't be helped, he had to see it through: tomorrow at the office all of today's events would be in the past, he would get his money, and that was the last they'd see of him...

Something began to drum heavily and rapidly on the ground and on the leaves of the elm, strange white streaks cut through the darkness. Valkov didn't realize that it was hail until it began pounding painfully on his shoulders and knees. The rain subsided, and you could hear the sound of the hailstones rolling down the slope of the bank into the water. The moon came out again, and everything around began to glitter: the puddles, the leaves, the hailstones. Slipping on the large hailstones, the size of cuckoo's eggs, Valkov went down to the river. A bright silver path of hailstones lay along the water's edge, and two strapping eels were crawling over it, as if it were dew-covered pea plants. Valkov barely kept himself from whacking them with the crowbar; instead he used it to throw them into the river, one after the other. It was then that he noticed how much the river had risen. The eels' heads were already coming up above the edge of the footbridge that Valkov had built above the sluice, so the river could be crossed there. It looked as though a little more, and they would start jumping over the dam. He ran onto the bridge, and got there just in time: a large eel, shooting out of the water like an arrow, nearly threw itself onto the narrow platform of the bridge. Valkov kicked it into the water, but right alongisde, another narrow head rose up; that one he shoved away with the bar, kicked another head, and slipped and fell, hurting his side on the boards. When he got up, he saw that a whole flock of eels was already crawling around the dam, and he dashed down...

Valkov was seized by fury. He was soaked to the skin, his side hurt, and his palms were bleeding from the jagged crowbar, and the eels kept pressing on; in their unquenchable, blind persistence they exposed their bodies to the blows, not just the prods now, of the iron bar, and kept coming, coming, coming. Something evil awoke within Valkov; he raced from the dam to the bank and back onto the dam, hardly aware in his rage what he was doing, and thinking only of one thing: to drive the eels back into the river. The cloudburst came beating down again, but Valkov didn't go for cover; he found the eels in the pitch darkness, he divined their presence as a more solid darkness. The short downpour melted some of the hailstones and washed the others into the river, and now the eels crawled out onto the bank only one at a time. It was clear that the endless horde of eels was trying to escape by a water route...

Now a lightning storm, without rain, was raging all around; the strokes of lightning would sometimes coalesce, and then dazzling domes would rise up over the earth. The deafening thunderclaps merged into a heavy avalanche of stones, a dry crackle, a glassy peal, as though invisible palaces were crumbling into dust. In the ghastly greenish flare of the lightning Valkov could see other, black, lightning bolts that the illuminated, frothing river was casting from its depths. The eels leapt out of the swollen water, slid along the rounded hump of the waterfall that was gushing over the dam, struck the edge of the bridge and fell back into the water. Sometimes they would manage to heave up onto the bridge a greater length of their body, and would hang there, squirming frantically, trying to crawl the rest of the way up. But Valkov would get there in time and throw them into the river. He had long since lost track of time, and couldn't have said how long this struggle had lasted: an hour, two, three, six hours. There were practically more eels than water in the river now; it seemed to Valkov that the river was swollen not so much from the rain or the water driven from the lake by the wind, as from those countless dark bodies that filled the entire narrow channel from the lake to the dam.

A huge, five-foot eel leapt out of the water and slammed down onto the bridge right at Valkov's feet. It looped its body and darted forward, toward the other edge of the dam.

"Ah, you damn monster!" Valkov yelled, losing control from wrath, and hit the eel on the head with the bar.

He struck again and again, until he had bashed the eel's brains out. Then, berserk, he began to beat the eel's long rubbery body; he hacked it to pieces, but each piece, as if endowed with a life of its own, continued crawling ahead.

"Damn monster!" Valkov said, not to the eel now, but to himself, and dropped the bar.

That moment witnessed a jarring return to lucidity. What was he striking out at with his rusty bar? At life itself, at its eternal, sacred law. The eels strive toward the distant warm sea in order to accomplish one of nature's great, pure, tender ends: to perpetuate the race of eels for all time. And he, Valkov, in his contemptible avarice, and for the sake of some Chuchukala's base designs, had barred their way, had condemned them to extermination and extinction. A chance passerby, a selfish stranger, he had crossed the local folk, who, through their labor, from time immemorial had, through their labor, come to be on friendly terms with nature, had learned to respect her laws, and therefore rightfully enjoy her bounties...

Valkov raised the bar high, with all his might drove it into a chink between two logs, and leaning all his weight on it, tried to tear apart that which he had put together, erected and made fast with such zeal and skill.

By a prodigious effort of his whole body, Valkov managed to separate the two logs, and insert the bar under the hook of an iron clamp. But when he tried to pull it loose, the bar slipped out of his hands and fell into the river. Without any hesitation, Valkov jumped in after it. The water was up to his neck, eels swarmed all around, he felt as if he had landed in a cluster of snakes. But he felt neither fear nor repugnance. They were his mute little brothers, and he must help them. He dove underwater, now feeling the eels' slippery bodies on his face as well, groped on the bottom until he found the bar, grabbed it, and began to make for the bank. The eels were in his way; he gently pushed them aside, muttering over and over,

"Let me by, brothers! How stupid you're being! ... "

Back on the bank, Valkov again went up on top of the dam, where it was easier for him to dismantle it. From out of nowhere he felt an influx of vigor; the heavy bar seemed to be lighter in his hands. He was amazed by this new, strange strength, he didn't yet realize he had risen to his highest potential, that at that moment he was both nature herself and the human reason that protects her...

A nearby lightning bolt suddenly lashed across his eyes, blinded him, convulsed him with an electric shock; Valkov fell, lost consciousness of his surroundings for just a moment, and when he came to, he saw a huge torch on the river bank: the elm was burning, set afire by the lightning. The wind had already blown the rain from it, and, dry to its ancient core, the tree surrendered to the fire with the speed of gunpowder. The trunk was blazing from the ground to the crown, the thick limbs burned, crackling and snapping, only the leaves turned to ash from the heat before they could even catch fire. Valkov remembered indifferently that he had left his jacket and the money there, and again took up his bar.

The dam gave way and collapsed abruptly, when dawn was already breaking. Valkov barely managed to jump to the bank. The pressure of the river finished the job that the man had begun. Valkov didn't see the eels rush into the breach and break through into the open water, leaving shreds of their flesh on the logs and boards. He painfully pulled the bar loose from his bloody palms, which had dried fast to the iron. One lonely eel was wriggling on the bank; Valkov kicked it into the river, and slowly, staggering, made his way over to the scorched elm. The ground under the tree was covered with soft ashes; Valkov sat down on the ground, leaning his back against the warm, charred trunk, put his wounded hands on his knees, dropped his head to his chest, and immediatley fell fast asleep.

In the morning the fishermen showed up at the river. They saw the wrecked dam, several dead eels on the bank, the burnt tree, and the man sleeping under it. Next to him lay a crowbar stained with dried blood, some sort of burnt cloth, and several bills, twisted into a black tube. The sleeping man's face was dead tired, his hands, dangling from his knees, were curled up like claws. The fishermen shook Valkov awake, so they could take him back to the village, but he didn't understand what they wanted of him, shook his head, plaintively mumbling something, and dropped back to sleep. Then they sent for the woman. She came, touched Valkov's shoulder, and he opened his eyes. Bending down, she took him by the shoulders and helped him to his feet. Then she carefully placed Valkov's arm across her shoulders, took hold of his belt, and led him to the village, into her life.

1963   Translated by Earl Sampson

The original ("Na tikhom ozere") first appeared in *Ogonek,* Nos. 15 and 16 (1963), 20-24 and 18-22 respectively. The present translation is of the edition included in the 1973 two-volume collection, II, 40-74.

Notes

1. The Sargasso Sea is a relatively calm area of water in the North Atlantic, northeast of the West Indies, noted for an abundance of seaweed.
2. The reference is to a design transferred onto the guitar for decorative purposes.

Olezhka Got Married

The light was born in the nocturnal blackness of the forest. From his window Bolotov saw the trunks of the pine trees behind the hunting shack become illuminated, the pine needles turned lightly and sparklingly green, the threads of a spider's web that was stretched between the trees gleamed; but he didn't get up and didn't even move. In spite of the obvious, he didn't believe he was seeing automobile headlights. Hunting usually started on Saturday at sunset—which meant there was nothing for hunters to do before the following day. The huntsmen, the nurse *cum* housekeeper, and the cleaning women would appear at the base only the following morning, and the generator that supplied light to all the buildings and moorings would start to work the next day. Right now there wasn't anyone else besides him, the boss, at the base submerged in darkness, and shouldn't have been.

With the calm of a bystander, Bolotov continued to observe the silvery-greenish light that was crawling out of the forest as an unterrifying marvel, a vision that appears to an extremely weary man before he goes to bed and dreams the dreams granted to every sleeping individual. Out of the darkness the light created trees, bushes, a steep slope in the rusty juniper above the standing water, and pale whisks of rushes; and all this looked completely different from the way it did in the daytime: it was taller, bigger, more imposing. Suddenly the light disappeared, and with it disappeared all the population of the nocturnal world, and Bolotov grieved for the light as though for someone close to him. He was beastly tired that day. Since morning he'd angled for fish in order to feed the drivers who'd brought the building material for the substation, then until midday he'd helped unload bricks, and towards evening he'd gone with the huntsmen to set up new duck blinds and barrels on the pool, then had thrown out nets for pike and carp to be used in the next day's fish soup and also to be sold to hunters, and finally, in complete darkness, he'd begun to knock together a duck house. Despite the unanimous opinion of experts, he firmly believed that it was possible to force wild ducks to nest along the shores of local lakes. Since funds weren't allocated for duck houses, he decided to gradually put together with his own hands over the autumn and winter the necessary number of little wooden houses which resembled huge sparrow boxes.

But the light appeared again, even brighter than before. As its two heavy rays coming from behind the corner of the hunting shack struck beyond the wharf, it illuminated the motor boats at the mooring, flickered along the quiet, dismal water, described a steep arc and settled on the speckled road and the flower bed with drooping asters and dahlias in a wide stripe that reached the walls of his dwelling. This soft yellowish light became blindingly unbearable at its source—the fishy goggle-eyes of two headlights belonging to a low-slung passenger-car.

Bolotov looked dully at the small car shedding the light, with its bumper, hood, and the darkness of the windshield flashing dimly, and each fiber of his overworked muscles resisted the fact that now he'd have to get up, leave the house, welcome the premature guests, show them to their rooms, and give them some tea to drink. He sighed, groped for his rubbers with his bare feet under the table, grabbed his padded coat, and went out into the road.

The driver turned off the large beams and switched on the parking lights. The car vanished except for two small yellow fires glimmering at ground level. Bolotov bumped against the brick ring of the flower bed, stubbed his toe, and lost a rubber. Fumbling around for it along the cold sand, he felt sorry for himself—old, tired, and alone in the dead of night, dependent on the caprices of strangers who took it into their heads to arrive before the proper time.

He finally found the rubber and stuck his foot into its cold interior. It surprised him that no one was getting out of the car. Small and low-slung, as if pulling its breath in, it looked at Bolotov with the half-blind flickers of parking lights. As Bolotov approached, the car lit up inside, laughter was heard, and behind the windshield appeared the unexpected and therefore especially dear face of Olezhka. There was someone else there too, but Bolotov saw only that face with its patches of youthful ruddiness, with huge, gentle, and gay eyes. And then he pulled in his paunch, stuck his thumbs under his belt, and in a thin old lady's voice sang out:

"Did thine-mine come to make poof-poof?"

Laughter was heard again—Olezhka's joyful, light, untroubled laughter. Bolotov had earned his living for many years hunting wild antelope in the Astrakhan steppes, and there he'd learned the subtleties of steppe speech. Olezhka, who laughed easily in general, went into ecstasy whenever Bolotov began to fracture the language 'in steppe talk.'

Olezhka got out of the car, still laughing. They embraced and kissed.

"How's your father?" asked Bolotov.

"An invalid of all-union status!" Olezhka gave a laugh again, but Bolotov felt a sudden chill in his shoulder blades.

"Is he really?"

"He's totally lost the use of his legs, and doesn't even leave his bed now."

Bolotov knew about the serious illness of Olezhka's father, but had been sure that Ivan Sharonov would get over the illness, as he'd overcome all the difficulties and misfortunes of his adult complicated life. The spring before when some Moscow hunters had brought the news that Sharonov wouldn't pull through, Bolotov had only snorted disdainfully. He didn't believe that there was anything in the world that wouldn't succumb to Sharonov's will power.

"All the same, how is he?" Bolotov asked again quietly.

"The old man? Fine!.. He sends greetings."

Olezhka's companions got out of the car: a tall girl with a shock of strangely shimmering dark hair, and someone with glasses of Olezhka's age, but so serious, so concentrated and intellectual, that Bolotov was slightly intimidated.

"I want you to get acquainted," said Olezhka. "The local commander and god of the hunt, Nikolay Petrovich Bolotov; this is Vadya Zelentsov, our shar-r-r-pest theoretician... And this," Olezhka turned to the girl and gave a laugh—his usual light happy laugh, "this is Nadenka, my wife."

"You got married?" cried Bolotov. "So I lived to see it! Congratulations, congratulations!" With both of his huge hands he shook Olezhka's hand and somehow involuntarily moved toward Nadya. He himself didn't know whether he wanted to kiss Olezhka's wife or simply to touch her precious shimmering head, or to leave his instinctive movement unfinished, but she shied away from him in fear.

"What's the matter with you?.. He doesn't bite," Olezhka burst out laughing.

"I'm only frightening on the outside."

Bolotov wasn't offended, but hurt. Life had left visible marks on his large face, which had been tanned from time immemorial. In the Civil War he came down with smallpox, which pocked his nose and cheeks; from behind a badly healed upper lip glistened a row of steel teeth—his own teeth were knocked out by the butt of a rifle in hand-to-hand combat at Elnya. From the left eyebrow, which looked broken, snaked a white jagged scar across his temple to the jawbone—the trace of a bear's paw. These were marks of war and hunting, but there was nothing repulsive in Bolotov's strong, masculine face. Normally he didn't think so either, but now he thought, "Apparently I'm getting frightening to look at in my old age." But even this melancholy conclusion couldn't cast a shadow over his good-natured feelings of tenderness.

"Your father must really be tickled pink?" he said to Olezhka.

The latter, his eyes laughing, looked at his wife, then at his friend,

"And what do you think, is my old man very happy that Nadya and I've worked out so well?"

"That's enough now!" said Nadya with a touch of annoyance.

The friend straightened his glasses and in a business-like acid tone, said, "Perhaps we can begin unloading, Oleg Ivanych?"

They lost more time than was necessary on unloading and settling in because of the muddle caused by Bolotov's eagerness to oblige. He took the travelers' things, dragged them onto the terrace of the main building, but realizing that the large living quarters were impossible to heat adequately, dragged their things to the adjacent building; en route he decided that the young couple would be most comfortable in his place, so he changed direction again, but after Olezhka's resolute protest, he again turned toward the small cottage which stood separately.

Genuine distress hid behind Bolotov's comic confusion. Old man Sharonov's hopeless illness and Olezhka's marriage merged for him in a single tangle, as though that was the way, and the only way, it should be according to the true and meaningful movement of life. Ivan Sharonov was passing on, but he'd lived to see Olezhka reach maturity, and now he knew that he'd be leaving not a green youth, but a man, and that the good Sharonov blood wouldn't die out in the world...

In the cottage it was bone cold, there was an inhospitable smell of damp firewood, which was piled up next to the stove, and the water in the wash basin was frozen. The kerosene lamp that Bolotov found in the kitchen after a great deal of effort finally released a long black tongue of soot up to the ceiling. That wasn't the way Bolotov would have wanted to welcome Olezhka and his young wife, but it had been their idea to arrive without warning, and moreover, earlier than the specified time. And, contrary to normal procedure, it turned out that they'd been issued a pass for overnight and the following day. Apparently Bolotov had been out of the office when they called from Moscow to announce the hunters' arrival.

"So how did you manage to get a pass for tomorrow morning?" inquired Bolotov.

Olezhka only laughed a little, but his friend with glasses pointedly said: "Well, what do you want, he's a Sharonov, after all!.."

Of course, had there been even one efficient person in the group, everything would have been put in order in a jiffy. Think what work was involved: to light the stove, turn on the generator, bring water from the well, and prepare dinner. But Olezhka distinguished himself by a rare lack of skill in everyday life ("He takes after his late mother," the old man Sharonov used to say tenderly), and there was no point whatever in counting on the others. Olezhka's learned friend sprawled serenely on the cot and kept blowing blue rings of smoke, and Nadenka was shivering, wrapped up in a shawl, and kept putting her palms to the cold side of the stove. They wouldn't likely be much use. He had to do it all himself, and that would take time—and Nadenka would become stiff with cold, Olezhka would grow sour, and their first wedding-hunting trip would be hopelessly ruined. Bolotov's chagrin and pity for Olezhka, his passionate desire that he feel happy, filled Bolotov with inspired insight. He went out into the yard, and making a megaphone out of his palms, he gave a loud shout:

"Anfiska! Anfiska!"

No one answered; the night pretended to be deaf.

"Anfiska-a-a!.." called Bolotov, "There's no sense in playing the fool!.. Come here, you devil's wench!.. Or I'll drag you here myself!.. Anfiska-a-a!.."

Again silence, false, ambiguous silence, after which something creaked somewhere. For several seconds Bolotov still remained alone among the almost invisible wet trees, then quick steps crunched along the sand, and a well-built, solid young woman in a colt-skin jacket, with a white wool shawl thrown over her shoulders, appeared beside him. In the darkness he didn't see the expression on her face, but he felt the heat of her flesh and her breathing and suddenly was intimidated, just like a magician who'd summoned up a spirit that was beyond his powers.

"What are you shouting for?" said Anfiska discontentedly.

And then anger flared up in him.

"You should be ashamed, wench!.. You're a soldier's wife. You have a family, a child, and where've you lost your conscience?"

"But why did you start shouting like that?" Anfiska was indignant. "I was late, so I lay down in the large hall. What good would it do me to rush off to the village since I have to come back before dawn?"

"I'll tell your mother-in-law everything," promised Bolotov. "Hunters have arrived. I put them in the little house. We need to bring some water, boil water for tea, in a word, you yourself know... And tell your boyfriend to turn on the generator."

"What boyfriend?" grinned Anfiska.

"You know which one..."

"I don't know anything!.. It's easy for anyone to insult a soldier's wife..." Anfiska started up whiningly, but with self-assurance.

Submitting again to the same somnambulant and shady insight, Bolotov said harshly:

"Here's what, soldier's wife, tell Pleshakov to give us some light immediately, or else I'll fire him..."

Despondence reigned inside the house. Olezhka was clumsily stuffing the stove with thick damp logs. With a hopeless air Nadenka was shredding paper for kindling, and Vadya was blowing smoke rings.

"Step aside, now," said Bolotov gaily, pulling the young couple away from the stove. He knew that everything would be fine now, and didn't want to waste words on comforting them. He emptied the furnace of its inedible wooden food, chopped some chips, and lit the stove. Anfiska, wearing an apron tied over her jacket, flew into the entryway like the wind, almost extinguishing the newly-created flame, grabbed the pail, and swept out of the house. Before she returned, even before Bolotov got the stove going, the electric lights came on...

Running home to his place, Bolotov brought over a jar of marinated mushrooms and another with pickles, and a large pot of sauerkraut and soaked apples.

"Now that's food!" Olezhka was delighted.

"The most legitimate snacks," said Vadya seriously. "If there were potatoes too!"

And the potatoes didn't have long to wait. When a nice dry heat filled the place and various kinds of foods from Moscow were attractively arranged on the table covered with a white tablecloth, Anfiska, serious to the point of stiffness, triumphantly brought in a large black cast iron pot, then placed a wooden salt cellar with coarse gray salt on the table.

"Boiled potatoes love coarse salt," said Bolotov, catching Nadenka's glance.

She made no response whatever, but digging around in her knapsack, found a small glass salt cellar with a little red cap. In general, she was reserved and silent, was Olezhka's wife. Now that he'd got used to her, Bolotov saw that her magnificently puffed hair was covered with some kind of sticky shiny spray that resembled mica, and it was beautiful, as were the black corners of her eyes which led like arrows to the temples, and the blue sleepy lids and the soft drooping lips in deathly pale-pink lipstick. Bolotov was a modern man, and although even to his simple taste Anfiska's wide, wind-blown, freckled, thick-browed and full-lipped face, untouched by powder or paint, was much more attractive to him, he gave the painted beauty of Olezhka's wife's face its due. As for Olezhka, he apparently possessed the same broad taste. Distracted from the bottle of cognac, in which he'd clumsily crumbled the cork, Olezhka looked at Anfiska as if he hadn't seen her before and said loudly:

"Oho! What a picture!.. The old man has good taste!.."

Bolotov flinched. It was awkward in front of Nadenka, and besides, the overly familiar "old man" didn't sit well with him. Even Ivan Sharonov, who was much older, never allowed himself such familiarity. But then he decided that Olezhka did it from a youthful desire to assert himself. He wanted to show his wife how independent he was, and his friend—the adult intimacy he had with the local hunting boss. Nadenka didn't even raise an eyebrow at Olezhka's tactlessness, and he, Bolotov, ought to act likewise.

Even though he'd known Olezhka when the latter was a teenager that didn't mean that Olezhka had to look up to him his whole life. There's nothing more stupid than putting on airs because of one's age; just think: what an achievement! Casting off his old man's haughtiness, Bolotov again felt light, gay, and excited. He took the bottle from Olezhka, uncorked it, poured the cognac into glasses, and said warmly and grandly:

"I propose a toast to the newlyweds!.."

"You should pour a drink for the girl."

"Anfiska doesn't drink..." said Bolotov uncertainly, and in good conscience added: "on the job... However, on such an occasion... Anfiska!.."

Anfiska came in, wiping her hands on her apron.

"Here, Anfiska, the comrades invite you to drink to their health, they got married recently, created a family..." He sensed a kind of didacticism in his tone, as if the example of these young people emphasized especially keenly the disorderliness in Anfiska's life. "Well, fine! To your health, Olezhka, to yours, Nadenka! Live long and happily!"

"Ciao!.." said Vadya.

Olezhka drank it down, screwed up his eyes, and began to prod with a fork a mushroom that was sliding away. Vadya drank his down slowly and put a little round of lemon in his mouth. Nadenka downed a small glass in one breath, and stared heavily at a plate of salmon, then took the pickle jar with both hands, and drank the light brine. Anfiska carefully drained her glass, coughed, smiled, and said: "Oh, such sweet vodka!" shivered, and thanking them, left the guests.

"Where are you going?" shouted Olezhka after her.

"She has to get up early for work tomorrow," said Bolotov severely.

"Cut it out!" said Nadenka.

Everything that followed left Bolotov with the vague feeling of incomplete joy. Perhaps this happened because of the discrepancy between his tender emotion and their coolness. Of course they'd already got accustomed to what for him was a fresh marvel. He felt like a guest at a stale birthday celebration: the hosts had celebrated the night before, and now found it tiresome to pretend to be gracious and interested...

Still and all, they'd surely gotten used to one another quickly! And they drank steadily, and no one cheated. Olezhka didn't know how to drink: after each glass he winced in agony, greedily poured water down his throat, and nibbled rather sloppily. His friend drank with a swagger, unhurriedly, holding the glass with two fingers, his glasses glinting mockingly; he ate little, just kept sucking on a lemon. But Bolotov soon noticed with satisfaction that Vadya was getting drunk quicker and worse than Olezhka. Bolotov saw in this the organic health of the Sharonov nature, which reacted to poison and even overcame it powerfully. Vadya still looked as severe and smart as before, with the thin neck constrained by a starched collar, the tie beyond reproach, and the straight part in his hair, but his tongue seemed to have turned to wood, and he began to repeat himself. Having said once apropos of some clumsiness on his part: "This has no cardinal significance," which elicited Olezhka's loud laughter, he took to interjecting the same embellishment whether it was to the point or not.

Nadenka drank better than anyone, even too well for a young woman; she drank the liquor down to the bottom in one swallow and with scarcely a bite to eat. Everything about her remained unchanged: the shimmering glorious sprayed hair, the heaviness of the eyes, the deathly scarlet of the lips, the reserve and the silence.

"You're strong," said Bolotov after the regular mechanical gesture with which Nadenka raised the glass to her lips, threw back her head and poured the golden liquid down.

"A fantastic broad," Vadya joined in.

"What did you say?" asked Bolotov

"He meant to say," Olezhka cut in with his usual carefree laugh, "that Nadenka is one of our best lab workers."

Bolotov loved people who knew how to work, and was filled with a trust in Nadenka. He drew the stool towards her, and began to recount how he'd met Olezhka when his father brought him hunting for the first time. Ivan Sharonov was already suffering from leg trouble even then, and the heftiest of the local huntsmen used to help him. But when Olezhka was present he refused anyone's help, and performed all the huntsman's tasks himself. He didn't want his son growing up a goldbrick. And truly, the father taught Olezhka to hunt so well that the boy was second to none in hunting. And Olezhka shot better than any other regular standing shooter, both when the birds were at rest and when they were in flight. Imagine—not only on the attack or during the chase, but when they were flying past, he could draw a bead on two silhouettes ahead as along a ruler!

"You see, Nadenka, you haven't made a misalliance!" exclaimed Olezhka.

"But that doesn't have car-r-r-dinal significance," intoned Vadya.

"You could change the record," Nadya addressed him for the first time.

"Yes, pr-r-r-incess!" Vadya bowed.

"Ivan Sergeich and I," continued Bolotov, not having understood Olezhka's remark, "served together in the Civil War in the same division, my first wife used to change his bandages..."

He remembered the thin gentle cheekbones of Nastya the nurse, and drifted into thought. She was his first love, his wife, although they hadn't had time to make it legal, and the mother of his oldest child. War, typhus, and starvation had so physically drained Nastya, who was delicate anyway, that in order to create a new life, she gave up her own.

"And when Ivan Sergeich and I met here," continued Bolotov after a short silence, "we didn't know at first that we were almost comrades in arms. We got to discussing the events of bygone days, he mentioned Ilovayskaya, and I recalled Ilovayskaya, he mentioned Perekop, and I . . . "

"Oh, haven't we had enough of these reminiscences, old man?" interrupted Olezhka with a touch of annoyance.

Bolotov decided that the frequent references to his ailing father were hard on Olezhka, and promised himself not to speak about Sharonov. But the veto he laid upon himself turned into a long and boring sermon. Heaven knows why he began to preach to the young couple about their offspring.

"When you think of creating an heir then this . . ." he tapped the bottle, "is a no-no! . . . You've got to be most careful . . . I'm an old man, there's no reason to be embarrassed with me. I won't waste words, but a week ahead of time you've got to give up drinking . . . If you don't, its traces will show up on a living creature. It's not a laughing matter . . ."

"Good that you warned us!" guffawed Olezhka. "When we decide to continue the Sharonov line, we'll take an antidote."

"Enough of this nonsense," said Nadya dryly.

"You're laughing for nothing," Bolotov was offended, "Any doctor will tell you the same thing . . ."

Olezhka didn't let him finish:

"Let it go, old man, you're getting touchy about each piece of nonsense. Better let's have a drink!"

So they did, and immediately Olezhka pestered: "Tell us, tell us about steppe life." But Bolotov, as ill luck would have it, didn't remember anything. Whether it was that he just couldn't remember a thing, or whether it was because such a serious mood had set in, all the humorous stories were totally forgotten. But could anyone shake Olezhka off once he decided he wanted something?

"Tell us about the 'shveters,' " requested Olezhka, laughing ahead of time. "It's a fantastic story!"

"How many shveters you have?" began Bolotov, recalling vaguely that he did indeed know such a tale. "I have one shveter . . . How do you mean, one? . . Three . . And so one shveter for you, another for the policeman . . ." Mangling the words as usual, Bolotov muttered as if in a fever, incapable of remembering what it all meant or who was demanding an account from whom about some kind of sweater, "And I've got one shveter . . ."

But Olezhka laughed so much that there was no point in making sense out of it. The strangest thing was that Nadenka suddenly burst out laughing and said with an eastern accent better than that of Bolotov himself:

"I've got one shveter!"

"Two shveters!" Vadya, usually serious, picked up on it, and for some reason took off his glasses.

"Three shveters!" Olezhka yelped with excitement, "See what the old man can do when he gets going?.."

Inspired by his easy success, Bolotov remembered a delightful story about how "Once upon a time, the shvan, crowfish and pike little by little took a whole lot of stuff to market..."

"Well, you really are impossible!.." said Nadenka when he finished his story to general laughter.

Olezhka got the urge to play pool. An old, broken pool table stood on the glass terrace of the main building. Bolotov ran out into the hallway and brought Nadenka her furcoat. He didn't let her throw it over her shoulders, but insisted that she put it on properly, with her arms in the sleeves, and he himself fastened each button.

When they left the house the late moon was floating high in the sky between clouds thin as smoke, and the night had become silvery. To the right, beyond the pines, the lake glimmered and was irridescent, to the left, the forest, which extended up to the hunting base, was shot through with a faint beautiful light. The sandy paths were as white as could be, and on the iron roofs of the buildings the light of the moon lay like fresh snow.

"Bright, isn't it?" Bolotov, who'd leaned down toward Nadya, uttered the words as he went out. He was as proud of the moon in all its shining as if it were his wedding gift.

"Uh-uh," agreed Nadenka, "I even thought that those were street lamps burning... Well, boys, it seems I've had enough," she said in a calm, rather cold voice.

"You're not sorry you came?" said Olezhka.

"And I'm not at all drunk," announced Vadya, and staggered right then—"Although this doesn't have car-r-rdinal significance..."

Bolotov's head was buzzing, but not from drinking—he was as immune to the effects of wine as a swamp ringtail is to small shot—it was from the excitement and joy that alternated with grief whenever he recalled old man Sharonov, and from his constrained tenderness for Nadenka.

Bolotov unlocked the terrace door. On the short pool table covered with an army cloth lay the heavy cold cues without grips and chipped plastic balls, also beastly cold. Bolotov racked the balls. Olezhka selected a cue, touched the sharp end against the ceiling—there was no chalk—and asked Vadya:

"Do you want to break them, signor?"

Vadya straightened his glasses and said, "Roll, marquis!"

They played American style; Olezhka pocketed one with his breaking shot, and then three more balls in a row. He didn't know how to light the stove, how to replace an electric fuse, uncork a bottle, open a can without cutting his hands, but to make up for that, he played pool excellently, was a good marksman, knew how to handle oars, a sail, and a motor expertly. He was very athletic, and wherever the excitement and spirit of competition were active, he displayed maximum physical skill, accuracy, and concentration.

Olezhka gave Vadya a resounding beating, and the latter accepted it as his due, and Nadenka, who saw her husband play for the first time, expressed neither surprise nor pleasure. Apparently among people close to Olezhka his superiority was taken for granted. Olezhka defeated Vadya also in the second game; the effect of alcohol circulating in him manifested itself in the unnecessary strength of his shots. One ball ripped the net and rolled along the floor with a crash. Bolotov picked up the ball and gallantly held it out to Nadya:

"You can place this on the little shelf of your husband's trophies."

Nadenka wanted to take the ball, but pulled her hand back quickly.

"Darn it, it's cold!.. Better let's go and have a drink!" she suggested to Bolotov.

"Mine-thine always ready to chug-a-lug, glug, glug," the flattered Bolotov answered in pure steppe speech.

"Wait, we're coming with you!" Olezhka shouted after them.

"Your little husband is jealous!" laughed Bolotov.

He heard Olezhka shooting the balls, hurrying to finish the game. They hadn't even had time to pour the cognac into glasses before Olezhka tore into the dining room, and a little later Vadya appeared.

They drank, and Vadya immediately got drowsy. Olezhka took him by the shoulders and led him into the bedroom. In the doorway Vadya turned an unexpectedly sober face to Bolotov—as if for a second it had come into focus only to get fuzzy again immediately, and said:

"We're physicists, not lyricists, please take that into account!.."

"Vadya's a weakling!" said Olezhka when he returned.

"But, you know, next to you everyone's a weakling," remarked Nadya.

"Only not you, girl!" laughed Olezhka.

They drank some more, and then the light went out; it was after midnight, the time the generator usually stopped working, but it was light in the room from the moon, and they didn't light the kerosene lamp. Bolotov's memory got clearer, and he poured forth a string of steppe stories, and then, dropping a fork, he bent down under the table to retrieve it, and saw Olezhka's hand on Nadya's silky knee. And that hand, pale and impatient, reminded Bolotov that they wanted to be left alone, that these young loving people who were greedy for one another had got tired of him. And how sensitive they were, if he hadn't guessed their frustrated desire!

"Well, I'm off," he said gratefully and sadly and got up from the table.

"Perhaps a nightcap?" suggested Olezhka manfully.

"No, thanks!" Bolotov was ashamed of his talkativeness, his excessive persistence, and wanted to leave as quickly as possible. "Good night to you!"

He closed all the doors tightly behind him and ran down the steps of the porch. Night greeted him with its light, wistfulness, and emptiness, and he slowly wandered over to the lake. The islands, the sandbar, and the by-pass of reeds stood out against the sparkling lake just like black worked on silver. Because the people around him had been so openly, so almost crudely happy, he felt his own uselessness, abandonment, and eternal solitude.

Well, what kind of life was he leading! His wife, Katerina Vasilyevna, came only during Borka's summer vacations. They'd tried living together, but it hadn't worked out: the closest school with a ten-year program was fifteen kilometers away, and Katerina was beside herself whenever Borka set out for school on skis. She thought that wolves would tear him to pieces, an elk would roll him on its horns, a storm would engulf him, the convoy prisoners who were making concrete would cut his throat, or "he would be crushed by a falling satellite," Bolotov would add when she became too alarmed. Borka liked such a "dangerous" life, and for a long time Bolotov set no store by Katerina's empty fears until he guessed the real reason for her agonizing alarm. She'd already seen the older ones, a son and daughter, leave home. The son was sailing under the command of a step-brother on one of the fishing boats of a whale flotilla, while the married daughter was working with an archeological party near Bairam-Ali. The daily small "good-byes" said to Borka reminded Katerina of the inevitable great separation, when he, following the example of the older children, would leave home, and this was killing her. Bolotov let them go to Astrakhan, where he had an apartment.

And why shouldn't he return to Astrakhan too? He'd find better and more agreeable work than here. What was keeping him here? The duck houses?... Think what a great problem that was—would the wild ducks nest around here or not? Were they worth his living without Katerina and Borka? And why had he tormented himself around here for so long? Well, there were more wild animals and birds now, hunting for black grouse and wood grouse, which had almost been destroyed by poachers, had been restored. Just think what an accomplishment that was! But couldn't someone else have done the same thing? Of course he could! This other person also could have fought in the Civil War instead of him, could have come down with smallpox, could have pursued the counter-revolutionaries instead of him. This other man could have hunted tigers in the Ussuri taiga and gotten a swipe across the face from a bear; the other man could have worn himself out hunting for antelope, and could have joined the militia in World War II, and lost his teeth and a lung—this other one could have done all that...

True, this other man would then have known the brief love of Nastya the nurse, and would have been left with a marvelous boy on his hands who grew up and became the captain of a fishing boat, and it was difficult to reconcile himself with that. And what was totally unbearable was that this other one would get quiet, housewifely, domestic Katerina! For she was the one who chose an elderly, pocked, and scarred man for an anxiety-ridden, complex and financially modest life, and she hadn't abandoned him in his misfortune when, covered with wounds, his mouth crooked and toothless, he dragged himself home from the hospital. That meant that she needed him just as he was, and no other way. No, he wouldn't give up anything to the other one, not even the duck houses. Screw it!..

Bolotov got the urge to see Olezhka and his wife and tell them that he was a happy person, and not lonely at all, not abandoned, and that he loved his life and didn't envy them in the slightest if they lived better, richer, more finely than he...

Maybe they hadn't fallen asleep yet? Bolotov turned back, and with the silent tread of a pathfinder slipped into the house and went past the cozily crackling stove, past the table glinting mysteriously with its empty bottles and dishes, and slipped by to the bedroom door. From there he heard quiet breathing—they seemed to be asleep.

"Olezhka!" he called in a whisper.

The door to the bedroom opened with a soft melancholy sound, but there was no one behind it. He'd forgotten to shut the door in the corridor, and a draft had blown this one open. On the bed right in front of him, strongly and beautifully illuminated by the moon, two heads rested on the white pillow. Nadenka lay on her back with her bare arm flung behind her head, as if preserving its precious shimmering even in sleep. Her sleeping face looked haughty, and at the same time simpler, more trusting, than in the daylight. Olezhka nestled down at her shoulder, his mouth open like a child's. There was something so wonderful, eternal in the youthful sleep of the two, that Bolotov lingered for a second before shutting the door.

He took this vision with him into the bright clear night, and suddenly it came to him passionately, terribly, that in the living room of the main building Anfiska was sleeping alone. He caught at his coarse gray curls and tugged hard at them. Surprised at his own distress and a little proud of it, he decided to write Katerina the next day: let her make whatever arrangements she wanted, let her even leave silly little seventeen-year-old Borka with someone, but she must come to him for ten days or so, or else— a divorce!..

It was still night when Bolotov took a flashlight and went off to wake the hunters. The moon had set, and the world had become dark again, but the gaps of emptiness between the faded stars no longer seemed so unfathomable and melancholy; daybreak was approaching. A little longer and the dawn would daub the east with yellow, and the edge of the forest would grow black, and slowly, solemnly, the mystery of sunrise would begin.

Stamping loudly on purpose so as to warn them that he was coming, Bolotov went up onto the porch, made his way to the bedroom, knocked, and receiving no reply, thrust open the door.

"Rise and shine!.. Rise and shine!.."

The beam from the flashlight slid along the gray woollen blanket, came to rest on the pillow in a bright even circle, and (as if on a medallion) two heads were outlined. Nadenka lay in the same pose, her bare arm flung behind her head, tirelessly supporting the shining aureole; his forehead pressed against her shoulder, off which the strap of her thin nightgown had slipped, lay Vadya Zelentsov.

"But where are his glasses?" the idiotic thought flashed through Bolotov's mind. But the glasses were there too, their temples gleaming on the stool which was pulled up beside the head of the bed. Bolotov felt a strange heaviness gathering in his right fist. He'd already stepped forward to unload the painful weight onto Vadya's delicate temple when, smiling and disheveled from sleep, in pajama bottoms and a sleeveless undershirt, Olezhka came out of a side room.

"But we just fell asleep," he said. "Hey, sleepyheads, rise and shine!.."

He looked at Bolotov and laughed.

"What do you want, old man, way back Oscar Wilde wrote: 'marriage is a three-way union.' "[1]

He took another look at Bolotov and added with a touch of seriousness:

"You don't have to look so horrified! You don't really think I'd allow such a thing?.. Vadya and I have equal rights—she's simply our co-worker..."

Simply a co-worker...

Nadenka started, carefully took her arm out from behind her head, screwed up her closed eyes, then opened them, began blinking them from the light beating in her face—Bolotov hadn't turned off the flashlight—and suddenly sneezed, as if from a ray of sun. Vadik made an inarticulate sound, moved his head, started up with a wild look, and reached across Nadya for his glasses.

Bolotov grasped the goings-on with difficulty. At first only disappointment gripped him: this meant that Olezhka wasn't married at all and all the good and comforting things he'd thought about old man Sharonov in this connection were untrue. Then shame rolled over him in a stifling wave, for yesterday, for all the toasts, congratulations, marital advice, and his idiotic emotionalism. What a fool these snot-nosed kids had got him to make of himself! Then he remembered Anfiska. How he'd pounced on the unlucky young girl who, at the end of her third year, had not borne the loneliness and misery at the side of an old and malicious mother-in-law, how he'd reproached her with the example of the 'newlyweds!' And painfully, vaguely, he thought again of old man Sharonov. All right, sometime or other he'd figure out all this dirty filth, but now there was more important business.

"Your passes are cancelled," he said hoarsely. "Please vacate the premises."

"Cut it out, Nikolaich," said Olezhka with a strained smile. "So we had a little joke, big deal!.. Weren't you ever young?"

The bitter smell of wormwood gushed into Bolotov's broad chest, then everything smelled of wormwood: clothing, the grip of a machine gun, Nastya the nurse's palms and neck. How light her little head, shaved after the typhus, was in its gauze kerchief!..

"Here's what," he said, finally turning off the flashlight; for a few seconds it was completely dark, then the darkness thinned out, just as if it had leaked out the window. "This isn't some brothel. And now, clear out of here while the going's good!.." Here he noticed the faint glimmer of Nadenka's hair, and her slender hands fixing her hairdo. Something paternal and compassionate welled up in him. "Doesn't your conscience bother you, miss?.. These two are curs... But you're a nice young woman... Perhaps they forced you in some way?.."

"When is this soap opera going to end?" said Nadenka, turning to Olezhka. "If I'd known, I never in my life would have come... "

"Now, now, go easy, old man," said Olezhka coldly and even a little dangerously. "Your mouth is full not only of steel, it seems, but of slag too! I don't like it."

"I don't give a damn whether you like it or not!" Bolotov turned on the flashlight with a click and whipped the beam across Olezhka's face; the latter involuntarily covered it with his arm. "Take this..." He changed his mind and said, "...lady, and get out!.."

Bolotov walked out and slammed the door. But he no sooner stepped on the threshold than he leaned against the wall—his heart was being squeezed as if with pincers.

"Olezhka's an idiot," Nadenka's voice could be heard. "Why did we have to lie and say we were married?"

"Yes, it worked out badly," agreed Vadya. "And is this moralist going to spill the beans?.."

"Never!" Olezhka interrupted assuredly. "He apparently considers himself a comrade in arms from the war and practically a friend of my father's... A pity the hunt's fallen through. But he'll pay for this, I'll make him remember this day!.."

"You'll complain to your father?" said Vadya caustically. "He'll skin you alive."

"Why complain?" answered Olezhka condescendingly. "It's enough that I'm a Sharonov..." And suddenly he said with an intonation inherited from his father, but repulsive because its strength and fury were immoral: "I'll eat this creep alive, guts and all!.."

Bolotov kicked the door open.

"Not a chance!... I'm hard-headed and hard-assed!" he said, terribly twisting his face, marked by smallpox, animal claws, and firearms. "Get out of here, scum!.."

"All right," muttered Olezhka, his jaw working unpleasantly. "Let us get dressed and we'll leave right away..."

1965   Translated by Molly Nelson and Helena Goscilo

Notes

The original ("Olezhka zhenilsia") first appeared in *Nash sovremennik,* No. 2(1965), 17-40. The present translation is of the edition included in the 1973 two-volume collection, I, 296-312, where it is dated 1964, the year of its composition.

1. Presumably Nagibin has in mind a comment made by Algernon in the first act of Oscar Wilde's play, *The Importance of Being Earnest:* "... in married life three is company and two is none."

The Abandoned Path

Did it really happen or did I just dream of that strange boy, surrounded by an aura of otherworldly gentleness and sorrow, like the little prince in Antoine de Saint-Exupéry?[1] I know he existed, just like the cobbled road overgrown with plantain, burdock, horse sorrel, and camomile; but even if the boy belonged to the world of dreams, he touched my heart infinitely more than many other people whose blatant reality is beyond doubt.

It often happens that miracles are found by our side—right under our noses, and we don't even suspect it! That day started with a small miracle: the low-lying dampish alder thickets that bordered the northern side of the fence to our summerhouse turned out to be fabulously rich in mushrooms.[2] The mushrooms grew in blade-like grass resembling sedge, grew not just in patches, but blended into unbroken fields of brown tinged with yellow. Little ones with a white lining of neat round caps grew side by side with giants that resembled umbrellas overturned by the wind, with a dewdrop in each funnel. I kept stuffing my shirt full of mushrooms, taking them home at a run, and returning to the forest for more.

Apart from the mushrooms, the alder thicket swarmed with frogs; as I stretched out my hand toward a mushroom stem more than once I'd touch a repulsively cold body that instantly slithered by beneath my fingers. One would think that the mushrooms and frogs were living in some mysterious union that assured them a rich existence.

As always happens during successful mushrooming, I became more and more selective: the large limp mushrooms no longer satisfied me—I picked only the small, rubbery-hard ones, and moreover, even among them I started choosing the best shaped and the cleanest, most robust ones. This finicky search led me into the depth of the forest. Soon the mushrooms became much sparser, then they disappeared altogether, but I had no regrets, surfeited as I was with the prodigal success I'd enjoyed. I got carried away wandering around the unfamiliar forest, whose appearance altered according to its distance from the summerhouse. Low-lying land was replaced by elevation, the ground underfoot became firmer, and the swamp grass ceded to ferns and mane's tail. Then the twilight alder thicket, which exuded dampness and mold, disappeared completely and birches showed bright milky-white, pearl-like asps became visible, and thick short grass spread out silkily beneath them as columns of dusty sunlight slanted down on the forest.

I shook the mushrooms out of my shirt and put it on, hopelessly stained and smelling pleasantly and pungently of the brown fungus, then went on ahead. An uneasy happiness possessed me: I knew that I hadn't gone that far, and yet I couldn't have gone farther from home than if I'd wandered to the farthest point possible along a familiar well-trodden track. The bright clean grove of birches and asps that had pushed its way in among the alder thicket was mysterious. Both the birches and the asps were confined to this small area. I knew the neighborhood well: from the direction of the Dmitrov highway and from the direction of our summerhouse, and from the direction of the swamp covered with tussocks that stretched forth beyond the horizon, the forest borders were entirely of alder.

The farther I went the more thickly grew the trees, wind-fallen branches obstructed the narrow gaps among them, the grass rose high, standing up to half my height, and the graceful pink flowers that resembled candles towered far above my head. It was increasingly difficult to make my way forward, and it grew rather dark because the light smoky-blue columns of light couldn't penetrate the tightly-knit mass. And it was here that I happened upon the boy, and the major miracle of the day came to pass.

Short, thin, with a narrow face framed in round glasses with thick tortoise-shell rims, he was weeding the heavily overgrown cobbled road (where it came from no one knew) as though it were a vegetable bed. Where he'd already cleared quite a broad strip, the protruding grayish cobblestones with a blue pink tint clustered firmly and compactly, but farther on, the road was lost in a thick verdure of weeds. The boy not only was weeding the road, but was fixing it along the edges, hammering the cobblestones into their sockets with a homemade beetle.

"Hello," he said, turning round and kindly looking at me with large brown eyes from behind round flat lenses that were as plain and transparent as windowpanes.

"Hello," I responded. "Why are you wearing glasses? They've got plain glass lenses."

"Because of the dust. When it's windy the dust comes up from the road, and I've got conjunctivitis," he explained with pride.

"What path is this? I've never seen it before."

"I don't know...How about helping me?"

I shrugged my shoulders and, bending down, tore out a thistle bush with dark red flowers and clinging thorns. Then I tugged at some long plant with dry sacs of seeds that looked as though they were full of cotton. The plant, which had gotten embedded in the soil with its long hair-thin roots, refused to give. I cut up my palms before finally tearing it out of the soil. Yes, this was really work! No wonder the hands of the boy with glasses were all grazed. My ardor at once evaporated.

"Listen, what do you need to do this for?" I asked.

"You can see youself, the path's overgrown." As he spoke, kneeling, he tore a root out of the soil with a sliver. "It needs to be cleared away."

"What for?" I persisted.

"What do you mean!... " He had a polite, soft, and patient voice. "The flowers and grass are destroying the path with their roots. The cobblestones used to be close-set, and now see what gaps there are!... "

"That's not what I'm talking about!... Why's it necessary that it not be destroyed?"

He carefully removed his glasses, holding them by the bridge; he wanted to get a better look at the man who was asking him such absurd questions, and dusty lenses only got in the way. Without the protection of the glasses his eyes proved to be almost imperceptibly encircled in red, as though someone had run the finest of paintbrushes over his lids. Apparently that was what he so sonorously called 'conjunctivitis.'

"If the path gets destroyed, it'll disappear and no one will ever know there was a path here."

"So the hell with it!" I said irritably. "It doesn't lead anywhere anyway!"

"All paths lead somewhere," he said with gentle conviction and, putting the glasses back on, set to work. "Judge for yourself, would they have constructed it if it didn't lead anywhere?"

"But since it's abandoned, doesn't it mean no one needs it?"

He pondered that; his thin face became slightly distorted, and he even stopped pulling out the flowers and the grass; pain appeared in his brown eyes—it's so difficult to implant the simplest and most obvious truths in another person's heart.

"Do we really know why the path was abandoned?... Maybe someone at the other end is also trying to clear it? Someone may be working toward me and we'll meet. Paths shouldn't be overgrown," he said firmly. "I'll clear it, no matter what."

"You're not strong enough to do it."

"Not alone, I'm not. But someone's working toward me and perhaps he's already come halfway... "

"You're obsessed with this path!"

"Paths are very important. Without paths no one would ever be together."

A vague suspicion stirred within me.

"Has someone close to you gone off someplace far away?"

He didn't answer and turned away.

"I'll help you!" I cried, to my own surprise.

"Thank you," he said sincerely, but without excessive fervor. "Come here tomorrow morning; it's too late today, it's time to go home."

"Where do you live?"

"There..." he waved in the direction of the thicket, rose, wiped his palms on a clump of grass, put his glasses away in his pocket, submerged me for the last time in the kindness of his brown eyes, and went off—a dirty, tired, frail, adamant pathbuilder—and soon disappeared behind the honeysuckle bushes.

The next day I set out for the forest at the crack of dawn. The impassable alders entwined with long grass were hazed over with mist, a dense vapor that turned to moisture as it settled on one's skin; they resembled a jungle or the bottom of a fast-receding sea. The rain that had fallen during the night had endowed all of nature with new and vigorous life: the pastor's lettuce had shot up and turned a brighter green; the mushrooms pushed up from the grass just as before, as though I hadn't ravaged them yesterday; an enchanted princess hid in each frog—they were so majestic, so full of arrogance and unwilling to step aside.

Wet from head to foot, I rushed through the alders, seized with a burning impatience and the excited anticipation of meeting the boy on the overgrown cobblestone road—his faith had already become my faith. I was convinced that I'd find the road with no difficulty; it was so easy, after all: I just had to keep on going straight through the alders and the birch and asp to the other birch grove obstructed by the wind-fallen wood, and there I'd discover the clean strip of bluish and pink cobblestones.

But I didn't find the abandoned path. Everything was as it had been the day before: the trees, the grass, the wind-fallen branches, the burdock undergrowth and the pink candles of the tall flowers, but there was no road or boy with brown eyes. I roamed the forest until sunset, exhausted, hungry, my legs cut all over by the grass and cudweed, but it was all in vain...

I never came across the abandoned road nor the country-road, nor even the path that had needed my rescue work. But with the years I came to understand the boy's exhortation in a different way. Many paths leading to different people originated in my heart: paths to those who were close and those who weren't, and to those whom it's impossible to forget for a moment and to those who are almost forgotten. Those paths needed me, and I kept watch. I didn't grudge the effort or my hands; I tore up completely the thickets and the stinging nettles, and all the other rubbish; I didn't let the weeds choke or destroy the paths and demolish them. But if I succeeded, then it was only because every time a corresponding movement started from the other end of the path. Only one path, the most important one, it wasn't given me to save, perhaps because no one stirred to meet me halfway.

1967   Translated by Helena Goscilo

The original ("Zabroshennaia doroga") first appeared in *Literaturnaia gazeta,* No. 41 (October 11, 1967), 6. The present translation is of the edition in the two-volume 1973 collection, II, 321-325.

Notes

1. *Le petit prince* (1943) of Antoine de Saint-Exupéry (1900-44), the French writer and aviator, is an allegorical fairy tale in prose advocating a humanism based on action and extolling the beauty of pure human relations.

2. Mycologists may appreciate Nagibin's precise labeling here: the mushroom in question is the Russian *svinushka,* which comes in two varieties—*svinushka tolstaia,* known by the Latin name of *paxillus atrotomentosus,* and *svinushka tonkaia,* known as *paxillus involutus.* The descriptive details Nagibin provides suggest that he has the latter in mind.

Both types, incidentally, are considered inferior in taste, and the fact that they probably acquired their name because of their popularity with pigs surely indicates something about their quality.

Throughout the story I have translated the word *svinushka* simply as "mushroom" to avoid using the unwieldly Latin equivalent.

Needed Urgently:
Gray Human Hair

Gushchin froze in amazement. There it was in black and white: inscribed with relish in thick black India ink on white, icily glossy drafting paper: "Needed urgently: gray human hair." And next to it were hanging yellowed and faded announcements notifying that 'Lenfilm' needed cleaning women, lighting crew, chauffeurs, hairdressers, electricians, carpenters, janitors, a barmaid, a technician for special lighting effects, and an accountant.

"This part about 'gray human hair' sounds rather terrible," thought Gushchin. "You have to be in an enviably serene and untroubled frame of mind to print such an appeal."

He heard a short little laugh. Standing beside him was a girl with an innocent childlike face and a luxuriant stiff hairstyle that was too grown-up and fashionable.

"Don't be afraid," said the girl. "It's voluntary, after all."

Transported from dim images of Auschwitz crimes, from semi-delirious visions of war that had suddenly swept over him, and into the childlike gentleness of her glance, her laugh and voice, Gushchin didn't understand the words addressed to him.

"Your gray hair's in no danger," explained the girl, a bit embarrassed.

Gushchin had the kind of attractive steel-gray hair that comes of early graying; it didn't age his forty-five-year-old, dark and sad face, but instead made it look more youthful. Something flattering lurked behind the boldness of the girl's manner and in her words, but he had been hurt, hopelessly hurt by his wife, and because of that he didn't feel either joy or pride, but instead, his sense of sorrow was even aggravated. That's what always happened when positive signals came to him from the outside world. It was simpler to live with the awareness that he wasn't even fleetingly interesting or attractive to anyone, a most untalented, dull fellow, totally deserving the fate of a domestic apostate.

"At least it's a good thing they don't need human teeth, nails, and skin," answered Gushchin sullenly, not feeling compelled to show either courtesy or wit.

A pained looked distorted the girl's face, aging her for a moment.

"I'm sorry," she said. "It was a bad joke. I'm a tactless idiot."

He felt sorry for the girl. The poor thing simply wanted to have a little joke with a stranger, and see what a fine mess came of it!

"Forget it, really! Everything's okay." Gushchin smiled. "So why *do* they need this hair?"

"For wigs." The girl smiled too, convinced she hadn't caused him any pain.

"And I thought it was for mattresses."

"For mattresses?"

"Yes. In German hotels they have celluloid horns hanging over the sinks where you can deposit the hair that falls out while you're combing your hair. Then they stuff mattresses with it."

"How nice! How sensible!" The girl shuddered. "And how revolting!"

The subject was exhausted and nothing was left for these two strangers who'd met by chance at the studio's notice board but to part and each go his separate way. In a moment the unknown woman with her innocent childlike face and grown-up luxuriant hair would leave, would disappear and blend in the bustle of the avenue with her thin white sweater and short heavy skirt that barely reached her beautiful womanly legs. And for as long as Gushchin would live, he would never again see her large, trusting, merry eyes, her mouth that aged instantly with suffering; he wouldn't hear her little laugh and gentle voice. Horrified at the loneliness that awaited him, Gushchin, the wimp, the fool, the ninny, suddenly rushed forward.

"Are you in a hurry? . . . Perhaps we could take a walk in the city? Only, of course, if you have time. I'm here on business, I have to stop in briefly at the studio—it'll only take five minutes, really . . . Then we could take a boat ride, and sit a while in a café, or go to the Summer Gardens . . ."

The girl looked at him with curiosity and something akin to sympathy. Gushchin saw himself through her eyes: a heavy, dark, cheap coat that was inappropriate for that time of year, a clerical collar that was too tight and round, a cheap tie that didn't go with the suit, shoes that had man-made soles and hadn't been shined in a long time, and a depressingly large, worn vinyl briefcase.

"All that at once! Just think: a walk, a café, a boat ride, the Summer Gardens! Did you leave out anything? After all, we could also go see St. Isaac's, and visit the monastery and the Volkovo cemetery, and then go to the Hermitage, the Russian Museum, and the apartment where Pushkin lived."

She was simply laughing at him, at the pitiful display of vim and vigor by the old gloomy man in the Moscow-made suit and the clerical collar.

"Excuse me," said Gushchin, and meekly, without any show of

offense, retreated to his proper place. "I lost my head all of a sudden. It's been a long time since anyone came up and spoke to me in the street. It suddenly seemed as if the world had become magically kinder."

The girl's face clouded over in a way that was familiar by now, as if it had aged. Evidently she had the rare ability to penetrate through the surface of words.

"Why are you talking like that? I'm not turning you down, after all. But I also have to go to the studio for five minutes."

"So let's go!" Gushchin said in a voice that feigned joy, since he was convinced that the girl would 'get lost' in the endless corridors of 'Lenfilm.' "What section are you going to?"

"The actors'."

"You?..."

"Yes, I'm just what's never needed at a studio—an actress. And you? I can't imagine. You don't seem the studio type."

"Why not? Judging by the notice board, the studio doesn't only have artists as employees."

"No," said the girl, shaking her head. "The studio makes anyone who falls into its orbit highly visible, like God does a thief. A studio accountant is closer to Oleg Strizhenov[1] than to another accountant in some office. You aren't a movie person; you're a serious and sad man who's accidently found himself in pseudo-Wonderland."

"To put it more simply, I'm an engineer. Specializing in ejection capsules. They sent me here at the request of the group working on *Flight into the Unknown*."

"I know that one," said the girl. "They're always ejecting. Are you from Moscow?"

"Yes. I've noticed that people from Leningrad immediately spot somebody from Moscow."

"Their folksy dialect gives them away," laughed the girl. "Well, so we already know about each other what you could learn from a form you have to fill out for a trip to, say, Bulgaria. Only the first line has been left blank." She stretched out her hand to him. "Proskurova, Natalya Viktorovna. Natasha."[2]

"Gushchin, Sergey Ivanovich."

They shook hands and entered the vestibule of the movie studio.

"You have to get a pass?" And proudly: "I have a permanent one. So we'll meet here, or better yet—at the entrance, in fifteen minutes."

Waving to the porter, who evidently knew her by sight, she ran along the corridor into the depths of the premises. Gushchin followed her with his eyes. He understood that he'd never see her again, but he didn't feel the old pain. She hadn't disappeared nameless, she hadn't faded away like a daydream, she had made him a gift of her name, and with it she had as if given him some right to her, the right to remember, to long for her, and to hope. He could know her and name her, talk with her in his heart and soul, his loneliness filled up. Fate had given him an unexpected and undeserved gift: he ought to bless charitable fate and not think about any more than that.

Gushchin waited a long time while the invalid guard filled out his pass with his injured hand, but he didn't rush him. Time didn't mean anything to Gushchin now, for the moment he'd experienced had stood still and become eternity. The complex interchange that was taking place at the moment between Gushchin and reality was not subject to the laws of time: Natasha's universe was being created in the claw of the guard, in the wet lashes of an aged actress who was being denied a pass, in the thin blemished profile of a long-nosed youth who was saying to his friend in a confident but small voice: "Hey, old man, the tape came out!", in the frightened braids of two schoolgirls, drawn to the sacrificial altar of art— in all that was small, pitiful, flawed, and yet dear, surrounding Gushchin.

This continued even later when, pass in hand, he finally stepped into the studio corridor, so intoxicated with Natasha that his head reeled. He thought: from whom are they protecting the studio so passionately, and he pitied the small stupid people who had instituted this waste of time—the system of passes; these people found their expiation in Natasha. The director of the toy movie *Flight into the Unknown* and the red-nosed industrial safety engineer with whom he had discussed the problems of ejection for the last time, and the haughty director's secretary who had validated his pass and his business travel papers, and the unsung geniuses who were crowding the hallways—all were innocent before the world and illuminated through the intercession of Natasha and her redemptive charm.

When he went down to the vestibule and saw the world of the summer street through the frosted glass of the entrance door, a world that no longer belonged to the studio, he suddenly lost his sense of resignation. He felt he didn't have the strength to throw open the doors. He loved this studio where Natasha's strange mysterious life went on, not even her whole life, but only a small and minor part, but as long as the doors didn't slam shut behind him a thin thread still connected him to Natasha. Suddenly it dawned on him: what if he went to the wig section and gave them his gray human hair? He would have the right not to leave the studio for a while yet and, who knows, maybe Natasha would play the role of a worldly woman of old in the wig made out of his hair? Even if she wouldn't act in it, all the same, he would be joining with her world through something intimate and concrete. And then, Gushchin smiled to himself, the next thing you know the studio will develop a need for human nails, skin, bones, entrails, and he'd give his whole self, like scrap—which he was, after all—to the glory of his beloved.

"It's absolutely incredible!" he heard a voice choking with helpless anger. "You ... You're simply an old philanderer!"

Before him stood Natasha, her dark eyes enormous and filled with indignation and tears, and in the lower part of her face, her lips with their corners turned down and the wrinkled chin of a quite old woman.

"I didn't believe you'd come," muttered Gushchin.

"You're so strange," said Natasha with annoyance, but already without anger. "You've probably been deceived a lot."

Gushchin shrugged his shoulders. Yes, I've been deceived often, and I've lost faith in myself and in those around me. I recognize everyone's right to deceive me. That's essentially just as immoral as the deception itself. But I can't explain to you, Natasha, how all this happened to me because I myself don't comprehend the mechanism of my degradation. Evidently it's a matter of gradation; day by day over a period of many years you learn to reconcile yourself to meanness—that's how they make a human organism immune to poisons. Before you know it, you're already able to swallow arsenic and worse poisons with impunity. If anyone at the front had dared tell me that I'd be living my present life without a murmur, I'd have shot the scoundrel on the spot ... or myself.

They walked along Kirov Avenue in the direction of the Neva river. The wind coming from the sea tempered the heat; it was easy to breathe, the avenue was shady, and the square in front of the bridge was filled with bright sunlight. Natasha asked Gushchin why he chose ejection capsules to specialize in. She understood that all occupations were equally respectable, but she wasn't able to grasp how a person comes to decide on such a rare and unusual specialization. In youth everyone dreams of making mankind happy; apparently he also thought to make his fellowmen happy through his work on ejection systems? Of course, Gushchin answered, after all, ejection is inextricably linked to space flight, and who in the twentieth century doesn't dream of space? Gushchin talked mechanically, understanding that she was asking only for the sake of filling up the silence that had arisen between them as soon as they had left the studio. Gushchin had not been ready for this new meeting with Natasha. She had found a place in his memory, in his dreams and sadness; but alive, and formidable in her charm and in the intensity of youth, she was too much for him.

I'm tired. You pay a price for constantly violating yourself. My soul is tired. I force it all the time to live according to a routine that's unsuitable for it. My wife was right, in her own way, when she said: "So why are you tormenting yourself? Almost everyone lives like this." She wasn't sparing with examples. I hadn't thought that the affairs of our acquaintances were so complicated. But it's all right—they live. But it doesn't work for me. I should have belonged to the minority that didn't live "like this." I didn't discover the freedom of indifference. I can't teach myself not to see in my wife the girl from Chistye Prudy with a face madly in love. She had loved me then much more freely and selflessly than I did her. I had been stunned by the war and by the emptiness of the apartment that the war had made desolate, by sudden loneliness, the impenetrability of the future; but she loved headlong, with all her adolescent strength. It was I who slowly learned to love her. But learn I did—and then was lost. Afterwards, when she began to disappear from the house and return later and later, I forced myself not to notice her smeared crumpled mouth, her eyes with their make-up running messily, the disorder of her dress, the smell of wine or cognac, and of cigarette smoke trapped in her hair. I would ask: "Where have you been?", giving her the chance to make excuses, or at least to lie convincingly and preserve the appearance of dignity in our already unseemly life. I thought that by doing that I was keeping her back from some ultimate degradation. I hoped to conquer her with patience, endurance, and faith in her non-existent honesty. She was the first not to be able to sustain this additional lie. I opened the door for her at five in the morning. It was winter, and from the stairway the penetrating cold hit me under my robe on my bare legs, and stayed with me for ever. "So where was I?" she got out hoarsely, almost menacingly, and for the first time looked at me with hate. It was clear that she was sick to death of me and my games of ignorance and trust. I fell silent, stopped asking, and no longer saw hatred in her eyes, only a condescending contempt, at times even something like sympathy and compassionate understanding...

She rarely came to Gushchin at night and never sober. He understood that it wasn't love that brought her to him, but a feminine defeat, an insatiability, and ashamed and cursing himself for his weakness, he took this meager pleasure from the woman whom he'd once loved with an exclusive love, and of whom he now was almost afraid. A person is never definitively unhappy; there always remains room for more misery. The worst part came when his daughter grew up. He had endured his life because of his daughter. She loved him with that hint of jealous devotion that girls often feel in their love for a still young, attractive father who's not spoiled by his home life. But the little girl grew up, penetrated the essence of their shameful family secrets, and with youthful mercilessness decisively took her mother's side, putting up a blank wall of haughty contempt between herself and her father. His wife treated him cruelly, but she wasn't a bad person. When he made timid attempts to penetrate beyond the wall, his daughter's eyes became small and hateful. She seemed unable to forgive her father his sense of insult, his weakness, and his submissiveness. She didn't love her mother, but took her as a model, thus winning for herself independence, freedom from control, and the ability to demand without giving in return...

"No," said Gushchin. "You're wrong; that's not de la Mothe, it's Quarenghi."[3]

They had crossed the bridge and were now standing at the edge of the Field of Mars near the Suvorov memorial, and Natasha, who'd taken upon herself the role of guide, had mistakenly ascribed to Vallin de la Mothe a tall, dull-green and ordinary enough house that had been built by the young Quarenghi.

Natasha argued with the over-sensitive pride of a native of Leningrad caught at not knowing her own city.

"Why are you arguing?" said Gushchin. "There's a memorial plaque on the side of the house that faces the square. It's clearly stated there that the house was built by Quarenghi. Do you want to see it for yourself?"

But to get to the house from their corner turned out not to be so simple—to cross the street directly was prohibited, and they had to take a sizable detour. Calculating on this, Natasha continued angrily defending de la Mothe as being the architect.

"If you want, I'll name you all the known buildings by Quarenghi and de la Mothe, both the ones that have been preserved and those that burned down, were demolished, or destroyed by time, or rebuilt so as to be unrecognizable." Here Gushchin let loose with several dozen names, not sparing the addresses of extant as well as defunct buildings.

"We don't have to cross the street," said Natasha, stunned. "I don't understand a thing. Does your knowledge extend to other architects too, or do you have a narrow specialization in Quarenghi and de la Mothe?"

"To all those who built in Petersburg," replied Gushchin, not without pride, "Be it Kvasov or Rusca, Rastrelli or Rossi, Felten or Sokolov—but Quarenghi is my favorite architect."

"Why? You think he's better than Voronikhin or Rossi?"[4]

"But I'm not saying he's better. I simply like him more."

"So who *are* you? An ejection specialist, an architect, an art historian, a tour guide, or the author of a guidebook to Leningrad?"

"An ejection specialist," said Gushchin, smiling. "You can check at the studio."

"So how do Quarenghi and all the rest fit in? You're not even from Leningrad, after all!"

"At times a person needs a refuge where everyone will leave him in peace. They've even thought up a horribly wretched word to call this salutary escape for the soul: a hobby. So then—old Petersburg is my hobby. Ugh, you'll say, that's repellent!"

And indeed, what a joy it is to discover a small volume bound in red Moroccan leather and examine the precise and austere photographs on silky, thick, nobly yellowed paper; an entablement preserved from the time of Elizabeth on an unobtrusive private residence on Kamenny Island, a portico of Quarenghian simplicity and nobility, left whole in the heart of a far from picturesque warehouse yard on Liteyny, the miraculously untouched lattice of an unrecognizable, rebuilt urban estate on Fontanka[5]—to examine all this and search in your memory for the corner of the city that shelters this or that relic, to recall the landscape of the place: the neighboring stones and trees, to imagine how it all looked in the old days. You no longer notice that you're alone any more; you feel lighthearted and pensive—the stone of the old buildings is far softer and warmer than the stone hearts of people hardened by egotism. But the greatest joy—not joy even, but lofty repose, a solemn peace—was afforded by Giacomo Quarenghi, a stout, ugly dwarf with a botched nose: the creator of supreme harmony. Others may be more powerful, magnificent, and richer in fantasy and inspiration; but the pure simplicity, the artistic scrupulosity of Quarenghi endowed everything created by him with incomparable nobility and perfectness. Quarenghi thought in terms of volume and didn't decorate surfaces. The light and shade on the face of the former Academy of Sciences, simple to the point of defiance, fill your heart with a strange sense of pride. You begin to believe that a man can't be humiliated as long as he feels a part of the world soul. You and Quarenghi and the sad Argunov, together with the grand Chevakinsky and the all-powerful Rossi,[6] against the great and small misfortunes of life, against the night, which relentlessly thrusts you into solitude, and against spiritual bankruptcy and grief.

"Would you like me to show you a unique Leningrad?" he said to Natasha hopefully. "I'm positive you don't know such a Leningrad!"

"Where is it—your Leningrad?"

"In the side streets, in small courtyards, at the backs of famous buildings, sometimes even right in the middle of Nevsky Avenue, only people don't notice it, like they often don't notice what's right beside them."

"But my dear Sergey Ivanovich, we don't have enough hours in the day!"

The cat's-eye of a taxi that had stopped abruptly at a signal light near them prompted Gushchin to a decision. He grabbed Natasha's arm and hustled her into the car. The driver was about to start grumbling that it wasn't allowed, but Gushchin said: "Straight ahead, man, and step on it!" with such confidence and joy that he immediately became quiet and shifted gear with a clang. The cab jerked forward and Gushchin remembered with horror that he had practically no money. There was enough for the taxi, of course, but how would he pay for a hotel?

Gushchin always traveled light. In order to rid himself of unnecessary reproaches, he gave his entire salary, down to the last kopek, to his wife. He didn't smoke or drink, he shaved at home, and limited his transportation costs to a single monthly pass. Only his rare chance extra earnings would he spend on books. And he had set off on this business trip with an exactly calculated amount in his pocket: 2.60 daily allowance and a ruble 56 kopeks for a room, and also some for the tram. But with the quick ability to calculate that he had developed in his lean student years, when out of his scholarship money and his small pay for part-time work at the train station he was able to find money for a ticket to the conservatory, or to MKhAT[7], for a small bouquet of flowers or a modest gift for his future wife, and for other unplanned expenses, he now figured out that by exchanging his sleeping coach seat on the 'Red Arrow'[8] for a non-sleeper on a passenger train, he could make ends meet, and he got rid of his anxiety over the ominously clicking meter...

Every collector, even the most unsociable and ancient type, wants to show his treasures at least once to another person. But Gushchin was generous and gregarious by nature; only the circumstances of his life had made him unsociable. And what else could he share with Natasha? His resentment and depression, his melancholy, or his understanding of ejection systems? None of these could be divulged. He shared with her his only possession, gathered in bits during long solitary evenings. And that's why Gushchin, a person who was sensitive to a fault, hurled the taxi from one end of the city to the other, dragged Natasha through gullies, old cemeteries, cluttered courtyards, building sites, and vacant lots, totally unconcerned about whether she found it interesting or whether she was tired. It was as if he knew that there would never be another tour like this, and in a well-meaning frenzy he wanted to show her everything. He already realized that Natasha knew only the famous architectural monuments, but was not familiar with those little traces and signs of a vanished antiquity that made up his collection, along with the numerous secondary buildings by Quarenghi. He deliberately chose his itinerary along Khalturin, Nevsky, Sadovaya, and Fontanka, and would cry out triumphantly:

"That's a Quarenghi!... The old pharmacy!... That's another Quarenghi!... The tinstone merchants' stalls!... Quarenghi—a hospital! ... And do you recognize this? Quarenghi, doggone it, the real thing!... "

His enthusiasm infected even the sleepy red-faced driver whose small ears were angrily pinned back against his shaved head. Catching sight of a house with columns, he immediately turned toward it without waiting for directions.

"Where are you going? We have to go straight!"

"But that one... that's a Quarenghi," said the driver.

Natasha laughed. It seemed that the expedition was no less a joy for her than it was for Gushchin himself. The only surprising thing was that during Gushchin's most passionate hymns to some frieze or portico, Natasha's lively interested face was turned not to the marvelous ruin but to him, Gushchin.

"Look, look—how beautiful that is!" Gushchin would exclaim.

"Beautiful," Natasha would agree.

"Really now, have you ever seen anything like it?"

"Never," admitted Natasha. "I didn't even know such a thing existed."

Sobriety came to Gushchin suddenly, as they were examining a fragment of the figure of an angel in a small garden on Vasilyev Island.[9] All that was left of the angel was a stone tunic and one wing—proud and beautiful, like the outstretched wing of a swan. Gushchin was freely imagining how the angel must have looked whole when he caught sight of a large metallic bird grazing in the grass. A coat of chain mail made of the tiniest close-fitting scales was thrown over the streamlined body of the bird. A golden ripple ran along the mail when the bird intercepted the rays of the sun.

"Who's that?" asked Gushchin, interrupting his discourse.

"For God's sake, Sergey Ivanovich, you don't recognize a starling?"

"But how enormous he is!" said Gushchin perplexedly.

The starling was as large as a pigeon, a tsar among starlings, a marvel of a starling! It was as if he reminded Gushchin of living life, of the singularity of this day that had been granted to him and that he'd squandered so wastefully on beautiful but cold dead stone.

"Perhaps that's enough antiquity?" asked Gushchin.

"As you wish; I'm not tired."

Gushchin dismissed the cab and they slowly wandered toward the Lt. Schmidt bridge.

"Are you single, Sergey Ivanovich?" asked Natasha sympathetically.

"Not at all! I have a family: a wife and daughter—grown-up, practically your age. And why did you assume?..."

"It seemed to me you had no one except..." she smiled faintly, "except for Quarenghi."

"That's true," said Gushchin morosely. "Though I don't understand how you guessed."

"Well, it's not hard," she said quietly, as if to herself.

"And you?" asked Gushchin. "You, of course, aren't single? You have a family, a husband?"

"I have no one. My father was killed at the front, and my mother died during the blockade. My grandmother brought me up; she also died, she was old. And no one's married me yet. But I'm not alone, Sergey Ivanovich. If you'd like, I'll show you my Leningrad.'

"It's not inconvenient?"

Natasha laughed.

"I was sure you'd say something like that. Of course it's not inconvenient."

Natasha's Leningrad wasn't far away—on Profsoyuz Blvd. They went there on foot and were silent almost the whole way, occupied with their own thoughts. Near the boulevard they came upon a small donkey under a huge fancy saddle trimmed with red plush; it was the kind of donkey children take rides on.

"What a little thing!" said Gushchin, unexpectedly moved.

"Thanks to the starling for being so big and to the donkey for being so small," said Natasha in a strangely touched and almost arch tone.

"What are you talking about?" Gushchin didn't understand and was embarrassed.

"Thanks to life for all its wonders," answered Natasha just as tenderly and strangely...

They ended up in an artist's studio. Almost half the spacious room was taken up by an engraving machine and a large barrel of plaster. Besides two easels, there was also a squat, very wide ottoman, a dozen stools, and a solemn Voltairian chair. Wire artifacts reminiscent of birdcages were hanging from the ceiling—models of atomic structures; shelves with plaster models of some strange exotic fruits stretched along the walls. They turned out to be internal human organs: kidneys, the liver, stomach, intestines, lungs... The artist believed that art had sufficiently celebrated only the visible manifestations of the human essence—the face and the body; no less magnificent and perfect in man—the crown of creation—were his entrails: the powerful stomach, capable of transforming any vegetable matter or meat; the splendid lungs, which suffuse the blood with oxygen, whether at the top of a mountain or in the depths of the earth; and the human heart, incomparable in its endurance, making it possible for this weak, naked, defenseless creature to bear what isn't within the power of the most powerful beast; and the divine genitals, which free man from seasonal dependence for the continuation of the species.

The paintings, drawings, and etchings testified that the volatile nature of the artist had professed a great number of beliefs. Suzdal icon painters, Italian primitives, French Impressionists, Spanish surrealists, native 'Itinerants,'[10] and abstract artists without any roots, one after another, or perhaps even at the same time, had captured his heart. But he remained boldly, enormously talented in every hypostasis. Plaster casts of hands that widened towards the base into a cone were hanging over the fireplace. Here there were the trowel-shaped hands of pianists, and the long hands of violinists with their nervous fingers, the powerful hands of sculptors and the weak undeveloped ones of poets, actors and scientists, inventors and artisans. Among these countless hands, the cast of a small narrow foot with dry ligaments pulled taut across its instep—the foot of a famous ballerina—looked strange and touching. After shaking hands with Gushchin, the artist immediately expressed his wish to make a cast of his hand.

"But I'm nobody!" objected Gushchin.

"That's as yet unknown! You have a good talented hand."

And so there was Gushchin sitting with his sleeve rolled up, and the artist, a huge, bearded, blue-eyed man who looked like Mikula Selyaninovich,[11] was putting plaster on his hand with delicate tickling movements of his powerful paws.

While the plaster was drying, the artist, his light brown head adorned with a garland of daisies, clambered onto the barrel and began playing a reed pipe. Two little light-haired boys immediately came out of the other room and began bending gracefully to the delicate flowing sounds. Gushchin felt in all this no affectation or desire to show off in front of a guest; the boys didn't even seem to notice his presence. That was how the family lived: the father sculpted, painted, drew, modeled and stitched, and in moments of relaxation he played the reed pipe and adorned himself with a garland so that at least for a short while he could feel like a carefree forest-dweller.

The artist put aside the reed pipe when it came time to take the plaster cast off Gushchin. He'd barely done this, with his inherent dexterity, when Natasha and his wife, a thin woman with a languishing face, brought in a round table top set with bottles and glasses. They placed the table top on two stools and the artist filled the glasses with amazing speed and without spilling a drop.

"To art!"

They all drank and the artist filled the glasses again.

"To women!"

Gushchin glanced at Natasha questioningly; such a pace was not within his powers.

"There's nothing you can do—it's a ritual," she said. "Otherwise it's a mortal offense."

"To love!" announced the artist the third time.

Gushchin drank the sweetish sparkling wine and felt a pleasant buzz in his head.

"Wonderful wine!" he said. "Like Caucasian Tsimlanskoye champagne."

"It's a Khvanchkara that's turned sour,"[12] explained the artist calmly. "It doesn't travel well."

Two young poets came and brought Kuban vodka. One of the poets was a boy of about nineteen, thin, puny, with golden bangs hanging to his brows and a round childlike face; they immediately begged him to read some verses. The poet didn't put on airs. He began reading the poem in a full baritone, surprisingly resonant, given his meager appearance. The verses themselves were impressive, sonorous, a little reminiscent of Esenin's "Pugachyov"[13] in intonation, but not at all imitative.

Then the handsome poet read. Although he was older and much bigger than his companion, Gushchin sensed that his poetic reputation was not as great. In a schooled, quiet but clear voice, he read a short poem about a solitary lantern and looked at Natasha with wounded eyes.

"Very nice," she said indifferently.

The poet flushed and turned away.

All this time Gushchin hadn't exchanged two words with Natasha. He talked with the artist, drank wine, and listened to the poetry, while Natasha whispered with the artist's wife, played with the children, exchanged short remarks with the poets, and also listened to their verses. But behind Gushchin and Natasha's surface disassociation there was a friendly intimacy. They acted like people who shared something and didn't need contact out of politeness. And the handsome poet most likely felt this. Gushchin caught his passionate somber gaze on him several times.

The wine, the unusualness of the surroundings, and all the impressions of the day descended on Gushchin in the form of leaden exhaustion. He drank some more toasts, admired something or other, answered someone, but all this was as if in a dream. Clear moments appeared now and then, and he heard the handsome poet sing a song about the country of Hippopotamia, accompanying himself on the guitar, and saw a hairy youth burst into the studio and immediately pounce on the host: "So, Vereshchagin's[14] a genius and a luminary?" In response to which the artist, tearing the collar of his shirt like ancient warriors before battle, stood up staunchly for Vereshchagin. And he also remembered his clear sober thought that people of his generation criticized today's youth for nothing: "They're better than we are, better because they're more independent"; he wanted to impart this thought to yet another guest—a sad Mephistopheles with a goatee, but just then sleep toppled him into a black pit.

The sleep didn't last long, but it refreshed him. He didn't open his eyes, thinking up an apology, and suddenly he heard the quiet voice of the handsome poet right next to him:

"So he picked you up on the street?"

"No, I picked him up," was the calm answer.

"I didn't know it was a habit of yours!"

"Neither did I."

"Nonetheless it's swinish to dress like that," said the poet with impotent spite. "War Communism is over."

Gushchin had missed the moment to wake up and so to put an end to further discussion of his person. Now what he'd heard demanded a response. But what was he to do—you couldn't fight the boy and moralizing was even more stupid. One thing remained: to doom himself to further eavesdropping by pretending that he was still asleep.

"That's strange," said Natasha. "I didn't even notice how he was dressed."

Gushchin didn't catch the tone of her voice; he thought he heard estrangement in the word "he."

"You usually notice."

"Well, yes, when there's nothing else to notice."

"Why are you mad?" asked the poet bitterly.

"Me? I thought it was you who were mad."

"Tell me, only be honest. How could such a, you know... dusty old man take your fancy?"

"I feel safe with him. I don't know how else to explain it. I feel protected."

"And with me you feel unprotected?"

"Well, sure, you're a first-rate boxer and can knock out anyone who pesters me. But I'm not talking about that kind of protection."

"Maybe he's a latent genius?"

"I think he's a good specialist. He knows his work."

"And that's it?"

"That's a lot. We've known each other about seven years and you've always been the same: an aspiring poet, an amateur actor, and a first-rate boxer. So *be* a poet, or become a professional actor, or at the worst, a champion boxer."

"You were never cruel; why all of a sudden?..."

"I never had to defend anyone!" interrupted Natasha, and Gushchin began to feel sorry for the poor handsome poet.

He was far from seriously considering himself the poet's fortunate rival. Natasha didn't like the poet for himself; but he, Gushchin, had turned up by chance as the focus of attention of a young, thirsting heart. His personal qualities were not the issue here. But he saw the real Natasha and his heart was drawn to her. Natasha didn't see him, but had made him up, rejecting her first impression. Perhaps the reason for this was his gray hair, the one that was "needed urgently" by 'Lenfilm.' But he didn't feel bitter; their meeting remained a divine gift all the same, as did the artist's studio,

Mikula Selyaninovich, his family and friends, and the poetry, and the songs, and the arguments—the very sound of young, ardently interested voices!

When Gushchin opened his eyes, the handsome poet was no longer in the studio; in his place sat a girl with a pale mermaid face and beautiful red hair. She smiled mysteriously at Gushchin, as if greeting him after a long period of separation. Natasha came up to him with a little pillow covered in thick linen from Vologod.

"You're tired, Sergey Ivanovich; let me put this under your head."

This was no longer a play of abstract powers, this friendly concern for an older exhausted person. Gushchin said, embarrassed and grateful:

"Thank you. I can't hold my liquor. I've gotten unused to it."

"No one can hold it. Even if they're used to it."

Obviously Natasha was thinking of the young poet with the unhappy pointed face, who'd gone to pieces, of the sleepy Mephistopheles, and of Vereshchagin's opponent, who was as red as if he'd come from a sauna. Only Mikula Selyaninovich, as befits a knight, was fresh and in good spirits, although he'd drunk no less than the others...

Natasha led Gushchin away from the hospitable home when the half-dead poet and Mephistopheles started making preparations for another vodka run.

"Don't be mad, Natasha," said the artist dolefully. "The boys just want to have a little drink."

"Drink away, but Sergey Ivanovich has had enough!" declared Natasha decisively.

The parting was touching. The artist hugged Gushchin, kissed him, and whispered, gritting his teeth:

"When you come here again, don't dare go to a hotel, come straight to us! If you hurt Natasha..." He didn't finish, but the unchecked tear that clouded his blue gaze replaced the words: "I'll kill you!"

Gushchin felt that that wasn't merely a threat, and he kissed the artist again on his hard red mouth, which was buried in a plush thicket.

Vera, the artist's wife, insisted that Natasha take a pie, some cooled tarts, and other food, and the boys clung to her skirt with desperate howls, and Gushchin saw that Natasha really wasn't alone in her big city . . .

Natasha lived on Rakov Street. They chose a roundabout way there across Palace Square and the Field of Mars. Here Leningrad was generously illuminated by spotlights that advantageously removed the palaces and obelisks from darkness, but this Intourist gloss deprived the city of its austerity, its proud independence. However, if you made the effort, then in the light blue haze over the spotlights, in the sharp whiteness of the illuminated walls, you could discover the Petrograd of 1917, when the revolutionary fighters had warmed themselves by bonfires at night. "The smoke of the bonfire and the cold of the bayonet... "[15]

Gushchin flinched, as if the point of this cold bayonet had touched him. Look out—your day isn't over yet, the coals in the bonfire are still glowing. Remember, remember that you really did walk along Palace Square arm in arm with a girl, Natasha; don't try to persuade yourself later that this was all a dream. And remember: she was with you all day long and the entire evening, and put up with you, and didn't send you away, although at times you were overexcited, depressed, inebriated, and towards the end went to pieces totally. She forgave you everything and remained kind to you, and it was, it was, it was, it was, and it is as long as it is. She's beside you, right next to you, all of her, her eyes, her tanned cheekbones, her gentle mouth, which aged when she was sad, her disheveled, expensively styled hair, her neck, shoulders—my God, all of her glowing with life, she's walking beside you, and you can touch her. And to his horror, he touched Natasha with his hand. She looked at him questioningly.

"Forgive me," muttered Gushchin, "I had my doubts all of a sudden that you were really here."

Natasha wasn't surprised; she said reassuringly:

"I'm here, of course I'm here."

Happy again, Gushchin began to thank Natasha warmly for 'her Leningrad.'

"What talented and good people they all are!... "

"Yes... " agreed Natasha absentmindedly. "But for some reason today I liked them less than usual."

"Why?" asked Gushchin anxiously.

She was silent for a while.

"How can I best put it... An actor's greatest accomplishment is to perform a monologue or a pause on the stage. At one time MKhAT was famous for its pauses. With my friends there are never pauses. They have to be doing something constantly: arguing, showing someone up, or reading verses, singing, drinking vodka, suffering, fighting, or running around to exhibits, previews, premieres... "

"But that's not bad, is it?"

"You know, their fussing stems from dilettantism. The dilettantism of their whole spiritual life. This, of course, doesn't apply to the artist—he's a master, a professional, supports a family, and still finds the strength to play, and for mischief... But I'm saying this needlessly... Thank God for all of them. Nothing to rouse God's anger over. Thank you, thank you!" she repeated, lifting her face. "I said that to God, so he wouldn't cause any harm . . . But you know, Sergey Ivanovich, *you* know how to maintain a pause; it's so marvelous to just be silent with you! . . . "

Natasha lived in an old house near the arcade. From her low gateway, resting against a stack of birch firewood, one could see the stylish wing of Mikhailovsky Palace, illuminated by spotlights. Gushchin thought that it was Natasha's sensitivity that had made him a gift of one of Rossi's finest creations as a farewell for him; Natasha wanted to adorn, if not brighten, their parting. If it had been another girl in her place, he would not be able to see Mikhailovsky Palace in these final minutes, its bright columns and austere fencing. Gushchin tried to put himself in an ironically exalted frame of mind in order not to fall into despair.

He touched her shoulder with his palm and felt the delicate warmth of her body through her thin sweater. Now she'd go and the happiest and most unexpected day of his life would come to an end. Oh, stay, stay! . . . [16] It will be so terrible—what will happen to me when your steps die out in the black gun barrel of the gateway. Nothing will save me, neither Mikhailovsky Palace nor all the wonders of Rossi, nor of Quarenghi himself! . . .

She took the hand that he'd laid on her shoulder and, since he didn't grasp her intention, pulled him a bit sharply so that he'd follow her. Above them hung the dome of the gateway. With inexpressible tenderness Gushchin gazed at this low-hanging, gloomy sky that witnessed Natasha's comings and goings; he gazed at the damp peeling walls and the old cobblestones underfoot. Natasha didn't want to part with him on the street, in view of passersby; she was drawing him still nearer to her life, to the threshold of her home. And here was the threshold, in the heart of a circular yard, not very large, smelling of decay from piles of birchwood. The yard was deep, like a well; a full moon hung over it, and its brilliance lay on the root-roughened logs, on the steep cobblestones, and on the bronze handles of the old doors.

Gushchin stopped at the shabby stone steps. And again Natasha's hand drew him after her. The massive tired door sang its sad song; in the dim light of small dusty lamps a staircase appeared, leading up into infinite heights captured by the darkness. Like all old apartment houses, the stairs were well-trodden and worn down, the rickety banisters had been rubbed black and silky by countless palms, but to Gushchin it seemed a staircase to heaven, and he followed Natasha, becoming short of breath not from the steepness of the stairwell, but from the intensity of his feelings and from gratitude. Natasha was doing him the greatest kindness—leading him into her home, and presenting him the joy of the last possible nearness to her before she disappeared forever.

Brass plates with names written in the old orthography flashed by, along with hopelessly long lists of residents, and mailboxes that were labeled with the names of newspapers; suddenly Natasha stopped next to some door, and Gushchin, his thoughts set on an endless ascent, almost knocked her down. Natasha laughed, unlocked the door, and they stepped into pitch darkness. The light switch clicked, and Gushchin found himself in a small entrance hall with a tidy coat rack, an umbrella stand, and an oval wall mirror with a small table under it. Clothes brushes and a small whisk broom were lying on the table. Gushchin was touched by these details of the life of a solitary person who takes care of herself; he had never seen so sensibly arranged an entrance hall, equipped with all necessities.

Natasha took the briefcase out of his hands and put it on the small table. With its worn, greasy fake leather, it looked glaringly out of place in all this cleanliness and smartness. Gushchin walked into Natasha's room as into a sanctuary, in a beatific, prayerful trance; he didn't recognize separate objects, didn't even understand their purpose. Only the scent of flowers penetrated the fog that clouded his senses; there were many of them all over, and there were also many photographs with the whiteness of unfamiliar disturbing faces, and many drawings and etchings.

A tormenting sadness that became unbearable was growing in him from the briefness, the fragility of this undeserved gift, and he wanted to leave as soon as possible so as to avoid prolonging his torment for nothing. He'd go, go to Moscow, return to his customary existence, and the sadness within him would abate, and it would become tender and joyful to recall this clean small apartment, the focus of Natasha's life.

Natasha went up to him, and with an unexpectedly strong arm encircled Gushchin's neck, drew him to her, and kissed him. This Gushchin couldn't bear, and he started crying. But not with his face—his eyes remained dry; he cried with his heart. And Natasha heard the dry soundless cry inside him. She pressed her palms against his temples.

"Why, dear, there's no need. I'm so at peace and happy with you, and you just won't believe it. Come, kiss me yourself."

Gushchin took her hand and kissed it. And then Natasha kissed his hand and said with terrible simplicity:

"Undress and get into bed—I'll be right there."

It wasn't joy—it was oblivion, a coma, a sweet death. And when Gushchin came to, Natasha, eyes closed, was lying on his arm and he couldn't hear her breathing. Frightened, Gushchin put his ear to her breast; her heart was beating strongly and rhythmically, but very quietly.

The moon had practically climbed in through the window, and flooded the room powerfully, making everything in it as distinct as during the day. The steadfast lucid gaze of a young man of about twenty-five was focused directly on Gushchin's face from a large photograph hanging on the wall at the foot of the sofa. Gushchin turned away, but the very same steadfast large eyes stared at him from the dressing table. Gushchin turned his glance to the wall, but photographs of the same young man were hanging there too: on some he was older, on others younger, and on one he was a child, a big-eyed boy with a high forehead and undefined soft lips. And this photograph dealt the final blow to Gushchin. Of course Natasha had been attracted to others, had been in love; but how hurt, how wounded she must have been by this man to hang his picture all over the room, to condemn herself to his perpetual presence. After all, if the feeling was gone, then it would be annoying and oppressive to constantly encounter the features you no longer loved. Did that mean that Natasha loved this young man with the steadfast lucid eyes even now? Then what had taken place between them was robbery. Robbery of true love. Should he leave? And what would Natasha think? She'd be convinced once and for all that she'd been involved with an old philanderer. Should he leave her a note? But could he really express all that in a note? Gushchin raised himself, and not knowing himself what he was about to do, stretched his hand toward the large picture hanging across from him.

"Don't touch that!" he heard Natasha's unfamiliar ringing voice. "Don't you dare touch my father's portrait!"

Father!... This boy was Natasha's father? But what was so surprising about that?—Natasha's father, who'd been killed at the front, could have been even younger than his daughter was now.

"My God!" said Gushchin. "And I was so worried! I'm sorry, Natasha—I suppose I really did want to take it away."

The tension left Natasha's face. She reached out toward Gushchin and with an already familiar strong motion, put her arms around his neck. In a turmoil of joy and mortal pity for Natasha and her boy-father, who hadn't found out what he'd left on earth, Gushchin abruptly parted with everything that bothered him, chained him, and made him feel destitute.

When dawn came and they broke their embrace, Natasha said in a voice weak with happiness:

"I fell in love with you right away... As soon as I saw you... You're remarkable, you're a marvel, you are Quarenghi!..."

Gushchin was leaving late in the evening. Natasha was making a film, so all day he wandered alone around the city in a kind of sweet half-dream, without noticing his surroundings or his favorite buildings, for even the harmony of Quarenghi couldn't add anything to his overflowing happiness. This joy kept him from feeling pain during their parting on the station platform—in some unfathomable way Natasha managed to see him off. Only later he realized that she had probably watched at the station for a long time, waiting for that shabby train for which he'd exchanged his ticket on the 'Red-Arrow.' Only when the platform started rushing backward and

Natasha forward, turning a strangely aloof and matter-of-fact face to the car that was slipping away, did Gushchin feel pierced for a moment with the realization of another's pain, but just then the train speeded up, Natasha disappeared, and happiness returned to Gushchin again.

Not knowing how to convert this triumphant joy into something concrete, he began to help passengers arrange their suitcases on the baggage rack. He threw himself into helping them with such eagerness that an elderly woman, who'd apparently known better days, said while hesitantly fingering her purse:

"How much do I owe you, dearie?"

Gushchin burst out laughing and put his shoulder to a basket that was falling out of the weak arms of a young pregnant woman.

And then he climbed up to the second berth, placed his soft folding briefcase under his head—an excellent pillow—and was instantaneously transported to the room on Rakov Street, filled with the moon as if it were the sun, and he boldly met the steadfast lucid gaze of the youth who'd been killed in the war.

He woke up at Malaya Vishera, roused by the silence cast over the station. Outside, the station fires were growing dim; the platform was located on the other side, and on this side the damp rails glistened, railroad workers were wandering about, tapping out a mournful tune on the wheels of the train, a lone freight car was moving by itself, an old man with a knapsack was relieving himself gloomily at the pumphouse, and this whole life, so hopelessly estranged from and indifferent to his soul, descended on Gushchin in the form of an aching melancholy. He turned on his berth and wanted to jump down, but at that moment the train pulled out, toppling him backwards into the bottomless well of sleep, and he was in Natasha's room again...

Gushchin didn't like Kalanchevsky Square. Its stations promised long journeys in three directions of the world: to the north, east, and south—to the farthest ends of the country. And people would get on the trains and go to the Pacific Ocean and to the White Sea, and to the shores of the Aragva and the Kura, but Gushchin didn't go anywhere. He'd been tormented by this possibility of distant travel which had vanished in vain for him not so much for lack of time and means—if the desire were there, both could be found—as out of spiritual inertia and an inability to break out of the daily grind, to break away from the drudgery of family life. He felt guilty before these stations—an ant from Moscow who wouldn't risk crawling out of the magic circle drawn by routine. But today he went out into the square without shame or guilt. He'd gone maybe not to the other end of the world, but on perhaps the most distant journey possible. And getting a better grip on the handle of the little luggage he had, Gushchin mixed in with the crowd of other travellers in a businesslike manner.

He lived at the Red Gates and didn't go into the subway for the sake of one stop. Passing under a railroad bridge, he saw the gigantic advertising stand of the Museum of Fine Arts, which took up the entire fireproof wall of a six-story house, with its silhouette of the equestrian statue of that soldier of fortune, Colleoni.[17]

He liked the sculpture by Verrocchio[18] very much. Colleoni was looking out at the world, or rather, over the world, over his left shoulder, which was covered in armor; his face, furrowed with wrinkles, was full of an indomitable unrestrained will. The soldier's mighty horse was a match for its master; it seemed to be stepping over the bodies of those who had fallen. Gushchin saw in this sculpture the unconscious revelation of the spirit of the Middle Ages, which time hadn't awakened to doubt or mercy. With his customary pleasure he looked at the pale green silhouette of the formidable horseman, discolored by sun and rain, and he suddenly realized that everything was over; his Leningrad experience had been summed up. The Museum of Fine Arts was as inseparable from Moscow as the Hermitage was from Leningrad. He could delude himself on Kalanchevsky Square: it wasn't Moscow yet, but rather an extension of Nevsky, and a road the length of a dream returned him to what had been left behind; but here he was captured by Moscow in earnest, from here you could no longer get away; and his home was nearby, and that terrible alien thing that for some reason was called a family. Gushchin stopped and pressed his hand to his chest; the leaden hoof of a monstrous horse had trodden on his heart. He stood, his eyelids squeezed shut, barely breathing, and the terrible horseman, having spattered him with unhappiness, like mud, continued on his way...

Gushchin lived strangely now, more strangely than he had before. On the surface everything remained unchanged: he went to work, and in the evenings he leafed through books about old Petersburg in solitude, but he did all this without thought or feeling. He looked indifferently at the magnificent pictures of the magnificent buildings, but they were no longer soothing. Natasha's face would surface relentlessly and sharply out of the yellowed pages. It would show through the pieces of drafting paper and the tracing paper, it fluttered before Gushchin in the bluish smoke at meetings and pursued him on the streets and in the subway. This girl was merciless, like Colleoni; she went after him, stopping at nothing, through dream and reality, through the street crowds and business talks; there was no escaping her.

In Leningrad he'd promised himself that he'd buy a summer suit and a good shirt and tie, but Natasha had ordered him not to change his appearance, which retained the touch of her hands and her glance. For this very reason he hadn't parted with his awful briefcase—the immutable third party in their relationship. It was hot and he was stifling in his heavy suit and clerical collar, which had turned into a noose from daily laundering.

Natasha gave him no peace. Everything around him was losing its primal nature, everything was becoming the reflection of Natasha, was seen through her and made itself felt through her; this fatigued and debilitated Gushchin. He asked: "Leave me alone! Since you aren't here anymore, then don't be at all!" But that didn't help.

He was returning from work on foot and he stopped at Chistye Prudy to watch some children feeding millet and sunflower seeds to the birds. Among the old native Moscow sparrows Gushchin came across some unfamiliar beautiful sharp-tailed little birds with chocolate-colored backs and opal stomachs. But all of a sudden a large bird landed heavily and resiliently on the grass, frightening all the small fry, and soiling its gray plumage in the sunset. Not a pink bird, but one that was turning pink, had brought a wisp of heavenly blue on each wing. It moved its round eye with its golden border and began to peck at the seeds sharply and authoritatively, a beautiful, wild, and unnatural visitor in the stone sack of the city. "A jay!" said the children in amazement. But Gushchin didn't get taken in; he saw that unique gold around the pupil, that fusion of tenderness and strength. "Natasha!" he whispered to the bird. "Why did you come here? It's dangerous for you here, Natasha! . . . "

Nevertheless, he didn't give himself away to his wife, and couldn't understand why she said in a cheerfully threatening tone one day:

"Now, confess—what have you done?"

"Just like me . . . " replied Gushchin listlessly.

"An old bird isn't caught with chaff," she said with concern and with the insight of a person who's guilty herself. "You're in love!"

Gushchin didn't confirm her guess, probably only because the word sounded insulting coming from his wife.

Now he caught her studying him every now and then with a suspicious assessing look. "That's all I need, for her to start envying me," he thought wearily. "Apparently I'm fated to pass through all the circles of the family hell." But she wasn't envious; she was only getting adjusted to him, and in her faded, once emerald-green eyes, now the color of bottle glass, there wasn't any bad feeling at all, but rather, a benevolent curiosity. It was as if she was trying to find something in Gushchin, to awaken her memory of him, but she didn't succeed in this, which troubled and upset her. Her insistent stare bothered Gushchin. He felt that she was penetrating into his last sanctuary—his thoughts. And to top it all, she suddenly stopped going out at night.

The burden was getting too much for him. And when Natasha took root in all people, animals and birds, became all objects around him, when every time he touched living or non-living matter he was touching her warm light flesh, then, not from lack of resoluteness, but out of despair, he sent her a telegram: "Is gray hair still needed?" The answer came amazingly fast: "Yes, yes, yes—urgently." The triple repetition of "yes" told Gushchin that she had been missing him as well. It amazed him that he too could be the source of pain for someone. In all these agonizing days it hadn't once occurred to him that Natasha was also feeling wretched, that she too was suffering; he thought that she should perceive her existence as uninterrupted joy; after all, it was so wonderful and joyous to be her!

But now that he'd learned the truth he became strong.

How simple everything becomes when a decision has been made! At work everyone agreed with him about everything, as if they'd already been expecting for a long time that Gushchin would have to change his fate radically. His wife didn't put obstacles in his path either, gratefully accepting all his terms. She only said with a kind of incongruous exultation:

"See, I guessed right away what direction the wind was blowing from. How important it is for a person to be right about *some*thing!"

And then, with fuss and confusion, she began to fit out Gushchin as if he were going to war: washing and ironing his linen and shirts, darning something, hemming. It was unpleasant for Gushchin to see her back bent over the unexpected and unnecessary work.

His daughter reacted to his leaving even more straightforwardly.

"Father's leaving us," her mother said to her.

"It's about time," came the calm and benevolent answer.

Gushchin had read that when Karl Bryullov[19] was leaving Nicholas' Russia forever he threw all his clothes off at the border and crossed over into a new life naked; he didn't want to take with him even the dust, even the smell of the country that hadn't become his homeland. He had a similar feeling. He pawned his old, but still sturdy suit, and bought himself a pair of summer trousers, a wool shirt, and sandals.

"How young you still are!" said his wife with surprise.

He left home with very little; everything he had was on him—in his pockets: documents, a plane ticket, a comb and a razor. He was breaking with his former way of life once and for all: with people who hadn't wanted to become close to him, with the cold apartment that was always empty, inhabited by indifferent things, with the poor clothing he wore on his body, even with his few beloved books and his eternal companion—his briefcase, rubbed and worn till it was thin as a petal.

He went out early—just after dawn—into the street that was wet from the street washing and he was struck by its emptiness, its hot freshness, and its calm readiness to lead him to happiness. He felt like a runner who'd reached the finish line with a full reserve of strength. Nothing stood between him and victory anymore. His well-cut clothes, which he could hardly feel, reinforced his feeling of lightness. Yes, his wife was right: he had kept his youthfulness, he hadn't worried himself to death over the small temptations of life; they kept him on ice and now, thawed out, he emerged cheerful and fresh.

My God, in about two hours he'd be with Natasha! And he'd get all of Leningrad as a dowry. He thought of Leningrad with such tender affection, as if Natasha had built the city especially for him, had put up the bridges across the Neva and the Fontanka, erected the Rostralnye columns, put the lattice work around every park, set up arches where the houses blocked access from the streets to the squares. Carefully, painstakingly, generously and tenderly, she'd created this inimitable city which henceforth and forever would be the city of their love. Blessed be the generosity of life that presents him his beloved set in such a frame!

At the corner he turned towards the house where so many of his days and nights lay buried. Leaning far out of the window, his wife followed him with her eyes. In strange, unnatural close-up he saw her puffy face with its enlarged pores, her faded bottle-glass eyes set in wrinkled eyelids, the defenseless face, not needed by anyone, of a prematurely aged woman. She watched him with avid and perplexed curiosity, without malice, without envy, as if looking at something unattainable, and although she was looking from above, it seemed as if it were from below—the look of a thrown horseman, of a bird shot down with an arrow. He wanted to wave good-bye to her, but suddenly made a strange swallowing sound in his throat and turned back.

1968   Translated by Irene Kiedrowski

Notes

The original ("Srochno trebuiutsia sedye chelovecheskie volosy") first appeared in *Znamia*, No. 3 (1968), 70-87. The present translation is of the edition included in the two-volume 1973 collection, I, 403-428.

1. Oleg A. Strizhenov (1929-   ) is a Soviet actor who played in such films as *The Gadfly* and *The Duel*, based on Chekhov's story with the same title. From 1964 to 1976 he acted with the Moscow Art Theater (MKhAT).
2. The conventional Soviet method of introducing oneself is to give one's surname first, then one's Christian name and patronymic.

3. Vallin de la Mothe (1729-1800) was a French architect who worked in Russia from 1759 to 1775. He designed the mammoth department store in Leningrad called Gostiny Dvor (1761-85) and the Small Hermitage (1764-7).

Giacomo Quarenghi (1744-1817) was an Italian architect who from 1780 resided and worked in Russia. A representative of the classical style, he designed such buildings as the Aleksandrovsky Palace (1792-6) in Tsarskoye Selo (Pushkin), the Hermitage Theater (1783-7), and the Smolny Institute (1806-8) in Leningrad (then Petersburg).

4. Aleksey V. Kvasov (1718-72) was an architect and urban designer who supervised the general plan of Petersburg (1763-9) and worked on projects for the city plans of Kazan, Tver, Astrakhan, and Kharkov.

V.V. Rastrelli (1700-71) was a marvelous Baroque architect, son of the sculptor B.K. Rastrelli. His buildings are distinguished by bold sweeps and straight lines united with striking ornamentation and rich sculptures and colors. Among his many famous structures are the Smolny Monastery (1748-54) and the Winter Palace (1754-62) in Leningrad, the Grand Palace in Peterhof (1747-52) and the Ekaterininsky Palace in Tsarskoye Selo (1752-7).

Yu.M. Felten (1730[2]-1801) was a representative of early classicism in architecture who designed the Old Hermitage (1771-84).

Pavel P. Sokolov (1764-1835) was a sculptor, considered a master of classical decorative sculpture (e.g., *Dairymaid with a Broken Jug* in the Pushkin Park).

Andrey N. Voronikhin (1759-1814) was a Russian architect in the Empire style, designer of the Kazan Cathedral in Leningrad (1801-11), and participant in the designs for the ensembles in Pavlovsk and Peterhof.

5. Kamenny Island is one of the islands comprising Leningrad, located to the north northwest of the city center.

Liteyny Avenue is a major avenue in Leningrad which runs north-south. Liteyny Bridge is one of the bridges linking the northern part of the city to the city center.

The Fontanka is one of the major canals in Leningrad which connects with the Neva River. The canal figures prominently in Dostoyevsky's *Crime and Punishment*. Fontanka Street (where Pushkin lived with his parents) runs along the canal.

6. The Argunovs were peasant architects: Fyodr S. Argunov (c. 1732-c. 1768) and Pavel I. Argunov (c. 1768-1806). The latter was the head of the architectural team that built the palace theater on the Ostankino estate of the Sheremetev family not far from Moscow. He designed a series of well-known interiors.

Savva I. Chevakinsky (1713-1774?/1780?) was a proponent of the Baroque architectural school who designed the Nikolsky Military-Naval Cathedral (1753-62) in Leningrad and who helped in the construction of the Ekaterininsky Palace in Tsarskoye Selo in the 1740s.

7. MKhAT (Moskovsky Khudozhestvenny Akademichesky Teatr) is the Moscow Art Theater, one of Russia's largest and most prestigious theaters, established in 1898 by K. S. Stanislavsky and V.I. Nemirovich-Danchenko. Innovative in its early phase, the theater staged many plays by Chekhov and Gorky as well as the classics of Russian drama. For an irreverent and hilarious view of MKhAT, see Mikhail Bulgakov's novel *Teatral'nyi roman*, translated into English as *White Snow*.

8. The Red Arrow is the Moscow-Leningrad night train.

9. Vasilyev Island is an island to the west of Leningrad's city center, linked to it by the Lt. Schmidt Bridge.

10. The Itinerants *(Peredvizhniki)* was the name given to a Russian art movement in the mid-nineteenth century which advocated a greater realism, an increased emphasis on the outdoors, and a more profound psychological understanding of the subject than shown by conventional salon art. Its best-known representatives were Repin, Kramskoy, Levitan, Surikov, Perov, Ge, Savrasov, Shishkin, and Vasnetsov.

11. Mikula Selyaninovich, an epic hero and plowman, is the protagonist of the epic songs *(byliny) Volga and Mikula Selyaninovich* and *Svyatogor and Mikula Selyaninovich.*

12. Khvanchkara is a Georgian sweet wine. (Thank you, Nina Mitelman!)

13. Sergey A. Esenin (1895-1925) was a masterly lyricist, the son of a peasant, who wrote with melodious nostalgia of the countryside, the peasants, and Bohemia. He was briefly (1919-23) associated with the Imagists. After an even briefer disastrous marriage to the dancer Isadora Duncan (1922-3), he found oblivion in drink, then suicide. The tone of the poem "Pugachyov" (about the eighteenth-century rebel leader) is powerfully dramatic.

14. Vasily V. Vereshchagin (1843-1904), one of the 'Itinerant' group, selected themes from history, and especially battle, for the subject of his canvasses.

15. The line is from a Pushkin-permeated poem by O. Mandelstam, dedicated to N. Gumilyov, entitled "Petersburg Stanzas" (Peterburgskie strofy) (1913). It is the last line of the fourth quatrain. (Thank you, Ivan V. Elagin.)

16. "Oh, stay, stay!" echoes Faust's final apostrophe to time in Goethe's *Faust*, Part II: "Verweile doch, [du bist so schön!]."

17. Bartolemeo Colleoni (1400-75) was an Italian *condottiere*, at various times in Venetian and Milanese service and from 1454 general in chief of the Venetian Republic for life, who gained fame as a pioneer of field artillery tactics. He was a noted patron of art.

18. Andrea del Verrocchio (1435[6]-88) was an Italian sculptor, painter and engraver of the Florentine school during the Early Renaissance. His most famous sculptures include *David* (1473-5) and the bronze statue of Colleoni in Venice (1483-8), one of the finest equestrian statues of the Italian Renaissance, which the Russian reproduces.

19. Karl P. Bryullov (1799-1852) was a Russian painter who lived in Italy from 1823 to 1835 and for the last two years of his life. His work entitled *The Last Day of Pompei* (1830-3) caused a sensation when it was shown in Russia (Gogol was one of its admirers).

Somebody Else's Heart

Kostrov stood at the window and looked out at the hospital yard, or rather, at the small corner of it that was formed by the peeling yellow wall of the surgical building and the rusty iron gate that was always locked; a short scrawny tree, bare after early spring, also inhabited this part of the universe. Kostrov didn't know its name. Behind the tree was a door that seemed to blend in with the wall, and next to it lay an urn fallen on its side. Up above, the even taut blue line of sky extended over everything. Kostrov looked at the hospital yard for a good half-hour, but this knowledge of what he saw neither broadened nor became more intimate. The yellow wall and the gate and the door, even the pathetic tree, remained alien to him. Perhaps only the sky struck some sort of weak chord in him, like a half-forgotten melody heard in his youth. He was unconsciously obeying the doctor's orders: leave behind everything that was part of your illness, once you're over the threshold; don't take anything with you—not us, your doctors, nor your memory of the hospital surroundings, nor of your personal torments, doubts and fears. That phase is over, you'll no longer have to confront what for so long was the fundamental basis of your life. Don't burden your head with unnecessary rubbish. Splendid advice! Kostrov acted accordingly: he didn't take in what he saw, didn't respond to anything save the sky, but, after all, it was waiting for him on the other side of that door just the same as it looked from the hospital window.

Yes, he'd freed his memory of every burden, even of gratitude to the person who'd saved his life. Why should he be grateful? The doctors had hardly saved him—Kostrov, the one and only, the unique individual—from death, had they? No, they'd performed an experiment that was ordinary and a bit terrifying in its daring. And he, Kostrov, surprisingly enough, turned out to be a marvelously tenacious guinea pig, an unusually lucky rabbit. He was the first laboratory animal to survive to the end, right through to his own distant death, which was from a distant cause. He survived and became the greatest sensation of the century: the first man with somebody else's heart.

He had predecessors, of course. A human heart had started beating in somebody else's breast more than once, but that illusory existence hadn't become life: after existing from several hours to several months, the breathing half-corpses had become corpses. They had all been only artificial carriers of somebody else's heart; the miracle of uniting the matter of one person with the matter of somebody else's heart had first taken place in him. Yes, it had taken place, there hadn't been the slightest doubt about that for some time, and he was being kept there not for his own good, but for the sake of science. At times, however, he thought that the doctor who was treating him didn't seem sure of his psychological strength and his readiness for life with somebody else's heart. "What are you afraid of?" Kostrov asked pointblank. The doctor had apparently expected this question, yet wasn't ready for it. His thick bass voice cracked at first with uncertainty: "Have you read the autobiographical story of Peter Freikhen, the famous Danish traveler?"[1] "No, I haven't heard of him." "He writes about a man who threw over the medical profession and became a polar explorer... A worker who'd been crippled in a wreck was brought to the clinic where this doctor was working. The agonizing struggle for his life went on for several months. There wasn't a spot on the poor guy left unscathed. They put him together, sewed him up, and stuck him back together by bits. And when he walked out the door of the clinic with the weak unsteady gait of a man grown unused to motion and space—into the world, sun, and life—all the doctors, nurses, and orderlies were in tears as they saw off this, as it were, newly created man. But this latter-day Adam began to cross the street and was killed by the first and only car in Copenhagen, which darted from around the corner. The young doctor became disillusioned with his profession, conceived a hatred for the city and went off to Greenland for good."

"Are you afraid that I'm going to lose the life that's been returned to me just as foolishly?" asked Kostrov. "In any case, I'm not in danger of dying under the wheels of a car." "Why?" asked the doctor, surprised. "The law of probability: the same heart can't perish twice in an automobile accident." Kostrov didn't know anything about his 'godfather' other than that he'd been killed by a dump-truck and was so mutilated that they were unable to identify him. The deceased didn't have any papers on him and nobody recognized him at the morgue. It was possible that this was all a myth cooked up by the hospital because the patient wasn't supposed to know where his heart came from, but for some reason Kostrov thought that they weren't deceiving him.

"You took my story too literally," remarked the doctor. "Traffic isn't the only thing fraught with danger." "Do you mean that my brains are scrambled?" "You've got a good mind, it's too bad that you're so unread and uncultured." "So you think I haven't read much?" laughed Kostrov. "If you're thinking of *King Solomon's Mines*,[2] then you've read too much, but I'm talking about real books that lead to an understanding of yourself and your surroundings ... All right, then, don't engage in moral self-analysis, forget about mythology that a generation of windbags have twisted out of that simple and vulgar organ called the heart. You've had an operation, no different from, say, a kidney transplant. Some day science will be able to transplant any organ; it will all be in the order of things. But you're the first of your kind and you'll have to live among people who're often curious, obsessed, or tactless; don't let yourself get bewildered, and remember: the heart that's beating in your chest so wonderfully and rhythmically is *your* heart. You got it lawfully. No mysticism or Dostoevskian melodrama. Now you should begin a new and marvellous life. You've never known what it means to be a completely healthy human being. Try to use this new life a bit better, you're the first person who's had the opportunity to live a life with a fresh start."

Kostrov never did understand what the doctor was afraid of. Evidently it was the clash between his new health and his mind, which had been poisoned by his long illness. "I don't have enough education to undertand all that," Kostrov decided. "I don't even know the words you need to think about it. But I feel that there is something to be worried about, only I don't know how to put it into words ... "

Kostrov had been sick since early childhood. As a matter of fact, he'd only been healthy the first year of his life, when he was safeguarded by the protective powers of his mother's body. But, of course, he didn't remember this year of his infancy. His first memory was of 'tonsilitis': compresses on his throat, the steamy dampness of sheets heated by his fever, a small table with medicines, a slippery thermometer under his arm, the doctor's cold fingers and the round end of a stethoscope moving up and down his chest and back. Later his tonsils were removed, the tonsilitis was gone, but it had already worked its damage: by the age of ten he suffered from rheumatic fever with constant relapses. Then came children's sanatoriums and a strange, ambiguous childhood alongside death, with constant separations from home and family, only part-time school attendance, and that with interruptions now and then of weeks and even months of complete rest, a childhood without soccer or a bicycle, where every movement had to be considered and every kind of fear was present: the sticky nighttime and the aching daytime fear invaded his mind in the midst of a little joy, a brief forgetfulness. He didn't know to what extent his friends shared this fear, children never talk about illness, but he knew that they, too, lived in fear, in constant awareness of their lack, inferiority, and isolation from other normal children. He developed a liking for reading trifling things, numbed himself with adventure novels like narcotics. He was lazy and careless about studying, because he didn't think that academic study would ever be of use to him. And he didn't go to an institute, but graduated with some simple drafting classes. All of a sudden his constitution became stronger. The constant weakness, perspiration, short-windedness and irregular pulse disappeared; now he could climb to the third floor without panting, and no longer woke up in the middle of the night afraid his heart had suddenly stopped. The body of a boy turning into an adult brought to light secret resources, and he seriously believed that this unique and unbelievable prize fell to him in order to save him. He got married and started studying for entrance into the institute; then when his twenty-third birthday was approaching, he became suddenly and abruptly worse, went to the hospital, then got dropsy, hemostasis in the large channel of the circulatory system, edema; then came the frightening verdict that could be read in the hospital personnel's eyes and the sudden recovery with somebody else's heart inside his chest.

With an astonishingly healthy heart—he was someone who could judge that. It would be interesting to know if the former owner of the heart had felt its perfection as a constant source of happiness or if he hadn't even paid any attention to it. After all, he, Kostrov, didn't take joy in his nose, ears, stomach, and lungs. But he felt his new heart all the time—it gave him calm, even, deep breathing and a pulse as regular as a metronome, a kind of joyful tickling behind his shoulders as if he were growing wings. So much lightness and strength had entered his body that he felt that all he needed was to get a good running start and jump, and he would fly. All the simple acts that had been so taxing before: to bend and tie his shoes, to get up out of bed after sleeping, to pick up something that had dropped to the floor— all of this had to be paid for with palpitations, a darkness before his eyes as if he were half-fainting, an unpleasant perspiration on his forehead—this all gave him pleasure now. "How easily people live, it turns out!" He had foreseen how many surprises awaited him once he left the hospital: to take a running jump onto a streetcar; to run up the staircase to his apartment, scorning the elevator; he could go to the swimming pool on Kropotkin Square in freezing weather and swim under the protection of its warm vapors; he could take up mountain-climbing; he would buy himself the tennis racket with taut strings that had so excited his imagination as a child, and a light sleek racing bicycle. He could roam the Moscow streets as much as he wanted, go to the country, pick mushrooms and berries, go on sightseeing trips, hunt, fish. He could work out and make his body as hard as iron so that it would be worthy of his new magnificent heart. He was going to get all he could out of life physically, he wouldn't smoke, but he'd certainly learn how to drink vodka and wine.

Kostrov thought that the doctor would want to see him once more before he left the hospital, but that didn't happen. Evidently he did that on purpose—he severed the ties, letting Kostrov enter his new life on his own. The doctor was probably right. Kostrov walked without the slightest confusion down the treadworn steps of the hospital staircase to his new life, into his mother's and wife's embraces and tears, into their hands, which fumbled helplessly over his face and shoulders. He rather regretted, nevertheless, that he hadn't seen the doctor one more time—something remained unsaid...

Kostrov didn't understand why the women were crying so bitterly, why their hands clung to him that way. Either they were afraid that he'd disappear, or doubted that it was really he. He'd become unused to them, he found their cold tears, wetting his face and cheeks, their moist lips, their appearance, untidy from sobbing, unpleasant. They kept hugging him, but he was looking out the glass door beyond which air and sunshine made themselves felt, and he was mad with desire to get out there as soon as possible. They finally calmed down; his wife found her compact, while his mother seized his bundle of things and headed for the street, where a taxi was waiting for them. After a short struggle—he wanted to sit with the cabby, but his mother insisted that he ride in back with his wife—they set off. His wife took his hands in her own in a tenacious clasp, and this abrupt tenderness seemed excessive to him. He experienced no inclination for touching, for a demonstration of closeness. He felt a closeness to the street, streetcars, trolleys, houses, the crowd, the balloon vendor, the ice-cream vendors, the bicyclists, children, shoeshine boys, the bare lindens and poplars, to every living and inanimate representative of the outside world. But this closeness didn't extend to those who were sitting beside him in the hard-seated box-like taxi. It felt as though both women, the old and the young one, had imposed the power of their tenderness on him by some dubious right known only to them. But he had come back from too far away to become a part of the old life so easily.

"Why don't you ask about anything?" his mother started tearfully. "You're sitting there like a stranger!.. "

"And what should I ask about?" Kostrov inquired with sincere surprise.

"Well, how we got along without you... How your friends are, how things are at the factory... "

"It's easy to imagine how you got along without me, but did I really have any friends? I don't remember, somehow. We used to have guests, but they all drank, ate, smoked, and made too much noise for me to feel their equal. And things at the factory, to tell you the truth, don't interest me at all. Mother's the director, so it's understandable that everything there is interesting and important to her, but an assistant draftsman really doesn't have to burden his weary soul with such concerns." Surprising even himself, he said aloud:

"I'm not going back to the factory."

"What do you mean?" his mother started up in fear.

"I'm going to prepare for the institute."

"Good for you!" his mother gave a childishly happy sob.

"So that's how upset she's been that I never had a higher education. And she never reproached me, not a single word. It's really great to have such a wonderful mom that will let her married son go to school and not work!" He looked at the back of his mother's head, at the thin gray bun lying on the somewhat worn sealskin collar of an unattractive man's coat and coldly reflected that his mother, who'd worked in a clothes factory her whole life, had never learned how to dress.

"Are you really completely well now?" his mother asked.

"Of course!" he answered absent-mindedly.

All at once he became uneasy: the car had left the quiet hospital zone and now was making its way along the Sadovoye Ring in heavy street traffic. He thought that the cabby was driving carelessly and recklessly. He had evidently gotten unused to the insane traffic in Moscow streets; besides which, he had rarely had to take a taxi, particularly during the day. The street swiftly absorbed them along with the other cars and trucks, menacing dump-trucks, buses, trolleys, speeding motorcyclists, and it sucked them into the narrow dark jaws of the tunnels, and he felt in his bones that it would end badly, that they'd be crushed, squashed, flattened like a tin can. His mother was saying something, probably sharing her usual bits of news, but he didn't hear her, he merely felt irritated by her voice, which seemed to be trying to distract him in the face of unavoidable catastrophe. And in an instant it happened: the car brakes screeched, he was shoved forward, thrown backward, he let out a heart-rending cry, and lost consciousness for a moment. When he came to, the car was quietly continuing on its way, but his mother's and wife's faces looked numb.

"I thought we'd crashed..." Kostrov mumbled.

"Oh, no," answered the cabby cheerfully, "it was just a pick-up getting in the wrong lane."

"You never used to be so nervous," his mother said despondently.

"I don't want to die again!" said Kostrov with a feigned grin. "One always worries about new things, and they did sort of put me together anew."

He knew that he wasn't saying the right thing at all, but he didn't understand the reason for his panicked scare...

...And there was his 'paternal abode,' a two-room apartment, where he and his wife lived in the larger room, his mother in the smaller one. Kostrov indifferently examined the light-colored Finnish furniture with the red upholstery, his drafting table with a piece of drafting paper tacked on it, the wide low double sofa that wasn't part of a bedroom set. It turned out that he felt no attachment to his home. He suddenly became saddened. When he'd come to believe that he would live, the image of home, familial love, safety, and comfort had begun to glow distinctly and tenderly in his mind, and without assuming the concrete form of faces and objects, it had settled in his heart like an undiluted warm clot. Evidently he had confused the future with the past. Exhausted as he had been by sickness into a kind of egotistic moroseness, he had had absolutely no capacity for being absorbed in family happiness, in that tearfully joyful love for those whom he held close—something of which he'd dreamed during his isolation in the hospital. It would probably come now that he would be able to live more peacefully, generously, and sincerely through his surroundings.

And again he sensed a peculiar falsehood in his reasoning.

"Is there something for us to munch on?" he said jokingly, wishing to dispel the unaccountable coldness of the reunion. "I've become as ravenous as a boa-constrictor."

"Oh, you!" His mother forced a smile. "You should see the dinner we've prepared!" And she suddenly burst out crying, the small tears pouring straight down from her faded greenish eyes.

"What's wrong with you?" asked Kostrov, hiding his annoyance behind concern.

"It's nothing... You must understand... What a joy it is!.. "

"Mama's lying too," he observed privately. "I wonder if my wife is going to lie..?"

It was just after eleven when they went to bed. Something hadn't worked out, although on the surface everything looked as it should. Dinner was a success, and there had been excited phone calls from his mother's friends and his own, and nobody asked any tactless questions, everyone was gentle and sensitive, but this didn't move him much, since he didn't feel in touch with people. They decided not to invite anybody, to spend this unusual evening as a family, but they broke up unexpectedly early because they ran out of things to talk about. His wife, taciturn by nature, sat as if sealed, and his mother, despite all her forced talkativeness, couldn't keep up the conversation alone. If only her son had asked about somethng, shown the smallest interest in her life, but he kept quiet and only now and then smiled absent-mindedly. And then suddenly, somehow tired out all at once and with a heavy heart, his mother fell silent, then took a deep breath, and mumbled heavily as if to herself: "None of that's important, the main thing is that you've come back,"—and she went to her room.

Whether he had come back was exactly what Kostrov wasn't sure of. To come back in the full sense of the word, he would have to come back sick, but there wasn't any sickness, and because of this he didn't perceive his surroundings as the stuff of habit, as forms of his existence.

"Shall I sleep on the cot?" asked his wife.

"Why?" laughed Kostrov. "Have you really become that unused to me?.."

He suddenly stopped short of inexplicable embarrassment. For an instant he felt as if he'd blurted out something indecent. He himself had become so unused to his wife that he no longer felt 'of one body' with her. From the corner of his eye he saw his wife unbutton her polyester blouse, remove it with a movement of her plump shoulders, and hang it on the back of a chair. He admired the soft contour of her neck and shoulders. Then she pulled her tweed skirt over her head: the heavy fabric moved over her body slowly. Kostrov was overcome with excitement. His wife's head got stuck in the material, which caught on her chin, her hairpins, and comb. "A pretty woman," thought Kostrov, "I'm lucky."

"Turn round!.. What are you gaping for?" his wife shouted.

Kostrov quickly looked away and only later did it strike him that such modesty hadn't been a part of their relationship before: his wife had been comfortable naked in front of him. This meant that his wife felt estranged from him as well. It surprised him that he thought about her with detachment. Did he love his wife? Most likely his illness had directed him there as well. He couldn't wait to take advantage of the gleam of hope in the darkness of the night, and had married the first girl who'd caught his eye. Of course, that wasn't love. But, did she love him?

Kostrov slipped under the blanket. It was nice to feel the taut coolness of the lightly starched sheets. And then the sofa sagged and a large woman's body stretched out next to him. He was overcome by an incredible, strange, shameful animal lust for that body. He turned over and violently pulled the woman to him.

She cried afterwards. Why do they always cry?.. She suddenly became talkative, which had been unusual for her before, especially in bed. She had never felt so good, so complete with him, but for some reason she wasn't herself, as if they'd done something forbidden, as if she'd robbed somebody. She touched his face with wet trembling fingertips, reassuring herself that it was he, the one person in the world whose duty it was to protect her, save her from all misfortune. But he, completely devastated, exhausted, and indifferent, couldn't respond to her. The storm that had replaced his former weak tenderness hadn't left him strength for considerate pretense. She carefully cuddled under his chin. And he divined that in spite of the tears and the confusion she wasn't unhappy now. Her trusting attitude and the warmth of her tired body and her deep even breathing were signs of a total and joyful experience.

But he lay with his eyes open, without even trying to fall asleep. Through the window he could see the city night, the illuminated sky; and the stars, barely distinguishable in the electric glow of the streetlights and advertisements, were carried even farther from the earth. And Kostrov thought that his real life was somewhere there amidst the most distant stars.

In the morning for a long time he closely examined the sleeping face of his wife, an ordinary and mysterious face, shiny with the moistness of sleep. It could have revealed something to him, or at least have prompted him, given him a hint, but the face was impenetrable, like a fresh sheet of drafting paper that had just been tacked down onto his drafting table.

She sensed his excessively fixed stare through her sleep and moaned quietly, discontentedly. He turned to the window again. There morning was breaking in an ashy-rose haze. As with every half-finished product, it was almost impossible to discern in this haze the shape of what it would became. An hour devoid of associations was no use to Kostrov. He would remain in isolation until the final break of day...

...Kostrov didn't understand himself or his place in the life that had been given back to him. At times he thought that they'd returned him to the wrong place by mistake. He couldn't stay home for an hour more than necessary. And not only because his new, healthy, magnificent heart needed exercise (it forced him to roam the city endlessly, it led him past the outskirts, to brown April fields and bare swelling groves), but also because he felt like an imposter at home. Of course, there hadn't been any mention of studying for the institute, but they didn't reproach him for his idleness. Both his mother and his wife treated him like some alien fragile treasure that had been given to them for safekeeping . His mother tried not to go outside the routine of everyday necessities; his wife, having grasped the main point of that night, didn't try to break the magic circle of vagueness.

He lived peculiarly. Flights of violent physiological happiness—from walks, exercising, going to the pool—were followed by wretched listlessness. He didn't feel comfortable at home with his family or visiting the homes of so-called friends. We think that people live in an enormous world, in an infinity called humanity. That's a falsehood: our life is a performance with a highly limited number of characters, the rest is the crowd, the corps de ballet; the chorus is something amorphous, almost conventional, which doesn't imprint itself on our consciousness as "the individual expression of a face." The people who made up Kostrov's circle had also been in his life many years ago, the majority of them had appeared in the days of childhood and adolescence. Each carried in him a small part of the past to which Kostrov was as indifferent as to the present. At times, particularly at night, before falling asleep or on the verge of waking, he was struck by the pleasant belief that the most important, the indispensable people would still materialize, that he'd simply forgotten about them in the nightmare of his illness and dying. But then he would suddenly remember that all his life's companions were present, if he didn't count those who'd sunk into eternity long ago: his father, who'd died of heart disease when Kostrov wasn't yet five years old and friends at the sanatoriums who'd died of the same thing at various times.

He was searching, in the same way that people and entire nations had searched, for the Promised Land. What kind of land it was—whether it had rivers of milk and honey flowing along it or whether it was choked by weeds like an abandoned cemetery—was immaterial, this is your land, the only one, in all others you're a foreigner.

He set his sights on all passersby, trees, fences, posters, store windows, snow-removal machines, the benches and urns on the boulevards, streetlights, the sparrows fluttering in the smelly stream of manure, the shaggy bags of crow's nests and the doves, puffed up with self-importance. Whenever he went to the stadium or pool, he never took the same route twice; he unfailingly took a new street, alley, or communicating courtyard, or at least a through entrance, even if he had to make a detour to do so. He examined the features of the houses and courtyards greedily, listening intently to himself to see whether an unconscious recognition would respond with a tug at his heart, with an excited rush of blood.

He hated his old dead heart, the source of all his suffering and torments; he saw it as a rotten, worm-eaten mushroom—a flaccid fungus, but it carried inside those tender, delicate memories about him that he needed to build up again in order to achieve a full recovery.

He had already guessed something about several things. For instance, he now thought that he hadn't loved his wife in his first existence. Had he loved his mother? He couldn't find the answer. It looked as if a person with an illness like his wasn't capable of real love in general; the constant fear for oneself, which allowed no respite, was too great. Perhaps in other people, however, the fear of an inescapable and imminent end didn't extinguish love for the life of others, but he, Kostrov, obviously didn't belong to that select number. Nevertheless, surely he hadn't lived only on fear and alienation? Even he had probably experienced bursts of unselfish joy, at least moments of happiness and goodness, when he forgot about his illness and loved something outside of himself. Those moments, imprinted in forms of the material world, were what he was searching for now, hoping through them to recreate his life's soul, to find a capacity for love and tears.

And these blinding bursts of joy, even happiness, sometimes occurred unexpectedly, inexplicably, catching him by surprise. They arose from the most unexpected and strange sources: once it was an old dovecote lightly powdered with April snow in a small courtyard not far from Ksenya Godunova's room on Chertolsky Lane. An ordinary dovecote—a wooden box, enclosed in a thick rusted netting. No matter how he racked his brain, he couldn't grasp the significance of the dovecote in his 'former existence.'

He understood that the joy he felt was above all joy in this very instinctive recognition; it didn't necessarily mean that the dovecote at some time had been a source of pleasure for him. If he had been a street kid, the symbol of the dovecote could have been figured out easily; but as a pampered child he'd never chased pigeons.

Maybe there was a mistake here: had the dovecote taken on the role of a symbol falsely, by association, so to speak, and the true meaning wasn't in it at all, but in Ksenya Godunova's room? Maybe at some time he had been moved by the sad and gentle image of Godunov's unhappy daughter,[3] not guilty of anything before God and man, but raised in the proximity of crime, and so doomed to a harsh retribution? No, he hadn't had any such clearcut relationship with Godunov's daughter. But what if Chertolsky Lane itself, after enticing him with the dovecote, had played some role in his emotional life? No, he hadn't been there before...

Later on he became convinced that both the direct and the roundabout methods of speculations weren't right. He had watched sparrows a hundred times: in flight, as they alighted, in a heated quarrel over food, and then suddenly one time, God knows why, he experienced an almost painful stab of happiness at the sight of a sparrow. What governed the experience: the place, the time of day, the light? He didn't find the answer.

Once, after working out, he was walking down the long hallway in the stadium to the showers, a terrycloth robe thrown over his shoulders. Four girls carrying small suitcases walked past him. His wandering gaze slid over the unknown girls and paused slightly on the round, freckled face and heavy gray eyes of one of them. She was by no means the most attractive of the bunch and stood out only on account of her sullen, rather 'shut-in' expression.

The noisy group passed him, overflowing with simple laughter, twittering voices, and a clean, soft girlish fragrance, and he suddenly wanted to see the girl with the heavy sullen eyes again. But the main door had already banged shut behind them and he had only a robe on. Several minutes later, while standing under the shower, he recalled the gray-eyed girl again and moaned with pain. A feeling of irrevocable loss, swift and stifling, seized him. And accompanying it and aggravating the pain, small soapy bubbles of happiness kept appearing and bursting near his heart. What was this gray-eyed, sullen, in no way remarkable, girl with the small suitcase to him? What kind of complex or simple ties had bound them in the past? And was it worth disturbing the past every time? And what if it was a momentary burst of being in love? But why would this feeling of being in love, just barely arisen, assume the guise of deadening melancholy and the hopelessness of loss? Fleeting love is a light feeling, the shadow of happiness and the shadow of sadness. But he felt as if a stake had been driven through his heart. Angry with himself, he turned on the cold water. It was as if an ice pack had been slapped on his temples, icy coldness crept from his neck to his shoulders, back, and further over his entire body, but the heartaching melancholy didn't subside; it was independent of the rest of his being.

Now his unaccountable searching had found a goal: he had to find the gray-eyed girl. She would help him unravel the knot. But this turned out to be a hopeless endeavor. Thousands of people walked through the winter stadium, dozens of different groups played there, and he didn't even know if the girl was an athlete. She might just as easily be a doctor, masseuse, nurse, student intern, or just a fan. Sullen gray eyes—for him this was a momentous feature, but everyone else to whom he turned just made a helpless gesture with a bewildered and derisive look.

The longer he searched for her, the more certain he became that the gray-eyed girl was not a conventional sign of some past experience: in the obscure past he used to meet her and know her name, she had meant something in his life...

A frightening thought arose in him: as soon as he acknowledged his former heart's right of memory, then the heart that was now beating in his chest possessed a similar sovereign memory. Nonsense, madness, myth, as the doctor who had cured him said. Now Kostrov began to understand the meaning of his vague apprehensions. But no, a heart isn't omnipotent, and having 'agreed' to live in another body, it was obliged to recognize all of its laws.

There was only one way to put an end to this 'mythology': to love his family, to have faith in his friends—then the fanciful images, with the pointless torments they inflicted, would be extinguished and a serious outward existence would begin, putting an end to this damned emotional lunacy.

He became a stay-at-home; he heaped attention on his mother and wife; he constantly reminded himself how they loved him, how much concern, patience, tactfulness, and forgiveness he received from them. And how meagerly he paid them for all their goodness. He began to live for what interested them; he asked his mother in detail about things at the factory; gave them presents of mimosa and snowdrops, helped them around the house; and finally, to make their happiness complete, he started to prepare for his entrance into the institute. He was shocked when once he accidentally overheard a conversation between his mother and an old friend of hers. His mother for some reason had decided that he wasn't at home and was speaking in the loud voice in which elderly people and people who are hard of hearing usually talk on the telephone.

"It's as if they substituted him... I don't understand anything, but sometimes I feel as if they gave us back a robot. He knows all the words and all the rules of behavior, but he's cold iron. No, no, I've got nothing to complain about, he was never so attentive and thoughtful as he is now. But inside he's empty, I don't feel him, I don't recognize my own blood..."

He didn't listen any further; he was stunned not so much by his mother's words, which revealed to him the similarity in their perception of each other, as by her cold tone. She talked about him as if he were a stranger who irritated rather than saddened her. He didn't say anything to his mother, didn't change his behavior, but his feeling of homelessness became unbearable.

... Kostrov was coming back from the library by subway. An elderly woman in a round fur hat and a coat with the same kind of collar got out of the next car at Sverdlov station. Her salt and pepper hair was gathered in a bun and lay neatly on the shabby sealskin collar that had a rust-colored tint. He recalled returning from the hospital: when they were riding in the taxi, he had looked at the back of his mother's head and had seen the same kind of gray bun on a worn fur collar. While he was standing by the door, Kostrov absent-mindedly glanced at the faces of the people who were getting in and out, but the elderly woman for some reason attracted his gaze. With an incomprehensible curiosity he looked at her reddish, sclerous, ordinary face, the tired eyes beneath wrinkled eyelids, the mole at the corner of her pale sad mouth. Her face was neither pretty nor kind, but something about it struck Kostrov. This tired, worn, unhappy, harsh face, which bore with extraordinary openness the burden of time, adversity, loss, and disappointment, snatched Kostrov out of the commonplace, set him spinning, carried him somewhere like tumbleweed in a whirlwind. And there was a terrifying fall into a bottomless depth, darkness, and the damp tightness of pre-existence, and then an unbearable light which he couldn't shut out by closing his eyes, and the taste of sweet milk on his lips, and that drugged blissful feeling you get when you're on a swing or take giant strides as in the best moments of early childhood, when the nighttime fears and the day's hurts have been driven away and great protection, great safety, are guaranteed by the closeness of the most indispensable and all-powerful being in the universe. And all this was contained in the one short word that involuntarily and pathetically tore from Kostrov's lips when he darted off, cutting through the crowd coming out of the subway car:

"Mama!.."

The woman heard this strange childlike cry, uttered in a man's rough voice. She wasn't familiar with the voice, and the cry wasn't directed at her, of course, but she turned round, nevertheless, with the habitual pained expression with which she responded to every reminder of her missing son. She saw a young man with a sweaty, crazed, apparently drunken face tearing out of the subway car through the crowd of pushing people. And even though she didn't deceive herself for a moment, the fact that this stranger was almost the same age as her lost son and that he was gadding about, exuding the crude strength of life, when the body of her boy had rotted God knows where, filled her with indignation.

"What's the matter with you, are you drunk?.." she shouted with revulsion.

A dense crowd surrounded Kostrov. Someone was already calling for a policeman and one stepped out of the attendant's booth with the heavy stride of a commander toward the pulsating crowd at the edge of the platform. Kostrov didn't notice anything. He saw only that the elderly woman was about to disappear from his sight—and shouted in despair:

"Where are you going?.."

The woman stopped as if she had been hit on the breast with a fist. She didn't understand what had happened and didn't attempt to understand it; she didn't know what awaited her—salvation or destruction. She recognized her son's heartache and rushed to heed the call.

1968   Translated by Helena Goscilo

Notes

The original ("Chuzhoe serdtse") first appeared in *Znamia*, No. 6 (1968), 105-114. The present translation is of the edition included in the two-volume 1973 collection, I, 430-445.

1. Peter Freikhen is a contemporary Danish hunter-explorer and fan of Herman Melville who lived in Eurasia, and lost a leg during an expedition.

2. *King Solomon's Mines* (1885) is a colorful adventure novel about South Africa by Sir Henry Rider Haggard (1856-1925), who also authored the African tales *She* (1887) and *The Ivory Child* (1916) and an assortment of historical romances with exotic settings.

3. Ksenya Borisovna Godunova (?-1622) was the daughter of Boris Godunov, Tsar of Russia during the Time of Troubles (1598-1605). She was to marry Duke John, the younger brother of King Christian of Denmark, but in 1602 he died of a sudden illness only three months after his arrival in Russia and before the marriage took place. Upon her father's death and the accession of the false Dimitry, Ksenya briefly became the latter's mistress and then was dispatched to a convent, where she apparently remained until her death. In a work ascribed to Prince Ivan M. Katyryov-Rostovsky (?-1640), Ksenya is described as touchingly beautiful, virtuous, and possessing remarkable mental faculties. Probably her greatest literary fame rests on her lament for her dead beloved in Pushkin's play *Boris Godunov*.

Shurik

We despised Shurik together. With gold silky curls to his shoulders, enormous blue eyes under thick long lashes darker than his hair, with a round chin, softly and rawly formed, he was loathsomely like a girl. Not only that, that nonentity, that momma's boy, wasn't ashamed to ask for the pottie in front of everyone. It didn't occur to him for that there existed the walls of the summerhouse, the fence, the trees, the balls on the flowerbeds, or if the worst came to worst, the wooden box for starlings in the summer lavatory hidden in the blood-red thicket of elder.

He was spoiled and petted by his parents, aunts, grandmother, and in general by all adults, which aggravated our aversion to him—an aversion caused by jealousy. This pathetic creature, who was afraid of frogs and field mice, who couldn't swim or climb trees or play skittles, was constantly held up to us as an example: Shurik never stole apples, didn't jump out of windows, didn't leap over fences, didn't dive into the Ucha from the steep slope of the bank, didn't disappear God knows where for whole days, didn't fight and didn't hit girls, didn't tear clothes, didn't lose his sandals, didn't come home with his nose smashed, his eye blackened, his knees cut up and bloody; he didn't bawl songs, didn't emit Indian, cowboy, and pirates' yells, didn't curse, didn't act fresh with adults and didn't shoot a toy pistol or a homemade Monte Cristo[1] from morning till night. No one ever complained about him. In a word, this boy, endowed with all negative virtues, was a perpetual live reproach to us, and the summer gang paid him back in full for all these humiliations. When picking mushrooms we tried to lead him into the depths of the forest and abandoned him there; concealing ourselves, we'd listen to Shurik "hallooo" at first, then call us in an increasingly thin voice, and finally break out into howls. Then we'd come out of our hiding place, and with an air of innocent amazement we'd reproach Shurik for intending to lose his friends and reward him with slaps. Our favorite entertainment when swimming was to drag Shurik into the deep water and to watch him flounder helplessly, choking on the water with silt in it and emitting bubbles.

Shurik endured all this with enviable meekness, and never complained

213

to the adults. That didn't stop us from teasing him with false accusations and beating him for imaginary denunciations. His defenselessness, patience, and lack of malice only fired the fierce ardor of his persecutors.

We didn't miss a chance to talk about how Shurik's presence didn't fit in with decent company.

"Yesterday he asked for the pottie ten times," Galya informed us.

"He eats semolina in the mornings," said Vera the sleepwalker authoritatively in a slow tragic voice.

The gathering responded with a unanimous groan: to eat semolina was considered not simply shameful, but criminal.

"I know why he's so curly-haired," said fat Ronya. "They curl his hair with tongs every day."

And although everyone knew that that was a lie and that Ronya with her two sparse braids thinner than a mouse's tail mortally envied Shurik's fluffy curls, a groan of wrath and indignation sounded again.

"There was a real scene yesterday!" said Big Vovka, choking with laughter. "Rex got loose and went straight for Shurik! And Shurik shook his finger at him like he was a kitten or something... 'Noo, noo, noo!... Or I'll slap your fanny!' " he mimicked, making a face.

"And what did Rex do?" inquired Katya the gypsy lazily, as befits a beauty.

"Said to hell with it and walked away. Who wants to get mixed up with a fool!"

I don't remember what my friends did, but I no longer laughed. Rex was an enormous and nasty German shepherd; they didn't even dare take him off his chain at night. It would have been interesting to see how Big Vovka or any one of us would have acted if Rex had lunged at him?... But Shurik shook his finger at the man-eater: don't do that, or you'll get your fanny slapped!—and the man-eater spared such a defenseless and fearless creature.

Something in me felt moved toward Shurik. I recalled with what a sweet trusting smile he'd meet us, his persecutors, in the mornings, as though hoping that all the ugliness had ended and that we'd start being friends with him. And how pathetically that smile died at our usual cruel tricks, which caused him emotional rather than physical suffering. How humbly he trailed after us to the river and the forest, keeping at a respectful distance not out of fear, but so as not to irritate us, so that we wouldn't chase him away. And suddenly I also realized that Shurik was indifferent to the caresses and raptures of the adults, and reached out to us alone.

How I'd like to say that from that time on I took Shurik under my protection, made peace between him and the kids, and that the little sufferer finally tasted the sweetness of friendship. Not at all. I belonged to the gang and involuntarily obeyed its unwritten laws. And the gang remained merciless to Shurik. The story with Rex perhaps intensified the hostility to him. How could such a sniveler, the pottie-user, the 'angel' of all the old women at the summerhouse retreat have been not afraid, not taken to his heels, not wet his pants? One would think that Shurik had mastered himself so as to have revenge on us all. Of course, such considerations were entertained in secret; aloud Shurik's behavior was explained as stupidity and shameful confusion in the face of danger. We got into the habit of shaking our fingers threateningly at each other and also at stray dogs, at the landlady's goat, which was apt to butt, at the massive bull that walked past the summerhouse fence to the common pasture every day: "Noo, noo, noo, or I'll slap your fanny!"

And Shurik left us alone. Not right away—it was clear that it wasn't easy for him to decide to do that. At the beginning he still toddled behind us half way, then only followed us with a long melancholy look, his small face under the cap of gold hair wry, and finally an awakened pride gave him strength; he left us alone for good.

I felt relieved: the necessity of persecuting Shurik oppressed me. But my friends started feeling the lack of something. An outcast was necessary so that the others, in recognizing their superiority, would reciprocate in forgiving each other all their shortcomings. Fat Ronya was the first to suffer for our not having Shurik at hand. Big Vovka started jeering at her. We still stayed together, but the inner unity of the gang collapsed: Ronya stuck to Katya and doomed herself to the dull role of a plain girl at the side of a beautiful girlfriend, I became friendly with Galya, and Big Vovka, a bullying, derisive boy, suddenly discovered some unusual virtues in the half-asleep Vera, the sleepwalker.

Shurik existed quietly and unobtrusively, like a mouse; we saw almost nothing of him. But once, on a Sunday, a day that I disliked, when even the adults became sickeningly affectionate one moment, then unrecognizably estranged the next, completely immersed in their own world, which was inaccessible to us—and the world rolled on, topsy turvy, in a mad crush, music, songs, dances, kisses, and quarrels—I wandered off into the birch forest at the edge of the garden and there discovered Shurik and his father. While still at a distance I heard their loud happy laughter; I neared them unnoticed, and proved a witness to a strange scene.

"Man-monkey!" announced Shurik.

He drew his head down into his shoulders, lowered his arms almost down to the ground, bent his knees, and began jumping, touching the grass with his knuckles, first in one direction, then another, and finally he made straight for his father. He bared his fangs, gave a snarl, and his father, who was sitting under a birch, fell onto his back in horror, and Shurik leaped at him, gnashing his teeth, and they started rolling about and laughing, like the happiest people in the world.

Yet he, Shurik's father, wasn't the happiest person in the world at all. His wife, Shurik's mother, was happy—a stately beauty with the same golden curls as her son, the same enormous blue eyes and a crimson mouth, slightly parted, that breathed slowly and audibly.

Though her mouth became crimson and her breathing sonorous only on Sundays, when guests came to visit her: a tall thin lawyer in a snowy white tunic and a stocky young engineer in a tussore silk jacket and an engineer's cap pushed onto the back of his head. They drank wine all day, the lawyer played the guitar, Shurik's mother sang and breathed heavily through her crimson mouth. Shurik was left to his father's care.

His father had a habit when listening to his interlocutor of inclining his head toward his shoulder in an excess of respectful attention. For this we gave him an idiotic English nickname—"Comma." At times Comma would behave in a funny way, sending his wife into a rage. For example, once he bought an enormous watermelon in Moscow, but didn't have enough strength to drag it the three kilometers from the station, and he rolled the watermelon in front of him with his feet like a football all the way. All the summer vacationers were invited to demolish that wonder of a watermelon. Comma solemnly cut the watermelon, which crunched and almost burst beneath the knife from ripeness, but inside, it turned out to be filled with dark water, which all its pulp had turned into.

Such incidents didn't occur that often really—Comma's main concern was not to draw attention to himself. It's easy to imagine my amazement at the sight of two quiet people—father and son—gamboling about so noisily in self-oblivion beyond the area of the Sunday festivities. And also I discovered that, contrary to general opinion, Shurik resembled not his mother, but his father, though their features didn't match.

"Well, and who'll we have next?" asked his father. "I think we've already had everything?"

"And now we'll have the man-fish!" announced Shurik and suddenly started swimming toward his father.

He didn't swim like a human—he couldn't swim like that—but like a real fish, making a smooth arc with a sharp push forward, moving his fins and his gills.

Of course, now Shurik's invention no longer seems so startling, but there was no famous Ichthyandr[2] then, and Shurik was the first to create for me—moreover, not on paper, but in reality—am amphibious human being.

I withdrew from the birches soundlessly, but I emerged over the fence a man-fish. I made all the motions much more unskillfully, more crudely, than Shurik, but the joy of staying in a strange form didn't decrease on account of that. My God, how my imagination worked in those moments when I moved, wriggling, along the path which ran around the summerhouse, what boundless sweet possibilities opened up before a man-fish! And as I got tired from the long stay in the depths of the water, I perceived fully the grandeur of the discovery Shurik had made. Now I became in turn a man-beast, a man-bird, a man-snake. We had often played at wild beasts, had frequently imagined ourselves as mustangs, monkeys, kangaroos, eagles—that was all nonsense: under another's skin the human essense was lost. But to exist in a dual form, to fit a human's assets and appearance with the splendor of his dumb brothers' characteristics—that was a bliss not to be compared to anything!

Nice Shurik, how alone he was if he had lit upon the idea of inhabiting various creatures and in doing so, conquering his weakness, his desertion, the barrenness of dull days! I'm going to be friends with him, I thought, not only this summer, but next; I heard he'd be coming here again...

Those good intentions weren't realized. Our summer vacationing old ladies, the shark-like Fates, while admiring Shurik, after their usual: "An an-gil! Yes, seriously, an an-gil!" inevitably kept adding, with a profound and gloomy conviction: "He's not long for this world." Now many beliefs that used to be considered ignorant superstition have been rehabilitated: a charm has turned out to be a suggestion that healed—hypnosis; mould—penicillin. Perhaps folk experience possesses the ability to penetrate within elflike beings to their hopeless frailty.

That fall Shurik died of membraneous pneumonia.

Poor, poor little man-fish!...

1968   Translated by Helena Goscilo

Notes

The original ("Shurik") first appeared in *Nash sovremennik,* No. 6 (1968), 52-56. The present translation is of the edition included in the 1973 two-volume collection, II, 278-283.

1. A Monte Cristo is a single-shot pistol.

2. Ichthyandr is the hero of the novel by the science fiction writer Aleksandr Belyayev (1884-1942) entitled *Man-Amphibian* (Chelovek-amfibia, 1928).

The Peak of Success
(A Modern Fairy Tale)

They came out of the National Palace located behind the high fortress wall that had been erected as far back as the Middle Ages and then built up over the centuries against the ever-increasing enemy powers that besieged it. When it reached the limits of fortification perfection, the wall was transformed into the city's scenery, for methods of attack had developed much faster than means of defense, and all its power, thickness, height, and the mass of loopholes for arms had become a sham before the crushing forces of the attackers' weapons. But the wall was beautiful: in its loopholes the sky seemed much bluer than the sky of the town—it was the sky of ancient tales and legends; the doves above its towers never descended to earth to look for food in the rubbish of the streets; the grass on the sloping descent from the foot of the walls to the wooden pavement of the square, the asphalt of the embankment, and the cast-iron railing of the park was incredibly green, with a metallic stormy sheen when the north wind blew.

They came out of the fortress gates, and the main tower, which bore the name of the Tower of Time, let fall a full resounding stroke; as though falling into the water—Guy thought he heard a splash—time absorbed the moment sounded by the chimes the way a river receives a stone. Guy listened intently, but the remaining eleven chimes were absorbed by his own ear, and the mysterious substance that contains our being no longer manifested itself.

"What an amazing and sinister invention a clock is!" thought Guy, looking at the enormous black tower disk with the gold arrows of its hands and the signs of the zodiac instead of numerals around the circumference. "It's the overseer of death who doesn't let us forget for a moment that the shagree skin of life is shrinking inexorably."[1]

As always, recently, the thought of death was unpleasant to him. Before, he didn't use to think about death in general; he failed to take it into consideration to such an extent that he never attended the funerals not only of relatives and those close to him, but also the few people whom he admired. He wanted to have his own funeral pass as simply, quickly, and inconspicuously as possible. Death is the end of life, and life is only interesting when the greatest miracle of creation—the human being—is working. As for the various nice pieces of nonsense about dissolution in nature and new forms of existence that come after the disintegration of our earthly shell, Guy didn't want to listen to such rubbish. Death is talentless, it's capable only of destroying, and Guy didn't want to have any falsely significant relations with it. But recently a fear had entered him...

Moore noticed the glance that Guy cast at the clock, but interpreted it in his own way.

"You're probably sad that the hour of your greatest and inimitable triumph is passing?" he asked in his greasy voice, to which he tried in vain to lend a shade of subtle irony.

"What are you talking about?" Guy didn't understand.

Moore looked rather wildly at his companion. He himself knew how to dissemble splendidly, but other people's dissembling—a forbidden device calculated to disorient those around one—exasperated him to the depths of his soul. Surely the beast wasn't going to pretend that he wasn't going mad with joy? Why's your face so pale even now, Guy, whiter than your starched collar?

You've acquired an unpleasant absentmindedness recently... Either you don't hear or don't understand what's said to you. Or rather, you pretend not to understand. Must one really pay for success with the loss of good manners?

Like a diver surfacing from the bottom of the sea Guy slowly returned to reality: there was a gleam of coral encrustations, seaweed quivered and curled, monstrous fish shook their bodies and fins, then the semi-transparent green of the water parted, the sun streamed in his eyes, and earthly reality took the form of the massive, satin-cheeked face of Professor Moore, with his brown, naked, and therefore somehow defenseless, eyes— the sleek pedigree, substantial, and unhappy face of an envier.

Guy squirmed inwardly—his new, recently-acquired perceptiveness was disagreeable. He didn't want anything new in himself; that only sharpened his sense of loss. He wanted to stay just the same as before, to the very last detail of his most profound essence and his outer behavior. He wasn't the least cheered at the sudden discovery that the well-known, almost renowned, Professor Moore, a member and correspondent of many academies—with whom he'd struggled together over one and the same problem for a little under a quarter of a century, known similar illuminations, failures, hopes and disappointments—that talented, strong patient man, as Guy thought, selflessly devoted to science, was seized with black envy. And feeling sorry for Moore, Guy did for him what he wouldn't have done for anyone else.

"Don't be angry. I'm really in a bad way—my wife's left me."

Moore was shorter; he stood, his eyes lowered, and the gaze of his naked brown eyes rested on his interlocutor's chest. He saw a dark, skillfully knotted tie, the high, short lapels of an excellently-cut suit of tightly-woven strong material, and in the buttonhole of the left lapel, the large (indecently large), gold (flashy gold!) medal with the inscription: "To the Benefactor of Mankind." My God, it had all happened!... And those festivities that he'd had to attend hadn't been just a nightmare! There had been trumpets and violins, and speeches, incredible in their sincere grandiloquence, hurried and breathless speeches, so that there weren't enough words or gestures, and the speakers finished with tears and a check for a million dollars and the special award of the Nobel prize—that was the first time it had happened since the founding of the Nobel Institute—and academic honors of all kinds, and finally, the peak of it all—the mark of universal recognition and gratitude—the gold medal "To the Benefactor of Mankind," with a diploma signed by the heads of all the governments existing on earth.

God, and to think all this could have fallen to his, Moore's, lot! But he'd bet on the wrong horse. Who'd have thought that success lay in the most uncertain route, compromised and rejected by all the specialists! Why had Guy clung so tenaciously to antiviruses? From the stupidity, tiredness, hopelessness, and blindness of a petty soul? Now it would be called by a bluff word—genius. But how had it happened that an average researcher who didn't seem to stand out from the crowd suddenly refused to give a damn about all the world authorities and moved forward all alone on an abandoned path? Then he really must be a genius, or if not a genius, then a fanatic, an obsessed, superior madman?... A fine fanatic, a fine madman, getting his clothes made by the best tailor and knotting his tie with the coquettishness of a restaurant fop! A genius doesn't have the mental time for such nonsense. A hundred percent banal man, an average *intelligent* is the most crass type nowadays. But he *does* have something!... Industriousness, persistence, and, of couse, a fairly good clear brain. Yet he did win his million by chance. It's not the first time such a thing's happened in the lackluster history of mankind. Columbus stumbled upon America, thinking, moreover, that it was India, and it's considered that he *discovered* it, that is, committed a conscious act of will. Guy also stumbled upon something... True, unlike Columbus, he stumbled upon what he was looking for. But Columbus was truly great in his fanaticism, faith, vitality, unselfishness, whereas Guy.... But who cares about all that now? Guy is the benefactor of mankind, and everyone else isn't worth a dime. Guy has made thousands of other researchers who have given their mind and soul to the problem unemployed. Now there's nothing for them to do. To adapt the new method to every possible variety of the disease is the job of the average worker at the newly-built "Guy's World Institute." That's the point—that Guy discovered a *universal* method for the complete cure of cancer!...

"But why did he tell me that his wife left him? What's that got to do with me? And what's that got to do with him, that an insignificant stupid woman, who for sure is howling with grief for having missed the boat, has left him. Now there's a really stupid woman for you—she threw a million dollars and the title of 'Mrs. Benefactor of Mankind' down the drain! And who is she, his wife? Probably God knows what, since I haven't even heard of her. He can't seriously be suffering from such a loss!... He threw me that bone to console me. As if to say, don't envy me, I'm an unhappy man too... That means he's guessed about my envy!..." Moore felt that he was suffocating. "What gall to tell me about this woman whom no one needs, what meanness to pretend to be unhappy in front of me, whose life he's made absurd, what boorishness to guess that I'm unhappy..."

There was an unpleasant pressure on the back of his head, and his temples were squeezed by a band. Don't be in a hurry to die! In a month a monument to this lucky fellow will be standing in Central Square, a monument during the fellow's lifetime, to "The Great Healer from Grateful Mankind," then you can come and croak at the foot of the monument in praise of the vile triumph of blind success!...

Moore turned round abruptly and without saying goodbye, strode off. It was an instinctive impulse of self-preservation. His whole nervous system and his circulatory system were on the brink; a few minutes more in Guy's unbearable proximity and something irrevocable would happen. By fleeing he was saving his blood vessels, his heart, his reason, perhaps his very life...

Guy didn't attach any significance to Professor Moore's departure, or, rather, his flight. As soon as he'd mentioned his wife, he had immediately withdrawn into his own pain and had become incapable of any intercourse. He didn't discuss his domestic misfortune with anyone and it was the first time he'd brought it up himself, affected as he was by Moore's envious suffering. Because he himself was suffering he simply felt pity for a man who was suffering...

His wife had become like a cancerous lump, and here his universal method didn't help. A lump can be ignored for a long time, but a single careless movement can arouse either an instantaneous sharp pain that passes quickly, or a long dull nagging one. He, however, constantly felt the presence of alien regenerated cells in himself, but at times he was able to not think about the illness, to switch himself off from it and live as if nothing had happened. At times the illness forced him to engage in self-analysis, to drag all his hidden pain into the open so as to give him the opportunity for a scientific analysis from behind some sort of barrier. And it was then that it was good to be alone. In general it's good when one's acquaintances leave, go away, don't turn up for an appointment, don't call by phone at the appointed time, forget about an arranged meeting. These unexpected gifts of freedom, time, the absence of involvement with nonsense—these are truly precious. How nice, kind and tactful you are, you inattentive, scatter-brained, careless people!

Mentally thanking Moore for his sudden departure, Guy forgot about him completely; he set off in the other direction along the city wall toward the river.

The river didn't color the life of the city; it wasn't its symbol, like the Thames, the Neva, or the Seine. Only tourist yachts occasionally disturbed its limp, flabby smoothness. The turbid water covered with a film of oil didn't reflect the sky and was therefore untouched by the play of blue and gold that showed lightly iridescent at the granite shores. But when Guy reached the parapet and leaned his elbows on the cold stone, a strange calm came over him, a sense of repose that was almost happiness. Right now he didn't want to indulge in self-analysis; he preferred to trust in the happy feeling serenely, without thought. He gazed at the water, at the opposite shore with its faceless modern apartment houses, the Gothic slenderness of its blackened cathedral, which seemed lower because of the height of the glass boxes, the low sad chimneys of its old tobacco factory—and the honeyed smell of pipe tobacco reached him.

If you looked at the water widthwise, it seemed motionless, as in a pond, but that was deceptive; the river had a current and sluggishly carried away to the distant sea the various objects that fell into it: a fragment of mast, an empty cask, a burnt log... When Guy was small, they often used to take him to the river; he especially liked to be there in the fall, when the crimson and gold leaves floated on the water; obedient to the imagination, they easily became the fleet of Marc Anthony and Octavian.[2] Now Guy could look into the past without pain. Rivers—this or any other one—had no meaning in his life without his wife. The sea had a meaning, lakes had a meaning, the mountains and forest had a meaning, certain streets in the capital and in other towns had a meaning, asphalt highways, wires, streetlamps, almost all animals, a lot of birds and fish had a meaning, books and churches had a meaning, and snow had a meaning, especially trees—city trees, orchard and wild trees, and also flowers, wild strawberries, wood nuts—all these had become taboo for his memory, but more than anything else dogs had a meaning; he couldn't look at them without an inner shudder—they had liked so many dogs together and had lost so many under the wheels of a car, or from the plague and other mysterious and implacable canine diseases. But a river had no meaning.

They hadn't swum in one, fished, sailed in a yacht, roamed along an embankment, or languished on bridges; they hadn't even had any acquaintances living in riverside areas. Good for the river, it had spared him from memories!..

He enjoyed the peace for a long time until he suddenly noticed that a sense of anxiety was arising out of his overly conscious peace. You can be at peace until you become aware of your tranquility. As soon as you become aware of it, everything falls apart.

... When she was little, she lived beside a river and would often run to it with the girls on her block. They used to fish scraps of thin elastic from balloons out of the littered water at the rotting piles of the old mooring— further up the river there was a children's amusement park, a miniature 'Disneyland.' They used to inflate the slack, limp rubber into balloons, and tying the balloon with a thread at its mouth, they'd let it float in the air. When the air caught it, the balloon soared sharply, high in the air, and drifted off toward the chimneys of the tobacco factory. And there, with a last flourish, it would disappear. And that was happiness. But once a woman who was passing by pulled the rubber that had just started swelling out of her mouth with disgust and tossed it away, giving her a couple of painful slaps on the cheek:

"Don't you dare put all kinds of rubbish in your mouth!..."

When little Benevenuto Cellini saw a salamander in the fire his father gave him a slap in the face so that he'd remember forever a miracle that fate rarely vouchsafes a mortal.[3] But the cruelty of the unknown woman didn't correspond to the slightness of her guilt, and Rena was left with only the pain of an undeserved hurt in the midst of pure joy. Guy saw clearly the horror, anger and mortal hurt in the round, slightly swollen child's eyes with the black deep pupil elongated like a seed, saw the wonderful child's sculptured head, with the strong little neck, the open rounded forehead and the dark tints in the soft chestnut hair and saw her dash from the river, which had become alien and unfriendly, into her own backyard in the rear of the decrepit old church... Perhaps she didn't even cry—she could hold back the tears when she was really hurt, and she cried easily over little trifles or without any reason at all, simply from the pressures of fate.

Something stabbed Guy's left eye, or rather, stabbed his brain through his eye. It was his medal reflected in a tear that had welled up; like a lens, the tear caught the light, to form a sharp knitting needle.

That was all he needed! From time to time his eyes grew damp, he sobbed—even in front of people—from any little trifle that wasn't at all touching at the given moment, but somehow in a complex way touched upon his unhappiness. It was abominable, self-indulgent; he had to watch himself.

Two schoolgirls in dark dresses and white aprons passed by, looked with puzzled derision at the sight of an adult crying, looked mysteriously at each other, and vanished for good. Guy unfastened the medal and slipped it into his jacket pocket.

A feeble melancholy wasplike buzz was audible from above. Guy raised his head and saw the bright cross-like shape of an airplane—like a darn in the blue canvas of the sky. The airplane was moving upward steeply, almost vertically, and at first seemed motionless. Its motion was betrayed by the white trail accumulating behind its tail. It was as though toothpaste were being squeezed out of a burst tube.

The white path stretched across the blueness and made a steep, smooth curve. Its appearance wasn't the play of natural forces; the airplane consciously and diligently was tracing the gigantic letter 'G' over the town. An advertisement—the most visible and corrosive kind, despite its relatively short duration—the airplane would not let up until it daubed the name of the advertised product over the whole sky. Then the weals would start dissolving and melting, but if one wanted to, one could make out the washed-out writing until twilight. Guy thought of the pilot sitting in the cockpit. Who was he, a former ace, a fearless fighter, a lucky man spared by the war who one day shoved his decorations in the bottom of a suitcase and like everyone else went to work for a company? Or was he a civilian pilot who'd flown enormous passenger jets all over the planet, but had been fired for some fault or because of his age? Or had he been a test pilot whose services were no longer needed? In any case, he was a man with a destiny and with experience, and not a greenhorn who'd fallen greedily upon the control column nor an aged mediocrity—only first-class pilots were allowed to fly over the city. Probably he disliked sullying the sky with the names of suspect creams, powders, typewriters, and strong aerated water that didn't quench one's thirst. Or perhaps it was a long time since he'd given a damn about anything as long as he got paid decently?

In a clean, defenseless blue, the airplane wrote out his name, and continued writing, to produce 'Guylin,'—in honor of the discoverer, and with his absent-minded agreement that was what they'd christened the new patented medicine—not for corns, nor for a cough, but for what was the scourge of humanity.

What vulgarity, what foul vulgarity! And deception to boot. In serious cases hospitalization and special treatment are necessary, and they want to impress upon the man on the street that any cancer can be cured with pills, like indigestion.

Apparently in the fog of initial rapture, Guy made more than a few slips. He agreed to everything, hardly hearing what was being asked, signed papers and could easily have signed his own death sentence. But the people who had kept pushing those papers at him—contracts, agreements, commitments—they weren't intoxicated and drunk with someone else's success and universal salvation; they knew very well what they were doing. Now he was reaping the fruit of his trustfulness.... Damn, they could at least leave the sky alone, they could spare the blue expanse!...

He hailed a canary-yellow cab and settled against the greasy back of the seat...

The nurse opened the door. Guy fancied he saw a derisive meaningful look on her big-nosed black-mustached face. And almost immediately he experienced what can be called 'the effect of a presence.' In an empty, gloomy expanse of the apartment, which had the odor of a vault, there arose a live warm heat; his skin felt it like the heat of a campfire at night. There was no point in dissembling in front of the nurse, and he let the moment linger not for her sake, but to evoke inwardly his wife's image, to prepare for the meeting. Was she reading, sitting in her favorite seat—an old leather armchair with a pressed seat which he'd gotten from his parents—under the lamp on a crooked metal stand, or was she sleeping, her face buried in a pillow, and breathing a moist stain into the pillow case, or was she standing at the window, her hand grasping a fold of the curtain as she looked at the dry summer roofs of the squat neighboring houses? No, this was too picturesque, and she hated picturesqueness more than anything in the world. She was as natural as an animal, and that was the best thing about her. Maybe she was drinking coffee from the small blue cup, breathing in short gasps because the coffee at once acted strongly on her heart? And when he recalled those short gasps, as though of fear, his heart started fluttering and became hot and moist. He pushed the door, stepped into the dank dining room with the drawn blinds, from there to the bedroom, then to his study, which was permeated with the odor of tobacco smoke, then in a semi-delirium he rushed into the kitchen, threw open the door of the nurse's stuffy sanctuary, and only then realized that she wasn't there.

"And what are you looking for?" he heard the nurse's masculine voice. "You don't think she'll come back, do you?"

The fact that the nurse had immediately guessed why he was dashing about the apartment was quite natural. But why was she looking at him with such an ambiguous expression? "Devil of an old woman, she's making fun of me! She's always poisoned my life. She didn't let me bathe in the river as much as I wanted, didn't let me go alone to the woods, she put galoshes and padded jackets on me when it was hot and dry, she snarled when my friends came to see me, and almost spat when she opened the door for my girlfriends. How many times did I blush because of her deliberate malicious tactlessness, how many dates did she poison for me, how many friendships did she ruin! Ever sullen, discourteous, peevish,—I was always afraid to ask for a cup of tea for my co-workers; she resigned herself to my guests, but for some unknown reason she didn't give a darn about my colleagues. And stupid! She always mixes things up, garbles them, asks what the telephone message is only when it's not a business call, ceaselessly chews on something, sucks, swills down tankfuls of tea with jam, chocolate, biscuits, and considers herself injured, forgotten. All my wife's gentleness (and she was indifferent to household things) couldn't shield her from the pushy and troublesome pretensions of the old witch. Of course, if someone fell sick, nurse would go for nights without sleep, would look after that person out of pure devotion, but we were rarely sick. And also, whenever there were difficult times, some kind of frenzied devotion would come over her, but in the quiet current of life she's unbearable."

He felt his anger disappear, and began feeling ashamed of his malicious thoughts. Some person for him to be picking on—a pathetic old woman who in the course of her long life hadn't acquired anything and had even lost her femininity.

She'd been looking at him like that —playfully, significantly—all the time from the day he attained fame. Her pathetic pride consisted of adding a certain irony to her admiration for him; how many times had she changed the sheets under the "Benefactor of Mankind," slapped him below his back for various misdeeds, washed him in an enamel tub. He himself had let himself be deceived, and with the baseness of a weak soul had brought down silent curses on the poor shabby gray head.

"I thought . . . " he began, and then saw that the nurse was bending over the gas stove. "I won't be having lunch."

"So what's the point of getting food!" sighed the old woman.

Guy made his way to his study and seated himself behind the enormous antique desk covered in green broadcloth. The flat green surface was densely littered with all possible kinds of knickknacks that gave a very feeble idea of the owner's personality. There was a tortoise transformed into an ashtray—a part of the shell was cut out, and the hole was worked with copper; a bronze matchbox, a silver glass full of color pencils and ballpoint pens which Guy never used—he wrote with an old Parker fountain pen that stained the inside pocket of his jacket with blue ink; three tasteless terra cota statuettes, to which he'd reconciled himself only because he didn't notice them; two little vases for flowers that never held any flowers; an old Swiss clock that had stopped for good a long time ago; a dagger in an embossed metal sheath; a box inlaid with mosaic containing plastic clips; a rectangular piece of glass with a picture of St. Mark's Cathedral sunk in the glassy depths; the seal of his maternal grandfather, an eye doctor whom he'd never known; a goose quill—a gift from his co-workers that was supposed to work; a bust of La Bruyère of mysterious origin; every time he encountered the bust beneath his hand, he swore to himself to look up in the encyclopedia what La Bruyère was famous for,[4] but he kept forgetting to do so; and a yellowish piece of quartz, last year's calender, a wooden statuette of a very fat naked woman, Gauguinesque in quality and duskiness;[5] of all the objects littering the desk only the statuette aroused Guy's sympathy; a school pencilcase with stubs of pencils and worn-down erasers and other junk; a postcard with a view of Majorca, and a broken table lamp. Guy had no idea where most of the objects had come from; they'd appeared gradually and unobtrusively, as though they'd accumulated from the air permeated with tobacco smoke. "I should throw them out," he thought for some reason. "Things are fine when they reflect the owner's personality or when they work on the memory, but like this— what's the use of them?... "

Not a single thing remained of his wife. She'd arrived without luggage and had left the house without luggage. A person unconcerned with everyday things, she didn't have any attachment to the material trifles of the world. She could be happy with some bright rag or mechanical music box and could pass up something genuinely valuable with the greatest indifference. As a rule the world of objects left her cold, and if it touched her, it was through some complex ties of association. Then the thing would appear to her as a symbol, and then she'd show some implacable childish greed. When she left the house, besides a few dresses, a raincoat and underwear, she took with her only an old summer parasol with a broken handle. Even in mild sunlight her face was immediately covered with freckles, and she couldn't do without a parasol. That was her style— complete naturalness, no airs or poses. She hadn't thought that her minor foresight would debase their separation. She hadn't left a note, simply told the nurse, "Tell Guy that I won't be back,"—and left. Where? He didn't know. She apparently rented a room somewhere. She hadn't gone to join some man, she'd left him. A man, likely, would appear later; perhaps he already had. She didn't know how to live alone, and then, what could she live on: her strange paintings didn't bring in a single cent and she wouldn't accept help from Guy. That didn't mean that she wouldn't accept help from another man. Guy didn't entirely understand her moral code; it's possible that there was nothing to understand, she was guided not by rules, not by principles and laws, but by instinct, by intuition—something smelled wrong to her and she would move away with distaste, whereas something that really smelled to someone else didn't bother her sensitive nose. That was the way she was.

But why did she leave? Guy had thought about that a great deal, rather, he thought about it constantly; when he stopped thinking about it consciously, his heart thought about it for him. In any case, there was no cause for the break. There was a reason, of course. Perhaps they'd lived too long without misery, but also without acute joy, and she'd tired of the sameness, the stagnation? Evidently for her their form of existence had completely spent itself. Guy worked a great deal and gave her little time, but that was the way it had been from the beginning of their life together, and then it had suited her. Only during the time he was falling in love did Guy totally neglect his work, and existed like some enchanted loafer, the lighthearted squanderer of time. When they weren't together, Guy would roam the streets or would hang around a café over a glass of cognac, gazing at the customers with unseeing eyes, and would count the minutes and the hours until the telephone call and the meeting. Her day was full, she was enrolled in art school, and besides that, there were some 'boys'—fellow students purely and rapturously in love with her, who needed some extremely delicate handling,—she could postpone a meeting with him indefinitely only so as not to hurt the 'boys.' Her devotion in friendship appealed to him, though he couldn't settle down during these 'last suppers,' the right to which belonged to an outsider. But later the 'boys' somehow dropped away imperceptibly. Guy surmised that the fine fellows had started saying nasty things about him and Rena had sacrificed the romantic friendships.

In that period he was like the prodigal son who'd returned to the native Penates.[6] He'd completely forgotten the city in which he'd been born and grown up. He realized, of course, that time had passed in the city: new houses and whole regions were being constructed and old ramshackle buildings were being torn down, public houses were being broken up, monuments were being erected, underground walkways and tunnels were proliferating, but he hadn't supposed that the changes were so great. Home, the laboratory, the clinic—his whole life passed in a closed circle. He'd set himself his goal early, while still at the institute (or rather, the goal found him, for there was no willful act of choice; he suddenly discovered that the choice was made), and everything unimportant that weakens and distracts a man from his business fell away by itself: friendly get-togethers and drinking sessions, roaming around the streets at night, the movies, concerts, theaters, restaurants, resorts, and the parody of sport that students liked so much—the painstaking tossing of a tennis ball on a court reddish with sand. After he started his own independent work, he stopped taking vacations and spent the stuffy summer in the deserted smoky city— for some reason he could think especially well and freely during that time. The ironclad order of his life was disrupted only once, when he was in charge of a field hospital during the war. But he was soon wounded and he returned to his routine: home, the laboratory, the clinic.

He wasn't a robot at all, programmed for once and all; he read a lot and with passion, he listened to music at home, and at times the irresistible need for Botticelli or Rembrandt, Van Gogh or Derain[7] came over him, and he'd go to the museum—that 'charged' him for a long time. Women visited him, and he drank wine with them, a lot of wine, so that his tired brain could switch off. And these women almost always fell in love with him because he was a strong and vital man; his coolness and reserve, together with an external amiability, attracted them, made them want to get close to his heart. Remembering Hemingway's words that morning intimacy with a woman costs at least a page of good prose[8] (which could be compared to a single good idea), he allotted only the evening hours to love, which didn't make his girlfriends cool at all. One of them succeeded in staying on for such a long time that he was already preparing to make her his wife when Rena appeared, and the woman, who understood everything right away, retreated in silence. She was a good, intelligent, and pleasant woman, he could have lived a calm, orderly, worthy life with her until he died. A real scientist's wife, as they used to say in their circle...

But Rena came, and his regular way of life, which had created itself, burst all its seams. White streets with trees weighed down with snow or wet streets ringing with glassy brittleness appeared, and some unexpected new houses and deserted or full-to-overflowing cafés where girls with long legs drank coffee with cognac. Once he chanced upon the street where he'd lived in his childhood, which had retained its former quietly provincial look; three- and four-story apartment houses, gray private apartments with dusty windows that never opened, enormous oaks in the yards, cast-iron posts at the gates, uneven flagstones of sidewalks (you had to walk on all the flagstones without stepping on the lines joining them, then the teacher wouldn't call you to the blackboard). He was disturbed by some small discoveries: a bookstore he'd forgotten or not seen at all, a magazine stand, a beer hall, a summer café beneath a striped awning, and underground crossings where he always got mixed up, exiting in the same place where he'd entered. And besides this, the city was the herald of Rena, for each time after he swallowed some cognac or some light bitterish beer, swallowed the streets and alleys, the old cathedrals and new hotels, his half-forgotten childhood and half-unnoticed present, he was getting Rena. However busy she was, she never cheated his expectations, during the time, of course, when there were no longer any 'boys.' At times he felt that she was ruining certain important bits of her own life: an exam, a drawing lesson, a visit to the studio of a venerable master or a new genius, a meeting with a girlfriend, a fitting, a student ball—but she didn't let him feel that she was acting out of self-sacrifice and she herself didn't consider it a sacrifice. But he didn't stay in debt, for he almost abandoned his work. A long time later, he got the feeling that it was precisely during those days of love and idleness that he came upon the right path, the path that led him to his discovery. Uprooted from his routine, he acquired freedom and subconsciously underwent a reassessment of values. He stopped holding on to imaginary things as if they were already an achieved success, stopped considering them landmarks en route to truth. With a regal light-heartedness and sense of irresponsibility he moved in a completely different direction, turned his back on years of persistent exhausting work; with a strange lightheartedness that saved him from despair, he cancelled out the past, and in doing so, unknown to himself he laid the foundation of his future triumph...

She wasn't responsible for all this, however. She wasn't interested in his work. For a long time she didn't seem to know at all clearly what his work was. Something connected with medicine... Her indifference touched Guy. She reached out to his human essence, ignoring that which gave him his livelihood and position in life. But there was a falsehood in this. It was totally possible that Rena had such a high opinion of him that she placed no significance on his position in science, but beyond ranks and degree (forget about them) there still existed his work, a search that merited attention even on the part of a person who was a stranger to scientific matters. Modern man, after all, lives under the tropic of cancer. But only the humanities interested her. The feeling for color with which he was endowed as if by a freak of nature touched her immeasurably more than all his scientific achievements, which then, however, were limited. Whichever way you twist it, there was a strange, inexplicable arrogance in her disregard for his life's work. Arrogance and narrowness. And also ignorance. The layer of culture in her soul was very thin in general. Preoccupied as she was with art, she wasn't at all distinguished by her erudition, and he had to acquaint her not only with Proust, Joyce, and Robert Musil, but also with Stendhal, Dostoyevsky, Hamsum, and even Dickens.[9] She knew today almost without knowing yesterday. Was she talented? Yes, she had a talent, but nothing else, neither diligence, nor assiduousness, nor the ability to finish her work, nor a conscious attitude toward creation. For that reason she didn't achieve anything and remained a semi-dilettante. But what did he care about all those insignificant considerations when she finally arrived! Indifferent to his worries and reflections, she responded acutely and tenderly to all changes in his appearance. When they first met in winter on a wonderful lush evening—a thick snow that had fallen unexpectedly early covered the roadway and pavements thickly, coated every bough, every spike of the cast-iron railing of the public garden, clothed the streetlamps and posts in sparkling caps, covered the fur collar of his winter coat and the nap of his luxurious hat in a gemlike grey,—she kept skipping, clapping her hands, and moaning tenderly:

"My God, what joy!... Such an evening, and you're so fantastically beautiful!... "

She repeated this tirelessly and skipped until she slipped and fell, and her fall wasn't clumsy, but sweet and soft, like a sign of confidence in the snow that was spread over the asphalt. He didn't even have time to help her before she jumped up and started skipping again and clapping her hands and fell again, and when this happened the fourth or fifth time she suddenly got hurt at the perfidy of the hidden slipperiness and her dark pupils lengthened in helpless anger, and in the corners of her eyes, at the barely noticeable bridge of her nose, a small tear was squeezed out. He laughed then, comforting her for her bad luck, but now, now he didn't feel like laughing. Dickens and Joyce, the whole crew weren't worth a damn vis-à-vis that pure manifestation of trusting life. And she succeeded through that. Where another would simply have fallen, tearing her stocking and hurting her knee, ruining her own and other people's mood, she unconsciously and unselfishly created a tender and moving circus with a profundity of experience that is alien to the spectacle of a circus...

Well, fine. So there wasn't a single thing on the desk that could remind him of her—superfluous trash that deserved to be buried in a rubbish chute. But that required some effort, and the trash wasn't worth it. To hell with it! There was nothing for him to do at his desk. The task of pain and languishing could be continued in bed.

He stood for a while in the shower, too lazy even to soap himself, wiped himself any old way with the fluffy towel, went through to the bedroom, and drew the blind, trying not to look out of the window behind which the unbearable word 'Guylin' flashed emerald, gold, and cinnabar in a mincing dotted line; the play of colors kept appearing to create the unattractive night tableau of the city together with other ugly words that glorified bandaids, cigarettes, dark beer, and tire-covers. And what was Rena's reaction to the fact that his name assaulted the eye on all sides? Perhaps the intrusiveness was offensive, as if he were consciously and tactlessly reminding her of himself all the time, or perhaps she was totally indifferent? Given her abstractedness and her blindness to everyday things, most likely she simply didn't understand that the advertisement of the usual dubious medicine had anything to do with him. How strange, unexpected, unfair and sickening it was, though, that the grubby paws of vulgarity had reached down to his pure activity!..

He got into bed, extinguished the lamp, and came face to face with the flat ugly mug of insomnia. During his whole life insomnia hadn't brought him a single useful thought, he hadn't made a single decision as he tossed in sheets that at first were repulsively cold, then repulsively warm. Everything intelligent and worthwhile that he'd ever thought up, through, or out, had come to him in the clear light of day. Insomnia shifted about in his brain myriads of short fragmented little thoughts (not one of them was formed into a real thought), a crowd of the most empty superfluous little memories, images that were dim and disturbing in their lack of clarity, and petty little terrors, interesting only to provincial Freudians. Insomnia brought him the most talentless hours of his wakefulness. Nothing changed with Rena's leaving. Insomnia cheapened even his suffering, which in the creased sheets under the stuffy blanket was changed into the small change of everyday affairs; during the day the eagle tormented his liver,[10] now the mosquitoes were exasperating him.

In his insomnia her leaving no longer seemed significant; she'd simply got bored. Her art wasn't going well, whereas he'd never been so busy as now, and evidently the contrast between her tiresome freedom and his absorption irritated her. And besides that, she'd simply got tired of him; the last years of their life were scant in joys. She was unfaithful to him more than once, in his insomnia no doubt remained on that score, and she was angry at herself for her act of unfaithfulness; she was basically a direct and proud person, her own unfaithfulness humiliated her, but she placed the blame for her humiliation on him. In general she considered him responsible for everything that happened to her. Touching, of course, but hardly fair. If she were to commit a murder, she'd seriously consider him, and not herself, the murderer. There was something childlike and at the same time depraved in this freedom from all responsibility. He was to blame for the fact that she'd become bored with him, not stimulated, that she couldn't paint, couldn't draw, that uncomplicated distractions with second-rate people became more pleasant for her than family life. Nothing special pulled her away, but everything in the house irritated her, everything pushed her out: the old nurse with her pathetic growling, and the need to keep at least some established order, and his work, and the telephone calls, and the old cat that by a strange coincidence vanished the day she left, and the viviparous fish in the aquarium that dragged behind them the thread of their experiments, the tiny, greedy and demanding creatures that constantly needed food and fresh water; the arrival of the postman with the newspapers, letters, invitations and bills (it was necessary to pay off the last), and all the rest that comprises the day. There were only two ways out: the first and dubious one—to change everything decisively, to do a stunning repair and remodeling job on the apartment and change the furniture, throw out the fish, kill the cat and the nurse, reconcile him to the fact that in the evenings she had to have 'people' who liked cheap music and expensive drinks—in a word, to win complete freedom, or what was more likely and simpler, to leave. She chose the latter.

She knew he was close to success, but that didn't stop her; on the contrary, it accelerated her departure. Here her innate good taste told. A departure at the height of his triumph would have seemed calculated, melodramatic and insincere, and besides, it would have attracted to both him and her the excessive sympathy of the people around them. Besides, it wasn't good to deal a man a stunning blow in the midst of happiness. He could console himself with how sensitively he was abandoned, how much tact, goodness, selflessness, and faith in him was manifested—she didn't take anything with her except for a few dresses and an old parasol with a broken handle. In the painful bustle of insomnia, nothing made the usual touching impression on his heart. Like a dog he shook his fur and turned from his right side onto his left to press his heart; perhaps it would calm down.

But her departure was also unkind, cruel, monstrously cruel. She thought only of herself: if some concern was to be discovered in her action, then it was only by force of a certain coincidence of interests. She wasn't a malicious person, but she was a cruel one. Long-term and constant feelings were not her element. Instant self-abandonment followed by icy cold—that was she. And without the slightest ability to control herself, her feelings. In some ways that was splendid, as all genuineness is splendid, but it was disastrous for a relationship, for human relations aren't merely fireworks, merely holidays—the everyday is unavoidable. She burnt out in the everyday. But she was sincere in each separate moment...

He was awakened in the morning by the sun beating in his eyes; it was ten. He experienced an instant of pure physical joy from the sun, the blue sky, the return to reality, and then the weakness, the limp lethargy that he used to experience formerly only from too much drinking, but that had become habitual now, returned to his body. Old age, it turns out, is akin to a hangover. Everything will have to be started all over again. The night before hadn't changed anything. And what could it change?..

He dressed, recalling indifferently that he was running late for the regular academic bull-session. "They'll wait," he thought listlessly...

He sat through three hours at the meeting, his ears turned off. Recently he'd discovered that strange ability in himself whenever he wanted to become deaf. He sat, his head clutched in his hands, and examined the grandiose superfluousness of the learned faces surrounding him, with their sclerotic bare temples, sunken mouths, bespeckled dead skin, but still greedy eyes flashing excitedly now and then from being face to face with Success. And the fairy tale fantastic success was he, Guy, the unhappiest person in the world.

Those gathered there had nothing to do with Rena, which in Guy's eyes lent them a frankly unnatural emptiness. He refused to give a speech, as they proposed, and, strangely enough, that created a good impression. Those around him willingly accepted that behavior, which smacked of arrogance, for it seemed sincere, natural, and in its frankness, even valid. But he was silent from misery.

But perhaps his lack of participation created an even more gratifying impression on the portly graying man with the matte olive complexion in the dark tweed suit. Guy distractedly took him for a government clerk.

"Indeed, 'speech is silver but silence is gold!' " said the man with satisfaction, showing the delicate pink gums of his dentures.

And he said something else about 'Guylin' and about money; of course he spoke about money, for as soon as he opened his magnificent artificial mouth one could hear the jingle of money. Guy didn't listen to him, struck by the unexpected discovery that he, Guy, like his learned colleagues, was totally superfluous at that meeting. The handsome olive-skinned gray-haired man—that's who was necessary. And all the scholarly trappings were necessary only for a reputable reference in small print on the new packaging of 'Guylin' or in some prospectus.

Guy had never stopped to wonder before about whose money he and hundreds of other researchers had thrown about for so many years. What was important was that there had been enough... But those who gave money weren't distinguished by a similar carelessness and they kept a strict account. Now the time had come to return with interest—incredible, fantastic interest—everything that had been spent. And each screw in the grandiose machine that had made profits was adjusted, and it went into action. And the only thing that he, Guy, had to do from now on was not to get in the way...

From the scholarly council Guy set out for the clinic. Strictly speaking, there was nothing for him to do there, but he had to occupy himself somehow. Twice en route he thought he saw Rena. And once he grabbed the driver's arm, forcing him to stop in a place where it was forbidden to do so, but the woman turned out not to be Rena, though she was very like her: the chestnut hair with a reddish tinge, the pretty smooth olive skin, like the kind you have in old portraits, the rather narrow-shaped slightly swollen eyes, and the slightly flattened bridge of the nose that made this young woman, as it did Rena, look like a Korean. And she had almost as perfect a skull: strikingly precise in form, with a splendid back of the head and a high forehead that was slightly narrowed at the temples. But by comparison with Rena the woman who was passing by was like flat champagne. How strange that despite the almost double-like similarity one gets such different people. No, the champagne hadn't gone flat, they'd simply forgotten to put the effervescence in it.

The second woman was also strikingly like Rena, at least she seemed so as she flitted by for a moment. But Guy suddenly became shy, and the woman disappeared in the crowd. It was possible that it was in fact Rena.

Guy's heart beat somewhere below his stomach, and his chest cage became empty, like the bird cage on the Day of Birds,[11] and some time passed before everything within him returned to its rightful place. He wasn't ready for a meeting with Rena, and such a meeting could happen at any moment—the existence of such meetings was created in the outskirts of the old town, where everyone was forever bumping into everyone else . . .

In front of the entrance to the clinic some woman rushed up to him and seized his hand and kissed it before he had time to make objections. Tears were flowing down her large-pored swarthy face, which was no longer young, with swollen bags under the eyes—she had sick kidneys. Choking, she babbled that he'd saved her son. Her mouth emitted a strong smell of acetone—she had diabetes. But her own illnesses didn't concern her at all, the main thing was that her son, her Wood, who'd arrived at the clinic with neglected cancer of the pancreas, should be alive and well. He was so young, so capable, he should live forever, but he!.. "What about him?" Guy interrupted. "He *will* live!... Unlike you," he almost added. Guy always remembered his patients well, he recalled Wood at once, a commonplace pimply young fellow whom he'd set on his feet before he realized that he was doomed.

Guy's appearance at the clinic yard was noticed by the personnel, and the doctors, the hospital attendants, and nurses streamed out onto the porch. They applauded—someone had invented that idiotic ritual, and all he had to do was appear in the clinic and at once he'd spark off ovations. This whim of the hospital staff, which was at such odds with his current spiritual state, irritated Guy. He wanted to stop them with an abrupt motion, when suddenly a warm wave rolled inside him, knocking against his heart. From what?... Guy looked at the people in the white gowns and white caps, and focused on the young face, expressionless as if asleep, of one of his many assistants. What was his name, now?... He remembered faces better than names, but he never forgot the names of gifted assistants. Obviously the young fellow wasn't one of the geniuses. Guy looked again at the rather pale face, the limp, grey hair, the sleepy watery eyes, and the warm feeling amplified and became more defined, as if his heart were muffled up in soft marten fur.

"Listen, my dear fellow," said Guy, moving toward the young man, "How's your dissertation coming along?"

The assistant started, wiped his smile off, and seemed to fold up.

"But you rejected my topic, professor!"

Guy immediately remembered the assistant's boring topic and colorless observations, but strangely, now the topic didn't seem hopeless to him at all.

"You misunderstood me!" he said cheerfully. "The topic only seemed to lack perspective; it's pregnant with possibilities. Come and see me, we'll talk about it."

Guy gave him a friendly nod and proceeded to the clinic. His fellow workers looked with envy and deference at the sleepy young fellow who, God knows why, had been honored with divine attention, while he suddenly felt something squeezing his temples, as though a tin nimbus were attached to them.

Guy made his way along the corridor, past the tall soundproof doors which led to the wards. "Until recently we only pretended to be healing cancer," he thought, "At best we delayed death—for months, sometimes for years, but we healed almost nobody completely. True, we often eliminated the pain, restored a good frame of mind and hope to people, helped them pass on to the next world with a smile—that's also not little. We were sooner monks than doctors, not healers, but comforters, and monks of inferior quality at that: God's servants promise paradisiacal bliss, but we promise only a return to the vale of life . . . "

Guy pushed the small door which led not to the ward, but to a corner that was tucked away; the old woman who had been the first to know the miracle of salvation that was the new method was located there. The dried-up, solitary, beggarly eighty-year-old woman had arrived at the clinic with a liver eaten up by cancer; the metastases had woven a spider's net in her insides. Her tender-hearted neighbors on the same landing had brought her there.

As usual, the old woman was eating something out of a plastic hospital bowl. When she saw Guy she swept a lifeless blank glance over him and continued eating.

"How are you feeling?" asked Guy.

Something like cunning flashed in the old woman's blank gaze.

"Better than everyone . . . And you promised me something . . . " she mumbled, dropping gruel out of her mouth.

The creature drained by old age and sickness whose soul had long ago been shrouded in oblivion could understand an amazing amount. She understood, for instance, that her salvation was a colossal victory for Guy. And each time she reminded him of what he owed her and she demanded bribes. Soft toffees were the dues he paid; she liked to stretch out the long goldenish thread as she squeezed the candy in her toothless gums.

"No complaints?"

"And what would I complain for?" mumbled the old woman. "I'm leaving you."

"How's that?" Guy asked absent-mindedly.

The old woman set aside her bowl, her naked blank eyes acquired consciousness and gazed at Guy almost with triumph.

"Here's how! I'm going to a private clinic!"

At first Guy noted inwardly the perennial revulsion of poor people for free treatment—probably it was outright degrading to doctor one's body for free, as if from charity, when others were spending a tremendous amount of money for it, —and only then did the sense of the old woman's words dawn on him.

"Aha! You've come into an inheritance?"

But the old woman wasn't joking at all. A representative of the company that produced 'Guylin' had visited her; henceforth the old woman's embellished portrait would decorate the label of the medicine. Of course, she'd be paid something for it...

Well, well! The company owners were getting at the root of it. It wasn't for nothing that the newspapers were rejoicing: "They'll go down in history together—the doctor and his patient!" There was a ridiculous truth in this—people remembered the old woman's name better than his. They seriously seemed to think that the old woman had earned something, that she'd *helped* Guy save her. It was as though through her, simple mortals participated in the Discovery of the Age. The masses' self-delusion gave Guy a bitter satisfaction. Let him enter eternity with the old woman, they'd be a couple, like Dante and Beatrice, Petrarch and Laura.[12] But now the business had gotten going in earnest: the company owners had correctly surmised that the cured woman was much more valuable to them than the healer. She was a guarantee of success. And just as earlier Gioconda had decorated a perfume store, the old woman now would decorate 'Guylin.' And you, Guy, step aside, don't get under our feet.

Laughter erupted from his breast, strained his throat, distended the veins in his temples. Sensing that he wouldn't be able to control himself, Guy ran out into the corridor. My God, he could save himself from all this phantasmagoria only through Rena, and she wasn't there!...

He wiped his eyes with a handkerchief. Sick people were loitering along the corridor. Many of them had already become yesterday's sick, others were fated to become that very soon. He'd saved them, but who was going to save him?... Everyone had applauded Bombard,[13] but how easily the enraptured world left him to his solitude and despair. And various ex-champions, the darlings of the masses, had fallen into penury and laid hands on themselves or had ventured to take on a deathly commercial feat only so as not to sink to the depths! No, people don't show indulgence for yesterday's idols. They show you consideration while you're in good shape and for that long and no longer, and then demand that you come up with something new, but a little more racy... People don't know how to help each other and don't try to learn to do so, that's why a person who meets with misfortune is so immeasurably lonely... Guy turned to his own concerns, and catching himself doing so, decided that misery was immoral, for it leads to alienation and hatred.

Simultaneously with these bitter thoughts (and recently the taste of all his thoughts was either bitter or sour), a warmth that was equivalent to joy rose and increased in him. Guy trusted this joy, for it couldn't be deceptive; all the same, the indistinctness of its source disturbed him. Mentally he ran through the day's events and everything that he recollected produced only a brief shudder of alienation. And then a sleepy expressionless face and a rather distracted grimace of lips crumpled in a half-smile flashed before him, and the joy inside Guy became confident. Ah, that's what it was—the assistant, what's his name!... He'd thought up an interesting topic, probably, a talented young fellow. How had he not noticed him earlier? How indifferent we are, how unperceptive regarding those around us, especially regarding quiet, unobtrusive people with a little gold nucleus inside. And he really should have seen at least his smile. What a marvellous smile! It may have been unattractive,—he had thick, flabby lips and an uneven row of yellowish teeth—a man who smiles like that can't be either bad or commonplace. Damn it, he should drop in on this nice assistant and support his difficult and bold decision. Even if his chosen topic leads to a blind alley, surely we *together* would pull through an M.S. dissertation? A search sometimes is more useful than the find. Guy felt a fierce determination. He'd help the assistant, help his marvellous smile, which was nice and a little pathetic.

Getting the talented young man's address in the office, he rode over to his apartment in the other end of town.

The arrival of the Benefactor of Mankind plunged the assistant into a painful confusion that verged on his not being responsible for his actions. He forgot to invite Guy inside, and for a long time they hung about senselessly in the entrance hall; he forgot to introduce him to his wife, a strong, plump, angry blonde, who at first didn't recognize the great man, but then fell into a state of quiet rage at her husband's fatuous behavior. And his behavior was, indeed, unusually fatuous: he couldn't smile, he couldn't do the little for the sake of which Guy had come to see him, personifying fate. The skin on the assistant's shaken face with its bulging eyes tightened so much, pulled the mouth that had dried up so much, that much as he wanted to, he couldn't give a smile, like a woman with an egg or paraffin face mask for the prevention of wrinkles, and he didn't feel the slightest urge to smile.

And Guy waited. "My dear fellow," he said, "You're a gifted and clever man, why are you so shy? Have more faith in your powers, more healthy drive, and, hell, you'll be all set!" But the lifeless mask loomed before him as before.

The wife tried to compensate for her husband's stupid ungraciousness. Repressing the rage boiling inside her and the desire to tear her idiot to pieces, she wrapped Guy in a net of affectionate gestures and birdlike twitters; and how she smiled! Tenderly, ecstatically, alluringly, and almost indecently. But after seeing in passing that moist white bone of her even teeth between her full crimson lips, Guy didn't look any more in her direction; he needed another smile.

"Head higher!" Guy made a last attempt to arouse the lump. "With such an adviser you won't fail! Tomorrow I'll be waiting for you in the departmental office!"

And now the assistant finally believed that what was happening wasn't a dream, ghastly in its seductive deceptiveness, that an omnipotent hand was holding him behind the collar, protecting him from adversity—his unattractive flabby lips twitched and crawled apart, exposing the yellow incisors.

"Goodbye!" cried Guy, feeling tears of joy, tenderness and sorrow begin to well up. "Till tomorrow, my dear man! . . . " and he ran out of the apartment.

"What do you think?" the assistant turned to his wife.

She was standing, her head lowered pensively. She was no longer angry at her husband, having unconsciously guessed that he'd somehow done what had been expected of him.

"You see," the assistant pressed ahead timidly, "Not everyone, it seems, considers me a flop."

"Nonsense!" his wife said abruptly, "You surely don't think that he bowed down before your genius? He sees through you. There's something wrong here, but what—I have no idea . . . "

. . . Guy carried the assistant's smile within him. He savored it this way and that, one moment blinking it away like a tear off an eyelash, to remain in a state of light-hearted joy that seemed causeless; the next he allowed it to appear again without protest—the weak grimace of unattractive full lips. And finally the smile pulled behind it the invisible trace, and that trace led him to a lake, a large oval lake that sparkled brightly in the rays of the sun that had already started going down.

The shore was overgrown with willows, but the one opposite was completely bare and hilly, with almost every hill crowned with an old abandoned monastery. This had once been the location of the country's religious center. To the east an enormous cloud without a clearcut line had been standing motionless for several hours. It had risen from behind the horizon, barely darker and more turbid than the dull blue of the sky, and up above, it had merged with it—at times it seemed as though it weren't a cloud at all, but the earth's smoky breath congealed in the air. But no, it was a cloud, of course, carrying not rain, but a downpour, a flood, a doomsday—just to glance at it sent a racking chill through one. The approach of something dire can be felt in nature: the birds fly low in zigzags, the seagulls and crows scream with all their might; behind, far in the distant low-lying damp field, lapwings sob and fish bite frenziedly at hooks that are practically bare.

Independently of the main cloud on the other shore, small blue-gray clouds pass by, sweeping over the cupolas of the monastery temples with their long beards of rain. But here there's sun, luster, and the kind of curly clouds one sees in cheap popular prints.

The shifting sheen of the lake told what was bound to happen. Instead of gold sparkling-wine ripples, streaks of dull silver spread along the still water. The birds fell silent and dispersed. The sky over the lake became deserted. And then, by wordless consent, they stuck their fishing rods into the ground and went to the pine forest which separated the lake from the highway. Their friend, an inveterate fisherman, cried reproachfully:

"Where are you going, they're biting fantastically!..."

He didn't get a reply. They lay down on the ground at the foot of a tall, mastlike pine on a soft bedding of old dead needles, and started kissing. They didn't exchange words of love, and didn't need that beggarly babble. And then there was a silent frenzied merging, and along the way everything that got in the way was cast aside. They didn't even notice how they got naked, they didn't remember that a forest path wound beside them, but evidently God protects those who are drunk and those who are in love. They didn't break their embrace even when the rainstorm that had been brewing all day broke. The crown of the pine didn't hold back the torrent for long, and soon cold jets started whipping their defenseless bodies. It got dark in the forest, and lightning shot through the dusk in short, sharp flashes one moment, and the next, cast a pale blue glow over the forest; then came the thunder, the universe caved in, and the eruption of water swelled—it was as though the lake rising up from the shore were attacking the wood with all its enormous mass. And joined together, they fell asleep to the sound of the storm.

They slept for a long time, but the storm had spent itself, and now the only thing left of it was a hesitant sparse rain and the distant dull northern lights; a clear bright light was already glimmering, and beside it, next to their cheeks, icy-cold bilberry bushes stirred from the dripping drops of water as if some nimble little beasts were poking about in them.

They regained consciousness, but lay for a long time in exhaustion, lacking the strength to pull on their clothes and return to the sobriety of existence, to their friend the fisherman, the fishing rods and the can with the bait. But no one passed by along the path. Only when they'd dressed with difficulty and he was trying with clumsy damp fingers to fasten a slippery button on the back of her dress did an old fisherman in rubber boots tramp by past them, almost catching them with the flaps of his heavy raincoat.

And later when the fishing was drawing to an end, chilled to the bone, without having dried off, they didn't know where to go. Their fisherman friend, with a glum face indifferent to everything besides fishing, had become tiresome to the point of making them shudder. They couldn't go to her place—her relatives had arrived from the provinces; his house was excluded from consideration because of the irritated comfortlessness of the nurse. And then she recalled her older girlfriend, a kind soul who had no reason to be embarrassed. She'd be concerned about them, would ply them with hot tea and raspberry jam, and could go to spend the night at the apartment of one of her adult daughters. And that's where they went. A short plump woman with grey hair and a black mustache that was thicker than his nurse's opened the door, an unattractive but kind and open woman, as one could guess right away. She held out a short strong hand to Guy, smiled with full lips, showing dark tobacco-stained teeth; and decades later her smile turned into a dissertation for an unlucky wretch of an assistant.

After he realized his reason for being drawn to the assistant, Guy didn't renege on helping him at all. That amortized reminder of Rena, of the best they'd had, didn't cause him any suffering, only joy with an aftertaste of sorrow. It would have been agonizing to meet Rena's elderly friend, but the assistant's smile acted like a weak dose of poison that heals instead of killing; one has only to increase the dose, and the poison becomes fatal ...

... Much of the ugliness that Rena introduced afterwards into their relationship was always more than made up for by their embrace under the rainstorm. "And would another woman have been so trustingly and unashamedly, so self-obliviously and extravagantly close with me?" he used to ask himself, and at once answered: "No!" But sometimes when that "No!" echoed within him with its customary joy, he would think soberly and coldly: but why not, actually? Another one could have, and not even one with an overly elevated manner. A lack of care and lack of caution are characteristic of women to a much greater degree than of men. It's a rare man who in his place would have dared such a frankly pagan act—from a sense of shame, a fear of responsibility, publicity. But a great many women would have followed whoever led them. But the lack of shame of some women on the lookout for adventures has nothing in common with the pure self-abandonment of a person who senses the weight of the stars and all the mysterious convulsions of the world. And he was trying to expose to doubt the best experiences of his life in vain. You won't save yourself through that. And besides, it's not worth saving yourself that way, cheapening the past. That's the self-defense of low and petty souls...

... Paul Homburg,[14] a Nobel prize laureate, a great physicist and once even known to a broad public—true, later he was essentially forgotten—arrived; his name was given to one of the quantitative effects.

Wallowing as Guy was in his spiritual misery, he nevertheless awaited the meeting with excitement and curiosity. For people of his generation Homburg was the Einstein of experimental physics. But after thirty years of stormy fame his name had stopped being mentioned, as happened with many who'd worked in the field of practical atomics, then soon after the end of the war it floated up to the surface in connection with some scandal and finally sank in Lethe.[15] Guy thought that Homburg had burned out a long time ago in silence and oblivion. But no, he was alive and even commanded a certain public interest; his arrival for a meeting with Guy received lively coverage in the press.

Guy was startled at the fact that Homburg was so hopelessly frail; he wasn't seventy, after all. From the railway carriage appeared a thin old man with long white hair almost to the shoulders that flew up at the least gust of wind and with a gray droopy mustache that was excessive for his wrinkled face with its large tearful eyes. Homburg bore an indecent resemblance to an old sick hare. His upper lip with its mustache twitched every now and then, and his chin quivered in harmony with it. He really wanted to kiss Guy, and the latter embraced him too impetuously out of embarrassment and lifted the light body that seemed hollow off the ground.

"Hello, my dear," said Homburg in a quiet but very clear, pure voice. "Hello, my dear man!"

"But where's your wife?" asked Guy, warned in advance that Homburg would come with his wife, without whom he could never take a step.

The upper lip with its weak white mustache jumped.

"Her stomach's in very bad shape," said Homburg mournfully. "Very, very bad shape... extremely bad!" His dark eyes filled with tears.

"Not cancer, I hope?"

"My dear fellow, after your discovery, you should say: cancer, I hope. God grant it's cancer, and not an ulcer, or worse than that—gastritis. An ulcer can be operated on wonderfully now."

"Forgive me," Guy was embarrassed, "I suffer from strange attacks of absent-mindedness."

The moist dark eyes looked at him with attentive sympathy.

"You're upset over something, my dear fellow?"

"My wife's left me," Guy said with a frankness that was unusual for him and suddenly realized that he loved Paul Homburg.

The latter extended a narrow liver-spotted hand with blue transparent veins, took Guy by the wrist, held it for a little bit, and let it go—he didn't have the strength for a handshake.

Homburg refused to give the newspapermen an interview. Guy did too. They drove off to Guy's apartment, where breakfast for two awaited them.

"How strange," said Guy to his companion, who was cowering in a corner of the car, "I've never seen your photographs, yet your face seems surprisingly familiar to me."

"Nothing strange about it, you've probably seen portraits of Einstein."

"Oh, of course!" cried Guy. "What a resemblance!.."

"Not so great, actually," Homburg smiled. "Once when I was sick I got really overgrown. And when I glanced in the mirror I saw my old teacher. Long hair and a mustache change a person's looks remarkably. Einstein had totally different eyes, nose, mouth; he didn't twitch and was much more solidly built than I am, but that doesn't mean anything—it's the general picture that's important. And I kept Einstein's mask. It's childish, of course, but I love him a lot. Sometimes I sit down in front of the mirror and talk with myself as I used to with him. We've got something to talk about!" Paul Homburg laughed.

Guy felt that one could be completely simple and open with this man without fear of doing something tactless. And he asked Homburg what had happened with him soon after the Second World War.

"My God!" Homburg was surprised. "I was sure that my story, which is overgrown with moss, has long set everyone's teeth on edge. But scientists with different specializations are separated from each other by an impenetrable wall. Moreover, you naturally don't read newspapers. Everything was completely commonplace. As I sweated in my laboratory I considered that I was helping to create a weapon against Nazism but not against the black-haired children of Hiroshima. A scientist working in my field should harmoniously combine political naïveté with moral irresponsibility. I violated the rules of good taste, I let myself have my opinion. And moreover, I expressed it quite loudly. People think I was treated divinely: I wasn't tried for anti-government activity, I was simply erased from the slate of life. They took everything away: the laboratory, the fruits of my labor, even my name. Who knows Homburg now? But they permitted me not to perish from hunger—I started teaching college. And recently they've even started inviting me to various scholarly gatherings.

I've fallen behind in modern science, I don't know its language, but I go all the same. Strange as it may seem, I still find it interesting to be alive. Even like this... You see, I've dragged myself over to see you."

Then changing his tone, lending it a certain solemnity, Homburg paid Guy the compliment he'd prepared in advance: how lucky is the scientist whose discovery brings people only good and cannot be used for evil purposes.

"Thank you. Though for some time I've not been so convinced that I've made mankind happy."

Homburg looked at him with surprise.

"You understand that the medicine will always be in the strong hands of this world and perhaps will increase their power over people."

"How unfortunate you are, my dear colleague, if you're already tormenting yourself with such thoughts. In your place I'd prefer to enjoy illusions."

"I really am unhappy," admitted Guy, "Tell me, strictly between ourselves, does He," Guy jabbed his finger upward, "exist?"

Homburg screwed up his eyes slyly.

"I'm absolutely convinced of it. Otherwise everything is too senseless. Better to think that our planet is an immoderately unsuccessful experiment of the keen old man."

"Old man? That means you believe in..."

"In the most primitive children's God with a beard and a circular nimbus."

"You mean not a Higher Intelligence, not the Primary Postulate?..."

Homburg waved his small liver-spotted hands. His upper lip jumped like that of a hare that had been given a scrap of paper instead of a cabbage leaf.

"No, no, no!... Why do you need all that nonsense? A light-eyed bearded being. A German. I'm convinced he's a German, that accounts for such a devotion to world cataclysms, comets, solar prominences, galactic explosions, and the steady expansion of the universe."

"But surely such an old fellow can't be omnipotent?" Guy asked seriously.

"My dear fellow, you know that everything in the world is relative. Of course, he can do somethng... You understand what the trick is? He thinks up riddles, and we're the ones who have to solve them. You think he knew Einstein's formula? Not a chance! In general he plays dice: whichever way they fall is fine. He didn't fight against cancer when the play came out that way, but I'm convinced that until you, he had no notion of how to treat cancer."

"And if one prays, does that do anything?"

"It's hard for me to say. I'm a special case. Whether unwittingly or not, I thwarted his expectations and didn't provide the lesson, so he's got a grudge against me. That's why I haven't asked him for anything serious in a long time. Only for the simplest everyday trifles, sometimes for household things and also for weather... But you're in a different position. Try it, it won't hurt, in any case."

For the whole remainder of the day and the evening they looked through photograph albums. Rena didn't care about taking photographs, but for some reason she was photographed a lot. Possibly that was because unlike most women she never cared about how she looked and she didn't prevent amateurs from snapping her as much as they wanted to. That was why there were so many choice photographs in which she looked natural and nice.

"That's us hunting," said Guy. "Rena shot a gun for the first time. And strange as it seems, she shot quite accurately. The huntsman for a joke hung his peaked cap with a coat of arms on the pole instead of dead crow, and Rena's shot blew it into scraps."

"I've never hunted or fished," said Homburg sadly, "I lost out on a lot on account of physics. True, in my time scientists in general didn't hunt or fish."

"No reason not to!... Here we are on a fishing trip. See, Rena's fishing directly with her hands? During spawning you can do that. The fish rubs itself against the reeds and loses all caution. You get your hands down and pull them out together with silt waterweeds."

"You don't say!" Homburg was surprised.

"And once Rena 'caught' a wallet. Some fisherman evidently leaned over the water and dropped the wallet out of his jacket pocket. Rena laid out all the contents on the bank to dry them out, and what resulted was a kind of one-man museum of a contemporary and neighbor of yours and mine."

"Interesting!" said Homburg, "It was probably a pathetic sight?"

"Yes," said Guy quietly, completely unsurprised at Homburg's perceptiveness. "The man didn't have a regular job and all of him was contained in his papers. He had a non-staff radio worker's identification, a temporary pass to a TV studio, and a piece of paper from *The Evening News...*"

Guy remembered all the other contents of the wallet. There was a urine analysis with traces of albumen and an excess of flat epithelium, a blood analysis with a high sedimentation, an analysis of the stomach fluids with an acid content of zero, and a certificate for a slipped disk. Either the man had recently had a medical check-up or he'd lain in the hospital. There also was crumpled paper money and change, the photograph of an unattractive tired woman with an inscription, "To my one and only," an editor's letter that announced the rejection of some manuscript, a copy of a complaint to the municipal office about the landlords who didn't do any repairs; in the secret compartment was a telephone number written with lipstick on a scrap of restaurant menu, and a laboratory report of a Wassermann reaction that was negative[16]—the short and sunny path of happy love; there was also a letter from his former wife, who threatened all kinds of punishment if he continued transferring the money for their son's support just as inefficiently, an overdue pawnbroker's receipt, and several photographs of the wallet owner himself; in one of them he was young, with tightly curled hair, in the other others—hard knocked by life, with a bald head...

While the papers were drying, the fishermen kept coming up and looking at this housekeeping activity, and they appeared displeased; either they thought that these were the possessions of a drowned man, or they were pained by the poverty of someone else's life, in which one so easily recognizes the poverty of one's own. And Rena, who had undertaken this 'exhibition' without any ulterior motive, suddenly scowled, dropped her gaze into the depths of her dark pupils, as if she'd gone blind, and immersed herself in that inconsolable gloom that always led him to despair. A lot of time passed before she squeaked in a childish rusty voice: "It's pathetic!..." And then she shed a few brief tears and recovered...

"Wonderful shape of the head," said Homburg: he'd come upon Rena's childhood photographs. "And what serious eyes!" He didn't turn the page for a long time... "Of course, the whole future person is already solidly present in the child, yes, yes..." He finally turned the page; there was a single photograph glued there of Rena as a young girl: the provocative toss of the head, the slightly dissolved soft outline of the face, and the same eyes—serious, deep, dark. In all the other photographs Rena remained unchanged: when she matured, her looks seemed focused at a standstill and weren't susceptible to the influence of time.

"I understand what her fascination is," said Homburg thoughtfully, "From the time she was an infant until she reached adult womanhood she was always feminine... There's nothing feminine left in my poor wife and hasn't been for a long time; the only thing that's timeless..."

Homburg grew sad. He examined the photographs attentively as before, and Guy, accompanying him with his gaze, discovered with tender emotion what a large role animals had played in Rena's life: dogs, cats, squirrels, tortoises, birds. She treated animals as equals, that's why she could not like some of them, as, for instance, the vivaporous fish. He, Guy, liked all animals, considering them all his younger brothers, and his love was grandly all-embracing, whereas Rena's was selective and therefore genuine...

"What does a man have besides a wife?" said Homburg. "Parents depart too early, and children too late, when relations are already hopelessly ruined. Friends? But that's such a rarity! A discovery is intimately close to you while it lives in your head, then it becomes a whore accessible to everyone. The only thing left is a wife, who gets old, grows weak, tiresome, peevish, stupid, and yet is the only one and the eternal one. It's only in her that you have proof that you're a personality or at least an individual."

"I don't have a wife theory," said Guy quietly. "But I'm unhappy, so unhappy that I simply don't know what to do about it."

"Marcel Proust said: real paradise is the paradise that you've lost.[17] You didn't see her as continuous happiness while she was at your side, did you?"

"Of course not. But what's important is something else—at times I'd forget about her existence. And that was happiness. I realize that now, when I can't shake her off for a single minute."

"You really love a wife in your old age," said Homburg and gave a sob. "Don't be angry, my dear fellow, I'll be leaving tomorrow... "

Guy didn't even try to dissuade him. They'd looked through all the albums and there was no point in Homburg's wasting time on official nonsense since he was so worried about his wife.

"It seems there's one thing left for me," said Guy, escorting Hamburg to his bedroom, "Plunge into new work as if into a pool. Come up with something grand. After all, all roads are open to me."

Something resembling pity flashed in Homburg's old eyes.

"Don't be deluded on that score, my dear fellow," he said quietly. "Our bosses are very adult people and not at all ones to get carried away."

Guy raised his eyebrows in perplexity.

"They know very well that no one's succeeded in breaking the bank twice."

"Really!... That means to them I'm a lemon that's been squeezed dry?"

"The Moor's done his duty... "[18]

"To hell with them! I have my own money. What counts is only that I work."

"That's something else," Homburg uttered in a melancholy voice. "When one's got money... "

"And what's your opinion, can one break the bank a second time?"

"You've got to believe it. But I don't know. I've taken large sums, but I didn't break the bank."

"But you have a wife," said Guy.

Homburg's sudden departure plunged the press into painful bewilderment. Everyone decided that the great minds didn't get along well.

Therefore there was no end to their surprise when before the train left the dried-up Homburg in a faded coat and the tall elegant Guy stood about a minute, if not longer, on the platform embracing and burying their faces against each other, their shoulders shaking. And then Guy ran with wet eyes to the very edge of the platform and Homburg kept leaning dangerously far out of the train, his upper lip twitching like a hare's...

After Homburg's departure Guy seemed to have some relief. He tried to pray, sometimes cried. He didn't pray that Rena would return—not for a second did he succumb to the delusion that meat which had been torn off the bone would grow back—but that she'd leave him for good, and he cried from pity for her, as though with the loss of his love she'd become weak, helpless, and not needed by anyone. He asked her forgiveness for praying to be guaranteed indifference and freedom. He said, fearing the bearded old man's stupidity, "God, I'm not asking you to give her back to me, that's pointless, for after coming back she'd never forgive me for her defeat. Only while we're apart I hold at least some place in heart, she doesn't know that I'm tormented, that I'm unhappy. But already I'm drawing to an end, I'm ceasing to be a human being. I'm a poor weak man, but I haven't done anything bad, I don't want any bitterness. Give me freedom!"

But he became somewhat alarmed at the thought that God would grant his entreaty and free him of Rena. This was equivalent to his life being maintained without his having a heart, a normal, peaceful, valuable and even more confident life, for such a decisively simplified organism was exposed to changes much less. Well, of course... Still, it's better to keep one's own fragile heart. If Rena won't be there, emptiness will appear, a terrible vacuum which nothing can fill.

Nothing brought even brief relief, he didn't know what to pray for, what to cry over. He couldn't live like that, but he couldn't get her back either, and he also couldn't get her out of his system for good. There was no way out. Rather, there was only one. He'd read somewhere that time could go backward. That meant that it was controllable. What he had to do was bring back the time when she'd been with him, and once he was in that past, to prevent her from leaving.

Having reached these views in his ravings, he realized that it was time to turn to a psychiatrist. But at the mere thought of medical fiction, as he privately called psychiatry, his blood coagulated inside him. An American doctor had invented the treatment not of people's sick souls, but of their behavior, trying to get a being with a fragmented consciousness to imitate in monkey fashion the actions of so-called normal people and in that way to become safe for those around him. A flame rages under the cranium, but the unhappy madman gets up in the morning, washes, cleans his teeth, and starts to knit a jumper or to do something else of that kind: simple and useful.[19] Then at the prescribed hour he eats, drinks, takes care of natural needs, strolls—all with the same unabating flame in his brain—and goes to bed. This psychiatric idyll—to achieve model external behavior in a person independently of his inner state—is horrible. However, the American at least thought up something new; the rest are still chewing Freudian cud in their minds. And if it turns out that you didn't feel a criminal passion for your mother and an ineradicable desire to murder your father, they fall into complete and utter perplexity. Totally regressive, but far from harmless, they mark time in the stuffy little world of carbonic baths, cold sponge-downs, and shock doses of insulin given to patients with sugar diabetes.

And Guy didn't go to a psychiatrist. He decided to treat himself. First of all he had to understand what love was—was this feeling so essential and important as to have one lose both oneself and one's life. After lengthy reflection and comparisons, the conviction grew in him that with the loss of his beloved he'd lost everything that had any meaning for him in the world. Now everything that he saw: a house, a tree, a bird, a dog, a bench, a mailbox, stairs, a cloud, a star—contained a hidden aftertaste of pain, or in the most complex, elusive, associative way, led him to Rena. Until Rena came, the surroundings had been as if covered with fog, everything existed, but there was nothing: not objects, not beings, but shadows of objects, shadows of beings. In Rena's presence, everything that populated the world, including him, ripened with the fullness of existence: with colors, odors, sounds, the manifestation of another, a higher idea. Love elevates an object to its own class; the loss of love turns an object into an image of pain, but until love comes, the object exists only as a sign of its own naked essence. Having brought his thought to that vague conclusion, he started examining whether in Rena's presence a tree really had been Tree, a fence, Fence, a bench, Bench, a star, Star. Yes, now it seemed that they had been. And how it had really been he'd never find out now, because his blood had become different. And if Rena were to return—she herself, full of love and of all that had existed formerly—would a tree be Tree again, a fence, Fence, a star, Star? . . .

What was the sense of conjecturing? She couldn't return the same person she'd been before, she also had different blood in her. She could return only in humiliation, and for the humiliation she'd pay him back through a tree's not becoming Tree, a fence, Fence, a star, Star. Perhaps they would become that for a split second, in the very first second . . . No, it was impossible to save him through her return . . .

Guy turned to books. Formerly he used to read a great deal, but then his work left him almost no free time. He didn't know how to read on the go. From his childhood he'd been brought up to respect books, the strange miracle that was much more mysterious and incredible than all the miracles born of Einstein's formula.

In Rena's room he discovered a pile of uncut magazines and a pile of books that she'd read, judging by the slovenly earmarked pages. Among them were authors who were familiar to him and new names that sounded so unusual and strange that it was difficult to believe in their importance. He started reading like a drunkard, but as a rule cast them aside in the middle, for he found no alleviation there. He became convinced that recently they had all learned to write, there was almost no bad prose, and even less very bad prose. The average level of 'stringing words together' had risen extraordinarily, all prosaists were in command if not of phrasing, then at least of intonation, which creates the illusion of a phrase; they all were in command of some trick that allowed them to stand out from others who were writing, yet there was nothing to read. An agitated, bitter, sweet depiction of life and human passions was substituted for by some mockingly-charming corrosive descriptiveness beyond which there was a void. Whatever fell into the modern writer's field of vision, whether it be an ashtray or a flower, was described with microscopic meticulousness and stupefying scrupulousness. Marcel Proust too knew how to describe in greatest detail some hawthorn or cake,[20] but he did it not for the sake of the hawthorn or the cake, but for the sake of the protagonist-narrator in whom the miracle of memory's birth took place. Proust was profoundly human, whereas the modern writer was inhuman. He treated you to a hawthorn in pure form, so to speak; it wasn't a sign of some higher life, but a hawthorn and nothing more, simply a hawthorn, to hell with it! And you couldn't reconcile yourself to that, you kept on seeking a second, major significance in the soulless glimpses of material details, you kept wanting to nestle with your pain against the sham of picturesque significance and found only emptiness. Cold glittering emptiness...

He gave up reading. Now his days were filled with the fear of death. Why days? At night the fear of death was stronger. Especially when you extinguished the light and pretended that your eyes, which were sticking together, the faltering movement of your hand, which didn't feel the switch right away, the yawns, which ceded to heavy breathing, guaranteed you instant sleep. But sleep vanished as soon as awareness of the impenetrable darkness pierced his brain. Horror compressed his heart; Guy would jump up, sit down on the bed, and moan very quietly. The outline of the window slowly cut through the dark, the pale flatness of the glass began to show, then what was behind the windows appeared. The horror receded, and misery would begin. It wouldn't leave till dawn, then he'd fall asleep, most often sitting up.

Fear of death had been completely alien to him before. He'd lived so seriously and profoundly that he didn't have enough mental time to fear death. But that seems to be a general rule: people who live badly fear death much more than people who live fully, joyously, happily. Now he had a special reason to be afraid of imminent death: he had to live so long before his blood changed, before his cells were renewed so that his whole organism, his whole psychic apparatus, became different, so that what belonged to today, the bad, would be totally overcome, and then he would be able to be with Rena again. Let them be reunited when they'd be very old, God knows physical closeness didn't disturb him much. But old people don't live long, that's why they're old people, and it's terrible that their new lifetime would be so short. Is it terrible? And if it turned out they had only one day, just one single day, but theirs, theirs, only theirs completely, surely that would be enough? In a day one can say all the words, cry all the tears, absorb the closeness of a dear being as much as one wants. And then, go ahead, take the bag of bones to the scrap heap. It had all come to pass, life had taken place.

But here greed awoke in him. One day with Rena wasn't enough for him, a year wasn't enough, a decade and eternity weren't enough...

...Imperceptibly—when a person feels bad, everything happens imperceptibly—fall approached, cold, windy, with a white dry granular snow overstitching the ground around the houses in the mornings. And the enormous building on Central Square that until then had been covered with tarpaulin was stitched over with granular snow, orphanlike and somewhat pathetic in its senseless bulk. The unveiling of the memorial to the Benefactor of Mankind still hadn't taken place. Guy kept delaying the festive ceremony under various pretexts. He told his acquaintances jokingly that he wanted to postpone that happy moment when all the capital's pigeons, fat, clumsy, and impudent, would settle on his head, as huge as a beer barrel, of pure gold, with a diamond wreath.

In fact, he found it hard to look a crowd in the eye: they would have to dam up the immense square with representatives of all the nations populating the globe. He was in the grip of a childish resentment against people. He understood that it was stupid, inhumane, sinful, but couldn't do anything with himself. He looked at the people who filled the streets, stormed the buses and trolley buses, dived into the dark maws of the subway and underground crossings, pushing, arguing, laughing, sometimes secure and cheerful, more often anxious, gloomy, and tired, and thought: surely this crowd, possessed with such immense energy, can help me? There's not a person to whom my discovery doesn't make a difference. If only one of them were to try and do something for me. Even if I yelled at the top of my voice: "I feel bad! Save me, people!"—no one would be able to help. The trouble was not the absence of desire, but the impossibility of rendering help. Your illness is incurable, and there's no point in getting angry at people, they're not guilty before you...

And then a small incident occurred, not even an incident—a few words were simply spoken which in an instant wrenched him out of his malicious prostration, giving him back to life, tenderness, and tears. The nurse merely said:

"You might take her her fur coat. Go on, it's cold."

My God, how simple that sounded: she was cold! ... Her delicate little bones were cold, goose bumps were scattered over her fine yellowish skin that was smooth as a baby's, her knees and those tender spots above the knees were freezing. She was huddled up and raising the collar of the raincoat in which she'd left home; she was protecting her chest and neck with a scarf, but she was still cold. The wind was blowing right through her, the dry white granular snow was falling behind her collar, making her cold, running down her back in thin melting rivulets. She'd left without thinking about the fact that she'd be cold, or perhaps she herself hadn't expected their separation to drag out until the cold weather came. No, she knew she was leaving for good, but out of a sense of delicacy she hadn't wanted to surround her departure with crudely material objects. When it got cold she probably thought he'd remember about her and protect her from the cold, but he in his swinish egotism, in his selfish preoccupation with his own sufferings, didn't even stir. The old nurse who was in her second childhood—even she remembered about a person who was cold.

So it was that that nonsense, that ungodly cold of early fall, took the veil of unreality off Rena and returned her to her real self; she became simply a person, live, vulnerable, who could get cold, and shivery and forlorn, who'd shiver in the wind, blow on frozen fingers, hurry into a warm room. Guy suddenly imagined her life without him totally differently: the daily little cares, the necessity of preparing food, calling somewhere, meeting someone, arranging her affairs. He'd pictured her in the sunnily mystical light of Beatrice, whereas she had the usual troublesome life of an average person, without special conveniences and privileges. She wasn't in need, she had enough to live on, but, of course, there was no question of another fur coat. He ought to do things in such a way that she'd get warm, without complicating it with any explanations, simply give her the fur coat of light, soft, beautiful fur and the fur cap and the fur-lined little suede boots. And that was all.

And here he experienced a burst of energy reminiscent in miniature of his earlier devastating push toward the goal—something like an atomic explosion in the conditions of a physics laboratory in an elementary school. With the speed of lightning, without giving anyone a single trump-card to hold, he found out all the circumstances of Rena's life, her address, her daily schedule, and even the fact that that evening she would be at the restaurant *Continental*.

He intended to take her things over the next morning, but toward evening the temperature fell below zero, and real snow—large, cottony flakes—began to fall, covering the windows in an impenetrable curtain, and he realized that he couldn't put it off; she'd be very cold when she left the restaurant.

Quickly and deftly he folded and packed up her things—it made a pretty, oblong package—dressed, called a cab, and set off for the *Continental*.

He hadn't been in the new bar which had opened recently at the foot of the television tower. Made completely of glass, the *Continental* was reminiscent of a giant aquarium. A milky light came through the semi-transparent blinds, and along it green, red, and black spots shifted lightly; it looked as if fish were swimming in milk. The bar had already won popularity, crowds besieged the doors. It was basically young people in velveteen and suede jackets. The restaurant was located between the 'art' block where the artists lived and the university, apparently gravitating more toward the former. "Though you can't tell today's students and the artistic bohemia apart," thought Guy. He'd look fine there in his evening suit! The entrance to the restaurant was blocked by the massive figure of an attendant in a double-breasted jacket with golden piping and a uniform cap; he sooner resembled a bouncer than a respectable doorman. The thick frontal bone protruded over his eyes and the short bridge of his broken nose. A former boxer, perhaps? He stopped those who were trying to get into the restaurant rudely: "Can't you tell it's full?"

Guy also received his share of boorishness, but didn't retreat. He told him who he was, gave his name and academic rank, but the former boxer seemed not to understand what he was talking about. When Guy tried to put money in his paw the boxer spread his fingers and the crumpled paper note fell in the mud. In despair Guy did something he couldn't believe himself. Seizing the double-breasted jacket by the sleeve—under the material he felt iron muscles—he cried:

"I'm Guy, Guy, you understand, Guy—the Benefactor of Mankind!"

Something like a contemptuous and comprehending smile appeared on the pancake-flat face with the broken nose.

"Had more than a few, haven't you, buddy? Get out of here!... "

Guy withdrew, downcast. Yet the bouncer kept soundlessly opening the door for some rather ill-favored people. Guy thought that he was letting through only those who'd reserved tables earlier, but then he caught the phrase uttered like a password by all the chosen ones:

"For Layo-Mayo!"

He realized what that meant when, his eyes roaming over the forbidden entrance, he saw the poster announcing the tour of the South-American jazz trio Layo-Mayo. Apparently Layo-Mayo were newly arrived stars, for Guy, who was observant where all sorts of nonsense in life was concerned, had never heard such a peculiar sound combination: Layo-Mayo. On the posters were depicted three young fellows in multi-colored shirts: a saxophonist, a drummer, and a contrabassoonist. The first with his skinny bent figure was reminiscent of a question mark; his big hands with long strong fingers looked like a strangler's hands; the second, an enormous bearded hulk with wide cheekbones, was squeezing a drum stick like a cudgel; the third was hiding his face behind the sounding board of a contrabassoon, leaving a coyly lowered gaze with lashes halfway down his cheek for all to see. Their line of business was easy to read: a schizophrenic, a bogatyr, and a tart. But that wasn't the point.

Guy retreated around the corner, turned his coat with the fleecy lining inside out, raised and tightly fastened his collar so as to hide his starched shirt and tie, pulled his fur hat low over his nose, and with the package in his hand extended forward, headed for the door.

"For Layo-Mayo!" he cried, changing his voice for some reason, and pushed his package under the bouncer's nose.

The fellow didn't even look at him: the great trio's name worked as reliably as "Open Sesame!"

Inside, the restaurant no longer recalled an aquarium in any way. Modern hardness and definitiveness of forms reigned here, incarnated in metal and stone, a vulgar human crowd, the odor of cosmetics, cigarette smoke, and some plants or other; somewhere in the distance the contrabassoonist was tuning his instrument; the heavy solitary sigh of the thick string fell mournfully into the even hum of the restaurant, which seemed artificially produced. The main event hadn't begun yet—the music box of the peerless Layo-Mayo was silent.

There was a complete mixture of styles here. The velveteen jackets of artists and casual student dress dominated; there were quite a few phoney hippies with hair washed in Dior soap, in scrupulously torn jeans acquired in a special store and expensive unpolished shoes. But one came across well-dressed people too: women with bare arms in long clinging dresses, men in evening suits. There was no need for Guy to be embarrassed about his splendid appearance. And at a certain moment he felt the daily, standard, automatic festive air of the restaurant begin to penetrate his soul and dissolve there with forgotten ease. To hell with it, life is wonderful in all respects: in its cheap music, in the icy-cold drinks, in the slightly languid and thick warmth of the air-conditioned air, in the thick beefsteak on red coals that became covered with bluish, light ashes so quickly, in all the details of that trifling existence that led him to that other one, totally non-trifling, when he'd feel the sharp elbow through the thin fur coat as he led Rena to the large glazed door looking out into the night of the snowy city.

His joyful excitement died, having barely appeared. In the surroundings there was no festive mood, not even that petty, superficial kind that any human assembly contains. The ill-assorted crowd was united in only one thing—its lack of contact. It seemed that all these people, even those who'd come there in pairs, weren't communicating with each other. It was as if they didn't know how they'd ended up together, and they didn't even make any attempt to understand it. Their surroundings made no difference to them, there was no opening up—everyone remained in his shell.

And then he saw Rena incredibly close: she was sitting at a side table in the main hall, half turned toward him, in the company of an unfamiliar ash-haired woman and two unfamiliar young fellows.

She was smoking, emitting the smoke vigorously, as usual. The smoke came out of her nostrils in two blue columns, and the ash fell on her sleeve, on the tablecloth, on the edge of her plate—everywhere but the ashtray, though she considered it her duty to tap the cigarette with her finger in the direction of the ashtray. All this was familiar to Guy, familiar to the point of making his head spin. So was her manner of not hearing and not listening to her interlocutor. One of the young fellows was telling some story, but Rena's eyes were fixed on her own distant point, and one sensed from the narrator's pathetically wounded glance that her inattentiveness was causing him pain. Guy felt liking, almost love, for the young fellow who'd replaced him beside Rena but who couldn't get her to listen to him. And had he been able to hold her attention? No. And yet in the beginning she used to listen to him and hear, later she only listened without hearing anything. But now she wasn't even pretending to be listening. Her face seemed tired and a little older, the skin had become dry, darkened and stretched on the cheekbones and around the mouth. Her short wiry lashes weren't made up, she wore her hair simply and smoothly. Usually she made up her eyes with something black and dark blue, extending their corners all the way to her ears, and she wore a fluffy hairdo, taking whole days to fuss around with the revolting iron rollers. Was her new indifference to her appearance good or bad? Perhaps she'd finally really started working and the daily nonsense that had fomerly filled the day's emptiness had peeled away? Or was it here that the influence of the young fellow with the wounded eyes, who loved naturalness, told?

For the last time Rena dirtied the tablecloth with ash, and jabbing the cigarette stub into the ashtray, extinguished it. As she did so, her distracted gaze slid around and for a moment crossed with Guy's gaze. He paled, smiled with trembling lips, and raised his hand. But Rena's face remained dispassionate, and her gaze slid further; and she turned to her interlocutors. She hadn't noticed Guy. Rather, she was so far from thinking about him that in the brief moment it took to see him, she simply hadn't recognized her former husband; his gesture and smile hadn't aroused in her a fleeting quiver of memory.

The awareness of his alienation, his complete and absolute exclusion from Rena's life pierced Guy to the very depths. She wasn't in step with him at all in his yearning, suffering, and regret for what had happened. She'd even forgotten to think about him! . . .

His forehead broke out in a sweat. Where had he gotten the idea that Rena was also taking their separation profoundly to heart and was inwardly searching for a way of returning, that what had happened between them meant something in her spiritual life? If he were to appear now, she would feel nothing but awkwardness and annoyance. He'd invented her for himself, and the woman sitting in front of him had no relation to the invention, perhaps only a certain surface similarity, and not even too big a one at that.

The young fellow finished his story and smiled pathetically. Those sitting at the table didn't respond in any way, as if he hadn't opened his mouth. And then Rena started speaking. She knew how to tell funny stories, sometimes maliciously, sometimes with a kind of belligerent good-heartedness, but always with a bite. Now there wasn't a trace of animation on her face. She spoke as though into a void, her lips moved mechanically of their own volition, and her thoughts were wandering far away. Only the young fellow with the pathetic wounded eyes listened to her; the other two sat with the same apathetic absent look. She didn't need anyone.

Guy realized what had taken Rena away from him, had taken her away a long time ago, hopelessly, forever; it was what was permeating the atmosphere of that caravansary more strongly than the smell of tobacco, perfume, and hothouse plants, what covered all the pale faces with a dull film and deprived the eyes of sparkle and the smiles of joy. Complete alienation, that's what it was called; the cold inhumaneness of the world, where everything is sold and bought, where an indifference more frightening than death rules.

And if one were to be serious to the end, then there was no reason to blame Rena. The same force that had deprived Homburg of work, of his life's goal, even of his name, that had plundered his, Guy's, discovery, had taken Rena away from him too. There was no point in rummaging about in all this, in tracing complex connections; it was enough to know that Rena was a small part, a victim, of that reality. He'd comforted himself before with the thought that, pleasantly protected by his work, he was living in a social vacuum. Nonsense! No one and nothing can be saved from the carnivorous dentures. And he was being chewed up, innards and all.

He summoned the maître d'hôtel with the starched chest.

"Be so good as to give this package to that lady there."

The maître d'hôtel bowed, showing the white crack of his parting.

"Excuse me, it the lady asks from whom...?"

"Say from Layo-Mayo." And Guy made for the exit.

He emerged onto the street, breathed in its thawed empty air and realized that everything was over. It had gotten warmer, the snow had stopped falling and was melting into blackness under the wheels of cars and the feet of the passersby.

Guy was completely disemboweled. All the painful tissue was safely distanced, but the area of defeat had turned out to be too great. To live with what remained in him was, in any case, impossible. Rena had taken the past from him, the last thing that he'd been holding on to. Now he knew: not only wouldn't there be anything, but there hadn't been anything. They existed in different systems of coordinates, in different dimensions, even in different times. They couldn't meet because they hadn't met before. He tasted the illusoriness of the past as the aftertaste of copper. Guy spat and burnt a black hole in the snow. That was what was left of the life they'd lived—the aftertaste of copper in the mouth.

He had an old revolver from the war. A childhood friend, a war correspondent who'd turned up by chance in their field hospital, had given him the revolver as a gift. He'd rubbed his foot sore until it bled, and had come in to ask for some plaster. They'd reminisced about their school years, their friends, live and dead, and his friend had given him the old revolver, which had never been cleaned and which he'd picked up God knows where. Now he found it in the bottom of his desk—heavy, dark, black, primitive and old-fashioned. It was impossible to believe that one could fire it.

There was only one cartridge in the chamber. Guy rotated the chamber, cocked the gun, put the barrel to his chest, and pulled the trigger. The hammer clicked, and Guy instinctively squirmed, but no shot followed. A misfire?.. Guy sat motionless for several seconds. The unsuccessful shot didn't change anything in him. He broke open the chamber again and realized what his mistake was. As one cocks the gun, the chamber rotates, and he'd not taken that into account when he'd put in the cartridge. He noticed how businesslike his gestures were, but that didn't surprise him. Before, he'd been unable to understand the act of a voluntary rejection of life and hadn't pitied suicides, considering them worthless. Now he knew that there was no reason to pity suicides, but for another reason. Suicide is the means of ending more quickly a life that has become completely unnecessary. One should feel happy for a person who's overcome blind instinct, the fear of physical pain and a certain rudimentary moral interdiction, instead of rotting alive...

... Guy didn't leave a note, and the official verdict was that the shot had happened accidently when he'd been cleaning his old revolver—a patriotic relic that he'd kept and cherished. Of course, no one believed that. The majority believed that he'd taken his life as a consequence of monstrous nervous and mental exhaustion. Only the very few who were better informed connected his departure from life with his wife's departure...

... Once the academician Moore, the director of Guy's World Cancer Institute, met Paul Homburg at an international congress. Their conversation naturally touched upon Guy, and Moore spoke sharply of the deceased:

"In my opinion he was an insignificant personality if he could commit suicide on account of some nonsense."

"Forgive me again, colleague, there's a huge difference. If my wife...were to leave me..." Homburg's upper lip with the hanging mustache twitched like a hare's, and his mournful eyes filled with tears. "I also would...also..." He gave a sob, and taking out a large checkered handkerchief, blew his nose like a trumpet, leaving his eyes wet.

Folding and putting away his handkerchief, he said with devastating conviction:

"You know, colleague, I've suddenly realized why you and everyone like you will never discover anything worthwhile. Precisely because you are incapable of committing suicide if your wife leaves you."

1970   Translated by Helena Goscilo

The original ("Pik udachi [Sovremennaia skazka]") first appeared in *Znamia,* No. 9 (1970), 60-89. The present translation is of the edition included in the two-volume 1973 collection, II, 184-232.

Notes

1. The reference is to *Le Peau de chagrin* (1831), an early novel by the awesomely prolific Honoré de Balzac in which the protagonist Raphael acquires from an antique shop a shagree skin that guarantees its possessor the realization of all his desires, but also measures his life and shrinks with the fulfillment of each wish. Since for each realized wish the payment is a fraction of one's life, the skin simultaneously measures not only the amount of time left to the possessor, but also the strength of his thirst for sensations. Balzac allegorically juxtaposes two mutually exclusive options: vegetation versus self-destruction through an unrestricted pursuit of intense experience.

2. Presumbly Nagibin has in mind the great sea battle near Actium in Greece fought between Marc Anthony (83?-30 B.C.), Roman general, friend of Caesar and lover of

Cleopatra, a member of the second triumvirate (the other two being Emilius Lepidus and Octavian) and Octavian (alias Augustus Caesar, 63 B.C.-A.D. 14), heir and successor to Julius Caesar, who defeated Marc Anthony and invaded Egypt.

3. Benvenuto Cellini (1500-71) was a Florentine goldsmith and sculptor, pupil of Michelangelo, and perennial vagabond, whose adventure-packed, vigorously-written *Autobiography* (Vita) (1558-62) offers a colorful picture of Western Europe during the Renaissance. The salamander episode to which Nagibin refers is one of the most famous moments in the work, and has been used by other writers as a dramatic illustration of a point, e.g., see Edith Wharton's comment: "It is useless to box your reader's ear unless you have a salamander to show him." Edith Wharton, *The Writing of Fiction*, New York, 1925, p. 50.

4. Jean de La Bruyère (1645-96), a French social critic and satirist, is known for his volume of character sketches, *Les Caractères* (1688), adapted from the Greek character sketches of Theophrastus.

5. Paul Gauguin (1848-1903), a successful Parisian banker, fled 'civilization' for Tahiti, where he married a native woman and produced exotic neo-primitive canvasses in brilliant colors populated by hefty rounded Tahitian women. He drew on Indian, Indonesian, and Egyptian sources for his style. W. Somerset Maugham's *The Moon and Sixpence* gives a fictional account of Gauguin's life.

6. The Penates, like the Lares, were deities in Roman religion who watched over a particular home or community. Vergil's *Aeneid* contains numerous references to both.

7. Sandro Botticelli (1444-1510) was a Florentine student of Fra Filippo Lippi. He enjoyed the patronage of the influential Medici family and later of the priest Savonarola. His paintings, usually of mythological or religious subjects or portraits, invariably poeticize their subject matter: every face is beautiful and angelic. His most famous works are *Spring* and *Birth of Venus*.

Rembrandt van Rijn (1606-69) was a Dutch painter who for about forty years in Amsterdam produced etchings and paintings consisting of landscapes, religious subjects, and chiefly portraits—among them, many self-portraits—which made wide use of chiaroscuro. Countless Rembrandt paintings (e.g., *The Night Watch* and his self-portraits) are renowned throughout the world.

Vincent van Gogh (1853-90) was a Dutch painter, an Expressionist (usually called a Post-Impressionist) whose dazzlingly vivid, swirling depictions of landscapes, interiors, and people brim with frenzied conflict and intensity. Influenced by the primitivism of Gauguin, with whom he had a stormy relationship, van Gogh led a life of violent, anarchic individualism which ended with his suicide after a lengthy stay in a mental institution. Apart from his paintings, of which *Sunflowers* and *Starry Night* are probably the best-known, he left behind a large body of correspondence with his devoted brother Theo that is well worth reading. Most of his mature works were painted in the last three years of his brief and arduous life.

André Derain (1880-1954) was a 'modernist' French painter who admired and drew on the vehement chromatics of van Gogh and joined Matisse, Vlaminck, et al. in the 1905 Fauve exhibition. His *Blackfriars Bridge, London* is representative of his style at this time. With the advent of Cubism, Derain turned to a more austere, 'classical' style, and after 1919, reverted to a naturalistic manner distinguished solely by its unimaginativeness.

8. The remark, so lamentably characteristic of Hemingway at his most callow and shallow, sounds as though it comes from *A Moveable Feast* or *The Green Hills of Africa*, but I was unable to locate it in either volume. Nagibin, too, does not recollect where it appears.

9. Marcel Proust (1871-1922) was a French novelist and neurasthenic suffering from asthma, who withdrew from the world to a cork-lined room. There he wrote the 16-volume novel *A la recherche du temps perdu* (1913-27), a Bergsonian monument to memory and time that also analyses all forms of love and gives a comic portrait of the upper and middle class of the Third Republic.

James Joyce (1882-1941) was a myopic Irish novelist, author of four books of fiction, a play, and a slender volume of poetry. Associated primarily with experimental prose, especially with stream-of-consciousness and neologisms, James is remembered largely as the author of the relatively simple novel *A Portrait of the Artist as a Young Man* (1916), the more complex *Ulysses* (1922), and the virtually impenetrable *Finnegan's Wake*.

Robert Musil (1880-1942), an Austrian novelist recently 'rediscovered' after years of neglect, is especially admired for his stylistically synthetic novel *Der Mann ohne Eigenschaften* (The Man Without Qualities) (1930-42), which attempts to assess experiences of which the traditional qualities and values no longer seem authentic.

Stendhal (pseudonym of Henry Beyle) (1783-1842) was a French novelist. He held several government posts, lived in Italy (1814-21), and pioneered the psychological novel, whose protagonist was usually defined against his environment: *Le Rouge et le noir* (The Red and the Black) (1830) and *La Chartreuse de Parme* (The Charterhouse of Parma) (1839). In addition to his novels Stendhal wrote a fascinating treatise on love, *De l'amour* (1822), famous for its theory of "crystallization," biographies of Haydn, Napoleon, and Rossini, whom he admired, and memoirs, travel notes, journalism, etc.

Fyodor Dostoyevsky (1821-81) was a brilliant epileptic Russian novelist with extraordinary psychological insight and impassioned religious convictions whose neuroses, financial difficulties, and familial trials did not prevent him from writing a series of constantly superb novels: *Crime and Punishment* (1866), *The Idiot* (1869), *The Possessed* (1872), and *The Brothers Karamazov* (1880).

Knut Hamsum (1859-1952) was a Norwegian novelist with some poems and plays to his credit, known largely for his first successful novel, *Hunger* (1890) and his *Growth of the Soil* (1920). His narratives are permeated with irony and ambivalence.

Charles Dickens (1812-70), a Victorian, was the most popular English novelist of the nineteenth century. Many of his novels, which are strongly autobiographical, indict the English society in which he spent a poverty-stricken childhood. Social commentary, sentiment, and unsophisticated comedy mark most of his novels, of which the most memorable are *Oliver Twist* (1839), *Dombey and Son* (1848), *David Copperfield* (1850, *Bleak House* (1853) and *Great Expectations* (1861).

10. The reference is to Prometheus, the Titan who stole fire from the gods for mankind. As punishment, Zeus had him chained to a rock in the Caucasus, where an eagle visited him daily to feast on the Titan's liver. Authors who have treated the Promethean myth—Aeschylus, Shelley, Byron, Gide—conceive of Prometheus as a symbol of free will and rebellion against tyranny.

11. According to Nagibin, the Day of Birds was a fantastic old Russian holiday, now discontinued, on which birds were released from their cages

12. Dante and Beatrice and Petrarch and Laura, together with Abélard and Héloïse, are probably the world's best-known idealized and idealizing lovers. Dante's collection of lyrics entitled *Vita nuova* (The New Life) (1292) is a hymn to his ideal Beatrice, later a symbol of theology in *La Divina commedia*. He fell in love with her when she spoke to him at the age of eighteen, nine years after he first saw her.

Petrarch's *Canzionere* similarly are inspired by Laura, whom he first saw in a church when he was twenty-three, and fell passionately in love with her, a love that presumably lasted until his death in 1374.

13. According to Nagibin, Richard Bombard was a doctor who, in the late 1950s and early 1960s, claimed that many people who are shipwrecked and die should trust nature and thus survive.

14. Paul Homburg is clearly modeled on Albert Einstein (1879-1955), the greatest physicist of the twentieth century, who is best remembered for his theory of relativity. Awarded the Nobel Prize in physics in 1921, as a Jew Einstein was deprived of his property and German

citizenship by the Nazis in 1934, and emigrated to the United States, where he became a citizen in 1940. His favorite pastime was playing the violin.

15. In classical mythology Lethe was a river in Hades, the underworld, whose water caused those who drank it to forget the past. As a logical consequence, Lethe has become synonymous with oblivion.

16. The Wassermann reaction, named after August von Wassermann (1866-1925), a German physician and bacteriologist, is a diagnostic test for syphilis.

17. The idea is central to *A la recherche du temps perdu.*

18. The expression is a Russian idiom, probably derived from Shakespeare's *Othello.*

19. It is likely that Nagibin has B.F. Skinner in mind as the 'doctor' with the behavioral solution to mental disturbance.

20. Proust's description of the eating of the *'petites madeleines'* (the little cakes) illustrates involuntary memory at work. As the protagonist of *A la recherche du temps perdu* consumes the cake soaked in tea, he involuntarily recalls an earlier time in his childhood when his aunt Léonie would treat him to the cake in her bedroom on Sunday mornings at the family house, Combray. The description occurs in the beginning section of the first volume of the cycle, *Un Amour de Swann,* and is later repeated.

Elijah's Day

This happened back when Podsvyatye was part of a large impoverished collective farm scattered among the lakes and forests of Meshchyora. Now there's a state waterfowl preserve in Podsvyatye. The village is located on the high banks of Lake Dubovo, which is really the natural overflow of the river Pra, and it looks off toward the Moscow region. A border marker stands on the shore of Podsvyatye, pointing with one arrow beyond the lake to the Moscow region, and with the other right to the Ryazan region—in the form of Podsvyatye—as if jabbing a finger at a chest.

Year after year, at the end of the summer, in late fall and early spring, I used to go there for the excellent and abundant duck hunting. In the spring we hunted them with live decoys as a rule, in the summer with stuffed decoys from noiseless flat-bottomed boats as they flew up into the air. In the fall, standing beneath stacks of fragrant, sedgelike hay on the shores of the lake, I used to shoot the plump northern mallards and other wild duck when they passed through on their way south.

But this time I'd arrived about two weeks before the hunting season. I wanted to catch sazan at Dubovo and crucian carp in the Ozerka, a reservoir as round as a kopek that's only a stone's throw from Podsvyatye. I had just paddled across Dubovo in a dugout and made my way over a small incline to Podsvyatye's only street when I detected the smell of a holiday in the air. Smell isn't even the word—it positively reeked of the overpowering fumes of the beer that was brewing in every house. It turned out that I'd landed in Podsvyatye on the very eve of Elijah's Day!...

Food was roasting, steaming, baking, stewing, and boiling in every house. Here and there, in the cherry and apple orchards, thin whitish clouds of smoke were rising timidly from stills of home-brewed vodka. From the Moscow side of the lake there came a steady flow of supplies: cases of beer, fortified wine, canned goods, and white bread. Podsvyatye doesn't have its own store; people row over to the Moscow side for bread, vodka, matches, and kerosene. That's faster and more convenient than trudging through two swamps and a forest to get to the collective farm store—and besides, the only things you can be sure to find there are matches and fly paper.

Toward evening every hut smelled of hot irons—everybody was pressing pants, riding breeches, tunics, jackets and field shirts, skirts and ladies' jackets. The men were borrowing boot wax and razor blades from each other; you could have lit a cigarette from the housewives' faces, which were red and glowing from the heat of the oven, the children were running around underfoot, catching slaps, a box in the ear, and hot buns, cracklings, and duck gizzards.

A slight lull came only with the onset of darkness. People seemed to realize that they could only do so much—they'd done all they could—and they calmed down wearily. On the mound of earth around Anatoly Ivanovich's substantial hut the men of the numerous Makarov clan had settled in, as usual, for an evening smoke and leisurely conversation. Podsvyatye is divided into two parts: Podsvyatye proper, and the Belikovs' farmstead. The Belikovs, like the Makarovs, have a common surname because of their close kinship. Their relations with the Makarovs are, to put it mildly, strained, as they had been once upon a time in Verona between the Montagues and the Capulets.[1] And a few years ago, when Klavka Belikov took up with Grisha Makarov, Afonya—the Tybalt of the Belikovs—drove a round of buckshot into Grisha's rear; if Grisha hadn't been wearing quilted pants and flannel drawers, Afonya would have completely destroyed the fellow. And Ignaty Petrovich, the head of the Belikov clan, denounced the seducer to the police, accusing him of stealing collective farm property. They held Grisha in jail for about six months and then let him go without even a conviction. In spite of such a favorable outcome, Grisha never approached Klavka again, and even steered clear of the Belikov farmstead altogether. From that time on, Grisha was stuck with the nickname 'Bachelor Boy.'

He was also among the smokers who had gathered on the mound around Anatoly Ivanovich's house; and besides him there was the oldest hunter in Podsvyatye, Dedok, Grisha's brother, the collective farm driver named Petrak, another driver, Ivan, and that infamous liar—the sixteen-year-old orphan, Valka Kosoy. In the lazy rambling conversation, the topic turned to the coming holiday. They started arguing about how much the collective farm would allot to the Podsvyatye work team. Carried away with his lies, Valka blurted out that they would lavish the better part of a thousand rubles on them. Petrak, who had voluntarily taken charge of the orphan, started to put the liar to shame, and I told Anatoly Ivanovich that I'd never noticed any particular religious fervor on the part of the Podsvyatians before.

"And there never was any," replied the gamewarden calmly.

"But look how you're getting ready for Elijah!"

"Like everyone else does. Nothing special."

"What does the holiday mean anyway?"

"Who knows?" Anatoly Ivanovich shrugged his shoulders indifferently. "Elijah's Elijah, that's all."

"On Elijah's Day the water's cold; you can't swim," said Valka Kosoy, spitting out a viscous glob of tobacco spittle.

"Who says you can't?" objected Anatoly Ivanovich. "Every year I swim right up till the first frost."

"The fever will do you in," noted the taciturn Grisha.

"What do you mean, fever?" said Valka, narrowing his eyes as he always did before some particularly remarkable lie. "I swim in ice-holes all the time. It's nothin'."

"Who is it that swims in ice-holes?" asked Petrak in a threatening tone of voice.

But Valka was off and running.

"All us walruses . . . we have to swim in ice-holes."

"Okay, walrus," sighed Petrak gloomily, "I'll remember that. Next time we go north I'll give you a good dunking."

"It'll be my pleasure," said Valka, paling.

"In the old days people used to say: 'On Elijah's Day, it's summer till dinner and autumn after,' " announced Dedok. "And here's another one: 'Till Elijah's Day there's a pound of honey in the hay; afterwards there's a pound of manure.' "

"So what are you celebratin'—the exchange of honey for manure?"

"Good Lord, what on earth are they yappin' about now?" broke in old woman Martynovna, Dedok's companion of half a century, who'd just walked up to the group. "On Elijah's Day they celebrate the first sheaf of grain. There's even a saying: 'Rye ripens for Elijah's Day and is gathered in for the Assumption.' "

"Wait just a minute, Martynovna," interrupted Anatoly Ivanovich sternly. "What are you talkin' about the first sheaf for, when the ears of rye haven't filled out yet?"

"I can't tell you about that," persisted Martynovna stubbornly, "But in the old days it used to work out just that way. 'No one's workin' in the field; the prophet Elijah counts the yield.' People wouldn't say it for nothin'!"

"So that means there's nothing for Elijah to do here," laughed the dark-complexioned, curly-headed Ivan, who was so unlike the rest of the Makarovs, with their light brown hair, gray eyes and pale skin, so quick to blush. "How can he count sheaves if the rye's not ripe yet?"

"What kind of rye could we grow, anyway?" said Petrak bitterly.

"Who ever used to sow rye in this miserable soil? Nothing grows here besides potatoes and weeds, and won't."

"On Elijah's Day they don't drive the cattle into the fields," said Martynovna sternly, as if reproaching one of us.

"But seems like I saw them drive the herd into the flood lands," noted Ivan.

"On Elijah's Day beast and reptile wander at will," Dedok recalled joyfully. "Wolf season opens; that means we'll go after the gray wolf."

"Hunting's not allowed yet," objected Anatoly Ivanovich, who'd recently been elected gamewarden for the umpteenth time. "Just let me catch you with a gun in the woods, and I'll register you for such beasts and reptiles that you won't get a whole lot of pleasure out of it."

"But, Tolechka, that's how they used to reckon in the old days," said Dedok, who in spite of his countless years was still an inveterate poacher, trying to talk his way out of it.

"In what 'old days'?" asked the gamewarden.

"In the days of damned tsarism," specified Dedok.

"In that case, there's no reason to go stirring people up. Young people are listening to you," said Anatoly Ivanovich, motioning toward Valka Kosoy.

"And non-union besides," added Valka, adopting the gamewarden's tone. "You're supposed to educate me, not teach me a bunch of garbage."

"Hey, that's enough, you're attacking an old man," said Martynovna, coming to her husband's defense. "Before Elijah's Day even the priest's prayers won't win a drop of rain; but after Elijah's Day an old woman can start a downpour with a wave of her apron... When Elijah comes he'll bring some rot... After Elijah's Day hail and thunderstorms are let loose... Ascension Day with rain; Elijah's Day with a thunderstorm..."

"Hold it, Martynovna, you're splitting our ears!.."

"And *you* just try to understand this. On Elijah's Day a fire always breaks out somewhere. That's why people celebrate Elijah—to pacify him."

"Seems like a lightning rod would be more dependable," said Anatoly Ivanovich, showing off his common sense and refinement.

"Martynovna's talking sense," said Valka in a bass voice, assuming the role of the young positive hero. "At this time of year, thunderstorms come often, and that's how people got started believing that the prophet Elijah drives around the sky in a fiery chariot. And our ancestors, fearing for the safety of their homes, cattle, and crops, tried to pacify Elijah any way they could."

"Well, I never!" said Petrak, getting carried away. "He talks like a book. You don't suppose he's lying, do you?" he added uncertainly.

"No, that's exactly right," declared Grisha the 'Bachelor Boy' authoritatively, and his testimony put an end to the discussion. People are always more inclined to believe quiet people.

But Anatoly Ivanovich's wife, the round-faced, black-eyed Shura, added the final word to the conversation.

"Our menfolk like Elijah 'cause he gets rid of all the prohibitions!" she said mockingly and, as far as I was concerned, mysteriously. But all the others, it seems, understood her and frowned a bit.

Only Martynovna was totally unaffected by Shura's remark. She slapped her smooth unwrinkled forehead, as if killing a mosquito, and said:

"I forgot all about what I came here for! Shura, can you spare some cinnamon?.."

As usual when a lot of food is being prepared, there's nothing in the house to eat. A meager kind of supper was put together toward nightfall when the long crimson August sunset had burned out, giving way to a greenish transparent twilight, and the stars had already come out and Anatoly Ivanovich had lit the kerosene lamp, which in an instant was enshrouded in a fluttering swarm of midges. The house was overflowing with food: pies, buns, and cheese tarts; jellied fish and pork had already thickened out in the entryway. There were also plenty of roasted and stewed foods, but not a thing could be touched. "That's for tomorrow!" Shura kept saying harshly. And nothing else appeared on the table except cucumbers, cans of stuffed squash and cold boiled potatoes. Evidently this scarcity was to offset tomorrow's abundance. And only in honor of the arrival of Shura's brother, the construction technician Mikhail from Alma Ata,[2] were we allowed to open a bottle of Stolichnaya vodka.[3]

"I saved up my days off on purpose!" Mikhail was jubilant as he presented his relatives with Kazakh sweets: dried melon that looked as if it were braided, dried apricots and currants. "It only took four hours to fly to Moscow, but I spent half a day getting from Moscow to you."

"You've become a real Uzbek out there in your Alma Ata!" said Shura, lovingly examining her brother's thin, darkly tanned face. "Will you be with us for long?"

"Till the holiday's over and then I'll head back. I've got to be at work on the sixth."

Footsteps and quiet voices were heard outside the windows, which were open wide onto the darkness of the street. Anatoly Ivanovich's younger brother Vaska, with his tiny little wife, twins, and baby, which he carried easily and carefully in its pretty bunting, paraded past the hut, heading for Bald Knoll, where there was a boat moorage. The relatives didn't exchange a single word, but went on down the street, pretending that they didn't see us through the illuminated wide-open windows.

"Where are they off to?" I asked.

"Vaska's wife is keeping him away from sin," Shura explained vaguely. "She does that every year... And Vaska always minds her," she added with a sigh.

"Well, here's to our reunion," said Mikhail, holding out his swarthy hand toward me with a full glass in it.

"To our reunion!" I replied and didn't ask Shura what kind of disasters Vaska was being kept away from.

The next day, which was quiet and totally unlike a holiday, I didn't even remember my question. Somehow I'd thought that the visiting would begin in the morning; we'd go to their house; they to ours—but nothing of the sort. The Podsvyatians traditionally spent this day in the company of their families, enjoying simple home-brewed drinks and pies. From morning till night, the pies filled with buckwheat porridge, potatoes, cabbage, fish, viziga, mushrooms, rice, and jam never left the table, which was covered with a starched white tablecloth. Nor did anyone clear away the small blue decanter of vodka in which wormwood had been steeped. There wasn't a single bold guzzler in our group. Anatoly Ivanovich was a confirmed teetotaler, Shura and I didn't count, and Mikhail had a strong constitution, although outwardly he was no Hercules: he was as skinny as if he'd been pulled through a ring, and he was dry and veiny besides. He didn't get all excited, didn't overdo anything and seemed not to have his eye on the little blue decanter, but gave his undivided attention to his sister's pies. He would alternately taste small pieces of first one pie, then another, and would give thoughtful and favorable evaluations of both the pastry and the filling, which delighted the humble and diligent Shura immeasurably.

From time to time various people passed by the window: first, Anatoly Ivanovich's brother, Senechka, carrying his little daughter on his shoulders, then Petrak in his new sky-blue nylon shirt, accompanied by his six heirs and his overgrown ward, Valka Kosoy, his cousin Grisha the 'Bachelor Boy,' with Nyura, his new fiancée from across the river, whose gaze was so deeply hidden in the eyesockets between her strong forehead and her stony, protruding cheekbones that she seemed to be sightless. But these figures brightened up the landscape only now and then; the street remained deserted, as on an ordinary work day when everyone went off to the farm and the fields.

I must confess I was feeling a bit disappointed that the holiday, which had required such a tremendous amount of fuss and bother, was burning out so dimly. True, I understood that everything still lay ahead, but the next day, too, passed uneventfully.

The Podsvyatians paid one another visits. In the morning we were invited to Senechka's. Anatoly Ivanovich's younger brother wasn't so young anymore. He'd finished his term of active duty a long time ago, had gotten married, and had a household of his own, but to the people around him he was still 'Senechka'; they didn't call him anything else even in the heat of an argument. Old Martynovna explained to me that in Podsvyatye people who were a little bit unreliable somehow got stuck with nicknames till their dying day. "And how did your old man get the name Dedok, Martynovna?" I couldn't resist asking. "But that's not a name!" objected the old woman. "He's Savely Petrovich. But if Dedok didn't play the fool so much with fish and game," added Martynovna, "maybe they'd call him something a little more respectful, like Gramps or Old Man. Here everyone works with an axe—can't handle any other tool, but Savely Petrovich is a carpenter and a cabinetmaker and the best woodcarver in this whole countryside. People used to come from Moscow to watch him and snap pictures. But just let a fish start splashin' or a duck fly up, and that old man of mine will take off like a bat out of hell. He don't like to know about laws or rules. He's a worse mischiefmaker than Valka Kosoy. It don't matter that he's getting on. He's Dedok, that's all—just Dedok..."

Senechka, too, wasn't reliable. I didn't know him real well, and I'm hard pressed to say just how his superficiality made itself known, but in all his behavior, his manner of speaking, his way of walking, in the foolish expression on his lightly freckled face with its gristly turned-up nose, one sensed that Senechka was a shallow person who lived without serious thoughts and without respect for the people around him or for himself. What Senechka especially loathed and scorned was science. Out on the mound around Anatoly Ivanovich's house, I had occasion to hear how he abused Dedok, who was touchingly delighted by the discoveries of man's restless genius.

"Science, science, all the time science!" said Senechka in a nasal voice, which was perpetually hoarse with a cold, and he spat caustically under his boot.

"But what about Sputnik?" objected Dedok. Though intimidated a little by the young upstart, he overcame his fear and spoke up like a real champion of scientific truth.

"Have you seen this Sputnik? Have I seen it? Has anyone? No matter who you ask, nobody's seen it. It's all a lot of nonsense, something they thought up for the newspapers."

"Go on yappin', but don't go too far!" cried Dedok in his thin voice. "People have seen Sputnik... it sails through the sky like a slow star, and they've heard it tickin'!.."

"Tickin'!.. It's the piles on your butt that's tickin'!" Senechka snapped out with such a clang that you'd think he was spitting out steel. "There ain't any science, so keep your trap shut!"

"And what about the compass?" babbled Dedok in pitiable confusion.

"Big deal—it's a magnet, but it still ain't science," explained Senechka condescendingly. "And it was invented maybe a hundred years ago."

"That's more'n likely true," Dedok, who'd been totally shown up by Senechka, agreed sadly.

What else could you call someone who completely rejects science and all its achievements? Senechka[4]—there's no other name for him. What's more, this nickname was pronounced 'Sinichkya.'

Anatoly Ivanovich didn't feel like going to Senechka's. It seemed to me that he was somewhat afraid of his younger brother.

"I won't go!" he asserted stubbornly, blushing so that a brick-red color spilled out over the collar of his field shirt with its clean undercollar, and it splashed from under his sleeves over his freckled arms, which were covered with rust-colored hair; and the thought occurred to me that the gamewarden must now be red all over, as if he'd been scalded. "You go ahead, but I'm going to sit home for a while and listen to the radio."

"The batteries are worn down as it is," objected Shura, "Why waste the radio for nothing?"

"They promised to bring a storage battery from Klepiky."

"It's not good to offend Senechka," insisted Shura. She didn't like her brother-in-law at all, but observed all the local customs—maybe because she herself was from the other side of the river.

"He's mean when he's drunk," said Anatoly Ivanovich, reluctantly voicing the real reason for his unwillingness to go to his brother's place.

"You can't stay home, Tolya," said Shura solemnly and sadly. "You know yourself you can't. With Mikhail here too... Can't you really see what an insult it would be to Senechka if we didn't go? And besides, he's harmless today."

"How do you know?"

"Just believe me!.. Well, have it your own way. I'm better off going to my mother's. Have a good time here without me."

Shura's mother lived on the other side of Lake Dubovo, as if in another world. Anatoly Ivanovich could easily cover twenty kilometers on his crutches, paddle to Klepiky in a dugout and to Kasimov in a kayak. But that was all within the boundaries of his native Ryazan region, while Shura was threatening to leave for the Moscow region; this geographic point meant a lot to Anatoly Ivanovich. How easy it would be to lose Shura on that alien unknown side of the lake! Anatoly Ivanovich didn't simply love his wife; in a moment of candor he confessed to me that all he had to do was think about another woman more vividly and he'd be hit with such intense nausea that he'd have to drink down two or three mugs of cold clean water from the river Pra in order to calm down his insides.

Sighing, he pulled himself up on his crutches. Shura took the bundle with the pies that had been prepared beforehand, Mikhail put a bottle of vodka into his jacket pocket, and we set off.

It was noisy and chaotic at Senechka's, and they were always running short of something: either glasses or knives, forks, plates, or places at the table. Various people kept coming and going, and in the extremely thick tobacco smoke, I couldn't make out their faces very well; it looked like the whole village, or rather the Makarov side (I didn't notice any Belikovs), had dropped in for a visit. Soon visitors who seemed to be from neighboring villages showed up, but they didn't stay long. They'd come in, take off their caps, exchange holiday greetings with the hosts and guests, pull up to the table for a minute, bang their wineglasses, poke someone else's fork into the cucumbers or pickled mushrooms—and that was all; they'd move on to the next house. It seemed to me that nomads like these weren't terribly well-respected. Nothing was said about them; the hosts welcomed them politely, entertained them cordially, but made no effort to get them to stay, even for the sake of politeness.

Senechka's behavior was unusually responsible and restrained, even stern. He saw to it that the guests' glasses were full, passed out hors d'oeuvres and pies, opened bottles and drank almost nothing at all himself. He'd only take a sip with each new guest and then leave his little wineglass on the windowsill.

His thinnish, sickly little wife Marya, who always had one foot in the grave, rushed back and forth between the oven and the table, never quite able to satisfy the fluctuating group of guests. She was one of those unfortunate housewives who can never manage things. They're inspired by the best of intentions, don't spare themselves, run their legs off, and try to be on time everywhere, but something always goes wrong: they'll overlook something here or let something slip there, and mess everything up elsewhere. They're always cleaning up, and yet the house is dirty; they forever cluck over the children, and yet the children run around with running noses, chapped skin, and bruises all over them; and all the while in the kitchen everything burns up, boils over, goes sour, turns out underdone or is left around till it goes bad. Either clumsiness trips them up, or they lack a connection between their head and their hands, or some kind of mysterious inner timidity gets them all mixed up. Most likely, the last was just what kept the diligent hard-working Marya from being equal to the task. Her fear of her husband, who was tricky and capricious when drunk, never faded.

This time, even though he did frown at various minor hitches, Senechka didn't needlessly abuse his wife and seemed to be satisfied that everything at his house was just like at other folks': the table was piled high with food and the front room was so crowded that an apple couldn't have found a place to fall; his neighbors and relatives didn't shun his house, and a lot of outsiders dropped in too. Senechka even spared Dedok, who'd been expressing his profound dissatisfaction with contemporary medical science for bringing the dead back to life so unceremoniously. He only remarked with a fleeting ironical grin:

"Don't even dream about that, Dedok. They'll only bring the bosses back to life."

"But why bring them back to life?" objected Dedok. "They never die anyhow."

We sat for a long time, but, oddly enough, there was neither music nor singing; it was just like a wake. I won't even mention dancing; everyone was too sober for that. You couldn't say they spared the bottle, but drunkenness just couldn't make its way through that padding of starchy, meaty, and greasy food.

Right before we left, Petrak showed up in his sky-blue shirt, all excited, and announced that the collective farm administration had laid out fifty rubles for the Podsvyatians, instead of the thirty they usually allotted to them for the holiday.

"Valka!" cried Senechka. "Where'd you get to?.. You promised us a good thousand!"

"Exactly!" retorted Valka coolly. "The Kasimov merchants used to come across with a good thousand in the old days—that's fifty rubles by the new price scale."

"Don't spoil my holiday for me," requested Petrak. "Try to get through just one day without lying."

"But who does the money go to?" I asked Anatoly Ivanovich.

"It's for everybody. Tomorrow we'll pool our money. We all celebrate together."

"Where?"

"At the Belikovs' farm."

I was surprised, but didn't say anything. At this point Shura started itching to get home: now it was our turn to receive guests.

Almost the whole village showed up at our place too. And here too it was noisy, crowded, smoky, and chaotic. Only Senechka's wife was no longer bustling around, but sat at the table in her new stiffly puffed-out dress, her thin arms with their large, toil-worn hands folded in her lap. She was so tired she couldn't eat or drink, while the quick and dexterous Shura dashed back and forth between the kitchen and the front room. But all the same, once again there weren't enough plates, cups, forks, or places at the table because it was beyond the strength of even the most capable hostess to manage with such a large and continuously changing group of guests. The main difference between the people at table here and where we'd been earlier was that everyone noticed Mikhail, as if for the first time, although he'd been over at Senechka's too. They tried to get near him to kiss him and clink glasses; they praised him for coming, and asked him about life in the south—about wages, living conditions, and the price of alcohol.

Then, when it was already dusk, we set out for Petrak's. Petrak, a collective farm driver, had the largest family and was the poorest man in the village. Collective farm drivers are usually well-off. But Petrak wouldn't take money on the side; his conscience wouldn't allow it.

Once he picked up me and two other hunters not far from the creamery. He was supposed to go to Derzkovskaya, but he agreed to drop us off at the ferry. When an elderly hunter offered Petrak a crumpled three-ruble note, he turned pale, and said, shaking his head:

"What kind of nonsense is this!"

"Come on, take it. After all, you made a detour."

"And all for nothing, it's plain to see!" said Petrak. He slammed the door of the cab angrily, nearly pinching the hand that was clenching the three-ruble note, and took off.

"Blockhead!" people would call him, but the second driver, Ivan, a shifty rascal and a scoundrel, sincerely considered Petrak a saint. And Petrak undoubtedly was, if, overburdened as he already was, he could take on still another burden—the task of making a man out of Valka Kosoy, an orphan who lived with his stupid and malicious aunt. Petrak regularly went to Valka's school for the parents' meetings, took Valka along hunting, taught him automechanics, and never let him get away with lying.[5] Now Valka was performing the duties of a majordomo in Petrak's house: he would meet the guests, offer them seats, and pour the wine, or rather, the smoke-colored home brew.

The spread at Petrak's turned out to be every bit as good as it had been at Senechka's and even at Anatoly Ivanovich's. His younger brother, Grisha the 'Bachelor Boy,' who was the leader of the Podsvyatye carpenters, was giving him a hand. Grisha was in charge of the carpenters, both in collective farm construction and when they went around the towns and villages as an artel. Every year they got together in a little artel and made their way to Moscow and farther south to the Tula and Kursk provinces, to the Ukraine, and sometimes they even made it all the way to the Crimea. Skillful craftsmen, sober on weekdays, reserved, not given to overindulgence, the Podsvyatians would come back with large earnings that enabled them to work for the collective farm for the rest of the time. Grisha was invariably elected head of the artel. The fellow combined the strength of a bear with the gentleness of a dove; he could never have lifted a hand against an offender. Besides, Grisha's outward appearance was so imposing that people rarely offended him. Grisha yielded nothing to his older brother Petrak in honesty and unselfishness. Grisha had broken away from Petrak long before, when he built his fine smart house with its tin roof on the outskirts of the village; but being a bachelor, he clung to his brother's family. All the Podsvyatians were troubled by the fact that such a kind, hard-working and well-to-do fellow was a bachelor. But if there was ever anyone who couldn't be called a slouch, it was Grisha. He made his first attempt to get married during the tender time of adolescence, when he proposed to his teacher. For this he was forced to leave school. But that didn't cause him too much grief because he was a poor student; but he was handy with an axe and a rifle. He got engaged before he left for active duty. His intended was a member of the Makarov clan, Dedok's grandniece, who spent every summer in Podsvyatye. She studied at the pedagogical institute in Ryazan and lived there in a dormitory. Well, what happened after that was what usually happens in such cases; maidenly loyalty couldn't stand the test of separation, and right before Grisha came back the people in the village found out that Polina was having a love affair with the movie projectionist, a married man. True, when Grisha came home, the frightened projectionist immediately turned into a stay-at-home family man, and Grisha generously forgave Polina for her unfaithfulness. But all the same, Polina turned him down under the pretext that now she couldn't respect him. Grisha never did understand this quirk of female temperament. Of the two of them, he thought, it was really Polina who deserved disrespect.

Grisha became consoled only when he fell in love with the quiet and gentle Klava Belikov. But we already know how that ended; Grisha fell, struck down by Afonya's shot and Ignaty Petrovich's denunciation. Once he was free again, Grisha kept a tight rein on his marital aspirations for a long time, but his unfullfilled family instinct gained the upper hand and Nyura from across the river appeared in the village.

Grisha's bosom pal, the cynical and scoffing driver Ivan, said they ought to pass Grisha around the whole region so as to improve the deteriorating race. In grade school compositions students write that Tatyana wasn't really in love with Eugene Onegin—she was in love with love itself.[6] This nonsense took on meaning when it was applied to Grisha. He loved his love and remained faithful to it through thick and thin. This man of steel, this knight, was preserving his virginity. He was saving himself for the mother of his future children. It's interesting that Petrak wouldn't allow Grisha to spend money on his nieces and nephews; he was apparently afraid that Grisha would transfer to them his tormenting desire for children. "Raise your own and spoil them to your heart's content!" he would say, angrily reining in his brother.

Now Grisha was sitting next to his fiancée in the place of honor at the head of the table. In spite of their totally dissimilar features—on Grisha's large fleshy face everything was outsized: big eyes, big nose, big lips; while all Nyura's features were small: tiny lips, tiny eyes and tiny button-nose—still the two were strikingly similar. Nyura from across the river, like Grisha, wasn't born of a mother, but was sculpted by the mighty hands of Vera Mukhina[7] for a never-finished ensemble—*The Collective Farm Workers.*

In Petrak's stuffy ramshackle dwelling there was probably more order than in any of the other houses. This may have been due to the fact that Petrak's wife, Nadyoga, was used to constant overcrowding, perpetual pushing and shoving, and endless confusion. She handled the guests as she handled her own six kids: she shouted at them, restrained them, and all but gave them a wallop. "How about a fork?" a guest asked. "What next?! Shovel it in with your hands," Nadyoga would answer.

The activity at the table was outstanding. No one got drunk, but they greedily guzzled down the drinks. Grisha, who rolled his 'r's' in his throat like a true Frenchman, had lost the letter 'r' altogether and was trying in vain to get it back again. Now and again he would call out 'Petwak' instead of his usual 'Petkhak.'

"Well, whaddya want?" his brother would answer lazily.

"Petwak," said Grisha plaintively, "what's a matta with me? I can't say yaw name, Petwak... Me, yaw own bwotha Gwisha... No, not Gwisha... Gwisha..."

Nyura from across the river nudged him in the side with a ten-pound fist in order to calm him down, but Grisha was inconsolable over the loss of this letter, which sounded like 'r' to him.

Senechka was drowsy and tried to fall asleep, laying his head down in a plate of jellied meat, but stubborn little Marya raised him to a sitting position again. Ivan, who was curly-haired anyway, had set his shock of dark brown hair all in ringlets and was now unusually handsome. Mikhail started speaking broken Kazakh:

"Leesten, my g-o-o-o-t friend, I weel make meence-meat out of you!" he would say every now and then, to the wild delight of Petrak's children.

True, the oldest of his six kids, Lyuda, expressed her pleasure with only a faint smile. She was standing with her back against the old sideboard, and she didn't budge from this spot the whole time. In the village they called her 'The Little Gypsy.' Thin, swarthy, with violet eyes—Lyuda wasn't a bit like the fair-skinned, light-haired Makarov breed. But then, there was something gypsylike in the dark hook-nosed driver Ivan too. Apparently, in the distant past some gypsy had overtaken one of the Makarov women, and a fiery streak had been mixed with the Ryazan blood. Petrak's Lyuda was so unusual a beauty you might think she hadn't been born on this earth. It wasn't goodness but sadness that radiated from her beauty. She was like a message from some other beautiful and inaccessible world, and it was impossible to understand what she was doing among us, with our noise and nonsense, vulgarity, boozy breath and earthbound sluggishness. And suddenly I understood Petrak, who constantly worried about her soul. Many people thought he didn't love Lyuda, and felt she was a burden to him, as if he didn't consider her his own daughter. And, indeed, he did feel burdened by the strange miracle of this little girl; he didn't understand what she was doing in his poor, difficult, ordinary life. If even my heart—the heart of an outsider—melted at the sight of her, what must a father's heart have felt, especially one so full of ineffable kindness and tenderness?

Suddenly, as if out of the blue, the guests started hurrying to leave. It turned out that they still had to visit for a while at Ivan's house, where his brother Boris, who'd come down sick, was sitting out the holiday; and then they were to go see Dedok and the homemade beer that Martynovna brewed a special way with various spices.

I felt all worn out and went home. When I woke up in what seemed to me the middle of the night, I saw a light in the clean front room. Opening the door of the storeroom a crack, I discovered a group of night owls sitting around the empty table. Shura, Anatoly Ivanovich, and Mikhail were carrying on a quiet conversation. Their faces were sober, kind, and a bit tired. The men were smoking and waving the smoke away toward the wide-open window. Shura was sewing a stripe, awarded for 'Severe Injury in Action,' onto Anatoly Ivanovich's dress tunic. A little star was gleaming on the 'Order of Soldier's Glory, Third Degree,' for which Anatoly Ivanovich had exchanged his left leg during his very first battle.

Mikhail was telling them about construction work and about life in Alma Ata. Anatoly Ivanovich, with his inherent distrustfulness, although without the teasing at which he was a past master, was demanding a more precise account of various details.

"Do you always get so much or only in season?"

"I'm telling you—all year round! We always have sun; construction never stops..."

"Okay, enough of your bullshit! Sun all year long—that can't happen."

"Now that's enough out of you!" said Shura, raising her voice. "What are you bugging him for?"

"I don't like it when people lay it on too thick."

"I'm not stretching anything," said Mikhail authoritatively. "I'm telling you the way it is."

"Listen, Tolya, what do you say we take off for the hot sun?" suggested Shura provocatively.

She was joking, of course, but Anatoly Ivanovich became gloomy:

"Go ahead if you want. They couldn't drag me away from here with a tractor..."

... In the morning there was a knock at our window. We saw a balding middle-aged man with a pale, official-looking face that was slightly damp with sweat.

"Interested in playing lapta?"[8] he asked softly.

"We're interested all right!" answered Anatoly Ivanovich, and taking his crutches, he drew himself up on his one leg.

"Please excuse me," the man said, recoiling from the window.

"Who's that?" I asked.

"He's the district organizer."

"What kind of organizer?"

"You know, for organized recreation for the village workers."

"They want to keep'm busy," said Shura in a somewhat mournful tone of voice.

In childhood I'd enjoyed lapta, and now I felt like taking a look at this age-old and almost forgotten Russian game. After a light breakfast with pepper brandy, I went out beyond the village to the playing field.

They were playing on an even mown glade at the bottom of the slope that was on the side of the Belikovs' farm. The teams consisted mainly of women and girls, but there were also a few adolescent representatives of the stronger sex.[9] The balding district recreation director was umpiring the game. As I walked up, Petrak's Lyuda was dashing across the glade, lifting her tanned legs high in the air like a colt, while Valka Kosoy, his mouth twisted in a rapacious leer, had managed to pick up the ball and was aiming at her. The fact that Valka was cross-eyed didn't keep him from being a good shot; he would shoot teals in flight and hardly ever miss. Lyuda knew this and was on her guard. When Valka hurled the ball, she veered sharply to the side and dropped to the ground. The ball whistled over her head, to the great consternation of Valka's team.

At this point there was a slight holdup in the game. Grisha showed up with his fiancée and demanded that they let him play. He'd evidently pulled himself together a bit since morning, but all the same, he still hadn't found the letter 'r' that he'd lost the night before.

"Make woom faw me!" said Grisha, smiling with a kind, shy, but now slightly stubborn smile.

One of the kids gave up his place to Grisha. This was against the rules, but the umpire for the match deemed it wise not to protest. Grisha took the bat in his mighty hands. But he'd lost his aim along with his 'r'; Grisha just couldn't manage to hit the ball. He wanted to distinguish himself in front of his fiancée and his heart hardened. He put all his monstrous strength into the final hit. The bat whistled past the ball and crashed into Grisha's forehead. The blow resounded with an echo. Grisha collapsed on the ground. Anyone else would have been killed on the spot by such a blow, but our hero was only knocked out. And at this point Nyura from across the river amazed everyone. She threw herself on Grisha's chest and in an unexpectedly thin, squeaky voice, so incompatible with her powerful build, she began to wail:

"Oh my God!.. But for whom have you left us, my shining falcon... my bright sun?.."

"Shut up, stupid!" said Petrak in a calm tone of voice. "Your falcon will come to. Valka, you take his legs. Got him? Let's go!.."

They carried away the athlete and the game went on...

... The Belikov farm—six sturdy huts—stood on a little hill opposite the church of Nikita Yalmansky, which had been turned into a potato storehouse. Only in the wintertime was it possible to get to the church over dry land; the rest of the time one had to go by water. Six long, flat-bottomed boats—the Belikovs' flotilla—were tied up at the mooring at the foot of a small hillock, and were always ready to sail. In a wing of the church there was a small grocery store. They also sold kerosene there. The Belikovs' farm, like the whole village, was actually located on an island. True, you could walk there through the swamps at any time of year except during spring flooding, but you could only drive there when everything was frozen or during the dry month of August, when the merciless sun drank up the swamp wash. To avoid walking through Podsvyatye too often, the Belikovs kept up their ties with the outside world and with their own collective farm primarily by water, although this way they had to make a detour.

The Belikovs lived prosperously and handsomely. Their short street was lined with poplars. Under every poplar there was a little bench. There were lilac bushes and flowers in their front gardens; in their kitchen gardens, which clearly exceeded the official norm, they had planted apple and cherry trees. From the farm there was a wonderful view of the river and the tall red brick church, from which for some reason they still hadn't removed the tarnished gold crosses.

The feasting took place on the grass and benches under the poplars. Groups would come together and break up; some preferred to enjoy their food alone, others in pairs. Here there was no gathering at the table to draw everyone together. Tablecloths were spread out on the grass; on the tablecloths there were dishes and tureens with various snacks, bottles of vodka and home brew, and jugs of homemade beer. A long table covered with pies had been squeezed into the front garden of Ignaty, the oldest Belikov. The hostesses would jealously sample the handiwork of their rivals, but they'd always judge fairly, without bias: "Nastya Belikova's pastry is just as good as last year's"; "Martynovna's is like clay—neither rich nor fluffy"; "You didn't spare the butter or sour cream, my dear, but your filling is raw and it's pulling away from the pastry."

The accordionist from across the river who'd been hired and was to be paid in money and food had settled down on a bench near the table. There was a glass of vodka and a dish of snacks in front of him. In Podsvyatye there weren't any good musicians. True, Grisha played the accordian and Valka Kosoy strummed on the balalaika, but that was only suitable for small private parties—not for such a grand holiday. The accordionist from across the river was a master of his trade. His face expressed his customary boredom, but his fingers were doing something incredible. He ran his fingers over the keyboard so quickly that it made your head swim just to watch him. He played as if into a vacuum; they didn't pay him much mind, but that didn't matter to him. He wasn't there to take part in the holiday; he was there to work. And the vodka he was drinking didn't make him a part of the general merriment. It was really fuel to keep the musical motor from breaking down. But at this point, Nastasya Belikova, a red-faced, rugged old woman, walked up to the accordionist and started stamping around the densely packed earth on her heels. The accordionist—totally oblivious—gazed through the obese Nastasya as though she were made of glass. And Belikova, looking angry, attacked the accordionist, demanding an explanation; but without waiting for it, she backed off and once again went on the attack. This was all a game; she really didn't care about the accordionist. She was having herself a good time. The accordionist indifferently switched from the dance music to "Dunay Waves"; resolutely straightening the hem of her skirt, Nastasya made her way over to the pies...

In a small meadow behind the wattle fence of the outermost hut, still within range of the music, some young girls were singing and doing a round-dance. In bright dresses, with wreaths of wild flowers on their heads, they were spinning around, now quickly, now slowly, raising their slender tanned arms to the sky, investing each movement with a joyful earnestness. And it was annoying when Senechka's Marya broke up their circle and, wildly contorting her thin face, stamped about, squatting and screeching shrilly. The round-dance broke up. Marya was pitiably hurt by the girls:

"Don't you want to dance?"

"Oh come on, Aunt Man'!" said Lyuda, walking up to her and putting her arm around her shoulders. "After all, you're a grown-up, and we're having our own fun."

And once again—why, I don't know—a feeling of sadness stirred in my heart at the sight of this girl. It was as if her presence made everything around her seem worthless—even your own inner life. You just didn't have the strength to rise to her level. It was a low blow to be so old, worn-out, intoxicated, and undemanding of fate when alongside you was this divine gift. You had to cast off the years and all your weariness to start all over again in a new role; but you just didn't have the strength, and that's why it was sad, so sad...

To this day I can't figure out when the quiet harmonious holiday, with its good conversation, music, and round-dance of girls in wreaths, with its benevolent sun, blue sky, poplars, flowers, glistening river, with its well-dressed, picturesque people, began to deteriorate rapidly, to fall to pieces, to turn into chaos. It seems to me now that it all started with Marya's clumsy act, which caused the insult to her and brought on new senseless acts. Very often commotion and disorder begin with the meekest people. And this is no coincidence. Perhaps Marya, restrained by Senechka, unseen and unheard in her everyday life, felt the liberating influence of the holiday more strongly than the others. On ordinary days she never took a drop of liquor in her mouth, but now she'd allowed herself a few shots and her lively heart had warmed up; it wanted something—something secret of its own that she herself couldn't even name.

But the cause itself really wasn't all that important. The outburst would have happened anyway for one reason or another. And in general it's a rare company, a rare gathering of human beings, that gets by without a scandal when people drink vodka. But usually the fire localizes and the holiday runs its normal course. Here, on the other hand, once things went haywire they never got straightened out again.

Leaving the girls in peace, Marya slowly dragged herself over to the accordionist; Nastasya Belikova was once again stomping around by his side. There was more than enough room, even if the whole village had joined in the dance; but to Marya it seemed too crowded, and she pushed old Belikova. Belikova, without changing the icily haughty expression on her face—an expression appropriate for an honored folk dancer—shoved Marya in the chest with both fists. Marya fell backwards as if lifeless; her skirt rode up, exposing her thin legs with their childlike knees.

"Take her away," Shura said to Anatoly Ivanovich.

Anatoly Ivanovich couldn't handle it alone; he called to Petrak for help.

The driver had been enjoying the holiday by himself. He was in the same sky-blue shirt, carefully shaven, his hair brushed and parted hair by hair. Having set down on some hemp a bottle of Kuban vodka and a bowl of pickles, he was leisurely downing glass after glass, crunching pickles with great relish, and smiling at his thoughts. Before each glass he would encourage himself, saying: "We're on our way, Petrachok. Let's go, old driver!" He was devoting this hour to himself, putting out of his mind his large demanding family, his house with all its holes that he'd never get patched up, the strange and sad miracle of his oldest daughter, and the pitiful liar, Valka Kosoy. But hearing his cousin's call, he immediately hurried off to help. Together they took Marya away.

Already within the bounds of Podsvyatye, they ran into Senechka. No one had seen him at the Belikovs' farm; whether he'd been strolling along the hillside, by the water or behind the white willows, wandering over to the other side of the river or to the neighboring village of Tyurevishche—one way or another, he'd reached his limit: his face was puffy; his sweaty forelock was sticking slantwise to his forehead. Senechka looked at his wife and the people accompanying her and didn't recognize his own kin.

"Ah ha! Strangers are leading you around!" he bellowed and darted into the house.

He sprang back out again with a double-barrel shotgun. Running up to Marya, he jabbed the barrels into her chest, and had already cocked the gun when Petrak grabbed it away from him and hurled it on the ground so hard that he broke the rifle-stock.

Shura and I came up just as Petrak was struggling with Senechka in the entryway, trying to tear an old Berdan rifle out of his hands. Shura's sensitive heart had warned her of trouble. Not wanting to leave me alone at the Belikovs', she'd asked me to go home with her, as if counting on me to help her in some way.

The thin, veiny, strong Petrak was second in strength only to his brother Grisha. He effortlessly broke Senechka's fierce resistance, disarmed him, and wanted to smash the second rifle, but Shura wouldn't allow it.

"Hold it, you half-wit! And just what's he supposed to hunt with?"

Petrak looked at Shura sullenly and spared the Berdan rifle.

"Bury it in the hay," Shura advised.

Senechka took off into the house; we followed. Marya was lying on the floor and seemed to be sleeping. I didn't even notice how the hunting knife wound up in Senechka's hands. He bent down over his wife, but Anatoly Ivanovich managed to intercept his hand. But he did it awkwardly—the edge of the blade caught his palm. Even though he was drunk, Senechka discovered his brother's slip and started twisting the knife out. Blood appeared. Shura threw herself on me and pushed me into the corner.

"It's kin fighting kin; you're an outsider—stay out of it!.."

There was no way I could get her off me.

Anatoly Ivanovich collapsed on the ground, pulling Senechka down with him. As he fell, Senechka let go of the knife and crawled off to the side on all fours.

I got free, and Shura helped her husband stand up. Anatoly Ivanovich got a handkerchief and wrapped it around his wounded hand. He gave Shura the knife to hide.

"Marya ought to be put to bed," said Shura, but we didn't have a chance to do that.

Senechka had managed to arm himself with a soldier's belt that had a metal buckle, and he lashed Anatoly Ivanovich as hard as he could with the belt. The blow came down on the stump of Anatoly Ivanovich's leg. The pant leg that was folded up around the withered stump made a loud slap. The gamewarden's face, ruddy by nature, turned deathly white; his hands on the crosspiece of his crutches became interwoven with taut veins. It looked to me as if he was about to bring the crutches down on his brothers's head, but restraining himself with an incredible effort of will, he said in a hoarse, shaky voice:

"Forty years I been in this world, and 'cept for a German, no one's ever lifted a hand against me! And this is what I get from my own brother!.."

He turned around and, thrusting his crutches far ahead of him, took a step straight for the doorway. Senechka overtook him in the entryway and once again walloped him with the belt. This time Shura didn't manage to, or maybe didn't want to, get in the way. I snatched the belt away from Senechka and with disgust felt the taste of his sour fingers in my mouth. He meant to rip my mouth apart, using the ancient method that had been put to the test by many generations of village fighters. I spit out his fingers, but of course wouldn't have been able to handle him, even though he was drunk, if Petrak hadn't come in at that moment, just in the nick of time.

You shouldn't think that Senechka was some kind of degenerate, flawed individual. On his healthy days, he was modest to the point of shyness; he was quiet more often, and smiled with his firm lips, which had been singed by strong cheap tobacco. The trouble was that every year he had fewer and fewer of these healthy days. But, after all, a person should be judged by his basic nature. And, since such days still did occur, you could say that Senechka's basic nature was good. It wasn't for nothing that he finished his term of active duty with a diploma, the badge of expert marksman, and lance corporal's stripes. In regional hunting, Senechka was ranked among the best wolf hunters. They even wrote about him in the newspaper. He was also a skillful carpenter, although recently the artel had been reluctant to take him on. Senechka was about three or four years younger than his wife, but judging by his appearance, you'd think he was a whole ten years younger; hard drinking had had no effect on his dry youthful face and lean well-proportioned figure. Sober, he wouldn't say a word against Marya; he'd take on any household job without shying away from even such notoriously woman's chores as laundry, ironing, and floor washing. His daughter adored him, and even in his very worst moments,

Senechka wouldn't allow himself to utter a crude word around her. But the little girl always guessed when her father wasn't himself and, squeamish and frightened, she steered clear of him, which painfully wounded Senechka. He was always tortured by his own drinking sprees and excesses. His torment and self-disgust were so genuine that the people close to him seriously feared that he might kill himself in one of those moments. I happened to have seen Senechka in various states, but I'd never even dreamed of anything like what came to light on Elijah's Day...

On my way to the Belikov farm, I ran into Boris Makarov, the driver Ivan's brother. He'd come down sick before the holiday and hadn't shown his face outside. I'd always regarded this reserved, serious, thoughtful person with respect and tenderness.

Boris was the only Podsvyatian who worked on the field crew. The rest either worked as carpenters or drivers, or, due to war disability, served as gamewardens, fishing supervisors or nightwatchmen. Boris could have either worked as a carpenter or joined the machine operators—in the military he'd dabbled in machinery—but to these, he preferred field work, which was unprofitable and, according to the local way of thinking, even a bit shameful for a grown man. He loved the smell of soil and the scent of hay, went out for the mowing as if he were going on a holiday, and would mow down nearly twice as much as any other mower. Incidentally, almost all the men went mowing, since in payment for this they were given hay for their own cows and were allowed to mow not only along the edges of the woods and sides of the road, but also in the meadows with their luxuriant variety of grasses. Boris took part in all the jobs: he worked in both the impoverished rye fields and in the thriving potato fields, and he even went out for the snow retention[10] that the other collective farm members hated so much. He especially liked it when something was done collectively by a group effort. "And what if someday we won't have the collective farm anymore?" his fellow villagers would ask, egging him on. "I'll go where they do!" "And what if there isn't one anywhere—if there's a universal agricultural factory?" "So, I'll have already kicked off by then," Boris would say confidently.

He regarded hunting and fishing more coolly than did all the other Podsvyatians, and if he did shoot ducks or net fish, then it was only out of necessity; you won't get rich on what you get for a day's work in Podsvyatye, even if you have a cow. But Boris worked just as energetically when it wasn't a working day and there was no pay at all. He was proud of the fact that in the work team ledger he had more checks next to his name than anyone else. Boris was a poet—a real poet of the collective farm village, though he didn't even write verse.

"I let him have it...bam! And he lit into me...pow! But I swung around and ...whap!" I heard Boris mumbling in far from poetic terms.

But Boris really did remind me of an old corngrower, not only in his love and devotion to the soil, but also by virtue of his sobriety. A glass or two on Sundays—this was Boris's norm. But now, red-eyed, with a puffy and somewhat greasy face, he was spouting a lot of the boastful nonsense that's typical of men who are always fighting and was so foreign to his serious nature. Maybe he really hadn't had all that much to drink, but for an organism weakened by illness and fever it turned out to be more than enough. He was still mumbling something and not letting me pass; but in all this verbal mishmash, I could only make out one thing:

"Ivan's kaput!.. Ivan's out cold.. Unnerstand?.. Kaput!"

He wrinkled up his red face, which was blazing with fever, as if he was about to start crying, and the wild thought crossed my mind that they'd killed Ivan. But my attempts to get at the truth were in vain. Animated by his drunken affection for me, Boris was hanging on to me by the button of my jacket, bringing his face up stiflingly close to mine, and muttering; now and then he would tip backwards, and only missed falling because he was holding tight to my button.

"I...y-o-o-u...unnerstand?..S-so!..Unnerstand?..Do you respect me? Spit in my puss...Right here!..And I looked after Ivan like my own brother...He's sleepin' in a ditch...Kaput! Let's get ourselves a little bottle!.."

"Don't you think you've had enough, Boris?"

"Impossible!" he said and even sobered up for a minute. "We've pooled our money!.." he exclaimed, and tearing my button off, toppled over into the burdocks.

I didn't have time to help him. A feeble cry sounded from over by the Belikov farm, and instantly realizing that I'd been waiting for this signal of the latest trouble, I started off for the farmstead. In a hollow, along the bottom of which stretched the dried-up streambed forming the natural boundary between Podsvyatye and the Belikov farm, I very nearly ran right into a flock of frightened kids who were rushing along the slope toward me. Lyuda was flying along in front, lifting her knees high in the air as usual, and throwing her head back. I called out to her. Breathing heavily, the girl stopped. Her violet eyes were burning brightly; there wasn't a hint of fear in them—excitement, alarm, almost ecstasy, but not fear.

It turned out that a father and son of the Belikov clan had gone after each other with axes. No one knew what set them off. They'd been staying aloof from the Podsvyatians, afraid that the latter would get down to settling old scores. They'd been drinking wine and chatting quietly, when suddenly they both went for their weapons. The son was a bit more agile than his father, and the latter didn't have time to take a swing before the son's axe pierced his father's body. At this point everyone started screaming wildly, and Lyuda and the other kids took to their heels.

"Did he kill him with the axe?"

This Lyuda didn't know. When she was running by, the old man was still on his feet and his son was straining to pull the axe blade out of him, as if from a gash in a pine tree. And suddenly I fathomed the thrill that Lyuda got out of what had happened, and I myself felt the rather eerie fascination of this bloody battle. There was something epic in all this: the battle between Rustam and Zorab, or, even closer to home, Ilya Muromets's battle with his enemy-son.[11] Senseless mischief had been elevated to the loftiness of a tragedy. It was bad to think and feel this way, and both Lyuda and I were guilty of a shamefully esthetic attitude toward the misfortune of others. I caught Lyuda's adult, conspiratorial gaze on me.

"How old are you?"

"Almost sixteen. My sixteenth birthday's coming up soon."

"Soon! You mean you've had your fifteenth?"

"I have. Word of honor, I have!"

Lyuda was waiting for something. But I had to hurry off to the Belikovs'. Why? I myself didn't know. In this kind of situation it seems that you can help out somehow. But still more likely, I was motivated by the irrational instinct that attracts us to a place where blood has just been shed.

The Belikov farm was still out of sight behind the hazel grove that screened it from the Podsvyatye side, but I was seized by a strange calm, as if someone had whispered in my ear that everything was all right. This invisible prompter was the accordionist. The sweet sounds of a polka—so incompatible with misfortune and murder—touched my ear like glad tidings.

The accordionist was playing, his indifferent untiring face inclined toward the bellows, while alongside him on the bench, their hands joined and their pale lids closed over their eyes, Dedok and Martynovna were humming in the weak voices of the blind:

> What're you dancing, Katenka?
> A polka, a polka, Mama dear!
> Who're you dancing with, Katenka?
> With an ohficer, Mama dear!..

It was strange to hear this prerevolutionary ditty, which had been sung in cities by the petite bourgeoisie, coming from the mouths of village people. And just then, my head spinning somewhat, I discovered Petrak in his sky-blue shirt at his former place by the tree stump. In front of him was the very same spread: pickles in a bowl, a half-liter bottle of vodka and a cut-glass tumbler. Petrak had firmly tied the broken thread of his holiday. He had to make up for the past, for the future, and for the break he'd been forced to take on account of Senechka.

"What's going on over there with Belikov?" I asked.

"Nothin' at all," Petrak, who'd never forgiven the Belikovs for the wrong done to Grisha, answered indifferently.

"Is he alive?"

Holding the little glass with two fingers, Petrak slowly emptied its contents into himself, put the glass on the stump, took a wrinkled pickle and greedily sucked on it with his lips.

"His kind don't die," he declared solemnly at last.

"Come on, how can that be?.. They say his son chopped him in half."

"That old devil—he keeps his pants up with a packed ammunition belt. And he don't ever take it off, the damned poacher. The ammunition belt's pigskin, and the cartridges are brass. Just you try and chop him in two! He damn near blew Afonka's precious skull all to bits. It's a good thing Nastasya managed to block the blow with the fire tongs. She disarmed them and led them off to sleep."

"Well, thank God!"

"If only they'd cut each other all to pieces," said Petrak vindictively.

Dedok and Martynovna were singing a new gentle song:

> All my girlfriends enviously
> Gaze at us all day.
> "What a truly wonderful pair!"
> All the old men say!..

"That's for sure—a wonder!" said Petrak, grinning, and filled his glass.

And at that point yet another wonder-couple entered the holiday circle: Senechka and Marya. They'd changed their clothes: Marya had on a clean white jacket and bright scarf; Senechka had pulled on a quilted waistcoat lined with rabbit fur over his field shirt. Both their faces were a little swollen, as if they'd been beaten with a wooden spoon. I'd never seen Senechka like that before. Yet he was strutting around like a peacock. But Marya looked submissive and unhappy; you immediately sensed that she hadn't come of her own free will—not that Senechka was trying to hide this:

"So I tell her: why don't you go out and join the folks? The money collection's more'n likely for everyone. Aren't we just as good as the Belikovs? Some fashion you've picked up—hidin' out from a celebration."

He was playing the part of the grumpy but thoughtful spouse. He dragged Marya over to the table and stuck a piece of viziga pie in her hand. He poured some vodka into a glass and ordered her to drink.

Marya tried to refuse; she said she had a splitting headache as it was.

But that didn't work! Senechka considered a swallow of vodka a remedy. Wincing in agony, Marya drank it down, choked, cleared her throat, and wanted to have a bite to eat, but Senechka wouldn't let her.

"Now, he'll tell you," he said, nodding in my direction. "Their famous poet said not to eat after the first drink." And he splashed some more into the glass.

Marya took a deep breath, as if she were about to dive into water, and drank it down.

"Now have something to eat," said Senechka, giving her his permission. "Eat and rest; you've earned it."

He himself took a drink too, but didn't stop to rest, for he'd sighted a new victim. This was an extremely quiet person, a former gamewarden who went by the nickname Strizh. He bore the surname Belikov, but was only distantly related to the farmsteaders, and had even built his miserable little house closer to Podsvyatye beyond the stream. Maybe Strizh had stayed at the party for the very reason that he didn't consider himself a Belikov and wasn't expecting trouble from anyone.

Senechka drilled Strizh with his eyes for a while, trying to remember something bad about him, and finally succeeded in doing so: about three years back, Strizh had caught Senechka in the preserve and had fined him ten rubles. They were supposed to take your hunting permit away for this kind of violation, but Strizh had mercy on his fellow townsman, accepting his word of honor that he wouldn't get into the preserve anymore.

"Why'd you beat me up last year?" Senechka starting badgering him.

"I've never laid a finger on you in my life."

"Never laid a finger on me! And how 'bout in the preserve."

"Last year I didn't set foot in the preserve."

"Well then, the year before last. Don't try to get out of it! You beat me brutally! In the eyes, on the head—wherever you could lay your hands on me!.." Senechka gave a sob.

"I'm twice as old as you," said Strizh, "and not once have I ever lifted a hand against a man. I took the fine—the legal amount and just a little something for myself. That's what they elected me gamewarden for. Your big brother Anatoly fines violaters too. And he takes their permits away, while I had mercy on you."

"Mercy!" screeched Senechka, calling on the bystanders to witness Strizh's shamelessness. "You hurt me in the head and busted my kidneys..."

"The hell with you!" said Strizh and taking his glass, made to leave in one piece, but Senechka blocked his path.

"No, you hold on a minute! What a slippery one! Mutilates a guy and runs away. That won't work!"

"And I say I never touched you! I never touched you, I tell you!" yelled Strizh, already close to tears. "Let me go!"

"All you Belikovs are worse than an ulcer for folks!.."

Strizh darted past Senechka; with one blow he threw off Senechka's arm and accidentally knocked him on his lip.

"You saw it!" Senechka cried out triumphantly, squeezing a drop of blood out of the corner of his lip. "What'd I tell you, folks? He's decorated me again! Looks as if he's knocked my teeth out!.."

Strizh covered his face with his hands, and crying with his whole back the way old men do, he trotted off.

Senechka pretended that he wanted to chase after Strizh, but he hadn't reckoned on attacking the old man. He wanted to stand his ground, to try Strizh's patience, to force him to hit him, thus proving his case before the people, to expose the barbarity of the Belikov breed.

"There, you see!" hollered Senechka. "He's spilled innocent blood, the snake! How long are we gonna put up with the Belikovs?.."

In a blaze of eloquence, he knocked the glass out of Petrak's hand with a careless movement. Petrak had remained indifferent to the spectacle enacted by Senechka, or possibly he hadn't even noticed anything, immersed as he was in his own secret inner life. But when the glass of vodka was knocked out of his hand and the precious liquid poured onto the ground, everything inside him went numb with rage. Without turning round, and without asking himself who was responsible for what had happened, Petrak dealt a violent backhand blow to the unseen mug with his knuckles. The blow was terrible; it wrecked Senechka's gristly nose. Senechka fell unconscious. Petrak saw his fallen friend, sighed, and hoisting him up on his back, lugged him home...

Senechka had left the celebration for good, but a holy place is never empty. Ivan arose from his slumber in the ditch under an old elm. He had woken up and discovered that his 'Victory' watch, a gift from his ex-wife, had been taken off his wrist. He valued it not as a memento but as a first-class mechanism—it kept time with the clock on the Spassky Tower to the second.[12]

Ivan was a hot-tempered fellow, explosive, with a southern temperament; and in appearance, as I mentioned earlier, he was the very picture of a gypsy: swarthy, angular, slim and strong as a knife, with sharp white teeth between dark firm lips. He wasn't even twenty-five yet, but he'd already managed to do more than his share of gallivanting. After the army he'd lingered in Moscow on his way home, and unexpectedly even for himself, he'd married a middle-aged dentist with a city apartment and a garden plot on the Old Kaluga road. He obtained a Moscow passport and passport registration and went to work for a taxi fleet. He arrived home for his vacation dressed in an expensive wool suit and felt hat and sporting a watch with a gold band. His wife wore silk pants, lay around in a hammock brought from Moscow during the day—something that had never been seen in Podsvyatye—and bathed nude in Lake Dubovo. In Podsvyatye it just wasn't considered proper for women to bathe in rivers, let alone stark naked. But Dedok explained that Ivan's wife was 'intellikhentsia,'[13] and, in the Podsvyatians' eyes, this not only justified the Muscovite's quirks, but earned her great respect. And great indeed was the disappointment when, after a half-year of marriage, Ivan came back to the village in a soldier's field shirt, boots, and a tankman's cap—but with the watch, albeit with an ordinary leather band. He turned in his Moscow passport and went to work as the driver of an old collective farm pick-up truck. He would answer the curiosity of his fellow villagers with one succinct phrase: "Got bored." Apparently it had gotten too stifling for a lake-country man in a city apartment and garden plot; he was drawn back to freedom and wide-open spaces. He gave himself up passionately to hunting and fishing, made money on the side without a twinge of conscience, caroused in grand style, and carried on light romances with girls from the local center.

But it wasn't the usual Ivan who now arose from the ditch—the merry fellow, ringleader, curly-headed mischief-maker, and favorite of girls and guys—but a stupidly spiteful troublemaker, out of his mind with a nasty hangover.

First of all, he stopped in at home where his sister-in-law Lyubasha was rocking her baby in a cradle.

"Where's my watch?" shouted Ivan.

"How the heck should I know?" snapped Lyubasha. "Don't shout or you'll wake the baby."

Ivan let out a long barrage of curses, grabbed a poker and stumbled outside. There he immediately ran into Petrak, who'd just had it out with Senechka.

"Gimme my watch, you goddam mother..!" barked Ivan, brandishing the poker.

In a hurry to grab what was left of the holiday, Petrak, without getting into any explanation, let Ivan have it in the teeth and proceeded on his way.

Ivan picked up a gold tooth that had fallen out onto the ground, spat out some blood, and just then caught sight of his bosom pal Grisha with his bandaged head.

"My watch!.." Ivan mumbled and jabbed Grisha in the shoulder with the poker.

At any other time Grisha out of the infinite goodness of his nature would have ignored his friend's rudeness, but he'd just lost his bride and was downcast! All the same he didn't start beating Ivan, but just squeezed him in a bear-hug and let him go. Ivan collapsed like a heap of rags. Grisha smiled disconcertedly and set off to look for his bride. He never did find her. Nyura from across the river—no one knew how or why—ended up in an empty threshing barn beyond the village with Ignaty Belikov's nephew Vaska, whom she'd seen for the first time in her life. They left the barn towards morning, leaving behind an unextinguished cigarette butt in the haydust. The threshing barn burned to the ground, but none of the Podsvyatians noticed the fire, even though the wind was chasing the black smoke over the village. Only the next day did a stranger stumble across the ashes and bring the sad news to Podsvyatye. They generously attributed the fire to the irascible Elijah...

For a long time Ivan couldn't get up. Later it turned out that his rib had been cracked by his friend's powerful embrace. But the sight of Shura walking hand in hand with her Alma Ata brother gave him the strength of despair. He threw himself at Mikhail, wailing, "Gimme back my watch, you snake!"

In his time Mikhail had worked for the police department, where he'd learned the techniques of judo. He immediately knocked Ivan down, and as he fell, Ivan took Shura down with him. Recounting what happened after that, Shura would say:

"I don't know how it happened, but the three of us wound up on the ground. The menfolk were beatin' each other up, and I was between 'em. They tore my new dress. After Misha caught Ivan by the forelock, he tipped his head back and hit him in the throat. Ivan started wheezin'. Misha went off to play lotto, and I ran home to change my clothes. I'd just changed my dress when Ivan burst in, covered with blood, frightful to look at, his eyes like the devil's, and holding the poker in his hands. What was I gonna do? I was alone—none of the menfolk were around. I tell him: 'Go ahead, beat me, kill me, but we didn't take your watch. Honest to God, we didn't take it!' He didn't say anything and started makin' a search. He turned everything upside down, threw the bedding on the floor. And I just prayed to God that Anatoly wouldn't come. He could easily kill someone for offendin' me. Ivan finished searching and stood up panting. Well, I thought, now he'll start in on me. Just then, thank the Lord, Grisha and Boris walked in. Both of 'em were in good spirits, chucklin'. And Boris says: 'Vanya, are you looking for your precious watch? Here it is. When you were sleepin' in the ditch, I took it off your wrist on purpose so it wouldn't get lost.' Ivan took the watch, smiled and said, 'Why the heck didn't you warn Lyubasha? I searched all over for it.' Right then they made up their minds to go to the other side of the river; Grisha thought his bride had hightailed it home..."

Grisha paid dearly for this trip. He fell asleep in the boat, but his thoughtful friends dragged him over to the doors of the club and laid him down in the bushes to sleep it off. In the middle of the night Grisha was awakened by the light of a flashlight beating down into his eyes. He hadn't even managed to sober up when two terrible blows plunged him into a long spell of unconsciousness. When he finally came to completely it was already broad daylight. Ivan, badly beaten, was asleep next to him. Grisha shook his friend awake; they went down to the river, cleaned out their wounds and swam across to their own side of the river. Ivan had gotten what was coming to him for starting a brawl with the folks from the other side of the river. They added Grisha in by mistake, having taken him for Petrak. Petrak had refused to transport stolen hay. This was a relief to the goodhearted Grisha; it had tormented him to think that someone could feel such hatred for him.

Toward evening I stopped in at the Belikov farm again. Everything had quieted down there, calmed down as if after a storm. The accordionist had cleared off for home; the guests had dispersed—those who were still on their feet, that is. The rest of them were lying on the grass, arms outspread, eyes closed. Their lifeless faces were lit up by the crimson light of the setting sun, which hung like a pink ball over the sad earth that had let off steam and was cooling down. On the table, which was littered with cores and pie crumbs, a fire-red rooster was strutting around, tapping with its claws, and raising its wings in imitation of a hawk or kite. I'd seen all this before somewhere. Yes, in a painting by Vasnetsov—*After the Bloody Battle*...[14]

In the evening of the next day the inveterate smokers gathered as usual on the mound around Anatoly Ivanovich's house. Only Ivan and Senechka, who'd had such a rough time of it the previous evening, were missing. Grisha, in a white turban of bandages, was smiling a feeble smile that looked apologetic; the others were frowning, and often cleared the phlegm from their throats and assumed a look of manly businesslike concern. Something had gone foul in their modest everyday lives, and it wasn't going to be easy to come to grips with it.

The sky was clouded over; off toward Moscow, summer lightning flared up, thin streaks of lightning raced by like little snakes, and from time to time a large warm raindrop fell on one's hand or cheek. Boris was the first to break the silence:

"How are the Labor partymen doing over there?.. I haven't heard the radio in three days."

"They're fightin'..." answered Anatoly Ivanovich reluctantly. "But what for?.."

Valka Kosoy walked up and flopped down on the porch stoop.

"Ah, I can't take it, guys!" he croaked with an affected grimace. "I'm hoarse from that home brew!.."

"Valka!" Petrak's voice wasn't as persuasive as usual. "Are you yappin' again?"

"It's dogs that yap, Pyotr Nikolayich," said Valka, pretending to be hurt. "I got no reason to lie."

"Maybe there's some good in you, after all, since you didn't latch on to that vile stuff—that damned devil's brew!"[15]

Anatoly Ivanovich raised his head and glanced attentively at Petrak.

"That's it exactly—devil's brew! You found a good word for it... And how'd you come up with that, huh?"

"What are you talkin' about?" though flattered, Petrak didn't understand him.

"Why is it that nothing like this happens on other holidays? Not on May Day, November 7th, New Year's or Easter; even though folks drink themselves blind!"

"Some comparison!.. May's the first bloom, November's the October Revolution, New Year's is New Year's..."

"Easter—Christ rose from the dead!" prompted Boris with a grin.

"I wish!.. Easter is spring; everything comes back to life. But what's Elijah's Day for? Nonsense, and that's all."

"That means there's nothin' in our Elijah, no faith, no thought, no warm memory, and no gratitude?.."

"We already explained that to you," interrupted Dedok. "The rye ripens and they raise the first sheaf..."

"There's no point in blaming it on Elijah: it's your own fault," noted Grisha.

"And when they just start in on us poor devils?" muttered Petrak sadly.

"You need to control yourselves," Dedok said didactically.

"If only it didn't exist at all—damned vodka!.."

The men sat on the mound reproaching themselves, grieving, repenting. Transfiguration Day was still a long time off.[16]

1972   Translated by Joanne Innis

Notes

The original ("Il'in den' ") first appeared in *Literaturnaia gazeta*, No. 32 (August 4, 1972). The present translation is of the edition included in *Berendeev les* (M. 1978), 179-211.

1. The Montagues and the Capulets are the two warring families in Shakespeare's *Romeo and Juliet* whose long-standing hatred ultimately dooms the young lovers, Romeo and Juliet, as well as Tybalt and Mercutio.

2. Alma Ata is the capital of Kazakstan, in the Asiatic part of the Soviet Union.

3. Stolichnaya vodka is, according to connoisseurs and experienced drinkers, the best Russian vodka available.

4. *Senechka* sounds rather derogatory because of its association with the word for *hay— seno*.

5. For a more detailed treatment of the relationship between Petrak and Valka Kosoy, see the story "Petrak i Valka" (Petrak and Valka) in the two-volume 1973 edition of Nagibin's prose, I, 121-130.

6. In the next sentence Nagibin correctly dismisses the statement about the heroine of Pushkin's *Eugene Onegin* (1823-31) as nonsensical.

7. Vera I. Mukhina (1899-1953) is a Soviet sculptress known for such representative group sculptures as *The Banner of Revolution* (1922-3) and *Bread* (1939), and monuments of Gorky (1893-9) and Chaikovsky (1953).

8. Lapta is a Russian team sport with bat and ball not unlike American baseball and English rounders.

9. Presumably, male.

10. Snow retention is the accumulation of snow on fields for the purpose of increasing the earth's humidity and of warming the pasture and whatever else may be growing in the fields during winter.

11. Ilya Muromets is the epic hero (*bogatyr*) of many Russian oral epics (*byliny*) composed from the twelfth to the sixteenth centuries, e.g., *Ilya Muromets and the Nightingale Robber, Ilya Muromets's Quarrel with Prince Vladimir.* He had the dubious distinction of having a Soviet war plane named after him in 1913.

12. The clock on the Spassky Tower is the Kremlin's equivalent to London's Big Ben.

13. Dedok means "intelligentsia"—the term coined by P.D. Boborykin in the 1860s to designate individuals from a cross-section of society whose professional activities were of a socio-philosophical and often reformatory nature. These intellectuals came to be considered an artistic, social, and political elite.

14. Viktor M. Vasnetsov (1848-1926) was a Russian "Itinerant" painter who often drew upon subjects from Russian history for inspiration, e.g., *After the Bloody Battle* (1880), *Bogatyrs* (1881-98). Perhaps his most interesting works are the murals in Vladimir Cathedral in Kiev (1885-96).

15. The Russian is *chertogon,* a reference to the title of Leskov's story. (Thank you, Yury Markovich!)

16. Transfiguration Day is August 6th. (Translator's note.)

The Outsider

Kungurtsev was one of those craggy Siberians whose firm sense of order can offset the noise, turmoil, and ugliness of life around them. And his appearance corresponded totally to his inner essence: a large head set low on the shoulders, a finely-molded upright body with a prominent powerful chest. And yet this hulk almost lost heart, though the affair was personal, incapable of casting even the slightest shadow on the universe. Putyatin came to visit them with his new wife for the first time. Alyosha Putyatin was Kungurtsev's best and dearest friend. But no, it doesn't happen, or rather, it happens only in novels that one has several friends united not for life, but unto death. In fact, you can have only one Friend, the one for whom you'd go through fire and water and put your head on the executioner's block, whose blood flows in your veins; all other friends, if you have them, are at best good companions, but often the sacred word 'friend' is used sloppily for casual acquaintances and simply drinking buddies. And Putya was a real friend, although their relationship had not undergone the test of war nor of mutual favors in anything more significant than lending money or a car or getting a rare medicine. But that was precisely what mattered! "She grew to love him for his suffering, and he loved her for her pity—" there's the root of Othello's tragedy. One can love only for nothing; if one loves for something, then that's already a different feeling, also valuable and worthy in its own way, but lacking the fatality, irrevocability, and selflessness of authentic love. The same applies to friendship. You pulled me out of the fire, I sacrificed to you the woman I love—so we're friends for life. Nonsense! You shouldn't confuse friendship with gratitude or a sense of obligation. Friendship is when it's simply good to be with somebody just like that, when there's no pressure of any kind (demanding friendship is the false invention of edifying literature); friendship is happiness.

Kungurtsev liked everything about Alyosha Putyatin: his towering height, his healthy leanness, the brilliance of his dark brown eyes, his rather low lilting voice, the immediacy of his response to any impression. He was well-equipped for life, a strong and healthy man, a splendid hunter and fisherman who knew the taiga like his own back yard, and the fact that he was an eminent specialist to boot, the chief engineer of an enormous aluminum plant, was his own business. What was a greater pleasure for Kungurtsev was the way he cut his meat, drank vodka, laughed, chopped off branches, built a hut or a campfire, bawled songs, and occasionally withdrew within himself, into his seriousness and silence, when his eyes acquired a distant look.

It's wonderful to have a friend, but it's absolutely great if your friend and his wife are accepted by your family as one of them. That happens all too rarely. It was quite natural that uncle Alyoshka should be number one with the three young Kungurtsevs: he had the best hunting dog in the world (a six-year-old shorthaired gold medal winner), his own Volga (their father hadn't found the time to get a Zhiguli[1]), a Belgian rifle (their father had an old gun of domestic make from the war), he knew judo holds and could do yoga. With her harsh, prickly temperament, Maria Petrovna didn't have to open up her heart to the Putyatins. Yet she did, and how! When the Putyatins arrived, she immediately retracted her prickles, and became as soft as velvet. True, it was difficult not to love Lipochka (everyone called Putyatin's wife that, even the boys). An extraordinarily good-hearted giantess, excessive in everything (she was her lanky husband's height, but much broader, with a stentorian voice that could be heard above any noisy group seated at table), always cheerful and tireless; above all else she loved to be needed, to be useful to people. In her presence, others instantly became free to enjoy "sweet sounds and prayers," while she shouldered all the "daily cares."[2]

Whenever they turned up at the Kungurtsevs' house, the kitchen, the refrigerator, the cellar, and all the corn-bins were instantly placed without a word at her command. She adored cooking, decorating the table, waiting on guests—that was her element, her sphere of talent.

Maria Petrovna had no use for anything except her medicine. She was the head of a large local hospital where she was the chief surgeon, she took on the most complicated operations and was justly proud of the fact that patients were brought to her even from the town in that region. She was a God-given surgeon and an efficient organizer, but would exhaust herself so completely at work that she simply didn't have strength left for anything at home. It also didn't appeal to her. Her bustling, obliging mother, who was muddle-headed with age, did the housework. With Lipochka's arrival, the Kungurtsevs' rather incoherent way of life started to thrive. There appeared pelmeni,[3] which Kungurtsev could put away by the dozens, though no better than the thin and insatiable Putya—how could so much pastry and meat fit into his flat stomach?—mushroom pies were baked, as were pies with fish, cabbage, apples, bilberries, currants; vodka made with various grasses and berries was brewed; home-brewed beer and a refreshing drink from wild cherries were prepared, beautiful china and silver tableware—Maria Petrovna's trousseau—were brought out, and guests were always invited, for it was a sin to enjoy such luxury by oneself.

There was another reason why the Putyatins' Saturday visits were so desirable for Kungurtsev, and they visited almost every week, for they lived about a hundred and fifty kilometers away. In a good humor from the tasty and filling food—on weekdays she'd go hungry, not having time to take care of all her duties and drink a cup of plain tea, let alone have lunch in the dining room—fortified by a glass or two of homemade brandy, but most importantly, having rested in complete freedom from all her worries, Maria Petrovna recalled that she was a woman and didn't push away her persistent but submissive husband, as she did the other days of the week. Two days of total happiness provided by Lipochka's efforts seemed to bring her closer to those mysteries to which bystanders have no access. And that large woman, attractive in her own way—her hair, sprinkled with gray and cut short, made her look a little older—somehow merged strangely and tenderly with Maria Petrovna in Kungurtsev's perceptions.

And suddenly they were thunderstruck by the news: Putya had parted with Lipochka and had married someone else. How had he had the time, where had he dug up this new one, how could he bring himself to break off with Lipochka after living with her for so many years in love, happiness, and harmony, why hadn't he consulted his friends, and how had he managed not to give himself away?—Kungurtsev racked his strong head in the most painful bewilderment.

Maria Petrovna had a simpler attitude to the development: "He's found himself a young girl. You're all fine studs!" The last comment was totally irrelevant, but she wanted to vent her spleen, and Kungurtsev held his peace.

The picture grew less clear still when Putyatin brought his young wife to get acquainted with them. To be more precise, he dropped in for a moment at the Kungurtsevs' en route to Angarsk, where they were supposed to pick up Vera Dmitrievna's daughter. Kungurtsev decided that Putya had intentionally combined two tasks in one so as not to drag out the visit and to eliminate the appearance of a celebration. He felt obliged to introduce his wife to his old friends, but either he didn't anticipate special joy from the introduction or he didn't know how to behave and was afraid of inquiries about Lipochka, and rushed to leave after they had barely crossed the threshold and exchanged the first greetings.

Everyone felt constrained, tense, and uncomfortable, but no one lifted a finger to relieve the tension. Under some pretext they had hurriedly sent off the children and had shut the grandmother in the kitchen, fearing equally the ingenuous straightforwardness of youth and the lapses of old age. Vera Dmitrievna, Putya's new wife, behaved more naturally than the rest; actually, she didn't behave in any way, as though what was going on had nothing to do with her. She betrayed no embarrassment, no defiance, no personal interest nor marked indifference, and what was the main thing—she had no desire to make herself liked. And she wasn't so young either, about thirty-seven or eight. She had tired eyes, with crows' feet at the temples; her large mouth with drooping corners made her look younger and bloomed only when she smiled, but she didn't smile often. At rest her face was sooner sad; she didn't resemble a young seductress at all. Nor a Siberian: her brown eyes under wearily-dropping eyelids appeared completely black and grew light only when her lashes lifted; she had dark hair, an olive matte skin, and a frail build, but solid muscular legs. "Where are you from originally?" Kungurtsev asked the woman. "The Volga region." "Have you been in our parts long?" "In your parts," she smiled, "Almost all my life. My parents are Siberians. Father was a soldier, served in Saratov. And after the war he returned with the whole family to Irkutsk." So she turned out to be Siberian, after all, but Kungurtsev didn't want to admit it. Neither in coloring nor build, nor in habits did she correspond to the image dear to his heart. She didn't make it in height either—she was of medium height for a woman, but beside her husband and the Kungurtsev couple she seemed small. Not like Lipochka—the right wing of this troupe of giants. "So our heroic foursome has disintegrated," Kungurtsev thought sadly, as though that were the major loss.

Putya was so ill at ease, strange, and ponderous, that at first Kungurtsev was happy at his departure. "Yes, yes," he said, "Go on, otherwise you won't get back before dark." It looked as though Vera Dmitrievna was happy that they weren't trying to keep them. "I'm nervous, old man," Putya whispered confidingly to Kungurtsev, "I've never been a father before," which set his friend's thoughts in a different direction. Lipochka's strong womb for some reason hadn't given birth to a new being, though who knows whose fault that was. And perhaps the major attraction for Putya wasn't the mother, but the daughter? Frustrated paternal feelings had begun to gnaw at him.

Putya's trust helped Kungurtsev carry out an intention that he'd almost abandoned out of cowardice. Under some pretext he hustled him into the library: "How are things with Lipochka? Where is she? Does she need anything?" Putya answered angrily, but it was a fine anger: "She's not feeling any too good, you can understand that, can't you? She went away to her sister's in Tomsk. She'll be going to work. She said it'd be easier for her that way. She decided everything herself, including her own departure." "I should think so! You played around while she...she..." Kungurtsev choked. Putya gazed calmly and coldly at him: "That I didn't," he said and left the study.

After the Putyatins left, Kungurtsev shared his observations with his wife. "I don't know, I don't know anything, and I don't want to know!" she brushed him aside. "I love Lipochka, but I'll never take to this one!" "She didn't do much for me, either," said Kungurtsev. "She's cold, somehow, aloof, I don't trust people like that. Putya's doomed, ah, he's doomed!" "No," said Maria Petrovna, "She's not a bitch." This simple comment made a tremendous impression on Kungurtsev. He'd waited for Maria Petrovna to make Putya's wife smart. It wouldn't have surprised him a bit if he'd heard her say about the silent woman with the tired eyes and sad mouth: "She's a fast one! May she never set foot in this house!" But for all her hostility, Maria Petrovna had affirmed her acceptability. And this meant that relations between the families could continue. Of course, his friendship with Putya would survive any test, but it would have been incredibly difficult for them to meet! That could have happened, and it wouldn't have occurred to him to dissuade his wife, for he unconditionally subordinated himself to her opinions. He was a good judge of people's business abilities, but people's moral qualities often eluded him.

But now he decided to renew the custom of their Saturday get-togethers, especially as an unexpected disaster had fallen on his shoulders and Putya could prove useful. The secretary of the regional Party committee had called him and asked him to entertain a group of filmmakers who were shooting a big movie about Eastern Siberia. The secretary mentioned the name of the chief filmmaker, adding in a tone that precluded a negative response: "You've heard of him, of course?" Kungurtsev, who hadn't caught the name, muttered: "What am I, some kind of savage?" "So you realize who it is they're sending to you?" the secretary said impressively. After that there was no sense in asking why he, Kungurtsev, had to entertain the great filmmaker on his day off, to sacrifice his Sunday for him, and to feed and give him drinks besides, and to cater to him, and what was the main thing, to give him a sense of what Siberia and Siberians were like!...

Kungurtsev was the director of the largest abrasive plant in Siberia. The plant, which had arisen before the Revolution alongside the corundum-fields and had expanded with the Five Year Plans into an enterprise of national standing, had gathered a settlement around it that already had claims to the status of a town. The center of peasant huts, with the noisy cockrels, crooked vegetable gardens and brown-faced old women on their mounds of earth, was becoming overgrown with blocks of multi-storied houses, which contained stores, barber shops, tailor shops, movie theaters, schools, kindergartens, and nurseries.

The plant dominated the district. Because of it, a station appeared on the railroad that stretched through the entire country, and an asphalt highway connected the station with the settlements, and other roads—concrete and dirt—ran in all directions from the plant gates; because of it, roofs bristled with TV antennas, posters annouced to the community the arrival of tours from the capital, and a stadium and swimming pool were being built. If the plant's existence were curtailed, then all life here would fall apart and then would completely abandon this bare land which didn't yield any crops.

It was natural that the plant director be the tsar and god of the area over which the smoke from the plant chimneys spread. His realm included the transparent, swift, cold river with its dried-up river bed, which divided the town in half, the islands, overgrown with wild currants, the water meadows, blue with forget-me-nots, the taiga, full of mushrooms along its borders, and the wood itself—full of hazel-grouse, ravines and gorges choked up with bird-cherry trees. Who if not he should entertain the distinguished guest and amuse him with Spartan Siberian pleasures!

And here a crafty scheme occurred to Kungurtsev. The filmmaker would come from Irkutsk by electric train, he'd have to be met by car. And if they were to have a picnic and camp out overnight, a car was essential. So that meant that the chauffeur of his company car would have to work on Saturday and Sunday. He, of course, would give him a holiday to compensate for it or would pay him overtime, whichever he preferred, but the director had never yet used the car for his personal needs. True, he'd been assigned an official mission, in a sense, but it was awkward, all the same. And Putya was glad of any opportunity to spin the steering wheel one more time. He'd been driving for many years, he'd gone through three cars, and yet his thirst for the steering wheel was that of a beginner. If a man's a natural-born driver, then whatever position he may occupy, his real joy is to drive a car. In calling on Putya for help and not simply inviting him over, Kungurtsev felt as though he were less guilty before Lipochka. Besides, he needed Putya not only as a driver but as a good table-companion, for Kungurtsev himself was of a silent breed and didn't know a damn about movies.

He expounded all these considerations to Maria Petrovna. "Why are you pulling this stuff?" she smiled. "If you want to see Putya, then call him to your heart's content." Nevertheless, when he called Putya, who was overjoyed to distraction and talked wildly enthusiastic nonsense, Kungurtsev changed the invitation to a request for help. Putya immediately calmed down, deciding that he alone was being called for the purpose of waiting on the guests from Moscow. "Don't worry, old buddy, it'll all be taken care of," he said in a deflated voice. Then Kungurtsev realized that he'd outsmarted himself in his devotion to Lipochka, but sticking stubbornly to his devious ways, he said: "Keep in mind that they're coming at 10 A.M., and there are three of them—that means you'll have to drop by our place first, and then go without luggage to the station." "As good as done!" Putya cried happily. "I'll drop off my women, and then go to meet the train. Expect us at nine sharp. Cheers."

No, he'd not done too bad a job thinking that one up: he'd avoided a direct invitation to Putya's wife, had eliminated any unpleasant overtones, hadn't sinned against Lipochka, and had involved Putya in his problems right away, which ought to give the latter a moral uplift: Kungurtsev was convinced that Putya was wilting under the fetters of a bad conscience.

Putya arrived on time, as always, with his wife, stepdaughter, and dog—his magnificent Romka. Kungurtsev and Romka, who hadn't seen each other for a long time, were happy to the point of tears to see each other. The sheen of former tranquil times lay on Romka's warm gray-blue short hair with brown spots. Lipochka had doted on him, but Romka, a real hunter, and not a spoiled domestic creature, recognized only one master. He even accepted food only from his hands, and whatever he was busy doing, he always remembered him, would run up and gaze into his eyes as if wanting to check whether he was behaving as he should be and whether there were any orders for him. Whenever he was hurt out hunting, he would be doctored by Putya, allowing only him to examine his wounds, to clip the extra hair out from between the pads of his paws, to brush out his coat, to wash out his eyes. But when Putya was away for a long period he tolerated Lipochka's ministrations; only he wouldn't accept food because he would be pining away madly for his master, but he drank water and let himself be walked and brushed as though he knew that he had to keep in shape. And he had an endearing habit: once in a while he'd lick Lipochka's hand as if to let her know that he admitted her right to be with him and his master. Each such tender fervent lick made Lipochka's large body heave with happiness. Capable of loving unreservedly herself, she was grateful for every kind gesture sent her way, irrespective of whom the gesture came from: an adult, a child, or an animal.

Kungurtsev instantly realized that the new mistress and her daughter had not succeeded in making contact with Romka. Vera Dmitrievna simply didn't notice him, and the girl only made the dog nervous by pointless demonstrative cries. Olechka looked much older than her fourteen years: tall, dark-skinned, fully developed physically, and showing promise of becoming a beauty, she bore little resemblance to her mother, having apparently taken all the best from her father. Uncertainty was mixed with arrogance in her behavior. When the Kungurtsev boys threw themselves at Romka with howls of affectionate longing without paying any attention to the beautiful newcomer, she twitched her shoulder scornfully, tossed her head, prettily stretching her profile, and loudly affirming her power as mistress, shouted, "Romka, settle down!"—and the dog crawled under the table with a servile downward slide that was alien to him. The shout turned the brothers' attention to the guest. And how quickly the oldest and middle one realized that the chief wonder of the day was not their old jowly, salivating, golden-eyed furry friend, but the mysterious dark-skinned stranger who suddenly turned out to be uncle Lyoshka's daughter. Only the youngest remained faithful to Romka, but even he at the end of the day beside the river, when the forest campfire was shooting sparks through the darkness, suggested to Olechka that they run off to the Baikal-Amur Trunk Line.[4]

Kungurtsev's boys represented three different hypostases of the human spirit: in the oldest, an enormous powerful Hercules, who seemed a trifle crazed from an excess of strength, the flesh triumphed; the middle one—depite all his vain attempts to imitate his older brother, which sidetracked him to the vanity of physical rivalry—became himself when he stood stockstill over some machine, a draft, or a riddle of organic life; he belonged to the realm of thought; in eleven-year-old Benjamin flourished the soul of the family. He rarely let his brothers tempt him into their devilish games; he was always his own independent being, reigning in the summits above and listening to the music of the spheres; his relations with people, objects, and phenomena were carried out with subtlety and mystery that were inaccessible to the others; he could be painfully pitiful in his inability to fit in according to the customary earthly yardstick, but he also could irritate one, the pot-bellied small-fry, with his arrogant alienation, and as was the custom from Biblical times, he was loved by his father with agonizing tenderness and fear. But even this soul abiding in mysterious regions betrayed Lipochka, powerless to resist the magic of feminine charms.

Vera Dmitrievna didn't merely ignore the dog. From time to time he would run up to her, and smelling the master's scent on her, with a short sniff would push under her hand with his nose, but she didn't respond at all. Kungurtsev decided that the dog wanted a drink.

"We forgot his bowl," said Vera Dmitrievna distractedly.

"He has a bowl here!" exclaimed Kungurtsev, to stress that Romka was a member of the family.

But Vera Dmitrievna didn't make a move. Kungurtsev brought him water, the dog sniffed the bowl from a distance, but didn't drink.

"You don't like dogs?" Kungurtsev asked Vera Dmitrievna with a rather unpleasant smile.

"Not much, to tell the truth," she replied calmly.

"And your daughter doesn't either?"

"I wouldn't say that. But she was frightened by a big dog when she was a small child. She even began stuttering and I used to take her to a speech therapist."

"How can one not like dogs? A dog, after all, is the best thing man's created."

"Alyosha also thinks that. I don't find it convincing. They've taken a splendid predatory animal, natural in all its habits, and have turned it into a toady, a sycophant, a slave. What's so moving about that? But man is so vain..."

"A toady, a sycophant?" Kungurtsev interrupted. "You should see patrol sheepdogs, what kind of sycophants are they!"

"What are you talking about?" the woman said with reproach and disgust. "Those are prison-camp dogs."

"To hell with them!" Kungurtsev flushed. "And hunting dogs? What brains, what devotion!..."

"Devotion—again for man's benefit. And brains? It's simply a sense of scent and training for the chase, as I believe it's called?"

"And Romka?" Kungurtsev wasn't listening to her. "Is is really possible not to love Romka, Romulya, the beauty, the smart dog?"

She shrugged her shoulders:

"A splendid dog... I never had a dog, either in childhood, or... later. One probably needs to get used to loving them." This sounded conciliatory.

"Don't try to wriggle out of it, don't!" Kungurtsev snarled inwardly. "That's not the Siberian way. You've said you don't like dogs, so stick to your guns, don't try to justify yourself, don't dodge it, don't be sly!..."

"Perhaps you don't like animals in general?"

She shrugged her shoulders again, the corners of her mouth turning down.

"I feel sorry for them..."

"I'm not talking about pity," Kungurtsev pressed, feeling that he was becoming unseemly in his persistence, but unable to control himself.

"Why are you badgering her?" Maria Petrovna got angry. "So she doesn't like them! Calm down! She likes people," she added with an enigmatic expression.

"I don't quite understand what that means," Vera Dmitrievna said quietly. "That's too abstract."

"If you worked in the hospital, as I do, for a while, you'd understand!"

"Possibly. But I've worked in an office, and such a—how can I put it... sweeping feeling didn't well up in me. People are varied, there are good ones and there are bad ones. Though what is a good person? For some he's good, but for others he won't do at all."

"Well, one can confuse any issue that way," said Kungurtsev.

She obviously had herself in mind: now, she was saying, for Putyatin I'm good, but for you, not very. The conversation was acquiring a dangerous tone.

"Well, and if instead of 'people' we say 'the people,' will everything become clear then?" he said, pleased with his own resourcefulness.

"Without question!" she smiled slightly. "But I think that's necessary only for leaders and heroes, and the average person can make do with a narrow circle. Those whom I do love, I love very much, and can only regret that there are few of them. To love is so pleasant, you know."

"Lipochka, though, loved everyone!" thought Kungurtsev, without noticing the almost overt mockery of her final words. It didn't escape Maria Petrovna, however, and she peremptorily put an end to the argument:

"Okay! To each his own. Whether we love people or not, the table needs to be laid."

"I'll help you," said Kungurtsev. "And Vera Dmitrievna will too."

"Of course," she answered politely, but without enthusiasm.

"Keeping house isn't in your line?" Kungurtsev inquired.

"To tell the truth, no," And she felt it necessary to explain. "We had a difficult, disorderly household. I don't know whether Alyosha told you."

"He didn't tell us anything."

"We led an irregular life. But that's not of interest to anyone. Better tell me what I have to do."

"Have to!"... Had Lipochka asked that! She just rolled up her sleeves, tied an apron on, and began poking about until the house shook! This woman, of course, was at their house for the first time. All the same, a real housewife would go to the kitchen, peek under every pot lid, shove her nose in the oven, inspect the refrigerator, and immediately know what to do. But Maria Petrovna didn't let the guest into the kitchen, and had her set the table:

"Tablecloths, dishes, and tableware are in the sideboard."

The Kungurtsevs themselves plunged into the impenetrable fumes of the kitchen, where stout Anna Ivanovna, cornflower-blue eyes popping out of their sockets, was suffocating.

"Rest a bit, mom," said Kungurtsev.

"I don't know whether what I've done will suit you," the old woman said plaintively. "I don't have Lipochka's talent."

"Shhh!" hissed her son-in-law and daughter.

Of course she didn't have Lipochka's talent: one thing was burned, another undercooked, a third overdone, but they didn't have the talent either. They bumped into each other, getting in each other's way, grabbed the salt-cellar or the vinegar at the same time, forgot to slice some bread, to make the mayonnaise dressing for the salad, to put the pod of red pepper in the bottle with the diluted spirits. As a group they couldn't manage what Lipochka had done alone easily, cheerfully, and unobtrusively.

A dog's bark and noise in the entrance hall announced the guests' arrival. Kungurtsev went out to meet them, but the newcomers, children, and Romka, who'd gone completely berserk, had gotten tangled in a fantastic knot. Then Putya's strapping figure blocked the whole mess.

"Military mission accomplished!" he reported, and as over Kungurtsev's shoulder he caught sight of his wife taking care of the table, he cried gaily: "They've already set you to work?"

"It won't hurt her," Maria Petrovna growled, gravitating toward her husband.

"That's the way it should be!" rejoiced Putya, happy that his wife had been drawn into the Kungurtsevs' routine.

He dashed toward her, clearing the way. And somehow the knot at the coat rack immediately disentangled itself; the children pressed back against the walls, the oldest caught Romka by the leash, pressed him close, while the great filmmaker, in a grey suit, very small, very thin, and very old, rushed straight in Kungurtsev's direction with a hand raised high, the five fingers spread wide for a handshake. Of course, he hadn't known of Kungurtsev's existence at all until a vagrant's fate cast him in this godforsaken hole, but his transport seemed so sincere, so irrepressibly loving, as if he expected to find here the light of truth and spiritual healing. The grip of his extended bony paw, with the liver spots of old age, proved unexpectedly strong. "A cameraman!" guessed Kungurtsev. "He's used to dragging a camera around." And he responded to the handshake in Siberian fashion. It ended in a draw, and they emerged pleased with each other. The chief filmmaker was handed over to Maria Petrovna, while Kungurtsev was introduced to the fat bald business manager of the group, Buryga, and the pretty assistant Lenochka. Extremely slender, with a largish head, an absolute child in appearance, Lenochka was quick to inform them that she'd graduated from a film institute and was really entitled to be a second director, but had chosen to be an assistant just to work with such a master. "So he's a director!" realized Kungurtsev.

Taking advantage of the slight confusion that usually precedes the start of a feast, Kungurtsev drew the assistant Lenochka aside and said in a conspiratorial undertone:

"It's somewhat awkward to ask ... " he faltered slightly. "But what can you do, our honored guest, he, excuse me ... "

"I don't know," said Lenochka quickly and blushed. "I don't assist in those areas."

She'd concluded that Kungurtsev wanted to know whether the fellow wanted to go to the bathroom.

"That's not what I'm asking about," Kungurtsev, even more embarrassed, assured her. "You see, I rarely go to the movies, I never watch TV and I'm not in the swing of things at all. What was the last film he presented ... "

"Bless you!" Lenochka interrupted almost indignantly, "Why, the African epic, of course!"

Kungurtsev clapped his forehead penitently. In fact he didn't know anything about documentaries at all, if one excluded the newsfilm that was shown before each feature. But of course, an old diehard wouldn't concern himself with such trifles.

"And how do you address him?" he asked with interest.

"Chief. Ever since the Institute—I finished my training under him. But the whole studio calls him that. After all, he's the founder... "

And at that point they were summoned to table.

The eminent guest was seated at the head of the table, with Maria Petrovna on his right and Putya on his left. Kungurtsev sat beside his wife so as to be able to contemplate Putya freely, Lenochka sat beside him, and farther down, all the children, with Buryga, Vera Dmitrievna, and his mother-in-law opposite. And when everyone finally had taken his seat and Putya, leaning across the table, stretching into the farthermost corners like the jib of a crane, had poured vodka, wine, and the berry drink into everyone's glasses and goblets, Kungurtsev with a swelling heart became aware of how he'd not seen enough of Putya during this whole last period, how he'd missed his dear leanness, his head with its slight hollows at the temples, his warm brown eyes, his long agile arms and soft-sounding voice.

But this wasn't Putya's day, and the first toast made was to the newcomers. Cleverly playing on Siberian laconism, relegating to the profound subtext those gifts with which they in whose honor the feast was being given had enriched the country's art of film, subtly and enigmatically singling out the chief without pronouncing his sacred name, as though there were a taboo on it, Kungurtsev gave his toast a kind of mysterious brilliance. But the director didn't disgrace himself either, in his answering toast linking the Siberian expanses with the boundlessness of Siberian hospitality, and singing the praises of House, Family, and Host, whose name he doubtless had already forgotten. With that, the ceremonial part ended.

Everyone fell on the food, while Kungurtsev abandoned himself to an affectionate examination of Putya. How deftly he managed everything: he didn't forget about the director, he joked with Maria Petrovna, kept heaping the plate of his neighbor Buryga, who was putting it away as though he'd just been released from starving Ethiopia, yet had time to eat and drink himself, drew the young people into the conversation and didn't allow the general conversation to fizzle out. Putya knew a lot; he didn't deal in hot air. He could talk about fishing for grayling and salmon, about hunting for wild ram and Siberian elk, about Siberian flowers and herbs, animals and birds, about cars and airplanes, about water resources and minerals in the area, about prospecting and construction work, about the problems of the Baikal-Amur Trunk Line and the latest technical advances, about world science, and about Decembrists in Siberia, which was his favorite topic. Putya didn't talk about things he didn't know or didn't know well. And he listened willingly to what others had to say. But the main thing was that this was the Putya whose side had pressed so many times against Kungurtsev's side during freezing nights spent in the open during a bear or deer hunt, with whom he'd met the dawn and the sunrise, with whom he'd engaged in daredevilry and had almost drowned on trips down the river and with whom it wouldn't be frightening to greet old age.

But Kungurtsev's efforts to enjoy gazing at his friend came to naught. The great filmmaker required too much attention, mainly because he didn't require anything, kept refusing everything, and implored everyone to ignore him. Pressing his thin hands to his chest, he adjured them not to pour any alcohol for him—he didn't drink, blood pressure, ischemia, not to keep putting food on his plate—his sparrow's stomach couldn't hold the food. They had to cajole, to flatter him, almost to grovel at his feet: "At least try the salmon, it's smoked in a special way, it's got an aroma!" For a long time he'd grimace, wailing: "Why so much? You're awful!"—then he'd eat it with enthusiasm, praise it unrestrainedly, and appeal to the business manager Buryga, who, his mouth stuffed, would nod and goggle his oxen eyes. And they'd start all over again: "We pickled the mushrooms ourselves, you've got to try them!" Again a lengthy resistance, then the energetic motion of thin jaws: "Divine!"... "And now a cabbage dumpling, this piece is meant just for you."—Just as with a small child. And the main thing was that he ate everything, and drank, as it soon became apparent, no worse than anyone else. After he declined with horror the homemade pepper-brandy—a pod of hot Bulgarian pepper was thrown in diluted spirits—he kept pouring himself the inoffensive red cherry brandy with the air of a good child, but in the same considerable quantities.

The unkind thought occurred to Kungurtsev that the brandy would lay the director out and they would go down to the river on their own. But this elf-like, or, as his mother-in-law would say, gutless, man possessed an enviable capacity. He didn't get drunk, but became increasingly kind, glowed radiantly, and seemed to expand strangely, absorbing everything outside of him. Small, frail, with a weak, rather husky, voice, he subjugated the company at table to his will. Chekhov somewhere has the thought, I think, that on stage it is those surrounding him who play the king by rendering him a king's homage. The manager Buryga, tearing himself away from getting his fill, and Lenochka, pecking away like a bird, also 'played' king, in Lena's case this stemming not from an assistant's servility—but from worship before a master who had been her teacher besides. They involved first the children in their games, and then the adults at the table. And now everyone was 'playing' king, and he, without wanting to himself, towered over them and expanded. As host, Kungurtsev was happy that respect was being paid his guest, but he began wanting more of Putya for himself. The latter was an insignificant courtier and preferred to retreat into the shadows.

Tired from working with his jaws, the manager Buryga sighed noisily and announced for all to hear that the Baikal was perishing.

"Why?" the director clasped his thin hands.

"They've permitted them to transport oil by barge, and during the loading a certain percentage spills into the water. And the Baikal's a closed reservoir."

"As far back as I remember," commented Kungurtsev, "The Baikal was always perishing. Yet it hasn't perished."

"They saved it at the movies," said Putya, laughing, "Do you remember how the movie *At the Lake* ends? With a glass of Baikal water as pure as an infant's tear."

"Even now they give water like that at the cellulose works," commented Lenochka.

"Only to visitors," said Vera Dmitrievna, who'd been silent until then. "You can't fool the locals."

"As far back as I remember," repeated Kungurtsev, who didn't like the conversation. "The Baikal was always perishing, yet even the salmon has been restored."

"Some salmon!" said Putya. "Real salmon melts in its own fat!"

"Nothing will happen to the Baikal," announced the director in an unexpectedly distinct, clear voice, as though he were reading from a book. "The Angara will carry the oil. The barges will be loaded below the source."

"And how about unloading the oil, or isn't there any leakage with that?" Maria Petrovna intervened.

Why did she have to interfere? The question hung in the air. The director half-closed his eyes; after every effort he needed some time to recuperate. Kungurtsev himself hadn't followed the problem, and Putya, who knew everything, sat with a vacant and absent expression. And Kungurtsev realized then how difficult his friend's life had been recently. He was losing himself and his wide-ranging avid interest in life through the agonizing division, emotional confusion, and the constant lies, and you couldn't avoid them, however honestly you wanted to handle the matter; silence, too, was a lie, after all; evidently he didn't read anything either, and understandably, had lost touch,—he, who was used to being always on top of events. Poor, poor Putya! It's hard to reverse the direction of one's life in one's old age. And Kungurtsev suddenly wanted to do something good and kind for Putya, to do it immediately. He rose and said loudly.

"Vera Dmitrievna, your health!"

She raised her brows in surprise, bowed slightly in his direction, and drank a little of her wine. Kungurtsev emptied his glass at one go and put it on the table with a bang.

Catching a marinated mushroom on his fork, Kungurtsev caught sight of Putya's face, which expressed not the simple gratitude of a friend for the attention accorded his wife, but something wretched: a kind of slavish devotion. "Do you want me to bark? Do you want me to crawl at your feet? You give the order, and I'll kill!"—such was the degrading readiness that he read on Putya's face, distorted by an ugly grimace of gratitude. And it was like a death sentence to Lipochka. It would have been better had he not come up with his toast. Especially since Vera Dmitrievna hadn't accepted his sop. Possibly she was indifferent to the Kungurtsevs' attitude or perhaps it was emotional apathy, callousness, or, what was even worse, a contemptuous self-confidence? But Alyoshka!... He had sold himself with all his innards for a single kind gesture to his wife. Such a thing hadn't ever happened between them. They took everything from each other for granted, without gratitude and without offense. To think they'd come to this!...

Kungurtsev grew gloomy, tuned out of what was happening around him, and forgot his duties as host. When he floated back to reality again, he heard Lenochka, who'd become somewhat drunk, trying to explain something to a sober and imperturbable Vera Dmitrievna across the table:

"He's seen so much!... Where hasn't he been!... All the greatest events of history have passed before his eyes. He filmed the first World War, the Provisional government, the assault on Perekop, Douglas Fairbanks and Mary Pickford's visit to Moscow. He filmed Rasputin's murder..."

"He didn't film Golgotha?" asked Vera Dmitrievna.

"Now, she's nasty!" thought Kungurtsev.

"No. That event was exaggerated later. And at that time he was filming Tiberius on Capri," Lenochka replied smoothly.

"Good for you, girl! A good retort!" Kungurtsev approved.

"He saw so many great things that he started appreciating only the simple life," continued Lenochka. "He said that only the everyday has a real complexity."

"There's a fine old guy for you!" Kungurtsev was delighted.

After the mass of hors d'oeuvres and mushroom cabbage soup with dumplings, everyone refused the cutlets. They had some jellied currant juice with honey cakes and Putya sent the cork from the champagne bottle flying to the ceiling.

"Now I understand what Siberian hospitality is," said the director, clinking glasses with Kungurtsev.

"Huh, my dear, if you'd visited us earlier, you'd really understand what Siberian hospitality is, you'd find out how sweet each mouthful of food can be when it's coaxed with an affectionate timely word! It's possible to stuff yourself like Buryga in any cafeteria, but to set a real table is a subtle art which few master. We had someone who has it, and who got all of us to dance to her merry tune. As people filled their stomachs, wings would grow at the back of their shoulders, everyone got up from the table feeling pampered, respected, kinder, and you didn't even feel heavy from our nourishing dishes. They were all like the crew of one ship. But now everyone goes his own way. One belches, covering his mouth with his fat hand for the sake of appearance, another is casting a pall on the company, a third isn't participating at all, the main guest is dozing, and the hostess is happy that the cutlets are left, so that it won't be necessary to cook supper, the host himself has melted like shit in a thaw. Yes, there's also a Friend who's sold himself with all his innards for a dishonest toast. Well, okay, it could be even worse... "

Noticing that he'd become despondent, Maria Petrovna seized a moment and whispered in his ear:

"Our guest is crazy about you. At last, he says, he's seen a real Siberian."

"I'm a cream puff, not Siberian stuff!"* thought Kungurtsev.

Preparations for an expedition to the woods were predominantly a male job, and Putya especially shone here. The habits of a confirmed traveller, hunter, and fisherman are telling. But that day he outdid himself. Everything moved with incredible speed and ease in his hands. The women were still fussing about in the kitchen with the dinner pans, bowls, and saucepans, whereas he'd already packed and loaded the car with blankets, pillows, dishes, thermoses with coffee, folding metal chairs, a plastic bag with bones for Romka and 'a thousand little things' that are essential for camping out at night in the taiga.

Everything was finally gathered together, and the first party, consisting of the driver (for some reason he started calling himself 'driver' in English—from an excess of joy, perhaps?), Vera Dmitrievna, the guests from Moscow, and Kungurtsev, set off. First they had to drop by the wharf and get a tent and an inflatable rubber boat from the boathouse. At the last moment Romka raced out of the door with a howl and scratched with his front paws at the side window, begging to be taken along. Kungurtsev, who was sitting up front, opened the door and took him on his lap; he was pathetically thin and light. The dog was trembling, and whined at intervals, shattered by his master's unprecedented betrayal.

For some reason Putya 'the driver' took them the long way round, past the hospital where Maria Petrovna worked, the new movie theater, and the swimming pool that was under construction. Kungurtsev was about to point out his mistake to his friend, but realized that Putya purposely had

* The original has a rhyme and rhythm that create an effect which the translation cannot duplicate: "Slabak ia, a ne sibiriak," literally, "I'm a weakling, not a Siberian."

chosen the roundabout route in order to show the Muscovites the Kungurtsev domain from the best vantage point. Putya maneuvered so deftly that several times the buildings of the factory plants and the factory offices and the new entrance gate were visible close up from a very good angle.

Kungurtsev was both disarmed and a touch irritated by his friend's naïve attempts to impress the movie diehard, who had seen everything there was to see, with the spectacle of an average factory. But here the director revealed that he really possessed uncommon powers of perceptiveness and professional experience. With his old, tear-filled tipsy eyes he caught sight of the blackened one-story building of the former office in the depths of the factory complex, which had been the payroll office before the revolution. This building had been preserved deliberately on the factory land side by side with all the reconstructed buildings as a monument of sorts. Putya had a favorite word—to 'dig,' by which he meant a high degree of sharpness, quick wits. The old director immediately dug everything regarding the office.

"Good for them that they've preserved this rundown old shack, let people see what it all began from." And he started showering Kungurtsev with brief, precise questions, all of them about what was essential and important.

The manager answered willingly, though in his usual unhurried manner. Suddenly the director fell silent. "No more questions?" Kungurtsev asked with a smile.

The old man didn't reply; he was asleep, laid low in a second by weariness and everything he'd drunk at dinner.

He awoke at the dock—that was the fancy name given to the shelter of planks belonging to the local boat owner who had motor boats and rowing and sail boats. Opening his eyes—which in the murkiness and dimness of semi-wakefulness took in the car's interior, and, on the outside, the boathouses, the wide, fast-flowing river, the taiga on the other shore, and the sky wherever there was no earth—he rejoiced at his return to this wonderful world.

"I seem to have dozed off?... Your teacher is clearly getting old, Lenochka."

Kungurtsev and Putyatin emerged from the boathouse, each dragging a heavy orange sack. There was a tent in one, a boat in the other. It looked as though nothing else would fit into the overstuffed car, but Putyatin, confident and cheerful, combining a herculean sweep of movement with precise eye measurements, moved something over, squeezed one thing, kneaded another, the car seemed to expand, the passengers in the rear became molded into a large lump, and the two enormous bags were fitted in.

Putyatin backed, almost driving into the river, swung around, made it up the steep slope in first gear, and leaped over the creaking wooden bridge onto the other side. He drove the car along the winding forest road, over the knotty roots of the pines and spruce, with the cones shooting out from under the wheels, then turned sharply toward the river and headed down into the tall green grass of the floodland meadow. The car went through what resembled a green tunnel and halted at the water's edge.

They unloaded the car quickly, Kungurtsev and Putyatin inflated the rubber boat, after which 'the driver' went off to get the others—Maria Petrovna and the kids.

They seated the director on a folding metal chair and Kungurtsev dragged the rubber boat into the water and started loading the bundles and baskets into it. The director reflected that the preparations for a modest picnic on the taiga shore were so massive and fundamental that they would have sufficed for a whole movie expedition. But it would take infinitely more people and time for a filmcrew to pitch camp. Here Kungurtsev accepted only fat Buryga's help and sent Lenochka away to pick forget-me-knots. Vera Dmitrievna went off into the depths of the shoreland where the pink lances of the tall willow rose were swaying. Romka raced along the shore like a maniac, running into the water up to his belly, frightening the yellow finch warblers off the willow bushes. The director closed his eyes in the quiet peace, but as often happened, memory supplied something that didn't accord at all with the surroundings. An arena covered with blood, the enormous bull's shoulderblades and back pierced with banderillas, the cushions over which the sweating and pale matador with a bloody wound in his groin stumbled. It had been in Toledo, when Dominguín,[5] gored by a horn, couldn't finish off his last bull. The director opened his eyes. He'd seen too much blood in his life, and not only during the war. Blood flowed everywhere where people attempted to do something outstanding, whether it was building a hydroelectric power station, bullfighting, storming Everest, or finishing the marathon at the Olympics, when the winner collapsed with a haemorrhage of the throat. He too had shed more than a little blood of his own under various circumstances. He'd grown to hate blood's color, smell, and salty taste. The interior of the rubber boat in which Kungurtsev and Buryga had seated themselves was also the color of blood. The director turned away. The sight of the thick green sedge-like grass was pleasant, as was the sight of Romka's spotted body flashing in and out among it, and the pink rose bay which bordered the meadow, and a woman's white blouse. But a little time passed, and he had to sink down on the bottom of the boat's bright red inside, as though in a puddle of blood. It was loathsome to the point of making him shudder but he didn't betray himself in any way.

The strong current caught the boat and carried it off. Kungurtsev plied the fragile aluminum oars and steered the boat toward the opposite shore. His shirt became undone, revealing his hairy tanned chest streaked with sweat from the neck to the gray mat of hair. His strong abdomen moved up and down. The little director, huddled in the bottom of the boat, followed the oarsman's movements with pleasure, succumbing to a faint misery. What's better than youth and health? Fifty-year-old Kungurtsev seemed young to him. "How old am I?" thought the director, and couldn't remember. He hadn't been able to for a long time. And what if he'd always existed? And always would? In the rarest exceptions nature grants its favorites eternal life. He knew several famous people who'd firmly decided never to die. Why shouldn't he become one of them? Little is necessary for that if you're one of the elect—only to avoid obvious idiocies. Titian,[6] now, had achieved immortality, but hadn't saved himself from the plague— that was his own fault. And he'd seen a shepherd in Mengrelia who'd lived for several centuries and had long stopped keeping count of the years. But it seemed a bit early for him to forget his age. "What sclerosis!" the director thought in delight. He had no fear of sclerosis because he knew that in the film studio and in the editing room he could handle his job as though he had a twenty-year-old's arteries. Sclerosis bypasses a person's professional skills, while everyday idiosyncrasies even enhance old men. But one should agree only to immortality, longevity is rubbish. People thought that he'd been born ages ago, but he remembered as though it were yesterday how his mother used to soap him in the child's zinc bathtub and he would slap himself on his taut, slippery little belly. Everything final is transient, like a flash of lightning; only immortality is protracted.

Something nudged against the director's hand, with which he was holding onto the rounded side of the boat. It was Romka, who was swimming after them, with his chocolate muzzle thrown up high above the water. But when he reached the deep stream, the dog realized that his master had stayed behind on the other shore, and he turned back.

When they were already close to the other shore, a long boat, which had pulled out from around the island overgrown with wild cherry trees, cut across their path. An old man and woman sat in the boat. They were floating along with the current, and the old man barely moved the scull. The bottom of the boat was stacked with woven baskets filled to the brim with wild currants—red and black. When they drew level with the rubber bubble of the inflatable boat, the old man lifted his cap off his bald white head and the old woman smiled cordially.

"Good evening," said Kungurtsev, "Congratulations on your success. Did you pick them on the islands?"

"We did," confirmed the old man, and the boat glided past.

Kungurtsev helped the director climb up the steep slope of the tall bank. Here behind the old pines, which had submerged the streaming reflections of their crowns in the river, was a circular glade, bright green in places, elsewhere grown brown from being scorched during the long hot summer. On the brown surface, larch 'butter' mushrooms were shining with cinnabar, and had blended into big flat cakes. And one had only to strain one's eyes to see between the roots of the pines on the edge of the forest the heads of other mushrooms, opal-pale and smooth, which had pushed through the ground and the coniferous carpet. Kungurtsev suggested that Lenochka and Buryga pick mushrooms, and in the shade which was cast by the claw of a pine, he again set up a throne for the director.

The director obediently sat down on the folding chair, as though sunk in himself. He liked submitting unquestioningly to someone else's judicious will. He felt that he'd never in his life felt as good, tranquil, and protected as that day, when strangers took it upon themselves to take care of him. A colorful nutcracker landed on a charred stump opposite and with its round little ocher eyes started examining the colorful man trustfully, and with interest. And the director started examinig the nutcracker with his faded eyes, which hadn't lost their vigilance, however. They caught each other's fancy—the bird and the man. And it was a pity that an invisible enemy frightened off the nutcracker.

Kungurtsev unpacked the bundles, spread the inflatable floor of the tent on the ground, and discovered that the foot pump, which had started malfunctioning a long time ago, now was completely useless. He'd have to inflate the equipment orally. But that could only be done with two people blowing from each end—one man couldn't possibly manage it. Buryga the mushroomer had disappeared in the growth, the old director was useless, even if he were to breathe his last into the mattress; he'd have to wait for Putya. And remembering Putya, Kungurtsev realized with horror that he'd forgotten his wife on the other shore.

God, how could he have done that? When he was bringing the director and Lenochka over, Vera Dmitrievna was gathering bunches of tall rosebay. He had caught sight of her light blouse with a distracted gaze, as though unseeingly, but either he'd not put two and two together, or . . . Of course, a man must answer for everything that he so generously ascribes to chance: sudden absent-mindedness, an ambiguous slip of the tongue, clumsy gestures which hurt someone,—those are all signs of the latent life which is inside us, a more sincere and authentic one than our external conscious behavior. He had seen fit to propose a false toast in her honor, but had forgotten to take her in the boat. He hadn't left the faceless Buryga or the smallest part of their equipment on the shore, but he'd forgotten his friend's wife, pretending to himself that he hadn't recognized her light blouse amidst the pink flowers!...

He was a fine one! What could he tell Putya? But he didn't have time to think up anything, because Putya himself stood in front of him in swimming trunks and rubber boots, completely dry, only the toes of his boots glistening with water.

"And have you walked across the Jordan on water, like Christ?" asked Kungurtsev, stupefied at his own effrontery.

"Some fishermen brought me across. And it looks as if you forgot about us?" said Putya in a strained voice.

"How'd I know that you'd be so fast!" Kungurtsev caught Ariadne's thread[7] and moved forward confidently. "Did you find your flower girl?"

"What flower girl?" His voice was still strained.

"Your wife, who else? She got so carried away with the rosebay that she forgot about everything in the world."

"Aha!" Putya said with relief, like a man who was ready to accept any lie if it contained just the semblance of likelihood. "She picked an enormous bouquet, but it wilted immediately. Okay, I'll fetch them all right now."

"And then we'll swim?" said Kungurtsev joyfully.

"Of course!..."

The nutcracker, which had abruptly left the charred stump, had had time to cast a spell on the old man. Its round shining ocher eyes doubtless emanated a bewitching power, for after it disappeared strange things began to happen. First a naked man in boots appeared, turning the director's thoughts to reservation Sioux, the pitiful remnants of a once-powerful proud tribe, now dying out without a murmur. He'd filmed them once and smoked the pipe with the sick old half-drunk chief. Then the Sioux vanished, but a man and woman in modern clothes appeared and started pouring mushrooms on the ground beside him. Soon a whole mountain arose and he became frightened that the mountain would certainly collapse and bury him underneath it. Here was that stupid fortuitousness that makes selection null and void. Titian perished from the plague, Konyonkov[8] from a draft, and he—from a mountain of mushrooms. And at that moment it did, indeed, fall, without causing him the slightest harm. And immediately he saw a crowd of people, among them some very young ones, who were executing some wild, apparently ritualistic dance around a young girl with long dark legs. Then the Sioux returned and he and a stout gringo lay down on their stomachs and started inflating an enormous flat hide from two ends. The hide distended, panted, expanded, swelled dangerously, but the director suddenly stopped being afraid. Something of the kind had already happened with him more than once: the heart of the forest and an animal ready to spring, and someone's eye getting his temple in the sights, and someone aiming from a bow, and someone's hand swinging an axe. But the present becomes the past so quickly that one has only to endure everything for a split second—and one's saved, for the bullet, arrow, brandished axe, and yawning maw are in the past.

So he didn't move, didn't change position, only closed his tired lids, and when he opened them again, instead of a billowing beast, a neat little orange hut stood there, and something warm and appetizingly aromatic was shoved into his hand.

The lees of exotic visions receded, and the leisurely, secure, solid Siberian life continued. He took a cutlet in one hand, and a dark blue glass with a golden rim in the other. The Sioux, who'd changed into the likable Putya, began pouring drinks from a bottle in which was floating a red pod of pepper.

"Putya," said the gringo Kungurtsev, reproachfully, "We *do* have the cherry one, you know."

"No, no I want to do it like you!" the director exclaimed and with unexpected agility tore out of the chair and pulling himself up short, appeared before them as a well-built elegant lean gentleman. "To the taiga!" said the director and tilted the contents of the glass into his mouth.

Kungurtsev followed his example and choked disgracefully. He'd thought that he was drinking the pepper vodka that they'd had at dinner, but Putya either by mistake or through gratuitous boldness had dropped a pod of pepper into the undiluted ninety percent spirits.

"Fantastic!" said the director. "It simply takes your breath away. It's strong and tastes great. I won't say 'no' to another glass."

They repeated the round, and the producer lowered himself into the chair with a satisfied look and began muching on the cutlet.

"Have you gone mad?" Kungurtsev hissed at Putya, drawing him aside. "He could croak . . . "

"You don't understand a damn thing. This old guy's made of iron. He'll outlive us all. And I've prepared some spirits for after our swim. Shall we get to it?"

"What do you think?" said Kungurtsev in a happy voice.

He knew no greater pleasure than swimming in the icy water of a mountain river. But except for Putya no one ever agreed to join him.

Putya ran off to get the towels, and Kungurtsev, who somehow seemed to have regained his youth, wanted to invite Buryga, who happened to be nearby, but he stopped short when he saw his glassy stare and the powerful workings of his jaws, demolishing a cutlet shoved in a loaf of bread. Buryga held another cutlet and a half-loaf in his hand.

"Old filmmakers," Lenochka's soft voice sounded, "have a secret rule: leave nothing for the enemy. It means demolishing free grub without a trace."

Kungurtsev smiled a bit forcedly. That kind of wit jarred on him. Lenochka's green eyes sparkled. All she had to do was drink a little and instead of an enthusiastic proselyte of the tenth muse another person awakened in her: observant, mocking, with a touch of malice. And it was very easy to imagine what she'd become once the freshness of youth fell from her sharp features and difficult adulthood with all its inevitable disillusionments came. "God grant you a good husband, my dear," Kungurtsev wished her from his heart, but not out loud, of course... "If your husband was so bad, why didn't you leave him earlier?" asked Maria Petrovna.

"And have you seen many women who left their husbands without anyone or any place to go to?" answered Vera Dmitrievna. "Not to mention with a child and a wretched profession like mine—that of secretary-typist."

"All the same, dear, it's strange, you know... "

"I assure you, it's not strange at all."

The water in the quick-flowing river didn't warm up in the course of the day and it was easier to enter it very early, when the air was piercingly fresh and the grass was crocheted by the morning frost, than in the warm early evening hours caressed by the sun. The bitter cold froze one's toes, rising to the heart and squeezing it, almost choking it. Kungurtsev and Putyatin, both naked, stood in the shallows, their arms crossed as they hugged their bodies, and shivered, glancing at each other a little wildly and with hatred, for a witness was an obstacle to retreat, to flight, and suddenly, by tacit agreement, but always simultaneously, they dived headfirst.

Burned by the cold, they almost lost consciousness and came up numb with cold but happy, yelping and laughing. Their hearts were already fighting for their existence, powerfully driving the blood through their veins, with each second adding a zest that turned into coltish delight. Two sedate men, no longer young, were behaving like village kids. "I'm going underwater!" one announced triumphantly and, his white behind flashing, dived to the bottom. And he knew that the other had already imitated his exploit without wasting a moment. The water was clear and transparent, so it was unnecessary to close their eyes. They could see the yellow sand and the pebbly rocks and the bubbles of the springs which pulsated up from the bottom, the slanting shoal of small fish, and infrequently, a big fish gleamed like a mirror; in the lightly greenish darkness they made out each other's bodies, now bronze, now bluish in the light, and they began the agonizing battle of determining who would be able to stay underwater longer. Their hearts sank, their glazed vessels were ready to burst, but, cursing each other's stubbornness, they remained there until the water itself pushed them up to the surface. And they invariably surfaced at one and the same moment. You'd think that that experience sufficed to quench their desire for a similar contest, but scarcely had they regained their breath when they would start diving for distance. And they'd continue until spasms and shudders shook them. But suddenly one of them seemed to withdraw and with a concentrated air started looking for something by the shore. The other at once started examining the base of the rose willow on the tussock-like island. The result of this intense search was some slimy snag or a half-rotted wooden rowlock. The found object was tossed into the middle of the river, and with panicky howls Romka dashed out after it. From the very start of the river games he had languished away on the shore, whimpering quietly; he was most strictly forbidden to crawl into the water while the gods were enjoying their swim. Now his golden hour had come. And his beloved master and his master's beloved friend in turn tossed him sticks, snags, branches, roots, trying to throw them as far as possible and at the same time in such a way that they'd be conspicuous to Romka. It never occurred to the faithful dog that they were competing again, and he served both with equal diligence.

For the first time in the years of their outings together to the river Kungurtsev felt that Putya had an edge on him. In health they were on a par, Kungurtsev was a trifle heavier, Putya a trifle more agile, and in general in all their activities they ran neck and neck. But today Putya dived farther, and he found more sticks and threw them with greater success. The lifting capacity of added wings helped Putya, and it was only a pity that these wings would melt before he reached the sun. And when, without drying themselves, in wet trunks—this also was part of the ritual—having only swallowed the burning spirits, they set off for the camp of nomads, Kungurtsev gave voice to what had been seething in his heart:

"What *is* going to happen with Lipochka, Alyosha?"

"Don't," said Putya, and shriveled all over, like a baby monkey. "Don't ... Lipochka is *my* sore spot."

And Kungurtsev fell silent, disarmed by the miserable words.

It was light on the river, only the fiery tongue from beyond the forest licked at the undersides of the white clouds which slowly drifted across the light blue sky. But higher up, in the clearing, the evening shadows were thickening, the grass and the needles darkening. In the far distance in the depths of the taiga the ominous August sunset showed crimson without lending any reflection to the twilight thicket.

The women cleaned the mushrooms, peeling the slippery skin off the heads of the pine 'butter' mushrooms with their nails like a stocking, and scraping the dry skin of the larch variety with a knife. They threw the cleaned mushrooms into a ten-liter saucepan. The saffron milk caps and the other variety they threw aside, intending to do something special with them.

"Give me that pail, dear," Maria Petrovna requested.

"You keep calling me 'dear' all the time. Am I really so dear to you?" inquired Vera Dmitrievna.

... Something bad was happening to Kungurtsev. The fresh cold water, the wild masculine games, the romp with Romka, the naked bravado, had turned into a quiet aching melancholy instead of the expected joy. What was responsible for that—the talk with Putya that hadn't materialized on the river or some more subtle loss which he himself didn't understand yet—was difficult to say—but if during their swim he'd thought that everything could still be put right, that the things that mattered were saved, now something else prevailed: nothing was put right, nothing was saved.

Putya's fatuous behavior intensified his melancholy. Putya probably sensed that his friend didn't feel quite himself, but instead of adjusting himself emotionally to him, he started crudely playing the hero around the campfire now. From time to time he'd dive into the thicket and return with gigantic armfuls of brushwood. The branches scratched his bare skin, but he didn't notice anything, completely in the power of his stupid triumph. He dragged enormous branches and cut off pieces of them with a small sharp axe, so that the sound rang through the taiga. He was really impressive, and if he wanted to attract his wife's attention with his exploits, then he succeeded completely. She laid aside her knife, took off her apron of newspaper, and went up to Putya. And Kungurtsev realized that all his melancholy, all his emotional desolation, stemmed from this small quiet woman with the tired eyes and sad mouth, who carried herself so unobtrusively but spoiled everything.

Kungurtsev turned away and started building the camp fire.

Maria Petrovna came up to him:

"Don't be crazy, go and dress."

"And Putya?" That sounded really childish.

"Well, Putya's so heated... He could even go to the North Pole without pants now."

"That's true," Kungurtsev said in a cheerless voice.

"Why are you so depressed?" Maria Petrovna gazed intently at her husband. "Are you envious of him, or what?"

"What's there to be envious of?"

"What do you mean? He's a newlywed. And you have the same old goods."

"I wouldn't change with him."

"I should hope not! Yet there's reason for envy. Okay, go on with your work, we've started the fire late. And I'll bring you your things in a second."

Such solicitude was not characteristic of Maria Petrovna, and it touched Kungurtsev and put him on his guard. Apparently he seemed pathetic to her. And what about the cracks about his envy of Putya? Couldn't she tell, couldn't she feel how alien that woman was to him?

Before vanishing completely, the sun expiring in the depth of the taiga flooded the area with a mysterious strange light. Trees the color of old unpolished bronze rested their crowns against the gilded bronze of the sky. People's faces and the folds of their clothing showed bronze in the bronze air. And then it was as though a switch clicked off. The pitch darkness lasted some minutes—the low moon barely standing over the earth emitted its pale light through the taiga, it spread through the mist which until then had been invisible, and the clearing was wrapped in silvery smoke. In this pearly fluttering drizzle now and then the long streaming body of a young girl in a white dress appeared and immediately dissolved, melted. And dark patches—three of them—showed through in the mist and without becoming distinct, disappeared. Mother and daughter adhered to different tactics. The adult woman worked in the interest of alienation, the little one defeated the enemy camp, turning the three mooncalves of the divine king into slaves. Awkward, sluggish, and obsessed, they tried helplessly to grasp with their spread arms the white phantom, the moonlight on the mist. From the bottom of his heart Kungurtsev felt sorry for his louts, whose hearts, regardless of the difference in their ages, had awakened simultaneously.

In the meantime the campfire didn't want to get going. It smoked, stank, shot out sparks intermittently, but the flame didn't rise in a column, faltering in the damp fuel instead.

"I thought a taiga camp fire was something majestic," said the director in a damp voice which sounded as though he had a cold, and moved up to the feeble fire, "A Gothic cathedral of flame."

"One has to court a campfire," Kungurtsev replied, a trifle embarrassed.

"Like a woman?"

"Like the most obstinate woman."

The director's mild reproach made Kungurtsev give himself a shake. He rebuilt the campfire: he put the drier stuff at the bottom, the damper on top; the thickest and wettest logs he tossed aside—they'd do when the camp fire was ignited and started roaring. It was strange—there'd been almost no rain, the summer in general happened to be arid, yet the brushwood was rather damp from the heavy dew. He packed some dry moss and some old newspapers into the campfire, and getting down on all fours, he turned himself into a forge. Reluctantly, lazily, threatening to go out, the campfire nevertheless got going, finally caught fire completely, and shot skyward a column of flame from which sparks of birch bark escaped and soared above the trees, endeavoring to become stars. Kungurtsev added some firewood.

"Good fire," the director said gently, "Like in Cuba. Ah, Cuba!..."

But Kungurtsev wasn't satisfied. The thin dry branches burned well, but he saw that the flame was licking the thick logs feebly. The wood smoked, became blackened and charred, and finally the campfire managed to place a crimson butterfly on the rib of a log. It crawled toward the base of the log, fluttering its wings, crawled over onto the bark, twirling ash-colored fleecy clouds on it, and then imperceptibly disappeared. And the campfire again struggled for a long time to place a new fiery butterfly on the log, and again its presence was brief. For a campfire to stay alive, good dry fuel is essential. Putya had played the hero to no purpose long enough—dragging up the wind-fallen wood that had rotted through in the ground and the damp wood that was lying about in the ravine.

Putya turned to the real task with great zest. Vera Dmitrievna volunteered to help him. Kungurtsev took the buckets and headed for the river to get the water. They needed to boil some water for tea and to cook the mushrooms so that they wouldn't turn wormy by the following morning. When he returned, the campfire was roaring, and on the edge of a wide crimson circle rose a pile of dry twigs and Putya, still naked, crimson from the flames and damp with sweat, said, as he toyed with the axe and twisted his mouth in concern.

"Whether you like it or not, Pavel Leontyevich, we'll have to fell a birch. For a campfire this dry stuff is like husks, it won't be enough supplies for the night."

"But who'll give you permission to chop down a live tree?" answered Kungurtsev in alarm.

"You, Pasha, are the king and god of these blessed parts."

"Don't flatter. It'll do no good."

"And don't you play the hypocrite. Look at how many fresh stumps there are. You'd better have it out properly with the forest guard, or he'll let the whole taiga go for vodka."

Kungurtsev sensed that Putya wanted terribly to chop down a big tree and not only for the sake of the campfire. At any other time he'd not have allowed it under any circumstances, though the factory personnel committed outrages in the forest at will, but now he thought it petty to refuse Putya.

"Damn it. Just choose a dead one."

"You must be kidding!" Putya became brash at once and stepped out of the light of the campfire.

Vera Dmitrievna followed him.

Soon the thud of the axe was audible, then the rustling and crash of the falling tree. The noise swelled menacingly and drew closer; it seemed as though the tree would fall right there on the campfire and the people sitting around it. But no, it fell somewhere in the depths of the darkness, and only the wind created by its fall bent the flame. And in those moments the darkness became even thicker, enveloping the clearing and the forest. And it was impossible to understand how the children could roam about in the bushes and trees without breaking their limbs and putting out their eyes. You'd think that they'd been fitted with special sensory radar, like bats. And yet it was frightening to see them appear for a moment in the red light of the campfire and break through the darkness of the thicket. And somehow during this mad running about the youngest Kungurtsev had had time to suggest to Olenka that they run off to the Baikal-Amur Trunk Line, and she, to tittle-tattle to her mother.

Vera Dmitrievna in turn told Kungurtsev about it when she and Putya dragged up the birch tree he'd chopped down. Putya, of course, had gotten not dead wood, but a fresh old tree. He started chopping off the branches with the same devil-may-care sweep that had marked all his actions that day. Vera Dmitrievna had drawn Putya into her age group, which wasn't Kungurtsev's, Lipochka's, or the old Putya's. Now he'd become younger than all of them by a whole generation, and this was yet another of Vera Dmitrievna's sins.

For the first time that day, Vera Dmitrievna turned to Kungurtsev, and it could have been taken as an attempt to get closer. But he proved emotionally unprepared, and limply inquired what reply Olechka had given "his idiot." The use of "idiot" showed his irritation, which Vera Dmitrievna either didn't catch or didn't pay attention to. Olechka had said that she'd promised his older brother. And again Kungurtsev wasn't up to making some sophisticated gesture or a light phrase.

"You're a dangerous family," he began, then, catching himself, retreated to the theme of the 'new generation,' felt ashamed of the tedious, inappropriate moralizing, and fell silent.

...They drank tea out of the enormous aluminum kettle, and Maria Petrovna, stiffening the muscles of her strong character as she did before a difficult operation, chased the rowdy children into the tent. Lenochka made her way there too; and the drowsy Buryga had gone already before her. Upon learning that Kungurtsev always spent the night by the campfire, the director decided to keep him company, and nothing could dissuade him from it.

"It's warmer here than in the tent," he said, "And toward morning we'll scatter the embers on the ground, spread out the canvas sheet, and we'll sleep wonderfully for an hour or two. That'll be enough for me, in any case. An old man shouldn't sleep too much."

"And have you ever slept by a campfire?" Kungurtsev asked in surprise.

"Yes... Many times. The first time was in Ryn-sands, the nights there were very cold."

Kungurtsev hoped that Vera Dmitrievna would also bed down in the tent and that Putya would join them, but that didn't happen. Dragging up a whole pile of brushwood and stacking a pile of logs so that there'd be enough for the whole night, Putya finally dressed and went off with his wife to the other shore to sleep in the car. Romka insisted on accompanying them.

A great loneliness engulfed Kungurtsev. He tried to think about the fact that the next day would come, there'd be sunrise and the pearly, smoke-colored dew, and a morning swim with Putya, and the glass of burning spirits, the mushrooms filled with onion and the boiled saffron milk caps with vinegar, there'd be long hours of sweet idleness and the children's mad games, and the old fellow, who was unlike anyone else, having lived through so much in his life, and whom he was already coming to love, but for some reason all those thoughts didn't bring him any comfort, let along joy. The sense of loss didn't grow any duller, it pressed more firmly into his heart.

A strange headless creature with a patched back and rump jumped out of the forest and coming into the light of the campfire, acquired a solid body and became Romka—wet, whining quietly and occasionally howling. His silvery coat on his sides, belly, and paws looked phosphorescent, while the chocolate patches merged with the darkness of the night.

"Romka!" called Kungurtsev quietly.

The dog prostrated himself on the ground and with a humility that didn't accord at all with his dignity, crawled up to Kungurtsev and started licking his hand with a warm tongue.

"Did they chase you away?" Kungurtsev guessed. "Oh, you poor dog..."

Could that have happened before? Putya had often slept in the car with Lipochka, but Romka had always shared their bed. They used to tell, with laughter, how the dog would grow heavy with sleep and fall on them. Putya used to call such nights 'Morpheus in hell.' But, of course, the new madame Putyatin didn't want to have Romka, wet, smelling of dog, with them in the car at all. "And then, they *are* newlyweds," Kungurtsev grinned unhappily.

Romka was shaking with cold and hurt. He didn't notice that his coat, turned toward the fire, was steaming and crackling from sparks.

Kungurtsev covered him with a corner of the canvas and pressed his shivering body to him.

"It's okay, Roma, it's okay, boy, we can do without them. Sleep, old fellow, and dream of rabbits."

"The 'driver'—your friend..." the director's faint voice reached him as though from an infinite distance. "Why is he so happy...and so unhappy?"

Kungurtsev was silent for a while, not knowing whether he should reply to the question. But his Siberian's respect for age triumphed.

"Probably because one shouldn't build one's happiness on the misery of others."

"Come on!" The voice sounded as far away and very calm. "That's the only thing all of us do. Happiness that isn't bought at another person's expense simply doesn't exist. When you embrace one woman, another one, sometimes unknown to you, is crying into her pillow. That's so obvious..." he said in a tone that was almost apologetic.

Kungurtsev was silent, and the director suddenly lost the desire to convince him of anything. For some reason he again remembered Dominguin and the arena strewn with pillows and stained with blood.

"Listen," he said, "Didn't you ever stop to think about why a matador's terrible wounds—and the horn most frequently gets the groin—never cause the loss of his masculinity?"

"To tell the truth, no," Kungurtsev replied.

"Okay," thought the director, "Things are fine with matadors." And things seemed to be fine with him too. He was going to live forever. He'd shoot this film about Siberia, and tens and hundreds of films more, he'd shoot a film about the Golden Age of man. He'd receive a lot of prestigious prizes, awards, and cups. Only he'd never see his mother's dry little hands, so like his own; but he didn't like his own hands. And he said, without knowing to whom, but firmly believing that he'd be heard:

"If there's just one chance in a million that I'll see mama, you can take your stinking immortality. Immediately!"

...Putyatin turned on the engine, closed the windows tightly, and turned on the heater. In about fifteen or twenty minutes the chilly interior of the car would get warm and it would be possible to undress. He got the bedclothes out of the trunk, laid back the seat.

The meadow was swathed in mist. The latter stirred, tossed and turned, wove and unraveled its whitish mane; cold little sparks flashed in it; it had already swallowed up the river and the shrubbery at the riverside, had covered the other, high bank; only the tops of the pines were distinctly etched in the dark cloudy sky, in the yellowish glow of the dissolved stars. The mist spread across the meadow, it was about to envelop the car, to fill the whole area with its unstable surging substance.

Putyatin lit a cigarette, drew deeply on it a few times, brushed his hand across the perspiring window, and saw that his wife had lain down without waiting for the car to heat up. He extinguished his cigarette, undressed, threw his clothes in the trunk and climbed in the car.

"Oh, how cold and wet you are!" said Vera Dmitrievna, but didn't move away, and pressed her weak body against him.

He embraced her, started kissing her greedily, only now realizing how he'd missed her during the long day that had stubbornly kept them apart. And that complex, vague, occasionally tormenting thing that would wash over him, however firmly he held himself, at once fell away, like a scab from a wound that had healed long ago, and only the truth of love, closeness, and happiness remained.

It got hot in the car. He switched off the engine, lowered the side window, and lit a cigarette. The smoke he expelled curled in a blue spiral into the milkiness of the mist. Then he stretched out again beside his wife. And not for the first time he marvelled at her quietness. While he turned around, looked for cigarettes and matches, smoked, closed the window, and settled down again, she didn't move. In general she made do with a minimum of movements and gestures; the people around her seemed to bustle around jerkily, as in old German films. But what lay behind that— discipline, extraordinary reserve, or constraint, brought about by a difficult life and habitual self-control, he didn't know, for until now he'd hardly touched her inner being.

"Your former wife, apparently, is a good woman," she said.

Putyatin didn't understand whether it was a question or a statement.

"Of course she is!" For some reason there was a note of vehemence in his voice, and he hurried to compensate for it with conciliation. "And very helpful to those around her."

"I understand," she said. "I'm not nearly as helpful. It'll be hard for your friends to get used to me."

There was no sense of injury here, nor a desire to put a wedge between him and the Kungurtsevs, and still less, jealousy of the wife he'd left. She wanted to digest the day which they'd spent side by side with his friends, and she even expressed an indirect assurance that they'd have to reconcile themselves to her. She didn't want to deprive her husband of the friendship, but she didn't construct any illusions for herself, looking seriously and soberly into the future.

"Don't think . . . " said Putya, "They're good people. Very good and reliable."

"I know. Although not as helpful as your former wife. In general there are few helpful people. But there are still fewer real friends and you shouldn't lose them. For example, I haven't ever had friends. Or maybe only when I was a child."

"What about your daughter? Surely she's a friend to you?"

"No," said Vera Dmitrievna with that uncanny simplicity that both attracted and frightened him. "She loves me in her own way, but it's her father who was her friend."

"What, didn't she...?"

"She saw everything... Well, not everything, of course, but a lot, and that worked in his favor. In the favor of her unfortunate, sinful, enigmatic father, who was destroyed by a universal callousness. And then, you know, he's very good-looking, and his defects are to his advantage. He has flashing, sort of gem-like eyes, and nervous, abrupt, yet graceful gestures. He's always animated, elevated, and gives the impression of being a most sincere person. He lied all the time, from the first day of our life together. I think you can forgive everything except lies. He was firm and constant only in deceit, in lies that were stupefying and that drove me mad. He was a fanatical liar, and would sooner have climbed the pyre than admit to his lies. It was a kind of honesty turned inside out."

"But didn't Olechka herself decide who she was going to live with?"

"Yes... I think the instinct of self-preservation played a role there. And then—there's also your car."

"Come on!..."

"Seriously. She's a young girl, after all. A vain, silly, frivolous young girl. She looks older than her age, but she's awfully childish. You can't imagine how flattered she is by everything: the car, the dog, your wonderful guns..."

"You're maligning her."

"Why?... And then, it's to be expected. She never had any good toys. But that's not the important thing. I don't believe much in various methods of upbringing, but I do believe in a person's charm—let's call it that. And I hope that she'll appreciate the owner of the things which have attracted her so much."

"I don't know how to act with children..."

"There's nothing to know. You're not at all obliged to take care of her, thank God! Just be yourself..."

"How much prejudice there is in human relations, how little desire to get through to another person's real self," thought Putyatin. "Even the Kungurtsevs, who are the people closest to me, all made up their minds about Vera beforehand. And whatever she does, it won't melt the ice. To her credit, she didn't even try to make up to them, she remained herself, without the least challenge, incidentally. If anyone curried favor with the Kungurtsevs, it was me. But perhaps my mistake lies elsewhere—should I have pushed Vera onto them all? Lipochka was so much a friend of theirs, and who gave me the right to make the decision for everyone? Don't play the hypocrite, my friend! When she was leaving for Tomsk, the last thing Lipochka was thinking about was the Kungurtsevs. It's something else with Pasha. He loves his Maria Petrovna devotedly, but he needs a wife who doesn't work professionally. What he values in a woman above all are purely domestic abilities. He can't stand going to other people's homes, he loves entertaining at his—hospitably, plentifully, generously, sweepingly, in a word, on a level which only Lipochka could attain. He thinks he's missing Lipochka, but he's missing her dumplings . . . "

"Listen, can you cook at all?" he asked, recollecting belatedly that his wife couldn't have followed his train of thought and that his question would strike her as strange, at the very least.

"Depends what you call cooking. I can make soup, of course, and cutlets, but where did I have the chance to learn to make all kinds of exotic dishes? Apparently you still don't have any notion of what our daily life was like."

Not for the first time he felt convinced that it was impossible to catch Vera Dmitrievna unawares. She was always ready to give an answer, being totally unsurprised at and unopposed to the twists of other people's thoughts. He couldn't find an explanation for it, but ascribed it to that same inner integration that didn't allow her to slacken, to retreat into her personal mist. She had had a lot to answer for, and she was always equipped, like a soldier before battle. "My poor dear little soldier," thought Putyatin, swallowing the lump in his throat.

"I can prepare an omelette *aux fines herbes*."

"What's that?"

"An omelette with vegetables, cheese, mushrooms, and lard."

"Where'd you learn that?"

"A colleague taught me. She went to France on a student exchange. She lived a whole year there and cooked an omelette *aux fines herbes*— every day. It was cheap and nourishing."

"You won't buy Pasha with an omelette *aux fines herbes*," Putyatin decided sadly, and said aloud:

"Are you going to cook it for us?"

"Of course!"

Carefully, as though everything around them were made of glass, she turned to her husband and slowly, tenderly, kissed him hard on the lips.

Putyatin had never felt a woman so piercingly before. This wasn't enjoyment, but something else, an exquisite torment which you couldn't prolong or stop, and then a collapse, an exhausting fall and a return to consciousness in melancholy devastation.

It was hot, humid, stuffy. He moved away from Vera, sliding over to the very edge, to the side of the car. The misted windows exuded cold. He imagined that Vera wanted to embrace him, and his cooling body flinched in convulsive protest. Right then it would have been unbearable for him to touch any woman. But she didn't touch him; she merely pulled the sheet over herself, and apparently fell asleep at once.

The mist pasted silver foil over the car windows. Beyond this mist, beyond the great night spreading over thousand of kilometers, Lipochka, driven out by him, was sleeping, or rather, languishing sleeplessly. So big, strong, full of warmth and concern, of readiness to sacrifice herself for everyone who entered the boundless sphere of her kindness, and suddenly become totally alone, not needed by anyone. But no, probably she was needed by her recently widowed sister, but could that really satisfy Lipochka's heart? She wasn't guilty of anything, of anything before God and man, and all at once she was deprived of everything that had comprised her life's meaning: the man she'd loved devotedly, her home, friends. And was it easy to start a new life when one was over fifty? Putyatin gave a sob, and froze in fear. But Vera was sleeping, her breathing deep, long and regular. He stopped holding back his tears. He wept quietly, and begged Lipochka's forgiveness, and thanked the Kungurtsevs for not having accepted Vera. It wasn't his place to judge them with cheap cynicism; instead he should bow at their feet for their loyalty to Lipochka and their loyalty to his former self.

Ah, if the past were to return! He knew it was impossible, and he grieved and wept, and fell asleep like that, with a wet face, a weak, precarious, transparent sleep, when the surroundings don't go away, don't disappear, but penetrate the thin veil of visions and you don't even know that you're sleeping. You retain memory of yourself, you're conscious of the position of your body, the feeling of the bed, all the smells and noises, and only your closed eyes are turned not to the outside world but within— to the floating images of dreams. He knew that he was lying in a compact car, he could feel beneath his side the hard hump that joined the back of the front seat to the back seat, he could hear the river rumbling at the boulders and the breathing of the woman sleeping beside him, and he embraced her shoulders. And in the first instant he wasn't surprised to encounter beneath his palm the plump shoulders of Lipochka, on whose account he'd just wept silently. Then doubts arose, he couldn't believe it, but his palm was not mistaken, what was under it was too familiar. There were the two large smallpox marks, each the size of a three-kopek piece, which he'd never confuse with any others. And he smelled the scent of her warm dry skin. It was incredible, incomprehensible, but she'd come, evicted the chance intruder, and taken her place beside him forever. And it was then that he gave a cry of horror and despair, wanted to jump, but struck his head hard and fell back.

"What's the matter with you?... Calm down!" he heard an alarmed voice.

He didn't understand to whom the voice belonged, and awkwardly rearing up, with his feet braced against the dashboard and his head against the back seat, sagging ridiculously, he stared into the darkness, and moaned piteously.

"Calm down, dear!... It's me... me, Vera... "

"It's really you?... Ugh, God!" he breathed out the last of his fright.

"Was it a frightening dream?"

"Couldn't have been worse... " he muttered.

1976   Translated by Helena Goscilo

The original ("Chuzhaia") first appeared in *Novyi mir,* No. 6 (1976), 13-37. The present translation is of the latest edition, included in *Berendeev les* (M. 1978), 140-178.

Notes

1. Zhiguli—a make of small 'economy' car produced by the Volga Car Plant (VAZ) since 1970; Volga—a pricier, medium-sized car produced by the Gorky Car Plant since 1956.

2. The phrases are from A. Pushkin's poem "The Poet and the Herd" (Poet i tolpa, 1828), which constrasts the inspired creator divorced from "daily cares" to the uncomprehending insensitive mass of men who thrive on everyday activity.

3. Pelmeni are Siberian dumplings filled with meat or potatoes or cabbage.

4. The Baikal-Amur Trunk Line is a railroad in Eastern Siberia and the Far East which started being extended in 1974.

5. Luis Miguel Domínguín was a popular Spanish matador exaggeratedly admired by Hemingway and gored in the groin by a bull during a bullfight in Valencia in 1959. Hemingway was a spectator at the fight and later wrote about it in an article for *Life* magazine. Nagibin recounts the incidents of that period of Hemingway's and Domínguín's life in his fictional narrative, "One to One" or "Mano a mano" (Odin na odin).

6. Titian (Tiziano Vecellio, c. 1477-1576) was an Italian painter at the forefront of Venetian art during the High Renaissance. Renowned for his vibrant use of color, he produced many paintings on secular and religious themes, the most famous of which include "Danaë" (1554) and "Venus and Adonis" (1554).

7. Ariadne's thread refers to the myth in which Ariadne, a daughter of the king of Crete, Minos, and Pasiphaë, gave Theseus, son of the Athenian king Aegeus, the thread by which he escaped from the labyrinth built by Daedalus that housed the half-bull half-human Minotaur. Deserted by Theseus on Naxos (the topic of Richard Strauss's opera *Ariadne auf Naxos*), she became the bride of Dionysus. Ovid and Apollodorus offer slightly different versions of the story.

8. Sergey T. Konyonkov (1874-1971) was a Soviet sculptor who worked primarily in marble and wood and had a fondness for subjects drawn from folklore (e.g., "Nike" [1906], "Stribog" [1910]), though he also contributed to more conventional Soviet sculpture (e.g., "Liberated Man" [1967]). Extraordinary longevity is the only thing he and Titian have in common.

The Runaway

Kirilla Trediakovsky, the priest at the Astrakhan Trinity Church, married off his son, the chorister Vasily, against the latter's will. The fellow was going on twenty-one, the skin on his face was shiny from a surplus of ripe vigor, blood gushed from his nose without rhyme or reason, but the fool had absolutely no desire to enter into wedded matrimony with the worthy girl. In the clergy, people got married early; after all, if you hadn't wedded before being elevated to the priesthood, you'd be a bachelor to the end of your days. It goes without saying that Father Kirilla saw his eldest son as a priest into whose hands, in accordance with custom, his well-to-do parish would pass. Father Kirilla presumed that he had not long to wait for that, not at all because he had an intimation of imminent death; he was just mortally tired both in flesh and spirit, and he dreamed of taking vows and quietly spending the remainder of his days in the blessed calm of the cloister. His parish was hardly poor, but Father Kirilla's large family, though it was not in dire straits, had never known comfort. Another priest in his place would have done well—among his parishioners, besides fishermen and the usual laborers, there were quite prosperous people: shopkeepers, boat and seine owners, middle merchants, minor officials, and district clerks. Everyone had need of a priest for weddings, christenings, requiem services, blessing boats, shops, and new houses—but Father Kirilla couldn't make a profit off God, which is why he earned the derogatory nickname of 'the cheap priest.' He wanted to believe that having received his father's inheritance, his first-born Vasily, a taciturn, secretive, incomprehensible fellow, wouldn't be so generous and would squeeze some juice from his tight-fisted flock. Then they'd remember 'the cheap priest,' the over-scrupulous Father Kirilla, who in order to feed his family, now had to maintain a vegetable garden and an apple orchard and vineyard as well.

The garden began right behind their home and sloped gently down to the river Kutumu, and although the men in the Trediakov family had turned themselves inside out there, because of a debt of forty-eight rubles, they'd had to return the land across the river to Osip Plokhoy,[1] of His

Majesty's fishing office. God marks off a rogue; it wasn't for nothing that this sturgeon and sterlet fisher bore his abusive name—he'd skinned the poor people alive for a rather unimportant debt that he could have gone along with easily, considering his wealth. That had happened three years earlier, but things still hadn't improved for Father Kirilla's family, the more so as the vegetable garden left them didn't feed them very well. Droughts had taken their toll. From year to year, every summer the earth dried up, cracked and turned to powder, and no matter how hard Father Kirilla and his sons worked, they couldn't give the earth its fill of water.

But still and all they lived, didn't starve, ate bread and on holidays— fish pies. And if his eldest son's wedding had been done in a surprisingly modest way, it wasn't because of poverty—it would have been quite possible for proud Father Kirilla to arrange a more festive holiday, but his soul wasn't inclined toward generosity when he'd practically had to force his son under the wedding crown. He didn't want to get married, the nitwit, he wanted to go to school! It wasn't enough that he'd worn out the seat of his pants for ten years at a Catholic school run by Capuchin monks, and he'd already known how to read and write when he got there—he decided to go to the Kievo-Mogilyan Academy, and the reticent wallflower had even gotten a passport from the County Chancery. And he hadn't told anyone a word. By accident Volkovoynov, the clerk who arranged the document, let the news slip to Father Kirilla at a christening at the shipowner Frolikov's. It wasn't exactly that he let it slip: he congratulated Father Kirilla on having a brainy son who had such a thirst for learning. He thought, clerk that he was, that the son was headed off for Kiev with his parents' permission. But could it really be that you can give out passports without asking the parents? The son was still awfully young, he couldn't live by his wits. The aristocracy, the Capuchins, and the crafty knaves had great influence with the Vice-Governor Kikin too. Vasily himself was too simple and clumsy to have done something like that.

Kirilla Trediakovsky wasn't at all a foe of education; in his youth he himself used to read the Church Fathers, sampled Daniil's lofty eloquence, even used to take the high-flown Quintilian[2] in hand, since he knew the fundamentals of Latin, but heavy family cares had torn him away from books and made him live for the sake of his daily bread. He didn't see any other fate for his first-born son either. Learning was fine if a person was a wealthy aristocrat like Prince Dmitry Kantemir,[3] who had passed through Astrakhan with Tsar Peter on his way to Persia and who'd fallen ill here, but for a plain person it was useless and even harmful, since it distracted one from the serious life outside, stuffed one's head with superfluous, burdensome thoughts, and sometimes even destroyed you altogether. A poor man who'd learned too much either became a hopeless drunkard, fell into heresy or sedition, or went out of his mind. Many times Father Kirilla had come across pathetic people like that, who, having gorged themselves on the indigestible food of bookish wisdom, had turned into simpletons or idiots. There were lucky ones, of course, for instance, the famous Nikon who from God-forsaken Moldavia had ascended to the Patriarch's throne. But besides great learning, Nikon had a special talent for exercising power, for suppressing weak people and catching strong ones, none of which Father Kirilla saw in his own son. But even Nikon, princely and powerful as he was, ended badly. He got too wise, poor fellow, and because of his great mind and knowledge he wanted to jump higher than his own head and wound up incarcerated. Of course, under Tsar Peter a common person could rise to the greatest heights, not through book learning—that's what Dutchmen and Germans were made for—but by virtue of military valor or, in civil matters, a special skill with regard to factories and manufacturing, trade and crafts, or the happy ability to crawl into any crack without the help of soap, to worm one's way into the confidence of those who hold power, which gives a person the fastest and most reliable success. His ingenuous and clumsy son had no disposition for any of these things: he was a literate person, a bookworm, and nothing more. Nor was there in his stars the brilliant fate of Feofan Prokopovich,[4] the priestly poet and sly fox who had grown so close to His Majesty the Emperor. Not a chance of that! Therefore, it was incumbent upon him to take the well-worn path of the priest's son and toss that scholarly foolishness out of his head.

Hearing about the passport, Father Kirilla, using a firm hand that was used to the shovel and hoe, knocked some sense into his son. As usual, the latter didn't even attempt to justify himself, enduring his punishment in silence and wiping his bleeding nose—only a dull haze came over his dimly-blue eyes. Father Kirilla, who knew how to read people's eyes (at confessions he'd learned how to catch the truth in the darkness of slithering pupils), could never understand what his first-born son was thinking about. If you sent him out into the garden, he put the books aside and obediently sprinkled the beds; if you sent him to the vineyard or on some other errand, you got the same unmurmuring obedience, but Father Kirilla thought that his son had never seemed to answer him with inner agreement. There was neither love for his parents nor pity for his brothers and sisters in him; not even in his quiet, frightened mother did he show so much as a crumb of spiritual interest. Father Kirilla was greatly vexed by his wife's habitual, hare-like fear, which was transformed into mortal terror if she in some way failed 'to please' her husband. But, after all, Father Kirilla, who was severe, harsh, and quick to punish, not only had never laid a finger on her (he beat his sons, flicked his daughters on the forehead with his fingertips, and whacked the servants on the head), but he hadn't even raised his voice to her. As soon as he had sensed this inexplicable spiritual meekness in his radiant, snow-white, touchingly sweet bride, he had enveloped her, as if with fluffy fur, in his own kindness. But his quiet wife knew that there was another soul in him too—rough, impatient, and embittered by a hard life, and as though not believing in the reliability of the warmth enfolding her, she shook constantly without getting warm. Apparently Vasily had inherited something of his mother's meek, unintentional, and unconquerable stubbornness. He submitted to his father's will without a word, but didn't recognize his rightness. Father Kirilla suspected that in her heart of hearts, his wife took their son's side; had it been her choice, she would have left Vasily to his empty and ceaseless studies. But the choice wasn't hers, and Father Kirilla mercilessly drove his son into church choirs, the garden, the orchard, and the apiary. And it was he alone who decided Vasily's entire fate: he even picked a bride, Feodosia, for him. She was the daughter of Fadey Kuzmin, the watchman at the Astrakhan District Chancery.

In spite of his modest position, Fadey Kuzmin was a rather prosperous person. Apparently he knew how to do what Father Kirilla couldn't at all; it's not for nothing that popular wisdom says that it's the person who adorns the position, not the other way around. You'd think that a Chancery watchman wasn't worth much in comparison with the priest from the city Church. But he was! Fadey gave his daughter a dowry the likes of which the Trediakovskys had never even dreamed of. He had wanted to give money for the wedding, too, but Father Kirilla sharply rejected it: "We're having the wedding at our house, using our resources. And you know that you're not giving your daughter in marriage to a princeling."

And strange to say, everything seemed to turn out as Father Kirilla wanted: his son remained at home—along with the church and the garden, an end was put to his studies, and the date for the wedding had already been set, and from then on everything would take care of itself, but Kirilla's soul was alarmed and troubled. In his mind's eye he didn't see his son as a priest and the inheritor of his place; he couldn't form that pleasant picture at all. At times it seemed to him that his son didn't believe in God at all, and if he did believe, then it was in some special way of his own. Even when he was singing in the church choir his hazy-blue gaze wasn't enlivened by warm faith; his soul was absent from the church. That was a source of no little suffering for Father Kirilla, but what depressed him even more about his son was something else: the taciturn, obedient, meek oaf with a round, inexpressive face distinguished by two warts, and a stout body—where wasn't there fat on him!—was not only a secretive, stubborn fellow, but a person *possessed*. This was what frightened Father Kirilla and made him doubt the solidity of all his victories. And that was why he arranged a niggardly and un-Russian wedding feast. After all, would the marriage work out, was it true that he had yoked Vasily and forever tied him to the clump of ungenerous Astrakhan soil where the Trediakovskys were to live until the end of the world, transmitting the cathedral church parish from father to son?

But really, it is very rare that a person is governed by a single, indivisible emotion; usually nearby there's a glimmer of another one, sometimes its direct opposite. And in Father Kirilla too, in spite of his firmness of conviction, rooted in his great and bitter spiritual experience, his knowledge of people, and submissiveness before his own unlucky star, there was concealed the hope that a check on his son, possessed by the demon of idle learning, would be formed or found.

Father Kirilla wanted to believe that Vasily's young wife would become such a check. Father Kirilla had known Feodosia when she was still a long-legged, freckled, snot-nosed little girl—they'd been neighbors; he'd glimpsed her when she was an adolescent as well, when it's absolutely impossible to judge about the female sex: the unstable lump of flesh can take the form of an angel just as easily as that of a devil. Then the Kuzmins changed their place of residence and Feodosia no longer crossed Father Kirilla's path, but he heard from people in passing, and without asking for details, that the Chancery watchman's daughter, on entering her maidenly maturity, had blossomed with a rare, subtle beauty. Once, on the street, Father Kirilla received a low bow from a young woman in a downy Astrakhan kerchief which she clasped to her throat with a slender white hand. Burdened by his eternal worries, Father Kirilla nodded absent-mindedly, but suddenly, succumbing to an inner impulse, he turned around and stared after her, which was not terribly fitting for a worldly person, and for a clergyman was absolutely outrageous.

She was thin to the point of fragility, supple in the waist, light in step, not rushing and mincing, but floating, flying, and Father Kirilla regretted that he hadn't noted her features. But he remembered something like a burning sensation on his cheeks, as though a burning wax candle had been brought right past his face—it was the momentary fixed stare from her bright, honey-colored eyes. "Isn't that the watchman Kuzmin's daughter?" suddenly dawned on Father Kirilla, and a strange sadness compressed his heart.

That was just who it turned out to be. Father Kirilla recognized her immediately when he came to the Kuzmins' house a year or two later. Of course, she had changed: while retaining her delicacy of body, she no longer seemed frail and feeble; there was a sort of subtle and agile strength in her. "You won't blow her out like a candle," Father Kirilla thought with pleasure, "She's a strong one!" You felt that her slender white hand with its long fingers could lay hold an any object, be it a needle, oven prongs, or a husband's collar. And her face was worthy of an icon, such was the purity and sternness of her gentle features; it was only the gaze from those honey-colored golden eyes that was altogether earthly: it was merry, passionate, and caressing.

And Father Kirilla's thoughts turned gloomy: why on earth would such a beauty as Feodosia marry his nit-wit son, who could boast neither of his appearance nor manners, and of whose wealth there was no point in speaking? Fadey Kuzmin had let it be known ahead of time, through a talkative woman who had been sent to him for the object of feeling out the territory, that he would consider it an honor to become related to Father Kirilla's family, but he wasn't about to force his daughter into anything. That explained to Father Kirilla why Feodosia, a prize catch, had remained unmarried so long. Of course there had been proposals, it couldn't be otherwise, but the grooms hadn't been to her liking. It's well known that girls are picky, and if not compelled by parental will, they're ready to spend an eternity picking and not choosing. But what could draw Feodosia to that eternal student, the poor priest's son who had rotted his brains with learning? True, his Vasily was a local attraction of sorts: he'd been marked out by Tsar Peter himself when he stayed in Astrakhan. A person who loved to get personally involved in every little thing that seemed to him essential for the good of Russia, Peter Alexeyevich not only traipsed through all the shipyards, curing factories, salt works, and warehouses, but wanted to see the young Latin students as well. Of all of them Vasily alone was favored with the Tsar's attention. Seizing his reddish forelock and shoving it back on his forehead, Peter looked deep and long into the youth's hazy-blue, serious, patient eyes and, nudging him in the forehead with his broad palm said—either in praise or consolation—"An eternal toiler!"

No one understood what the Tsar, a seer of men, meant, and Father Kirilla didn't understand either whether the Tsar's prediction boded good or evil for his son. 'Toiler' seemed to be good; it would have been bad if it had been 'lazybones,' but 'eternal' sounded like a sentence, meaning that he would never have rest from the labors of the righteous and wouldn't taste his deserved peace and quiet in his declining years. But that was another matter, and you couldn't dispute that the Tsar's mark lay on his son. True, it was not likely that the ambiguous sign of the Tsar's attention could dispose Feodosia's unengaged heart in Vasily's favor. But, then, who knew? That Prince Kantemir, left behind by the Tsar's convoy because of his illness, took an interest in the work-loving youth and asked to have him brought to his bedside. A long conversation took place between the seminarist and the Moldavian who had been abandoned by the Tsar, and although the Prince didn't grant Vasily any place in his personal entourage, the latter made friends with the Prince's domestic secretary, Ivan Ilinsky, a man well on in years, of great erudition and considerable weight. Maybe there really was something in his absurd Vaska?...

It would seem that there was: to Father Kirilla's great surprise and joy, the beautiful Feodosia immediately responded by agreeing to the marriage to his first-born. "I remember Vasya when he was still a boy. He was quiet and thoughtful. He never fought with the other boys and never played. He wasn't like anyone and seems to have stayed like that." That was the utter truth.

When he was little, he never left his mother's side, and as soon as he learned to read, he barricaded himself from the whole world behind books. Father Kirilla burned with un-Christian wrath when he saw what a dawdler, a lump, a sissy his first-born was growing up to be. There was nothing boyish in him. And he didn't know how to stand up for himself at all. In the school run by Catholic monks the children were like children, the rote memorization didn't prevent them from messing around, fighting, chasing pigeons, swimming, fishing, and later on, experimenting with wine and tobacco. Vasily had never ever participated in anything of the sort. If they hit him, he stepped to the side, sniffing in offense, didn't hit back, and when he got it on the snoot, he tilted his head backward and waited patiently for the bleeding to stop. And it wasn't that he was a puny thing: he was broad in the chest and sacrum, with large arms grown strong through garden work. "Why won't you pay 'em back in kind?" Father Kirilla harassed his son, in spite of the Gospel precept about the right and left cheek. "You're a boy." "I'm not that kind of boy," came the quiet response. Then what kind...?

His son opened up a little bit much later, when he was already a young man. Once, in the presence of Father Kirilla, he had gotten into an argument with a schoolmate about the meaning of a poem by Feofan Prokopovich. The subject of the argument didn't interest Father Kirilla, but he was struck by the stubbornness with which his son defended his opinion. Under his crushing pressure his opponent, a good-natured, shaggy-haired fellow, quickly lost all his positions and dreamed only of an honorable retreat. But, not sparing his friend's self-esteem, Vasily trampled him with his feet, demanding a complete capitulation. One didn't sense either triumph or gloating joy in him; what he was defending was more important and dear to him than all the friendships in the world. Without hesitation he could sacrifice the only person close to him for the sake of a few cursed rhymed lines! It was then that Father Kirilla found another word for his son besides 'possessed'—'elect.' People live in accordance with chance and circumstances, traditions and rules, the bidding of their elders or personal benefit, and feelings as well, but Vasily seemed to be under some other authority, and worldly statutes had no power over his soul.

To the honor of Father Kirilla's spiritual sobriety, he didn't detain his son for long on the lofty heights to which the latter had been elevated by the parental ambition smouldering under the stifling mass of need and disillusionments. Avoiding the temptation of even momentary hope, he immediately returned the usual sobriquets to his son: 'nitwit,' 'clumsy oaf,' 'ninny,' 'bookworm.' But suddenly he was wafted by a breeze unlike the usual pungent Astrakhan air, reeking of fish, salt, and hides; instead, there was the sweet fragrance of angels' wings. This refreshing current was born in Feodosia's unexpected and inexplicable consent. Evidently there was a certain radiance from behind his son's broad shoulders if a marvellous girl was ready to link her fate to his.

Everything was simpler than Father Kirilla had thought it would be. Endowed with bright intelligence and a straightforward soul, Feodosia knew that her time had come, that she needed to marry if she wanted to live a good womanly life. There's nothing more pitiable and pathetic than old maids, and the threat of a lifetime of solitude already hung over her. She needed love and affection and she herself needed to pour out the force of her love onto someone. She could no longer be just a loving daughter. But the young men who came to her with proposals revolted her either because of the early spoilage written all over their hypocritically pious mugs or because of their greedy youthful lust. Uncleanness of thought went along well with inarticulateness, oppressive cerebral laziness, the odor of tobacco and cheap vodka. Among those seeking her hand there occasionally turned up dashing, sharp-witted young fellows with clever tongues, but she was frightened by their early independence and self-confidence. Feodosia wanted to subjugate herself to a husband and do everything for him, wash his feet and drink the water,[5] but only at her own discretion. With tenderness and kindness you could wind her around your little finger (that was exactly how her father had behaved), but her gentle and strong soul instantaneously rebelled against the slightest compulsion or pressure.

She had been well disposed toward the quiet, meek priest's son since her childhood. She had run across him in later years, too, and he in no way spoiled the impression he gave of himself. She liked his predilection for books, too, although she herself, while literate, didn't like to read. Well, and Vasily's looks weren't repugnant to her, either. Of course, they'd be better without the warts, but what are you going to do with them if God gave them to you, and his complexion was clear, he was nicely and firmly built, and his wide, steep brow reflected tranquillity. She knew that she could easily get used to him and even come to love this pure and meditative person.

If his son had received the news of the marriage with even a drop of gratitude, Father Kirilla would have thrown a wedding the likes of which had never been seen in the Astrakhan clergy. He wouldn't have stopped at anything: he'd have mortgaged his house and land and sent his family out into the world to fend for themselves. But Vasily's whole revoltingly submissive look seemed to say, "Your word is law, father, if you so command, I'll even marry a serving spoon or a broom." What an idiot! His elderly father had found him something marvellous beyond description, and he turns up his snotty nose. Well, if that's the way it is, there's no point in setting off fireworks. We'll have the wedding in poor man's style. Of course they prepared plenty of all sorts of dishes—it's never otherwise in a Russian Orthodox home—and there was enough to drink: Yakov, Vasily's youngest brother, imbibed so much liquor while gawking at the new bride that he slid down under the table. They dragged him away, and the wedding continued in a quiet, orderly manner. And, nevertheless, Father Kirilla remembered this modest holiday as a gift from God, as the most beautiful moment of his life. And the reason for that was the bride. She was so attractive, so angelic looking in her white gown (it was too bad that after the ceremony they'd removed the veil that hovered over her gentle head like a cloud), her every languid movement so captivating, and her golden-honey-colored eyes sparkled so, her little pink mouth opened slightly to form such a trusting, tender half-smile, that the old priest's young heart almost wept from inexplicable and melancholy ecstasy.

The whole time, even while they were in church, he'd been watching Vasily jealously and malevolently. He caught an instant when that dummy shuddered, screwed up his lusterless eyes as though they'd just been dazzled. The bride had touched his arm while putting on the ring, and in the threatening proximity he'd seen her radiant face. But he immediately relapsed into a somnolent stupor, obediently and listlessly doing everything that he was supposed to, and at the wedding table he behaved as though he were doing his duty and filling in for someone who had failed to show up. And when they cried "A kiss!" he looked around each time, expecting the person whose place he was taking at the table to appear and claim what was properly his. But no one appeared, and Vasily, suppressing a sigh, would turn woodenly to his young bride. She would already be waiting, trustingly and gracefully would extend her palms to form the shape of a pitcher, take his face in them and kiss him on the corner of the mouth. Father Kirilla envied his son terribly and cursed him for all he was worth for his coldness.

But it wasn't exactly that Vasily remained cold toward the enchanting girl who had practically materialized out of thin air and been betrothed to him; it was just that he didn't believe in his own participation in what was happening. His father had undertaken another of his usual business deals that seemed profitable to him—how many such deals there'd been: he'd buy a melon patch and bit of land near the garden, only to let them go soon for half-price; or he'd buy a share in a fishing vessel, not thinking to do it until the end of the season, when they stopped catching sturgeon; then he'd invest his torturously accumulated money in a shifty businessman who'd lost his shirt, about which everyone in Astrakhan knew except the smart, truly smart, Father Kirilla, who was hopelessly undone by his passionate, presumptuous nature. And this undertaking of his—to marry his son, bind him hand and foot to the Trinity Church, the garden and orchard, to all the dark, sad life here—would also fail, just like his other projects. After all, Vasily had to study, to find out everything and to understand about words. Why he needed to do that, Vasily had never even wondered. Why did one breathe, eat, and drink water? Simply because without those things a person couldn't live. But, Lord knows by whom, he'd been given yet another need: to know about all words. That's not really such a rarity: people committed to something can be found all over the world. They can't live just like that: some need to draw a brush across a canvas or wood, some to think about the nature of things, some to gather herbs for medicines, and there are those who spend their whole lives looking for the philosopher's stone or trying to build a *perpetuum mobile,* or endeavor to give man wings, or preserve the noise of their time for the future. And if you deprived them of that, they'd fall sick and die.

Moreover, Vasily couldn't recognize that Feodosia belonged to him, that the words "husband and wife are flesh made one" related to him. Could it really be that she'd go into the bedchamber with him, undress, exposing all the indecency of her nakedness, lie down in bed with him and commit that shameful and mysterious act that he often found himself dwelling on in the insomnia of oppressive spring nights? It was terrifying even to think about it. He wouldn't dare touch her. The Lord wouldn't permit it. And, indeed, his father had seen to it in his worldly calculations that the pure turtle-dove not be profaned. That was why he didn't even attempt to be tender or even simply attentive to the young one, though he fulfilled everything required by the ceremony and even responded by touching his dry lips to the warm smoothness of her cheek and the living, moist corner of her lips. During the entire wedding feast he kept his soul on ice.

Vasily melted only once, when an elderly grey-haired gentleman from Prince Kantemir's suite who had been brought by Ilinsky the secretary and who travelled all over the frontiers of the Russian state collecting ceremonial songs, folk tales, and legends, asked permission to sing a wedding song that he had recorded among the coastal dwellers. One could suppose that this gentleman had dropped in here, too, in the hope of hearing a new song, but it was quiet at the chorister's wedding.

It was well-known, remarked the guest, that all wedding songs are sung by a chorus. I'll perform this ceremonial song by myself, however, so that you might become acquainted with the customs of the northern peoples. And he started up in a pleasant, reasonably high voice:

> Oh how one of us at the feast is handsome,
> Oh how one of us at the feast is beautiful.
> How handsome is the newly-wed prince,
> The newly-wed Prince Vasilyushko,
> His face is like white snow,
> His cheeks like a red flower,
> His brows of black sable...

Truly, it's the figure of my son, Father Kirilla thought spitefully. The face, the cheeks, the brows—all copied right from him. He realized that these were general, age-old, traditional traits for the groom in a wedding song, and not those of a specific person, but he couldn't stifle his irritation. Then they importuned the singer for a song for the new bride. He didn't make them beg him for long:

> The gray turtle-dove
> Has a golden head,
> Gilded,
> Woven together
> Of various silks, various silks.
> Brothers, if she
> Were my wife
> In the summertime, in the summertime
> I'd drive her in a golden carriage...

"Oh, yes!... Only a golden carriage would be right for her beauty. A gold and diamond one!" rang out in Father Kirilla's breast.

"Father Kirilla," he heard his wife whisper frightenedly and reproachfully, "Come to your senses, my dear! You, our breadwinner, aren't the one who's getting married!"

For the first time in their long life together his wife had gotten up the courage to raise her voice, and even with a reproach. The dear soul stopped her fierce ruler in his tracks. He must be a sight if such an ingenuous creature had penetrated his secret thoughts. How had he given himself away? Or perhaps his shy mate wasn't so terribly ingenuous after all, and took in plenty from her mouse hole? Oh, well, decent one, take yourself in hand, and most importantly get your eyes off the bride! Calm me and forgive me, Lord! You know that it's not vile lust, but ecstasy and sadness that have mastered my withered, but still living soul. The Lord understands everything, but could you possibly explain anything to people, even those close to you? And slowly, with an effort, he averted his gaze from the bride.

And for the first time during the wedding feast Vasily grew lively; red roses even blossomed on his face "white as snow." He was talking about something and seemed to be arguing with Ilinsky or the folk-song collector. But did he *have* to? How could yesterday's student permit himself such things with important learned gentlemen, though the latter didn't tell the brazen fool off. They were listening with attention and even interest. His son wasn't expressing his thoughts terribly well; he kept breaking off, mumbling and trying to find the right words. Well really, if you're going to enter into a serious conversation with people who are older and better off than you are, then at least know what you want to say, bird brain, and don't hem and haw and stutter: hit the nail on the head. But apparently Vasily's inarticulateness didn't anger these indulgent gentlemen. They were listening, furrowing their brows in concentration, and nodding significantly. Well-well, now, what were they carrying on about?

"...don't know how many times I've observed," said Vasily, "that there is much more melodiousness in base poetry than in the verse of someone even like Feofan Prokopovich."

"Folk poetry *is* lyrical. It doesn't exist in any other form," Ilinsky smiled.

"But isn't any poem a song?" Vasily said with a surprised and stupefied look. "Well, not that it is, but it should be?"

"You don't mean to say that elevated poetry of a didactic or odic genre needs melodiousness?" remarked Ilinsky a bit haughtily.

"Of course not!" replied Vasily, flustered. "That's not what I meant...I can feel it, but I don't know how to express it..."

"If you don't know how to, then don't go sticking you nose in. Sit still and shut up!" Father Kirilla thought with wrath.

"Darling," he heard his wife's voice, quiet as grass, "you ought to gaze at Vasily more tenderly. You have the look of a wolf in your eyes. That's not good!"

Father Kirilla almost spat from vexation. What had come over her, to call her husband to order? Whence such courage? Perhaps she saw support in her married son and his bride, the poor thing? Well, no matter. But what was happening to him, what were these storms making his insides quiver? He rested his forehead on his broad hand.

"...I think that it has to do with the difference in the methods," Vasily argued. "Syllabic poetry only demands the same number of syllables in each line, but folk poetry is based on another sort of harmony."

"That poetry, if I may say so, is very poor in rhymes," Ilinsky said sternly.

"Oh, is that so?" the song collector interrupted. "You'll find very clever rhymes in folk poetry, too. Most often the ends of lines are rhymed, but sometimes rhymes occur at the beginning or in the middle, when the line is divided into hemistichs."

"That's not what the question is!" Vasily cut in abruptly. "What if one were to give high-born syllabic poetry the melodiousness of folk poetry?"

"Why not try it," the guest advised good-naturedly. "Perhaps you'll discover a new method."

"A kiss!" Father Kirilla thundered, himself surprised at what he'd said.

2.

... For a long time they lay awake on the far sides of the wide and horribly narrow wedding bed—the slightest movement, and you'd at once roll into the heat of the other's terrifying body—under sheets that were at first cool, but now hot and damp; their heads sank into the scorching pillows. From the partially opened window there came a salty freshness, but it brought no coolness.

Vasily was thirsty; he wasn't accustomed even to small doses of liquor, and his mouth was dry and burning; his mother had taken care to place a small barrel of kvass with a pitcher floating in it near the headboard on his side, but he was afraid to move his arm. With a rough tongue he licked his lips and palate, but that brought no relief. But his head was clear; the intoxication had evaporated immediately, as soon as they rose from the table and he suddenly realized that all of this was serious and in a moment they would be led off to the bedroom and left alone, eye to eye, in the darkness that was shot through by the flickering icon lamp and the weak light of the stars in a moonless April sky.

"Well, what's wrong with you?" a whisper broke the silence.

Vasily heard Feodosia's light, rapid breathing, heard the buzz of mosquitoes and the rasping of the wood-boring beetle, far-off voices outside the window, the regular squeak of a poorly-fastened shutter, the mysterious colloquy of the old house's floorboards where someone seemed to wander through all the rooms all night long.

"So are we going to lie together?" Feodosia whispered in a tone of mild reproach. "After all, I'm your wife, Vasya. The Lord God has united us."

"What do you want?" Vasily forced out hoarsely, through parched lips.

"Well how do you like that?" she laughed. "He even asks! Can you really be so stupid that you don't even know why people get married?"

"I don't know how," muttered Vasily.

"Oh, you sweetheart!" she said melodiously. "Did Adam and Eve know how? Why, it wasn't for nothing that the Lord God drove them out of

Paradise. They found out how, that's what that means. Lie closer."

But Vasily didn't make a move, because he already knew beforehand that this was all pointless, that he wouldn't have the courage to touch her, and if he did, then it would be to no purpose, and because of his pathetic, vile weakness he started to cry. At first quietly, covering his mouth with his hand, biting his fingers so as to use bodily pain to drive out the other pain, and then loudly. He buried his face in his pillow, his back heaved, and he didn't immediately sense that Feodosia had lain up close to him. She embraced him and comforted him; with unexpected strength she parted his hands, and with the hem of her nightshirt she wiped away his tears and even dabbed at his nose, as if he were a little boy; then she took off her wet shirt and threw it on the floor. She put his head on her breast, and pressed herself to him, filling every indentation of his hunched-up body with her own, and in return he began to penetrate her, trembling all over, but calming down at the same time. He again recalled that man and wife are flesh made one. Now he understood those words, for he himself could no longer tell where he was, where she was, where his arm was, where hers, where his leg was, where hers. And she managed to conceal her pain; it was only in the morning, when he saw the bloodied sheet, that he realized how much he had hurt her inside, but she hadn't given any sign of it, didn't yell or grit her teeth; all she did was think about him and help his coarse and clumsy efforts. And in the morning he also realized that she no longer found it painful, but delightful and good, just as he did, and that she sought their union, and that they were truly flesh made one.

On that first wedding night, lying in pain, in blood, with a scream clenched in her breast, Feodosia came to love Vasily with all her large heart, to love him with that enormous, sacred, devoted, self-sacrificing and boundless love of which only a Russian woman is capable.

She had gotten what she wanted: a pure man who hadn't been loved by others, who hadn't know others' embraces and others' lips, a person who was fresh and strong because he'd preserved himself, a man who belonged to her entirely and wholly.

Toward the morning the birds burst into song. The window was flooded by a pink light. They were mortally tired and happy.

No one woke them until evening. Father Kirilla had ordered the young ones not to be disturbed. He was exultant, at once forgiving his son for all his foolish behavior during the engagement, marriage ceremony, and wedding feast, his stupid dourness and ingratitude toward his father. After all, it had turned out that there was no mental defect, no damage; it was just that the flesh in him had not yet awakened, he was a child encased in a grown man. But one night had turned the child into an adult male. It wasn't in vain that Father Kirilla had so placed his hopes on the fragile Feodosia; she had sprinkled his son with the living water of love. Now perhaps he would turn toward a serious life, learn to be responsible for his wife and future children. At the thought of grandchildren, who wouldn't be long in coming, since the young bride had taken the business so well in hand, Father Kirilla felt the chronic, hard lump that had been crushing his heart dissipate. "Soon I'll marry you off too," he promised his younger son Yakov, "and I'll give you in marriage"—he thought of his eldest daughter Marya. He had a knack for arranging marriages, he'd fix things up well and reliably for all of his children, and together, a large, harmonious family, they would raise themselves up from want. Well, and if anyone wanted to live in his own house, he was more than welcome, we couldn't compel anyone, and the shrinking of the family has its own profits. Because of his joy, though it was as hot as could be, and there was much work to do in the garden, Father Kirilla decided not to disturb Vasily—let him enjoy his young wife to the point of devastation. Well, then he and Yakov would have to get down to work. Which was done after overcoming Yakov's minor rebellion caused by his rage at having to work for his older brother as well, while the latter lounged around in bed.

It wasn't until the fourth day that the young ones, following tradition, favored the bride's father with a visit; but the proud Fadey didn't take offence, rejoicing as he was at his daughter's happy look. Feodosia was radiant with joy, her mouth had blossomed, her eyes had blossomed, her breasts grown rounder, her figure grown firmer and her whole body grown ripe, although she and her husband, like desert hermits, had eaten nothing, not going near the tasty dishes that the priest's wife had prepared. It was another sort of hunger they were appeasing, for truly it is not by bread alone...

And on returning home, they again retired to their room, but not for long; in a day or two the bride's fresh young voice began to be heard in the other rooms. With sense and understanding she asked the women of the house about domestic affairs, trying to find her place in them. But Vasily Kirillovich hardly showed himself: he apparently couldn't part with the wedding room. He listened to the spring birds, dreamed and stretched, drank cold kvass with raisins, and impatiently awaited his wife's return. At any event, that was the way the people in the priest's house imagined things. And indeed for a while that's the way it was. Feodosia got to know him and understand him, grew more expansive and filled out the expanse of his being with herself. Not with anyone and never again would he be so happy, and what more could one wish the poor man? The path before him was plain and straight: he'd become a priest, praise the Lord God just as his father did, watch over human souls, cultivate his garden and orchard, and raise his children. He would teach them everything that he himself hadn't had time to learn, and at the appointed time he'd leave this world, having done what a man should do. Having done everything?... Yes, if one didn't establish other, extraneous goals for himself. But he did. He wanted *to know,* to know everything about stringing words together into lines of poetry; he had an inkling of something new and unknown for Russian poetry. Unknown today, but tomorrow you might look and discover that it had become known. It might and it might not, but if it did, then it wouldn't be because of his work, but through the intellectual and spiritual efforts of some other unselfish person. But he didn't want anyone else to do his work, just as he didn't want anyone else to embrace Feodosia.

But these were all just words that he mumbled to himself as he loafed around in the little bedroom, listening to the singing of the birds and the buzzing of the May bug, and their bitterness melted away at the mere thought that his wife would soon return and nestle up to his chest. And if things became too impossible, he'd throw himself on the bed, bury his face in the pillow, and so greedily breathe in the scent of her hair that his heart would stop.

Once, as he let his arm slip down off the bed, his fingers came upon a tattered little book on the floor near the wall. Either he himself must have brought it here in his remote adolescent days, when he looked for solitude in this large house that was full of people and cares, or his sisters might have hidden it there as a prank. The old book smelled of dust and decay, and the dried-up pages had turned yellow. Ovid. *The Metamorphoses.*[6] There had been a time when he was inseparable from that book, seeing in it a model of wisdom and verbal beauty. But you grow out of books, just as you do clothes. What use had he for a dense Russian reworking of Roman verses when he, the best Latinist at the Catholic school, could enjoy Ovid's Muse in the original, just as he could Catullus, Horace, Terence[7] ... The Monk Marcus Antonius, discovering a rare memory and zeal in him, gave him a decent training in Greek, which the school didn't teach. But it wasn't only classical languages that he knew: he read Italian fluently, and German and French fairly well; without the last of these it was absolutely impossible to be initiated into the world of contemporary poetry. Its center of concentration nowadays was France, just as it had once been ancient Rome, and in the Middle Ages—Florence. And carried off to the heights by his ardent youthful imagination, he dreamed of transplanting the fragrant flowers of French poetry to Russian soil. And in general he was easily ignited by others' fires. He would quickly grasp another's thought and could not only convey it in the words of his native language, but develop it, broaden it, and embellish it with something of his own that had been dormant at the bottom of his soul, waiting for an impulse from outside. But now all these majestic thoughts had gone up in smoke. He needed once and for all to toss the disquieting names of poets and philosophers out of his head: they would be useless for a priest-gardener, model husband and father of numerous offspring. Matins, mass, vespers, church holidays, christenings, weddings, funerals, memorials and confessions—that was the life awaiting him till the end of his days, and the Bible was the only book he needed. He ought not to fool himself on that count; he needed to forget about even thinking about scholarly studies for his own pleasure: they were beyond the powers of a poorly educated, intellectual half-wit; he would need to study more, to imbibe others' wisdom. That, then, was the price for the hot, sweet nights!

His dear, tender, affectionate Feodosia had cast Homer and Ovid, Dante and Tasso, Ronsard and Fénélon[8] into the dust with a single movement of her white shoulder. But the moldy smell of the old book aroused in him a mortal longing for the downcast idols and his former burning thirst to learn everything, and having done that, to give expression to what had happened, which, though still vague, he hoped for in the future. He needed to flee, to flee immediately, because with each day it would become more difficult. With each hour Feodosia's gentle power over him was growing firmer, and there would come a time when he wouldn't be able to flee, and that would be the end of him. He wasn't made for the quiet happiness of a life that flowed along slowly and imperceptibly. He could fool himself for a long time, but sometimes he would realize that he'd sold his soul for a soft bed and a woman's body that would grow cold with the years, and then he would either lay hands on himself or become a hopeless drunkard, the unhappiest and most horrible person on earth, and people would be terrified to look at him. He wasn't rejecting Feodosia, or more accurately, he was rejecting her only for a time—when he became the person that he ought to be, he would return to her. But strange to say, for some reason he didn't believe he'd come back. He knew that Feodosia would wait for him, remain faithful, and he knew that he wouldn't love another woman, and he knew just as firmly that his departure was forever. But all of that was in the future, through the haze of years; right now he was only faced with one thing: being able to leave. After having slapped his son a good number of times, Father Kirilla hadn't seen fit to take away his passport, the document that stated he was free, that the runaway could not be seized upon parental demand and forcibly returned home. He would leave for Moscow, enter the Slavonico-Greco-Latin Academy, which was called, as in the old days, the Zaikonospassky School. Earlier he had wanted to go to the Kievo-Mogilyansky Academy, but Ilinsky considered the Moscow institution, of which he himself was a graduate, a more fitting one for a Russian youth. In Kiev the Polish, Catholic spirit was strong, but Moscow was the stronghold of Orthodoxy, the heart of Russia. And besides which they'd begin looking for him in Kiev, of course, where earlier he had planned to go, and when they didn't find him, they'd lose interest.

Twirling the half-decomposed book in his hands, Vasily discovered that he was sizing up his chances for escape in a business-like manner and realized that his decision was irreversible. He lay down on the bed, pressed his face to the pillow that retained the scent of Feodosia's hair, and began to weep quietly from the depths of his being.

And later he arose, dressed, splashed his face with water, and set off for the city. There his actions were distinguished by such exactness that one might have thought he'd spent his entire life in flight. He immediately made for the wharf, found out that at the beginning of June an artillery command of seventy men was setting out for Moscow—to Saratov by water, and from there on by land. He couldn't have hoped for anything better—with military people he would be safe from the brigands who prowled the banks of the Volga. He quickly made a deal with the tipsy, good-hearted artillery captain, who idolized learning, showed him his passport so that he wouldn't think that he'd gotten himself involved with an escapee, greased the palm of the also tipsy, but threatening cook, so that he could eat from the soldiers' pot, and no longer doubted that he would reach the capital without dying from hunger or a bandit's knife...

...He left the house at dawn. In his bag he had only two shirts, a pair of socks, a razor, and a few favorite books. His holiday garb, his fur coat, and his gilt watch—a wedding gift—he left for Feodosia: that wasn't much help, but after all, the family could take care of her. He himself was in much greater danger of want, but he wasn't worried about himself. As he was writing her a farewell note, Feodosia, in her sleep, had sensed the uncommon emptiness of the bed, cried out, stretched out toward her husband's place, but fell still without completing the motion—she had spent the whole day working hard in the garden along with the men, and she lapsed back into a deep sleep.

Vasily, who had frozen in alarm, realized that she wouldn't wake up, finished his note, leaned over toward his wife, and instead of the former subtle fragrance, he smelled sweat and dirt. So that's how the aroma of their youthful feeling would have vanished, replaced by the stale breath of everydayness. A saving thought, but it didn't make things easier. He hadn't expected this to be so painful. It was as if he'd been stabbed in the chest with a knitting needle—it was difficult to breathe. How firmly they'd been bound together by their honeymoon, truly a honeyed month. With that pain he made his way out into the orchard, repeating to himself: "Maybe I should stay, stay, before it's too late..." He imagined that he heard the squeak of a window frame. In a second the beloved voice of Feodosia, who didn't expect any vileness from him, would call to him, surprised and trusting, and right then Vasily made a leap that a mountain goat would have envied. In spite of the needle in his chest, he jumped over the fence, raced through empty streets, down the hill, and didn't come to his senses until he reached the wharf, when he realized that he'd imagined everything. The artillerymen were already loading the boat, exchanging listless and unnecessary curses in the darkness of the new-born day.

The last moments of parting with the city weren't bitter for Vasily. He calmly looked at the ships and fishing boats crowded around the wharf, at the warehouses, at the nets hung out to dry, with glittering fishscales in their opening, at the fat gulls circling above the dirty, smelly water; his soul was unmoved by the crosses and cupolas of the city's churches that flashed blindingly under the sun and the flocks of pigeons rising in the pale high sky. Thinking of Feodosia after the mind-boggling goat leap made him somehow uncomfortable. At times his mother's sad face floated up before him and he wiped away the vision as if it were a tear. He didn't want those whom he'd left to have power over him. He already belonged to the Zaikonospassky School, Homer, Dante, Fénélon...

3.

Vasily Trediakovsky, who had set off in flight right from his wedding bed, was committing an act which, though outrageous in its cruel audacity, was hardly an unusual phenomenon in the Russia of that time. During the era of the Petrine transformation many Russian youths were to be found in flight. The sons of nobles fled the double yoke of uncommon discipline and impossibly difficult studies at the navigation schools to which they'd been sent by force, having been plucked brutally from their warm parental nests; the children of clergy and minor civil servants fled from divinity schools and academies, not wishing to link their lives with religion at a business-minded, practical time; uneducated youths of all social strata fled naval and military service and every sort of instruction; peasant sons, recalling the glorious days of Stenka Razin,[9] who was executed on Red Square in Moscow but celebrated in songs, fled from arbitrary masters and formed gangs of brigands. But along with all of this there was another sort of flight. That stubborn coastal-dweller, the pride and glory of Russian learning and all arts, Mikhaylo Lomonosov, paralleling the fate of Trediakovsky, his future colleague at the academy and sworn enemy, fled from the far North to the same Zaikonospassky School. Future scholars and scientists, explorers, poets, artists, military leaders, naval commanders, great sons of Russia, the creators of her strength and glory, fled from their warm families for the torments of education, near-starvation, exhausting prohibitions and drills.

It goes without saying that the abandoned wife and relations of the

Astrakhan couldn't perceive their misfortune in a broad historical perspective. When Feodosia came to from her deep sleep, she found the note left her by her husband, realized that she would no longer have Vasily at her side, let out a penetrating scream, and fainted. They rubbed her temples with vinegar for a long time, but it was only when her mother-in-law extracted a tarry substance from a little iron-coated chest and forced it through Feodosia's clenched teeth that the poor woman recovered her senses. While she was unconscious there seemed to have taken place some sort of process that helped her to acknowledge what had happened: she awoke a different person—quiet, concentrated, calm, and seemingly lucid. She herself didn't understand what had taken place in her. Having lost her surroundings and herself, it was as if she had continued to read and reread her husband's note until she memorized it and understood its meaning, which had escaped her at first.

"It's not you that I'm running from, but myself—the person that I have become under my father's hand. Until I acquire all the knowledge I need, I won't return. Forgive me if you can. And don't look for me. If it is God's will, we'll see each other in time. Either I'll come myself or summon you to where I am. Your husband Vasily."

Your husband . . . He hadn't abandoned her or left her; as before, he was her husband before God and man; he had simply gone away to study, just as other husbands left for the sea or the war, for the conquering of distant lands, or by command of the Sovereign, for service to Russia in foreign countries. No one had given Vasily Kirillovich such a command other than his own soul, but that command was no weaker than the Sovereign's. And if that was what he needed, then that was the way things must be. And there was no point in wailing and gnashing her teeth; she must wait, keep her husband's place sacred, and arrange everything so that when the wanderer returned he would have a home, coziness, and comfort awaiting him. Of course she would be lonely, especially at nights; she had grown so used to his warmth, caresses, and slightly agitated breathing. But she could cope with that; after all, she was strong.

Feodosia recovered so quickly, and even grew merry, that the others in the house were amazed, and Marya, the runaway's eldest sister, cast reproaches: "What an insensitive one she is!" "You're a fool," said her mother, sighing. "She wants to preserve herself for her husband." And, making the sign of the cross over her daughter-in-law, she added: "And so you take care of yourself, my child." "Mama, you seemed to expect Vaska to take off," remarked Yakov, who, for all his dull-wittedness, was distinguished by a strange acuity. "I didn't expect, but I thought it was possible," the old woman replied quietly. "What do you mean—you thought it was possible?" thundered Father Kirilla. Stunned by his son's flight, he opened his mouth for the first time. For some reason his wife didn't take fright, but answered almost haughtily: "I'll tell you what I mean! He had a different way of seeing, not the local way." "What nonsense are you talking, silly woman?" "No nonsense at all, my benefactor; I'm the one who carried him, and I only feel with what's inside." "And why didn't you speak up then?" Father Kirilla erupted in fury. "But who would have believed me? As it is I'm taken for a fool—if I'd said anything, I'd have been completely disgraced. But you just wait, daughter, wait . . . "

And Feodosia began to wait. Oh, it's a difficult job—waiting. Feodosia sensed that with her perspicacious heart right away. It has to be admitted that Feodosia was perspicacious only with regard to herself and to people who possessed a pure, radiant core; where human soot and shadowiness were concerned, she lost her keensightedness. But as regards herself she knew everything perfectly well. And so she knew that she must plunge into work right up to her ears so that there would be no energy for nostalgia and lonely thoughts, and so that her sleep would be dreamless. When Vasily Kirillovich returned, let him see that he was awaited by his own home with clean, attractively appointed rooms, full grain bins and stuffed pantries. He'd see how capable and domestic she was, that she hadn't gone to pieces, hadn't dissolved into a muddy puddle, like a snowbank in March, but had taken care of herself for her beloved and taken care of his place. She must not be thin and pale, with tiny, cried-out eyes; he had produced the flowering of the woman in her, and it should continue even if only because of the strength of her loving memory. She would take care of herself, wash in the morning dew, which keeps the skin smooth, eat richly and well, even though she had no appetite, and dress elegantly for holidays—that also helps preserve a woman's youthfulness. She had to use the three or four years that his studies would last to her advantage, not her loss. It was certain that in Kiev, Moscow, or Petersburg—wherever the dear ended up—Vasily would have plenty of beauties to feast his eyes on—and she mustn't let his own wife seem ugly to him.

And Feodosia began smiling at people again as she had during the time of her brief happiness; she once again became courteous and pleasant to everyone. And, trying to cheer up the rest of the disheartened household, she kept repeating: "But he'll come back. He'll come back for sure." In reply to which Father Kirilla only grunted and turned his dark angry-sad eyes away. Yakov smiled derisively, the sisters puckered up their fastidious mugs, and only the old priest's wife whispered barely audibly: "Believe, daughter, believe!"

Feodosia was grieved by Father Kirilla's changed attitude to her. Earlier she had felt that her stern father-in-law liked her, and that had made her happy. She liked it when people liked her. But now a wall seemed to have grown up between the two of them. She knew of no fault on her part; indeed, if you were going to go looking for guilty parties, then it was the Trediakovskys who deserved rebuke. They ought to have looked more deeply into their Vasya's soul before entering into matchmaking. He wasn't mature enough for family life; what sort of husband could he be?—he, a student as yet uneducated; why constrain him? He should have studied all the sciences first and satisfied his itch for learning; then it would have been worth thinking about marriage. But nobody took him into account; Father Kirilla made all the wise and far-sighted calculations, and he really had looked far into the distance, but he lost sight of what was right under his nose. Vasily's mother had noticed, but she was deprived of a voice in family affairs. No, it would be better not to look for guilty parties, but to close ranks in their common misfortune and to bear jauntily their shame, neighbors' silent reproaches, and any other difficulties; but she didn't sense any support from anyone in the household except the taciturn mother; all she felt was alienation and ill-will.

Father Kirilla had very firmly determined for himself who was responsible for the disgrace that had befallen the family. The guilty one was Feodosia, in the strength of whose enchantment he had believed blindly and made a colossally stupid mistake. Father Kirilla understood perfectly what his wife had said; he was just acting the part of a person surrounded by deceit. He himself had constantly and instinctively sensed the unreliability of Vasily's submissive manner, but he hadn't taken the necessary action. And when he saw Feodosia he'd dropped his guard completely, immediately persuaded that she would collar Vasily and make a husband, father, and bread-winner out of him. And everything that had followed the wedding had confirmed his belief. He was proud of his perspicacity, life experience, and knowledge of people; and what a filthy puddle his worthless son had landed him in! Father Kirilla was too proud to admit his own defeat, and a guilty party was found at once—Feodosia. What good were her honey-colored eyes, silken hair, lithe figure, the enveloping caressingness of her voice and movement if she'd been unable to domesticate Vasily, to sew firmly to her skirt the overgrown boy who was out of his mind from the bliss of the bed? That meant that her outward perfection was a fraud; there was spoilage somewhere, a hidden wormhole, as in a piece of fruit that looked delicious from outside but was rotten within. Father Kirilla despised Feodosia, as though he knew her to be guilty of a secret vice or to have a vile disease. This squeamish contempt saved him from hatred. And when she asked him to let her have the garden land so as to build a home there and feed herself from that same land, Father Kirilla didn't refuse, but demanded cash for the parcel of land.

Feodosia suggested payment by installments: she would pay every autumn after the harvest. "In that case I'll die before I see the money," Father Kirilla smiled dismally. Feodosia objected reasonably that Vasily Kirillovich would return before then and make complete payment or else give back the land and live as before in the single large household. "We don't know any Vasily Kirillovich any more and don't want to know him. Whether he returns or not is of no interest to us. I offered you the land at an extremely low price because of your poverty; Prokopy the potter would give me fifty more." Feodosia was saddened by her father-in-law's words, but she didn't refuse the land. She sold everything from her dowry that she could get along without: her wedding dress, pearl necklace, pearl ribbon, silver necklace hung with two crosses, four yards of velvet, a damask skirt, a piece of embroidered cloth, and after a short mental struggle—two antique Latin books in pigskin bindings. Books and what they brought with them had sullied her fate, and Feodosia regarded them with superstitious trepidation. Vasily Kirillovich hadn't had time to find out about these books, which lay at the bottom of her hope chest, and Ilinsky paid such a price for them that one would have thought they were printed on Chinese silk and bound in gold. Besides which, she didn't want any books in her house; good riddance to them—they led to no good. And as long as Vasily Kirillovich was absent, she felt calmer without them.

After coming to terms with the artel carpenters about how much the construction would cost, she discovered that she still didn't have enough money and so she turned to her father for help. After paying for the land she still needed 101 rubles and 50 kopeks, and her father had money. Fadey laid out the needed sum without any objections, but he demanded that she sign a promissory note. "Papa, dearest, why do you need a note?" asked Feodosia, surprised. "You don't imagine that I can pay back so much money? But when Vasily Kirillovich returns, we'll make payments as often as we can. Don't you believe me?" "I believe you, daughter. You I believe. But it's your family that I don't trust. If your husband could play such a dirty trick, what can you expect from them? If they were people, would they try to drag money out of you for the land? Well, and so you go ahead and build, but by law the land all belongs to them. But he's taken it into his head to deal with you as if you were an outsider. He ought to blush on his son's account, he ought not even to raise his eyes in your presence, but he, the viper, the rogue . . . !" "Don't, papa," Feodosia asked tiredly. "Why swear and take sin on your soul? I understand you. You need to watch over your own interests if I should pass away before you do." "Stop that! What kind of nonsense are you talking? Children can't pass on before their parents, can they? God forbid that I should outlive a child of mine. It's something else that I'm afraid of and yes, I do want to protect my interests there . . . but no, what interest am I talking about?" He cut himself off with a ringing voice. "This ... this," he pounded the left side of his chest with his fist, "is what I want to guard. If you can't stand it and take off after your runaway, that family of yours will take everything. The plot of land and the buildings. And do you think that I've saved all my life, kopek by kopek, so that that niggardly priest should profit?"

Feodosia had nothing to say to that. Her soul just gave a quiet sigh. She had scarcely begun to live, and how many cruel, base, evil, dark things had fallen on her in a heap. No, people weren't at all in a hurry to disclose that charm that she had seen in them in the rosy days of her maidenhood.

The letter of debt was drafted in due form, the clerk Volkovoynov assisted, the land was acquired, and Feodosia began to build a house. With enviable speed there appeared on her plot a cottage with an entrance porch, stables, a vegetable cellar with a wattled cover, and an irrigation system. Feodosia put up a fence around her plot of land, planted apple trees and plums. Amazed by her business-like zeal, Father Kirilla felt an involuntary respect for the abandoned girl and once said good-naturedly, "Don't you think it's going a little too far to wall yourself off from your family?" "Not a bit," Feodosia answered calmly. Because of all the things she had to take care of she hadn't even had a chance to look around when a year had already passed since her husband's flight ...

4.

... That time had flashed by just as imperceptibly for Vasily Kirillovich. He had lost the sense of its rapid passage even while on the boat, when, settling himself down on the stern behind the cables, he opened the volume of Lucretius Carus again, after a long separation. The banks of the Volga slipped by, at first as flat as a plate, licked clean by the river's waves and blown completely bare by the wind; then green, gently rolling; the sky was flooded by the crimson of dawns and sunsets; curly clouds, white as steam, scudded along; at times, dark clouds frowned and emptied themselves of thunderstorms or light showers and sun showers shot through with rays of sunlight—then Vasily Kirillovich would seek cover under a bast mat and continue reading, and if it really poured, then he would descend into the foul-smelling hold. The rain would let up, the sky would be belted by a rainbow, but, indifferent to the beauty of the external world, Vasily Kirillovich kept his eyes glued to the book until the last ray of sunset was spent and night spilled stars and a full moon into the river. Then he would lie down on the warm deck boards, his bag under his head, curl up, and fall asleep at once. He tried not to think of Feodosia, and he was successful: during the day he had the book in front of him, at night he quickly passed out. But all he had to do was let up his guard, and the sharp needle at once pierced his chest, his eyes brimming over with tears.

He didn't draw close either to the soldiers or the younger officers, although they treated him affectionately, as though he were one of God's unfortunates. The captain couldn't have cared less about him. He drank vodka and caressed a dark, slant-eyed girl who had ended up on the boat for some inexplicable reason, and at stops he walked along the bank with her. None of this interested Vasily Kirillovich in the least, nor did the rest of human vanity which burned out within itself without becoming the property of the ages in the way that the printing press granted to vital phenomena, thoughts, and feelings, just as the calligraphic handwriting of assiduous scribes did in ancient times.

At Saratov the detachment left the ship and set off for Moscow on foot, marching not in formation and with frequent bivouacs and camp fires. Vasily Kirillovich learned how to read while walking and didn't mind the march at all, devoting just as much attention to Russia's steppes and forests as he had to the great Russian river. Toward the end of the journey, when in the distance glittered the golden crowns of Moscow's forty times forty churches, Vasily Kirillovich discovered that the artillery captain's companion had changed strikingly: from a slant-eyed thin dark girl she had turned into a plump maid with light blue lakes on her round, bun-shaped face and smooth hair the color of millet straw. Pondering this marvel, he realized with embarrassment that the fickle captain had acquired a new sweetheart; it was amazing how easily that was done.

Moscow stunned the young provincial with its multitudes, noise, movement, and deafening bells. Here you needed to keep a sharp lookout and to keep your ears open, because if you were the least bit inattentive you could be trampled by a carefree rider, wind up underneath a carriage; or a crazy muzhik, bringing pickles, sauerkraut, or spiced apples to town might knock you over with the shaft of his sledge.

The old capital's confused look was compounded by the fact that something was always burning somewhere. And that wasn't surprising: the city was almost completely wooden, the buildings stood in higgledy-piggledy clusters, and people were always baking or frying something in the streets, passers-by lit their pipes, showering sparks all over, and there was ample opportunity for a fire. Vasily Kirillovich was mortally afraid of fires, though he'd never in his life seen a large fire close up. But in books he'd come across descriptions of devastating fires, in Moscow and elsewhere, and the printed word had an unlimited power over him. And so the freethinker from Astrakhan began secretly praying that Moscow wouldn't burn down until he finished his course of studies at the Slavonico-Greco-Latin Academy.

Vasily Kirillovich found his way there without difficulty. True, passersby hadn't heard of the Academy, but everyone knew the Zaikonospassky Monastery, since it was located in the busiest part of Kitay-Town, near Red Square.

Vasily Kirillovich reached his destination quickly, but at the gate he suddenly grew timid and at once lost his certainty that his knowledge was sufficient for entry into such a high institution of learning. And in order to calm himself and regain his faith in himself, he decided to take a walk around Kitay-Town.

His legs seemed to direct themselves through the thick crowd toward the strong smells from the trading stalls. He was shoved in the back and sides, almost got knocked off his feet—the people in Moscow were impatient, quick, and impolite. He soon realized that it was impossible to get out of the way of the shoves and proddings; there was only one salvation—to become just as annoying a pedestrian to those around him. He raised his bag a bit higher, tensed himself, spread his feet wide, and bent forward a little so as not to be knocked over by too abrupt a collision, and set off to brush up against everyone in his way. There was cursing, cries, threats, surprised, offended and respectful glances, and, miracle of miracles, it began to be much easier to make his way through the crowd. But after all, the people whom he knocked up against couldn't tell others to beware of this fellow from Astrakhan—that he didn't give any quarter, but meanwhile a certain respectful void had formed around him. Was it possible that a crowd knew how to communicate without the help of words, like insects, by means of humming and buzzing, and to relay information in this insect language?

Satisfied with his small victory, Vasily Kirillovich continued vigorously on his way, and with every step that brought him nearer to the trading stalls from which came an aromatic smell of fried meat, baked dough, tripe and fish, he had an emptier and emptier feeling at the pit of his stomach. He'd already stocked up that morning by eating quite solidly from the soldiers' pot and he was obliged to get by on that food until the next day, since he had pitifully little money. To avoid temptation Vasily Kirillovich turned off from the trading stalls into a lane where, near the wide-open doors of a little church, there was a horde of grotesquely ugly beggars. Only on cathedral frescoes depicting hell had Vasily Kirillovich seen such repellently sweet mugs as on these tramps, cripples, and holy fools at the church. Frightened, he cut a wide path around the group of paupers and caught sight of a log building surrounded by clouds of steam behind a low fence. He realized that this was a bathhouse when a naked woman, her flesh as red as if she'd been flayed alive, leapt out of the steamroom, grabbed a bucket of water and overturned it on herself. These movements were accompanied by the hoots and merry cries of the young men clinging to the fence. The woman parted her hair down the middle, tossed it away from her face, stuck her tongue out at the fellows, spread her legs indecently, and juggling her buttocks, went off to the bathhouse.

Vasily Kirillovich was dumbstruck. He knew that crazy steambath enthusiasts threw themselves into the snow in order to cool off in the wintertime, but after all, it was summer now: the bucket could be kept in the washroom, and there was no need for women to show their nakedness to mockers who surrounded the bathhouse. That meant that it was done on purpose, for the sake of obscenity and not at all by fallen women, but by respected city women who came to clean themselves. In Astrakhan many fantastic tales circulated about the old and new capitals, but Vasily Kirillovich couldn't even imagine anything of this sort. His sense of shame was wounded. Himself as red as if he'd come from the steamroom, he rushed away from the bathhouse, and just then someone gave his bag a strong tug from behind.

Vasily Kirillovich turned around. A strapping fellow with a broken nose, wearing a cape that looked like a crow's nest, was trying to pull his hand out of the mouth of the bag where it had gotten stuck.

"What are you up to?" Trediakovsky said, glaring at him.

"And what are you up to?" the fellow asked audaciously. "Your eyes are popping out of your head, hay-seed! This ain't your Svinyachi village, you know."

"What do you mean—Svinyachi village! I'm from Astrakhan."

The fellow extricated his hand. "Are all of you in Astrakhan fools? Or just the whole city?"

"Go away," muttered Vasilly Kirillovich, amazed at the brazenness of a fellow who tried to rob him in broad daylight and then even made fun of him.

"What do you have in that bag there?" asked the fellow.

"Books."

"Valuable ones?"

"They're valuable for me. I study from them . . . "

"So you're a seminarian!" the fellow guessed, his voice resonant with contempt. "I thought so. Your mug all puffed up like it was worth something. All right, get out of here, you flap-eared seminarian, don't lead people into sin for nothing."

Vasily Kirillovich had already realized that it would be better not to get involved with this loudmouth and was happy to move on. His walk around Moscow hadn't given him the pleasure that he'd expected. Later, when he'd settled in, lived there a while, and made acquaintances with long-time residents, the city would surely reveal itself to him in another aspect.

Moscow was staggeringly rich in churches, palaces of the nobility and merchant quarters; there were public parks and all sort of amusements, but you had to know the right approach to Moscow, and he lacked such knowledge. And so he walked back toward the Slavonico-Greco-Latin Academy.

The institution of learning that bore such an ornate name was located in an old wing of the Zaikonospassky Monastery, which stood behind the icon stall on Nikolsky Street in Kitay-Town. All he had to do was to take a step behind the old, crumbling monastery walls, overgrown with grass and birches, and the annoying Moscow noise was at once cut off, as though the monastery stood in an empty field or woods instead of the busiest section of Moscow. The sleepy quiet and odor of decay, close to the smell of old books, filled Trediakovsky's soul with a blessed calm, and he believed in this place, believed that things would be good for him here. And he wasn't entirely mistaken.

He was accepted at the school without difficulty, since he was considered well prepared, and he was enrolled in the middle philosophy class. There was only one impediment, but a serious one: he wasn't taken on as a government dependent and would have to support himself. But that was taken care of, too. They helped him find lessons for grub and a small salary, as well as clean living quarters at an old woman's place. What more could he need? He got his books, sharpened his goose quills, and bought some tallow candles for a kopek. At his very first lesson in the classroom he heard, "The great blind man Homer was the most keen-sighted of men," and he burst into tears of joy...

5.

... Feodosia's first year of waiting passed rather easily. The next one didn't begin badly, when she acquired some ramshackle furniture and furnished the house, giving it a homey, comfortable look. But little by little her longing was growing. True, the unprecedentedly rich harvest of apples and especially plums (in the hands of the old garden keeper, Father Kirilla, there had never been such abundance) made her happy—not because of greed, but because of the demonstration of her abilities. But when the autumn wind began to drone, bringing first dust and sand, and then dry, granular snow, being in the attractive, empty house grew tedious. And her sisters-in-law, whom she lured to her place with Chinese tea, plum brandy, and delicious apple jam, couldn't take the edge off her loneliness. There was no contact with the rest of the Trediakovskys. Father Kirilla simply couldn't forgive her his disappointment, and his wife, after showing uncharacteristic obstinacy on the day of the loss of her son, was expiating her pathetic revolt by servility toward her husband. As for Yakov, not even his shadow could be glimpsed in the environs of her house after an unsuccessful nocturnal visitation when he broke the window frame, stole into her bedroom, but was evicted in shame. Feodosia had lost all her girlfriends, saw her father rarely—there was some sort of barrier between them—and the image of her runaway husband, embellished and elevated by her longing, appeared before her more and more insistently even in daytime hours: the dust rag would suddenly freeze in her hand, the raised wood chopper would hang suspended in air, and her gaze would fall into a void, and it was especially terrible at night; then she would squeeze the pillow against her breast, pull the blanket up between her legs and howl from longing and the torturous yearning in her hot, dry body.

The third year it became altogether unbearable. The longing and sorrow were more and more often replaced by bitterness toward her runaway husband. How long could one study, after all? Others learned from the Psalter right at home; they could barely read and write, counted with their fingers, but they became important men, controlled large businesses, and caravans of their vessels plowed the Volga and the Caspian; others, educated in poor seminaries, were now archpriests and spent their time very enjoyably in their own homes with their children and domestic servants. What was Vasily Kirillovich planning to study to become, after all? The tsar's main advisor, a chancellor, maybe the tsar himself? Her eyes sparkled malevolently through a gush of tears. It was all foolishness—you couldn't study right off to be the top person. You ought at least to become something, and then acquire knowledge, and not just from books, but from life itself, from people, from your activity among them. And what if he wasn't studying to become something, but just because, for himself, in order to know more than anyone else? In that case a whole lifetime wouldn't be long enough? Thank God that no academy would keep a student on for his whole life. There was a time limit for any studies, but what was that limit, and would she have enough strength to endure it?

She noticed a certain recent change around her; the air had grown different. It was as if an ordeal had ended, and the residents of Astrakhan recalled the grass widow cordially. Earlier no one had come to visit her except her sisters-in-law—the idiot Yakov didn't count—but now a day didn't pass but one or another animated woman dropped in and would begin to describe the grand merits either of a merchant of the second guild, the vigorous spouse of an ailing wife who hadn't risen from her bed in many years, or a minor official and widower with the most serious intentions: either to marry her if the old marriage could be annulled, or to live together by loving consent, with written guarantees. Other Astrakhan suitors, not resorting to the help of talkative women, turned up in person—sometimes in the vegetable garden, sometimes in the flower garden; one had even knocked at her bedroom window late at night, and with such endurance that Feodosia's head began to spin.

The behavior of her fellow citizens had its point and its profundity. Unconsciously, without discussing it among themselves, they had changed their attitude toward the married widow. Earlier they had respected her grief and admired her faithfulness to her husband who had vanished, but the years passed, the runaway gave no signs of life, and the unspoken consensus was that Feodosia, a young, strong, independent woman, was free from any obligations. It was as if she was being invited to return to life.

She, too, spent more and more time pondering the ambiguousness of her position. Her husband was off God knows where, maybe he'd even found another wife, and if he hadn't, then a momentary consolation on the city streets would be more than enough. But more likely he had long since left this earth; how long would it take for a poor, defenseless person to die in an alien place? And her sacrifice made absolutely no sense. For whose sake was she supposed to lead a monastic way of life and spoil her irretrievable youth? In the hot, sweaty work in the orchard and garden, in the constant whirl of unwomanly cares, she had grown all dessicated and dark, as if she'd been tanned, and she no longer resembled her former self in face, figure, or manner. This new, dark, vivid, un-Russian, Gypsy beauty of hers was more sriking than her former radiant, azure good looks. It wasn't that she'd been burned by the sun—a tan fades in winter—like a snake, she had changed her skin. Her witch-like Gypsy face, flooded with a smooth, even, nutty swarthiness, gave off heat that could be felt at a distance. But her soul remained the same—faithful, tender, loving—and Feodosia couldn't turn it toward betrayal. The soft core of Feodosia's nature was hidden from those around her: the extraordinarily estranged severity of her eyes that were no longer honey-colored, but almost black, radiated warmth in a hidden smile that didn't touch her rosy lips.

Feodosia's strange new beauty turned the heads of young and old alike. But only a few old-style righteous people approved of her unapproachability; the majority of the populace was enraged by it. Such unnecessary firmness was irritating, like a reproach to human weakness. But people's gossip, reproachful glances, and the malicious comments thrown her way didn't bother Feodosia in the least. She didn't take offense at bad people, because she considered that their being in God's world was accidental, and she firmly believed that at an appointed hour wonderful, kind, gentle people would take their place and remain forever.

But she needed to defend herself from those who were earnestly seeking her attention, and their numbers were growing alarmingly. Feodosia acquired a huge, coal-black hound. The hound never barked; he roared with a terrible noise that began in the depths of his huge body, grew, filled his throat with a slavering growl, and tore free of his mouth with a furious, thundering howl. Often this was followed by a leap and the wild wail of a mortally frightened person. For some reason Feodosia thought that the fright would put an end to everything. But once, looking outside, she saw the hound chewing on a piece of fresh meat that had made his face all bloody and using his paw to try to dig a clump of blue material out of his mouth. Soon afterwards she heard a rumor that the public prosecutor's son had lost a piece of his thigh in a run-in with a wild bull. Through not very complicated ratiocination Feodosia realized what animal had inflicted such a painful mutilation on the bold youth.

Apparently other residents of the town realized this as well; the people of Astrakhan were sharp-witted, and they poisoned the black guard. But that happened just before Feodosia's departure. She had found out that Vasily Kirillovich was alive, well, and studying in Moscow, at the Slavono-Greco-Latin Academy, and she decided to go to him in spite of his interdiction; but after all, any interdiction loses its force over the years. Besides which, she'd been told that Vasily Kirillovich was living in dire poverty, and she cast off her last doubts. This news was brought by a former classmate of Vasily Kirillovich's at the Capuchin school who had accompanied the archpriest of Astrakhan to Moscow. He had run into Vasily Kirillovich on the street and hadn't recognized him at first, so thin and ragged did he look. But when he recognized him, he took his gaunt fellow-Astrakhanite to a tavern, where Vasily Kirillovich wolfed down five portions of tripe. "But how did he get it all in?" his schoolmate wondered. "He's as thin as a skeleton, his stomach clings to his backbone."

Feodosia's heart was shattered into pieces when she imagined the hungry, gaunt ragamuffin wolfing down foul tripe from a tavern. In the heat of the moment she decided to sell the house and use all the money to feed Vasily Kirillovich, but she reconsidered in time. Perhaps Vasily Kirillovich, worn out by Moscow poverty, would want to warm up in the coziness of home, near his family? She sold the remains of her dowry, sewed the money into an underskirt and, coming to an agreement with merchants who were on their way to Moscow with their wares, soon departed . . .

6.

. . . Trediakovsky learned of his wife's imminent arrival while sitting in a tavern with one of his pupils, Novichkov, a noble's son, whom he had recently been preparing for enrollment in the Navigation School, which was located in the "magician and sorcerer" Bryus's tower, otherwise know as Sukhareva Tower. A tall, vain youth, whose knowledge of the maritime elements was based on Patriarch, Chisty, and Ostansky Ponds and rather dirty Moscow riverlets, he dreamed of the sea, frothy waves, sails, masts, yard arms, and more than anything else—strong rum, which sailors consumed in quantities impossible for mortal landlubbers. He had read about all of this, syllable by syllable, in the only book in his father's library; the other ones, stamped in gold, contained bottles of domestic and foreign wines. Accustomed since childhood to intoxicating beverages, he had discovered his father's storehouse of books early on. But once, taking from the shelf a heavy volume that promised an acquaintance with an as yet unknown nectar, instead of a good bottle he found to his surprise printed pages and a multitude of pictures of ships. He taught himself to read from this book and fell in love with the sea for good. But, lacking a talent for arithmetic—he didn't even know simple mathematical operations—he had already twice flunked out of the naval school in spite of all the indulgence of his professors whose favors were curried by his father. Hired in exchange for food, old clothing and a few bronze coins, Vasily Kirillovich was supposed to pound the basics of the exact sciences into the young noble's head—a head that was lively, but lazy and incapable of the least bit of exertion.

Vasily Kirillovich, who had once been a student of the superb mathematician Timofeyev, was full of knowledge, but he didn't know how to deposit this knowledge in his pupil's lackluster memory. He lacked the teacher's gift and made any questions unnecessarily complicated. The future sailor didn't respect his teacher, but he pitied his gauntness and the cold glitter in his eyes, and from time to time he took Vasily Kirillovich to a tavern, where the latter enjoyed tripe to the accompaniment of a mug of frothy beer, and the host—rum, which gave him the sensation of the rocking of the sea, and sometimes even seasickness. Half-crazed from prolonged hunger and two sips of intoxicating beer, the usually taciturn Vasily Kirillovich would become talkative and boast endlessly of his academic successes. Recently he had been allowed to be present at debates where the older students showed off the art of dialectics, and he was extraordinarily proud of this. Novichkov was amazed and amused that his tutor attributed such great importance to empty theological arguments out of which no truth was born, where each person simply asserted what he thought without even trying to persuade his opponent of anything. But Trediakovsky was delighted by the honor that had been given him, and Novichkov, who wasn't stupid, discovered that the modest Latinist, who was not of this world, who wore a caftan with worn-through elbows and pants so rotted away at the crotch that it was embarrassing, who didn't understand titles and ranks, possessed a fair amount of vanity.

Vasily Kirillovich himself recognized a fair share of literary ambition in himself. He wrote poetry and plays, dreamed that his works would become known to Russians, and firmly believed that sooner or later that would happen.

Always hungry, but knowing how not to think about food, warm only in the summer time, lacking any joys other than spiritual ones, Vasily Kirillovich was happy every day, for he was doing what he loved. And suddenly into this beggarly life, stripped of everything that makes youth wonderful, into this remarkable, full life aimed at great goals, something terrifying had intruded: Feodosia was coming.

Vasily Kirillovich learned of this from a fellow who happened to turn up at the tavern. He was a distant relative of Vice-Governor Kikin's who had gone to Astrakhan in the hope of arranging a cushy position with his uncle, but his stern uncle hadn't liked him. As soon as he caught sight of his nephew's red nose, he ordered that a return travel document be issued to him. The nephew drowned his failure in wine, to which young Astrakhan nobles treated him generously, found out about all the local news that he didn't need, and, with a seventy-five-pound tub of freshly-salted caviar, he left the city that had disappointed his hopes. In Moscow he continued to nurse his sorrows, wandered into the tavern near the Kitay wall, met his friend Novichkov, sat down at his table, was introduced to the gaunt Latinist, heard the name "Trediakovsky," and right away, out of his idle and steel-trap memory, set forth the news about the abandoned Astrakhan beauty who had set out to find her husband.

Trediakovsky choked on the tripe and with an uncertain voice asked when and with whom Feodosia had started on her journey. Sensing that the news had not only not made the beauty's husband happy, but thrown him into confusion, Kikin's nephew, obeying the logic of human baseness, depicted the matter as though Feodosia would arrive in Moscow at any moment with the merchant train, if she wasn't already waiting for her husband near the gates of the Zaikonospassky Monastery. Having poisoned a stranger's blood and finding a certain comfort in doing so—he'd really given it to the fellow from Astrakhan—Kikin's nephew left the tavern.

Novichkov honestly couldn't understand his tutor's despair. "You ought to be happy. Take a look at yourself, at what you look like. Your wife will make you look decent again. She's apparently a decisive woman." "That's the whole problem," said Trediakovsky morosely. "She'll destroy what I've built. And there's still so much that I have to find out!" "But what for?" "Obviously not for a rank," was the gloomy reply. "I have to, and that's that!" "That's the way it is with me too," Novichkov said pensively. "Everyone pesters me about why I need the ocean, since I've never seen it in my life. How should I know why? I need to! Otherwise there's no life." "But enrolling in navigation school is a tight squeeze," taunted Trediakovsky. "You're a big, tall lad and can't master the four rules of mathematics." "I'm talking about the sea," Novichkov deflected the reproach without taking offense. "Is your wife beautiful?" he asked strangely. "Yes, she is!" and Trediakovsky suddenly recalled Feodosia, just as she was in real life. "That's the trouble—she's beautiful and good. I ran away while she was sleeping, otherwise I wouldn't have been able to. But I wouldn't be able to at all a second time. A man isn't made of wood. I'm in a bad way. No, I can't cope with her. She's up to her ears in love, in love with me . . . don't smirk!" (Novichkov wasn't even thinking of smiling; his face was serious and thoughtful.) "But it has to do with love, not me. She's in love with love, and thinks she loves me. But just try to explain that to her!" Trediakovsky didn't himself know why he'd opened up so much to this coarse and dreamy nitwit. "The sea, the sea!" said Novichkov. "The same old thing! . . ." Trediakovsky failed to understand and was a little offended. "Everyone has his own sea," Novichkov said quietly, "and it's terrifying to lose it. There's nothing more terrifying." "You're right . . . and you're smarter than I thought," Trediakovsky replied, surprised. "You're altogether smart. Remember my words—you'll be an admiral."

Vasily Kirillovich proved to be a prophet. Novichkov, without getting into the Navigation School after all, would take off for Petersburg, enlist on a ship as a plain sailor, having concealed his noble origins, would go through the whole hell of duty with rope's ends and blows to the teeth, mockery and bad water, work his way up to officer's rank, plow up the seas and oceans and end his life as a rear admiral.

"It looks as if I can help you," said Novichkov, frowning, as if he'd tasted something sour. "It's vile, of course, revoltingly vile, but I don't know the woman. But if I get to know her, I might put her onto your tracks or grab you by the scruff of the neck and drag you to her. But I don't know her. It's you I know. And I hear your sea. In a week our relatives the Burnashevs are sending their youngest son to Holland to learn ship building." "Can it really be that the nobles are still obeying Tsar Peter's commands even after his death?" inquired Trediakovsky, amazed. "No," Novichkov shrugged his shoulders contemptuously. "They're happy as can be to return to their swinish old ways. True, not all of them, though hardly because they're obeying the 'powerful shade,'" he recalled Trediakovsky's poetic turn of phrase. "The Burnashevs' eldest son also studied there and ended up a bigwig. Now he's in England building frigates. He's rich. They hope that fortune will smile on their younger son, too. He's a snivelling cry-baby, grew up near his mother's skirts, but he's harmless enough. His uncle's going with him. I'll persuade them that an illiterate uncle isn't enough. Mityayka Burnashev isn't very bright at schoolwork. Do you know Dutch?" "I'll learn it—it wouldn't take much. It's close to German."

"Excellent! You'll help the shipbuilder. He's a dullard like me, but without a sea." Novichkov gave a meager smile. "The Burnashevs are very stingy, but you'll get room and board." "If that got me out of this situation ... why I'd be satisfied with nothing but air"—Trediakovsky grimaced because of the tears rising in his throat.

Two days later Trediakovsky was rolling along in a carriage together with the Burnashevs' tearful scion and his gray-faced uncle, who gave off a sweet aroma of cognac. On the Moscow streets and even when they'd passed the gates and all around there unfolded fields, birch groves, and fir groves, Vasily Kirillovich cowered in terror: he kept imagining Feodosia's troops in hot pursuit. At any moment now armed horsemen would gallop up, grab the Burnashev horses by the reins, throw open the doors of the carriage and thrust a document with blood-red wax seals on it—an order from the Holy Synod or the General Prosecutor to return to his legal wife. But no one stopped them except the guards who patrolled the western borders of the Russian Empire. The travellers presented their documents and travelled on to foreign lands without obstacle.

During the whole long trip through Great and White Russia, the Polish land and the German princedoms, the young Burnashev wept inconsolably. It was amazing that the youth, who was thirsty for all sorts of impressions, could remain so indifferent to the motley foreign life that flashed by outside the carriage windows, to the palaces, castles, fortresses, cathedrals, churches, bridges, gardens, to the beautiful cities with well-dressed people who filled the world's silence with the sounds of unfamiliar speech that was variously melodious, sibilant, and barking. As inattentive to his surroundings as the self-absorbed Trediakovsky was, nonetheless even he forgot about his cares, laid his favorite books aside, and spent hours looking out the window. But the self-centered Burnashev whimpered, unable to tear himself away from the comforts of home with mama's overindulgence, girls' caresses, a feather bed after a heavy dinner, and papa's pipe tobacco, smoked in secret in the servants' quarters. He livened up only at mealtimes, when his uncle, with a conspiratorial look, opened the next square bottle. It was amazing that the beardless youth was so devoted to wine, which quickly wove his tongue into a knot, made his eyes cloud over and plunged him into a long, uneasy sleep accompanied by muttering and sorrowful exclamations. Vasily Kirillovich, though irritated, had the sense to keep quiet. He had enough of his own worries.

7.

But he needn't have been alarmed or have fled from Moscow—Feodosia wound up in the hands of the chieftain Kiriak who earned his living by banditry on the lower Volga.

This is how it happened. The merchant caravan sailed from Astrakhan one fine morning to the accompaniment of ringing bells that promised success and joy. They travelled smoothly and rapidly, a taut southwesterly wind filling their sails. Feodosia had never in her life sailed on a river, not even in a rowboat, and she enjoyed the journey, which disclosed all around views of endless, flat land, sand islands overgrown with thorny shrubbery and gently sparkling flowers, all the little details of river life. She liked her hosts: they were sedate, elderly merchants who regarded their female companion with sympathy, but without offensive pity, inviting her to their dinners of sterlet soup, fresh caviar, fish pies, and cornbeef. She liked the ship's crew: they were merry, darkly tanned fellows, cat-like in their agility. Feodosia was ecstatically happy about everything, and she believed that she would find her husband and be joined with him forever.

But at Saratov misfortune was already lying in wait for the travellers. There they were supposed to transfer to carts and set off for Moscow accompanied by a small convoy, but they weren't allowed to disembark. There had been an outbreak of the plague in Astrakhan, news of which had travelled faster than they had. The merchants tried in vain to come to an agreement with the wharf authorities, offering them generous 'recompense,' but the authorities wouldn't even hear of it. Nor were the merchants successful in getting a meeting with the city authorities, who they thought might be more agreeable; the orders regarding people arriving from the plague-struck city were remarkably strict if a bribe, the master-key to all doors in Russia, didn't work.

There was nothing they could do: they left Saratov and headed back up the river. At Volsk, from where there was a cart road to the Moscow high road, they put to shore. No one prevented them from disembarking. The terrifying news had reached Saratov with the speed of an arrow, but it hadn't yet crawled to this backwater town. The only thing that surprised the local people was why on earth the merchants saw need to make their trip longer and more difficult—from Saratov it was closer and the road was better to boot. But the most respected of the merchants, the grey-bearded and dark-eyed Emelyan Isayev, whose manner resembled that of a boyar rather than of a trader, explained with an air of importance that they 'played tricks' on the Saratov high road, which sounded quite likely in the turbulent times following Tsar Peter's death. True, a carter from Volsk who happened onto the conversation remarked that they played pranks, and very nasty ones, right in their region, but he was attacked with curses and threats and driven away. For the local business people the appearance of the wealthy merchants from Astrakhan was a gift from heaven. The merchants needed carts, horses, and men to serve as guards; they were generous in what they were willing to pay, since delay would cost them even more.

If only they'd listened to the drunken carter! Many of them probably recalled his words when, above the crowns of the tall old trees in the dense Trunov forest, the first stars pierced the light sky, as blue as in the daytime, and a high-pitched whistle clove the quiet, a shot rang out, giving off an orange flash, and a smoky stench of saltpeter stifled the bitter smell of the forest. Instantaneously, as if that was all they'd been waiting for, the armed guard scattered and disappeared. Dark-complexioned bearded men leapt out from behind the trees and began throwing the merchants, who didn't even think of resisting, to the ground and unloading the wares from the carts.

Feodosia sat in the rear cart and observed the proceedings as if they were a puppet-show. A terrifying show. She saw the valiant Emelyan Isayev cock his pistol, but he didn't have time to fire; an enormous shaggy-headed fellow in a red-calico shirt slashed him across the head with his saber; she saw the same fellow slash at the decrepit old eunuch-faced merchant Churikov, who had fallen to his knees; she saw the God-fearing fishseller Mukhanov, always the first person in Astrakhan to give donations for churches, killed by a musket-shot. And then the shaggy-haired brigand noticed her, pulled her down from the cart, giving off a pungent, fox-like smell. She caught sight of his agitated, rotten eyes close up and lost consciousness. Much later, when she came to in a warm room, on a wooden bench stuck away in a corner under a weakly flickering icon lamp, Feodosia learned from the mistress of the hut, a dessicated quick-eyed old woman, that she had been rescued from the clutches of the shaggy bandit by the chieftain Kiriak. "You're lucky, my girl, that Kiriak had time to take a look at your face," the old woman said in the melodious voice of a singer of tales, "and was captivated by you. You shouldn't interfere with Semushka when he's all fired up. He'd do in his own mother, let alone an older comrade. He's a cruel man. Other men only kill when they have to. Kiriak, though he's heftier than anyone else, only kills when there's a battle, but Semushka enjoys bloodletting. Kiriak's as healthy as a wild bull and nimble as a caress, but he took a real beating from Semushka before he got the better of him. Right now he's lying all bandaged up in the next hut." "And what about Semushka?" Feodosia asked for some reason. "He's calmed down, drinking vodka to celebrate taking a rich booty." "And nothing will happen to him?" "Why should anything happen? He was within his rights. He could have taken you or chopped you up—it was his choice. It's Kiriak, girl, who went against tradition." "I'm a married woman, not a girl," Feodosia corrected her. "You were," said the old woman coldly. "Your husband is back there in the woods." "What are you talking about, granny? Those were old men who died there. My husband is young and lives in Moscow." "So that's how it is!" exclaimed the old woman, surprised. "You mean you're not a merchant's wife? Our people don't much like merchants." "I'm a watchman's daughter, and my husband's a seminarian," Feodosia announced. "Granny, where have they brought me to?" "To a hut, can't you see? And the hut stands in the midst of a village. And the village—in the midst of Russia. Makhonka's the name of the village; it has fine houses. The plague killed all the people. Neither gentry not the authorities show their noses here, and so our people are resting from their labors." Feodosia was amazed that the old woman spoke of these brigands and murderers as if they were just ordinary men; you might have thought they'd returned from mowing instead of a cruel deed. "Granny, tell me, dear, if I'm not a merchant woman, but just one of the common people, will they let me go free?" "I'm not the one to know that," said the old woman, pursing her lips.

8.

Vasily Kirillovich was walking late at night through the "merry" quarter, as sailors lovingly called the part of town near the port. The local residents, following the sailors' tradition, called it that too, but out of contempt. Here there was a tavern in almost every building; here there dwelled unbearably beautiful girls who were accessible—only not to Vasily Kirillovich, with his empty pocketbook; rooms and corners were rented by the day, by the hour; music thundered until very late; multicolored streetlights hung like garlands reflected in the filthy dark water of the canals planted round with thick-trunked short fir trees. Vasily Kirillovich rarely came here, in part because of a lack of interest in such amusements and in part because of a lack of money, but his protégé, who had gotten completely out of hand, never left the area. Vasily Kirillovich no longer tried to drag the future shipbuilder out of the drinking establishments or away from the girls, and besides—that wasn't his responsiblity anyway. And the uncle, himself an overly enthusiastic admirer of wine, considered that the lad was behaving as befitted a young Russian gentleman. "He'll have time to trouble his head later; let the boy have fun while his blood is still playful and his hair curly. Our nobles have been trained like that for ages, and look what a powerful state they've assembled. Any of our provinces could fit ten Hollands in it, even if these wild Dutchman with their model behavior know arithmetic through and through." There was nothing he could say in reply to that, and what did he care about the young stallion anyway? But in Vasily Kirillovich's character there was an importunate love of order that smacked of pedantry, and besides—he regretted the time that was slipping through the young man's fingers senselessly and without meaning. You could buy any book in Holland— even a French, English, or German one: anything that writers couldn't publish or were afraid to in their own country, was published without any obstacles in Holland, sometimes under a fictitious name. Nowhere in Europe was there such freedom as in this country, which had overthrown Spanish dominion and which hated any violence against the individual personality and any repression of thought or spirit.

And yet Vasily Kirillovich wasn't completely satisfied with the life there, and not at all because of the young Burnashev. Things were genuinely good there for those learning practical skills: shipbuilders, mechanics, carpenters, navigators, merchants, all sorts of businessmen and people in the exact sciences—but the spiritual center of Europe remained Paris. Everything created by the human spirit came from there: philosophical ideas, solemn, severe, playful, and captivating poetic images, elegant new literary systems.

Vasily Kirillovich wandered quietly along the canal, watching the narrow fir leaves settle on the water that was gaily colored by the streetlights, and, swept along by the wind, sailed like little boats out to sea; from the doors of a tavern came loud music and the sounds of women's laughter, raucous swearing, drunken songs, and the hopelessly alien quality of this life made Vasily Kirillovich sad. He didn't know himself what had brought him here; in any event it wasn't concern for the young Burnashev. Vasily Kirillovich knew the city poorly, didn't trust it, and felt afraid late at night: there were too many coarse sailors, too much excited multilingual speech, too many drunken bearded faces, too much tattooed flesh, too many shameless, importunate beggars and blind men who were a little frightening in their impudent pushiness—they seemed to be the only ones who knew exactly where they were going.

But now it was unusually quiet here: vice and merriment don't like autumn, and at the first breath of cold wind they hide under a roof, near the fire of a hearth, over which barley beer is warmed up.

Vasily Kirillovich's absent-minded gaze discovered that he had two shadows. One, constant, greatly elongated, ran from the right, stretching out over the stone pavement, climbing up the walls of houses: weak and indistinct, it was produced by the full moon. The other one, fuller, dark and short, slid along from the left; it arose behind his back, drew up even to him, ran on ahead, and then seemed to disappear, later to turn up behind him again. This shadow was created by the street lamps. Suddenly he caught sight of yet another shadow—also from the left, on the canal side—but this shadow didn't catch up with him: it stayed a little bit behind, thin, tiny, as though it didn't exist at all. But then he lost it, so it really was the shadow of another person who had fallen behind or turned off toward the canal railing; but the delicate shadow arose again, and with horrow he realized that this was a woman's shadow. Feodosia had tracked him down. And that wouldn't be hard; after all, he'd told everyone at the Academy that he was leaving for Holland with Burnashev. For some reason he had been certain, miserable fool, that Feodosia wouldn't have the courage to follow him to foreign lands. As if there existed an obstacle for her tenacious love! And now she'd found him. Lord, how wonderful life here had seemed, and he'd even dared to complain! Now this life would come to an end, they couldn't both feed themselves here. That meant back to Moscow or worse than that—to Astrakhan... And now wishing to hasten the moment, frightening as death, Trediakovsky turned around abruptly, and his gaze tumbled into a void. A tiny shadow that seemed rolled up into a ball lay at his feet; it was his own—a third shadow, probably from the illuminated windows on the upper stories. Thank you, Lord, you again had mercy on me! Still and all, this ought to be counted as a warning: Feodosia could turn up unexpectedly any day—the only salvation was in flight. And the next day he fled with a hunk of bread and a dozen books in his shoulder bag...

If Vasily Kirillovich had had a clearer notion of the journey facing him, he would perhaps have stayed in Holland in spite of the risk of being overtaken by his wife. Setting out on his journey of many days without a farthing in his pocket, he consoled himself with the thought that the world wasn't without good people, that he'd get along somehow. But as soon as he passed the borders of Holland, he found himself in a country devastated by endless wars. The destitution of woeful Flanders nearly exceeded the havoc in prostrated Russian villages in times of crop failures, but Russian poverty is kind and merciful: in even the poorest peasant family a traveller would find a piece of bread, a bowl of nettle soup, or mashed potato and onion, or at the very least they'd give him some kvass to rinse his insides with; but from the people here you couldn't expect anything; sullen and embittered, they either turned away in silence or angrily drove you out. They wouldn't let you into their barn, let along their home for the night. Perhaps they were more indulgent towards their own beggars, but the foreign tramp put them in a rage. They had endured so much from Spanish and French soldiers and German and Swiss mercenaries that every foreigner seemed a fierce enemy to them.

Vasily Kirillovich ate grass, sour berries, rotten forest nuts, some sort of mushrooms, and shook out the kernels of cereal from ears that remained in the fields; he sold his shirt, his caftan, then his hat, replacing it with a piratical kerchief; he parted with his wedding ring and his cross, exchanged his shoes with buckles for wooden clogs, but the money thus gained he spent only partly on food, using the major portion of it to pay for rides on passing carts, traps, and wagons. Better to endure hunger in order to get there more quickly. He didn't notice their entering France. Externally nothing had changed: it was the same havoc and devastation by fire, the same sullen faces and poverty. Closer to Paris the picture grew different: there were fewer soldiers, the cities and settlements were more intact, and the people friendlier. But Vasily Kirillovich, who had lost faith in his fellow humans, got along on his own non-existent resources.

One morning the servants of the Russian Ambassador, Prince Kurakin, found living relics at the embassy doorstep: a grotesquely wasted man, black from the sun and dirt, his face overgrown with stubble, was sleeping with his head on the stone threshhold. When they shook him, he shuddered, twitched, tried to rise, but couldn't, and from his parched mouth issued piteous sounds which were barely recognizable as Russian. They lifted him up, carried him into the house, washed him in a tub, fed him, and forced him to drink a large tumbler of vodka with salt and pepper. Prince Kurakin himself expressed the wish to see him. They took the vagrant under both arms and led him to the Ambassador. He fell in a heap of rags at the magnate's feet, gave his name, and begged not to be driven away.

Prince Kurakin was such an aristocrat, so wealthy and so powerful at court that he recognized himself the equal of only a few elect people who traced their origins to Varangian princes and who, moreover, had maintained their fortunes. Other people, without regard for title, rank, or position, he considered 'common rabble,' in which fact the Prince's peculiar sense of democracy made itself felt: a destitute representative of the ancient house of Obolensky, the Petrine 'aristrocracy,' a wealthy merchant, a workman or a barker were all equal before his contempt. But among the 'common rabble' the Prince distinguished gifted, knowledge-able, and eccentric people. The perceptive diplomat realized at once that the newcomer encompassed within himself all three qualities: in spite of his youth, this was a very educated, thinking person with God's spark in him, and moreover, he was as eccentric as they came. Trediakovsky's fate was decided. He was not only given refuge, clothing, and regular financial support, but the Prince even condescended to discuss his scholarly activities with him, advised him what courses at the Sorbonne were worth attending with which professors, who of the 'maîtres' should be avoided—scholastics, pedants, and donkey ears; which performances to see at the Comédie Française and the Italian theater, which sights to get acquainted with. The Prince allowed Trediakovsky unlimited use of his remarkable library. Vasily Kirillovich couldn't hold out, burst into tears, and tried to kiss the Prince's hand, but the latter wouldn't permit it...

9.

Feodosia was ill the rest of the summer, the whole fall and winter. She alternately tossed about in a fever, not recognizing the old woman and not remembering where she was and what was wrong with her, or faint from weakness, she sat by the window, looking at the boring outskirts of the village, where lay a huge puddle, which, after the first frosts, was covered by a thin layer of ice, later freezing through to the earth, turning from black to a dull green and finally hidden under thick snow, like everything in the wide-open spaces. Granny Akulina said that there'd never been such a snowy winter in these parts. Illness has a remarkable way of concealing time. Feodosia, going back and forth from unconsciousness to a state of shadowy semi-wakefulness, didn't notice the days, weeks, and months fly by. When she finally came to her senses, she began to get used to her weakness, learned how to walk, hold a spoon, swallow watery food, drink hot herbal decoctions and keep them down. When spring was on its way, she began to grow stronger from day to day, and even Akulina was amazed at how quickly this creature, who had seemed about to depart for the other world, was becoming filled with energy.

It now seemed to Feodosia that she had invented her illness so as not to die from grief and disillusionment. Akulina's words "Kiriak took a look at your face" had imprinted themselves in her soul. She understood very well what they meant: having been captivated by her, he went against the gang's code, took a comrade's booty away from him, and paid for it with blood. In so doing it was as if he had acquired the rights to her. Kiriak also spent a long time recovering: his wound festered and refused to heal. With his arm bandaged, he would come to their hut and silently look at her. His sullen face, overgrown with whiskers, with its inquisitive light-grey eyes, for some reason didn't frighten her. He would say something to Akulina in a half-voice and leave. No one else appeared in the hut; apparently Kiriak had forbidden it. Only a hefty woman from time to time brought firewood, flour in bags, lard, and fresh meat, without crossing the threshold of the room.

But Feodosia observed the brigands through the window. And she found it strange that, like Granny Akulina, she no longer regarded them as bloodthirsty murderers, in spite of what she'd witnessed in the forest. She knew that only Semushka had a taste for blood; the others found no joy in killing. They were ordinary peasants, weighed down by constant worries, back-breaking labor, and fear for the morrow. The outlaw life didn't much resemble the one portrayed in songs. There you had valiant skirmishes, gold, pearls, precious stones and sables, beautiful maidens madly in love with their dissolute swains. But here it was drag yourself out to an ambush every day, in rain, wind, and penetrating cold, when your teeth chattered and you couldn't hold a rifle in your stiff arms with their swollen joints, and you knew ahead of time that you wouldn't gain anything from your waiting except a pain in the chest and back. The success with the merchant train was the only one for the whole summer. In the fall things improved a little thanks to wealthy people from Astrakhan fleeing the plague, but the majority of them took the water route to Samara and beyond. Kiriak boasted that in the spring he'd seize a vessel and go make mischief along the Volga, as the unforgettable Stenka Razin had done. Of course that was empty bragging, since Kiriak didn't have enough forces: that was why they operated in the backwaters instead of on the fertile Moscow-Saratov high road where the gangs prospered. At the beginning of winter, on the fresh sledge road, they'd seized a train of peasant carts taking quitrent to the master in Borisoglebsk, but the take wasn't great: dressed poultry, frozen veal, about a dozen suckling pigs, barrels of home-canned goods, a lean purse.

At that troubled time banditry in Russia had reached extraordinary proportions. The weak government detachments that were occasionally sent in demonstrated little zeal. The more so as the bandits didn't ask for trouble; they immediately hid in the woods, allowing the commander of the punitive expedition to send the authorities a victorious report: the gang has been dispersed, order restored. The detachment marched back, to the accompaniment of a drumbeat and clouds of dust kicked up from the dessicated earth, and the bandits, abandoning their hiding places, again moved towards the cart roads.

Although Kiriak's detachment didn't see gold and sable, they made ends meet, and the family bandits—almost the entire gang was made up of local people—helped out back home by sending things there or delivering them themselves. Banditry was something like seasonal work: just as in other villages the men, instead of tilling the fields, worked as carters or carpenters, made felt boots, served in taverns or bathhouses, sold hot mead or dog-meat pies at city markets, so the local peasants left their infertile, dry fields, scorched from all sides by hot winds, for the bandit's craft. There were many people with grudges involved here too. Kiriak's young wife had been raped by their landowner-master, and she had laid hands on herself. Kiriak strangled the master and fled into the woods. Bogun, the chieftain's right-hand man, had settled accounts with the lady landowner. At her order he had been hung naked in the stables and flogged, while the lady watched, nodding her head, as if counting off the strokes, and later began to moan and writhe, but from some sort of inner pleasure, not from pity. Bogun, in his turn, hanged the naked lady from the same beam, and flayed her so that her skin, like a snake's, peeled off in shreds. Other men fled from lesser offenses, from destitution or hunger; there were those who had lost everything in fires too, and, of course, people who'd gone astray and didn't remember where they were from, like Semushka. Some of the men went back to their villages to help their parents and wives at plowing or haying time, but the majority of them stayed together in a firmly-knit group.

Having recovered from her illness, Feodosia nearly regained that vigorous tranquility that had once possessed her in Astrakhan. Yes, she hadn't succeeded in reaching her husband on the first try: man proposes, but the Lord God disposes. She had another trial facing her, but she'd endure it, make it through all right, and find her beloved. She had lost much time as well as the modest gift that she'd been taking to her husband—money: Akulina had evidently felt it in her skirt and ripped it out—but she was a little closer to her goal. Now she had only one task: to get away from the bandits. Who knew what further tribulations awaited her, what disasters, terrors, temptations, and difficulties would fall her way, but she had to overcome everything—whether through patience, bravery, or craftiness—fly like a bird, run like a wild animal, glide like a fish, or slither like a snake, and reach Moscow.

That meant that she needed to keep herself in check, to watch and listen carefully, and make more inquiries of the talkative Akulina so as to find out everything she needed for her escape.

To her vexation, Feodosia soon discovered that the wordy old woman didn't give away a single thing. She absolutely bombarded Feodosia with all sorts of information about the brigands, about their personalities, habits, domestic circumstances, about successful and unsuccessful raids on gentry estates, encounters with soldiers, about various bold and cruel deeds, but this all took place in some vague far-away place and time, seemingly beyond the world's end in the year one. No matter how Feodosia approached the old woman, she just couldn't drag out of her where their village was located, what roads led to and from here, in what direction the Volga lay, or whether there were any towns or large settlements nearby. Without taking her forget-me-not, baby-pure eyes off Feodosia, she would begin to babble incomprehensible nonsense, and Feodosia would close off her hearing. Good Granny Akulina was a real bandit witch: smart, clever, and implacable; put her to the stake and she still wouldn't give anything away.

It seemed to Feodosia that Granny Akulina was watching her every step on the sly. She decided to test her. The bandits were at work, the few women who lived in the village were busy in their gardens, and Granny Akulina was sorting through the potatoes in the basement when Feodosia unlatched the hook and went outside for the first time. There was no one in sight, only chickens wandering around. Feodosia passed the outskirts of the village and set off down the road, avoiding the enormous spring puddles that swarmed with tadpoles. Her legs, unaccustomed to walking, grew stronger with every step, and the pure air of the fields cleared her lungs. Feodosia looked around, but no one was following her. Even the zealous Akulina hadn't stirred. It was hardly likely that she trusted the girl—she was probably counting on her weakness. Feodosia didn't want to abuse her guardian's patience and so she returned home.

"It's wonderful out in the field!" she said to Akulina.

"Dress more warmly," Akulina advised her solicitously. "The weather's capricious, and if you fall sick again Kiriak will bite my head off."

The old woman often emphasized her special responsibility for Feodosia and the chieftain Kiriak's guardianship. Feodosia formerly went cold all over as she guessed the meaning of these hints, but now fury awoke in her: "And he'd do well to bite it off!" "So that's how you show me your thanks," the old woman started up tearfully. "Aren't I the one that nursed you, didn't sleep nights?" "Oh, so you're my benefactress too? And stop going on about your Kiriak." "Why? He's a good man, a just man..." "He's a bandit!" Feodosia cut her off. "Don't joke like that, girl, Kiriak is good and kind, but when he's angry, watch out." "A lot I care! And stop calling me 'girl.' How many times have I told you—I'm a married woman." Akulina turned around and muttered something coarse; Feodosia heard "Kiriak'll free you from those marriage ties—and handily."

Now she took longer and longer walks every day, training herself for long, fast hikes. And then, when Granny Akulina had left the yard for some reason or other, Feodosia thrust a piece of lard and a rye scone under her jacket and set off down the familiar road.

After two versts[10] or a bit more the path turned off into a forest, which was convenient for Feodosia: now she couldn't be seen from the village. The road was neither well walked nor well travelled, but all the same she could clearly make out cart tracks through the mane of spring grass, which meant that the road led somewhere, that people used it. Feodosia remembered the bandits: what if she were to run into the returning gang? But no matter how noiselessly the forest people moved, they had wagons and horses and all sorts of equipment; she'd hear them ahead of time and vanish into a thicket. The forest was quiet and calm, and the alert jays groomed their bright feathers under the sun. Small birds flitted back and forth with a dry rustling sound, like that of a dragonfly; a woodpecker bored away furiously at a birchtree, shaking up the poor brain in his little red head, and a cuckoo cuckooed sadly and only occasionally, as though not trusting itself. Feodosia didn't have the courage to ask the cuckoo how many years she had left to live; the bird's voice was weak and fading, and she needed to live a long, long time in order to make up for all the lost years of love with her one and only.

The farther she penetrated into the thickening forest, the hotter and stuffier it became. A damp coolness wafted from under the old trees that sheltered dense shade. The lilies of the valley smelled sour. On the side of the path there were yellow dandelions and elegant blue wildflowers. Feodosia had an urge to weave a garland, and the tips of her fingers even itched, so impatient were they to touch the flowers' slender bodies. She barely managed to overcome temptation: but she needed to reach a village by nightfall, since it would be frightening and cold in the woods and she might be struck by fever again. The path stretched through the woods assuredly, at times bending around a wet hollow or ravine above which rose a white, wild-cherry haze, and came out at a shallow, rather wide stream with low banks overgrown with sharp blades of grass. Feodosia looked across the stream at the tall brown moss through which horsetails poked through, and she couldn't make out a road. After thinking a moment and making a guess, she set off to the left along the water's edge and soon found the road which looped along the bank and gradually moved away from the stream. Feodosia was at a loss—the road seemed to be turning back. But no, things were purposely jumbled here, so as to confuse any outsider who, either by evil design or by accident, wandered into this forest preserve.

She set off along the clearly defined cart tracks and at twilight, having suffered her share of fear, she found herself on the edge of a glade directly across from a village that was strangely quiet and empty, as though abandoned. If only that were so! She'd spend the night in the first house she came to and head off again in the morning. Just then she saw the figure of an old woman near the porch of a far cottage. Feodosia hurried in that direction, and a revolting weakness in her knees almost tumbled her to the ground.

"All tuckered out?" grumbled Granny Akulina. "Come in and have supper. I'm putting on the samovar for the second time."

Now Feodosia realized why they didn't guard her and why they let her walk wherever she felt like going. But all the same, a road, a real road that led out of this trap, had to exist somewhere. After all, the bandit gang didn't come and go through the air, and besides, the former residents of the village must have had some contact with the outside world. Maybe she should have gone along the stream in the other direction or waded across it and tried to find wagon prints in the thick moss. All roads lead somewhere, and that meant that this road, no matter how these people who feared pursuit had tangled it up, had a real direction, and she just needed to be able to untie the knots. You don't get anything right away, but today she had come a little bit closer to deliverance. And most importantly, there was no reason for her to be secretive. Akulina was so certain that she couldn't leave here that she granted her complete freedom.

And on the following day, right before Akulina's very eyes, Feodosia again set off on her way. Everything was just as it had been the day before: the jays, the woodpecker, tiny little birds, and the cuckoo—only the dandelions had managed to turn into fluffy balls. When she reached the stream, she went in the other direction, fighting her way through meadowsweet and flowering nettles. She walked for a long time, the nettles scorched her all over, she grew tired and was about to turn back when on the other side of the stream, on a sandy bald spot, she saw wheel tracks full of water. Taking off her footwear, she crossed to the other bank through the scorchingly icy water, rubbed her numb legs, and drew on her boots, but about fifty sazhens[11] later she had to take them off again—she once again found herself before water. It was impossible to tell whether this was the same stream that looped like a rabbit trail or some other one. Farther on the path went through a dry glade, straight as an arrow, along the whole length of which a sunbeam lay outstretched. In its embrace the dull feathering of the thrushes who scurried above the glade took on the burning, brilliant colors of a pheasant and little silver balls seemed to burst—those were the bright corneas of flying beetles flashing in the sunbeam. And Feodosia seized that beam, floated along its dusty forest radiance, and arrived right at the back of a village. Granny Akulina was waiting for her by the wicker fence.

"All tuckered out?" the old woman asked kind-heartedly. "I cooked some milk porridge for you."

"Don't scream, don't cry, don't collapse on the ground," Feodosia encouraged herself. "I'm closer yet to Vasily, closer by one cursed deceitful road which I couldn't have escaped anyway. And maybe there are many such roads here, but just the same, one of them will turn out to be real and lead me to freedom. Tomorrow I'll set off again..." But she didn't have a tomorrow; during the night one of Kiriak's men appeared and ordered everyone to leave for the woods. A punitive detachment was approaching.

No matter how Peter's death had weakened the state apparatus, the wheels that he had set in motion were still turning, and the regime was protecting itself. Powerless in everything else, it hadn't completely unlearned the ability to repress and punish. From between the breaks in the thickets, the bandit wives who were leaving for the forest, along with Feodosia and Akulina, saw black, motionless smoke that covered like a cap the village that the punitive division had set on fire.

10.

The forest life began, in grass huts and dugouts. The brigands subsisted on an easy business that wasn't dangerous: they robbed marauders from Astrakhan. The plague continued to rage, destroying entire families, and the empty homes were pillaged by local people as well as those who had come from outside, who, in the hopes of finding something to live on, boldly penetrated the infested city and left with substantial booty. No one tried to stop them; the authorities had long since left Astrakhan.

"It's likely that they plundered my house too," Feodosia thought without the least regret. "But what was left: spoons, ladles, beds, and some clothes." It was strange, but it didn't occur to her that the plague might have deprived her not only of her property, but of people close to her as well— her own father. No, in her mind they all remained intact and unharmed. She didn't want to burden her soul with any extra cares, with any alarm or pain that would distract her from thoughts about her husband, with whom she must be reunited. In Vasily Kirillovich's fatal inaccessibility her love for him hadn't exactly grown stronger—one couldn't love more strongly than she did—but had acquired traits of ecstatic worship. Even his flight aroused delight in her. He hadn't fled for profit or gain, but to bring himself harm and troubles, exclusively for the sake of knowledge. Who else was capable of that? Everyone thought only of his daily bread, wealth, and all manner of earthly delights. He was an unusual and great person; it wasn't for nothing that Tsar Peter had let his gaze rest on him.

She thought about Vasily Kirillovich's studies and regretted that she hadn't understood them better. Why was he attached to rhymed lines that turned into a song, but weren't one? He called them verses. But why speak in rhyme, and moreover in a singsong voice, if you weren't planning to sing, or lament, or praise the Tsar of Heaven or an earthly man? With plain speech, the sort used in conversation, you could express everything more easily and clearly. She didn't understand that and it tormented her. Once, longing desperately for Vasily Kirillovich, wiping away the warm tears that were coming to her eyes and torturing herself with unbearable thoughts about her husband's gauntness and the impoverishment of his solitary life near Moscow learning, Feodosia spoke aloud something that she hadn't had inside her, as if she were reading something traced in the air:

> I'll meet you, my darling, my dear one,
> I'll feed you sweetly and richly.
> I'll succor your poor flesh
> With the tastiest and most satisfying food.[12]

She began to feel funny, joyous, and a little ashamed for some reason, and in the trembling void of the forest air she read other letters that only she could see:

> My poor heart weeps and hopes
> That love will warm it up again,
> That the horrible torments will be forgotten
> And that you'll still teach me happiness.

Feodosia was undoubtedly a poet, and a better one than Trediakovsky, but she never found out that eternity was speaking through her lips. It turned out that you could tell about your feelings more tenderly and more sincerely in rhymed verses than in plain conversational speech, and that this comforted the soul better than tears did. When Akulina entered the grass hut, she recited:

> It's hard to go cold,
> It's hard to go hungry,
> But it's even harder
> To wait for your beloved,
> To wait and never get to see him.

"Lord have mercy!" the frightened Akulina crossed herself, deciding that Feodosia was reading someone's fortune.

Sensing the alarm on the part of the old woman who feared neither people's judgment nor the Lord's, nor government torture chambers, Feodosia realized that Akulina only believed in the forces of the underworld, and she began to terrorize her. The verses composed themselves easily, playfully; they splashed about near her heart, and all she had to do was blink away the surrounding ephemeral things and read from the book in the sky, ringing lines about anything you wished: love, sadness, clouds, the wind, a nuthatch darting along the brittle willow upside down, even about the repulsive Akulina. Once, staring her straight in the face, Feodosia said in a sepulchral voice:

> I'll sharpen a little knife,
> And get Akulina's blood,
> Destroy the old witch's innards,
> And shove her into hell.

Akulina ran out of the hut with a loud sob and returned with Kiriak.

"Why are you scaring Granny?" he asked sullenly.

"Why should the old fool be scared?" Feodosia replied freely; she hated the old woman and didn't wish to conceal it. "I'm reciting verses."

"What are verses?"

"Well, things like a song... Only instead of singing them, you say them."

"Well, say one."

And Feodosia said one, only it was about her heart, not Akulina.

"Why do you still love him so much?" Kiriak asked tonelessly.

"And how could I not love him? He's my darling, my one and only. There was no one else and won't be."

"That's as God decides."

"God has already decided. After all, we were married in church."

"How is it that God allowed him to run away?" Kiriak snickered maliciously.

"His father, a priest, dreamed of transferring the parish to him. But he didn't want to be a priest, he wanted to study."

"That he didn't become a priest—that I approve of. But why would a married man want to study?"

"You're a little fool, Kiriak," Feodosia said almost affectionately. "People study so as to know everything. How God's world is ordered and what each creature's appointed place in it is. And when you find out, when you've read wise books, you reach a higher meaning."

"And will yours get there?" Kiriak said incredulously and with the same sullen mockery.

"Mine certainly will! " Feodosia said triumphantly. "He's stubborn."

"The hell he'll get there!" thundered Kiriak. "I'll tell you who's the biggest fool on earth—it's your husband. He had higher meaning right beside him, but he heard bells beyond the hills."

"You're talking nonsense," sighed Feodosia, who had already realized that the conversation was heading toward what she so wanted to avoid, and pitiable idiot that she was, the storm had seemed about to pass on by, but no, it wasn't over yet.

"That meaning is in you, Feodosia, and only in you!" Kiriak began in a passionate, sincere voice. "If you were mine, could I possibly abandon you? Not for all the treasures... "

"Get out of here with your treasures," Feodosia cut him off intentionally coarsely, hoping to extinguish the fire that was flaming up. "And get this straight about treasures. Vasily Kirillovich went for a life of poverty, not for treasures. For him all of your treasures are—ptooey!" She spat and rubbed it in with her foot.

"You can be nasty," Kiriak was surprised.

"Yes, I can. Not for myself, but for him. I could kill, scratch out someone's eyes, cripple someone; I could do anything. Make sure you understand that, Kiriak. I could kill myself, too," she added calmly.

"But why be smarter than smart?" said Kiriak after a short silence. "We had a fellow in the village who read all the divine books. He got smarter from day to day until he turned into a complete idiot."

"What's the point of talking to you? You won't understand anyway. Do you even know how to read?"

"Yes I do... a little, from the Psalter. And I know arithmetic."

"You're a real scholar!" laughed Feodosia.

"Say that one once more. About your heart."

> My poor heart weeps and hopes
> That love will warm it up again,
> That the horrible torments will be forgotten,
> And that you'll still teach me happiness.

"Yes," sighed Kiriak. "If you fell in love with me... " he fell silent, as though frightened by his own thought, and then went on, quietly and sincerely. "I would take up learning... "

Feodosia didn't respond; Kiriak's naïveté didn't move her in the least. Her woman's instinct told her that Kiriak, bold on forest paths and in his treatment of his co-conspirators, a man who didn't love blood but who had no fear of it, was indecisive with women. He adored his deceased, disgraced wife, was faithful to her memory, and his drunken prowling with girls on the make didn't mean anything to him. He had genuine feelings for her, and that was why he had been timid, but today he had crossed a boundary that was difficult for him and dangerous for her. Now it would be open warfare. It was even more difficult to escape from the forest than from the village; there at least there had been some hope of finding a road, but the mysterious bandit paths in the forest were absolutely invisible, and if she went blindly, she might lose her way in a thicket or get torn to pieces by a wild animal.

She began to watch the bandits and their comings and goings, but she couldn't discover anything; the dense, thick moss didn't retain tracks. Now, at every meeting with Kiriak, she asked him to let her go peacefully.

"You can forget about that," he would answer gloomily.

"Why do you need me? I know what you need, but I can't love you. I can't. And even if I weren't a married woman, I still couldn't love you. You smell of blood, Kiriak, and it makes me sick."

"Stepan Timofeyevich[13] killed a lot more people than I have, and the Queen of Shemakhan loved him," Kiriak said pensively.

"You're no Razin. What a comparison!"

"And I'll up and throw you into the Volga, and you'll understand what a Razin I am," he said just as pensively in his husky voice.

"Into the Kozye Swamp!" Feodosia laughed mockingly. "Where is there the Volga around here?" But she herself hoped that in the heat of the moment he'd give away their location.

"I'll go away to the Volga," Kiriak continued his waking dream. "I'll put people on boats and spread a Persian carpet under you. Oh, what a time we'll have!... "

"Console yourself with fairytales, Kiriak, and release me. I don't like you. And the longer you keep me here the more hateful you'll become."

"Well, we'll see about that," Kiriak's swarthy face turned pale.

"You don't want to be like that landowner-master... "

"Shut up!" screamed Kiriak, and in that tortured cry Feodosia gathered assurance of her own safety.

It only seemed to Feodosia that she understood people. She really could trace a person's spiritual path for a long while, but the enigma would be revealed to her only if there was a preponderance of good and kind impulses at the core. Even in evil, dirty games that were so alien to her nature, she could grasp a great deal, at times demonstrating a rare perspicacity, a sort of inconceivable instinct for what was absent in her own experience, but only to a certain extent; wherever human spite, viciousness, or simply unbridledness began to run free without restraint, Feodosia became as naive as a little child. She thought that she could disarm Kiriak with her sincerity. If he simply wanted to take her, he could have committed that inhuman deed long ago. She had been as good as out of her head for a long time. Anyone could have ravished her weak body that was incapable of resistance, and she wouldn't have even known about it. But Kiriak apparently needed something else. But perhaps the memory of his dishonored wife was stopping him? No, he wanted the feeling returned; he wanted things between them to be by common consent, and outrageous as it sounded, legal. Once when he was very drunk he mumbled something about a "forest priest" who could dissolve her marital vows and bind her to him, Kiriak. And she wasn't afraid to tell him about her disgust, considering that although Kiriak, in a rage, might strike her or wound her with a knife, he would refrain from rape, if only out of pride. It was more likely that when he got tired of the struggle, the humiliations, and the unsatisfied passion, he would drive her away.

Kiriak turned up in various moods: kind, hoping for something; more often irritable, angry; sometimes he was even pensive, downcast by the strange riddle of a young, beautiful, and moreover, defenseless woman, abandoned by her husband, who could so stubbornly resist a force that was capable of crushing her like a bug. He hated and respected that strange strength in her. His comrades' mockery behind his back didn't bother him in the least. Kiriak was probably the chieftain precisely because he spat on the opinions of those around him. Their womannish gossip was so insignificant in comparison to his pain that he didn't even attempt to shut their filthy mouths. A string stretched too tightly breaks. The chieftain's string broke too.

After having a great deal to drink, Kiriak came to the sleeping Feodosia's hut. He threw back the blanket, pulled up the nightshirt on the woman, and leapt on her with his heavy body. He did everything silently, with coarse simplicity, as if this were the way things had always been with them.

Feodosia awoke from the stifling weight and heat. At first instant she didn't understand a thing, but then it was as if molten lead had flowed between her thighs, and in order not to die, she looked beyond into another universe and recognized her one and only. He had heard her longing and call from across thousands of versts, returned, sought her out in the dense forest and immediately given her the love that her body had missed so desperately. An incomprehensible delight seized Feodosia; never had she opened up to her beloved in this way.

"Darling, my dearest!" she moaned through clenched, gnashing teeth. "What happiness!"

Kiriak, who knew how strong an enraged woman defending her honor could be, had not forgotten, even in his state of drunken resolve, to thrust a knife into his boot leg. He expected a rage, curses, tears, and a struggle; but what had happened was beyond his understanding. And to his unexpected, earthshattering happiness was added a tear. Devastated, without feelings, without desires, without thoughts, he rolled off the woman who was making quiet moaning sounds, crawled out of the hut, and fell into a sound sleep.

And in the morning, when he came to his senses, he washed himself in spring water, combed his hair and beard, put on his blue glazed cotton shirt, took a gold chain and a string of pearls, and presented himself to his pale, large-eyed, and strangely remote beloved—remoter than the farthest stars, she had awakened, but not yet arisen.

"Take them," he said, dropping the chain and pearls on her chest. "I know that you're worth much more. But give me some time. You'll be dressed like a tsaritsa, my beautiful darling."

"What's with you, Kiriak?" Feodosia asked in a weak, shaky voice and cast the jewelry aside with disgust. "Why are you giving me these things?"

"And who else would I give them to? You're my one and only. Don't reject them. There isn't any gold good enough to pay for your love. The Tsar himself doesn't have enough treasures. Accept them as a gift from my heart."

"What are you talking about, Kiriak?" she torturously strained her smooth brow, gathering it into a wrinkle. "Have you been drinking this morning?"

"No, my little dove. I confess that I was drunk yesterday. I drank for courage. Can you believe it—I was afraid to approach such a little thing. If I'd known that you would take pity on me... "

"I won't take pity. Don't even dream of it."

"What do you mean?" The chieftain's low voice turned rudely hoarse. "Have you forgotten in your sleep, or what? I was with you."

She stared at him attentively, as if trying to understand something.

"You're slandering yourself, Kiriak," she said calmly and as if with regret. "You're all covered in filth and blood, but you're not guilty of that sin. That landowner raped your wife, and you're taking someone else's blame on yourself. Your mind's been harmed from vodka."

The blood rushed to his eyes with such force that he pressed them with his fingers, fearing that they would burst.

"Leave my wife out of this," he said hoarsely. "Why drag her in? The landowner was satisfying his lust, but I'll give up all my kingdoms for you."

"What kingdoms?" Feodosia laughed disdainfully. "You don't have anything except a stolen chain. You're homeless beggars. You didn't even turn into a real brigand. You're a petty thief and a frightened murderer. You don't have any talent. None at all. Well, why are you keeping me here, be good enough to tell me." Her voice softened, sounding almost compassionate. "We fooled you in spite of everything. My darling found me, we cuddled all night while you were sleeping. And we're going to have a baby who'll look just like his papa—strong, white, with warts here and here." Feodosia touched her cheek and upper lip with her little finger.

"What nonsense are you talking?" Kiriak said with pain. "What husband, what warts? You slept with me! Me!"

Feodosia laughed haughtily.

"You see this?" A knife flashed in her hand; apparently it had fallen out of his bootleg. "Just come near me and I'll slash you across the eyes. And if you call for help, I'll kill myself."

"She's lost her mind!" Kiriak realized with horror. "Oh, the poor creature!... And why did I ruin the woman?... But what could I have done? Salvation for her was death to me. That's the way it turned out. Not by man's or God's design. I feel mortally bad for her and for me. Could I have thought that would happen? She might yell a little, well, maybe scratch my face up, pull out some hair, well, put up a fight and gradually calm down. After all, she's no virgin. But to commit suicide? She's not that sort. She's like my... But how she loves that wart-covered monster of hers!" Kiriak thought with a sort of ecstatic envy. "But he, that priestly maggot, betrayed her for books. You didn't get happiness, Kiriak, you only ruined a pure soul. If there's anyone genuinely miserable, it's you."

Kiriak called to Akulina and ordered her to gather up Feodosia's things. He wanted to give her money, and she took exactly as much as she had lost. It seemed as if this was another Feodosia; she was blind to her surroundings, to the chieftain, and only took note of Akulina, whom she treated haughtily, as if she were her servant. At the chieftain's admonition, the old woman didn't snap back, but humbly repeated, "Yes, ma'am," "Just as you say, ma'am." Akulina changed her tone when they left camp. Then she yelled at Feodosia, told her to hurry up or swore at her when Feodosia quickened her pace too much : "Why are you racing like a madwoman? I'm no spring chicken, you know. You'll have time to find your scarecrow." Feodosia did not reply to her, as if not hearing, and she walked just as she felt like walking. When they reached the wharf, Akulina again talked up a storm and bustled about. Feodosia remained just as aloof as before and didn't even respond to the news, related by Akulina, that the plague was nearly over in Astrakhan and that the people who had left town had now returned. But those words must have gotten through to her, and she drew some conclusions. That evening, when Akulina, who had run herself ragged, came back to the inn where they were staying and told her that no one was going to Moscow either by land or by water and that she'd have to sail to Saratov, Feodosia said in a low, heavy voice: "What Moscow? What Saratov? I'm going home." That turned out to be as easy as anything: on the following morning Akulina arranged passage for her on a boat loaded with refugees from Astrakhan. On parting, Akulina suddenly grew emotional: "Forgive me, girl, if things didn't turn out right!" "God will forgive you," mumbled Feodosia and made her way, on shaky legs, up the gangplank to the ship.

Feodosia did not remember how she reached Astrakhan or found herself at home. A strange illness that had begun in her after the night when Vasily Kirillovich had come to her, threw her, unconscious, on the bare bed boards. She didn't come to herself until the next morning. A terrible burning sensation seared her insides: it began in her stomach, rose upward, filling her chest; her heart seemed to be melting; her parched throat contracted convulsively and wanted to expel something vile and revolting; a bitter-tasting lump burst in her mouth, and no one would bring her any water, thought Feodosia, but she wasn't thirsty. And she didn't want anything at all, not even for the burning sensation to pass.

Her sister-in-law Marya showed up with her baby. Feodosia wasn't happy to see her. Weeping quietly, Marya told her that the whole family had died of the plague, one after the other, except for Father Kirilla, who had gone to the monastery and accepted the tonsure under the name of Kliment. Feodosia was silent. She listened indifferently to the news that her father had survived, too. She only asked, "Was there any news from Vasily?" "How on earth could there be?" Marya said whiningly. "We've been cut off here. Maybe there'll be something now." "No," said Feodosia, "there won't be." She fell silent for awhile, compressing her dry, cracked lips. "You know what, Marya? You'd better go. I might have the plague." "The plague devoured itself," said Marya, who had forgotten how to be afraid. "Its power is ended." "It'll devour me and then be over," Feodosia pronounced with prophetic certainty. Afterwards Marya said that she'd brought it on herself by talking about it. The plague, which really was on the wane, rallied its forces to carry poor Feodosia's life away.

The Lord eased her passing. When the darkness at times subsided, Feodosia was again filled with her love and not at all tortured by the fear of death. She both knew and didn't know that she was dying. She was certain of one thing: she couldn't die without seeing her beloved. He would return from far away, even if only at her last hour, her last breath. And if that happened, she wouldn't die, she couldn't die if he were nearby. She would take him by the hand and death wouldn't have the power to sever such a bond. She didn't know when she died. And, in fact, did she really die, having poured all of herself into love and faith which remained on earth to nourish the universal human heart?

11.

Father Kirilla, otherwise known as the monk Kliment, heard about his daughter-in-law's return and prepared to go to see her, but the news of Feodosia's death, which Marya sent to the monastery, kept him where he was. Out of his whole large family the only people still alive were this daughter, who had always been distant, and his grandson, whom he hadn't had time to come to love. Why hadn't God taken him along with those who were dear to him on earth? He was old, worn out, useless. Perhaps he had to expiate an evil act or an injustice committed by him through ignorance, for Father Kirilla was unaware of any consciously evil acts in his past. He wasn't a righteous man, but he'd always tried to live honestly and truthfully; he hadn't deceived, fleeced, orphaned, or slandered anyone. He'd exerted himself for his family and served people as best he could, without gain or cunning. But God knows better whether a weak person of this earth is guilty or innocent and summons him to answer at the appointed hour.

In the unexpected return of Feodosia, whom in his mind he had long since ceased to count among the living, Father Kirilla saw a sign from God. This was his sin before the Lord. He and his whole family had been entrusted with a pure young soul, and how badly, negligently, and cruelly they had treated it. He was charged with expiating the family's guilt toward Feodosia. He felt both a desire to live and a strange strength in his old, decrepit body; he longed for difficult, sweaty work, and caring for another person. But the Lord God took Feodosia, depriving him of the joy of expiation and setting him a new torturous riddle which Father Kirilla didn't even attempt to solve. He no longer had anything to live for. He lay down on his hard bed and entrusted his soul to God. Since he was dying, the Trediakovsky name would forever disappear in Russia and soon be expunged from people's memories. Marya bore her married name, and he'd never in his life heard of any other Trediakovskys. It was a good, sonorous name, borne by people who served the Church, city and village priests who accompanied men from birth to death, and there had been priestly Trediakovskys who had seen the field of battle, blessing troops going into action against the Tatars, steppe nomads, and Poles. From now on the Russian people would have to manage their affairs without the Trediakovskys. The old man didn't recall his prodigal son, because he'd long since buried the very memory of him. And with these mournful thoughts he passed away...

12.

Meanwhile, Vasily Kirillovich, far removed from Russia's hellish sorrows, had grown strong, and with an expanded chest he breathed in and still couldn't get enough of the invigorating Parisian air. In the whole long and difficult life of this first Russian intellectual, a life filled with backbreaking toil and unequal struggle and immensely generous with all sorts of evils: hostility and non-recognition, mockery and malicious jibes, humiliations and beatings—yes, yes, the all-powerful cabinet minister, former governor of Astrakhan, and patron of the Catholic School, Artemy Volynsky, gave a savage beating to the Secretary of the Russian Academy of Sciences!—in a life niggardly with success, warmth, and rest, in that martyr's life there was only one bit of blue sky: the Parisian days under the reliable hand of the Russian Ambassador. And even after Prince Kurakin's sudden death his patronage continued to bless Trediakovsky.

Outwardly, Vasily Kirillovich changed almost beyond recognition: the skeleton-like tramp disappeared, replaced by an imposing young dandy with a smooth, ruddy face unspoiled by two warts stamped on it like beauty spots, with a lively and observant gaze. Yes, Vasily Kirillovich was no longer immersed in himself; he had learned to see the world and to find himself a place in its vortex. But how could one have remained blind and indifferent to Paris, the Champs Elysées, the banks of the Seine, where chestnuts blossomed and old books that gave off a divinely moldering odor were sold, to Notre Dame with its sad gargoyles, to the Louvre and the Palais Royal, to the fragrant gardens where enchanting women with well-dressed children took walks, to the old stones of the Sorbonne, that center of wisdom from whose old stones emanated a disquieting chill. Vasily Kirillovich, the eternal captive of an ascetic power of spirit, came to know the joys of material blessings: refined food on Sèvres china, subtle wines in crystal wine glasses; he was admitted to the nobles' table, although his place was at the lower end of it.

Prince Kurakin was one of the most outstanding dandies of his time, and Vasily Kirillovich wore his hand-me-down coats, camisoles, and jackets, which the Prince only donned a few times, and a drop of Burgundy or a carefully darned little hole made by pipe tobacco hardly mattered, and in the same way he became the owner of the Prince's pants, overcoats, stockings, shoes with silver buckles, and hats which the fops on the Champs Elysées might envy. In a word, he was well-fed, well-dressed, and well looked after; the blue-eyed Marie washed and ironed his shirts, oh, how she ironed them!

Change jingled in Vasily Kirillovich's pockets, but he wasn't a spendthrift, using money only for theater tickets and books that were so delightfully cheap at the Seine booksellers that he spent only the slightest bit. His Highness the Prince and his successor sought conversations with the incredibly well-read student who had a good memory—a walking encyclopedia—and who had his own interesting way of thinking, though at times it was a bit clumsy, and who had gone beyond some of the professors at the Sorbonne, which he continued to visit regularly, in order to perfect his knowledge of French and classical languages.

He worked with rapture. He translated Paul Tallemant's book *A Journey to the Isle of Love*, which had enchanted exacting French readers for more than six decades,[14] and he wrote verses in Russian as well as French, which had become like a native language for him. He drank in Boileau's strict system[15] with delight and was thrilled by Voltaire's marvellous style,[16] enchanting cynicism, and bold atheism, which permanently shattered his religiosity, already weak to begin with. French freethinking and moral freedom had a beneficent effect on the dreamy soul of the versifier from Astrakhan. He began to despise Church Slavonic grandiloquence, cast off the heavy fetters of didacticism, and came to believe with all his soul that the poet was free to sing of other, radiant foundations of existence. His vague youthful suspicions that in their songs the people were closer to true poetry than the acclaimed servants of the fatherland's ponderous muse, headed by Feofan Prokopovich himself, became that certainty which leads to discoveries. Of course, he needed Russian and time in order for his guesses, intuition, illuminations, and painstaking mental search to be cast into an elegant system, but the foundation had already been laid.

At this happy, useful, and just slightly banal time of his life Vasily Kirillovich forgot Feodosia, her love, and his pain forever. He didn't simply forget it, but cast it away, as he had his entire past. He lived for the present, naively assuming that the rest of his life would be illuminated by the same sunlight; he had no way of knowing that this was but a short pause before his endless Russian Golgotha. Happy with his cut-off memory and his calm faith in the future, he dissolved into the present moment, made luminous by the victorious image of the magnificent Duchess of Bourbon.

Yes, Vasily Kirillovich was experiencing a passionate attachment. The greatest beauty of the court had captured his heart. It took him a long time to realize that, but gallant French poetry opened his eyes. When the impoverished seminarian's notions about the elevated didactic goals of poetry, which seemed to serve the greats of this world and the edification of lesser powers, had come crashing down, and when it was revealed to him that genuine poetry was a conversation about love and that he who was not in love was not a poet, he found to his delight that he was not deprived of this first and most important characteristic of a poet. For a long time and on the sly from his own heart he had been madly in love with the young lioness of Parisian society, a living legend, the dark-eyed beauty from the glorious house of Bourbon. Yes, an abyss stretched between them, but love had wings, it mattered not that his chosen one was a celebrity, wealthy, and spoiled by the attentions of the most outstanding gallants of France and all of Europe; nothing could hinder the poet's love. Audacious, inexhaustible, he didn't tire of caressing the object of his passion with the faded gaze of Slavic eyes, covering her angelic face with thousands of imagined kisses.

They had shared tastes. They both worshipped Melpomene, and every evening at the appointed hour Vasily Kirillovich met his chosen one's sedan chair at the steps of the Comédie Française. Since the beauty had not guessed about the fire that had been lit in the foreigner's soul, and in general did not even suspect his existence, Vasily Kirillovich had no need especially to hide himself among the crowd of gawkers, beggars, and thieves who constantly besieged notables near the theater; he could make his way right up to her litter, breathe in the intoxicating fragrance of her perfume, and listen to her silvery laughter and her slightly husky voice. He often recalled a famous line from the poet-musketeer Cyrano de Bergerac:[17] for someone in love any wound is fatal, for it strikes the whole heart and only the heart.

But, fortunately, that turned out to be poetic exaggeration—otherwise Vasily Kirillovich would have ended his days on the pavement in front of the famous theater and would not have given Russian literature the syllabo-tonic method of writing poetry, many scholarly works, and his own creations and translations. How often we underestimate human observation, how little we know of that interest which our modest person arouses in people who are complete strangers to us. But, when, making way for the Duchess' sedan chair, the young swarthy-faced porter gave a fist in the face to Vasily Kirillovich, who had not at all been trying to push forward, the poor poet could have sworn that he had done it on purpose. He had espied Vasily Kirillovich's figure in the multifaced human throng that besieged the Duchess' litter every evening, and something had occurred to him: perhaps it was that the audacious slave was jealous of his mistress and the young foreigner.

And what if the noble woman noticed him?... But he didn't want to think about that; the thought, no matter which way it turned, always ended up in a cul-de-sac. It was enough that the alluring image controlled his hand, which clutched the pen when he transferred his poetic daydreams to paper.

Vasily Kirillovich had a weak nose; the blood continued to ooze when he took his place in the gallery; from there, if you bent over, far below, you could see the Duchess of Bourbon's bared elbow and the delicate mounds of her breasts as she sat in her loge. He vowed to himself not to end his madness—that was beyond his powers—but to bridle himself so as not to fall under the irate porter's muscular arm. Vasily Kirillovich kept that promise. Now he kept at a respectful distance from the sedan chair and alertly watched all his enemy's moves. He no longer asked for trouble and calmly grew weak from the love which lent ever new colors to his poetic efforts in the gallant Gallic style...

Trediakovsky was inferior to both Lomonosov and Sumarokov[18] in poetic gifts and simply in the ability to write poetry, but it was in him alone, out of all his contemporaries, that there sounded a tortured lyric note. And that note broke through all the ungainliness of his ponderous verse—pure, from the heart, sincere—in his poems about Paris, in the song about a little ship setting out to sea, in the cry for his distant native land, and completely unexpectedly, in bits of hideous rhymed nonsense. This awkward poet was not entirely consumed by didacticism, and although when he returned to his native land he was cured in amazingly short time of his French light-mindedness and poetic irresponsibility, nonetheless, under all the layers of didacticism, pedantry, hypocrisy, and faithful flattery, there remained in him a living spring. And it might have been from there that the Castalian Spring spouted forth. He raised a flute to his lips, his soul sought an outlet in the elegy, but he deafened himself with the drum beat of the ode. He failed to recognize his muse and passed by it blindly. And after all, it was near his heart—poetry itself, love itself. Oh, if he had abandoned the Duchess of Bourbon, along with the laundress Marie, who knew how to iron so well, and all of gallant, literary, theatrical, scholarly Paris, which had already given him everything that it could, and returned to Astrakhan, fallen at Feodosia's tortured breast, bathed it even with his last tear, then Russian poetry would have received its first lyric poet.

Obviously, that was not his fate. And Russia received her lyric poet all in good time...

In this story there are neither people who were right nor people who were to blame. Each remained true to his own goal, to his destiny: Feodosia, doomed to love and only to love, and Trediakovsky, preordained to give his native poetry a new system and lay the path for Russian Classicism. He sacrificed the goals that had been set before him no one knows by whom, and Feodosia's love, and family happiness, and his own self-respect, dignity, and honor; he was trampled by nobles and court toadies, the Monarch's malicious laughter encouraged his most spiteful enemies to abuse him wholeheartedly, but, like Feodosia, he did not retreat. Great was the courage of this weak and defenseless person. Salt was poured in his wounds, and not a single hand was raised to wipe away the dark sweat of the eternal toiler.

In truth, literature is a cathedral built on blood.[19]

1978   Translated by David A. Lowe

Notes

The original ("Beglets") appeared in *Nash sovremennik,* No. 10 (1978), 71-113.

1. "Plokhoy" means "bad." [Tr.]

2. Quintilian (Marcus Fabius Quintilianus) (A.D. c. 35-c. 95) was a Roman rhetorician and teacher, the style of whose treatise on oratory entitled *Institutio oratoria* some critics consider florid.

3. Prince Dmitry Kantemir, father of Antiokh D. Kantemir (1708-44). Like his father, the son was a distinguished statesman who denounced opposition to Peter the Great's reforms and was ambassador to England, then minister plenipotentiary in Paris from 1736 to 1744. Often regarded as Russia's first secular poet, Antiokh Kantemir wrote a *Letter* (1742) on the syllabic system of versification, but is best known for his satires, especially "To His Own Mind" (K umu svoemu).

4. Feofan Prokopovich (1681-1736) was an Orthodox theologian and archbishop of Novgorod who by his administration, oratory, and writing collaborated with Peter the Great in Westernizing Russian culture. He assisted in organizing the Russian Academy of Science, penned religious tracts, and delivered the funeral eulogy for Peter the Great. Many consider the eulogy the classic example of Russian oratory.

5. A Russian folk saying. [Tr.]

6. Ovid (Publius Ovidus Naso) (43 B.C.-A.C. 17?) is the Roman poet known mainly for his *Metamorphoses,* a collection of exquisite mythological and legendary stories in verse centered around the theme of passion. The author of countless lyrics on the theme of love *(Amores)* and a treatise on the art of seduction, *The Art of Love* (Ars amatoria), Ovid was banished by Augustus possibly for the latter work and for an unestablished indiscretion to Tomis on the Black Sea. A. Pushkin's narrative poem *The Gypsies* (Tsygany, 1835) celebrates the gifted exile.

7. Gaius Valerius Catullus (c.84-c.54 B.C.) was a splendid Roman lyric poet with a frustrated passion for Clodia, the wife of the consul Quintus Metellus Celer, that caused him endless torment but inspired his best poems, the *Poems to Lesbia* (Lesbia being his 'poetic' name for Clodia).

Horace (Quintus Horatius Flaccus) (65-8 B.C.) was a Roman poet who enjoyed the patronage of Maecenas, Augustus' chief minister of state. Probably Horace's *Odes* are his most outstanding work, though his *Satires* (Sermones), *Epistles,* and *Art of Poetry* (Ars poetica) are marked by the same stylistic beauty and verbal economy. An advocate of the golden mean and of wisdom over passion, Horace presents a contrast of sorts to Catullus, with his impassioned outbursts of hatred and love.

Terence (Publius Terentius Afer) (195-159 B.C.) was a Roman comic poet and dramatist, adapter of Greek New Comedy, author of plays whose ideal is moderation, and whose audience were the educated classes in Rome. His best-known plays are *The Woman of Andros* (Andria, 166 B.C.) and *The Brothers* (Adelphoe, 160 B.C.).

8. Homer is the poet to whom the *Iliad* and *Odyssey*, the two incomparable Greek epics, are traditionally attributed. They are conjecturally dated c. 850 B.C. Most recent scholarship has concluded that Homer, who presumably was blind, composed the epics orally.

Dante Alighieri (1265-1321) was the Italian poet (an exile with political and military experience) who composed *La Divina commedia*, which offers his comprehensive view of man's temporal and eternal destiny.

Torquato Tasso (1544-95) was an Italian poet who authored *Gerusalemme liberata* (Jerusalem Delivered, 1575, published 1581), the most famous Romantic epic of the Renaissance, and other, lesser works. Tasso himself became the subject of Goethe's poetic drama *Torquato Tasso* (1790) and Byron's dramatic soliloquy *The Lament of Tasso* (1817).

Pierre de Ronsard (1524-85) was the pre-eminent French poet of his day, celebrated for his odes, his love sonnets, and his leadership of the literary group know as the Pléiade. Of the many collections of poems he produced, the best and most famous are the *Odes* (1550), lyrics in a Pindaric vein, *Amours* (1552). and *Sonnets pour Hélène* (1578).

François de Salignac de La Mothe Fénélon (1651-1715) was a French churchman and man of letters, author of the Homeric imitation entitled *Télémaque*, which, in defiance of all logic and 'taste, was the most popular French work of the first half of the eighteenth century. Now, however, Fénélon's voluminous works are read only by specialists.

9. Stenka Razin (Stepan Timofeyevich Razin), a folk-hero among Russians, led a major Cossack and peasant rebellion on Russian's south-eastern frontier during Tsar Alexis' reign (1670-1). He was defeated, captured, and executed on Red Square in 1671.

10. Two versts is the equivalent of about one and a quarter miles.

11. The verses here and following are rhymed in the original Russian. [Tr.]

12. Fifty sazhens is about 115 yards.

13. See footnote 9.

14. *Le Voyage à l'isle d'amour* by Paul de Tallemant (1642-1712) may have enjoyed popularity among early-eighteenth-century Frenchmen, Trediakovsky's contemporaries, and readers of eighteenth-century Russian literature who actually read Trediakovsky's translation, but contemporary specialists in French letters consider the work obscure and forgettable.

15. Boileau's strict system refers to the guidelines for literary composition that Nicolas Boileau (1636-1711) set forth in his *L'Art poétique* (The Art of Poetry, 1674). Dubbed the 'Legislator of Parnassus,' Boileau, a poet and critic, was the self-appointed codifier of literary rules and practices during the period of French classicism dominated by Molière, Racine, and La Fontaine. This treatise, which established a hierarchy among authors, literary subjects, and styles, advocated decorum and balance, and was much narrower and more dogmatic than Horace's *Ars poetica*, which Boileau took as his model.

16. Voltaire (pseudonym of François-Marie Arouet) (1694-1778), the French satirist deservedly famous for his keen inquisitive intellect, ironical skepticism, and ability to popularize the most advanced philosophy in a century of revolt against restraint, is remarkable for his lucid, witty, vivid style, perhaps best exemplified in the philosophical tales *Zadig* (1748) and *Candide* (1759) and in his *Lettres philosophiques* (Philosophic Letters on the English, 1733/4).

17. Savinien Cyrano de Bergerac (1619-55), French soldier, swordsman, and satirist-dramatist, achieved his greatest fame as the gallant, brilliant, but shy and ugly hero with the extraordinary proboscis in Edmond de Rostand's play *Cyrano de Bergerac* (1897).

18. Mikhail V. Lomonosov (1711-65) was the Russian poet whom Pushkin called "our first University" because of Lomonosov's prodigious knowledge of philosophy, chemistry, physics, prosody, and literature. He wrote poetry, treatises, essays, etc., and founded Moscow University in 1755.

Aleksandr P. Sumarokov (1717-77) was a Russian dramatist and poet who helped found and became the first director of the first Russian public theater (1756-61). He composed nine tragedies, fifteen comedies, and libretti for ballet and opera, and translated parts of Boileau's *L'Art poétique*. A proponent of classicism, he constructed his verse tragedies according to the principles of French classicism and took his themes from Russia's history (e.g., *Dmitry the Pretender*, 1771, *Mstislav*, 1774). The few who read Sumarokov today, however, bypass his drama in favor of his poetry: odes, elegies, eclogues, songs, satires, and fables—which is more varied and impassioned than one might expect from such a confirmed classicist.

19. As is Russian history! The reference may be to the Church of the Savior on the Blood (Spas-na-Krovi), which was erected in 1882 on the site of the assassination of Alexander II on the embankment of the Ekaterininsky (now Griboyedov) Canal in Leningrad. (Translator's observation, editor's wording.)

Afterword

Nagibin's Own Comments about the Stories Translated in This Volume*

1. "Zimnii dub" was written in early 1953. In his books *Literaturnye razdum'ia* and *Razmyshleniia o rasskaze,* Nagibin tells what led up to the story. Memories of forests in the winter, village children going to school, and a nurse at a sanatorium who fussed with her son for being late to school blended into a conversation with the writer N. Atarov about how Russian should be taught, and in time, the story took shape. "Zimnii dub" is Nagibin's best-known work. It was made into a television film as an aid for teachers of Russian and came out in a reader, *Rodnoi iazyk* (Native Language), for the fifth grade. Noted actors frequently read it on stage and on the radio, and a film short based on it won Grands Prix at film festivals in Munich and Prague.

After the story was first published in 1953, it was discussed at length by Z. Kedrina in *Literaturnaia gazeta,* No. 48 (1953), and was also treated in reviews by Anna Mlynek, *Moskovskii komsomolets* (October 19, 1955), Evgenii Vorob'ev, *Novyi mir,* No. 11 (1955), Leonid Khaustov, *Neva,* No. 7 (1955), Arkadii El'iashevich, *Zvezda,* No. 10 (1957), and Nikolai Atarov, *Nash sovremennik,* No. 12 (1972).

2. Everything in "Nochnoi gost'" actually happened. At one time, Nagibin was fond of going fishing in Lake Pleshcheevo and staying at a lodge with an ideal of a Russian grandmother named Julia. It was there that he met the prototype of Pal Palych, the night guest. Even the incident of the penknife that gives Pal Palych away is true.

After its publication in 1955, the story was reviewed by M. Cherkasskii, *Neva,* No. 5 (1957), Iu. Surovtsev, *Oktiabr',* No. 6 (1957), Inna Borisova, *Druzhba narodov,* No. 4 (1959), Nikolai Atarov, *Literaturnaia gazeta,* No. 122 (1960), Lidiia Fomenko, *Znamia,* No. 9 (1973), and Irina Bogatko in her study *Iurii Nagibin* (1980).

In 1958, "Nochnoi gost" was made into a film of the same name by Lenfilm studio. V. Shredel' directed; the noted actor I. Smoktunovskii played the title role. The film was well received and is still shown in theaters and on television.

3. "Posledniaia okhota" was written in the mid-1950s, when Nagibin was fond of duck hunting and went several times a year to the Meshchera lowland, which Konstantin Paustovskii also praised. This swamp country is in Riazan' province just beyond Moscow province and it includes a part

of Vladimir province. Sergei Esenin was born there and went to school in the little town of Spas-Klepiki, near Lake Velikoe and the Pra River, where Nagibin hunted.

"Posledniaia okhota" is part of the Meshchera series and is based on real persons and events. The main character, the older hunter Dedok, also appears in Nagibin's story "Novyi dom" [and in "Molodozhen" and "Il'in den"—H.G.].

After "Posledniaia okhota" came out in 1955, it was reviewed by A. El'iashevich, *Zvezda,* No. 12 (1959), and was discussed by Nikolai Atarov, "Chelovek iz glubiny peizazha," *Nash sovremennik,* No. 4 (1970), by Nina Briabina in her review of *Na tikhom ozere i drugie rasskazy, Nash sovremennik,* No. 9 (1967), by Oleg Smirnov in his review of Nagibin's *Izbrannye proizvedeniia, Novyi mir,* No. 11 (1973), and by Irina Bogatko in her book *Iurii Nagibin* (1980).

4. The characters in "Molodozhen," as in all the Meshchera stories, are based on real people, and Nagibin calls them by their real names. The only exception is the negative character Voronov, whom Nagibin has disguised somewhat and given a different name. The incidents in the story are also based on fact.

The story, which was published in 1956, was discussed by Inna Borisova in her review of Nagibin's *Skalistyi porog, Druzhba narodov,* No. 4 (1959), Nikolai Atarov in "Chelovek iz glubiny peizazha," *Nash sovremennik,* No. 4 (1970), and Irina Bogatko in *Iurii Nagibin* (1980).

"Molodozhen" was made into a film short by Odessa Film Studio, with V. Isakov directing.

5. The only part of "Ekho" that is not fictitious is the setting. The story takes place in Koktebel', which is now called Planerskoe, and the surrounding countryside with Mount Kara-dag and its Devil's Finger, where there are a great variety of echoes. Koktebel' was founded by the poet and artist Maksimilian Voloshin, a friend of Marina Tsvetaeva, Mandel'shtam, and other Russian poets.

The young people in the story have no real life models, although in Vika, the girl who collects echoes, there are a few features of Nagibin's Akulovka friend Galia; and in the boy there is a little bit of the young Nagibin.

Published in 1960, the story was discussed by V. Favorin in his review of Nagibin's short stories, *Ural,* No. 10 (1962), by Evgenii Nikolin in his review of *Chistye prudy, Neva,* No. 7 (1963), and by G. Brovman in his review of *Zelenaia ptitsa s krasnoi golovoi, Moskva,* No. 4 (1966).

Nagibin also wrote the script for a film entitled *Devochka i ekho,* based on this story. The film was directed by A. Zhebriunas, produced by the Lithuanian Film Studio, and won a Grand Prix at the Cannes festival of children's films and Silver Wings in Locarno.

6. Nagibin heard the tale which serves as the basis of the story "By A Quiet Lake" from a Belorussian friend, now deceased. Nagibin went to Lake Naroch' in West Belorussia, where there is a professional fishermen's association which catches eels. The fishermen there told him a great number of interesting facts about the habits, life conditions, and reproduction of that mysterious fish, but nobody had ever heard the tale that prompted Nagibin to travel there. So Nagibin altered the story in his own way, creating a new hero—Val'chikov, the carpenter from Meshchera; in short, he fictionalized the events while keeping the general humanistic concept of the original story. Everything that happens to the eels in the story is absolutely true.

The story was published many times, and was broadcast over the radio, with a sequel. It enjoyed considerable success with readers. The publishing house "Khudozhestvennaia literatura" printed it as a separate book with illustrations, and it was reprinted in many anthologies of Nagibin's works, including the 1973 two-volume edition. It will also appear in Volume 2 of Nagibin's *Collected Works.*

The story was made into two movies: a Russian one entitled *The Dam,* which was awarded several film prizes, and a Polish one called *The Epiphany.*

Critics who have discussed the story include N. Atarov, L. Fomenko, N. Briabina, and I. Bogatko.

7. Another of the Meshchera series, "Olezhka zhenilsia" is based on a story Nagibin heard from the director of a hunting camp on Lake Velikoe. Although Nagibin changed the style and the names of the young people, the plot and attitudes correspond to those of the director's account. Nagibin's play *Pozdniaia osen'* is based on this story and has been performed in a number of theaters in the Soviet Union.

The story, first published in 1965, was discussed by Lidiia Fomenko in her review of Nagibin's *Izbrannye proizvedeniia, Znamia,* No. 9 (1973).

8. One of the series of stories that make up the book *Leto moego detstva,* "Zabroshennaia doroga" is the only story in the series in which something has been invented. Even here, though, almost everything is taken from life, the forest full of mushrooms and the abandoned road that Nagibin suddenly comes across in the woods. But the boy with glasses clearing the road is made up. He occurred to Nagibin as an ideal of good and selflessness and is a composite of various people Nagibin has met.

"Zabroshennaia doroga" was first published in 1967, and was discussed in Galina Drobot's review of the collection *Chuzhoe serdtse,*

Literaturnaia Rossiia, No. 9 (1970), M. Makina's review of *Chuzhoe serdtse, Moskva,* No. 6 (1972), and Lidiia Fomenko's review of Nagibin's *Izbrannye proizvedeniia, Znamia,* No. 9 (1973).

9. Everything in "Srochno trebuiutsia sedye chelovecheskie volosy" is fictitious except for the title. For a good while, an advertisement worded in that way was posted on the doors of the Lenfilm Studio. As soon as Nagibin saw it, it suggested a story. Gushchin, his wife, and Natasha are composites of people Nagibin has known. The artist, Mikula Selianinovich, goes back to Nagibin's old friend Iurii Vasil'ev, an original and talented artist. In the story, Nagibin described his family, home, and studio; and Vasil'ev had no objections.

When the story came out in 1968, it caused a lively controversy. Readers seemed to like or dislike it very much. The main bone of contention was the ending, why Gushchin should have stayed with his old and faithless wife. The first to attack the story was L. Mil' in *Literaturnaia gazeta,* No. 18 (1968). The most favorable review of the story was that of Vladimir Shaposhnikov, *Sibirskie ogni,* No. 9 (1974), who pointed out the moral intent of the whole story, especially the ending. Other discussions of the story include Lidiia Fomenko's review of Nagibin's *Izbrannye proizvedeniia, Znamia,* No. 9 (1973), and Oleg Smirnov's review of the same work in *Novyi mir,* No. 11 (1973). In 1979 the story was made into a television movie called *Pozdniaia vstrecha* (A Late Encounter), directed by V. Shredel', with A. Batalov in the leading role.

10. A contemporary fairy tale, "Chuzhoe serdtse" (1968) tells of a man who receives a heart transplant and later comes to sense that he has acquired not only the heart but also the feelings and memories of someone else. The story is, of course, entirely fictitious and is of special importance to Nagibin in that it convinced him that he could, after all, make things up. Afterward, he relied on his imagination for a whole series of stories, including "Ty budesh' zhit'," "Pik udachi," "Sredi professionalov," "Son o Tiutcheve," and "Miagkaia posadka."

Perhaps the best discussion of the story is that of Irina Bogatko in her book *Iurii Nagibin* (1980). M. Makina also reviewed the story in *Moskva,* No. 6 (1972).

11. One of the same series as "Zabroshennaia doroga," "Shurik" is based entirely on fact: the summer home in Akulovka, the charming, lonely boy badgered by his playmates, his game of 'fish-man,' his untimely death, and Nagibin's belated regret. The story was first published in 1968 and has been reviewed in the same places as "Zabroshennaia doroga."

12. Like "Chuzhoe serdtse," "Pik udachi" (1970) is a contemporary fairy tale, but a more complex one. When it first came out, it met, as "Srochno trebuiutsia sedye volosy" had, with heated controversy. The

sharpest reviews were those of Lidiia Lebedinskaia, *Literaturnaia gazeta,* No. 15 (1972) and M. Boiko, *Literaturnoe obozrenie,* No. 1 (1976). The most favorable discussions were those of Lidiia Fomenko, *Znamia,* No. 9 (1973), Oleg Smirnov, *Novyi mir,* No. 11 (1973), V. Sakharov, *Nash sovremennik,* No. 1 (1976), and Irina Bogatko, *Iurii Nagibin* (1980).

Television versions of "Pik udachi" were filmed in Budapest and Bratislava, and it has frequently been translated.

13. "Il'in den" differs from the other stories in the Meshchera series in that it does not deal with hunting and it shows an unattractive side of the country people Nagibin is so fond of. The holiday in honor of the prophet Elijah marks the end of the summer and the beginning of autumn. Although most of Nagibin's characters follow the old tradition and celebrate by drinking too much, the principal character, the hunter Anatolii Ivanovich Makarov, a disabled veteran of World War II, maintains his dignity. He is a model of the virtues Nagibin finds in the Russian character. Makarov is based on a real person with the same name.

The story first appeared in 1972, and is discussed by Irina Bogatko in her book *Iurii Nagibin* (1980).

14. "Chuzhaia" goes back to a trip Nagibin took to Eastern Siberia and is set in a factory settlement near Irkutsk. Although the taiga and the characters in the story are taken from life, the incident is fictitious. Nagibin imagined what would happen if the wife of his host's best friend were an outsider, a stranger to his old friends. From there, he constructed a story about the subtleties of human relations, about the difficulty in approaching strangers. Later, it turned out that the couple Nagibin had used as his point of departure resented being put into his story.

"Chuzhaia," which first appeared in 1976 and later was made into a film, was discussed by S. Sivokon' in his review "O liubvi i ne tol'ko," *Literaturnoe obozrenie,* No. 12 (1979), Galina Drobot, "Poznanie cheloveka," *Literaturnaia Rossiia,* No. 16, (1979), V. Korobov in his preface, "O proze Iuriia Nagibina," to *Odin na odin* (1980), and Irina Bogatko in *Iurii Nagibin* (1980).

15. "Beglets" is the last in a series of stories entitled "Vechnye sputniki." (Nagibin remembered belatedly that Merezhkovskii had already used the title.) He has worked on the series about ten years and considers these stories the most important he has written, an opinion shared by Irina Bogatko, V. Kholopova, Dora Dychko, and other critics. The collection deals with writers and composers, from the archpriest Avvakum to Ivan Bunin.

Two of these stories, "Beglets" and "Ostrov liubvi," have to do with Trediakovskii. In the entire series, Nagibin takes considerable liberties with historical fact, a practice to which some critics have objected. But Nagibin stresses that he is writing fiction, not history. The part of "Beglets" about Trediakovskii himself is based on fact, the part about his wife Feodosiia is fictitious. Almost nothing is known about her except that she tried to persuade her husband to return after he had left her to go study in Moscow and that she died in Astrakhan', of cholera or the plague.

Irina Bogatko discusses the story, which first appeared in 1978, in her book *Iurii Nagibin* (1980).

Translated by Richard N. Porter

---

*Data that overlapped with information contained in the Introduction or Interview have been deleted.

Interview[1]

Q. Let's begin with a self-assessment. Which of your stories and tales do you consider your best, and why?

A. If I'm to be completely honest and sincere, then I have to say that I'm almost always interested and involved in whatever I'm writing at the moment, regardless of what it's worth. With the passage of time, however, I begin to find former works unendurable. I have stories, such as "Winter Oak" and "Komarov," which are better known than those I wrote later when I started writing much better. Even abroad these early works are pretty well known—they've been translated into numerous languages. But personally I'm not fond of these stories and don't think they're worth much. So I have a qualified response to your question: what I like are those works with which I haven't yet lost an inner link. What I've been writing recently about the past, for instance, is much closer to me than my earlier stuff. Among the stories I consider the best is "The Fiery Archpriest"—it's about Avvakum. But I say this without much conviction because I've already started moving away from it, and even now my link with it is weakening. There's another story of mine, called "An Evil Squint," about Apollon Grigoryev. It's a complex piece written in a difficult manner, and not particularly popular, but I like it a great deal more than better-known stories of mine, such as "The Pipe," which has even been translated into Swahili.

Q. What is your opinion of your story "The Outsider," which was published in *Novy mir,* No. 6, in 1976?

A. That's one of the stories with which I've still retained that inner link that I'm talking about. I haven't grown indifferent to it yet, and I'm certainly glad I wrote it. It's received a considerable amount of attention in our country, incidentally. There was a film made of it, but I didn't write the script—E. Volodarsky and V. Shredel wrote it.

Q. You didn't want to write the script yourself?

A. No, I didn't. I considered it—well, let me tell you all the facts. When I was writing that story my mother was dying. I was writing then simply so as not to think too much about what has been the greatest loss in my life. I wrote to avoid tormenting myself over what was confronting me immediately. So I didn't want to touch that story later with—well, how should I put it?—with dirty hands. Besides, I wasn't convinced that the story would transfer well onto the screen. Although now there's a point of view that maintains that one can make a film even of Church books. Perhaps to some extent that's so.

I've done lots of work on various films, but Bella Akhmadulina did *Fresh Ponds* (Chistye prudy) and Volodarsky and Shredel did *The Outsider.* I'm used to doing the screenwork myself, but in this instance I didn't. In any case, they did a crude job, but the film somehow came off anyway. There were some good actors in it—I. Savina in the main role, and Obolensky. But the script was cut up, and the ending was eliminated altogether. All in all, it's a pretty bad film, though Obolensky, who's an experienced actor in the tradition of Kuleshyov,[2] has some good moments and gives an interesting performance. And Savina has intonations at times that are worth watching.

Q. In general, though, would you rather the film hadn't been made?

A. Yes, I would. Critical articles that came out afterwards claimed that the film didn't compare with the story, so I haven't exactly suffered a moral loss in the whole affair, but—

To return to your original question—of the stories with a contemporary theme, the ones that are the most alive for me are the two latest—"Two Stories," which came out in *Novy mir,* No. 3, of this year (1979).[3] A story that is somewhat less recent but one of which I'm fond is "Elijah's Day." It was published earlier in a drastically shortened version, and now for the first time it's finally come out in full in my latest book, entitled *Berendeyev Forest.* It'll probably get here to the U.S. soon. The volume came out in 1978, published by "Sovetsky pisatel." The story is about drunkenness—about a fantastic, hopeless drunkenness that can't be compared to anything. A book of mine came out in Hungary, by the way, which adopted *Elijah's Day* as its collective title. I'm pleased with that story to this day.

Q. What significant differences do you yourself perceive between your early and your later works?

A. I think they can be distinguished from each other pretty easily. I know that some people think that earlier I used to write better, closer to the reader, in a sense. I certainly wrote more simply, perhaps you could say more sentimentally. I'm not a fan of that part of my work now. I've started writing a lot about the past, and in a somewhat more complex manner, without the kind of tenderness you'll find in "Komarov," for example. In my later works there's more thought, more culture.

Q. To what period do you assign the shift? The early 1960s?

A. Maybe the late 1960s. Elements of what later entered many of my stories and is visible in my current cycle, appeared then for the first time. The late 60s include my stories "Muteness" and "The Typist Lives on the Sixth Floor," which are about the nature of creativity. That's what occupied me then. These aren't general human concerns, and before the late 1950s I wrote about things that many found of more general human interest.

Q. Why? Why the change? What motivated it?

A. I don't know. How does one explain such a change? Can one? Maybe a critic can. Irina Bogatko, who wrote a book about me that enjoys a general acceptance in our country,[4] has a hypothesis about this question. But I'll try to answer it myself from my own perspective. A man gets older; I'll soon be sixty. In his youth a man lives more by feelings. (What I'm saying is primitive, I know.) As he gets older, a man begins to live more through his mind. Probably his passions are fading, they're on the wane. A man starts working through his head, he discovers he has one, so to speak. And probably what happened to me is that I was drawn to analysis then; I increasingly had the desire to know, to understand. Amazement and joy at life are very simple. At the start one writes with one's feelings alone— simply in order to write. Then later you begin thinking about why you're writing. At least that seems to play a role here.

Q. A rather different kind of question now. Of the Russian prosaists of the nineteenth and twentieth centuries, which have inspired you the most?

A. I find a great deal of enjoyment in the works of Andrey Platonov, of course. There are so many— It's not a question of imitation, but I do have a great deal of regard for Bunin. I don't imitate him the way, say, Kazakov does, or the way Antonov imitates Chekhov, but I'm strongly drawn to him. My favorites, though, are Gogol, Dostoyevsky, and Leskov. They're the three for me. Others that I like include Lermontov the prosaist, Chekhov—though, strangely enough, I like him more calmly.

Q. I'm surprised that you didn't include Tolstoy. Now the reverse, however—is there a writer you can't stomach?

A. Hmm—at times, Saltykov-Shchedrin, though his *Golovlyov Family* is a fine work.

Q. And of the European writers? Which ones are you especially fond of?

A. Proust above all. Also, Joyce, but not *Portrait of the Artist as a Young Man*. I'm attached to *Ulysses* and *The Dubliners*. I also like Dickens a great deal, and Jean Giraudoux and Jorge Borges, Cortázar, and Márquez. They're all giants. But above all Proust, Joyce, and Giraudoux. And of our writers, Andrey Platonov. I could even say that I studied from Platonov and Jean Giraudoux. They're polar opposites, in a sense, but I feel a great awe before both of them. They both performed linguistic miracles. I saw a lot of Giraudoux staged in Poland, by the way. Mrożek too.

Q. Yes, I'm constantly struck by how diverse and high in quality Polish theater is. I'd like to turn to a specific writer now—Hemingway. In your "Kenya Notes" you state apropos of Hemingway: "I am enraptured with the virility of Hemingway, who looked life, and death, too, right in the eye." (Hemingway would have been delighted to read that!) What precisely does Hemingway's so-called virility consist of? To tell you the truth, I find Hemingway's treatment of the problem of death in his major novels stilted and strangely insincere, and he seems to simplify and narrow the whole issue. Everyone in his books speaks so unconvincingly whenever the question of death arises, that I feel extremely uncomfortable—especially for Hemingway.

A. It's interesting that you, too, should ask me about Hemingway—I've been asked that question more than once. I'll try to explain my feelings about him. When I was younger and was passionately fond of hunting and fishing, I admired Hemingway much more than now. Then killing animals became hateful to me, and at the same time my enthusiasm for Hemingway dwindled. His ideas, his personality, his preoccupation with virility—they all began to push me away from him. You know the newspapers wrote that he wore false hair on his chest—as though "physical strength" of that kind proves something. And I began to feel rather skeptical about his love involvements, too.[5] For example, he never forgave a woman for slighting him; he almost conceived a hatred for Dominguín[6] because Ava Gardner, who had been his mistress, took up with the bullfighter. Hemingway couldn't forgive a woman whom he'd presented with the gift of his love for getting close to, becoming intimate with, another man. The same thing happened with Rossellini,[7] the director who married that marvellous actress—she's Swedish—what's her name?—Ingrid Bergman.[8] Hemingway hated him too. In any case, the period of my profound regard for Hemingway is long past. Toward the end he was a deeply disturbed and unhappy man.

Q. Are you familiar with Heller's novels? What's your opinion of Joseph Heller? I know that his *Catch-22* is very popular in the Soviet Union.

A. Yes. My feelings toward him are mixed. I think *Catch-22* is an excellent novel, very human, and Heller writes profoundly, intelligently there, but—what's the name of his second one—?

Q. *Something Happened,* though many reviewers claimed that nothing in the novel did, on any level.

A. Exactly. There's little in that novel to like. It's artificial, somehow, and creates an unpleasant impression, not at all like *Catch-22.*

Q. I think you'll find his latest, *Good As Gold,* equally disappointing. He uses precisely the devices that worked so successfully in *Catch-22,* but now deals with the idiocies of government, and somehow the impact is much weaker than in his first novel. Now a question that sounds frivolous, but is really serious. If you were washed up on a desert island and had to live there in isolation for several years, which five works of world literature would you need to have with you?

A. I can't name books, but the authors I'd need would be Proust—definitely. Also Dostoyevsky, Gogol, Joyce's *Ulysses,* but no, it's impossible to limit oneself—

Q. My final question is: do you believe, as does the boy in your story "The Deserted Path," that all roads lead somewhere?

A. In the most general sense, yes. Belief, of course, comes more easily when one is younger...a person changes with time, life becomes more complicated...

Recorded and translated by Helena Goscilo

1. Because parts of the interview recorded poorly, it was impossible to distinguish clearly and completely Nagibin's rapidly-delivered replies to about ten additional questions. These have been omitted so as to avoid misrepresentation.

2. Lev Vladimirovich Kulishyov (1899-1970) was a Russian film director, film theoretician, and pedagogue, who in 1939 became a professor at the All-Union Institute of Cinematography (VGIK), founded in Moscow in 1919.

3. The stories in question are "Silent Spring" (Zamolchavshaia vesna), pp. 106-112, and "Moonlight" (Lunnyi svet), pp. 113-117.

4. Bogatko's most recent and lengthy study of Nagibin and his oeuvre is the 111-page volume entitled I. Bogatko, *Iurii Nagibin (Literaturnyi portret),* M. 1980.

5. Nagibin's view of Hemingway may be seen in his fictionalized account of the last period of Hemingway's life, a story fusing facts, rumor, and imagination, entitled "One on One" or *"Mano a Mano"* (Odin na odin), *Znamia,* No. 5 (1979), 78-111. For additional information about Nagibin's opinion of Hemingway, see the interview he gave in Norman, Oklahoma on 26 April 1979, Dragan Milivoević, "Nagibin's View of American and Soviet Literature: An Interview," *Russian Language Journal,* Vol. XXXIII, No. 115, (1979), 132-33.

6. Luis Miguel Dominguin, Ava Gardner's lover and Hemingway's "friend," was probably one of Spain's most outstanding matadors.

7. Roberto Rossellini is the post-World-War II film director famous for such films as *Open City* (1945) and *Paisan* (1946), which ushered in the Neo-Realist revival in film. His relations with Ingrid Bergman caused her ostracization from Hollywood for over a decade.

8. Carlos Baker, Hemingway's foremost biographer in America, does not even hint at any physical intimacy between Hemingway and either actress in his thorough (697-page) book, *Ernest Hemingway: A Life Story,* New York, 1969. Nor does Hemingway's last wife, Mary Hemingway, in her lucid and unflinching memoirs, *How It Was,* New York, 1976.

Bibliography

For a list of works by and about Nagibin see Ellen Cochrum, *A Bibliography of Works by and about Jurij Nagibin: 1940-1978, Russian Language Journal*, Vol. XXXIII, No. 115 (1979), 137-204. Because that list omits several items published in 1978, the bibliography compiled here covers the years 1978-1980. Anyone interested in earlier publications should consult the Cochrum bibliography.

I. Separate Editions of Nagibin's Works

Nagibin, Iu. M. *Berendeev les. Rasskazy, ocherki.* Moscow: "Sovetskii pisatel', " 1978.

_____. *Rasskazy o Gagarine.* Moscow: "Detskaia literatura," 1978.

_____. *Zabroshennaia doroga. Rasskazy.* Moscow: "Sovremennik," 1978.

_____. *Odin na odin. Povesti, rasskazy.* Moscow: "Roman-gazeta," 1979.

_____. *Tsarskosel'skoe utro. Povesti, rasskazy.* Moscow: "Izvestiia," 1979.

_____. *Zamolchavshaia vesna.* Moscow: "Biblioteka Ogon'ka," 1979.

_____. *Sobranie sochinenii v 4-kh tt.* Vol. I. Moscow: "Khudozhestvennaia literatura," 1980.

II. Nagibin's Works in Periodicals
1978

Nagibin, Iu. M. "Beglets. Rasskaz." *Nash sovremennik*, No. 10 (1978), 71-113.

_____. "Etot schastlivik Kheili." *Novoe vremia*, No. 34 (1978), 27-30.

_____. Foreword to Filipp Berman's "Belyi pukh. Rasskaz." *Literaturnaia Rossiia*, No. 11 (1978), 18, 19.

_____. Foreword to L.V. Karelin's *Izbrannoe.* Moscow: "Moskovskii rabochii," 1978.

_____. Foreword to E.I. Kuman'kov's *Moskva... kak mnogo v etom zvuke...* Moscow: "Sovetskii khudozhnik," 1978.

_____. "Geroi zhivut riadom." *Vecherniaia Moskva*, No. 160 (1978), 3.

_____. "Mal'chik na byke. Rasskaz." *Literaturnaia Rossiia*, No. 7 (1978), 12, 13.

_____. "Moskva moia..." *Vecherniaia Moskva*, No. 32 (1978), 2.

_____. "Nemnogo o Bazene. Retsenziia." *Inostrannaia literatura*, No. 1 (1978), 265, 266.

_____. "Ne toropis' v pisateli. Ocherk." *Literaturnaia ucheba*, No. 6 (1978), 136-143.

_____. "Obraz rodiny. Stat'ia." *Pravda*, No. 324 (1978), 6.

_____. "...tak khorosho i strashno. Zametka." *Literaturnoe obozrenie*, No. 9 (1978), 11.

1979

_____. "Chekhov redaktiruet. Stat'ia." *Literaturnaia ucheba,* No. 3 (1979), 189, 190.

_____. "Dva rasskaza." *Novyi mir,* No. 3 (1979), 106-117.

_____. "Dva starika. Byl'. " *Ogonek,* No. 15 (1979), 28, 29.

_____. Foreword to B. Kravchenko's "Dvoe. Rasskaz." *Literaturnaia Rossiia,* No. 9 (1979), 6.

_____. Foreword to N.S. Leskov's *Levsha.* Moscow: "Detskaia literatura," 1979.

_____. "Letiashchee so stseny slovo. Stat'ia." *Sovetskaia kul'tura,* No. 24 (1979), 5.

_____. "Odin na odin. Povest'." *Znamia,* No. 5 (1979), 78-111.

_____. "Samaia vazhnaia vstrecha," *Voprosy literatury,* No. 2 (1979), 191-198.

_____. "Slovo o Platonove." *Literaturnaia Rossiia,* No. 33 (1979), 11.

_____. "Telefonnyi razgovor. Rasskaz." *Ogonek,* No. 1 (1979), 14-16.

_____. "Tochnyi adres. Retsenziia." *Knizhnoe obozrenie,* No. 26 (1979), 9.

_____. "Vernost' idee avtora. Stat'ia." *Sovetskaia kul'tura,* No. 3 (1979), 9.

_____. "V gostiakh u Dzhonsa, professora. Ocherk." *Literaturnaia Rossiia,* No. 39 (1979), 22, 23.

_____. "Vorobei. Rasskaz." *Literaturnaia Rossiia,* No. 8 (1979), 12-14.

_____. "Zastupnitsa. Otryvok iz p'esy." *Rabotnitsa,* No. 11 (1979), 23-25.

_____. "Zastupnitsa. Povest' v monologakh." *Nash sovremennik,* No. 11 (1979), 63-81.

1980

Nagibin, Iu. M. and Vladimir Gusev. "Chem slovo zhivo? Dialog." *Literaturnaia gazeta,* No. 1 (1980), 6.

Nagibin, Iu. M. "Dorozhnoe proisshestvie. Rasskaz." *Oktiabr',* No. 11 (1980).

_____. "Dostoinstvo zhanra." *Literaturnaia Rossia,* No. 3 (1980), 8, 9.

_____. "Eshche raz o boe bykov. Rasskaz." *Ogonek,* No. 15 (1980), 22-24.

_____. Foreword to Evgeniia Pozina. *Literaturnaia Rossiia,* No. 24 (1980), 18, 19.

_____. "Ital'ianskaia tetrad'. Putevye zametki." *Novyi mir,* No. 4 (1980), 110-125.

_____. "Izuchenie bez chteniia?" *Literaturnaia gazeta,* No. 12 (1980), 5.

_____. "Koshka, golubi i Tintoretto. Etiud." *Literaturnaia Rossiia,* No. 12 (1980), 23.

_____. "Letaiushcie tarelochki. Putevoi ocherk." *Nash sovremennik,* No. 2 (1980), 135-178.

_____. "Miagkaia posadka. Sovremennaia skazka." *Literaturnaia Rossiia,* No. 26 (1980), 12, 13.

_____. "Morelon. Rasskaz." *Nash sovremennik,* No. 4 (1980), 65-72.

_____. "Moskovskii rasskaz." *Sbornik posviashchennyi olimpiiskim igram.* Moscow: "Moskovskii rabochii," 1980.

_____. "Net problem? Rasskaz." *Literaturnaia Rossiia,* No. 6 (1980), 12, 13.

_____. "Pozdravliaem iubiliara. G.S. Chikovani—70 let." *Literaturnaia gazeta,* No. 13 (1980), 6.

_____. "Prekrasnaia loshad'. Rasskaz." *Literaturnaia gazeta,* No. 9 (1980), 7.

_____. "V plameni chistom i svetlom. Rasskaz." *Smena,* No. 10 (1980), 9-11.

_____. "V poiskakh Lassila. Rasskaz." *Sovetskaia Rossiia,* No. 178 (1980), 4; and *Znamia,* No. 12 (1980).

_____. "Zastupnitsa. Monologicheskaia p'esa s prologom i epilogom." *Teatr,* No. 6 (1980), 173-191.

III. Criticism of Nagibin's Works

1978

Amlinskii, V. "Pozdravliaem iubiliara. Iu. M. Nagibinu—60 let." *Literaturnaia gazeta*, No. 15 (1978), 4.

Bogatko, Irina. "Luchshee u nas. Retsenziia." *Literaturnaia gazeta*, No. 9 (1978), 4.

Cochrum, Ellen Joan. "Jurij Nagibin's Short Stories: Themes and Literary Criticism." *Dissertation Abstracts International*, No. 39 (1978), 313A-314A.

Gerasimova, Liudmila. "Segodniashnee i vechnoe. Retsenziia." *Literaturnoe obozrenie*, No. 12 (1978), 45, 46.

Grinberg, I. "Energiia rasskaza. Stat'ia." *Neva*, No. 1 (1978), 181-192.

Gusarova, I. "Kniga, kotoraia vospityvaet serdtse." *Znamia*, No. 11 (1978), 247-250.

Ivanova, Natal'ia. "Pri svete nastoiashchego. Retsenziia." *Druzhba narodov*, No. 9 (1978), 263-266.

Pistunova, A. "V derzhave moei liubvi. Retsenziia." *Literaturnaia Rossiia*, No. 19 (1978), 20.

Porter, Richard N. "The Uneven Talent of Jurij Nagibin." *Russian Language Journal*, No. 113 (1978), 103-113.

Reshetov, Nikolai. "Postizhenie zhizni. Retsenziia." *Smena*, No. 19 (1978), 19.

1979

Drobot, Galina. "Poznanie cheloveka. Retsenziia." *Literaturnaia Rossiia*, No. 16 (1979), 14.

Korobov, Vladimir. "Donesti, ne raspleskat'." *Sovetskaia kul'tura*, No. 2 (1979), 4.

Milivoevíc, Dragan. "Nagibin's Views of American and Soviet Literature: An Interview." *Russian Language Journal*, No. 115 (1979), 128-136.

Sakharov, B. "Prostor mechty. Retsenziia." *Oktiabr'*, No. 12 (1979), 195-197.

Semibratova, I. "Chudesnyi i zagadochnyi grazhdanin budushchego. Stat'ia." *Literaturnaia gazeta*, No. 7 (1979), 8-13.

Sendich, Munir. "Jurij Nagibin, *Carskosel'skoe utro*. Review." *Russian Language Journal*, No. 115 (1979), 243-249.

Sivokon', S. "O liubvi i ne tol'ko. Retsenziia." *Literaturnoe obozrenie*, No. 12 (1979), 44-45.

Sosina, N. "Bez kompromissov." *Sovetskii ekran*, No. 1 (1979), 20.

1980

Bogatko, Irina. *Iurii Nagibin. Literaturnyi portret.* Moscow: "Sovetskaia Rosiia," 1980.

Bogatko, Irina. "Vo imia chelovechnosti. Stat'ia." *Komsomol'skaia pravda*, No. 79 (1980), 4.

Korobov, V. "Shchedrost'mysli i chuvstva." *Oktiabr'*, No. 4 (1980), 216, 217.

L'vova, E.L. "Novoobrazovaniia v proze Iu. M. Nagibina." *Russkaia rech'*, No. 1 (1980), 47-52.

Pistunova, A. "Chistye prudy. Ocherk." *Sovetskaia kul'tura*, No. 28 (1980), 5.

Ukhanov, Ivan. "Dobryi master. Portret pisatelia k 60-letiiu." *Literaturnaia Rossiia*, No. 14 (1980), 11.

Compiled by Yury Nagibin and Richard N. Porter